DREAMERS OF THE GRAIL

Dale Geraldson

Stone Ring Press
www.stoneringpress.com

Copyright © 2011 by Dale Geraldson
Published by arrangement with the author
Cover art by Maria Talasz

Library of Congress Cataloging in Publication Data
Geraldson, Dale
Dreamers of the Grail / by Dale Geraldson
p.   cm.
ISBN 978-0-9829712-2-2
1. Perceval and Galahad (Legendary characters) Fiction.
2. Knights and knighthood – Great Britain – Fiction.   I. Title
PS3600.0333   2011
813'.57-dc21   2010940094

For Questing Fools Everywhere…

PART ONE: FOOLISH YOUTH

The water looked so peaceful, drifting under the bridge. The girl loved watching its ceaseless flow, quiet but indomitable, with no one to answer to, no one to judge it.

It was Galienne's favorite spot, this bridge which spanned the cool river Wey. It offered her a view of the small tradeships unloading their treasured cargoes, of the town's children running about in the busy streets, of the comings and goings of Astolat's citizens. She cherished these glimpses, especially when she knew the people she watched. Growing up in the city, she felt she knew every last foot of it.

At least she had a break from her labors. Her mother, Elaine, had been helping her to close the seams on a new tapestry, and Galienne stuck with it diligently, but continued to have trouble finishing the work. It would have to wait until later. Her fingers already had thick calluses which were all but immune to the poking of needles, even the fine and sharp ones Elaine preferred. Elaine was the finest seamstress in Astolat.

Galienne looked about the city. The sight of the perimeter walls always comforted her, even though tales of the Garmani invaders breaching those walls dated to the years just prior to her birth. Astolat lay at the east end of Arthur's domain; Londinium was the only city closer to those lands the Garmani settled and plowed as their own. She had never met a Garmani before, and her mother's stories made her curious. She sometimes wished she could seek out some Easterner to befriend, but couldn't of course. The local populace would not tolerate that, such was their loathing of the foreigners.

Galienne wondered what the outsiders would be like. Being of Cymru stock but Roman civilization, almost all of the people she knew had much in common with her: a sense of order, ornate architecture, strict laws, regular hygienic habits (one of the legendary bath houses was right in Astolat, and Elaine would sometimes take Galienne to visit it as a special treat). The men kept their faces shaved, hair combed, pride swollen. The women were always shown their place: hearth, field, or shop. It was difficult to keep a secret in Astolat. Galienne had tried to keep two of them.

It was one thing for her to study Latin; almost everyone in the land spoke Cymru, except for the Garmani, with their gruff dialect, and the Picts to the far north. Galienne had even heard a few phrases in something Continental: French, she surmised, and she wanted to learn that, too. But girls weren't supposed to learn; they were supposed to master their family trades, and hope for suitable marriages to better their stations in life. But *Latin!* That was the tongue of the educated, and the educated were male.

She grinned, overlooking the city. She felt her own pride as her eyes took in the steeple of the Astolat cathedral. That was where the Bible lay. Books were priceless; this was the only one Galienne had ever seen. Not even her best friend Lupinia knew how much time she spent in there. Bishop Baudwin, the patriarch of Camelot itself, performed the Mass here last Christmas, and was intrigued to find this girl standing at the dais hours after the service, gently inspecting the holy text. It was an immense tome, leather-bound and hand-stitched, the pages thick and fibrous, each lovingly illustrated and painstakingly copied from an original.

"Six monks labored almost a year to produce it," the voice behind her had said that day.

Galienne had immediately withdrawn from the masculine tone, stifling a yelp. "I-I'm sorry," she said. How would Elaine scold her for this?

"It's all right, child. Tell me, do you know how to read?"

She was so taken aback by the question she could only shake her head.

"Well then, perhaps we could work on that," Baudwin added. Galienne thought he was teasing her, all the way up until he stood next to her, and inquired as to her favorite Book.

"I'm sorry, your Worship. I don't know. Your sermon sounded lovely, but I just didn't understand much of it. All that Latin."

And he laughed, and she was unsure how to respond. Then he grew more serious. "Everyone who attends a service should be able to comprehend its lessons. Come. I have some time now. Let us start."

He was elated to have such an eager pupil, and never seemed to care that she was a girl. She discovered that the nuns learned to read, but never admitted to him that a nunnery sounded quite dull to her. Baudwin stayed in the city for several days following that first lesson, and Galienne took to the new skill quickly, craving new knowledge. She had been to Camelot on occasion, accompanying her mother as she periodically took her wares to the grander marketplace, and always sought out the bishop for additional study. He continued to encourage her. Even the local priest, the spiritless man who preached to Astolat's crowds on holy days, was ignorant of the girl's practice; he thought she came to pray.

Such was the first detail she wished to keep secret, but no one else knew about the second one. She had good cause for hesitancy: the local young people, even Galienne's own mother, taunted her for wanting to learn to read, and the curious girl could only imagine the ridicule she would invite if people learned of what she could see.

Her visions still terrified more often than comforted. Galienne liked not to think about them at all, but they would not go away. Indeed, they occurred more frequently recently, and with greater clarity. The most recent one was of the two knights, leading the beating back of a Garmani revolt to the east. She could not see King Arthur dispatching them, nor those who saw them on their way as they left Camelot behind. But she was able to make out the details of the pair of them as they rode on, rallying the Romanized landholders on to quash the Garmani upstarts before the flames of rebellion had any chance to fan. She could have even picked out their shield designs, were either of them to cross over the bridge toward her now.

But who were they? she craved to know. That was the unfair part. She used to think that she just had an overactive imagination; after all, considering her mother, that trait surely ran in the family! But still…the visions always were so real, more vivid than dreams, more lucid than a storyteller's yarn. Galienne could make out so much detail, and all it left her with was the desire to know more.

Which was heresy, of course; wanting to know more than one's fair share, or receiving sendings from some demonic source were sins, to put it mildly. What would people say? She couldn't let Elaine find out, or bishop Baudwin. Maybe she could tell Lupinia.

Galienne's best friend was what her mother called a free spirit. Never one to judge, always one to listen, and certainly out for a good time, Lupinia came from a well off merchant family, dealing with the profitable but odoriferous leather trade. Practically, this meant she got to go to Camelot often, partly to help her father, and partly to gain the attention of suitors, especially knights. Both she and her father wanted her to marry well; Galienne never thought that would prove difficult.

But how might Lupinia respond to all this? Galienne was supposed to meet her here on the bridge, so maybe she could tell her then…

"How long have you been here?" the familiar musical voice chimed.

Galienne turned toward the sound. "Lupy! Finally. Where were you?"

"Working." *Flirting with someone,* Galienne thought. "I was helping Father get ready for his next trade trip, and just singing." She grinned, the luscious locks of her dark hair swirling about her curved face. "And you haven't answered my question."

"I've been down here a while, since that ship arrived."

"You still want to take that boat trip, don't you?" Galienne nodded. "That's a trade ship. Father's used that one before. Looks like they're taking on a load of grain." That was all the small talk Lupy wanted. "So, what are we doing tonight?"

Galienne shrugged, not really wanting to respond. "I just thought we'd take a stroll down by the bathhouse, and maybe get something to eat." She knew Lupinia adored baths, anything to help get the smell of leather and tanning away from her. Neither of them had much love of the urine and guano from various species which often went into the creation of good leather.

Lupinia brightened at once. "You mean casually walk by all those sexy bathers, and loiter about in a local tavern?"

Her friend blushed. "I don't want to spy on anyone. But Mother and I just sold those dresses we finished last month, and she's actually given me some of the money. I haven't eaten outside the house since –"

"Since we flirted with those squires in that place on East Gate Street."

"You flirted with them, not me."

"Oh, dear little Galienne. You know we share the same faith. When are you going to let yourself have some fun? God doesn't care. I think He wholeheartedly approves."

"Lupy, you know that's not what we're taught."

"Well, whatever we're taught in church might affect our souls. But I'm telling you, why shouldn't we be allowed a bit of joy in our lives, too? You spend too much time listening to your mother."

Galienne hated that, because she knew her friend was right. "You commit no sin tonight, is that clear?"

Lupinia crossed herself, grinning. "None of the seven deadlies from this young angel, I promise. Now, what was it you wanted to talk about?"

The younger girl sighed as they started walking through town. *If you only knew. But can I tell you the truth?*

* * *

Sixteen dozen miles northwest, a young man was angry and tired, perched atop one of Cambria's endless grassy and rock-strewn hills, feeling the sweat tighten his skin as it already began to dry. The day finally was beginning to cool, and Perceval watched the huge deer sprint further and further away, until it disappeared into the labyrinth of what the native Cymru proudly called mountains.

I should have had it, he thought; *I know my aim is better than that. And I never should have left Dindraine alone with the sheep.*

The herd animals provided enough on which to live. They might be used by the family in their village of Oerfa, or traded to one of the other neighboring raths. Perceval took pride in his mother's trust, though today was the first time he relinquished control to his younger sister. Dindraine had gone into the hills with him enough times, so why shouldn't she be able to do the job herself? Besides, the prospect of bringing down the stag was just too much for him to resist.

His skin felt warm and snug now, and he stood up again. He knew he had to return to Dindraine before nightfall, and the sky was already beginning to glow, no longer orange and blue, but the deepening reddish-purple of a summer sunset, extending outward forever. He glanced upward. *Where do the clouds go?* he wondered. *How far does the land go, before the world ends? Can the birds fly there?* He smiled. So often he wanted to be anywhere but the tiny rath in which he had been raised.

"*Ble mae'r gwaywffon, twpsyn?*" was the sound which brought him back from the realm of the birds.

He only then noticed that he had wandered clear back to the hill where he left Dindraine and the herd; he had passed the time daydreaming, mostly recounting his failed hunt. It rubbed at him, especially since Perceval knew how to kill; he was blooded by the hunt already, once leading a snarling boar to the rath so the warriors could dispatch it. His mother had threatened to kill *him* for that stunt.

"What?" was his delirious reply, his mind still fantasizing.

"Your javelin, bone-head. Where did you leave it?"

He hadn't even considered it. Then he remembered: he last saw it falling somewhere near the stag, after his hasty and surprisingly inaccurate throw. Curses! Now he would be in trouble. He couldn't believe he forgot; had he really been that out of it? His family was not known for their rich coffers; javelins cost. It was already too late to look for it, and he didn't think it would last long exposed to the weather. He shook his head. Dindraine seized the moment.

"Ha! You foolishly leave me here to watch the sheep, and you go and lose the javelin. What if some wolves attack us?" Dindraine had never even seen a wolf, though she often resented how their mother kept harping on about how *responsible* Perceval was, and now this.

"There are no wolves out here, you ugly little hag." This insult, of course, was one of the older brother's retorts to his younger sibling's prodding. While he had only rarely seen wolves and never worried about them, he likewise had never seen a hag, nor knew of any, except maybe for the witch who lived outside the village. Kundry she was called, although the villagers stayed far enough from her to avoid having to call her anything at all.

"Am not. I'm telling Mother what you called me!"

"You started it."

"Uh-*uh*. *You* did. You did, by chasing something you could never catch, and by being so stupid in the process."

Perceval misjudged the act accused of idiocy. "It wasn't stupid."

Dindraine could hardly believe it. "How could losing the javelin not be stupid?!"

"I meant chasing the stag. It wasn't stupid. Haven't you ever chased after anything you couldn't catch? Not even for just the excitement of it?"

There was little reply to that. Dindraine opened her mouth, instinctively expecting to throw something back at her brother, and could feel her cheeks warm when nothing came out. "Well, no," was all she managed.

"I really thought I could have bagged it, that's all. I'm sorry I left you here. I just got too excited." Perceval was in no mood to continue the bickering, especially since they had to get the sheep from their grazing hill back to their evening pen, or else maybe his sister would get to see some wolves after all. He felt defenseless without the lost weapon, though he never understood how some of the people he knew hated wolves; they'd never bothered him or his family before.

"Let's just get back. It's getting late," he told Dindraine, not looking at her.

"But tell me about the hunt."

"I don't want to," he answered, less than proudly.

"Please," she whined, giving him her best imitation of the sort of look he might get from their dogs when they wanted treats. "It's the least you can do, after running away."

"Fine," he conceded as they started to walk. "But let's get the others first."

They called the dogs, Cabal and Dannedd, who never seemed to tire. They came trotting over, encircling the sheep along the way. Dogs and humans finished regrouping their woolly responsibilities, and silently turned towards home.

Wouldn't Mother have been proud, Perceval thought, trying to ignore his earlier considerations of her rebuking him for this, *if I could have only caught up to the beast, and brought it down.* It was just like him to be primarily concerned with what his mother would think, and he never even considered just how he might have managed to haul such a sizable carcass back to Oerfa.

"It had sixteen points, I'm sure of it!" he told her excitedly.

"You'd need four hands to count that high," she chided him. He briefly considered smacking her. "Why did you want it so badly?"

"I wanted to be like it, just run with it, all the way to the end of the world, maybe. Does that make any sense?"

Dindraine nodded, enjoying that image as much as her brother. They often spoke of what life might be like if they could leave Oerfa behind. "How did it get away?" she asked, not wanting to think about home right then.

"Oh, I got close to it, hiding behind a tree, and then stepped on and broke a twig, of all things. The noise scared it off. Hey, it's not funny."

Dindraine couldn't help laughing at him, picturing him giving chase to something much faster and stronger, alerted to his presence by his own clumsiness. "It sounds like it was teasing you."

"Teasing! How?"

"Perceval, that thing could have changed its mind and come right after you. It didn't. It's like it wanted to see how close you'd come."

Perceval thought about it. He wondered if a stag could be that bright.

The surrounding countryside ignored his storytelling. They hiked through a valley isolated from most of the known world by mountains and rugged hills. The Plimlimmons lay westward; Mother said to never go there. Snowdonia perched far to the northwest, and they thought they could actually see it sometimes.

Perceval remarked about how good the cool wind felt at their backs. He almost felt cold now, with the sweat in his clothes still drying. His thoughts returned to his conception of the end of the world. It did not sound bad to him at all, especially right then, to just keep on walking and walking until the world ended, if for no other reason than to enjoy the view along the way. He wondered what it would be like to actually get there; he was just feeling tired of home. What would the people be like at the world's end? How exactly did it end, gradually, or all at once? Was it just dark there; was that the end? Or did everything just go there to die?

Oerfa lay a bit removed from most civilized centers, in the middle of the old Pagan Belinan's chiefdom of Powys, which encompassed eastern and central Cambria. He largely kept the peace while clinging to the old ways, even though he looked to the future, much as his counterpart to the southeast; Perceval had never even heard King Arthur's name. The Cambrian tribes were fiercely independent, even from each other, and the hills had mostly kept out the Romans and their cities and their monotheistic religion, while the young ruler of Camelot had better affairs to attend to than trying to quell thousands of folk who shared his blood. Oerfa, the tiny rath, was typical of the lifestyle of the Cymru of the hills.

The youths were now barely two miles from the *rath*, still meandering along silently. Only the occasional *bah* from the sheep, or a yelp from one of the dogs as it ran off to bring straggling herbivores back into the herd announced their presence. Sometimes it just felt too peaceful to talk. Perceval and Dindraine were like that: they shared a bond in which neither had to say anything, and yet both knew more or less what the other was thinking and feeling. Their mother sometimes felt jealous of this. Perceval finally broke their mutual silence.

"Stop. Cabal! Dannedd! Come here, boys." The commands came quietly, and the dogs put themselves in front of the herd, expertly stopping the sheep.

"What is it?" asked Dindraine, whispering. She trusted her brother's judgment, at least when he looked as serious as he did right then.

"Look, right over there," Perceval said, pointing north. "Do you see it?"

Dindraine followed his finger and squinted. "What?" she demanded.

"Keep your voice down. I don't want them to hear us."

"Who?" she looked again, her intrigue rediscovered.

"Stay here with the animals. I'm going over to get a closer look," Perceval commanded.

"At what? I'm coming with you." It wasn't like him to act like this, and just run off alone, twice in one day no less.

Perceval could hear his mother's words echoing: *a man has to take care of his family*, not recognizing the Roman stereotype which portrayed females as needy and helpless. He looked at Dindraine. Her eyes were wide and pleading, yet determined. She would not be easily swayed. Actually, when he thought about it, he could hardly believe that she had not tagged after him and the stag.

He pointed again. "There are some people over there. I want to know why they stopped, without going into the village. They must not be from around here."

"I can take care of myself, Big Brother." Dindraine sarcastically slurred the last two words, then immediately regretted it. What if he said no, and tried to force her to stay? Then again, how could she be forced, if he went himself?

But there was no effort to stop her. Big Brother hung his head down, and she knew she had won. Behind him, she could finally see the faint, rosy glow of a campfire, over on the next hill. She wondered who might be over there as well. Not wanting to rub in her victory, she listened to Perceval.

"All right, let's both go. The dogs can handle the sheep." Dindraine likewise tried to sound calm, while her brother called the dogs over, pointed towards Oerfa, and commanded them to go home. These two were quite well trained; they wasted no time, and started up the sheep with more ease and grace then most human shepherds could have exhibited.

Brother and sister waited silently, hearts thumping almost audibly, while their companions and livestock went. Cabal held up the rear, and he stopped and looked back. Perceval met his glance, thinking that those canine eyes seemed so smart, so *human* sometimes. The dog looked a bit sad, but his master and friend pointed again towards Oerfa, and Cabal turned around and continued.

It seemed to take hours to reach the hill with the campfire. It wasn't very far, but Dindraine and Perceval were not taking any chances. They reached the base of the hill and paused. Dindraine smiled; she always did love excitement as much as her brother. They had to cross the distance between hills in the open, which would have given them away instantly in daylight, but now they were just shadows under the light glow of a moon far more accommodating than the blazing sun had been.

It was completely dark now; the sun had finished its westerly departure, another infinitesimal part of its endless cycle. Perceval might have thought it lay somewhere beyond the world's limits, had he even noticed it. Dindraine and Perceval actually *crawled*, zigzagging their way uphill, mindful of their shadows and the scratchy noises the terrain made beneath them; it sounded as though the tiny rocks and grasses, and running and flying insects, protested this invasion.

Then the intruders were close enough to see three shadows, and hear several horses grazing, hoping the sound would muffle their own. The only source of light now was the campfire, and even it was so small that one could still see the stars above if one was sitting close to it. But the two youngsters didn't notice them, finding their own heart thumps quite distracting enough. Perceval wondered how the men could not hear his alarmed chest, as its pounding echoed behind his ears. He stopped, and tried to listen. Dindraine was just a few feet behind him, belly to the cool ground, trying to get within whispering range of her brother.

Perceval motioned for her to lean her head towards him and listen, finally acknowledging her presence to his rear, giving her at least a modicum of comfort. He whispered that he could understand them, though their voices had some twang to them (he did not know about regional accents, but at least the visitors spoke Cymru). Brother and sister leaned toward the rock, listening.

"How does he fare now?" came the voice of a man who sounded to Perceval like he was in charge.

"Still feverish, but otherwise all right, I think," was the reply from a male voice still lined with the scratchiness of one's teen years.

"Sir," said the same voice, "Do you think we'll be safe out here? I like not to think of us stranded, in case it comes back."

"Oh, come now, Clydno," said a third voice, also sounding rather young, but with a touch less trepidation. "We're safer here among the hollow hills."

"That's just it!" Clydno all but cried out. "What if there are more like it? It's said these hills are full of all manner of evil, and my master would be better suited in a Christian house of healing."

Perceval found the ensuing silence perplexing. He could not see the healthy knight, Sir Yvaine of Gorre, flash his friend's squire a glare which hinted at menace. Yvaine was a Pagan by birth and inclination, and while he respected the wounded knight's other faith, he was not inclined to try moving again, not after dark. The horses had a difficult enough time navigating this terrain in daylight.

"I agree with your diagnosis," Yvaine told the young man. "But we will stay here tonight, and be off at dawn. For now, just stay at Lamorak's side." *Be well, brother knight. By Lleu, was she worth this? Or this "creature" of yours, that none of us have seen?* Yvaine let his thoughts wander for a few moments, watching Clydno wipe the sweat off his master's brow. Lamorak had indeed received punishment for pursuing his quest so fervently. The "barking beast," as he so called it, summoned him out of Camelot, with his friend Yvaine along for the ride. Yvaine, the good-natured and reckless adventurer, came along for the fun of it, and now did not want to acknowledge the possible truth of Lamorak's claim.

His own squire spoke now, giving no small sense of relief to Perceval and Dindraine, who by now thought they were likely discovered.

"Sir, why do you smile?"

Yvaine grinned even wider. "I was just thinking, Vonnet, how much better we all might feel if we had brought Chat du Soleil along."

The squires both chuckled at that. "Can you imagine?" Vonnet asked. "Your lion could have helped Sir Lamorak beat anything that came his way, that's for certain."

"What's that name again?" inquired Clydno, eager to take his mind off Lamorak's unconscious and labored breathing. The three of them discovered the knight several hours after he gave chase to something they did not see. But Lamorak remained adamant, not slowing down when shouted at, and took quite a severe beating from... something.

Yvaine's humorous nature didn't like considering the absence of tracks near his friend's body when he and the squires arrived, other than those a horse would make. They could only hear the noise, like the baying of dozens of hunting hounds, and they reeled from the stench. Lamorak still smelled awful, like he had tangled with something already dead.

"It means sun-cat. It's a Continental name." Yvaine traveled the mainland extensively, though not for some years. He had returned home to find life at court more conservatively Christian than ever. "Its strength but gentle pride reminded me of our King. Arthur wanted to keep him personally, but decided it was enough if he stayed in the Queen's menagerie sometimes." The squires nodded.

Still behind a boulder, confident that there were four men and six horses at this camp, Perceval mouthed "What's a 'lion'?" to his sister. She didn't understand his question, and didn't know the answer anyway. But then she stifled a gasp, terrified of being discovered, as she watched her brother suddenly move out from behind the rock into the circle of the campsite.

Years later, Perceval would never be able to tell just *why* he started crawling around like that. Whichever the reason, it never mattered in the least. Fate would pick up the pieces of decisions to its own liking.

"Greetings," Perceval offered presently. As he stepped towards the fire, he noticed the prone form of Sir Lamorak. He looked badly hurt, his chest rising and lowering rhythmically but belaboredly. That was all Perceval had time to notice before hearing the reflex-quick sound of metal sliding against other metal, and he found himself facing another.

"Who in blazes are you?" demanded Yvaine. "Do you want to get yourself killed?"

Perceval was dimly aware of the words, barely looking at the knight's face. A young face, no beard, and weary but excitable at once. Yvaine was shorter than his Orkney kin, but still stood proudly, with thrusting jaw and curled copper hair mostly hidden beneath his mail cowl. And Perceval was at once rooted to his spot. The fire danced and flicked shadows upon the Yvaine, making his arms and legs shine! Like his skin was covered with silver. And the sword. Perceval had never seen one so long. The villagers in Cambria used shorter weapons, when they could afford them.

"Speak," Yvaine commanded, more calmly, seeing this was clearly no ambush, unless it was led by the most tactically stupid person in Britain. He sheathed his sword, noticing the way this young inquisitive man, the age of his own squire, followed the motion as the weapon slid home into its protective scabbard. His smile once more returned; Yvaine's lips constantly were in that position, even when angry. "I didn't mean to frighten you, but I'm asking: who are you?"

"He is Perceval, and I am his sister," came a new voice from behind one of the larger boulders between which Yvaine had opted to encamp. The men turned and saw a determined girl, standing with clenched fists. "Surely you can see we mean no harm to any of you. We saw your fire some distance yonder and merely were curious about who might be out here." *At least they speak Cymru.* Please *let them be friendly.*

"At least one of you talks," Yvaine noted, prompting laughter from the squires. "Come. Sit by our fire. We have no food to offer other than dry biscuits and fruit and what little water our skins still have. But you are welcome to join us."

"If I may, Sir," Perceval began finally. "What is that metal skin you wear?" He did not see Dindraine raise her eyebrows at him, nor turn to shrug to the strangers.

"This?" Yvaine said, pinching a section of chain link, meticulously forged and shaped by the finest armorsmiths in Logres. "It's mail, of course. Haven't you ever – " he began, pausing after seeing the younger man's intrigued but perhaps pained expression. "Here," he offered, sliding closer to Perceval.

Perceval stroked the mail, feeling its artistry and power. His eyes stole down to the sword. Yvaine unsheathed it again, handling it carefully to Perceval.

He grasped the proffered hilt, feeling his arm muscles tighten just to keep the blade aloft. It felt cool and invincible. The smith in Oerfa could hardly match this kind of work! He let it swing back and forth in his palms; it felt almost to possess its own will. When he raised it up, Yvaine intercepted his hand.

"Not just yet," Yvaine commanded. "You see these two with me?" He pointed, indicating the squires.

Perceval nodded. Yvaine introduced them. "This is Vonnet, my squire. He is an apprentice knight. And this is Clydno, who serves in the same capacity to my friend." Dindraine and her brother peered over to where Lamorak lay, his mouth open and his breathing slow. The fire flickered in the sweaty drops on his forehead. Dindraine was concerned at once; she winced at the man's stench.

"If I may, Sir," replied Perceval. "What is a knight, exactly? Is your friend there one also?" He gestured towards Lamorak.

Dindraine rolled her eyes. What foolishness was her brother up to now?

Yvaine and Vonnet shook their torsos slightly from laughter. Clydno chuckled once, and never took his eyes from his ailing master. "A knight?" Yvaine asked, incredulously. Perceval nodded, looking innocent or stupid, Yvaine could not tell.

Vonnet, used to picking up the proverbial slack, offered the obvious answer, which would not make his master appear foolish if this "Perceval" was only humoring them all. "A knight, of course, is a mounted, armored warrior who lives by a sacred code and serves his lord, as we serve the knights."

"And in this case," Clydno added, though not turning away from Lamorak, "the lord in question is Arthur of Logres, right and fair ruler of all Britain." He had been saying it with those exact words since he turned six.

Dindraine, not wishing to look as naive as her older sibling, wandered over next to Clydno and Lamorak, overcoming her initial reaction to the odor and looking the knight up and down for injuries. The squire noticed her, and offered as much of a smile as he could, given his feeling of dread.

Perceval tried to piece it all together. He looked at Yvaine. "So you serve Lord Arthur," then turned to Vonnet, "and you serve him," and looked back to Yvaine. "And both of you are apprentice knights." Perceval understood something of apprenticeship, though it bothered him that the closest he had come to one himself was tending the sheep. *Warriors. Men with the finest weapons, and huge horses.* He looked at the immense destriers, at least eighteen hands in height, and he wondered again about the lands that must lay beyond these hills for them to ride. His family even had a horse in Oerfa, but it could not go very far, simply due to the terrain.

Yvaine saw that the younger man was, after all, truly, surprisingly, ignorant. Not stupid; indeed, he displayed remarkable curiosity for a commoner past the age of becoming a page or squire. And the questions! The lad never stopped asking of Yvaine and Vonnet. He seemed most befuddled by mention of the grand Round Table, insisting that tables were always rectangular; Yvaine laughed even louder at that. Perceval wanted to know everything about these men: Yvaine thought of earlier days, training and living with Margawse, Gawaine, and others.

No, this is not the time to waste on thoughts of your vengeful cousin or his bloody manipulative mother, my aunt, Yvaine thought. He did not look forward to the likelihood of having to take a side: Lamorak, on the one hand, his friend who spilled blood with him, most recently helping to quell a Garmani uprising in the southeast, and whom Chat du Soleil actually liked. On the other hand lurked Yvaine's own cousins, vindictive because their mother had taken Lamorak, son of their father's slayer on the battlefield, into her bed. Why weren't they angry with her instead? Or were they? Or were they afraid of her, a supposed sorceress?

Yvaine silently chided himself for daydreaming too much, having allowed Vonnet to take over answering Perceval's interrogations. The latter still twirled Yvaine's dagger playfully when they were all distracted by Lamorak's sudden moaning.

"What did he say?" Clydno asked Dindraine, who knelt hunched over him like a doting parent, soothing his brow with a dampened cloth.

"I don't know," she answered. "Something about his father, maybe. Sir Yvaine," she called.

He was already behind her, coming to kneel next to the little group. Only Perceval and Vonnet stood, the one feeling out of place, the other ready to respond to any orders he might receive. He soon heard one. "Vonnet, another water skin."

The squire responded immediately. Lamorak babbled a few syllables. "Father... can't kill, it knows... she's... coming for me..."

When Vonnet brought the water over to them, Yvaine demanded a supply status. "Down to two skins, Sir, and barely a day's rations, assuming we can get Master Lamorak to eat anything."

"How long since he last ate?" Dindraine prodded. Perceval was shocked. Their mother had taught them it was usually both more tactful and proper to hold their tongues in the presence of people they did not know well, never mind how forward he had just been himself. Mother sometimes seemed afraid of saying too much to anyone.

"Since before he was attacked," Clydno answered. "Two days ago."

"Two days?" Dindraine said, incredulously. "We have to move him to a place where he can rest, and get some proper care."

"Out of the question," Yvaine replied without hesitation. "We've already made camp here, and besides, there may be some danger of inf-" and he cut himself off at that point.

"Of what, Sir?" Perceval said, finally joining the conversation.

"Nothing. I just think it would be dangerous to move him."

Dindraine was closest to the man's sick friend, most able to breathe in the noxious vapor he carried. "Do you mean for him, or us?"

"How's that?" her brother wanted to know.

Yet all eyes were on Yvaine now, ignoring for the moment the delirious knight wrapped in his dark wool traveling blanket. Yvaine was not in the mood to argue. "Look," he began. "You can all smell him. I believe he'll be fine, with time and care, but what I mean is that there may be some risk of contamination." Yvaine didn't believe this himself; but to bring his friend to any settlement while still ill meant risking discovery by those Lamorak had angered, and besides, common villagers might be prone to panic upon seeing the nature of these particular wounds. At any rate, Clydno would feel better out here, since the only human habitats in this region were Pagan.

You must get better, brother, Yvaine thought. *You must be able to confront those who would oppose you again. I will stand at your side: you, who never put differences in faith before friendship.*

"I admit I don't know too much about the spread of diseases," Dindraine continued. "But if there was much real danger of that, wouldn't the three of you be showing some signs of this as well, after more than two days?"

None of the men had any answer for that. Perceval refused to be outshone by his little sister. "Please, Sir Yvaine," he began. "We can take him home with us. Our mother is an excellent cook, and I know you'd all be welcome there."

Yvaine looked at Lamorak, still writhing occasionally, looking as though suffering some unmentionable nightmare. "Where is your home?" he sighed.

"At the base of some of our famous hills," Perceval replied. "There's not another village for a dozen miles. We should know. We visit the other *raths* sometimes."

Sounds perfectly isolated, Yvaine mused to himself. *And* "raths"*? How much more Pagan could they be?* He was intrigued.

"How did you get him this far?" Dindraine wished to know.

"We assembled a litter for him," Clydno told her, proud that he had done most of that work while Yvaine and Vonnet searched for the Beast that day. "I still have the pieces for it on one of the horses." By now Clydno figured any settlement, even a Pagan one, had to be better than hills full of faeries.

He found support in Yvaine, who warmed to the idea. "It will take some time tonight, since the horses will have to watch their footing. We'll have to walk instead of ride." No one cared about that in the least.

While Dindraine and Clydno readied the litter and the others prepared to lift Lamorak into it, Perceval, feeling guilty, nonetheless resumed his questions. "Sir Yvaine, could you tell me more of this search your friend undertook?"

Clydno felt the urge to cross himself at the mere mention of that, but was already gripping his knight's legs. He exchanged a worried glance with the other squire. Yvaine paused before answering, still hesitant to share what he wasn't sure he believed himself.

"Old Lamorak here was, excuse me, *is* trying to finish a quest begun by his father many years ago, in a land not far from here. He wishes to kill something monstrous."

Perceval felt a bit guilty for not grasping one of Lamorak's limbs, hoisting him into the litter, where Dindraine and Clydno wrapped his blanket about him and tied the canvas litter closed. It was already tightly secured to the back of Lamorak's prime charger, an almost ebony steed who still had a nervous twitch in his eye.

"Where could this monster have come from?" Perceval demanded.

Yvaine wondered if these two peasants would understand the significance of his answer. "Probably from way up north, in the great wasted region."

"Wastes?" Dindraine asked, finally comfortable with how Lamorak was secured in his temporary traveling bed.

"Dead lands," Yvaine continued, not really wanting to do so. "Where the faeries come from and go to." Only Perceval noticed how Clydno shuddered at that. "But enough of that for now. Shall we be off before it grows any later?"

They began the trek back, each person leading a horse except Vonnet, who cared for two of them. Perceval loved it, leading such an animal as this! He just hoped Cabal and Dannedd got the herd home safely.

Dindraine shared the lead of the party with him, and finally murmured her concerns to him. She didn't want the others to hear. "I want to talk to you."

"What is it?" he wondered aloud, mimicking her virtual whisper.

"What's all this about you suddenly wanting to be a knight? What makes you think you can do something like that? You're not even nobly born!"

"What does that have to do with it?"

"I mean knights are of noble blood, foolish brother! You must know that, surely. And what was with all those idiotic questions, anyway?"

Where had she learned to become such a nursemaid? "What was so bad about my questions? I wanted to learn about what these men do, that's all. I think I should be a knight, one of the best and bravest warriors around. You'll see. You and Mother will be proud."

"But that's just it," she continued, then looked around quickly at the others, making sure she wouldn't be heard. "Perceval, Mother hates knights, in case you'd forgotten. That's why I'm so surprised at you; the only reason she'd welcome them is because Sir Lamorak needs help. I thought you were asking all those questions because you wanted to poke fun at them."

"Why would I want to do that? That makes no sense. Dindraine, tonight I met the men whose example I wish to follow. Can you understand that, since I didn't have a father to look up to?"

"Of course I can, but neither did I have a father around. And besides, Mother said you shared her feelings about knights with her."

That stopped him cold. "Remember?" Dindraine probed. "Come on, brother, it's time to get your head back out of the clouds."

Then Yvaine was upon them. "Is there a problem, you two?"

"N-no," Perceval told him feebly. "Of course not, Sir Yvaine. I was just thinking."

Yvaine smiled. "That could get you in trouble if you're to become a knight someday." The squires laughed with him.

Dindraine recognized the befuddled look on her brother's face, which meant he was trying to juggle too many thoughts at once. She opted to change tactics. "Sir Yvaine, how fares your friend with the travel so far?" She went over to the litter, checking on the man.

Why would Mother lie like that? And since when can my sister act like a healer? Perceval wondered.

"Well enough, I believe," Yvaine responded.

"He's saying something!" Dindraine yelled.

Yvaine was at her side instantly. "What's he saying?"

The others all watched Lamorak now. He writhed in his stupor. "M-my Lady! Must warn... my Lord, beware... Blessed Christ, what is that thing?!" They heard the pain in his voice; conscious or no, Lamorak was clearly terrified.

Clydno could not help himself; he made the sign of the crucifixion across his breast, silently murmuring a half-forgotten prayer from childhood. Perceval could only feel pity for the knight, while Dindraine wiped sweat from his cheek.

Yvaine wanted answers. "Warn who?" he asked his friend, for a moment actually expecting a response.

"Sir Yvaine," Dindraine said, though she was just as curious, "we're quite close now. Our mother should have some hot food waiting for us all, and your good friend can get the rest he needs."

Yvaine looked at her, then to Perceval. The younger man nodded, slowly but confidently, still awash with all that occupied his inquisitive mind.

"Lead on," Yvaine gently commanded, watching as the litter moved again.

Again the siblings took the lead, resuming their talk. "Who do you suppose he had to warn?" Perceval asked his sister. She only shrugged with her eyebrows.

He didn't want to ask the next question, but knew it was inevitable. "Did Mother really tell you that?"

"About the knights? Yes. She told me all about Camelot and Logres, and all the wonderful knights and ladies and court life." Dindraine stifled a chuckle at her brother's pained glance. "And she told me not to talk with you about them, said it would just upset you."

She let it go at that, for the moment. *He looks like he's about to vomit*, she thought. *But he* must *have known, surely. Don't all*

boys wish to grow up to be brave knights and run around killing enemies?
To Dindraine it seemed part of the natural boy-thing to wish
for, even in the wilds of Cambria.

Yet the nagging question remained. Mother had deceived him, both of them, for reasons unknown.

They walked on, leading the horses and the questing party, noticing how the faint moon cast their small wavy shadows
about them. Dindraine watched them dance with the excitement only the young can exhibit in response to them.

The feeling of Perceval's hand as it took hers surprised
her. His grip was warm and strong, with a slight edginess to
it. Their other hands still held reins, and for a time the pair of
them simply relished the sounds. The crickets chirped noisily
and carelessly, and the water of the nearby Severn continued its
eternal race to the sea. The river would soon cross southward
in front of them, and the group's leaders knew exactly where it
could be safely forded. The pair of them had crossed at that
location perhaps hundreds of times. The ford was their special place, to where they would come when they wished to be
alone, and they had shared countless thoughts while sitting on
the rocks which remained in the water's path as though stub-
bornly trying to stem its flow. But Dindraine had always obeyed
Mother's dire warning: no details of knights discussed with her
brother.

The ford was shallow enough that even Lamorak's litter
made it across with barely a touch of dampness to show for it.
Perceval proudly showed off the tracks left by dogs and sheep.

As they continued on for the last segment of their journey, a sudden wave of dread struck Perceval. He could not allow
himself to daydream anymore. Again he took his sister's hand,
and said simply, "I love you, Dindraine. I always will. It's just
that something really bothers me. Do you know what I mean?"

"Mother," she replied as softly. "And I love you, too."
She kissed him on the cheek playfully.

Mother lied to us. She got the entire rath, even my sister, to lie to me. Perceval hated that thought. He demanded a reason. His mother was such a loving person; how could she have done that?

"I truly wish this, sister, more than I've ever wanted anything."

"I know," she said slowly. She admired the knights, was intrigued by their squires. Dindraine had yet to learn how it felt to be so impassioned, but she did comprehend how people loved what they did; she knew such souls in Oerfa. She didn't want to consider what was likely coming from her brother next, though.

"Do you understand that I'll have to leave home if I am to become a knight in the service of King Arthur? Sir Yvaine said his castle is very far from here."

Afraid of choking up in front of him, all Dindraine could do was nod, yes. She swallowed hard. "How soon do you think you'll have to go?" She hated choking on tears in front of him.

"I don't know. When our guests leave, but... hey, you're crying!"

He took her gently by the shoulders, pulling her close to him. She kept her arms down at first, then finally raised them to return his embrace. She fought to control her feelings, but at last let herself sniffle. They stood there together until the others rejoined them. Perceval loosened his grip at the men's approach, and Dindraine rubbed her reddened and swollen eyes.

Perceval pointed for the others to follow. "There! Can you see it now?" Oerfa lay just a bit further for them, though none but Dindraine detected the lack of excitement in his voice.

She never saw the pair of glistening tears which escaped her brother's eyes as they walked.

* * *

Lupinia felt she could spend the rest of the night right there in the bath. Even the rest of her life sounded fine then. "You see, my dear?" she teased Galienne. "This is what I meant."

Her friend had to concur. "You're right. This is lovely, even better without any adults around."

"Hey, we are the adults. And there's no sin here tonight."

Not yet, anyway.

Galienne blushed at both comments. She didn't see herself as a grownup, not like her parents. And she did not wish any talk of sinning. She was taunted enough about that. "No, you're right."

"Even with the men in here looking about?"

Galienne would not be drawn in so easily. "Yes, even with them. I'm sure their intentions are all flawlessly noble." They both giggled.

The Astolat bath house was one of only a handful throughout Britain. Aquae Sulis was the Roman's pride and joy, much larger than Astolat, attracting citizens from across the Empire during its glory. King Arthur and his queen, Guinevere, both loved the site, and the town had grown since he came to power. There was another such location in southern Cambria, one more way North. Astolat's was smaller, but no less luxurious. People often had to wait hours for the privilege of entering, and were then admitted according to rank, coin, or both. Lupinia's connection to her father ensured that they only had to stand idly for less than an hour. That gave them time to finish their supper: baked lamb and vegetable pies bought with Galienne's earned pay and Lupinia's allowance.

"Thanks for coming," the elder Lupinia added, emerging above the surface of the steamy water after a full body soaking. "It's good to be on our own."

Galienne moaned her assent, not wanting to think of anyone else.

"My father and I return to Camelot soon. Maybe you could come with us again," Lupy added.

"Oh, I'd love to! How soon?"

"Not for a couple of weeks yet. That's why I wanted to ask now, so your parents don't make plans for you, if they haven't already." She tried to bite off the last words, mumbling them instead. She overstepped her bounds.

"Lupy, please don't. You know what my situation is."

Her friend couldn't resist that. "But I'm not sure I do. I sometimes wonder if you even know what it is." She watched Galienne's face. "I'm sorry. I've no right to go prying like that."

"Often, I still just wish that they could be together, that's all. Mother wants it so. Why would someone do that, Lupy? Why does he run off?"

"Isn't that what men should do periodically?" she teased, fantasizing a courtly love affair. "I guess your father is just always away on campaign."

Galienne was not about to let that go. "What campaign? We're at peace, and have been since before you and I were born."

"I just meant he must be busy." Lupinia wanted to change the subject. "And besides, surely you heard about the uprising east of here."

Galienne looked surprised now. "I thought that was just a riot. Weren't the Garmani just irritated about the King's taxes?"

"Oh, yes, like always. But it was bad enough this time to grow into almost a full rebellion. Arthur sent the Round Table members to take care of it."

Galienne couldn't tell if her friend was just giving another overly dramatic description of events. Lupinia was enough of a romantic that the mundane often grew into the thrilling through her telling. "How do you know about it?"

"Because I pay attention, silly girl. A Garmani revolt upsets trade, it makes the citizens panicky, since we're so close to their lands. Your mother may not have noticed, but your father undoubtedly did. He was probably there."

Nice of him to stop and visit, Galienne thought, then felt guilty for it. Still, she knew so little about the man, about whom her mother kept talking like he was the Second Coming incarnate.

She flushed again, feeling her face grow hotter than the soothing bath water. *Stop those thoughts. That's heresy! He's just a man.*

"Well, obviously nothing like that came of it," she told her friend.

"Of course not. I heard who was involved, though."

"Lupy, you always seem to know who's involved. I learn more from you about life at court than I could ever gleam from actually visiting Camelot."

Lupinia laughed at that, playfully splashing some water at Galienne. There were only about a dozen other people in the bath this late, and nobody cared what they discussed here. The bath house was a place to soothe and relax, its stony walls built over Roman brick foundations at Arthur's expense. "What do you wish to learn next?" she tempted.

"I wouldn't even know where to start. I imagine you could give me descriptions of all the Round Table members, and their ladies, and who's betrothed to whom."

"It helps to know," Lupinia added, grinning. "And I only would know about ten or fifteen of the Round Table knights."

Galienne splashed her back. "You would not!"

"Would too! How else can I expect to become a wealthy court lady?"

"You're already rich!"

Lupy snorted. "Father takes good care of me, indeed, but he and I both want to see my station improved. I can't stink like leather forever. We go to Camelot for trade, since I'm better with money than he is, but it's the best place in the world to meet bachelors."

"Like who, for instance?" Galienne had to admit she was curious.

This was her friend's territory now. "Well, I personally think Sir Trystan is about the most beautiful man I've ever seen, but," she lowered her voice to a conspiratorial whisper, "his heart belongs to someone else, whom he can't have."

Good Lord, how does she know this? Is she just having me on?

"Don't look at me like that. I know what I'm talking about. He's completely sweet on his uncle's wife. The lady Isolde, from Eire-land, and her looks rival the Queen's own. Ugh! How horrible it must be for him. Can you imagine the humiliation? What must family gatherings be like?"

Galienne shrugged, bemused, while her friend continued. They often talked of life at court, but Galienne hadn't realized how much gossip her friend really knew. "Or mighty Gawaine, the King's right-hand man. He had a love once, but she's never returned to Camelot. He looks brutish, but who better to protect you?"

"Doesn't he have some brothers?"

"Oh, yes! Gaheris is still single, so far as I know. The others are too young, more like our age." Galienne rolled her eyes. Why did men have to be older than the women when they married, when the women were young and supple and the men started to show signs of age?

"Oh, and there's Dinadan, though he's not very endowed." Galienne looked aghast. "I mean he's not very rich! I'm surprised you caught that, my friend. That poor knight is a bit of a practical joker, though, which sounds good."

The younger girl took a reprieve from this news to completely succumb to the water, opening her eyes as she sank herself below it. The sensation was cleansing, her every pore welcoming the engulfing wet heat.

She broke the surface. "Aren't you glad you came out with me now?"

She smiled at Lupinia. "Indeed. So, tell me, since you know so much: who led the counter to the Garmani those weeks ago?"

Galienne was less than surprised to learn that her friend knew that, also. "I believe the main members of that party were Sirs Lamorak and, oh, let's see, Yvaine."

She opted to keep humoring Lupy, though she was a bit curious. "Who on earth are those two?"

"Yvaine's the world traveler. He's seen the Continent, and is Gawaine's cousin. Lamorak is," she pondered it for a few moments. "I can't remember where he's from. Somewhere in Cambria, I think."

"That would explain it." Galienne shared her friend's basic prejudice: Cambria was regarded by the "civilized" populace of Britain as a wild holdout of bygone times, little better than the land of the Picts northward. That the populace of Astolat and Londinium shared the same blood and old culture as the tribes was conveniently ignored, a bias made stronger by centuries of Roman civilization.

They giggled again, the water with its purported healing properties beading off their bodies. Galienne recalled the talk she so wanted to have with her friend, and was so afraid of starting. She chose an unusual approach.

"Lupy, do you know anything about heraldry?"

Lupy raised her brows. "Not really, but I can identify some of the designs. The shields and banners are always so colorful and proud."

"Do you have any idea what the arms of those two knights, Yvaine and Lamorak, look like?"

She did, and not just a rough idea. Lupinia gave a colorful description of Yvaine's shield design, with a similar background to Gawaine's, as they were kinsmen. She'd never seen Lamorak's, but relayed what she had heard.

The color drained from Galienne's face. It was *them*: the knights she saw in the vision! Not any dream, but an actual, vivid vision. She had seen them charge into Garmani lands, leading the lesser knights and the Logres footsoldiers to an easy victory, hacking and looting the bodies as they slew. She shivered. She actually *saw* it all!

"What's wrong?" Lupinia queried, concerned.

Galienne shook her head unconvincingly. "It's nothing. Forget I asked."

"It's obviously not nothing. You look terrified."

"Look, it's all right. Please, Lupy." *I'll tell you later. Someday.*

"Fine, then. Let me know if you change your mind." Galienne nodded. "Listen, I meant what I said."

"What's that?" she said faintly. The fear was starting to recede.

"About coming with me to Camelot. We'll go check out the scenery, take your worries away, and just have fun for a few days. How else can we improve our lives if we don't go out to take our chances?"

Galienne smiled in agreement, but still felt the fear. How could she see what she saw?

* * *

Oerfa was not a large community, and it felt even smaller now to Dindraine and her brother. This was home, the center of their lives, and Perceval knew that he now wanted to leave it behind. He had always wanted to follow the clouds and let them lead him where they would, but now he just felt sad, this business with their mother facing him.

The *rath* itself was active as usual for this time at night. The wattle and daub huts all glowed from the fires built within them to heat and light up the night (not that heat was required after such a warm day). Oerfa lay securely situated among four hills, each of which went several hundred feet to their summits. The tiny village was entirely surrounded by a ring of eight-foot high wooden posts, each sporting a sharpened tip to discourage eavesdropping. Land devoted to grazing and minimal farming lay beyond this protective ring.

Just south of the hill nearest the ford, adjacent to the village, stood a small forest. It still seemed huge to the youngsters, since they were many miles from the large Cambrian forests, like the Arroy. Nestled halfway up a hill beyond these light woods was Kundry the witch's abode. She was content to keep to herself, and the villagers for the most part ignored her.

They neared Oerfa's peaceful collection of thirteen huts of earth and wood, in which lived a clan called Gwydd. Its assorted members were listening to a night's entertainment: Tathan the bard was musically telling another of his endless stories, although they had to get close to discern which tale he might be sharing. He had left years ago in hopes of becoming a druid, traveling to the sacred island of Mona to the north, but was judged to lack the requisite natural magickal ability, or so he said. Still, the villagers loved him, and never tired of listening to the stories of Arianhrod and Bran and the mystical land of Annwn. His tales were largely restricted to the myths and legends of Cambria and the Cymru peoples, though Donngal had brought with him the Irish stories of Cu Chulain and the Morrigan, and so many others. Tathan indeed knew about knights and ladies and castles, but his silence regarding these matters had been purchased by Perceval's mother.

Such was Oerfa, total population thirty-nine, plus several dozen sheep and even a trio of horses, each owned by a different family. All save Tathan, Donngal the Irishman, Perceval, Dindraine, and their mother were related by blood or marriage. Their *rath* was just one of hundreds existing across Cambria, relatively

untouched by foreign influences. Everyone, however, partici-
pated in the seasonal festivities; the Summer Solstice had passed
several weeks before, and they were approaching Lughnasadh,
to mark the harvest season. There was not a large harvest in
this settlement, but Cymru seldom passed a chance to partake
of festivities, and these souls taxed Gwyddnyn the brewer's abilities regularly. Fertile Mother Earth had aged into a dying crone,
and there was a mass storing, baking, and brewing of grain for
the Lady who would replace her in the spring, after the shadowy
death of Samhain.

　　　Perceval and Dindraine led their guests between two of
the hills, noticing the familiar glow from inside the perimeter
of dead but protective elms as the inhabitants prepared their
evening meals over small fires. The *rath* welcomed the strangers,
saw them set up camp in the pen of Perceval and Dindraine's
mother. The party relished listening to the bard continue, even
anxious Clydno. Presently, the youths missed their guests, hearing Tathan outside their hut relating the story of a magickal cauldron. They had heard this tale before, and paid little heed to it
now. The cauldron could supposedly grant new life to those
who perished heroically in battle, the bard said, and it was kept
safely away by three trios of maiden guardians in the Underworld kingdom of Annwn. Apparently a great king had gone
off to claim it, and at this point in the telling his ships were being
destroyed by the Underworldly sea leading to Annwn.

　　　Perceval reserved judgment as to the legend's truthful-
ness. He indeed heard a good share of mythology from this
minstrel Tathan, but he remained skeptical about it generally, as
with all spiritual affairs. After all, he had never witnessed any of
the Cymru deities emerging in Cambria to work their wonders,
nor did he know anyone who could claim so. Who cared what
the gods did? He was as far removed from them as he could
imagine. What might the gods care for the pursuits which had
engaged his time for the years of his life? Actually, living in

Oerfa was not quite so dull as Perceval's attitude at that moment would make it seem. He already had learned much which was lost in the cities, where nature was forgotten, built over, struggled against.

Perceval could build a shelter from the trees, just by using their dead branches and shed leaves. He could ride a horse, milk a cow, and tend sizable groups of sheep and even shear them for their valuable wool, a tradable commodity in the hills. He could train a dog to stay with him while he hunted down prey. He could make fishing hooks from twigs and use woven grasses for lines. His appetite for learning was enormous.

Dindraine followed him endlessly, like the dogs. They even went to the neighboring villages together, sometimes learning some new trick or skill from the local residents. They always knew Mother became edgy when they traveled at all; they assumed she was just concerned for their safety. Dindraine, for her part, had learned a bit of herb lore, and already could identify a large number of local flora. She knew which plants could be used for eating, spicing, healing, and which should be avoided. The bit of the healer's touch she knew came compliments of Tathan, imparted to her and her friend, Nia.

But this was no time for fond recollections. They were both angry and afraid from their mother's response to their curious guests. They had set about seeing Lamorak nestled securely off to the side of the house, which lay just beyond the *rath*. No more did he moan or make any sound beyond his breath. While Clydno had balled up an extra blanket for him to use as a pillow, Perceval and Dindraine's mother fetched a thin red ribbon from her precious chests. She brought it over to the knight and tied it about his head, muttering, "I fear I'm not much of a healer, but I can offer faith. He'll be all right, I'm sure."

As she fastened the ribbon and Clydno tucked the pillow under his master's head, she had recited the prayer. "In the name of the Father, of the Son, and of the Holy Spirit, let the fever go from thy head, the wounds from thy body, O knight, and be thou healed." She added an "amen," echoed by Clydno.

"Thank you, gentle lady," Yvaine offered weakly, feeling exhausted now. "We are in your debt." They had left in silence immediately afterwards.

Now Dindraine looked nervously at Perceval while their mother ladled up the evening meal: garlic roasted trout and potatoes with herbs, and apple juice spiced with cinnamon. The drink was the children's favorite, easily come by in the Severn valley. Dindraine normally would have pounced on the liquid, but suddenly did not want to be there for what might ensue while she drank. Yet she really didn't want to miss it, either, and was too hungry to give it much further thought. Mother had worked hard at preparing the meal, just like always. The smell of the food made them forget about their prone houseguest.

They all began eating, Perceval barely touching his food, playing with it instead, wishing his humble supper knife was three feet longer like the swords knights carried. Dindraine almost inhaled her share down in grotesquely large gulps, while their mother ate daintily, with the most delicate table manners.

Perceval couldn't stand it any more. "Mother," he began, while at the sound Dindraine raised her head and stopped chewing, a wad of mushy potatoes in her cheeks.

He looked back at Dindraine before continuing. "Mother, why are you so opposed to their being here?"

"Does it matter? I was worried about the two of you, that's all."

Perceval gestured to the sleeping form that Dannedd and Cabal had already taken to guarding. "He is Sir Lamorak. You wouldn't let me say that earlier, but that's who he is, and... Mother, what is it?"

The woman who bore and raised him paled before his eyes. He thought she would have dropped her spoon and its contents into her lap had her arms not already been resting at the table; she hadn't much appetite.

Perceval hoped he would never again experience the utter silence that immediately followed his words. It was the kind of dead silence which is really *too* quiet, because it's only a matter of time until something shatters it, as if the silence craved disruption.

Just above this quiet, they could all just barely hear Tathan's voice from outside, but it was incoherent to them now, only adding to the tension. For him to project so much, he must have reached quite an exciting part of his story. Perceval again doubted that tale of the cauldron.

Dindraine just watched, trying to anticipate the next action, terrified of whatever form it might take. She finally noticed her unswallowed food and promptly sent it down to her stomach, with some help from a swig of the apple juice; she was afraid of choking on a combination of the food and the silence.

It was really only several seconds before Mother spoke; for the two younger people it might as well have been days. "I-I beg your pardon, son, but what exactly did you say?" *It can't be him. I won't look at the man, not now.* Her voice sounded as scratchy as his had, like she was choking on her words.

He tried to sound as strong as possible, but his voice came nervously, almost pubescent. "As I say, Mother, Sir Lamorak. Traveling with Sir Yvaine and their squires. They've come all the way from, oh, where was it now?"

"Camelot," Dindraine added, finally finding her voice, and appreciating her brother's obvious invitation to the discussion. "Yvaine told me a little while ago that Lamorak is from these parts, and they've come looking for something."

Mother froze, jaw hanging agape; mouths dropping to the floor in utter shock was truly a family trait. She looked away, not bothering to compose herself. She glared at Dindraine, who looked down at her bowl, as though staring at her dinner could lighten the situation. Dannedd, named for his huge teeth, came over to her drooping hand and licked it. Aside from that, there was the agonizing silence.

Perceval's mother finally looked back at him. "The King's own knights," she started. "The very finest in the world. What did you say to them?"

"I, no, we," Perceval said, Dindraine looking back up at the mention of her inclusion in matters, thankful even though the gesture might bring her trouble later.

Perceval went on, "We simply talked with them about who they were and where they were going. It seems they have some vicious monster to kill." Perceval smiled at the last few words. Unlike his usual agnosticism, he was almost ready to consider the creature; the promise of fortune and glory could make one believe a great many fanciful things. Desire for knighthood talking or no, he thought there might be something to some of those stories after all.

Perceval thought he might as well finish what was on his mind. "And, Mother, I wish to be a knight. I want nothing else and nothing less than that. If I present myself to the King at his Court, I'm sure he'll see that I am worthy of it. Well, I think I'm worthy. Or at least I could be." The words came out fast this time; he was determined to settle this once and for all.

He managed to look into her eyes, and he thought he saw anger, but more than that, fear as well. He did not want to hurt her, but his mind was made. *And*, he thought, *she has kept this from me so long; she must have seen it coming.*

"Well, then. How quickly you've decided your destiny!" she snapped. "What do you think you know about this, anyway? You have no idea at all of what you're saying. You ignorant, foolish child! Have you even stopped to consider how I would get along without a son?"

There it was, cold as month-old snow, the guilt he had anticipated. And a disturbing lack of reference to how well Dindraine would fare without a brother. "Mother —" he began.

"Don't 'Mother' me boy! By Saint Albans, you're not leaving Oerfa and you'll never be a knight because you're needed here, not out in the wilderness running about waving weapons at things. And, that, dear boy, is the end of the discussion."

During duress, this woman swore in the names of those closer to her true religion. As for Perceval, he hated to be called *boy*. Cymru males prided themselves on becoming men, and Perceval was already blooded by the hunt.

Dindraine sat totally silent, watching the scene like a prowling cat. She would remember all of this. A vague sense of finality about the whole episode crept into her soul. She resumed eating, and found some comfort in petting Dannedd while she sat at the table. She was not at all surprised when her mother rose and stormed out of the hut, knocking over her chair in the process, and almost tripping over the poor knight as well.

Perceval did not wish to confront the woman again. He contented himself to picking up the crude dishes and remains of the food, taking them over to where he could feed the well-behaved dogs. They eagerly set about lapping up the leftovers, and licked the bowls clean in seconds. Perceval felt drained, but then it had certainly been a rare day. He and Dindraine stretched out on the bed and lay there, not talking, with the satisfied pets at their feet. Dindraine was wondering just how much her mother loved her, and Perceval was thinking about the clouds.

And both of them watched Lamorak in his slumber, wondering silently about tomorrow.

"We should go after her," Dindraine said at last.

"Why? So she can yell at us again?" Dindraine liked how, even through his anger, he still included her in his thoughts.

"I think we need to confront her about a lot," she added absently, making another brief check of Lamorak. He actually did seem a bit more restful, like he knew he was safely within shelter.

"I know we do. I'm just not sure I'm ready."

Dindraine finally allowed herself to relax about the injured stranger next to her on the floor. "You're ready to become a knight, aren't you? How could dealing with Mother be any worse?"

He looked at her, his eyes smiling. "True enough. Let me ask you something."

"What?"

"Do you believe in what I'm doing?"

"I'm not the one who really has to."

For all he teased her, Perceval had to admire his sister's maturity. Or perhaps she viewed things from a certain perspective he lacked. "I mean it, Dindraine. What do you think of all this?"

She gazed again at the knight. She would not weep again; that wasn't what her brother needed right then. "Perceval, I believe in you. I even want to go with you, but Mother always said how knights don't travel with ladies."

"I wouldn't even know," Perceval admitted, knowing he had much to learn about the path he'd chosen.

"Then we have to talk with her, now, while all of this is still out before us. I don't want to pretend any more. I want to grow up and become something."

"Like what?"

"I don't know yet. It's just that I see you here, tonight, full of this fire that you've never had before. I want to feel that, too."

"I think you will. Look at the way you handled Lamorak here."

"Oh, that was nothing. While you were learning to hunt, Tathan showed me something of caring for the sick. I don't know much at all, really, just some of the signs."

"But you looked after him so well. You were great."

"Thanks," she said, with a twinge of the family sheepishness. Then, with sudden seriousness, "If you become a knight and then get yourself killed, I'll never forgive you."

"Never. You and Mother will be proud of me. I promise."

Beside them, Cabal and Dannedd came over to stand guard over Lamorak's prone form. Nothing would disturb him while they remained there.

"Come on," Perceval said, standing. "Let's go get this over with."

They weren't surprised to find their mother had refrained from going into the *rath* itself; she was never one for close company like that. Besides, Tathan could still be heard strumming his beloved harp strings, and Mother had always considered him too nosy. The knightly visitors lay encamped near the sheep herd, and so she had wandered outside the perimeter of both *rath* and farm, and her children found her just sitting near the west hill.

"Mother," Perceval began, trying to sense if her mood had changed.

She didn't stir at first, but when they tried to gain her attention, she slowly stood, brushed her hair out of her face, and fell into Perceval's arms. She didn't sob, but just let herself become dead weight against him.

Dindraine stood next to them, awaiting her own turn to comfort her mother. For now at least, she did not care that her brother always seemed to be the first to receive her affections; she only wanted this to be resolved. Besides, she was still trying to believe that this woman had deceived them both so. She *loved* the old talks about Camelot and the other faraway lands, about the fearless knights and the colorful tournaments and markets. It always sounded so exciting, such a change from the farm girl's life she had led. She was not the only member of this family who craved something different; what would her mother's response be when she learned that she could lose her daughter eventually as well? *No,* she thought: *lose* is not the right word. *Release, that's it.*

Her mother began to collect herself emotionally, still hanging onto Perceval, her insides starting to untie themselves. Her previous tears were already beginning to dry, though she certainly did not want to release her son yet. *Not ever,* Dindraine thought. *Her hold on us is strong; but she'll have to let us go.*

"Oh, son," Mother said, "I tried so hard to keep these foolish ideas from you. There is so much more to a man's life than being a knight. They think they own the world, when all they really do is die young." She lifted her head from Perceval's chest, gazing into his face while still clutching his shoulders. They felt tense to her, and very strong. She also tried to forget that this "little boy" in front of her was almost a fully grown man, already several inches taller than she, with a man's thicker muscles. She tried not to notice the coarse hairs on his face, that he shaved as best he could with stones, and concentrated on his eyes.

"Mother, I —" he began, then cut it off. Dindraine could see he still looked exhausted, almost ready to collapse right there on the hill among the sheep. He could have, too; he briefly considered how comfortable and deliciously cool the grass looked under the moonlight. But he knew they weren't finished yet. He had to make his mother understand, no matter how it might hurt her. He glanced at Dindraine, who sensed what he was about to do, and she nodded her support. *At least she's on my side,* he thought.

"Mother, look, please, I beg of you. All my life I've been told that this valley and some of the neighboring countryside and a few more villages and even some island to the west is almost the whole world. Tonight I find out that I was mistaken, that there are people traveling through these parts who are from far-off places, places that I want to see. That I *need* to see. Don't you understand that? Did you think you could keep me locked up with the sheep my whole life? Is that what you wanted? To have a son who was so much of an idiot he didn't even know about lands to the east and south?" He had to get everything out at once.

His mother released him completely during his tirade, and ashamedly looked down. She no longer wished to see his face at all. That only fueled Perceval's anger. The more he thought about what was on his mind, the more upset he became. She had *lied* to him! And so had all the other villagers, for that matter, probably at her request. No wonder they used to look at him like he was the village idiot. That was precisely how he felt.

He forced himself to sound calm, his expression a mask devoid of any hint of emotion. "I am leaving. With your support or without it. I wish to be a knight. All my life I wished I could leave this place, and go off and do something great. And now I have my chance, and all you want to do is keep me here! Dindraine can tend the sheep. *Anyone* can tend the blessed sheep. All they do is walk and eat." He waved his arms up and down twice during this, as if trying to fly.

From around him came the sound of several sheep *bah*-ing their displeasure at his remarks. Dindraine almost laughed. *Anything to break the tension*, she thought nervously. Her brother had never been this worked up before, not that she could remember, anyway.

"Mother, " he started again. He looked at her as his flailing stopped. Maybe he had said enough. No, he still wasn't done, although he could feel some of the anger leaving him. The sight of his mother standing there in front of his rage, clenching her fists to resist crying, was taking the fight out of him.

He sounded just slightly more relaxed. "I'm leaving, Mother. When the knights depart, I shall kiss you and my lovely sister good-bye, and I shall be off. And in one year I shall return to tell of my adventures."

He already *sounds* like a knight, Dindraine thought, almost proudly. And she had never heard him refer to her as lovely. *What a heart-breaker he'll be.* She almost laughed again, then stifled it on the thought that he had already broken one. Dindraine would miss him terribly, and wondered how her mother would cope with his promised absence. Not well. Indeed, she resumed resistance.

"You can't go!" she protested, her already red, swollen eyes tearing up again. "You're my only son. I already lost your father and brother this way. Please." It was not like her to beg. Plead, often; argue, definitely, but not grovel.

"I already told you I will return soon." Perceval crossed his arms, not wanting to be further defied. He already considered the debate to be ended.

But, wait, he frowned; *what was that she just said?* "Brother? What are you talking about? If ever I deserved to hear the truth about my father, about my family, now is the time."

She looked to Dindraine and found no support; they really were brother and sister, even if they were really only halfway related. She was not about to also tell of Dindraine's father; she already had to confront one rebellious child tonight, and another would be unbearable. She would not talk so quickly again. Not after tonight. Not ever again, to the likes of these two. She gave them everything, and they slapped her in the face for it.

She noticed Perceval, still standing there, arms crossed and flexed, demanding an explanation without asking for one verbally. "Oh, very well, I'll tell you," came her hostile consent, knowing she really did owe them both the truth; *children have a right to know about their true lineage,* she thought. *Fine, if that's how they want it, then the truth they shall receive.*

"Your brother was only a child when I was forced to leave home. I no longer know of his whereabouts, and it has been many years since I left. Your father was a great knight." *And a king, but you don't need to know that now.*

Perceval's eyes were wide, and his arms fell to his sides. Seeing his relaxation, and that Dindraine had crossed over to her brother's side, their mother continued with the whole story. Occasionally Dindraine looked over at Perceval, with an incredulous expression, but he never acknowledged her glances. He was far too engrossed in this old tale to pay attention to anything else. He looked just as dopey as when he had listened to Yvaine. No, that wasn't quite it. Dindraine thought her brother always looked dopey; dreamy, yes, that was it. And somehow he looked a bit older as well, with the face of a man. She could tell this was all going straight to his head. And who could blame him? She confessed to herself that she did not fully understand this apparently uniquely male infatuation with the sounds of clanging metal, but she did believe that a person should be free to follow his dreams.

Or hers, she thought. She was trying to listen to her mother, telling of love won and lost, of a kingdom that had actually shaken off the yoke of paternal rule, and the evil which later terrorized it, and found herself distracted by her own daydreaming. She was most intrigued by the part about a rebellion being led by women, although her mother's voice suggested that she thought it inconsequential.

Dindraine heard a wonderful story once, from Tathan (who took her aside and told it to *her* and her alone, bless him), about a Cymru woman far to the east, who rebelled against the *Romans* of all people! She loved that story. She tried to imagine that tribal queen, riding her chariot defiantly through the lines of shocked Centurions, taking her own revenge for their thievery of her land and rape of her daughters. Dindraine smiled. Yes, the righteous revenge was definitely the best part. And now her mother's story was winding down.

Perceval wasted no time responding. He had sat down on the grass while listening, mother and sister following his lead, and they were in a small family circle, meeting together for what might be the last time, for a while. At length he addressed her. "Mother, the knights we met this very evening were after the same beast as my father, the one you just described. They said it was a truly terrible sight, and they had come all this way from Camelot to hunt it down and kill it like the plague it is."

Plague? thought Dindraine.

Mother hardly heard him. She was visibly nervous, her hands clasped tightly into her lap. "You must promise me one thing, my son," she said. "You must swear to me that you shall never reveal your true blood to anyone. Your father Pellinore, bless his soul," she said while crossing herself, "had certain enemies, people who would all too gladly kill you if they knew who you actually were." *Such is the way of chivalry, damn it to hell.*

"But why?" came Perceval's ignorant retort. "Why would knights, men of honor and reputation, kill me because I am the son of a certain knight?" He was beginning to wonder just what the implications might be for his noble status. "Sirs Yvaine and Lamorak would never do such a thing."

His mother cringed at the mention of their names. Perceval thought she was just still showing her offense at her son's decision. But Dindraine saw right through it: her mother knew something else that she desperately wanted not to tell.

"Just swear to me!" Mother commanded, her face noticeably reddening in the moonlight. Perceval leaned back slightly, as though he could dodge the harshness of her imperative.

"All right," he surrendered, hoping to calm her.
"Let me hear you say it."

He thought about it, and it occurred to him that he did not really know how to swear an oath. He thought this might be good practice for knighthood, however. He said, "I do hereby most solemnly swear," mimicking part of another of Tathan's stories, though he could not recall which.

His mother cut him off with a wave of her hand. "No, no. That's not how. That sounds like something you heard from that old bard. Try this: 'I swear by my name and soul under the eyes and ears of our Lord Jesus Christ, that I shall obey my mother's words.'" She brought the waving hand to her breast for the ritual.

Perceval slapped his hand to his chest with all the rigor of a Centurion, and repeated the words. Dindraine sat in silence, apprehensive by the display; she never thought her mother such a devout Christian, yet here she was, invoking the name of their deity.

No wonder those Pagan women revolted, she thought; she knew something of this new religion, and she didn't like it. How could a woman follow a sacred path which degraded her by definition? She recalled another story of how the Christians viewed creation (thank goodness for such a well-versed bard, and it was a good thing for her Tathan never succeeded in his druidical studies!) What was it they called it? *Jensis,* or something. And there was a total paradise, with just one happy couple, but it was the woman's fault for it ending. There was something about a snake, too, but how could a woman and a snake destroy utopia? Whatever a snake was; Dindraine thought it sounded despicable. Hadn't the Romans followed this strange religion? And wasn't it about making people feel guilty for "sinning," even if they had yet to do anything?

Such was not the case. Perceval took this all very seriously, considering this crude ceremony a precursor to the status he hoped for, though he did agree with his sister in her assessment of this religion. But he did not want to make any mistakes, especially on his first day of what he was already thinking of as his squirehood. He had not bothered to consider that his mother had tricked him. He had sworn on his immortal soul (if what the Christians and Pagans alike said was true) to heed his mother's "words," and her words were far from over.

"And now then, dear boy," she said, "if you are to be off in such a hurry, it is my responsibility to prepare you for your journey, to the best of my ability."

"Please tell me, Mother. Let me say first how pleased I am with your acknowledgment of my departure," came his proud answer. Dindraine thought he was trying too hard. She also speculated that all of this was too easy; she and Perceval had expected more of a contest with their mother about his decision.

Instead, she continued with her hasty lesson. "These are the things I believe you must know, if you are to be a knight." Her eyes no longer looked so worn; indeed, they seemed almost eager, for the first time that evening.

"First," she said, "whenever you come upon anyone needing your aid, do not hesitate to give it, especially if the needy person is a maiden or girl." *Does she think he'll only encounter virgins?* Dindraine thought, supposing virgins would be the most likely in need of help; she snickered to herself.

"Second," Mother went on, "when you arrive at Court, proceed directly to the main hall (you shall have to ask directions; I have never been there), and ask that the King personally make you a knight."

Perceval nodded gravely. He looked entranced.

"Third, remember that one of the knightly benefits is the right to partake of the hospitality of others, so do not feel ashamed to indulge yourself when opportunity presents itself."

"You mean such things as food, drink, shelter," Perceval said.

"Yes, and anything else you may find of which you may be desirous."

What happens if he encounters a consort of those same needy maidens? wondered Dindraine. She knew her brother was still a virgin, and the thought of him randomly groping people because her mother had seemed to prescribe it was too much. She marveled that Perceval had not found the humor in all this, or at least not shown some embarrassment at what must surely be his other most heartfelt desire, after knighthood; he looked the way she imagined any eager-eyed candidate for knighthood must look: motionless, erect, and oblivious to everything else that might be happening. Like one of their sheep.

"Finally, you must promise me that you will stop and pray in any church, abbey, or holy place you encounter." This last demand sounded the most unusual; *why should he bother praying, especially if he is not the religious one in the family?* Indeed, Dindraine and Perceval had never cared much about religion at all, *any* religion. This all seemed so unnecessarily formal and presumptuous; who cared if a knight prayed, or to which god?

Perceval now looked confused, his brow curling into a slight frown. "What is a church, Mother?"

His mother's jaw lowered. Dumbfounded, she replied, "You will know such a place by a prominent cross somewhere upon it. It shall be obvious. You do remember what I told you about the cross, don't you?"

Perceval nodded. Their mother had not minded finding a heathen village in which to settle after fleeing her old life those many years past, especially since Oerfa's few residents took a liking to her right from the start. Yet she never forgot her childhood beliefs, hoping now that God (*her* God, not these infernal Pagan lesser deities) would protect and bless her son until he returned.

And he *would* return. Her son was literal-minded, and if he really followed this strange advice, he would be laughed back to Oerfa in no time. She did not care. One way or another, she would keep her son.

She leaned across the tiny circle, placing one hand on Perceval's shoulder and the other on his cheek, and said, "Never forget what I have told you this evening, and never forget that you have sworn an oath to obey me. Do not repeat your vows to these other men you have brought to the *rath* tonight, for a knight's oath is his own to keep. If you follow my instructions you shall yourself be a knight in no time, and then you may come to visit your lonely mother."

Apparently she thought Dindraine would not likewise be lonely in Perceval's absence.

"Thank you, Mother," he offered. He embraced her and they rose, Dindraine standing and following as they walked down the hill toward the hut.

* * *

Galienne, many miles to the southeast, was just out of church, and only wanted to be alone. She was so afraid! Was God punishing her?

It should have been another normal Son-day service, with that drone of a priest hammering away from his pulpit at the ornate dais within Astolat's holiest building. Galienne was proud of her faithful devotion, singing loudly with her mother all the hymns selected for that morning, songs taught to children for generations. She was proud to know what the archaic Latin words meant now, but would still not translate the verses for anyone else. Too many of Astolat's youngsters already ridiculed her for that, and Elaine would just not understand.

Lupinia was there, too, sitting two pews forward with her father. Galienne once thought the man would have made a good match for her mother, but Elaine would not have that, either; she was obsessed with Galienne's father. But today was not for dwelling on what might have been. Galienne was too busy enjoying the beauty of the warm, sunny day, engrossed in the sermon's lessons.

And then she began to see some of the congregation in extremely different circumstances, just by glancing at them.

The priest carried on, and she saw him struck down by a Garmani axe, with hordes of the barbarians streaming through the city's walls. She shook her head, focused on the words, and looked again. "…as a man thinketh in his heart, so is he…" She heard the voice clearly, not caring about the translated passage; she knew the Book well enough to recognize the text of Proverbs.

The priest looked fine: no head wound, no death scream. Galienne glanced next to her, at Elaine. Her mother smiled back. But something in Galienne's mind made the smile a deathly grimace: suddenly her mother appeared floating on the water, holding a weapon. But there was no wound to her body. It looked as though she drowned, then floated downstream.

Galienne's breathing sped, and she willed herself to look away, towards the double doors leading outside. They were to the rear, and Galienne caught the curious gazes of some of the other parishioners. *What are you looking at, spoiled brat?* she almost thought she could hear them say. *What's the matter, child? Have you never before seen the deaths of people?*

She looked forward again. *Please, Father, let Bishop Baudwin know how to better face these visions! Will these things come to pass? What am I to do with this knowledge?*

Presently she was at the bridge once more, watching the water flow. Perhaps that was part of why she so loved this place: the water always looked the same, lively and free.

She still couldn't tell anyone else about these things. Not her mother, not even Lupinia; only the bishop. It was like when Lupinia confirmed her vision of the knights who recently passed near the city. She wondered if she could recognize them if she saw them. What on earth might she say? *I saw you ride by, you know, even though I was miles away, and I might stand accused of witchcraft for even telling you.*

Thank God Baudwin has never betrayed my confidence. She thought King Arthur had located the most honorable representative of God in Christendom for his ability to listen, and to judge very carefully. He took one of the better known biblical passages most gravely: "Judge not, lest you be judged in return." Even he had been suspicious of her tales at first, until she offered him proof.

She still clearly remembered their talk that day, last year. It was an even larger gamble for her, to speak of politics openly, but Baudwin knew the girl to speak her mind. "King Marcus' nephew will continue to betray him with his wife."

The bishop of Camelot was stunned, but made sure she could not hear so in his voice. "Continue? I was unaware this had already happened."

"Why then do you think that the High King always sends the nephew off on some urgent mission whenever Marcus and his lovely Isolde visit Camelot?" Galienne didn't even realize this nephew of King Marcus was the same "beautiful Sir Trystan" Lupinia mentioned to her in the Astolat bathhouse.

Baudwin considered it, knowing that Isolde had a reputation as the loveliest woman in Britain. Sure enough, Marcus himself gave confession during their last visit, when he made known his suspicions. The bishop thought he sounded like a man looking to justify removing his nephew from Dumnonia forever, by having an influential person in Camelot know ahead of time. Whatever the case, Baudwin's own suspicions were laid aside. Since then he had worked to help Galienne deal with her visions; he still sought a constructive venue for them. Neither of them wanted people seeking her out, wanting to know the year they would die, or whether it would be a good planting season. It was easy for him to keep her secret safe.

But even around the bishop, she remained cautious. She saw her father, she saw the King and Queen. She had envisioned a time when people with such insight would be tortured and executed horribly as heretics, and she believed in her faith as fervently as she knew how! Would God permit that? How could His followers face such atrocities, and when might this all happen?

But what to do now? She was terrified, didn't know where else to turn, and wanted nothing more than to return to Camelot again to talk with her confidant.

Sometimes she had nightmares about these things. Galienne never felt sure of which visions would truly come to pass, and which might be simple dreams.

The problem was, how could she differentiate between the two?

PART TWO: THE ERRANTS

Brownie was the name Dindraine had gi en to the tall and strong sumpter her mother bought for them four years earlier. Mother said she wanted them both to learn to ride, even though there were only so many places horses could really go in Cambria: most of the hills were so treacherous as to forbid their safe passage by horses. The expansive, arterial network of roads built by the Imperial invaders was the best way to navigate the area, on horseback or foot.

Perceval and Dindraine both eagerly took to the saddle back then, arguing over whose turn it was to ride next. Brownie put up with it stoically, and took a liking to both children, although she never became very fond of the dogs, especially Dannedd, who usually ran along just to try and scare her.

Perceval thought Dindraine and his mother handled his departure with relative calm. There were no more tears shed, just the hands of three dozen people waving as he rode off eastward for the road which would take him to Camelot. He appreciated how the whole village had shown up to see him off, and on such short notice, though such attention made him anxious; never mind that people leaving Oerfa was a rare experience and they tended to send everyone off the same way. He had the family horse, and a handful of imperial silver denarius coins from his mother's precious and previously unknown stockpile.

Besides him, of course, Yvaine and his entourage had already left, earlier that same morning. Mother complained of sleeping not at all the night Lamorak spent in their hut, and she insisted that if they were to stay longer, the wounded knight would have to join his comrades in the pen. This he did, for just one more night. He looked better earlier this morning, rested, but still out of it as Yvaine and the squires led him off in the litter. Yvaine did not wish to further antagonize his hostess, and Dindraine made sure her mother was not present as she presented him with some prepared dressings and a salve. She agreed Lamorak already looked much improved, but was still silently furious at her mother's insistence that the knights leave so quickly.

Accordingly, Dindraine and her brother had precious little time to spend with their guests that second day. Perceval did talk with Yvaine long enough to hear more tales, and reinforce his new obsession. Yvaine told him of Arthur's conquest of what was now Logres, and the ensuing peace.

"But how do all the Round Table knights busy themselves, if there's no war?" Perceval asked.

Yvaine laughed. "Let me tell you something of tournaments and courtly love affairs, lad," and so he did. Perceval beamed. "You'll be a fine knight," Yvaine said, thinking, *he already knows how to have fun.*

This was not merely a week-long ride, but a week of totally new sights and experiences. Perceval rode east; Yvaine headed northwest. Perceval's dream had materialized; he felt like he was riding on the clouds at last! He barely noticed Brownie's steps. She was eager herself, having spent too little time roaming.

His mother had prepared him as best she could: he had her money, her cross, and her love. He lightly rubbed the cross again, wondering just how God might intervene in the lives of mortals (*or the gods*, he thought, confused by the multiplicity of deities he had heard about). He tried to imagine what a miracle must be like. He had heard of wondrous, impossible things happening, supposedly by the hands of the divine: lightning flashes in the nighttime sky, animals who could talk like people, and endless riches for the one lucky or persistent enough to track a rainbow to its end. It sounded like nonsense to him. Life itself felt miraculous enough.

He also had a new javelin. Melangell had entered the barn two nights earlier as he and Dindraine had readied Brownie, and she gave him one from her own stockpile, free of charge. He thanked her profusely, promising to master it and keep it always at the ready. She had come to groom her own horse Windrider, and wished Perceval luck. He thought it funny that she had never really spoken to him much before, yet showed a genuine interest in his affairs during the night. She joked with him that if King Arthur needed a new smith, she'd gladly accept the offer.

So now he was ready, he thought. Mother had given him a store of dried food, fruits and nuts, and bread and salted lamb, enough to last many days, and he had two rolled up blankets and extra clothes to keep behind him atop Brownie. He reminded himself that he had promised to return after a year, but was too preoccupied to think much of it.

Dindraine and his mother had both kissed and embraced him farewell, Dindraine stepping up on her tiptoes to peck his nose. He loved that gesture; it was her way of telling him that she was his best friend, and that she would sorely miss him. It had all transpired so fast!

At Brownie's side marched Cabal. He was the only one to truly start whimpering as his master began riding. His yowling grew so piercing and so pitiful that Perceval's mother had gestured for him to follow, yelling "keep him safe" as he followed.

He loved his mother for that. Dindraine would still have Dannedd, who, while perhaps the less friendly of the pair in general, would gladly die for the girl. Besides, he thought, a huge dog at his side would impress a measure of both wealth and protection. Who knew what awaited them in these hills?

Mother went over the directions time and again, until Perceval memorized them. They were simple enough; he would stick to well-traveled major roads, even the Royal Road to Camelot itself, once he drew close enough. His mother had not liked the idea of his probable encounters with many folk along the way, but at least the roads were the safest way to travel.

Of course, this particular route would take him through some dense parts of the Arroy Forest, and except for the roads, few dared to travel such parts. Perceval did not mind this in the least. He would get to see more trees and bushes and wildlife than he had ever imagined, and he would finally get to set foot on flatter land as well. The Cambrian hills ended where the heavy forests began, and he could not wait to get there, to get to *any* of this great land. His smile had never been so deeply etched upon his face.

Cabal barked at him occasionally, and constantly wandered just off the road to sniff at something. That was fine with Brownie, content to just walk as long as Perceval would take her. All three of them enjoyed the change of pace and scenery. Perceval was simply glad to be alive, to feel the light wind rustling his long hair, to yell as loud as he could and not worry about who might hear him, to stop whenever he wanted to do whatever he pleased.

He began by following the Severn around the hills until it met up with its other branches. It was easy to navigate this way; the river meandered between the various rolling hills, the occasional wild animals drinking from it or running scared at his approach. All the first day was slow but pleasant going, since he still had to be careful with Brownie.

Near dusk, the road appeared, like a lost friend rediscovered. It consisted of rocks a foot or so across fitted together, wide enough to accommodate a good six riders at once. Perceval was intrigued with the way it just came to a dead halt; its builders had chosen not to extend it further west. Perceval decided it would be a wonderful place to make camp.

The first night under the stars, with just Cabal and Brownie to keep him company, would remain one of his favorite memories. It seemed that no one else existed in the whole world, and the three of them could just stretch out and enjoy themselves. Cabal promptly brought down a rabbit, and Brownie contented herself with grazing on the local flora. Perceval managed to build a fire by rubbing two sticks together in the manner he had learned as a child, and dismembered the hare with his small knife, saving his food stores. Cabal liked the meat cooked. Perceval thought he had never tasted sweeter flesh. When the two of them finished the rabbit, Perceval sighed, munching on some nuts while petting the contented dog. The sound of his crunching might as well have been the only noise in the world.

He slept with Cabal on the rolled out blankets, using one as a mattress and the other as cover. When he lay down beside his animal companions, listening to the familiar insects chirping and evening bird cries, he counted endless shimmering stars until he fell asleep.

The next day they hit the road. It was easy going, and Brownie appreciated not having to gauge every step she took. Perceval beamed when he saw the castle late in the day, not even a mile from the road.

It seemed like Rhun must surely have been the largest fort in the world, but Perceval would come to learn that it was actually among the smallest. It consisted of a tower surrounded by a circular wall, inhabited by a mere handful of beings. From a distance Perceval wondered if the villagers were mistaken, if this was not the glorious Camelot itself, despite its lying twenty or so more days away. He was not at all disappointed when he found out it was merely an outpost of Chief Belinans.

The chief was not here, to be sure, but he had left a castellan in charge of the garrison. Two guards on the wall hailed Perceval as he came into their view.

"Ahoy there, good traveler. And who might you be seeking, eh?" asked one of them, sounding excited by the prospect of company. Or a new enemy to kill.

The other guard nudged him in the ribs, and said, unheard by Perceval, "Fool! Don't you know you only say 'ahoy' when aboard ship, and not when you're on top of a hill?"

Perceval watched them bicker, and waited until he was within easier earshot to attempt a reply. They looked at him when he called, their ranting interrupted.

"Hello! My name is Perceval, and I am on my way to Camelot to become a knight," he shouted, after trying to think of something important to say.

The two guards stopped elbowing each other. "Camelot, eh? That's a long way from here, now, isn't it?" asked the same one who could apparently not distinguish land from sea.

"Yes, I realize that," Perceval said, remembering his mother and hospitality, "and I would like to request shelter and a hot meal this evening."

"So who are you really, now, 'Persuhvill'? We're hardly in a position to grant such favors in this part of the countryside, so why don't you just run along?" This from the first one again, clearly the more obnoxious of the pair.

"But I am going to become a knight, and sit at King Arthur's own table." Perceval was concerned; shouldn't he be shown some respect? Hospitality alone prescribed a warmer welcome than this.

The guards looked at each other and began laughing, hard and coarse; they sounded much like Yvaine had three days ago. The men cackled, pointed, and vainly tried to speak.

Perceval was angry; it had been in fun when the others had done this some nights past, but these, these *guards* thought him a buffoon!

Then the half-laughs, half-throaty coughs ceased. Perceval could hear a deeper voice, from within the wall of the shell keep, but muffled and unintelligible to him. He wondered if perhaps that was the guard's superior talking with them about their carrying on so. He hoped they were being suitably chastised.

Perceval tried to understand what was said, watching the two bumpkins gesture and babble to the deeper voice; they had turned their backs to him now. He thought the pair was rapidly losing face, then felt surprised by the consideration.

Face? Tathan used to speak of that. Cymru honor and pride. Why didn't Perceval listen more closely to those tales? It sounded like more knightly virtue, which Sir Yvaine had described as leading to glory. Or something like that.

The guards interrupted his thoughts. "Excuse me, sir, but our master has instructed us to bid you welcome. Won't you come on up to the gate? You are invited to spend the evening, if you like." Perceval thought the second guard at least had some manners; no more reply came from the first one. *And "sir"?* That was what they called knights. He had never been called that before, but liked it.

He rode up to the wall, noticing that the two guards had disappeared, and that the wall was probably only twice as high as himself. This no longer looked like such a domineering fortress, but more like a big stone hut instead. Still, Perceval leaned over to brush his hand against the wall as he rode by it. He had never felt a mason's product before, and he immediately loved the cool hardness of it. These walls certainly had the wattle and daub huts of his home beat.

He gripped the frayed leather reins with both hands again, and saw the gate. It was iron, black as night (where it was not reddish-brown from rust, looking much like the stains of dried blood), and he had never seen so much of the metal in one place before, not even in Melangell's forge. He wondered how many smiths poured their efforts into its creation. He liked how he could look right through it, but it would still keep out everything except arrows and small animals. He tried to imagine how much a place like this might be worth; certainly more than he had.

He dismounted Brownie outside the gate just as it started to slowly rise, creaking along hinges rusted almost to brittleness. Staring at him through the gate was the keep's entire compliment: castellan, the two guards, and twelve others, all men, all wearing local clothing, all looking like they could stand to bathe. And smelling like it, too. Even Brownie winced at the odor of this motley bunch. They wore simple clothes of basic colors, their tunics and loose-fitting breeches done in plaid or spiraling bright and colorful patterns. They did not look like knights.

"Well met, young man!" came the greeting from a man who looked large enough to wrestle down a colt. He was fully bearded, and Perceval felt embarrassed by his lack of heavy facial hair, a source of Cymru male pride, part of the "face" Tathan had vaguely mentioned or the glory Yvaine had tried to explicate. This man was dressed a bit differently from the others: beige leather covered most of his body, with small cracks at the joints. Perceval had never seen cuirboillic armor before, and thought the man moved a bit stiffly in it. He wore a once-white tunic under this, and attention was drawn to the polished and shiny belt buckle around his waist, looking like it was holding in too many extra pounds of flesh.

"I am Amlyn," he continued, "Chief Belinan's castellan here at Castle Rhun, and I am at your service. Do come in, and tell us about your travels." He motioned for Perceval to enter the gate, and he walked in, glaring up at the tower. He had never seen anything so high! It had to be twice the wall's height, with battlements around the top, and windows.

Once inside, the more courteous of the two guards approached Brownie, chirping as he led her away to the back of the tower, where they had a tiny stable. Cabal followed this man, seemingly wanting to watch over the horse, or just to pester her. The men laughed; they enjoyed seeing a dog. No other dogs were here, since they were just extra mouths needing to be fed, and the men themselves lived off the meat they hunted, and very little else.

Perceval was unsure whether he liked being the center of attention like this; they all gawked at him, as though they had not seen another person in years. He wanted to say something, anything, just to break the silence.

"Well, Amlyn, to be truthful, my travels are really just beginning. I have lived all my life in these hills, and I am journeying to Camelot, so that I may become a knight in the service of the King of Logres."

Some of the men glanced at each other, snickering. Amlyn looked surprised. "You mean you've never been to the great city of Camelot before, and this is your first time out of these hills?" The men laughed, sounding good-natured about it. But they still stood there staring.

As though he could sense Perceval's discomfort, Amlyn introduced his small band, identifying them as "so-and-so, son of someone else," in the Cymru fashion. Each man smiled warmly as his name was indicated, and each lightly slapped Perceval's shoulder in salutation. These were traditional tribal warriors, who had an allegiance to Belinans, the Cymru who could unite the local tribes.

The outpost was part of that unity; the tribal warriors looked a bit out of place here. Two different lifestyles had attempted to blend: these tribesmen had come out of the wilderness to staff a location which represented the future. Rhun was really a way for Belinans to show off his face to the local people.

Perceval knew he would never remember everyone's names, except perhaps for the guards, Gwyn and Elffin. He recognized Gwyn right away, the one who greeted him sarcastically; Elffin had just returned from tending Brownie. He would try to hang onto these names as best he could, though; his mother had taught him that he could never know when he might need to remember somebody.

Dusk had already arrived, and the bunch of them retired to the warmth and safety of the tower, the men breaking up into tiny groups, discussing who deserved the most credit for the successful catching of a boar that day, or who had the most attractive and strongest woman back home, or even who might be bested by their visitor if they started their favorite evening pastime again tonight.

The smell of the inside of the tower was disarming; Perceval had never encountered food as pungent as the boar, now a glistening brown hulk roasting on a fire on one side of the tower's interior. There were two long tables with accompanying benches on either side opposite this huge fireplace, a rack against another wall with a variety of melee weapons, and a stone staircase in a corner leading up to the second floor where the men slept. The upper story was a large room strewn with all manner and color of shaggy rugs, some furs and others woven, upon which the odoriferous group slipped into unconsciousness each night. It was not much, but they did not need much, and for now it was home.

Amlyn took a quick liking to his guest, listening to Perceval tell some of the group about his life back home. One thing the Peace of Britain had helped generate among the quarrelsome tribes was a sense of unity as an individual people, different from Romans, Irish, Picts, and particularly Garmani. Now many of the old tribes people referred to themselves simply and proudly as *Cymru*. Cambria was populated by a good five dozen different tribes, relatively indistinguishable from one another to the outsider. There were still the timeless squabbles between this and that tribe, the sheep and cattle raids, the disputes about hunting territories and rights, who slept with whom, and who was ruler of what. Yet despite their quarrels, they generally felt that deep down inside, a Cymru was a Cymru, and thus worthy of respect. So Perceval was welcomed.

The men were a loud, boisterous bunch, and Perceval had to strain both to hear and be heard. Amlyn told him that they were so few because they were so isolated, yet he was proud of his assignment; Belinans himself had entrusted him to keep the peace and a watchful eye on things in this remote part of Powys.

Cabal entertained the men with his antics; he rolled and sat and extended a friendly paw in return for some of the meat. Perceval felt at ease, hoping that the Round Table provided the same sense of fellowship.

"By the way," Amlyn mentioned, "it is the custom of this house that whenever we shelter a man for the night he should participate in the competition which sometimes follows supper."

The boar was quickly vanishing. Perceval was intrigued. Competition? Knights thrived on competition. He liked the sound of it, and considered it a chance to prove himself. "What competition is that?" he queried. Maybe a tournament, like Yvaine described.

"All in good time, lad," Amlyn answered. Next to him, a couple of the men were looking Perceval over and laughing to each other. He did not mind; he would excel in this event, whatever it was, and no one would laugh at him again.

He looked around the room. The men were gathering up their wooden supper bowls (they used no utensils here), sopping up spills with hard bread and eating it, and were already lifting one of the tables and moving it around so that it was against the wall opposite the weapons rack.

Amlyn, Perceval, and Elffin were the last to finish. Elffin liked their guest also; he figured that anyone should be made to feel welcome while traveling through the countryside, especially if alone. He really listened to Perceval's stories of being a shepherd and his family and the people back home. He even felt a bit embarrassed about having laughed at the young man earlier; Perceval seemed very sure of himself, and such a person might succeed on perseverance alone, if nothing else. Elffin had not seen his own home now for months, and was growing weary of Rhun. Any news from the outside was good news.

Some of the others were now clearing off the second table, then moving it, with its lengthy seats, to the side in front of the first. Perceval noticed how the room seemed much larger without the oak tables and benches taking up its middle.

With this done, Amlyn casually strolled to the center of the room; the men, including Perceval, lined the walls, all ready to listen to the castellan.

"And now then, fearless warriors of the tribes of Powys, may we commence, in honor of our guest," he gestured toward Perceval, who tried to smile but only managed to raise his eyebrows, "a demonstration of strength and cunning."

Cheers and extended fists shot up at once. Perceval cheered, but was now feeling out of place again, especially after someone behind him imitated the sound of a bleating sheep. Just what did this competition involve, anyway?

Amlyn slowly, methodically, turned in place, raising his fist to his chin. A light chuckle arose in the men; they had seen him do this many times, and all were wondering how the selections would go tonight.

He pointed to one man, a lanky, nearly seven-foot blond named Brugyn, whose chest and forearms were covered in inky blue, swirling tattoos (about a third of these men were in the habit of wearing garments for the torso only when the weather absolutely demanded it). He grinned when pointed to, and was cheered and clapped on the back as he stepped out next to Amlyn.

Again Amlyn turned, slowly, fist to chin, and everyone except one person knew whom he would point to next. Yet Perceval was not surprised when it was him. Again came the cheers, though not quite so enthusiastic, since they were, after all, applauding a stranger who had yet to prove himself.

And now the chance to do just that presented itself.

Perceval cautiously came to the center of the room. Cabal came over to his master when he saw he was the center of attention, and licked his hand. The men roared with laughter. Perceval blushed, but was pleased his dog always looked out for him. With a light hand motion he sent Cabal over to where Elffin stood. Elffin knelt with the dog and kept him out of the way of the contestants.

Amlyn took the hands of Brugyn and Perceval in his own, raising them above his head. "Let the games begin," he uttered, the cheers picking up yet again.

He spoke softly to the two men, explaining that this was a friendly wrestling match, with no promise of broken limbs or ruptured parts. Brugyn looked like he should drag his knuckles when he walked; Perceval nervously wondered how he might best such strength.

Amlyn continued, just to the two of them, "The match is over when one of you is pinned to the point of no longer being able to recover. I'll stomp my foot on the floor when I see that. Ready?"

Brugyn nodded, intently watching Perceval. Perceval glanced at Amlyn, nodded, and then met his opponent's stare. Brugyn's eyes looked as cold as the iron that composed the keep's gate, and he clenched his fists and then released them, revealing sinewy, large, and perfectly defined arm muscles in the process.

Amlyn stepped back near the circle of applauding men. Perceval thought of the days when he had wrestled straying sheep to the ground, and how he held them with total control while they were sheared. He was mentally picturing the moves, trying to forget that this was no sheep in front of him now.

Amlyn raised one arm; Brugyn and Perceval could see it out of the corners of their eyes. Then he dropped it, and the match began.

Almost instinctively, the two of them circled around the room, widdershins, moving smoothly yet deliberately, each trying to guess how the other would move, and how to counter that move. The men shouted strategies and encouragements.

Brugyn chose to close the gap first, his confidence leading him into Perceval's mid-section. Brugyn wrapped both arms around Perceval's waist, lifting him, while his momentum carried them both clear across the room. The men standing in their way had to move out of the way, and Perceval felt the wind go right out of him when his back hit the wall. *So much for Brugyn following the rules*, he thought, knowing he had never received such force before. Perceval knew the only way to ever have any respect in this hall was to beat this man, but now he lay there on his chest, Brugyn climbing on top of him, when Amlyn approached, pulling the bigger man off.

"Come on, Brugyn," Amlyn said. "You know the match has to stay in the middle of the room." Brugyn complied, smiling, and strutted back to the center.

Perceval thought he might never enjoy breathing again; he was gasping deeply, wondering how much of a blow ribs could take without breaking. He knew he would ache come morning, and he got to his knees, looking back to the circle of men. Some were applauding him, and all were insisting he get to his feet and finish the match, win or lose.

He put out one foot to stand, feeling a sharp jolt go through the bottom of his lungs. Putting both hands on the outstretched knee, he hoisted himself up.

The men seemed impressed. Apparently not too many were ready for more after being thrown into a wall by one of their biggest. Perceval walked slowly to the center, meeting Brugyn and Amlyn there.

Amlyn looked at Perceval, his eyes asking if he was all right. Perceval nodded, raising his head to look at his opponent. This time he would be ready.

Amlyn again left them and raised and dropped his hand, and again they started their ritualistic circling.

Brugyn looked pleased; he kept grinning at Perceval, taunting him. Perceval tried to ignore him. He was a bit tired, after riding all day and getting his air taken away; he just wanted it to be over now. His breath was raspy, and soon Brugyn began another charge.

This time the giant of a man came with his arms outstretched, as though he wanted to choke Perceval. But the latter's feigned exhaustion had been timed perfectly. Perceval ducked right under Brugyn's arms, and braced his legs as the larger man collided with him. This time Perceval kept his head down, and Brugyn's groin ran right into it.

Brugyn groaned in a voice higher than his own, and this time Perceval wrapped his arms around his opponent's waist, and spun around his own center of gravity, refusing to let go. The man seemed to weigh a ton, and Perceval knew he had only bought a few seconds for himself with that stunt. Every muscle he could feel complained for rest during the tackle; it felt as though the pressure in his forehead and cheeks would make his whole head explode.

But in a moment, Brugyn was down, and Perceval scrambled to shift his control and somehow pin the man, who was likely to be furious for being caught like that.

Brugyn was sprawled on his chest, Perceval's arms still encircling his middle. He was going to kill this little bastard for that! Never had a whelp like this taken him down. He was dimly aware of the men cheering. *Let them cheer,* he thought angrily; *let me hear them after I squash this boy.*

But the boy was quick, and stronger than he had antici-pated. Brugyn could feel his right arm being wrenched around, and his first instinct was to roll over.

Perceval took full advantage of his position; he was kneeling over Brugyn, remembering how sheep were best held when their joints were immobilized, so that they could not rely on strength to get away. Now he was concentrating on the el-bow, while holding Brugyn's thick meaty wrist with both hands. He had to hold on; he could not think of any strategy which might work if he slipped off the wrist.

Perceval leaned forward while Brugyn tried to roll over on his back. Finding that such a roll was impossible with his arm pinned so tightly. Perceval had actually halfway climbed over the man, trying to keep the wrist in his grasp. As long as he held it, bracing Brugyn's forearm next to his upper arm, and the whole arm pulled towards his head, Brugyn could not move. All he had to do was maintain the hold.

Brugyn bucked on the hard floor like a wild horse being ridden for the first time. Perceval knelt with one leg onto the left arm, putting as much of his weight onto it that he could spare. Now both arms were locked up, and Brugyn was in pain from resisting the holds. The other men howled; they had never seen anything like this! They had seen Brugyn beaten only very rarely (by visiting warriors), and never by one who looked so unfit for the task.

Amlyn walked over to them, peering down at Brugyn, who, despite the pain and pressure when he did so, continued to flail beneath Perceval.

Brugyn tried one last time; he yelled and tried to sum-mon any strength he still had, but Perceval was not to be budged. The holds were too well executed.

Beaten, Brugyn returned Amlyn's glance, and simply nodded.

The heel of Amlyn's boot smacked the floor, and the men ran from the circle and embraced Perceval, trying to hoist him off the larger man. He wondered how they could still have any voice left from the shouting, and he shooed them away for the moment.

As they began backing off, Perceval loosened his grip on Brugyn's wrist, then climbed off him, and finally knelt at the man's side. He extended his hand to Brugyn. Brugyn, while fiercely proud himself, took the gesture for what it was: a sign that there were no hard feelings, if he was willing to accept that.

They stood up together, and Brugyn nodded to his opponent. He would have to confront his own anger, and deal with the loss of face.

Perceval could barely believe he had done it! He had never really grappled with another person before, only animals, but was elated by how easily it seemed to come to him. He was again breathing heavily, and this time there was nothing false about it; he was really tired, and he regrouped with the other men in the circle. Elffin sent Cabal to him, and he was still petting the dog when Amlyn called out the next two combatants.

Perceval had never received much opportunity to bond with his fellow males back in Oerfa. His mother had protected him so, forbidding him to participate in any dangerous activities. He thought of her now, sipping a fresh mug of mead and wiping the sweat from his forehead. Maybe deep down she had known all along that her plan would never work, at least not for his whole life. He had learned to hunt, after all. Had she really believed it was possible to keep someone totally isolated from the rest of the world, especially if people from the rest of the world periodically stopped by?

He thought of Yvaine and smiled, watching the two newly selected men fumble their way around the floor, trying to dominate each other. The knight would have been proud of him, of his leaving home to seek his dream and his already best-ing another warrior. He was tired, but would sleep well tonight. He had won with grace.

But so far he had not received the opportunity to lose with grace.

The night wore on, the voices becoming finally hoarse. An outsider might have fled the premises from the pungent masculine odor alone, but the men's own senses had deadened to it. The winners of each previous bout were being given the opportunity to go another round, this time with someone new. They rarely got as organized as single elimination rounds; instead, each victorious man could choose among the other victorious men, and that would be the end of it. At least for tonight. Amlyn used the matches whenever they had visitors to help morale as well as stamina and prowess, and his men loved it. If nothing else, it helped pass the time, and the shrewder among them stood to profit if bets were placed.

Perceval was the first victor, so it was his option as winner and guest to select his opponent. He went into the middle of the room with Amlyn, and circled slowly until he pointed at Gwyn. Gwyn had valiantly overthrown one of the others, and looked like he could go another round. Perceval felt confident. He was not about to lose to this man who had greeted him rudely that afternoon.

The match started just as before, and Gwyn kept faking his entrance, dodging in and out of Perceval's space, just out of reach. Perceval was startled when Gwyn went right toward the floor, scampering towards Perceval's legs. He stood in place, unsure of what to do next, and Gwyn's own motion was sufficient to topple Perceval's weight right out from under him. He had been lifted slightly, being knocked off balance, by Gwyn's wrenching behind his knees.

He landed on his tailbone, wincing in pain, not knowing that was such a sensitive area. Slightly dazed, he barely noticed Gwyn slip an arm up around his shoulder, trying to connect it behind his back with the other hand. This second hand reached up from behind Perceval, the arm wedged in his crotch. He had never imagined such a move, especially not from Gwyn. He had no idea how to counter it.

Gwyn's hands were locked together behind Perceval's back now, against the floor. At first Perceval thought it would take little effort to break the hold, or to roll out of this somehow, but he found he could barely move. Gwyn had one of his arms pinned under his body as well, and every time Perceval tried rolling, Gwyn matched the movement by shifting his own weight, inhibiting further motion. They made several of these partial rolls to and fro, Perceval aware of how much energy he had already expended in his efforts.

Amlyn stood over them now, Perceval looking up into his face. The older man looked sympathetic yet judging, and he knew that the foot belonging to that face would soon stamp the floor unless he did something. He tried to get up, clenching every muscle in his abdomen and torso, his facial muscles likewise straining and reddening in the effort. He imagined he must look like Brugyn had earlier. Gwyn still had him locked up, but maybe he could still get out of this.

It wasn't working. Gwyn rolled up with him just slightly, but kept his hands fastened. He shifted his weight again to counter Perceval, and then Perceval's head landed hard on the floor, his vision immediately blurry.

He did not remember Amlyn ending the match, nor Gwyn getting up. He would only ever recall laying there, too dazed to feel ashamed, with Cabal licking his face.

After a few minutes he realized he was sitting on one of the benches, with Cabal and Elffin at his side. Elffin was patting his head with something cool. Elffin took the cloth away, rearranged it, and Perceval noticed it was dampened with a reddish mixture of water and his own blood.

He was still reeling, and now looking around the circle for Gwyn. He wondered how often injuries occurred in this building, then dismissed the thought; after all, these men were warriors, and bodily risk was part of the game. Another match was taking place on the floor, Perceval's small blood stain gone.

Leaning on Elffin's shoulder, he stood, his head throbbing clear out to his ears. Yet he stumbled as ably as possible over to Gwyn. Some of the men noticed this, as did Amlyn, who temporarily put a halt to the current match, which was so far undecided anyway.

The whole room fell silent; everyone wondered what would happen when Perceval found his previous opponent. Gwyn saw him coming and did not retreat, merely watching to see what came next.

Perceval looked at him, rubbed the back of his head lightly, and then smiled while he clapped Gwyn on the shoulder. "I'll get you next time," was all he said.

Gwyn actually smiled. The men were pleased. Perceval could lose with grace too, at least when his life wasn't on the line, and only his pride. His gesture was a symbol of his own sense of honor; neither he nor Gwyn had lost face, to their mutual beneficence. Sitting down again, he was surprised to finally recall some of what Tathan had said of face. *Honor's what makes a person noble and great, lad. It's the feeling which corresponds to respect. You earn respect, and then your own face is enhanced. Some people make much ado of honor, thinking every little insult or jest dishonorable, but I say be true to yourself, and respect, then honor, will follow.* Perceval thought he had been about eleven when he heard it, and it had taken this many years for the learning to actually begin.

And a knight, he mused to himself, *earns more respect than I think I can even comprehend. May I be worthy of it.*

A little later, the errant had no trouble at all falling asleep with the other worn out men.

* * *

Elaine's work room at home in Astolat was surprisingly well organized, considering the detail of her craft. The home she shared with her daughter was a second-story apartment: an older wooden edifice away from the heart of town, with the shared shop space of the clothier's guild beneath their feet. People who worked with fabrics, dyes, needles, and threads tended to have chaotic labor environments, but Elaine insisted upon keeping this place immaculate. Galienne felt she spent more time cleaning this room than actually working in it.

Still, today she could at least work on the family craft, and it pleased her this time. Too often she grew bored with the work, and Elaine knew this. She tried to persuade her daughter to persevere until she could master the advanced twill patterns, and thus be able to spin any fibers into workable threads. She looked over Galienne's work. "That looks good, though you need to readjust the shuttle."

Her daughter was rarely appreciative of criticism, even constructive. "But I just got the warps set right. I can finish this length of weave as it is."

"Yes, though you can still set it up to complete the entire length."

Galienne looked behind the loom, the delicate wooden apparatus with its movable shuttle to separate the threads so they could then be woven into each other and form fabric, and at last noticed the excess thread she did not see previously. "All of that for today, then?" she complained.

"Please," her mother said, knowing that keeping her daughter interested in this labor had grown more difficult lately.

"How were the baths today?" Galienne said.

"Delightful, as always. You know what the Lessons say of cleanliness."

Next to holiness, Galienne pondered. She took that as granted, though she wondered if she was wicked for thinking

God would have better things to worry about when Judgment came. Her mother loved the bath house as much as she.

She kept working. Over, under, over, under, the threads wrapped around each other, past the shuttle, and the sheet of fabric took form. Galienne much preferred this to spinning. She could most easily spin with silk, since its smooth fibers blended into thread readily. Such fiber had to be imported, though, and was so expensive she'd only worked with it a few times before. More common were wool, linen taken from flax plants, and hemp fibers, but all were rougher and more cumbersome. Thus, the weaving: the random and haphazard threads had no order or pattern. The woven fabrics, products of her hands and the motions of the shuttle, were lovely to behold and delicate to the touch. The goal was marketable goods, clothing which would be more elegant than the common homespun they both usually wore themselves.

The pair of them worked side by side, quietly as usual. "May I see the tapestry?" Galienne said finally.

"Of course. I admit I'm rather pleased with this piece, although I'm not sure it will be ready in time for Pentecost."

Elaine's daughter admired her labors. The tapestry portrayed a map of the whole Island, with legendary figures and creatures dotting the landscape, which also showed hills and rivers and forests. The fabric was soft but tight.

"Speaking of that," Galienne began.

"I was wondering when you would raise the issue. I think you should go."

Galienne looked dumbfounded. "You mean, you'd let me go? Alone?"

"You wouldn't be alone, child. Lupinia's father already spoke with me about it. It seems she really wants you to go with them. Besides, I know she'll want to get away from him for a while, and go hunting for those favorite knights of hers." *And perhaps you'll see your father.*

The younger of them blushed. "So maybe I should too, right?"

"Did I say that? But you could hardly do better than in Camelot, and I –"

"Oh, Mother, maybe you should go with them!"

"I'm just saying, love, that you're almost of marriageable age, and I know you don't want to be doing this your whole life."

"Well, then perhaps I should keep at it, like you, and just devote myself," she caught herself. "No, never mind, forget I mentioned it."

"Forget what?" Elaine prodded. She at least could sense when her only child was troubled.

"Mother, I have no wish to talk about this again."

"We should. I just wish you could know him the way I do."

"The way you did, don't you mean? Where is he, Mother? Does he care about us at all? I never even see him!"

Elaine could still picture her favored knight, vulnerable without his armor, in her arms. He would still come around, he was just so busy these days, and...

"Mother, you're doing it again!" *Some father I have. The absent knight!*

"Look, Galienne, why don't you just go to Camelot with your friend? Maybe you'll even see him there."

"Oh, please! He won't be there, and even if he is, what on earth would I say to him?"

"Galienne, what would the bishop say if he heard you speak this way?"

She stopped, fuming. *Like I could even get to my father if he's there. And she has no right to bring up bishop Baudwin.* "I don't know, but I'll likely stop and visit him anyway."

"I'm glad you can, Galienne. He's a good man." Galienne hoped she meant the bishop instead of the knight, but had no wish for confirmation.

They looked over the tapestry again. Galienne had to admit it was one of her mother's finest pieces. It would fetch a handsome amount in Camelot.

"Mother, are men unreliable?"

"Why would you say such a thing?!"

"Do you really have to ask? Just consider the man you love." *Don't ask me to take him any more gifts. And I refuse to speak of those stupid boys who keep teasing me outside the church.*

"Galienne, I mean it. What would the bishop think?" She instinctively dropped her voice. "I think he would remind you that we are the unreliable ones."

Her daughter hung her head. *So Mother and I are to blame for my father's not wanting either of us.* "I don't understand it. Why is that?"

"You already know this, child. We can't really understand men the way they understand us because of original sin."

Galienne knew the ancient story of the loss of Paradise, could almost recite it in the old Latin, not that Elaine realized that her skill had developed so much. "I just want to understand, that's all. Is that truly so terrible?"

"Come here, Galienne." She obliged. "It's not our place to understand. Men are better at that, and that's why we need them. For their strength, and their bravery. I weave and spin because I have a gift, and that should make men interested in me, but there's only one for me. You know that."

"Mother, he doesn't recognize us. He doesn't care. And what about your strength, to keep doing this work day after day?"

Elaine did not have a ready answer for that. "He knows how much I care, daughter." Galienne just shook her head. "He does, I tell you!"

The daughter simply backed away, not wanting to push the issue any further, not this time. They had this conversation on innumerable occasions already: the great knight, the unrequited love. But they never, never mentioned Galienne's birth, or the circumstances behind it. *One night of perfect passion,* she could hear Elaine say, *how could such love be sinful?* her voice sounding somewhere between wistful and proud.

Her flippant attitude about that made Galienne want to throw up. She was a bastardized child, carrying the taint of sin which no baptism could cleanse. That was why she wanted to understand the Book, why she spent so much time in the church. Elaine knew the implications of such sin; her daughter thought that the reason why she devoted so much thought to the man, and not as much to the girl.

All that time in the holy place was the best way to get clean. At least, that was how Galienne felt.

And as for the great knight, he was gone; that was what mattered. And maybe it was heresy, but she wanted to be strong and brave, too.

* * *

Perceval thought about last night. He had shown Gwyn the proper respect, but he was now angry that he lost. He had sorely underestimated the other man, and he promised himself he would never again consider someone to be an easy opponent, merely due to their appearance. He figured he had at least learned something then. He also disliked losing, even if he saved face in the eyes of the others. Winning might not be an end in itself, but it seemed to give a sense of satisfaction.

Glory, Sir Yvaine had bespoken. Losing just sent you back to the start.

No, that isn't quite true, he thought; he had just learned from losing, after all. He felt confused by this; how could there exist such an emphasis on winning if losing could still be profitable? Was that not so eagerly pursued by the knights? He wondered how knights dealt with loss. The tournaments he had heard of had winners and losers; how did the latter feel? How were they regarded afterwards?

He figured now was not the time to worry about it. In the meantime, he was glad Elffin reminded him of the horseshoes. Melangell gave him a full set when he had been readying Brownie, telling him that the mare would need to be shod once they reached the road. Elffin took it upon himself to put on the iron crescent-shaped shoes last night in Rhun. Perceval had never heard the click-clock of horseshoes on a road, but he liked it at once, knowing that all knights were familiar with it. And the shoes comforted Brownie.

Elffin and Amlyn had greeted him in the morning, while most of the others kept dozing. Amlyn gave the impression that Perceval would be genuinely missed, offering the blessing, "May She watch over you," as he left. Perceval did not reflect on the Pagan wish, grabbing what leftovers he could find before setting off with horse and dog.

Cabal was almost as eager to leave as Perceval himself, but not because of the company they had kept the previous evening; he simply liked to be outside and free to roam. He would wander off the road to follow the lead of any enticing scent, even though the majority of such odors led nowhere fruitful. He would then run to catch up to Perceval and Brownie, who stuck solely to the safe and predictable terrain of the road.

The trio traveled well together. Perceval had worried that perhaps he or the animals might grow lonely while en route to the fabled Camelot, but so far this had not been the case. He wondered how many nights they would spend alone outside, and how many they might enjoy in the company of others, under the added safety of constructed shelter. He was not disappointed by the lack of traffic on the road today, thinking (correctly) that he was still too far west to have many encounters. So he rode, peacefully admiring the rises and declines in the Cambrian geography.

It was two days before they arrived at Beacon Ring, and it would be months more until Perceval learned its name. He was simply intrigued by the appearance of what looked like an old fort of some kind.

Perceval had never seen a hillfort before, not even a tiny guard post such as this, although the Cymru had used them as garrisons, commerce centers, and storage facilities for centuries (and before them, the Picts, and before them, who knew). They also served as strongholds for the Legions, though this one was long deserted.

The place had been named, unbeknownst to Perceval, for its ability to serve as a signal post in addition to a small garrison. Perceval, however, loved it simply for the view if offered. He could tell it was a steep but relatively easy climb when he first saw it some miles back. This hill was not especially treacherous, covered with grassy and shrubby landscape clear up to its summit, and not the outcroppings of rocks of assorted sizes so predominate throughout Cambria. He wanted to get to the top right away, even if it lay off the road.

He was considerate enough to dismount Brownie before doing so, and she clearly appreciated the gesture. Cabal was thrilled; he ran off in front of both of them and scurried his way upward. Perceval lost sight of him just over the summit (much like he had lost sight of a certain large deer recently), but after a few seconds, Cabal popped his head over the edge and barked to them. Then he reared up his head vertically, and let out a long, baying howl. Perceval found it soothing, although Brownie looked around the area as though trying to ascertain who or what might have heard Cabal's intonations.

Perceval made it to the top, leading the mare. None of them breathed heavily, despite having climbed several hundred feet in a matter of minutes. The fort itself was comprised of two deep, roughly circular ditches, from behind which the former residents could take advantage of attackers having to navigate up and down and up again, having to pay more attention to their footing and less to those who awaited them. Perceval noticed that the ditch "walls" probably worked quite well, although he wondered why there were no huts up here; it did not occur to him that the place had been uninhabited for generations.

His thoughts about the site dissipated along with his breath in a deep gasp, when he turned and looked out at the scene below him. Back out to the west, half the Severn valley was laid out panoramically, as if for his enjoyment alone. Perceval could trace the silver line of the river itself, winding jaggedly and reflecting the light from the sun which was now arcing down to the sea. He noted how the river had not seemed to make such sudden turns when he was next to it; he was trying to get used to seeing his homeland from a bird's view.

His breath came slowly and evenly. He tried to trace their route thus far, his eyes navigating among the large and small bumps of hills. He only got a little way; already he had come far enough that Oerfa and its tiny valley had been swallowed up by the larger terrain features. He smiled. He had truly gone where the birds go, beyond the hills. He had visited other villages before, even further from home than this, but never had felt such awe in the face of Creation's artistry.

Perceval had never felt so free. It exhilarated his soul.

Cabal howled into the vastness again, still not getting a reply, yet refusing to quit trying. Brownie walked over to the center of the fort, and seemed very peaceful as she nibbled upon the tender grasses that had grown on it since the departure of the prior residents. Perceval thought the site perfect; he wasted no time getting camp set. He was excited by the thought of sleeping here, completely forgetting the old stories about the hollow hills.

So he was ill-prepared for the dream he had, if it truly was a dream; when he awoke he did not feel sure.

Cabal finally found one of his peers when Perceval and Brownie were just getting settled for the night. The horse's ears twitched toward the sound of a high- pitched wailing coming from the east. Cabal kept up the conversation for a few minutes, continually being answered by the wolf. Perceval finally had to order him to shut his mouth and come to bed. He stalled but finally came, laying next to his master. Perceval was fascinated by how, now prone, he could only see the inside of the hill fort and its earthen ramparts, and the darkened sky above. He was a bit nervous at the isolation now, and he lay his head on the unrolled blanket, hoping his companions would not sense his anxiety.

Sleep came for him, and it was much more populous than the hill fort.

He was in a great stone place, like the tower of Rhun only far more cavernous, and he could see two people with him. He did not recognize them. He knew they were both friends, one a husky bearded man, scarred from innumerable battles, and the other a disarmingly attractive woman, with flowing blonde hair and eyes the color of forest green. He could not recall their names.

He felt embarrassed. Looking at these people, he noticed they were stark naked. He quickly looked down at himself; sure enough, he was as natural as they. He ashamedly covered his penis with both hands and pretended he could not feel it swelling in the presence of the woman, her hard, lithe body standing unashamedly in front of him. Perceval could not help but sneak a look at her full, supple breasts, capped with delicious looking nipples. His face felt very warm.

They were in a hallway, and started to walk together, the woman between the two men. She took the bearded man's hand, and gently pried one of Perceval's hands away from his ill-concealed privacy. Her hand was warm and sure. They walked slowly down the grand hall, towards a conservative source of light near the end. They stepped deliberately but patiently, as though every step was judged.

Abruptly the scene ended, the hall's end never reached. Perceval could not tell where these people had gone, but he had left them.

Now he saw another person, another man. Actually, he was just a boy, even younger than Perceval himself. They stood in the woods together, Perceval not knowing how he came to be there. The boy smiled at him; no, it was more of a snarl. He wore black metal armor of a type Perceval had never before seen, with finely hammered plates covering the mailed joints, and around his neck was a long hissing creature, also black. The boy pulled a sword out of the scabbard at his waist, and brandished it menacingly. Perceval backed up, looking at the boy while feeling around himself for a weapon of his own, but none could be found.

Perceval lost his footing while walking backwards, and toppled down hard, wincing in apprehension and discomfort. His tail bone still hurt from the match with Gwyn, but he could not take his eyes off the boy, who came towards him.

Yet the boy no longer looked at Perceval, but past him instead. Perceval stole a furtive glance behind him, and was struck motionless by the image of a man, also with a sword and similar armor, and a weary look suggesting emotional as well as physical exhaustion. His armor was duller, however, and no creature encircled his neck.

The two phantoms wasted no words or gestures with each other; the man simply drew his own sword, a shimmering blade which Perceval swore glowed with its own life, and charged at the boy.

Perceval almost felt sorry for the little menace now, but the sentiment dissolved as he turned back and saw the boy return the charge, lunging at the man with adult strength and ferocity. And adult hatred.

They raised their swords high above their heads, and cleaved each other's brains in right above where Perceval sat. The mass of so much blood and gray ooze fell almost noiselessly to the ground at Perceval's feet; he had never been privy to such gore.

He woke up instantly, at first not noticing the cool sweat all over him. He was still in the ancient hill fort, and Cabal and Brownie looked at him eagerly. Cabal had to lick his face just to get his attention.

At first he only wanted to calm down. The images of the successive dreams were running through his mind in a chaotic, vague blur. Who *were* those people? The young woman and the bearded man; and the child and older man who killed each other without so much as a word? He could not recall their faces now.

His heart still raced, but at least the dream images receded, all save one, which left a hunger for womanly flesh remaining. Perceval wondered what it was like, to lay with a woman. He missed talking about his thoughts with Dindraine; the two of them had always been able to share just about anything, even their feelings about a topic of which neither knew much beyond mere biology.

His body was finally relaxing now. He felt at ease once more, and since his former erection was no longer influencing his thoughts, he again considered the males from the dreams.

The man with the beard was in excellent condition. Beyond that, he could not recall anything. *No, wait*, he corrected himself; he was scarred in many places. He must have had to fight a great many souls. He was probably a knight.

The child, so malicious looking. Perceval thought the whelp would have swung at him rather than the older man had the latter not arrived. How could someone so young be so full of anger? Perceval felt discouraged. He had never known anyone like that. All the people in Oerfa were fairly happy; none of them seemed to possess this kind of bitterness. And what on earth was that hissing creature with the forked tongue around his neck?

And the older man. Perceval thought he too had been bearded, with the scratchy blonde hair yielding to grayness. His sword was brilliant, reflecting light in colorful patterns. Perceval thought he saw every shade of a rainbow in the sword's shine; he wondered where the man obtained such a wondrous weapon.

Of course, he had been all too eager to attack the boy; actually, he moved first, without any noticeable provocation.

Other than the hatred.

The dreams still puzzled and worried Perceval, but as he lay in the hill fort, watching the swollen moon and the speckled stars, he noticed how tired he was. Sleep was soon to come again.

And fortunately, the rest of the night passed with no more vivid mental messages.

* * *

Brugyn was surprised to find Perceval gone when he awoke that morning. He supposed that his own head throbbed primarily from having taken in too much of the mead that the residents of Rhun consumed in voluminous quantities. He decided to walk downstairs, to see what food might be hiding down there, and to check if there were any special duties for the men that day.

When he entered the main hall, some of the others were there. Amlyn was speaking with some of the men at one of the tables, both of which had since been set up in their original alignment.

"Morning, Amlyn," he muttered groggily. He was almost awake now.

Amlyn responded with a nod and a wave; he apparently was quite into whatever the men were talking about. He was not

really a "chief" in the strict sense; the men who had been gar-
risoned here had just taken to calling him that. The Cymru had
few, if any, significant titles for a man who was responsible for
this many others. His was the closest to royal blood of them all,
and had also earned their respect as a frightful warrior and compassionate father-figure. Both were needed away from home at
this outpost.

Brugyn arrived at the pile of bowls and dishes left from
the night before. Not much remained: nothing at all, really, unless he counted the saucy smears which were the only sign of
food having once inhabited these containers. Even the smears
had finger streaks through them already; where food was concerned he was one of the later risers, even though most of the
household still snored contentedly away above his head. They
would have to hunt again soon; that was the only possible pressing duty of which Brugyn could think.

He didn't really want to eat again just yet, anyway. His
head still hurt. How could Perceval have gotten up this early
and been off already? It would have taken a full battle to rouse
Brugyn up after an evening like the previous one. And besides,
the young man had taken quite a lump from Gwyn's tackle. He
shrugged. Brugyn had reached that state in a man's life when he
still thinks of himself as almost indestructible, yet has become
old and wise enough to know when to trust his cautionary instincts. Perceval had to still be too young to know not to wander
out in the woods after what must have been a light concussion,
but Brugyn admired the lad's persistence.

He arrived at the populated table, the men not slowing
down the discussion on his behalf, but listening and talking most
attentively.

"– would never allow that kind of chaos again. He's
the new Emperor, of all things! The last thing he can afford
is to have the tribes fighting, especially when we're right next
to his own kingdom." This from the opinionated Gwyn, who

showed no hint of pride at having bested the man who had bested Brugyn.

Amlyn offered his own answer. "But I wonder if he's realized just what he has done throughout Cambria. His armies have never penetrated far into these hills, and his own men are not from here, but from the imperial lands. By forcing the tribes to become several larger kingdoms, instead of the pockets occupied by this or that tribe, he has allowed us to see how strongly we might function together. Recall the events on the Continent. Vercengétorix united so many of the tribes that they helped repel the Romans for a time."

"For a time," one of the others responded. "Yet Caesar still hauled him back to Rome and humiliated and murdered him before the Empire!" They all had heard the ancient tales of the likes of Vercengétorix, the war hero who with his charisma and chariot had indeed united warring Gaulish factions of Cymru into a single fighting force to be reckoned with. But they were eventually destroyed anyway.

The men mulled it over for a few seconds, Brugyn taking the time to sit down among them. Then he said, "Amlyn, do you mean that the tribes should try and rebel against the High King? We may be fine fighters, but his men cover their chests with iron, and ride fast horses. They can cut their opponents into crow food with a single charge on those animals, and –"

Amlyn interrupted him, with a simultaneous hand wave and the sound of his own commanding voice. "I am certainly not suggesting anything of the sort. It would be too stupid and too destructive. My concern, brothers, is what will become of Cambrians, be they from my tribe or another, when this 'High King' is no longer in power."

One of the younger men of the brood spoke up, barely containing his excitement. He was simply another hot-blooded warrior ready to prove something. "An overthrow, then? Is the Emperor to lose his throne?" He was clearly not listening. He reminded Brugyn of his own righteous rage; it had been tempered a bit since.

The chief continued, "Oh, eventually, all kings must lose their thrones." He could see that his men, as he had grown to call them and to think of them, had no interest in hearing him speak like a bard offering a tasty riddle. "What I mean is, this particular king has no heir, and is rumored to have a barren wife."

That earned their interest, although Brugyn had a question. "Why does he not take a second wife?" Cymru, men and women alike, had an ancient tradition of sometimes taking more than one person as a spouse.

Amlyn was quick to answer. He had studied the ways of the people of Logres for much time now, even talking to monks and knights who made their homes (temporary ones, he hoped) on the fringes of the Cambrian wilds. "Because Artos is a Christian, and keeps his court accordingly. The people of his kingdom have adopted the Roman ways as well as their religion, and have yet to see the instability of taking a life alien to their own." He referred, of course, to the native Cymru life, never mind that their ways had been largely unknown in Logres since the coming of the legions centuries before. And Amlyn carefully used the High King's Latin name. He knew those listening to him now would not forget it.

He wanted them to remember something else. "Brugyn, look you at Gwyn, and at the others, your brothers and comrades in arms. You have hunted together, sat at meat together, laughed together. Yet you men who live under this roof, provided by our Chief Belinans; you hail from half a dozen different tribes. This fort is a show of power for Belinans, who gives homage to Artos. The High King wants the Cymru tribes united as one, but some don't think that possible."

When he saw he had their undivided attention, he added, "Just see you all remember that, down the road."

Brugyn would remember it well, just as soon as his hang-over left.

* * *

Lupinia's father was running short on temper. Lord, would there ever come a woman who could actually be ready to depart at an appointed time? His late wife had possessed this undesirable trait of tardiness, and clearly passed it to her daughter.

He checked his inventory again, more to pass the minutes than to reassure himself; whenever he made a trading trip, he double-checked what he took, then had his daughter check it again. There were dozens of pairs of shoes, sandals, boots. He had worked with a variety of leathers to produce them. Cattle hide was cheapest, and simpler to produce in large quantities, partly because of the size of the beasts themselves. Better still were the imported breeds, both for their meat and milk, and their hides. But he also used deer, and the occasional snake. These creature's skins came at more of a price, but were also more decorative, especially the long reptiles, just the sorts of items to make for good selling in Camelot. Some of the other members of the tanners' guild would be jealous!

There were also belts, belt purses (the smaller ones were more difficult, composed of ears or scrota), carrying sacks, even some breast plates of leather armor. Lupy's father was most proud of the latter items; he often tested pieces of the boiled protective garments against the edges of slashing and bashing weaponry. A few good strikes would always puncture it in the end, but it was surviving those first blows that usually made the difference. Squires practiced in this cuirboillic, and many peasants could afford it, even if they didn't have much need.

The wagons stood ready, as did his guard and entourage. The men looked as impatient as he felt; they knew his daughter's proclivities.

In fairness, it was actually Galienne who made them late in leaving, though it wasn't her fault, either.

Lupinia had arrived at Elaine's home promptly, heading straight upstairs above the shop into the apartment. The mother of the household was absent, Lupinia not knowing where, nor caring. Elaine often looked down her nose at the girl, from jealousy, Lupy knew.

But where was the woman's daughter?

She had not long to wait. Lupinia lovingly inspected the rich tapestry, and quickly scanned through the most recent dresses. She wished her friend would wear one of them sometime, rather than her commoner clothes. The classy men were attracted by class. Still, the work was good, and therefore the money. So maybe someday, if she could convince Galienne that it was hardly a sin to try and look one's best (*Why else put on your finery for Son-day?*), the poor girl might have a better chance.

She heard heavy breathing from below, which the guild-keepers ignored, and then saw a sweaty, panting Galienne emerge into the upper floor. "What happened?"

"I, I –" she started, then had to catch her breath.

"Calm down," Lupinia said, easing her arms around her friend. She regarded Galienne as the little sister she had always wanted. Her breathing slowed. "Now tell me, where did you just come from?"

She wiped her eyes. "The church. The priest didn't notice me, but the boys outside did."

"What did they want?" *How did they make you so upset?*

Galienne did not wish to tell her friend the truth about her habit of reading whenever she could. That Bible was so important for her. "They just teased me for being in the church so much, that's all."

"Why would you want to even be in there on such a lovely day?" Lupinia preferred to avoid its stuffy interior whenever there was no sermon to be heard.

"I just feel peaceful in there. I wanted to pray before we set out for Camelot." *Is it still a lie if all I do is leave out the details?* she wondered.

"They didn't hurt you, did they?" Lupinia was not about to tolerate that.

"No, Lupy, I'm fine. They just teased me, and chased me most of the way home."

"Then they're just bullies, not even worth your time. Are you ready to go?"

Galienne nodded. She had a carrying sack with extra clothes ready near the bed. Elaine bought it for her from Lupinia's father, as an Easter gift last year.

Lupinia helped her to stand, watching as she gathered her things. "Let's be off, then. Father's waiting for us. We're probably late, but he won't mind."

"I'm sorry," Galienne added. Lupy shook her head. "No, now we'll have none of that. These young idiots just don't know better, that's all."

Then they heard shouting from the street. "Stupid girl! Girls can't read! Why don't you stay in the house with your needles?" The voice was quite young but noticeably boyish, and a pair of other voices laughed at its comments.

"Come on!" Lupinia shouted, bolting for the wooden stairs. Her friend was reluctant to follow, but did, with a bit more prodding.

They stood in the street now, the trio of boys having walked on further, though one turned back to make a lewd gesture with his hand at Galienne. She blushed, not fully understanding the meaning anyway, and turned away, trying to pull Lupinia after her.

But Lupy would not budge from the spot. Instead, she looked to the ground, locating a fist-sized rock in the walkway. She picked it up, and hurled it as hard as she could at the boys.

It hit one of the less attentive ones in the back, and he fell down, whining.

"Stay away from us!" Lupinia commanded, then made as though she meant to keep picking up rocks. The boys ran off. It took Galienne a few moments to overcome her shock long enough to laugh. "I can only imagine what your mother would say!" Lupinia said.

"Thank you. Why didn't I ever think of that?"

"Because your mother taught you not to fight back."

Galienne made to leave, but this time was stopped. "Galienne, what did they mean, about you reading?"

The younger girl flushed again. "I just like looking at the Bible. It's so beautiful. Maybe I could learn to read someday." *I hope that's not a lie, either.*

"Yeah, maybe," Lupinia chuckled. She knew almost no one could do that, though she and her father did have good heads for figures.

They walked along. "How did that feel?" Galienne said of the throw.

"It was marvelous! It was like testing Father's armor with the mace. Did you see them run? You should try it sometime."

* * *

Perceval slept peacefully the next time. He was still getting used to waking to Cabal's slobbering on his face instead of the more familiar crowing of the several roosters which proudly prevented late-sleepers back in Oerfa. Already the sun was warming him, evaporating the cool beads of dew on the grass within the fort. He was pleased; it would be another good day. So far he had been quite fortunate with the weather.

Perceval and his quadruped companions were still climbing over the second rampart of the hill fort when Perceval looked back towards the center of it. *The hollow hills*, he thought, and shuddered. Was he visited by the faeries last night? Were they responsible for placing the dreams in his head? He tried to remember anything he might have heard from Tathan, and found he could not look away from the hill fort. Something about it seemed irresistible to him.

The faeries have their own haunts, and such places must be paid their proper respect. He could hear Tathan's warning voice. How much did that bard know? Perceval never really considered this before; after all, the man studied with the druids, of all people! Had Perceval dismissed the man's musings just because he had not attained druidical status?

They were supposed to be very wise, those tribal religious leaders, and capable of magick beyond definition. Perceval had never seen magick actually working; he found no cause to believe in the miraculous. He could, however, remember a story about a druid who walked across a field of battling Cymru; such was the man's status and respect that all fighting ceased until he was across the field! Then it resumed again, the warriors returning to their favored pastime of sending one another to the Otherworld.

Or to be reincarnated, Perceval thought. The Ancients had also believed that the spirit of a person often came back, to inhabit another body. Or to haunt someone or something, like this place. The new physical body did not even have to be human. Such belief could motivate its adherents to acts of untold bravery. Or stupidity, depending upon one's outlook.

Perceval fidgeted nervously, although he still could not quite look away from the site. He thought that it might be only a matter of time before some faerie or spirit or who knew what came bursting out of some cave within or beneath the hill fort to attack him. Or curse him. Or make him age prematurely, maybe a decade a day. He had little idea of just what powers such beings might be capable.

Enough! Those things aren't real. Perceval closed his eyes, turned his head. He concentrated on the sounds, and determined to return straight to the road as soon as he opened his eyes. He heard Cabal's panting, Brownie's throaty head jerks, the far off cry of a bird. He opened his eyes. The day was still bright and beautiful, and Cabal and Brownie looked at him curiously. Not looking back, he led them down, ignoring the vista of the Severn valley all the way.

As the day continued, his thoughts of the hill and how it made him feel began to recede. He was still troubled by how he felt as though the hill had controlled his thoughts and feelings somehow, as if it were alive. He thought that ridiculous; how could a hill be alive? He tried to think of other things.

So far his only human contact had been with the men back at Rhun. He guessed he must still be too far west to really encounter the caravans and parties of knights he heard about. That was fine with him. He still loved the newness of the sense of isolation. Cabal and Brownie proved ample companions, and for the first time in his life, his mother was not looking over his shoulder, offering advice and warnings and judgments. He loved her, but did not miss her.

It was another two days before he found some other people. And the place was marked by a cross, just as his mother promised.

Actually, by several crosses. Perceval was intrigued to see them, looking forward to more human contact, with no one but a dog and a horse to talk with. He did not mind nor even hesitate to talk to them, but it was more rewarding to have one's own remarks returned by additional speech.

Just earlier that day, the trio had reached a point where the hills simply became flatter and flatter, until the land was barely hilly at all. Perceval figured they must be rapidly nearing the forest which his directions had promised (*which one comes first?* he wondered; *is it the Arroy?*) He stopped Brownie when she got to the summit of the last big hill, and he looked down at the flat land below. He knew he must be about where he once thought the world came to an abrupt halt, and he was unsure if he could continue. What if his earlier sentiments had been accurate? What if Tathan only made up all those stories, just so people would pay attention to him? He suddenly hated Tathan; for all his talk, what did he really know? What good were legends and myths and the stories of dead heroes if they couldn't even help overcome fear of the unknown?

A fear such as, what if the flat lands led to the Other-world? Or worse? *No, that's ridiculous, fool. Hell and the Other-world sound so implausible.* He reassured himself it was just fear of the mysterious. Camelot lay beyond the Cambrian mounds, the goal, the prize. Still, childhood fears were not always eliminated by mere reason, so he sat there, watching.

Cabal was the one to save Perceval from his trepidation. The dog looked up once at his master, wondering what the hold-up was, then bounded down the hill, and just kept running. Perceval cried out to him, but his yells fell unnoticed.

Yet the land did not swallow Cabal. Nor did any faeries or any other weird creatures. Perceval shrugged. He knew he should not resent Tathan; the man was only trying to help. He just had to accept that this was all still new to him. *Maybe this fear is what creates the old bard's stories.* He had wondrous new things to experience. As he rode down, he wondered how he could have let himself get worked up like that. And he considered how he would fare in the forest.

The abbey came into view shortly after that. Cabal returned from his initial wanderings. He was new to this too, but his drive to explore led him with no worries about the cosmological implications of where his nose might lead him.

The abbey itself looked like another small castle, although larger than Rhun. There were three buildings right next to each other, connected by the same walls. One had a narrow tower at one end, with a cross atop it. The others were higher (unless one counted the added height of the steeple), encircled by battlements. The last looked more like Rhun's tower. A short stone wall had been erected around the building cluster. Perceval wondered what good the wall was; at only several feet in height, it would be comparatively useless against attackers.

He knew his mother would have loved to see this house of God. Well, a house of the *Christian's* God, at any rate. Once again he did not want to think about how many deities there might be. To him it seemed as though everyone had their own, just like the guardian angels he had heard his mother speak of sometimes. There was the God worshipped by Christians, and the Goddess adored by Pagans, and individual lesser deities and saints of war, wine, love, lust, crops, cattle, weather, wishes. Many peoples had brought their divinities to the Britain.

This added to Perceval's antagonism: how could someone keep up with such a multitude? How would it ever be possible to keep track of which god might be pleased, and which might be offended, possibly with the same action?

Perceval found it odd that the sight of a mere structure could elicit such mental wanderings. In that sense it reminded him of the hill fort, and of the rocky spot on the river where he and Dindraine used to go to be alone and talk.

He thought he would like the abbey though; it looked like a fortress and yet it was devoted to religion. He wondered to what extent knights followed this duality.

As he drew closer he could see a pair of young men wearing dark brown robes tied at the waist with light rope. They were kneeling next to some kind of rounded stone planted vertically into the ground. Their hands were flatly joined together in front of them, their heads bowed.

Perceval rode up to the wall, and Cabal barked a greeting to the men. They ignored the noise until they finished, then rose, and looked at Perceval. He noticed now that the tops of their heads were completely shaven, and he wondered why anyone would shave their heads, much less only one specific area of them. But he would not ask them; he could hear his mother admonishing him for asking questions of his hosts.

"May we help you?" inquired one of the monks. Finished with their task, they both walked over to Perceval. They wondered what this stranger in their land wanted; he was obviously no knight, but did not look like a tattooed savage, either.

Perceval thought this was like the initial greeting he had received at Rhun, except these two seemed kinder. "Yes, please," he began. "I am on my way to Camelot, and seek lodging for the night," he groped for the words, "and a chance to pray." He hoped it did not sound as stupid as he thought; it was the first time he had ever asked someone permission to pray.

The monks came through a small gate nestled in the easily-jumped wall. "That would surely be fine. I am Brother Dyfed. This is Brother Merin. He cannot speak to you, as he is under a vow of silence. Please do not be offended."

Perceval raised his eyebrows. Brothers? They looked almost nothing like each other! And a vow of silence? How could anyone not talk? Perceval himself found it difficult not to talk, even when his only listeners were Brownie and Cabal.

Still, he had promised his mother that he would stop at any such place he found, if only to please her. Besides, despite his growing fondness of sleeping outdoors, he also liked being under shelter for the night. Sometimes he just wanted to feel safe, and God's houses were supposed to be havens.

"I offer you humble greetings, Brothers Dyfed and Merin, and I thank you for accepting me." Perceval dismounted, and noticed neither of the men offered to take Brownie's reins. So he led the horse to the gate, Cabal walking with them.

"Abbot Uren will be done with his class soon," said Dyfed. He spoke with a dry monotone, and was tall and thin beneath his robes. Perceval thought the man barely ate.

"Class?" inquired Perceval, motioning a request for Brownie and Cabal to be let free to wander the grounds.

Dyfed replied with a gesture indicating that it was fine, and said, "He teaches us all. There are only twelve of us here, plus six nuns, whom we rarely see. He teaches the Scriptures to us in Latin."

This was all going over Perceval's head, who wondered what nuns and scriptures and Latin were. Yet he did think to ask, "And how is it you both are not there with him?"

Immediately he regretted it. He had no business asking these strange men personal questions! He just hoped his remark would not be found offensive.

But Dyfed did not mind. "When you first rode up we were praying at the grave of one of our Brothers, who passed into the sanctity of Heaven this past winter." He pointed toward the tombstones. At least Perceval now knew what they were, without having to proffer another bumbling question. In Oerfa the dead were buried with no more marking than a stone or perhaps a freshly planted tree. The druids believed one's spirit could later inhabit such a tree, and the place might become sacred as a result; the trees were even selected according to one's character, such as a mighty oak or a gentle elm. Watching the tombstones, Perceval started to believe that maybe it wasn't wrong to ask questions, although perhaps occasionally impolite. *Besides, Mother, the departed Brother is dead; why should he care what questions were asked in his absence?*

"I'm sorry," added Perceval, apologizing for both the death of a nameless soul and for his drifting from the conversation into the rich realm of his thoughts. Death was another issue with which he would have to wrestle, later. He only knew how he hated for any creature to have to suffer needlessly.

Yet like the druids, the men now with him believed in a second life, although it was entirely spiritual, not physical. Perhaps that made dealing with the death of their friend easier.

"Please do not be sorry," offered Dyfed, "he is in God's care now, and I am sure he is happy and at peace."

Merin nodded his assent. Perceval smiled sheepishly, and let them lead him on a tour of the facility.

"This is the chapel of Our Mother, Saint Mary," Dyfed began, indicating the building with the tall steeple. "We've been fortunate enough to receive the talents of a painter from Viroconium nearby. Come see."

The three of them walked into the long chapel, the building Perceval had noticed first, with its oaken cross-topped steeple above, reaching up toward the heavens. Inside it was dim, and they had to wait several seconds for their eyes to adjust. Gradually a row of seats appeared, each long enough to hold maybe five worshippers. Three people were seated together on one of the benches, their heads bowed in the presence of another cross at the opposite end of the chapel. This interior cross was painted gold, and differed from the exterior further in that there was a sculpted man attached to it. Perceval tried to remember the lessons his mother imparted. Anxiously, he fondled the cross hanging beneath his tunic.

The painter's work was behind the cross. It showed two naked people, a man and a woman, genitals covered by giant leaves, in a garden of trees and flowers. It was a lovely scene, although the woman's eyes had a concerned look to them. In a corner of the scene, near the woman's feet, was a long, black ugly creature, like the thing around the little boy's neck in Perceval's dream.

It was deadly quiet inside. One of the people sitting turned to Perceval, and he saw it was a woman. He had not noticed that before, as they wore white cowls over their heads, covering up all but their faces. Perceval was certain it was a woman; she had a younger person's tender eyes, and Perceval could see the outline of two firm breasts under her black robe, and was instantly embarrassed. He knew he wasn't supposed to become aroused in a chapel!

He looked around again. There were cross-shaped divots in the stone brick walls, which let in the only light. There was also a large podium beneath the hanging life-size cross, and something curved and wavy atop it, but from his vantage point Perceval could not determine what it was.

He looked at Dyfed and Merin. Dyfed gestured towards the pews, indicating that it was all right for him to sit and pray. He was anxious about it, but felt nonetheless obligated.

Cautiously and slowly, Perceval strolled over to the pew closest to the dais with the open Bible on it, beneath the gold cross. The nuns barely noticed him as he walked past, involved with their own quiet worship.

The cross was almost right above him now. He had never seen an actual crucifixion scene. He knew little about the carpenter turned preacher and teacher named Jesus who had been killed by the Romans, those same villains who had swarmed over the Isles shortly afterward, and never understood the full meaning of *how* Jesus was executed. Looking at the grisly cross, he felt almost ill, gazing up into the sorrowful, pained eyes of the wooden but golden Savior hanging above him. He lowered his head, trying to imagine a more horrible way for someone to die. It seemed to him a description of the hell his mother had mentioned.

He knelt just in front of this forward pew, conscious of all these eyes that must surely be watching him. The floor was cold and hard, and his unaccustomed knees quickly began to feel sore. He wondered how anyone could remain in a penitent position for very long.

With awkward, unsure movements, he clasped his hands together, flattened, like he had seen his mother do, in front of his chest. He bowed his head slightly, and finally thought he was ready to pray.

But he could not think of anything to say.

Perceval thought that if God was listening, he should really say something, *anything*, otherwise God might be offended for a mortal having wasted His time. Yet he also thought God would not be interested in hearing about his pilgrimage, nor his dreams or wrestling matches or nights outside. Besides, wasn't God supposed to know everything anyway?

Just what should one *say* to God?

Perceval simply whispered his hopes for attaining the status of knight, and asked that God look after his mother and sister. It was all he could think of.

He finished with a befuddled attempt to cross himself. He could not remember the order of the points of the cross as one drew them across one's breast. Was it up, down, left, then right? Or up, down, right, then left? What about down, up, *no, forget it,* Perceval thought. He would not make himself look foolish in here. He silently rose, hearing his knees crack to disturb the holy silence as he did so, and returned to where Dyfed and Merin stood.

The nuns had left. They were very stealthy; Perceval did not even hear them. He was amazed how one could be so quiet in a place which was already almost totally silent to begin with. And now standing with the monks was a tall, heavyset, almost completely bald man. He was dressed like his subordinates, but Perceval could tell it was Abbot Uren just from his glance. His look was one of radiating self-confidence. And maybe a slight distrust, too. He eyed Perceval curiously, as though the lad had just committed some minor blasphemy in front of the altar. Perhaps he had.

Perceval hoped not. Now was no time to be dubbed a sinner, or worse.

"Welcome, my son," Uren said gruffly. Even his voice sounded authoritarian, as though he were used to not only giving orders but also having them promptly obeyed. "I am Abbot

Uren, and I am in charge of this fair and humble abbey, by order of Archbishop Dewi himself. In the absence of a bishop, he has had to personally appoint individual abbots to this diocese, which includes this part of Powys." The abbot sounded vaguely guilty about this, but Perceval seemed not to notice.

Perceval was actually surprised by the amount of information he had just received. This man was clearly proud of his position, appointed by an arch-something. Perceval did not even know what that was, but it sounded hierarchical enough to be worthy of respect. *But what did he mean by "this" part of Powys?* Powys was a single land, all of it ruled by Chief Belinans.

"Thank you, Abbot Uren. Please permit me to humbly request lodging for this night, and I shall be off come sunrise," Perceval said.

"That is easily enough granted, young Perceval, and may I in turn ask what it is which brings you through this area?"

How did he know my name? wondered Perceval. He must have been told by Dyfed. Yet he was unsure if he even offered it to the monk. He saw no harm in telling his story, though.

"Surely," Perceval began confidently, "I am journeying to Camelot, so that I may be made a knight in the service of King Arthur." He was getting used to saying that. He was also pleased to notice that these men poked no fun at him for his honesty, as had Gwyn and Elffin on the battlements of Rhun. Indeed, all three of them, even silent Merin, were totally serious in their manner. He had not seen these men smile at all. Granted, Dyfed and Merin were mourning someone when he first approached the abbey, but still, it made Perceval a bit edgy.

"Well, then, young man," said Uren, "let us adjourn to our humble hall, and partake of the Lord's blessings." He motioned Perceval to follow him, and the monks brought up the rear. "And perhaps you'll be good enough to share a story of your travels thus far."

Perceval was at least glad to be out of the chapel. "It would be my privilege." He felt easier about talking now, having been invited to do so. He felt as though he had done something wrong in the chapel, and yet he could not help but wonder whether God really cared about the intricacies of one's manner. After all, it seemed proper that the actual *content* of one's prayers was what really mattered. If a person was honest with him- or herself under the eyes of God, then how could God be anything other than pleased? But then, what if God really *did* care about the mundane aspects of this, and what if Perceval really offended Him? The serious demeanor of the men in his company suggested a lifestyle of strict obedience and homage.

But then, is a knight's life different? he wondered, walking with the others into an adjacent hall, which was just as simply decorated but cleaner than that within Rhun's walls. A knight, he reminded himself, was sworn to live according to the mandates of a lord, and a lord was a mortal, fallible human. Not a deity at all. What of the really religious knights? To whom would they have pledged their loyalty? To the higher matters of the spiritual life, or to the worldly concerns of the individual lord? Perceval considered how he might actually fit into this grand scheme of chivalric behavior. As long as he got to be a knight, and go off on quests for greater glory, he did not really care. The rewards of the quest outweighed all other concerns. Yvaine would have agreed with him.

The feast hall, such as it was, included a series of narrow windows along each long wall. There were half a dozen tables and accompanying benches lined up precisely in the hall's middle; they looked as though unmoved for some time. Perceval thought it odd that the room had more benches and tables than necessary to accommodate the few people who lived here; perhaps they often had visitors.

In two adjacent corners stood two dark wooden crosses (with no agonized likeness of Jesus on either of them, Perceval was pleased to note), and at the far end was another door which he assumed led to the outside yard. It was barren but well kept, and totally empty of people. And again, there was the silence.

Uren noticed Perceval's detached look. "This sparse room is our dining facility. I realize it is not spectacular, but we here at Haughmond Abbey have dedicated ourselves to lives of sacrifice and as few material considerations as possible," he said with just enough pride to make his point.

Perceval still had trouble averting his eyes from the twin crosses, barely noticing the abbot's voice. Beneath his tunic, he felt a dull but steady throb, and was unsure if it was his own cross or his heart. He did not think the cross could possibly have a life of its own, but something about this place made him wonder. What had his mother said about the unrepentant? They were unfit to even enter a holy place, much less perform a sacrilege in it like praying out of mere guilt.

No, no, Perceval insisted, and thought, *I've done nothing wrong, committed no sin.* His fists had clenched, one of them around the small cross. *Why does mother automatically assume the worst of people?* he asked himself. *It seems as if she* wants *me to fail in my chosen task.*

Perceval slammed his eyes closed, wincing. Uren, Dyfed, and Merin were concerned, and the two monks flanked the younger man, ready to grasp him should he suddenly collapse.

But the younger man did not. He was so wrapped up in his own confusion he did not even notice the others. His mind sped along, images of knights and maidens and monsters filling it, and he saw them with closed eyes, whether he wished to or not. For the first time he was starting to doubt what he decided.

But what of the King, whose peace and prosperity worked for the benefit of this whole land, and who needed the service of knights for his goals and protection? Yet even all this seemed overshadowed by the deities, the Holy Old Ones, who passively watched these pathetic mortals as they scampered about like so many rodents, killing each other over what they thought was right.

Who *was* right? His mother? The King? Both? Neither? And what did those dreams mean? Had he truly been visited by some kind of spirit in the hill fort, since he never before had dreams that were so fearful and confusing?

Perceval, still barely aware, allowed himself to be gently led to a nearby bench and seated. He opened his eyes, and saw Uren returning from having retrieved a copper goblet filled with cool water.

Uren sat opposite Perceval. "Are you quite well, my son?" he said, concerned but not quite alarmed.

Perceval opened his dry mouth, thought he might not manage actual words, and simply nodded his head. He took the goblet and drank slowly, swallowing tiny sips of the pleasingly clean and clear water. The liquid sensation helped to diminish his anxiety.

Still, he wanted some answers.

"I am, Abbot, thank you," he said, "but I was wondering if you might offer some help with my confusion." He hoped Uren would be willing to talk, that he would not have other duties awaiting him, like his Bible class.

"'Confusion,' dear boy?" Uren said, "What would you like to discuss?" He sounded ready to hear a confessional. He dismissed Merin and Dyfed with a glance and a hand motion, and they bowed and silently retreated from the hall. Perceval was now alone with Abbot Uren, who sat opposite him.

"Well, Abbot," Perceval began, "I'm unsure of even how to voice my apprehensions. I've been thinking a great deal lately."

Hearing one's intimate thoughts and concerns was nothing new to the abbot. He had several others right in this abbey to worry about, to say nothing of the hundreds he had come into contact with since he took this position. Savages, most of them, and too many who were unrepentant.

Uren knew that all these old legends and lesser deities were mistaken faces of the One, True God. It wasn't just that the natives were sinful; they remained ignorant of God's nature. Uren considered it his task, sanctioned by the Church, to help save them, through coercive conversion or at least baptism.

He knew that evil was very real. Yet surely there could not be evil in the nervous, fidgety young man now seated across from him; how could one so young be despoiled? He was just another of those in need of the promise of salvation.

"About what?" he said at last.

The fidgety young man squirmed around on the bench. "About my mother. And about becoming a knight, which is what I want more than anything else in the world. And about my sister. I wish she could have come with me."

Perceval was trying to relax, and did find some comfort by Uren's reaction: he sat there, motionless, his face fixed in a glance Perceval could only describe as caring. Like a father. Perceval briefly considered his own father, who had not lived to see his son pursue his dream.

"Clearly you love your sister. What of your mother? You mentioned her but did not express any sentiment." Uren kept his voice even.

Perceval looked around the room nervously. He still had to confront the guilt. He had, after all, just gotten up and left, and his mother had been totally unprepared for it. "She's lovely. Very caring. She would die for me. I know that sounds vain, but I truly believe it. She was sad to see me go; she even tried to forbid me outright." He was surprised by how much he said. *And sad?* he thought; hell, his mother had been *devastated* by his departure. He suddenly wished the year was up, and he could return to her and comfort her.

"There is no vanity in speaking the truth, Perceval," Uren said. "She sounds as though she were like any other mother, simply trying to keep her loved ones safe." Uren, too, knew of sons leaving to become knights and never being heard from again.

"Yes, but —" Perceval began, his eyes beginning to hurt. "But she acts like she won't see me again. I left so quickly, there was no time to really discuss it."

"Why don't you tell me how you came to be so desirous of knighthood. Perhaps that will help me to understand what has happened with your mother." Knights could be used to enforce Church aims, the abbot knew. This young man needed guidance now.

Perceval, eager to change the subject, if only temporarily, obliged the man. He told Uren of how he and Dindraine were out for the day, and how he saw a strange looking campfire. Uren was genuinely interested in hearing the tale, especially the part about the Barking Beast that Uren had never even heard of. *Surely there could be no such thing!* he thought, but did not say; he did not want to appear as though he doubted Perceval's story.

Uren also enjoyed the details about the talk with Sir Yvaine, and the caring for Sir Lamorak. He knew how well respected the knights were, and could see how they had so influenced Perceval; he was pleased the boy chose to trust him.

Perceval was a good storyteller; he left out no major details and only hesitated when he got to the part about the conversation with his mother.

"I know she loves me, and always will, but I am not her property, like another of her sheep. I want a chance to do something great, something for the benefit of everyone; she only would have kept me from that."

Perceval had never before thought of what he was doing in terms of some destiny, but felt empowered by his soliloquy nonetheless.

Uren sat back on his bench slightly, never taking his eyes off his guest. The lad was already quite remarkable! Here he was, wandering alone through God's wilderness, unafraid of anything except the possibility that he might never become a knight; and he barely seemed to consider that at all! Uren's heart went out to him; he hoped the lad would get what he wanted. And it sounded like his poor mother had become too overprotective of him for his own good.

Uren also took time to consider the story of Perceval's dreams. Uren's own beliefs would suggest that they were omens, perhaps even literal foretellings. He honestly had little idea just what was implied by the virtual ménage-à-trois, besides its obvious sin of the flesh, although the latter dream at least had some symbolism he could comprehend. He told Perceval his feelings.

"I thank you for opening yourself to me, Perceval," began Uren, "and I think both your story and your intentions are marvelous. I can empathize with your apprehension in the chapel earlier; praying is part inspiration and part vocal skill, and I do not believe there is really a wrong way to go about it. After all, God is always listening."

"Thank you, Abbot," Perceval said. The nuns, brothers Dyfed and Merin, and the other monks, were beginning to make preparations for the evening meal. They would not make any special allocations for their guest, but they would partake of his company and feed and house him so long as he helped out. They went in and out of the room, setting bowls, spoons, knives, and linen napkins on the tables. Perceval could already smell lots of bread and vegetables.

Uren was oblivious to the others working, and continued. "Son, I think that dream you had was about you and your own father, the man you never had a chance to know."

Perceval looked up at him, interested.

Uren went on, "I think maybe the boy that so scared you was yourself, and that other was your father, and you had at each other because there was so much you both wanted to know about each other but couldn't. So you took your frustrations out on one another in the only way your dream thought possible."

Perceval still looked at him, bewildered.

"What I mean is, I think all the guilt about your mother, and your missing your dear sister, and your desire to be something your father was, all came together at once. That's what happens in dreams; things get worked out for us, and then we have to figure out the meanings from what we remember of them the next morning. And nightmares usually tell us of our sins." The tone never changed.

Perceval liked the explanation. It made sense, and Perceval tried again to recall details of the dream.

"I still worry about what to believe, Abbot," Perceval said. "Here I sit awaiting my supper in a holy sanctuary, of which my mother would no doubt approve. Yet the people in my home are Pagans. Dindraine and I have never really cared much one way or the other. The people in Oerfa celebrate the Festivals, but aside from that don't take their beliefs too seriously. Maybe it's the lack of a druid to look to their needs. And my mother has spoken only little of it to my sister and I since we can remember. What am I to believe?"

Uren looked him straight on and simply said, "God assists those who assist themselves. That was how I came to be here in the first place; I believed in the core goodness of people and I wanted to believe in the possibility of eternal life. I think that's what everyone wants, in the end." He truly believed his words; such was the righteousness of his work.

Dinner was basic but satisfying. Dyfed spoke with Perceval about knighthood, and about the requirements of the church regarding their monks. Perceval was glad he had chosen another path, but thought he could at least begin to understand why people would give up so much to be a part of something greater than themselves. He slept very peacefully that night.

* * *

They had lost the trail, completely by the looks of it. Such was the frustration in pursuing something which clearly did not wish to be caught.

Or did it?

Yvaine stopped beneath the shady canopy offered by a copse of trees, many miles northwest of where they had met Dindraine and Perceval. Lamorak lay there, his robust strength helping him heal quickly, but occasionally babbling.

"We, we can't *kill* it!" he exclaimed.

By then the anxiety of trying to hunt this creature, whatever it was, had begun to tax Yvaine's patience. "But shouldn't we keep tracking it?" Now he wanted to know what it truly was, what it was doing.

Lamorak proffered no response, relapsed into rest. Their squires almost exhausted their spare horses trying to keep up with them. Yvaine felt the burdensome weight of impending defeat beginning to settle upon his shoulders, as though adding to the bulk of his armor. He also felt guilty for being the only person in the group wearing such protection.

"Vonnet, any sign of it?" Yvaine inquired of his squire. "Maybe it doubled back again, towards you." The squires had just ridden up; it was difficult to maintain the knight's pace, guiding two horses not one. Besides, squires were not allowed to ride in front of their masters.

"Nay, Sir. We haven't seen it since you spotted it this morning." Vonnet tried not to look as sheepish as he felt. He and Clydno, Lamorak's assistant, were both growing weary of them bolting at the slightest hint of the Barking Beast. It was running them all ragged in the rough terrain, the horses especially, though neither of the menservants dared mention it to Yvaine. Poor Clydno had enough concern just ensuring his master's wounds did not deteriorate.

Worse, Clydno had *seen* the damnable thing! He certainly thought it worthy of the tales and fear bespoken of it.

The first sighting occurred just six days after they had met that young boy and his lovely sister, Vonnet recalled. They rode further inland, to the northwest, trying to track the untraceable. The creature left no tell-tale signs. So they followed what they could, whatever they thought might be some indication of its passing. But disturbed branches and vague hoof prints could belong to several different species, and they didn't know exactly what this thing's tracks might look like in the first place.

Clydno, who froze in place with the exception of a quick crossing of his breast and an even quicker silent hail spoken to the Virgin Mary, thought that such a hellish thing might not even *leave* tracks. That consideration was numbing. He hoped he had adequately prepared his soul for the journey into the next life if they should actually cross paths with the Beast.

But there it had stood, its unholy sound finally giving it away as it looked at him. *As it looked at us all,* Clydno had thought, *as though judging us.* A bloated body sat upon what looked like a stag's legs. The body could have been that of a pregnant cow; how could those thin legs support such mass? From the gruesome torso sprang what could only be described as a snake's head. Only Yvaine had ever even seen a snake, and then only on the Continent during his prior escapades. But he confirmed the appearance as such, based on Clydno's description.

But the size! Surely no snake could have had such a head, big as a man's own, with the forked hissing tongue, no less. None of the small band wanted to give much thought as to just how such an abomination might live. Only Yvaine considered himself to have the answer, and so far he had only shared it with Vonnet. To try and ease the boy's mind.

If only Yvaine's own mind could be similarly soothed. He insisted that the only response was to chase after it, the only knightly course of action, anyway. Maybe it, too, could be frightened.

Looking out at the scene below their vantage point, Yvaine began to wonder how it might be that they had seen so few people since crossing the ambiguous line into Cambria. Aside from Perceval and Dindraine, they had only encountered a smattering of tribal warriors, who ran to hide. No merchants, no knights, no unruly peasants, no settlements. It was as though word of the Beast had gotten out, and people fled its path.

But if it couldn't be tracked, then how could the people possibly know which way to flee? Maybe they would have run right into it, so to speak.

This bothered the knight, who had for the first time all but forgotten the intrigue and potential vendetta awaiting his friend at Camelot. This quest, with its hair-raising uncertainty and challenge: this was what made a knight!

They kept scanning the wilderness. Only the spotty areas of forest suggested any life besides themselves. It was the loneliest place on earth right then. The only sound was the quick breathing, of four men and six horses.

Yvaine pointed. "There! Movement, down below. Do you see it?"

The squires followed the line indicated by the outstretched fingers, looking powerful and functioning as a single huge digit in their mail housing. All they could see below them, however, was another area of trees. Lamorak grumbled from his litter behind Clydno, seemingly aware of what was happening.

But the trees were only a large cluster. Not enough to be called a forest. Nothing could hide in there for long.

Following Yvaine's lead, they all rode down, urging their protesting horses onward to find the object of their quest.

To his surprise, Yvaine wondered again what might be responsible for such a nightmare appearing in the first place.

What causes a rift between the two Sides of reality? He considered. *Disharmony. There is a disturbance in the Balance.*

His mother taught him to view things from this perspective. All life was part of a sacred balance; Morgan had even said that the whole existence of the druids was focused on the maintaining and preserving of this balance, despite stories suggesting otherwise. Any right action had a corresponding wrong action. Any good had its opposite evil. Love could not exist without hate, and peace had no place without acts of war.

Those were the examples he could most easily understand. Yet his childhood was filled with other learnings, perhaps too obscure or demonic for the Christians. Life itself existed on two sides, This Side and the Other Side. The residents of the latter were called faeries, and the thing they pursued simply had to be among their number. Certainly no friendly faerie, but faerie just the same.

Wasn't it? And what about it made it so "evil" in the first place? For the first time Yvaine considered that he had listened all along to Lamorak's interpretation of the creature as inherently evil, pure and simple. What if it wasn't? Suppose it was here to make up for some previous imbalance?

It was too much to think about right then. He had to duck his head to avoid being swept off by a low-hanging branch. Just another of the Mother's ways of keeping things in balance; knock a vain knight off his mount, and he'll regain proper respect for that mount. Or so he thought. He tried to amuse himself with such thoughts whenever he could. Like now.

The others had done an admirable job of keeping up with his rugged pace. And now they had to stop, or at least slow considerably, so their horses could navigate the treacherous ground beneath them.

Still no sign of the Beast, however.

The squires dismounted and looked for tracks anyway.

* * *

"Forgive me, Father, for I have committed sin. Three months have passed since my last confessional." Galienne felt privileged to entrust the person in the other half of the confessional booth with her most sensitive feelings. She did not usually feel the apprehension of these visits, as did so many of the faithful. Today was an exception, however.

Bishop Baudwin knew her voice at once. Most younger voices came to him weepy and full of trepidation, when they came to confess their doings at all; he considered Galienne quite outgoing for her visits. "Speak truly of what is in your heart, my child, and know that God hears your entreaty as well as I."

The chamber was richly carved, nested within the magnificent cathedral of Saint Dubric's, securely in the heart of Camelot. The journey from Astolat proceeded pleasantly, Galienne and Lupinia delighting in the sights and sounds taken in from the trades wagon of Lupinia's father. The elder girl teased the men-at-arms escorting the party, encouraging her friend to join her. The men took it in stride, knowing they could relax their guard once west of the Garmani influence nearer the small city. Presently, Lupinia's father was engaged with his trade concerns, and his willful child took her leisure in the Queen's garden adjacent Pendragon Castle, admonishing Galienne to "not give in too much to the good bishop's prescriptions."

Foolish Lupinia, Galienne thought. Her soul needed more guidance than her father was clearly willing to supply himself. "I am afraid, Father. My sins include envy and sloth." She lowered her voice, guiltily. "And hatred."

Baudwin knew this girl better than that. "Come, my child, could it indeed be as bad as all that?"

From any other male she would have found the question patronizing. She stayed on track. "I have grown envious of my best friend. She is so lovely, and her father is always there for her. She's so comfortable around men, and me, I'm just so, so, out of place."

"Perhaps you are young yet to concern yourself with men."

"But my mother says I'm almost old enough to be married already. And I don't know what to say to men. The boys where I grew up always said I was too smart for a girl, and they didn't like me because I wanted to play like they did, instead of remaining indoors and learning to spin and stitch."

"Why would you wish to be more like them?"

"I don't know, Father. I just know that I want to do something other than follow my mother, who works all the time. She's very good, but she takes her work too seriously. She wants me to learn what she knows, but I have trouble concentrating with it."

"Is that why you seem to consider laziness one of your sins?" Baudwin had heard this from the girl before; she was too hard on herself, wanted so intently to live up to the demands of Scripture. She saw it as approval, though he had never told her: to win approval in God's eyes would translate to approval in those of her own father. Her earthly father. Or so she seemed to think.

He heard a deep sigh from the confessional chamber. "I just don't enjoy the work the way she does. My mother can sit and move that spinning wheel for hours and hours, talking or singing, and be perfectly happy. But it's so dull."

This one has never been content with where she was. "We are at our best, our most fulfilled, through our labors. You should realize this by now. What else would you do with your life if you have no wish of a husband, nor to follow into your mother's work? You do know that almost no one breaks with that tradition, unless to enter a convent."

That was what really terrified Galienne the most. What would she do if there was no way out of her family's lifestyle?

She could hardly enter her father's profession, and didn't want to follow her mother. Did she really tell him she had no wish for a husband?

The bishop continued. "My child, this is the way in which things are. How else are we to know our proper place and thereby fulfill God's will?"

That was too much. "Tell me, Father, please, do you come from a long line of priests or bishops?"

He took a moment before responding. "I believe I see what you mean. No, actually I did not. My father was a cobbler, but very devout." Another pause. "And, before you ask, I have remarkably little talent for stitching leather."

Now they both tried to stifle giggles. "In that case, how were you free to pursue your own passion?"

"I entered a monastery after failing as an apprentice. The rest fell into place after that. My family grew to love what I was doing. My father believed it would help them all be closer to God."

Galienne reminded him of why he considered her so perceptive. "So you chose your own calling?"

He exhaled. "I found my calling, though you could say God called me to it."

Then what is God trying to tell me through the visions He sends? But she was not about to discuss them again here. Baudwin was compassionate and understanding, and had heard about them before. "Then how do I find my calling, my place? According to God's will."

Baudwin was unsure if she intended the last part as statement or question. "You will. Through your faith, you will. Though I must admit, I'm not certain you're truly guilty of envy or sloth."

"I do help my mother with her work. I just don't wish to keep doing it forever." *Actually, the worst part is just listening to her.* "But I still envy my friend. It's like she toys with men, and they all go for it. She has them, what's that saying, wrapped about her finger. I think if she said the word 'jump' that they'd vault into their saddles."

"So she prefers knights?"

"Oh, indeed she does. So does my mother." Now she paused. "Perhaps that's why it's often difficult to listen to either of them. I just sometimes wish –"

He knew when she was hesitating with a difficult subject. "Wish what?"

"Father, sometimes I wish they would pay attention to me, too. Just a little." She felt her face flush again at the thought, all but ashamed. "How sinful is that, to want someone of the opposite, of the opposite –"

"Sex?" he prodded, unable to contain a smile, glad she couldn't see it.

She nodded to herself. Then, "Yes. How can I want something like that if I'm not also considering marriage? I feel like such a whore, even if my thoughts are otherwise pure."

Baudwin did not want this to continue. Sitting just a few feet from him was the most sinless female he had ever encountered. He marveled at how she turned out, this child of Elaine's. Merlin would have found her quite intriguing. He decided to try quite an unorthodox approach. The Archbishop might condemn him on the spot for this; he prided himself on reminding women of their station.

"You're not a whore. That requires action, far more impure than these mere thoughts, which are completely natural for anyone your age." Baudwin was almost sweating when he finished; Rome may have fled the Island, but its spiritual influence was still strong, especially after Eire-land's recent conversion. The Pope had already sanctified Patricus for his actions.

He did not notice Galienne's deep sigh of relief. Could the bishop be right? He had to be! Her thoughts felt so unclean, like when she and Lupinia spent the evening in the bath house.

It was the only acceptable place in which men and women alike could roam freely, barely dressed. And her mother approved. That still seemed strange, but the baths made everyone feel pure. "Thank you, Father. That comes as a huge relief. I did not want to believe it, but I was unsure."

"That is all right, my child." *And your mother no doubt had some say in your opinion of yourself.* Baudwin was not a parent himself, never would be, but he could still not fathom the guilt that some parents passed on to their children. His main difficulty was trying not to see the girl's mother as a whore herself.

But it was only one man, he reminded himself.

"Only one sin to go, Father," Galienne added to his thoughts, wondering what he would have her do to cleanse herself of her wickedness.

"Hatred," he recalled. "You hardly seem capable of it. Whom is the recipient of this evil?"

"My father, I think. I really don't even know him. How can I have such an opinion of someone I barely know, whose face I have trouble picturing?"

Baudwin felt obligated to consider the usual sources of such sentiment. "Does he beat you? Or your mother?"

She shook her head, the difficulty of speaking about *him* making her forget that the bishop could still not see her. "No. I'm not even certain he's a bad person. So many people adore him, and I have never understood why."

"Could it be envy then, instead of hatred, of the sort you mentioned regarding your young friend?"

Galienne mulled it over. *That would be better than despising the man outright. Still, he's never there, for either of us!* "Possibly, but aren't fathers supposed to want to watch their children grow, and to provide for their wives and families?" *Thankfully Mother didn't debate my refusal to bring him another gift.*

"So they are. *Abundant dulcibus vitiis.* Have you ever had the chance to speak with him of this?"

And say what?! she wanted to scream. "Never privately. Always has there been someone at his side." She admitted her additional envy only to herself; others always seemed to have access to that man, never Elaine nor Galienne. "And I do try and remember that no one's perfect, Father." She liked hearing him speak Latin, a reminder of her own efforts.

"If you'll permit my saying so, my child, this does not truly sound like hatred, merely regret. That is not a sin, merely unfortunate. I hope you can find the opportunity to speak with your father." He of course was unable to see her flinch; she'd rather do an extra penance or three than talk with that man.

She requested her actual penance, never waiting for him to begin prescribing it. She always felt he let her off lightly: three hours of steadfast prayer within the cathedral each day before she returned home, plus two afternoons helping the stable boys. She wouldn't mind that, really, so long as those boys didn't tease her, too. Additionally, she would spend two days as an errand-runner for some of the local nuns. Galienne had received that sentence before, and never informed the bishop that she actually enjoyed speaking with the nuns, even when they were short with her, and made her perform strenuous physical labors; that kind of work felt, well –

How does it feel? she wondered, at last leaving the chamber with Baudwin's admonishing prayer still in her ears.

Cleansing, she answered herself.

* * *

Perceval awoke early again, felt awkward as he uttered farewell to the silent group, and received a parting blessing from Uren. It felt like the one Amlyn proffered days earlier, though referring to a different deity. The prayer told of the Lord's Kingdom and Power and hollow name and trespassing. Perceval had little idea what it was all about, but he bowed his head and listened to the others, who murmured the verses in perfectly rhythmic unison. At least it wasn't in Latin.

Perceval was glad to be out of the abbey so early, his traveling companions eager as always to see him, especially after sleeping outdoors near the cemetery. The abbey was peaceful and part of him would miss it, but only a part.

The rest of him was far too excited to devote to a lifetime of humility as those people had done. He wondered about Merin though, who had greeted him mutely but with an expression suggesting graceful peace. Perceval wondered if the man's face had ever wrinkled.

He soon forgot his anxiety about prayers and crosses and focused on the open road. Which was soon closed, indeed swallowed whole, by the onset of the vastness of the Forest Arroy. He was upon it within the span of a few hours.

Nothing could have quite prepared Perceval for the utter spaciousness, paradoxically mingled with the sheer depth and density, of the great forest. It appeared as just a long and thick green line on the horizon at first, and Perceval thought it interesting, but hardly consequential. It was not until he stood face to face with the immense living entity that he began to appreciate the fears and stories of the villagers back home when they had said the forest could engulf you completely, and the Great Powers That Be help you if you got lost inside it.

Perceval, Brownie, and even Cabal stood and paused on the road, which clearly penetrated its way into the mossy, leafy, verdant darkness. It was the most daunting thing any of them had ever laid eyes upon; how could anyone be expected to wander through that clogged mess, teeming with untold species of predators, and natural traps of holes and fallen trees ready to take advantage of the unwary? How did the Legion's engineers lead a road through it in the first place?

Cabal whined slightly. Perceval noticed him, and looked down at the nervous brown eyes, which were almost, but not quite, as dark as the creeping, eerie green *thing* looming ahead of them. Perceval was not about to go back, not now; he had come too far to simply give up because of a bunch of intimidating trees. Besides, his confidence had boosted since Cabal led him down that final hill, showing how the world never really just ended.

The whole place was *alive*, and Perceval's awareness of this wreaked havoc with his nerves. He remembered how Tathan used to speak of the druid's regard for all trees, especially certain oaks, as sacred, and knew that they were living creatures with their own agendas. This place was not just living, but also home, to who knew what.

Fondling the cross proved to no avail, and the feel of its hard coolness was not very reassuring, either. Perceval released it, feeling it gently bounce once against his chest. He thought he heard some rustling from the trees to their left, but he must have imagined it, since neither Brownie nor Cabal took notice.

He wished Dindraine was at his side. Perceval was certainly no herbalist; to him there were just so many *trees*, more than he had ever imagined might exist anywhere. And they all looked alike to him, green and brown and daunting. They were so numerous and so convoluted that he had difficulty telling where some of them began and others ended; they sprouted all over like so many tentacles, ready to wrap themselves around anyone they didn't like.

Perceval remembered the times he and Dindraine had sneaked to the south of Oerfa to run and play among the forest-in-miniature which resided at the base of Kundry's foreboding hill. There were maybe five or six hundred individual trees there, and Perceval was proud of the time he could finally identify them (according to Tathan's descriptions, of course) as elms and ash and yews and even some oaks. But now the mishmash called the Arroy contained millions of them, to say nothing of their accompanying birches, maples, great oaks, pines (further up the larger hills, anyway), and every kind of deciduous tree ever heard of by even the druids themselves. Those little woods back home, fun as they were, were a drop in a pail compared to this. No wonder the people often said they were enchanted! Perceval again wished he paid more attention to such stories.

He sat there pondering the incredible living giant before him for many minutes, knowing that people had navigated their way past all of this before. How else could there have existed a road going through it? How else did Yvaine and Lamorak and their squires get so far west?

Cambria was completely cut off from the rest of Britain by this immense north-south-and-east expanse of forest, divided up haphazardly into sections with their own names, of which the Arroy was but one. Perceval knew the only way to reach Camelot was to go through it, and he was not about to give up on his task, fear of the green canopied mysterious darkness or no. He just didn't figure on how long it would take.

Perceval swallowed hard, his throat contracting as though he had tried to inhale a whole apple in one gulp, such was his trepidation. He could go on, or he could return. He was delighted when Brownie and Cabal offered no resistance; they either were calm themselves, or resigned to their master's bidding, wherever it might lead them.

He was also pleased by how easy it was to follow the road. Maybe the woods were not really enchanted; it was said that a person would know an enchanted forest by discovering that no matter which road he followed, he was sure to get lost and stay lost, until finding a way out by chance. Or staying there forever. Perceval did not intend to stay in there forever, and was surprised by how he actually began to find much of it quite enjoyable.

There were falcons and owls and ravens throughout, in addition to so many other types of birds, large and small, which he had never seen before. Squirrels and chipmunks, rabbits and raccoons, were often bold enough to peer out from behind the shelter of trees to look upon the intruders. Cabal even managed to summon enough courage, negating his earlier apprehension, to chase some of the smaller animals. He never went more than a few dozen yards, though, and barely left the road at all.

A small snake once startled Brownie so that she reared up and almost dislodged her rider, but it was harmless. Unless someone was a small rodent or frog, and there were plenty of them, too. Perceval was intrigued by the snake; he still did not know what one was, but was too fascinated to fear something that lightly hissed and slithered around quickly, without the use of feet or wings or fins. He thought those were the only ways a living thing could move itself, up until then. And he failed to connect the creature to what he saw in the land of dreams.

After a nerve-racking yet uneventful first night spent hidden among trees but with the road still within view, Perceval and his companions relaxed a bit. Maybe the great forest's bark was worse than its bite. No creatures molested them, no fellow travelers proved hostile (indeed, the only human contact amongst the trees was with a small caravan of miners and smiths, heading westward to tap into the vast mineral resources offered by the Cambrian hills).

The road was clearly marked and clearly avoided by most, judging by the relative absence of human and horse tracks, despite the reputation the High King's roads had for safety (an offense committed on them was considered an offense against the King personally, and was not taken lightly). That same small mining caravan was escorted by a quintuplet of knights, with sharpened long swords and dour expressions. They were mercenaries, governed far more by the promise of money than the attempted fulfillment of ideals, and while Perceval was intrigued and conversational with them, they were not the shining flowers of chivalry to which he aspired. Actually, they had so turned off Perceval that he avoided the shelter of two small castles along the way, thinking them likely inhabited by more of the same type of gruff knights of questionable merits. The castles were easily reached from the road, but looked dark, guarded and hostile; he wanted no part of them, and was content to sleep under the natural, more comforting shelter of the trees.

The forest was so dense that it completely shielded Perceval and the animals from the rain which fell during the course of an entire day and night; barely a drop hit them at all, and the mud which trickled down the road was easily avoided, although Cabal loved to tromp through it, getting filthy and then sending the mud flying every which way with the kind of thorough body shake of which only quadruped mammals are capable.

The initial fear and uncertainty gave way to a sense of awe and childlike curiosity as Perceval became bolder about which areas to explore. Not that he ever left the road for long, but he did often dismount Brownie, who could have all too easily tripped and broken a leg on the hazardous outcroppings of moss-covered trees and rocks which lined the road, that had lost all signs of having been disturbed so many years prior to make way for the marching Centurions. He would wander with Cabal to take a closer look at this melodic bird or that noble elder tree. It was pure pleasure, like when he and Dindraine used to run around outside the confines of Oerfa.

He wondered how she was doing; God, how he missed her. And mother. And the other villagers. How were they faring?

This playful mood remained largely intact, interrupted only by the occasional traveling group (no bandits on the High King's road, fortunately) until the trio made their way southward, through alternating forest and low hilly land, to the immortal Camelot itself.

* * *

The greatest city ever built looked almost like a shorter version of the forest at first. It appeared on the distant edge of Perceval's vision as another green line, rising up like a hill, then flattening out. Amongst this plateau could be seen, as he drew much closer, the unmistakable lining of battlements, flanked here and there by immense towers. Camelot was constructed upon a natural hill, which had been strengthened centuries previously by enormous versions of the same ditches and earthen ramparts which Perceval saw in Beacon Ring. Behind these defensive walls lay eighteen acres; it was only fitting that Arthur should choose it (with some cajoling on the part of Merlin, no doubt) as the site for his royal court.

The castles and fortresses of Britain and the Continent, be they mere wooden motte-and-baileys constructed from tree trunks or full quarried, concentric fortifications with walls as thick as the height of two to four grown men, all had one thing in common: they were erected for the primary (and usually sole) purpose of defense of some area of land. But not Camelot: this castle-city was visionary. Its several thousand residents not only lived here but thrived, and most actually resided on the city's slopes and surrounding countryside; want was largely unknown within its walls, the bravest and most able knights in the world would happily shed their life's blood defending it, and it contained wonders the likes of which had never been seen before.

There were not just one but two distinct castles within the site. The first was for the King and his entourage, which also housed the Round Table and Royal Palace, and contained banquet halls which could feed hundreds at once. The other was just as impressive, and reserved for the exclusive use of visiting royalty and dignitaries, such as the lesser kings of Britain and occasionally the Continent.

The safe and Roman-styled streets led people leisurely to the city's highlights: the Queen's Garden, in which those stricken by *fine amour* could be at one with their emotions and sometimes the recipients of their affections; the abbey and monastery located adjacent to a magnificent cathedral which sported actual stained-glass scenes of the lives of Jesus, Mary, Joseph, and the Apostles; and even a college where those of a more intellectual or spiritual focus could go to study from the fine collection of priceless books recovered from the Continent after the King's campaigns there.

Had Perceval known how to read, he would have memorized the colorful names adorning many of the buildings once he came within sight of them: Rhodri's Philters and Medicinals (word on the street suggested the house specialty was a potent herb from southern lands said to enlighten the spirit when breathed in smoky form); the Order of Masons and Builders; Gwern's Jewelry; a plethora of inns and taverns, guilds, a weaponsmith, a blacksmith and armory far better equipped and capable than Melangell's; healers, soothsayers, clothesmakers, leatherworkers, professions Perceval had never heard of, could not imagine the use for. But they were no less marvelous to behold.

Yet the magnificence only began. The city swelled to contain sumptuous quarters and houses within, and the prolific businesses which thronged the streets daily: artisans, butchers, farmers, craftspeople, and animal trainers (the latter even found sponsorship through the Queen's menagerie, which was rumored to contain not just stunning and proud beasts like lions and talking birds, but even winged lions and monsters straight from the realms of history or hell, depending on whom one asked). The common people of the Isle already had a saying about this place: if you could not find what you hoped to in Camelot, it did not exist anywhere. Royal cash and Merlin's foresight had combined to produce the greatest assemblage of construction workers in history, and the vision was realized in the space of a few short years! No one in this region of Logres could doubt the beneficence of the Pendragon's rule; all who opposed him initially were either conquered or subjugated, and there seemed no end to the wealth that helped support the King (from quelled lands, domestic and foreign, and the coffers of lords, ladies, and lesser monarchs).

And now here in front of Perceval was the object of his quest. His heart beat so strongly he feared it would bound right out of his chest, springing its way into the city without him.

He wondered how Brownie had the strength to carry him. Of course, she was not in such awe herself; to her this was probably just another hill, something to be climbed for the purpose of ensuring safety. She had no idea that soon she would be near the finest of stables, among others of her kind from lands afar, where oats and fruit, lavish attention, and flawless grooming were the daily fare.

As he drew nearer, Perceval noticed groups of children frolicking about, secure despite their games leading them beyond the walls, laughing and gaily screaming themselves hoarse. Not far from them knights practiced, doing things on horseback he never imagined. He was amazed, his head swimming; everyone was having the time of their lives, and they all delighted in doing this beyond the safety of the immense earthworks and fortress defenses. This was a true sanctuary on earth, he thought, never fully averting his gaze from the knights and their exercise. They reminded him of his mission, and for the first time he allowed himself to imagine just what would happen when he rode up to the palace.

How would he introduce himself to the King, then? What courtesy would he be expected to show the Queen? What about the other knights and ladies and nobles who might be present? Should he just casually stroll right on up and say, "I bid you greeting, esteemed King. Now would you please make me a knight?"

No, Perceval thought, that sounded pretty weak, to say nothing of presumptuous. How then would he gain the King's attention? He remembered how Yvaine spoke of great knightly deeds which one had to accomplish before one was judged fit to bear arms and fulfill a lord's justice. But Perceval did not like to think that the most impressive thing he ever did was to leave home and travel alone just to meet a man he had never seen before. Yet, that was a start. Perhaps something in Camelot would give him the necessary inspiration.

But it seemed there would be no great villainy to be vanquished, and even if there were, the other knights would likely scramble for center stage (Perceval allowed himself this occasional fantasy of thinking he had somehow already been knighted, pondering the doings of those *other* knights). Maybe the King would offer to send him on a quest of his own. *Yes, that must be the surest way,* he thought. His own quest!

Perceval continued to follow his way up the road which led to two consecutive gates, the first really not so much a typical gate as a cavernous archway dug into the hill itself, the second an immense tower always heavily guarded and more defensible by itself than Rhun. He was about to pass through the earthy entrance when he heard some shouting from the gate further ahead.

"Look out, dogs!" came the bellow of a large man wearing well-polished and maintained reddish chain link armor, covered with a crimson doublet and an embroidered shield design with a black field and some gold colored creature emblazoned over it. The whole knight emanated this loud redness, actually; something about his armor made it seem as though aglow. Then Perceval noticed what it was: small plates protecting the joints had been *painted* somehow, requiring a bit of arduous labor.

The knight reared his stallion charger up, knocking over two of the guards at the interior gate. From far behind him came other shouts, but Perceval could not comprehend them. Then the knight turned towards the source of the shouting, and yelled back, "Tell that false king that his queen's lands are forever forfeit, unless he produces a champion!" He snarled, adding,

"I demand this settled once and for all! By my blood, it is my right!"

He turned towards Perceval and charged out of the city, almost running the lad down in the process. Perceval had never met such an enraged look; he thought this knight would eagerly go after him if he wasn't careful, just from anger.

The knight galloped by, the people outside just now noticing him. Perceval looked back to the gate, where the guards mumbled and picked themselves up off the ground. Then he looked behind him at the rider, who began to slow, taking up a position amongst a bracken of trees. *Of course!* Perceval thought. *The knight could be challenged.* Perceval considered going after him right then, but thought better of it. He had no armor, little training, and he still had to gain royal attention.

He wondered how long the rude knight would wait. He rode up to the inner gate, looking at the furious guards. One of them had to be restrained by his peers so that he would not foolishly run after the red knight only to get slaughtered. The guards paid Perceval little attention. Such was the nature of Camelot that all were made welcome here, unless they were previously known enemies, and so people were free to come and go as they pleased. Besides, Perceval, Brownie, and Cabal hardly seemed threatening.

Perceval could see both of the immense castles more clearly now. He entered through the North Gate, and from his vantage point viewed the larger Pendragon castle, the King's own, in the far southwest corner. Majestic Keep, its equal in splendor if not in size, was firmly placed in the far southeast corner. Perceval at once considered this location absolutely impregnable; what force on earth could possibly tumble these walls? And Rhun? Castle Rhun was nothing, a mere splotch of hasty stone next to this.

There was another huge building, though certainly not as large as the castles, roughly in the middle, and Perceval knew it to be a religious center by the immense cross mounted proudly on top of it. The cross was the tallest single construction in here, save only for the tallest towers of Pendragon Castle. He could also see an area enclosed by a short stone wall, which held all manner of shrubs and flowers; this was just outside the main castle, and he could see several young people of both genders strolling through it, hands entwined, oblivious to anything else. The rest was an immense collage of brightly colored buildings of wood and stone, endless rows of homes and businesses.

And the Camelotian people: there was not a sad face anywhere. Perceval noticed a couple of young girls giggling at him and pointing, and he grew red instantly, looking away and at some other persons. Knights strolled around, wearing armor so brilliant it reflected the sunlight (he could only guess at the amount of sweaty labor armorers and squires put in to maintain such shiny hauberks and chausses). Ladies and gentlemen alike looked as though on parade, wearing such brightly colored woven fabrics that Perceval had not the slightest idea what might have been used to dye them. He only knew that dyes were rare and expensive; his mother had a vial of indigo coloring which she used on a dress she made for Dindraine when she was just a little girl, complaining sometimes about the shade's cost.

Music could be heard from several different directions as well. Perceval liked the melodic strumming of the harps and lyres. Off to one side a man and a woman danced to one of the tunes, circling each other and joined only at the hands, laughing lightly as though this was the greatest day of their lives.

It was so much to take in at once! Perceval reminded himself that he was here on serious business, and dismounted Brownie, leading the horse toward Pendragon Castle.

Along the way the same girls who had giggled at him approached Cabal, who was feeling as playful as they. The giggles became full laughs as the dog accepted their affections, rolling around on the ground while they stroked his belly and face. Cabal had not had such attention from anyone other than Dindraine, and he lavished it. Perceval finally had to call to him to catch up; the royal entrance was straight ahead. Besides, Perceval was still embarrassed by the girls' laughter, even though they were just having fun. They simply laughed that laugh of which only teenaged girls are truly proficient. Yet he noticed that the girls followed him toward the castle. What could they want?

"Hey, where are you going? Don't you know animals aren't allowed in Pendragon Castle?" asked one of them behind Perceval's back. He could hear her friend giggling at the question which clearly presumed his ignorance.

"Do you want us to watch them while you're inside? The dog already likes us." This from the same girl.

Perceval turned to face them. For the first time he noticed the physical details of each. The one he guessed had just spoken was the taller of the pair, her deep brown locks of hair enjoying the freedom of the light breeze; she had a dignified, sculpted face, and looked bright, both in an energetic and intellectual sense. Her clothes were the simple flowing robes of the majority of souls who lived in Britain, and it took the uncultured Perceval several seconds to avert his glance from her blossoming bust line.

The shorter girl looked more shy, aside from her almost annoying laugh. Perceval thought she was not as pretty as her friend, but also considered it to be more the result of what puberty does to a body, and not some inherited flaw. She still had the relative narrowness of hips and flatness of chest which all persons have while in their developing years, yet she had eyes the color of the richest of emeralds, and stood proudly, as though she had had quite enough of jokes about her height and slender build. Her hair length was indeterminable; the otherwise silky blonde threads had been pulled into an oppressively tight bun. Hanging from her neck on a leather strand was a carved wooden cross, even larger than the one which Perceval wore on his own chest.

The taller one was clearly not acquainted with shyness. "I'm Lupinia. This is my friend, Galienne."

The shorter one gasped. "Lupy, don't tell some strange boy my name!"

"Why not? He looks harmless. Besides, he's cute." Both Galienne and Perceval could feel their cheeks heating. "What's your name?" Lupinia continued, pleased to see a male blush from her words.

"P-Perceval. My name is Perceval. I'm from Cambria." His nervousness was at least helped slightly by these two speaking perfect Cymru. He had worried for a time after departing Haughmond Abbey that perhaps the people in Logres spoke Latin. Some did, but usually only for formality.

"Cambria?!" replied Lupinia, "Whatever could have brought you this far?"

Perceval was not about to let these two get the best of him. "I am going to be a knight. I just need to find myself a quest worthy of the King's attention, and, hey, what's so funny?"

Lupinia was choking on her laughter, much as Yvaine did weeks ago. "A knight? You? You look like a farm-boy!"

Perceval was just about to turn away when Galienne interceded. "Lupy, stop it. What's wrong with him becoming a knight? Maybe he's really a great person. Who can say what God may have in store for –"

"There you go again," Lupinia interjected, "I don't presume to ever know what God has in store for anyone. Look, Perceval, I apologize if I hurt your feelings, but even you have to admit you don't exactly look the part."

Galienne was not finished yet. "My mother told me that my father didn't 'look the part' either when he was younger, and now he's a great knight. Why he's the Queen's –" She bit off the words, remembering how she felt about him.

"Oh, please, I know the story already," said Lupinia. Then to Perceval, she added, "So, what do you say, 'future great knight'? We promise to take good care of your pets while you're trying to gain royal favors."

Perceval was in little mood to leave Brownie and Cabal with the likes of these two, even if the blonde was kinder than her companion. Still, he had to deposit them somewhere for a while. He doubted he could afford the royal stables' prices.

"Why not?" he asked both the girls and himself, "You can watch them. Just make sure they don't get into trouble, or take off anywhere. I'll be back soon."

"We'd love to," smiled Lupinia. Galienne was already stroking Brownie's chin; apparently she did know something of horses. Returning to his task, Perceval left the four of them.

As he got closer to the dominating Castle Pendragon, Perceval noticed a bit of commotion from within. People ran about, gossiping amongst themselves. He could overhear mention of the *"dastardly knight"* and the *"poor Queen"* and *"what the King will do to avenge such an insult."*

The hall was stunning, the inside decorated with perfectly carved and dramatically stained native hardwood. Perceval wondered how long it had taken to carve up that many trees. Ignoring the flurried activity, he focused on the actual building itself, noting how there were countless painted shields hanging from the walls. The most prominent knights and lords had the privilege of permanently displaying their personal arms here. On one wall, behind a huge feasting table, hung a single shield: a deep blue field, on which were painted three gold crowns, the King's own. Next to this was a shape he did not recognize; it looked like a shield, yet it was diamond-shaped. He had never seen a four-pointed shield before, if that was what it truly was. *No, wait.* Now he was understanding it. The four-pointed shape had the same heraldic design that the red knight wore on his own shield: the black field broken in the middle by the gold creature. A "lion" like Yvaine's? Something else, even deadlier? Perceval was no expert on fantastic or faerie creatures; this one looked as though it could easily and messily consume a horse, then demand seconds.

Perceval was confused, again. Why would *that* knight's arms be represented in here, if the man was obviously an insult to Arthur and his reign? It made no sense. The young traveler continued his scan of the furnishings in the mighty room when a voice bellowed above the droning of the other noises. He was sure the boisterous call specifically hailed him.

"You there, boy. What are you doing here?" demanded the gruff tone.

Perceval turned to face an obvious knight, though he walked with a noticeable limp on his right side. The man wore a tunic of the same blue as the King's shield, with a pair of golden keys emblazoned upon it. Maybe this man was the royal treasurer. His face sported a short but perfectly groomed blond beard, and the eyes bore in on Perceval with an accusing intensity.

"Excuse me, sir, but is this not the hall of the King? I have come to see him," Perceval said. The man had spoken to him in some unknown dialect; Perceval tried to sound as non-threatening as possible.

The man stared, disbelieving, turning his speech into Cymru instead. "You don't speak Latin; well you're an idiot, why would you? Of *course* it's the King's hall, doltish peasant. Now state your business, before I have you removed from here. The King has no time for you."

The doltish peasant would not be put off so easily. "But I've come to be a knight. And I was told that the King would make me one."

Perceval's antagonist exploded with condescending laughter. "Did you hear that, you all? Hah! This young churl wants to be a knight! This is too much!" The man almost fell over, he was guffawing so hard.

"What's that, Kay?" came another voice, from behind Perceval. The latter reeled around, happily turning his back on the man wearing the keys on his chest, and gazed upon a much more handsome and courteous looking knight.

"Lucan, look at this contemptuous boy," Kay said to Perceval's turned back, "he looks barely old enough to sport a beard, much less become a knight."

Perceval frowned. He *was* old enough! How old were men supposed to be to qualify as knights, anyway? And he was surprised Kay did not find insult in his turning completely away; he wondered at the older man's rearing. Perceval would have been offended by the same gesture.

Kay was too busy throwing cheap jests to care. Lucan spoke. "My dear Kay, if potential knights were judged solely by their pretty facial hair or their presumed contemptuousness, what makes you think you would have ever been dubbed?" Lucan's voice was devoid of the sarcasm it bespoke. Behind Perceval, Kay made a rude gesture. Lucan ignored it.

Instead he addressed the younger man in front of him now. "Tell me, boy, why do you wish to be a knight in the first place? And pay Kay no mind; he simply has his feathers in a ruff over what happened in here recently."

"Well, Sir," Perceval started, thinking he could feel Kay's breath on his back, "I want to go on great quests and quell the lands of all manner of villains. I have met Sirs Yvaine and Lamorak during my travels, and was told all I needed to do was to come to Camelot and make myself worthy in the eyes of the King."

Lucan raised his brow, impressed. Few candidates spoke this well of themselves and their intentions, and with such blatant honesty. Kay was still snickering behind. "And what do you think may be worthy of such attention from the King, who at the moment has his hands full of other concerns, and not the time to listen to you?"

Perceval looked back towards Kay, who still stood there, arms crossed, a vain and patronizing smile on his face. That look alone was enough to make up his mind, even though he thought someone else would already have jumped at the chance to avenge whatever insult befell the Queen.

"Please believe me, Sir Lucan, when I say I have something I wish to do which I feel will surely gain the King's favor. But I do not know how to proceed."

Lucan looked right past Perceval. Had he said the wrong thing again? He really must put a stop to these thoughtless exclamations, before he got himself into serious trouble. Like with the red knight. He still wasn't quite sure he wanted the job, but became convinced it would definitely impress Arthur.

"My lord," began Lucan, speaking beyond Perceval (even Kay turned to face the new addressee), "has the villain any takers yet?"

Perceval instinctively wheeled around to see this "lord," and froze when he saw the tall blonde man stroll into the room, followed by a rapturously beautiful woman who looked as though her clothes were stained with something, and followed again by several servants, ladies-in-waiting, and a trio of knights.

The tall man wore the most elegant deep violet robes, lined with the fur of some exotic spotted creature. His eyes suggested calm, yet it was merely a mask to conceal both his rage and the jealousy that, as king, he could not avenge the Queen himself. His face was lined with time's etchings and the responsibilities of leadership, yet he still looked strong enough to wrestle down a bull.

Arthur's simple reply was, "Aye, Lucan, he has, but I am still weighing my options in granting any of them the task. After all, Meliagrant has full protection when in my personal demesne, bastard scoundrel or no." He looked at his Queen, who stood next to him. Guinevere looked insulted but still proud and defiant, and also furious at the stain which had ruined her own clothing.

This was all happening too fast; Perceval wanted it to slow down. Surely that could not be the King and Queen themselves who had just entered! They looked like normal people. Just with better clothing. *Well, of course,* thought Perceval. *They are real people.* What did he expect, angels?

Perceval was beginning to feel as though he was the only one in the vast hall, despite the throngs of well-dressed, impeccably groomed people present, all of whom had fallen silent at the reappearance of their liege. The people formed a personal entourage, an assemblage of servants, advisors, and bodyguards. And they knew when to speak and when to keep their mouths shut.

"May I suggest something then, my lord?" inquired Lucan, "This boy here has traveled from far away, since he has already spoken with those who seek the Barking Beast, and he should like an audience, if you would hear him."

The cluster of beings simultaneously turned to Perceval, who felt himself swallow hard. He was sure he would pass out from fright right there and then.

From behind him came a gentle push from Lucan's firm arms, and the whisper, "Go on, lad, what have you got to lose?" Not a sound came from any other soul, not even Kay.

The King made no motion whatsoever; he was used to hearing the petitions of his vassals within his hall, and he was eager for any distraction from the dilemma he now faced. A knight, claiming blood relation (though bastardized) to the Queen herself, likewise had claimed her home kingdom of Cameliard. Its benevolent ruler, King Leondegrance, a loyal vassal and presenter of the magnificent Round Table as his daughter's dowry, finally passed away due to illness the last year. Arthur considered this Meliagrant a braggart and an insult to the institution of knighthood, but under the law he was perfectly safe within Logres, so long as he did not actually attack with mass force. To champion the Queen would be the easiest route, but he wanted Meliagrant's authority to be undermined, without risking his own. Lands, much less whole kingdoms, could not be just given up (especially within the range of Logres!) To lose such land would also mean losing face, losing wealth, and possibly losing popular support as well. None of these was acceptable.

And now this lad, who walked slowly up to him. What was on his mind?

Perceval tightened his innards as much as possible to avoid peeing away his fright right in front of everyone. What had that bastard Lucan done to him?

He has granted me an audience with the King, Perceval thought. *Wasn't this what I wanted so badly?*

That did nothing to stop his terror, however. Dozens of eyes watched his every motion, would hear his every thought made speech. It took almost a full minute to cross the hall to stand ten yards from its master and mistress. And now there he was, ready to make or break his dream.

"M-my lord," Perceval intoned, barely audible. Then he remembered; he was still standing. Quickly he bent one knee down to the floor and put most of his weight on the other.

He cleared his throat. It was now or never. "My lord," he began, louder, "I am Perceval of Oerfa, a small village in the chiefdom of Powys. And I have come to request such a deed which will make me worthy of the sacred title of knight."

The crowd gasped, all but Arthur, Lucan, and Kay. Perceval paid them no attention, and continued. "Sire, it has come to my awareness that a criminal was recently here, and paid you and yours no small insult. I humbly ask the right to champion your cause." No taking it back now. Either way, at least Perceval would know that he had tried.

The King remained silent, never taking his eyes off Perceval, though the onlookers fought off the urge to start murmuring, questioning, gossiping. That look felt physically heavy, as though Perceval were weighed down by it, and he tried to find solace in the unresponsive floor. There was something familiar about the King's stern face, too. Had he seen him before? No, of course not.

"Perceval," said Arthur. It seemed as though whole lifetimes had passed by the time he finally spoke. "I agree with you. I accept your courteous and brave offer. I want you to personally go and tell that very same knight that I shall never bow to his demands, as they are totally unfounded, and he is equally unworthy."

The gasping and conversing from the crowd instantly became so loud it could be heard outside, where a girl struggled to gain entrance. Galienne was trying to deliver a message of her own, and hoped she could negotiate her way through the masses to talk to the young man she had just met.

Still a bit dazed, Perceval forced himself upright on legs that felt leaden. The King's face showed hints of both gentility and firmness, compassion tempered by a duty to justice. He appeared deadly serious overall, and yet somehow looked at Perceval as a father might gaze at a son who has done something to make the elder man proud. Perceval would always remember this look; having no father of his own to impress, he marveled at how he had gotten everyone's attention in the royal hall in a matter of mere minutes.

But he could not hear Galienne, who still frantically tried to worm her way inside. "Perceval? Perceval!" came her cries, drowned out completely by the swarm of gossip descending through the whole castle. Galienne's weak voice was beaten back by the echoings of *"Who is this boy?," "What is the King thinking?,"* and even, *"He's just to take a message, not to fight."*

Undaunted and more confident, Perceval made for the rear of the palace; he thought only of his task, and had to get outside to make sure those two girls hadn't lost Cabal and Brownie. He made a quick mental inventory of what Brownie carried still: the two worn and old blankets, a change of clothes, his new javelin and the hunting knife, and little food. Not exactly the most knightly of weapons, but they would have to do against his opponent. *How does one come by a sword and shield?* he wondered.

But no, he reminded himself. *The King made me a messenger, not a cause-defender.* Perceval hoped combat could be avoided, but wondered if the usurping knight would wish to strike him down anyway, just for being the annoying bearer of ill news.

Galienne was still pushing her way through the gaping crowd, which wanted a better look at this brash youth who suddenly found his hands full. Kay and Lucan stood near the doorway, refusing to let anyone else enter until others dispersed. So far not many people had gathered outside the building, but some onlookers grouped to investigate the flurry of excited noise coming from within.

Kay fumed. Lucan the Butler was both amused and impressed. The latter knew the plan did not actually put Perceval in very great risk, unless, of course, he managed to anger Meliagrant into attacking him. Meliagrant had insulted Queen Guinevere, not only with his demand for her home lands, but also by picking up a silver goblet lined with gemstones and splashing its contents, some apple wine rumored to have been a gift of the Lady of the Lake herself, all over the Queen's front. She was livid. And now the insult would be returned by another: the King would deliver his final message, which was not only negative, but to be given by a commoner! The boy wasn't even a squire, so far as Lucan knew, to say nothing of a knight. Meliagrant would be steamed, all right. Lucan felt he should probably ride along behind just to see what happened.

Kay, still aghast at the nerve of not only Lucan but of this untrained boy, was in no mood to deal with the ever-growing mass of people outside who walked the fine line between curiosity and nosiness. Just now some whelp of a girl tried to get past him. He was not about to let her in, not until the assemblage here themselves dispersed, hopefully to see the boy get trounced.

"Please, Sir, let me pass. I have a message for the lad Perceval," Galienne pleaded. She had almost slipped by the seneschal when he laid his rough hands on her. Had Kay known her, he might not have been so hasty, but he had no wish to deal with more of the commoners, much less some girl who wanted to see the boy.

"Nay, I will certainly not," Kay said, "and if you have any message, it can wait until this 'Perceval' is outside." He slurred the name with the most malicious tone he could muster. It made Galienne cringe. It was almost more than she could stand for one day; she had already felt as though she was being watched by someone, and now this Sir Kay was proving most irksome.

Perceval was almost to the doors, trying not to listen to the gossip following right on his heels. He refused to look any of these people in the eye; let them see what he could do in the fields beyond Camelot first! Up ahead he saw what looked like Galienne struggling to get away from Kay, who had his arms all but wrapped clear around her from the rear. She looked distressed indeed. Perceval hoped nothing had happened to his quadruped companions.

"Perceval, it's Cabal," Galienne shouted, "Oh, let me go you ox! If my father hears of this –"

"Oh, do shut up, girl. Now get outside before I throw you out," and Kay wheeled her around and shoved her towards the exit, head first. She had to brace herself with her forearm just to keep from ramming her head into the heavy wall. No protests were forthcoming; as far as anyone could tell, this was just some griping lass who happened to pick the wrong time to try and have her petition heard. Those who saw what happened were surprised by the amount of fight this girl had.

Perceval, ignoring Kay, ran to Galienne, whom he had expected to find sobbing. Yet she shed not a single tear; she was too proud for that. She *would* give her message, and that was final.

"Perceval, I'm sorry. But Cabal, he, he ran off. I guess he got whiff of some great scent and just chased it. Lupinia and I lost sight of him."

Perceval was stunned. Had this girl withstood Kay's abuse just to deliver a message about a creature who always wandered, but who never went far and always came back? He almost loved her instantly just for caring that much, though he wondered as to Brownie's whereabouts. He needed his mare now.

"Galienne, please don't worry about Cabal. He's a big boy and can take care of himself. Now let's get you out of here." Perceval tried to pick her up, but she refused, insisting on getting up unaided. She was proud, all right. She looked back towards Kay, and by now the crowd was in their faces, some questioning, others cheering on the *"brave young lad."*

Perceval and Galienne headed the rest of the way outside, to where Lucan busily answered questions about the King's message to the Queen's protester. Towards the back of this second gathering of people, Perceval could see Lupinia, gently leading Brownie by the reins. *Maybe she isn't so bad*, Perceval thought. Ignoring Lucan and the people completely, he made straight for his mount.

"What took you so long?" asked Lupinia, "and what's with all these people? What happened in there, anyway?"

"Lupy, ask him again later. He's busy." Galienne was as intently focused as Perceval. She was tempted to tell him about what she felt earlier. He seemed so trustworthy, though she was unsure why. She contented herself to watch as he gracefully and confidently climbed on top of the mare, gripping the reins in one hand and securing the modest javelin in the other.

Perceval looked down at the girls. "What about Kay?" he asked Galienne.

"Oh, the Lord says that what goes around comes around. Kay will suffer a broken arm for the way he treated us today." She said it so naturally it startled her. How *dare* she speak like that! This was no time to discuss her gift with anyone. The feeling was getting to her; she would have to control herself.

Both Perceval and Lupinia stared at her, and Galienne withdrew from their confused glances. How could she have been so stupid? She never told anyone about her visions, except for the bishop. He had tried to convince her that she was not guilty of any sin for having visions of things which often came to pass, though she remained unable to find the courage to tell her mother about them, much less her father. Her father wouldn't have cared anyway. She at once felt nauseous. And what was that which she felt earlier, like someone's prying eyes? Well, no matter. Her companions were occupied, and they probably thought she was just joking anyway.

Perceval looked at her curiously when she said it, though he wanted to get out of there, to go and speak with this robber knight and false lord who awaited him beyond Camelot's security. He scanned the now huge crowd, looking for the man he hoped to swear his allegiance to, and bowed his head when he had picked out the elder man who appeared more casual than regal. He had never been more proud, and only wished Dindraine could see him right then. Without another word he urged Brownie up to speed and raced for the North Gate, hearing the mixture of cheers and shouts behind him.

Lupinia watched Perceval go, then turned to her friend. "What was that about a broken arm?"

Galienne continued to watch where Perceval had gone. "It's nothing. I was just teasing. When the crowd disperses, let's go look for his dog."

* * *

"Who are *you*, boy? Where is the King with a message for me?" barked the red-colored knight.

Meliagrant was a large, daunting man, who stood next to his personal pavilion, which was likewise dyed a bloody hue. Behind him stood his traveling entourage: four other personal knights and a half-dozen men-at-arms, all looking ready to pick a fight with anyone. Meliagrant reeked of travel and worse; Perceval could smell him even from atop Brownie, and he had never before seen a tent of any kind. He almost asked his antagonist about it when the man interrupted him.

"Well? Answer me, before I pull you from your mare and pummel you into the earth. What kind of man rides a mare anyway?" demanded the rude knight.

Perceval collected his thoughts, and began. "I have a message to you, Sir Meliagrant, from Arthur, the High King of Britain."

"And my message is delivered by a lowly squire? You tell that damned king of yours –"

Perceval saw his opening and immediately cut the man off. "I will tell him only of your defeat in a contest of arms, should it come to that. For I *am* the message. You are ordered to leave here at once, along with your men, never to despoil the lovely scenery surrounding Camelot again." *Maybe I take matters too far,* Perceval wondered. But he had to admit, insulting this man was fun. Yvaine would have been pleased.

Meliagrant thought the boy had some nerve, though he at least respected the lad's courage. He offered his answer. "I will not waste my breath on an insignificant servant such as you. Return and tell the king that I want a knight to –"

"As I say, *Sir*, it is I and no one else. Face me, or go."

The churl cut him off again, damn him! The deliberate slurring of Meliagrant's legitimate title was sure to anger him to no end. And it was starting to look like a fight; Meliagrant was not giving even an inch toward meeting the King's demands.

The red knight was equally colored beneath his armor now. The King could not even meet with him man to man, but dared to send this stupid errant in his stead! "You have interrupted my speech for the last time, peasant boy. Run that mare of yours down to that tree and meet my charge, if you possess nerve of equal strength as your tongue. Give your pathetic answer to your so-called king, or look down from the heavens as I ride with your head on the tip of my lance." Meliagrant was already mounting his own horse, a well-trained charger which also was a hot-tempered stallion. A squire handed him a lance, a sturdy one with a steel point set to kill. There was no going back now, unless Perceval wanted to face the same expectant crowd humiliated, the King further insulted.

He wanted no such thing. Even little Galienne mustered the courage to face Kay, and Perceval resigned himself to the belief that those who boasted the most were the worst performers, no matter the deed.

He felt caught somewhere between exhilaration and dread. He had his fight now; here was his undeniable chance to prove himself to the King and everyone else. He had nothing against this knight personally other than the latter's temper and a claim of which he even now knew little. He wondered how often knights found themselves in similar predicaments, fighting other people's battles. *No,* he reminded himself. *Arthur can fight, has fought, his own battles.* The knights were merely representatives of kingly intent and force.

The symbolic philosophizing would have to wait. Meliagrant, his face hidden beneath his visored helm, was charging him, and would surely kill him if he did not defend himself. Perceval arrived at the tree his opponent had indicated and immediately set about his own charge. It all still seemed unreal, like another dream. Yet the shiny tip of the knight's lance would impale, and did not care whether one thought it real or dreamy. Perceval had to forget his rationalizing.

Brownie was not used to running this fast, but she held her own in the face of the oncoming stallion. Perceval was glad she obeyed his subtle commands, administered though his hard leg muscles on her back. This would have to be timed exactly, especially since Perceval just noticed he had forgotten to demand a shield from Meliagrant's men; such was his chivalric right. The image of the hungry gold creature in the field of black came furiously. There would be no way to block the blow; at best he could get out of the way.

Still, Perceval never gave himself any time to doubt what he was trying to do. Never having jousted, he wasn't sure of the correct protocol. All he knew was that another man wished to run him through, and he had to get himself and his mount beyond the reach of the lethal lance.

The stallion and its fearless rider bore down on them, just thirty yards away now. Perceval gripped the javelin in his right hand, yet his enemy approached slightly to his left side, with the lance positioned over the stallion's neck, the pitch and gold shield covering most of Meliagrant's left side. Perceval was in no position to counter this at all, and almost out of time.

But then he leaned just slightly in the saddle, and Brownie obligingly veered barely leftward. The timing proved nothing short of perfect; Brownie moved left just enough to stay out of the stallion's violent path, and still put her rider into striking position.

Meliagrant let loose his loudest, scariest battle scream during the last few yards, hoping to achieve an easy kill, reminding any onlookers in Camelot that he would not be denied. The sound halted, becoming a soft moan of surprise as he was taken completely unaware by the younger man's tactic. When he saw the mare suddenly and inexplicably dodge to the inside of his attack position, he simply kept up the charge, and struggled to get his lance over his stallion's head so that it would still be usable. Stopping the charge against such a pathetic foe would have been cowardly, and Meliagrant was not about to be shamed.

But the lance was not usable in that position, and it was now too late. Weapon and shield were too heavy to be repositioned in under a second, as Meliagrant had situated both to attack from and cover his left side. And a second was all it took. Perceval, who now rode Brownie alongside Meliagrant's right and not his left, was in a totally advantageous position. He gripped the javelin as hard as he could, and tried to brace it against his side for the impact. He barely saw the action as the two horses passed each other, the javelin's sharpened head hitting Meliagrant solidly in the neck.

Perceval could not have hoped for a better shot, although he had actually aimed for the man's midsection, hoping to simply unhorse him. The motion was more instinct than plan. He led Brownie around to face his opponent, and turned just in time to see Meliagrant collapse from his stallion, one hand to his horribly mangled throat, his life's blood spraying from the wound in a fountain of hot sticky redness. It looked as though he desperately wished to just say something, his mouth gaping as though he were a fish removed from water. He continued to flail involuntarily for a few seconds after hitting the ground, his horse instinctively turning back towards the safety of the pavilion and the other men.

Perceval was stunned, though he had little time to consider his victory just yet, much less that he had just taken the life of another person. Of more immediate concern were Meliagrant's men. He was shaking, and could not afford to show fear, *but what should be done with the men?*

Perceval had an idea. He just hoped these were men of their word.

The unexpected victor was pleased to find them in a state of complete shock, even greater than his own. Some looked a few yards away toward their fallen master; others stared disbelieving at the peasant boy who had killed him.

The new champion addressed them. "Your lord's cause is as dead as he. As the winner of this combat I give all of you an option," Perceval commanded coolly from atop Brownie, willing his voice not to crack.

He now had the attention of them all. Slowly their heads turned to look at this young man giving them orders. All looked intimidated; even the other knights looked nervous. Of what other magick might this man be capable?

The intimidating youth continued, "You may either retreat to wherever you call home, never to return to this fair land, or you may go now back into Camelot and swear your personal allegiance to King Arthur as your new liege. Either way, consider yourselves bound by your decision. Now get out of my sight."

Within a matter of seconds and exchanged glances, the ten men all turned towards the great city. None ever saw anything like what just took place. All had feared Meliagrant, but now feared his better more. True, they each shared an amount of allegiance to the man who paid them and justified their fights and robberies, but none were much loyal beyond finances, and so none wished to wreak their vengeance. Besides, Arthur was supposed to be a just king; it seemed better to face his mercy and justice than to become his enemy.

Perceval, still straining to mask his own fear, watched them proceed, oblivious to the cheers which had begun along the city's ramparts. He was equally ignorant of Sir Lucan's approach, and watched only the encampment.

Meliagrant's knights seemed not to have their own heraldic arms. Instead, there were a number of three-pointed kite shields alongside a weapons rack next to the crimson pavilion, each painted a different shade of red. One shade in particular reminded Perceval of a rose. He had only ever seen one rose before; Tathan had a dried one among his few possessions, and showed it to a wide-eyed Dindraine and Perceval once, explaining that it was used by some to symbolize deep affections and desires. Perceval kept thinking about it as he rode over to Meliagrant's body, dismounting Brownie and setting about to remove the armor.

"Need some help with that, lad?" came the familiar voice from just behind him. He was struggling helplessly with the large chain-link skin, with no obvious separations in it. Perceval was glad he might be able to have some aid.

Lucan dismounted, walking over to him. "That was some piece of work! How did you know to do that with your horse in the first place?"

Perceval shrugged, still examining the armor. He really did not know, not consciously; it just felt natural to do it that way.

"Well, however it was, let me give you a hand," said the butler, and he proceeded to show Perceval the workings of chainmail. Fortunately, the armor was relatively sized, so that a person within an inch or so of Meliagrant's own height could wear it. Perceval was within a half inch, and of about the same physique as well. He failed to notice the good fortune of it.

Lucan's own squire arrived, and took over the task of helping the errant to actually don the spoil of his first fight. Perceval was entranced. He felt proud, and also shaken; he had no knightly training, and knew he needed it. He thought he was more lucky than anything else, the other, better trained and outfitted man lying dead beside him.

Finally wearing the scarlet protection, not truly red so much as dark, seeming to absorb the color of the surcoat, painted joint guards, and now blood, Perceval asked, "Sir Lucan, I am not a knight, I have no lord and precious little expertise.

Where does one go to study this sort of thing? Is there some place, someone, who might take me as an apprentice?" Perceval fidgeted with his hands, trying to get used to the feel of his new metallic epidermis, hoping he could later remember how to get it off.

Lucan smiled, remembering when he was so much like this young man, eager for nothing but practice. "Most of the knights in Camelot come from other lands and other lords, to pay their due homage. But there is an older man, who has trained several knights from around here, a veteran of the old battles."

"Where may I find him? Please tell me. I want to seek him out at once." Perceval did not care how pathetic he sounded; he felt desperate, unable to face the cheers from Camelot.

"Don't you want to receive the King's thanks for a job well done first?"

"I'm sorry, but no. I need to do this first. Please, Sir Lucan. Just tell the King I'll be back as soon as I'm able. I have to be trained as a knight before I can truly be a knight, after all."

"I will, Perceval. The whole court will be thrilled when you return. Of that I can assure you. I can't wait to hear what Kay has to say." Lucan knew he would answer plenty of questions this evening.

Perceval received his directions from Lucan, and rode away from the approaching crowd, come to congratulate him. They would have to wait. For now he was simply thankful that his aim with the javelin had been better than when he met the stag.

* * *

"There. There! Did you see her?" The woman's voice was eager, trying not to be so loud as to interrupt the otherwise solemn ceremony.

"Shh," commanded the older woman, her stern eyes looking into the perfectly clean water anyway. Whatever image might lay within was solely the domain of she who performed the magick. Her own visions were beginning to fade with age; being a crone had its disadvantages too, she supposed.

But she was caught up in this, felt young again; someone who showed remarkable promise had been found to come to this place, to look into this sacred pool of water herself one day. Hopefully.

Nimue pointed at the water, ineffectively gesturing for the Mother Crone to notice her. She could have sworn she saw the girl herself, running impossibly through the water, unaware of the eavesdropping. Maybe she just saw what she *wished* to see. No matter, though; wishes had a power all their own.

The third woman present remained motionless, looked virtually dead save for her perfectly upright posture, as she knelt before the Well of the Chalice. She did not hear the younger priestess' exclamation, and saw only the young girl whose image appeared in the ripple-less surface, so lively, so innocent. So ripe to become another of their sacred number.

The female trio were the only ones present on the tiny island, a mere outcropping from the surrounding marsh and swamp. Their boat was tied to a barely noticeable landing just twenty yards away. It was an elegant craft, just big enough to carry the three of them yet sporting its own tiny sail, the bow richly carved in the likeness of a swan's head. It sometimes seemed to possess a motion of its own, although Nimue, as the lowest ranking of the three, had guided them.

From Avalon they came, the second sacred island, never touched by Roman hands, and which was said to shift its very existence from This Side into the Other Side and back again. Such were the conclusions drawn by those daring or foolish enough to venture out in search of it. Not even the druids from Mona could come here without invitation, the women were that secretive. They had to be, from many years of experience. They found that mystery enhanced their reputation.

And their power. Girls showing significant promise and faith could be brought here just after their first blood cycle, to learn the ways of Goddess and Her unique magick. Years of isolated, dedicated study were required for the girl to grow into a priestess, and strict behavioral rules continued to govern her all her life. Yet the enchantresses complained about little, other than the omnipresence of foreign influence. It had come to pass that even many of those who shared the same blood, the same spirit, as these women, no longer trusted them. It was rare for one of them to oversee the sacred days, even in the more remote settlements.

But now they had an opportunity to gain more influence and respect as the healers and priestesses and magicians they proudly were. They could bring a new person to their island of apples, island of glass. Their home had many strange nicknames. It was actually a small, lightly wooded, very hilly place which stood as the summit of a number of tiny islands in this marshy, usually foggy locale. The buildings were much like those in Perceval's home: simple, functional, weather-resistant. The women lived off merely the vegetables and fruits which were never to be found in short supply. It was the ideal place to work, to train, to study. To perform magick.

The woman the populace of Logres called Fay stayed in her penitent position, head slightly bowed, looking directly at the child who was in front of her, yet many miles away. Her hands were perched above her thighs, the five digits on each stretched and rigid, as though she were the ancient prophet trying to part much larger waters. She thought much of prophecy right then, the five pairs of fingers acting as her senses, all to try and hold the girl's image as long as she could. Her left hand represented the feminine, the right the masculine; Morgan was surprised by how balanced her subject felt in this regard, and the two other women would note later that her hands remained at the same level throughout the Sending. Morgan wondered most of all what the girl might be thinking right then. Scrying did not always go unnoticed, especially by one who had the Sight.

She vanished. Someone came along and started talking to the girl and she disappeared from the range of second Sight. Only Morgan knew this at first; when her hands slapped down on her thighs, Nimue and Viviane knew it as well.

Morgan clamped her eyes closed, as though that might allow her to see the girl again. But the well had spoken its share this day.

"You seem to have found her. Nimue thought you did, certainly," said Viviane, her subordinate priestess nodding in affirmation. Young Nimue was thrilled, giddy even, to be part of this ceremony. The Mother was beginning to entrust more and more sacred matters to her!

Nimue obligingly helped Morgan to her feet, knowing that receiving the Sight could be very taxing on a person's stamina. Indeed, the older woman felt almost like dead weight in her grasp.

Her head clearing, Morgan thanked Nimue. Then she looked at her superior. Viviane simply said, "So it will be. Morgan, know that the Lady thanks you for your participation."

Morgan would never quite learn when Viviane's use of the term "Lady" indicated herself or Goddess. She was sure, though, that the ambiguity was a calculated part of the Crone's authority.

"Lady Viviane," Morgan began, "I regret that it is my task to return to Gorre. My husband awaits. As do the people; I must personally oversee the upcoming events." That was true enough. The Summer Solstice was rapidly approaching. Morgan had journeyed back south to the marshy, magickal island just after the fires of Beltaine died down. Thanks to Uriens' rule north of the Wall, those fires were lasting longer each year.

Uriens was a just king and a good husband, and the Camelot courtiers did not need to know of the older festivities.

Of course, Gorre bordered Lothian, up in Caledonia, just above the devastated lands. Morgan and Margawse, Lothian's queen, were not on the most pleasant of terms, and one never could be certain of where the other's loyalty lay.

"Surely I realize this, child. That is why Nimue will be going to escort the girl back here personally." Viviane's tone was not one to be questioned, but the hair on Morgan's neck shot up all the same.

"Mother, are you sure?" Morgan turned to look at the incredulous Nimue, who had just finished turning pale. "Nimue, I mean no offense my dear, but there must be someone more —"

"Experienced? Mature?" This from Viviane; Nimue looked as entranced as Morgan had just moments before. "Look, Morgan, I've no time to argue about this. The decision has been made, and you know as well as I that there is no one else. That's the whole reason we need the knight's daughter in the first place."

There was no arguing with that. Morgan devoted her very existence to furthering the cause of the Earth Mother. Even her marriage to Uriens, whom she grew to love (having joined with him and no other at Beltaine), was part of her dedication; the people were rediscovering their roots. She was defiantly proud of this, even if it distanced her from her Christianized half-brother and diabolic sister.

But the cruel irony was that no matter what the people's spiritual hunger, there were only so many priestesses and druids left. It was still just as difficult as ever to join the ranks of those who called Avalon home: demonstrable Sight and at least one accompanying Talent, such as healing or glamour (Nimue had shown much promise with the second). Also, the girls could not marry until becoming priestesses at the age when rich fortunate men became knights; they faced endless study and practice and memorization of rituals. Because of this strictness they had never quite recovered from the wrath wreaked by the Romans. They lived in the shadows now. The mists that shrouded their island sanctuary from prying eyes kept them safe, but also kept them from growing.

Such was the reason for a suitable marriage to an aging king in Gorre. Morgan would never qualify for crone status now; Viviane never married, never would. She could have easily; even in her waning years she had an undeniable beauty about her. She walked and talked with an elegance to rival any of the women in Logres. She had not lost any of her physical grace, the nourishment of Avalon keeping her body strong but supple. Her face had lengthened somewhat, showing her proud cheekbones even more prominently, and her forehead had begun to wrinkle from her normally severe demeanor. But she was still striking; Uriens could have been just as pleased with her as with Morgan.

Nimue still looked shocked, her own wrinkles years in front of her. Viviane spoke to her. "Nimue. Priestess. Enchantress. You are charged with the task of bringing this child to Avalon for fostering and tutelage. You shall leave as soon as your necessary preparations are made. It is ordained that the girl shall receive that which is reserved for the greatest of them all. It will be much like Arthur's own king-making."

The true source of Nimue's apprehension came out at last, the color beginning to brighten her face again. "Mother, the girl is Christian."

Viviane had not expected any hint of insubordination from her charges, but she was prepared to answer this regardless. "Correction: she thinks she is such, just as her father sometimes claims to do, and just as her mother would have her believe. But never forget you her true heritage."

Nimue surprised herself with her own objections. "Whose lineage is the more important for her then, her mother's or her father's?"

The crone was not quite as ready for this question. "Her father studied at Mona; he is half-druid. Her mother is only a token member of the Christian church. His influence will win out. And lest you forget, she has the Sight, indeed knows she has it. Such a gift is nothing from heaven; she will have tried to declare it blasphemous but even now she knows its power is undeniable. That alone should turn her loyalty to us."

Morgan was still unaccustomed to this kind of talk, wondering if it concerned religion or politics more. But Viviane was set, and Avalon in dire need of a new priestess.

So this girl would be the one. Nimue would see to that.

* * *

Sir Gornymant of Jagent Castle was a gruff, tough old veteran, who lived to train young men to be knights. And today he watched a younger man spar with his own son, Llascoit, using wooden practice swords and shields. His new student was energetic and passionate.

The cane-like beating sound of wood striking other wood stopped for a second, the would-be knights apparently thinking it was time for a break. Gornymant watched them breathe heavily in the courtyard below where he stood observing, but only for a few seconds. If they were to be knights, they would have to develop more impressive stamina than this!

"Perceval, remember to pivot and block him with your whole shield if needed. You keep leaving your side open, and his blade keeps finding your ribs."

"Thank you, Master," came Perceval's winded reply. He was tired; he and Llascoit had already been mock dueling for an hour and a half. His arms dangled like lead weights, and his leg muscles vibrated rapidly from begging his body for more oxygen. Perceval was glad his opponent and sparring partner looked similarly spent; he would have felt ashamed if Llascoit won by simply wearing him out.

Perceval had already been here for over a week, greeted by the lord of this modest castle as though he were royalty. Gornymant recognized the armor Perceval wore, although the plain red shield he bore proved a bit confusing, until Perceval fully explained what had happened since his arrival at Camelot. Gornymant was immediately convinced that whoever could best Meliagrant could hardly need further training, but conceded to the lad's request when he discovered at dinner that evening how impossibly ignorant he was. Not stupid, not at all; just, well, perhaps too literal.

Gornymant and his family listened attentively to the tale of this person raised in almost total seclusion, who one day just found the impetus to leave and seek his dream. Gornymant was pleased; he had not trained anyone new for some years now, and was delighted to take in this lad, a good partner for his own son, the latter only a couple of years older than Perceval and virtually ready for knighthood himself.

Gornymant himself was a veteran of many melees and skirmishes, and could well remember the time before the Boy King united the warring lords of Britain under the Pendragon banner. He was even with Arthur at three of his Battles of Unification, and fought valiantly at Badon Hill against the encroaching Garmani. He was a displaced Cambrian himself, and constantly craved Perceval's descriptions of his homeland. Gornymant actually heralded from the southern chiefdom of Deheubarth, and while he missed his old home occasionally, he had grown to love the countryside around Camelot. It was more peaceful and civilized here, and Jagent Castle had been Arthur's gift to him after Badon Hill. Gornymant had single-handedly hoisted the Pendragon banner after its bearer fell to Garmani savagery, and then carried the standard to the top of the hill while carving up several Garmani warriors along the way, which impressed the young King to granting a reward. The only condition was that Gornymant refused to train anyone of Garmani descent (no one even resembling a Germanic, thank you!); such was his hatred of them.

Since the great battle, Gornymant had offered to personally see to the training of those men, who while deemed worthy and full of potential, lacked either the financial or familial backing to rise beyond squire.

Like the young man in the courtyard below, who had a passion for life the likes of which Gornymant had only seen once before.

Best not to dwell on the past, he thought. The other similarly impassioned person was his loving wife, who departed this life as a result of a serious lung disease only two years after their second child, a daughter, was born.

Why is it that the innocent ones always suffer? he wondered. Arian had led a blameless life, and accompanied him while he fought alongside the new King. So why did she have to die, leaving him to raise two willful children alone?

No, that isn't true, he reminded himself. He had been graced with all manner of servants, part of his fief: cooks, grooms, squires, even a strict but compassionate minstrel who taught the children to read and to appreciate the vitality of good music and story. Thank God he had the help these years! Arian would have been proud to see her children grow this way. Llascoit was well on his way, and Llio had become quite a stewardess and maid of the castle, managing the affairs of the whole place, even though she was just seventeen.

Gornymant swore he could feel the spirit of his departed wife watching just above where he now stood, giving commands. Beneath him, Perceval and Llascoit resumed their efforts to try and hit each other.

"Keep your shield lower, Llas. You'll blind yourself if you keep trying to hide behind it that way."

Llascoit responded by adjusting his fighting stance, and he and his partner continued to alternate blows, most deflected by the shields.

Perceval loved all of this. His tiredness was the proud weariness that comes from dedicated work. He was learning all manner of knightly combat, from swordplay to advanced riding to jousting (genuine jousting, and not improvisational), all from this man who had taken him in. It was fun, even when he carried the bruises from Llascoit's wooden sword or the fast-spinning joust quintain.

It was also pleasant to not have to wear the armor, at least not today. It was heavy and bulky, and hot when he exerted himself at all. Brownie had snorted her lack of appreciation at her master's added weight when they left the field outside Camelot that day, but both man and horse would have to get used to it. Usually Gornymant insisted that all combat-related activities be practiced in armor, but today he eased up due to the heat. Of course, the training session lasted longer because of this leniency.

Perceval missed his dog, though. He hadn't even remembered Cabal until he saw Llio's own hound at supper that first night in Jagent. He could not believe he had been so quick to run off that he had forgotten to track him down! Still, he did not worry about it so much. He was occupied enough here in Jagent to not think about it very often, and when he did, he reminded himself that Cabal made friends very easily, and that he was last seen in the company of the two girls, Lupinia and Galienne. Both seemed trustworthy enough, especially Galienne. *Surely he would not leave Camelot,* Perceval thought. There was so much to do and see there. Besides, Galienne clearly loved the dog.

On the balcony where Perceval's tutor perched with his usual judging glance, Llio came into view. The former did not notice her until she called out.

"That's it, Perceval, give him a good lump on the head!" Llio's voice was sweet and playful.

And it distracted Perceval. He sneaked a quick peek up at her smiling face, and it was his undoing. Llascoit easily took advantage of the momentary hesitation and thrust at Perceval with the sword, bringing it up under his shield and catching him in the side of the chest. Perceval was lifted up slightly from the momentum and quickly found himself sprawled on the ground. He instantly tucked his head down, touching his chest with his chin. A man named Gwyn once taught him not to let his head go loose when hitting the floor.

He was trying to get back to his feet to meet Llascoit's charge, his aching thighs no longer able to spring him upright. His opponent brought the oak dueling stick high above his head; he had dropped his shield, and gripped the practice sword with both hands, as though it were the only thing worth hanging onto in this life, and was just about to bring it down when his tense body was interrupted.

"All right, that's enough for today," said Gornymant from above them. "Both of you come inside now and make yourselves ready for supper."

Llascoit still held the dummy sword with one hand, and extended the other to help Perceval to his feet. Perceval took the hand eagerly, considering that this man was the closest to a brother he ever knew.

They were all inside now, Gornymant having come down the immense carved rock staircase, Llio behind him. Normally she walked astride her father, but she knew this was knightly business, and Gornymant would reprimand her if she dared interfere with his instruction of the two younger men.

"You both looked all right out there today, all considered. Of course, you were able to train without the weight of your armor. Tomorrow you'll be wearing it, no matter the weather."

"Thank you, Sir," came the simultaneously reply of both errants, hoping their initial groan at tomorrow's practice forecast went unnoticed. They were already looking forward to some sleep tonight; they would need their rest to train in full armor in the morning.

"Llio, is supper ready?" asked the lord. He smelled the delicious aromas from the kitchen waft their way into the upper reaches of the castle.

"It is, Father," Llio said proudly. She had seen that some special dishes were prepared, as sort of a celebration of their new guest, who had already survived his first week's training. She was fond of Perceval; he was attractive in a rustic sort of way. Civilization had not interfered with his natural beauty, she noted, although she suspected that the same lack of civilization was what kept him so distant. *He is shy, yes, that's it,* she thought. Just shy. She often wondered what he thought about, since he spoke little to anyone, almost not at all to her.

"Freshen up, both of you, then come to supper," ordered Gornymant. Llascoit and Perceval went at once to the large painted porcelain bowl of water in the kitchen. The room smelled divinely of fresh herbs and simmering meats, and the bowl on a corner table contained fresh water used for washing just about anything, including the soiled hands of aspiring warriors.

The water was pleasingly cool as the two students plunged their hands into it, cupping them to bring some up to their faces. Their skin was still quite warm from the session, and the sensation of the water relaxed both young men. Full baths were rare occasions; even for a special family dinner like the one they would soon share, a basic rinsing of the extremities was enough. The two smiled at each other, feeling the water's

exhilaration, and then turned to leave the kitchen and its assortment of staff, busily working on finishing up the meal.

The feast hall of Castle Jagent was modest by most
knightly standards, but possessed the basic ingredients. The immensely thick and heavy wooden tables. The lighting from candle sconces (mostly mounted within the walls). The unwieldy
second shield hung high on one wall, painted with Gornymant's
arms: a blue field superimposed by a long sword. And the assortment of rugs (normally rolled up for feasts, to prevent stains).

The three men knew they were in for a treat tonight,
however, when they saw the embroidered tablecloth on the main
table (indeed, there were just two other tables in here, and both
almost always empty for lack of guests). The cloth depicted
scenes of the battle at Badon Hill. One side however, in front
of Gornymant's own chair, showed him and his lovely wife, their
hands clasped and their eyes locked on each other.

Gornymant of course recognized the cloth at once; he
had rarely seen it since Arian's death. He was momentarily angry at Llio; he did not wish Perceval and Llascoit to see him
start bawling like some scared babe. Arian had stitched every
last colored thread into this tablecloth, and when she was gone
Gornymant ordered the servants to lock it away where he would
not have to see it.

Llio rescued her father. "I thought it only appropriate
that Mother be able to welcome Perceval to our home, in spirit
if not in flesh." The room fell quiet, the family members thinking of the wonderful woman who once shared meals with them.
Perceval bowed his head in respect, thinking of his own mother
and wishing her well. This done, Llio led each man to his seat,
beginning with Gornymant and ending with Perceval.

The room did seem a bit empty, since the four of them
were the only ones who regularly ate there. The servants normally shared supper at their own table, off the kitchen near their
living quarters. Llio seated herself, and with subtle glances and

hand movements directed toward the kitchen staff, took command.

The meal was wonderful, the men all eating as though it would be their last chance to ever partake of food. The introductory course of pear tarts was delightfully received, and all currently worked on the second course of broiled chicken. Perceval loved chicken; it was a rare treat back in Oerfa and it pleasantly reminded him of the hills of his home. Llio had really outdone herself readying all this; Perceval wondered how knights didn't grow fat and listless with all the feasting they supposedly did. He knew that only his constant training would keep the gastronomy from eventually encircling his waist.

Gornymant sought a distraction from the memory of a woman who died too young. She had produced a remarkable likeness of herself and her husband on the cloth; he always felt pride in knowing the incentive for such a project had been pure love, rather than some sense of matrimonial duty, as was common in too many marriages.

"So, young Perceval, tell me: what do you think of your training so far?" He really did care what his student thought; he worked hard to ensure those he taught were capable fighters, but he also wanted them to be civilized, courteous, and, most importantly, able to think on their own and master their base emotions.

"Well, Sir, I –" Perceval tried to force something out, which was not coming. Near him, Llascoit looked lost in thought, as though trying to formulate answers to his father's questions, in case he was asked anything himself.

"Oh, come lad. I haven't asked you a riddle. I only wish to know what's on your mind."

Perceval loved the training, but it seemed cheap somehow to just blurt it out like that. "It's been excellent, Sir, better than I could have hoped for. Thank you again for taking me –"

"No, Perceval. That's not what I mean. Just tell me what you're thinking, and stop worrying about whether or not it's what I want to hear, because I'm telling you I want to hear it regardless."

Perceval cleared his throat, the flavor of the strong herbs of the roasted chicken swirling in his mouth, teasing him into wanting more. "Master, I love what I'm doing here. You've taught me swordplay, how to ride better, how to joust. You are my teacher and I am in your debt."

"There now, that wasn't so hard, was it?" Gornymant smiled, as did Llio. Llascoit still seemed to be searching for hypothetical answers to imaginary questions; he did not like to be interrogated any more than Perceval.

Amused but unfinished, Gornymant returned to the discussion. He had something to teach. He would be damned if he let them loose into the world without an education. Gornymant himself could read Latin, and actually acquired several books as part of his boon from the King. He would not let these two out of his sight until they knew more than just how to ride and hack and kill. He needed a lesson for them, something that would help make sense of all they studied.

"Perceval, take a look at the shield hanging behind me. Tell me, what do you see?" Obediently, all three youths looked up at the design.

Perceval wondered why the lord would ask him something so obvious. "I see a sword on a field the color of the sky on a calm summer's day." His words were poetic enough to win an affectionate smile from Llio, who offered him a reflective glance after dismissing the servants with a load of soiled dishware.

"Yes, you're right, you would-be-bard, but now try this. Close your eyes, keep them closed for a few moments, and open them again. Then tell me what you see." Perceval was a bit confused; this gentle man at the table hardly seemed the type who could mow down multitudes of Garmani like so many weeds.

Perceval obeyed and again looked at the huge shield. He considered the possibilities: a shield was a knight's defense, aside from his armor; it was most often painted with a knight's personal or familial crest, or coat of arms, and there were people who dedicated their lives to the study of this elaborate heraldry. He hoped himself to one day put his own design on the shield he liberated from Meliagrant but was unsure of a design. Yet what did his master want?

"It identifies you as lord of this house, Sir Gornymant," Perceval said feebly. He could think of nothing else.

Gornymant figured he would just have to spell it out. "It has three points. Men in other king's armies used circular shields, like the bowls on the table, or rectangular, like the Centurions. Why do you suppose the shields we use have three points, like a triangle?"

"A triangle, Sir?" asked Perceval, "What is that?"

Gornymant sighed. He sometimes forgot how ignorant this young man really was. How could anyone have grown up so stupidly, yet so full of promise? Perceval barely mentioned a word of his parents back home; only his sister, a storyteller, and two knights, were ever discussed by him.

Perceval still awaited an answer. "A triangle, dear boy, is a shape with three straight sides. The only difference between the shape of the shield and the shape of a true triangle is that two of the shield's sides are curved."

Perceval listened attentively, oblivious to the newly arrived course of poached snapper. Llascoit and Llio knew their geometric shapes, and kept eating.

"You still don't see what I'm getting at, do you?"

Perceval shrugged. He thought that any questions asked of him during his training would have to do specifically with the physical: he could already answer questions like *"How do you most quickly stop your horse when it's charging?"* and *"Which stance is superior for facing a left-handed opponent?"* But triangles?

"Perceval, the triangle is a sign of perfection, just like a circle. These shapes appear in so many places because of their usefulness. But the triangle goes a bit further, because it has, what?"

"Three points," answered Perceval sheepishly.

"Yes. Now, three of anything should be easy to remember. There are three of us here eating with you. There are three points on a shield. When you become a knight you'll likely travel with three types of horses."

Perceval responded, suddenly eager, "A charger, a rouncy, and a sumpter."

"Yes! That's it. Now we're getting somewhere." *Maybe I can finally get through his thick head.*

"You and Llascoit have been practicing at the quintain, which will ready you for jousts and battle with the lance, and also your riding and your swordplay."

"Those are the three main skills a knight needs to survive," Llascoit said, looking up from a bowl full of tasty snapper.

Good! thought his father. Knights worked better as teams; Arthur had taught many people that lesson.

"Right," said Gornymant, "but what good is a knight who only knows how to survive, and nothing else?"

Perceval and Llascoit looked at each other, dumbfounded. What else was there really, in the end, other than sheer, brutal, necessary survival?

Gornymant enlightened them. "Well, to begin with, before you both leave here you're going to also know how to run without losing your wind, how to grapple with someone so you can fight without a weapon in your hand, and how to swim so you can survive the water." Gornymant wanted them both prepared; he was tired of most knights dying young. One of his charges now was his own son.

Perceval was about to ask about swimming, since the only large body of water he had ever seen was the Severn's offshoot back home, and it could be easily waded through, never getting more than several feet deep. But there was no interrupting Gornymant anymore.

By now the four of them partook of the next course: artichokes stuffed with butter-soaked wheat bread. Gornymant kept eating eagerly, so that his breaks between points would be shorter. He still had much to say, but was not about to forego any of this wonderful food his daughter had supervised.

"I want you all, you too, Llio, to tell me any set of three things you can think of which go together. I want you all to think on this, and above all, to remember what you each hear at this table this evening. I want you all to be prepared for the world beyond these walls."

Llio listened, trying to ignore that she hated artichokes; she only told the cook to prepare them because her father and brother loved them. So she went first. "There's the Father, the Son, and the Holy Spirit," she said confidently. Perceval looked down, knowing his new family were Christian in faith, though they always seemed relaxed about it. Gornymant believed salvation was available to all.

"There are the three manifestations of Goddess, too: maiden, mother, and old crone," Llascoit added.

"Good, Llas, good. I see you haven't forgotten your heritage," said Gornymant. He was pleased his children could speak openly about religions that had been forced to integrate back in Deheubarth, and try to understand the merits of each, rather than bicker about who was right or wrong, saved or doomed.

"Or heaven, earth, and hell. And the otherworld, this world, and the underworld," quipped Llio with a smile. This was fun. Gornymant noticed how they treated this almost like a game. So much the better.

"Past, present, and future," Perceval said, finally having conjured his first trio. He had been lost in his own world of private memory, thinking of his mother and her stories about the life she had known before leaving home.

"What of the cycle of birth, life, and death, and its repetitiveness?" asked Gornymant. "Now do you see why the number three was considered sacred by the druids, who were the great teachers of the Cymru?" All at the table nodded.

"Three points on a shield; always remember that it starts there. There's one more thing I want to tell you about all this, lest you start to think that I somehow came up with all these ideas alone."

"What is it, father?" asked Llascoit, his eyes full of the eagerness normally reserved for much younger children hearing their bedside stories.

"One of my books in Latin is about an ancient teacher who lived many, many generations before we were born. It was in a land far from here, what our own forebears called the Land of Heroes. This man wrote about something that Christians have since adopted as part of our views: the creation of the ideal civilization. Not in heaven or the otherworld, but here on this earth."

The three younger people listened, ignoring the few remains of their dinners. Perceval was especially curious; he knew that sometimes stories got boring, yet he recalled that during his trip to Camelot he constantly thought of various things Tathan had once said. He knew he should listen now.

Gornymant continued with his primer in Greek thought. "This wise man also spoke of matters using groups of three. First, he said a person's soul, a person's character, consisted of three parts: reason, emotion, and appetite."

"So people were rational despite their being high-strung and hungry?" Llascoit said, half-jokingly and half-confusedly.

"No, Llas," Gornymant said, pleased that Perceval and Llio kept their snickers at his son's comment to a minimum. "He used them sort of as building blocks, like those that make the huge walls of this castle. The appetite is the bottom block, something that we all have, and that animals too have. It is the urge to survive, by meeting basic desires, like those for food, shelter, safety. Like what we discussed earlier about the knights. Do you understand?"

Perceval nodded. He really did want to understand it. So far it made sense; of course everyone had basic wants and needs. Why else was he here?

"The next block," said Gornymant, "is the emotions, the way we feel happy or angry, or love or hatred. Those are all emotions, and some of these we share with the animals also. Do you see?"

Perceval nodded again, along with the others. He knew well the feelings and expressions of the animals: their shyness or bravery, curiosity or caution.

"Well, the top block is reason, and this is where people want to differ from the animals. The wise man said that we alone have the power to judge right from wrong, good from evil, and to make decisions after thinking about our choices. So now do you see how these three work together to make each of us what we are? At least beyond the mere flesh of ourselves, that is?" To illustrate his point, he pinched a chunk of his meaty arm.

Llascoit and Llio could almost see the tiny gearwheels spinning in Perceval's head. *So reason is supposed to govern the others, like the roof that covers the building?* But it was more than that. It was like the building was here, like Jagent Castle, all around him, but it was useless without someone to run it, like Sir Gornymant. *At least it should be easy to remember*, thought Perceval.

Beginning with the very shield he liberated from a dead knight.

"Only one more point shall I make now about this old, dead, wise man. He said that these three properties corresponded to the three classes of people which would make up his soci-

ety. The people in each class would then correspond to one of
the personal traits."

"How is that, father?" Llio said. She was fascinated by
this, too.

"Well, child, there would be artisans, which would be
those who produced everything people need to survive, and they
would be most like the appetite. Farmers, cooks, cobblers, armorers, shepherds, and everyone else who practiced some craft
would be part of this class."

The mention of shepherds struck a chord with Perceval;
here was something he could really comprehend. But did that
mean he had to be mostly appetitive? He knew, after all, of having just one essential desire that overshadowed all others.

"Who would be the emotional types, then?" he said.

"It's not that they would be emotional types themselves,
necessarily. It's that what they did with their lives would be a
larger representation of what a person does when using emotions."

That remark gained some curious glances from around
the table. Gornymant hoped dearly he was getting all this right.
His Latin was excellent, and he spent many a night going over
this particular text, which he hoped was translated accurately
from whatever archaic language the old dead wise man had used.
Maybe they spoke Latin back then, too. Gornymant did not
know. What he did know, and truly had come to believe in all
the days that had elapsed since his fighting glory, was that there
was no substitute for learning. Not for anyone. He heard that
Merlin, when he had still been around, was always at Arthur's
side, constantly tutoring him in language, lore, and custom, in
addition to the skills normally considered most necessary for a
king: to be able to wield a sword better and mightier than all who
might oppose its blade. And his queen, too: she had studied the
old scriptures in a monastery as a child, and now was the stewardess of this entire kingdom. Gornymant had no doubts with

the need for this talk. And yet, even if it was not quite on the mark, what then? The wisdom of the Cymru themselves had passed on, generation to generation, through who knew how many centuries, and yet those very same beings had no written language.

"Let me explain," he said. "What is it that we often do when we feel strong emotion, like love or hate?"

Gornymant's children looked at each other, confused by the obvious answer right in front of them. Perceval spoke up, his answer sounding shaky.

"We act on the feelings. We embrace those we love and attack those we hate," he said.

"Right. That is precisely what the next class, the guards, the warriors, do."

More confusion. Llascoit, Llio, and Perceval were concentrating such that none seemed to notice the servants clearing the remains of supper from the table, leaving behind only a pitcher of wine and fresh goblets for the diners.

"How can warriors embrace those they love when it is their task to conquer their enemies?" questioned Llascoit. Perceval had the same thought.

"Listen, all of you, and remember the model of the individual. The warrior is charged with making the decision to embrace or attack. It means that the warriors simply have the task of keeping the artisans, and the other class which I'll get to, safe from harm. That is exactly why our own King has his Round Table: the best of the warriors receive the honor and glory of membership, and the King in return has them pledge to die for him, should he think it necessary."

"So then King Arthur himself decides what everyone else does, more or less," came Llio's response. "I mean, he can't keep track of every last person, but he sees to it that everyone knows their place."

"Well, of course he does. That's why he's king in the first place." Llascoit's voice sounded a bit harsh.

"Yes, Llas, but what you know now is that the King is civilization's equivalent of reason itself. He could not rule without the warriors and merchants supporting his kingdom, and he grants them safety and the promise of a fair and just rule in return." *There*, thought Gornymant, *hopefully that will get through.*

Perceval focused on his own thoughts. What his master said seemed to make so much sense. He had been an artsan, or artisan, or whatever Sir Gornymant had called them. He was a shepherd who wanted to be a knight. Uncontrolled appetite wanting to be willful emotion. It would take some time to work all this out. In the meantime, he was exhausted.

"My lord, may I be excused?" he asked.

"Yes, Perceval, but remember: it's considered rude to get up and leave before one's host has dismissed himself. Now off to bed, all of you." Gornymant actually found the lad quite controlled this evening; he often became unnecessarily vocal with his thoughts during the training, despite his shyness around Llio.

So why did he say that, then? Was it because Perceval needed to learn there was a time to speak and a time to listen? Perhaps. One had to be a good observer before becoming a good contributor.

All except Gornymant rose, saying their goodnights. Llio and Llascoit both embraced and kissed their father on their way out of the hall.

As for Perceval, he was already halfway back to his quarters. When he arrived he forgot to even shut the door, he was so tired. The last thought he had when he hit the feather-filled mattress was that he promised himself he would never forget what he heard here tonight.

Gornymant remained there at the table, sipping his wine, gazing at the lovely embroidery that his departed loved one so painstakingly performed.

He thought the evening went quite well. He just hoped his three charges would learn to think independently. Even the words of a teacher could be taken too literally sometimes.

* * *

Oerfa's knightly visitors were absent for several weeks by the time Dindraine and her mother finally had it out with each other. Both screamed and wept, and neither would admit to the sense of release it gave.

It started innocently enough, or so thought Dindraine at the time; she merely pried her mother for information about her own father and background, and instead got to hear more than she ever wanted to know about Perceval's.

And now Dindraine wanted to disappear just as badly. Her mother was troubled more deeply than she ever imagined.

Mother started by pointing out that she really was trying to understand, to control her emotions, but to no avail. Her whole body clenched as Dindraine approached her. Dindraine just let her talk.

Mother swore she would never quite fathom just what it was about knighthood that so attracted young men. It was dangerous, it was elitist, it constantly led to warfare, with the women and children and peasants suffering the worst of it. How could the men she had known be predisposed to pursue such a mindless way of life? Dindraine could offer no answer, wondering if her father, too, was a knight. So she waited for more explanation.

As for the older woman, she could not admit any possibility of overprotecting her children, especially her son. Her background permitted no such confession. Her own previous life had been one of privilege and power. When she was Dindraine's age, she dreamed of the prince who would come sweep her off her feet and marry her in his own castle. The memory of that grew so abhorrent to her that she started to feel nauseated just in its telling, but Dindraine kept insisting.

Pellinore was so beautiful that first day, she remembered, her emotions summoning her to a place out of another lifetime, a different world. Like his son so much later, he also had a momentous day. He had just come from wounding some hell-spawn thing that he said emitted a scream sounding like the baying of dozens of hounds; his first thought was that he had stumbled into someone else's hunting party, as the dog-noises could be heard a great distance. The other knights thought him mad, but the evidence still ran freshly from the tip of his lance. It was coated with a purplish ooze which would have resembled blood if not for the color. The smell was darker, also; it stank of death and decay, like a carcass left for the crows and flies. Yet he was oblivious to it. It was said to have been born of some unholy union in the bitter Wastes in the far northern reaches of the Island; the sort of place known to be the abode and haunting grounds of giants, dragons, goblins, and God alone knew what else. He only cared about finishing his quest to rid the land of the beast, perhaps from knightly pride, perhaps from not wanting the Wasteland evil to spread.

"But at what price?" the woman asked her daughter in the present, bitterly. Dindraine shrugged, then tried an answer.

"But think of them, Mother, of them all. Despite all the bad details of knights you've shared recently, I think even you know how majestic they look, perched upon their horses, ready to shed their own blood for the women and causes they love."

"You speak like your brother," Mother said. "They don't stay around when they should. When they're needed most, they can be found anywhere but home. Like that wounded man dragged into the village when the two of you came home that night."

"Lamorak," she mused, not noticing her mother stiffen at the name's mention. "But Perceval won't be like that. You heard him; he'll be back before we know it. We both heard his oath."

Dindraine's mother tried not to roll her eyes, tried to hold onto that piece of faith, like the cross she gave her son. "What did you say to him that night?"

Dindraine knew that tone: it was accusatory, and always had seemed much more reserved for her than for Perceval, more so lately in his absence. "Nothing he didn't think of himself. He had to wise up sometime."

Her mother pondered the words, then continued the old tale.

She grew up on a farm herself; it seemed only natural that once she had forsaken her entrance into the ways of knighthood, she should return to that simpler lifestyle. Her parents raised their own herds (the cattle being a true symbol of wealth to the country people, more so than any gold), even dabbling in the growing horse trade, on a farm outside Caernarfon.

She loved going into the town as a girl. It was a bustling seaport, with a thriving trade based primarily on the exporting of slate, and the view of the nearby holy island of Mona always pleased her, even if it had once been a training ground for the druids. Pellinore was to rule Gwynedd, northern Cambria, to take the place of the long departed emperor. And she desired him from the moment she first saw him, hoping it sinless, seeing him sweating atop his horse, proud of what he hoped would be the first of many injuries inflicted upon this "Barking Beast."

The Gales clan, of which Pellinore was clearly an up and coming member, had attempted to unite the various tribes of Gwynedd, much as their Roman predecessors tried to do (advantageous marriages and promises of farmland worked better than the scourging fires and swords the Centurions brought). The people of several clans merged into a single political entity, a new chiefdom, during the start of the reign of a teenager wielding a sword and a dream.

Pelleham, king in his own right and a loyal subject of Arthur eager to participate in the civilizing lifestyle mandated by the religion of the Mediterranean, had not much considered how the tribes might resent this intrusion into their ways. His son, a knight of the new Round Table, was just as culturally ignorant of the Old Ways; every effort had been made to eliminate the ancient rituals. Father and son considered Arthur's way to be the only way (never mind that the Boy King had a druid as his mentor), and the tribes resented it.

Some of these people even spoke nonsense describing the Beast as an omen, come to kill the Christian rulers. Cymru were fiercely proud, and the eventual uprisings began at the hands of some very displeased women; it seemed they particularly resented being told that Goddess was dead, replaced by an unreachable deity who preferred sin and damnation to Nature worship.

But such events still lay ahead of the dreamy young girl who grew up near Caernarfon. She next saw Pellinore at a festival some weeks later, looking much cleaner than the first time. It was to be a celebration of Christmas (although most of the people were celebrating the Yule instead, along with the Winter Solstice). The rulers and merchants, transplanted descendants of Roman citizens, never heeded the subtle differences, even going so far as to bring trees into their homes to mock the Pagan Yule logs, and decorating them with candles and trinkets.

Pellinore looked even better at the festival. He had shaved his beard and worn a silken sea-blue doublet, with matching leather breeches. She was so impressed by his clothes and their costly hues, and when his eyes first met hers she nervously glanced away. She could not believe it when he approached her, from behind his personal guards, and requested a dance.

This was the only part of the grand recollection she did not mind presently, and she pointed that detail out to the eager Dindraine: that one moment of pure joy as he led her around the town square in his arms. She could almost feel his touch again. *So many years ago.*

Gwynedd had since reverted to Paganism, under a new chief, who was anything but a friend of Arthur's. The Pendragon was content to leave the smaller petty monarchs (really tribal chiefs) alone, too concerned with maintaining his own huge demesne of Logres to worry about the Cambrians, who posed little military threat to him anyway.

She collected herself, watching her daughter's response, and returned to the festival. She recalled that it seemed to end so early, even though she already danced several times with the prince, and even shared some laughs over a goblet of spiced native wine with him. She could no longer remember what had been so amusing; she thought she was just caught up in the magick of that perfect moment. She had already learned that Pellinore had been initiated into the wondrous Camelot fraternity in return for Pelleham's sworn allegiance and his pledge to keep Gwynedd under Arthur's vassalage. It was perhaps a sound political move, but only infuriated the tribes people further. The King quickly learned that Roman ways did not always work; why else would they have abandoned their provinces the previous century with the cold, stark message: Look To Your Own Defense?

Pellinore had felt angry at first with the arrangement regarding his knightly status, but the members of the Round Table held tremendous power anywhere in Britain, and were respected (if not actually liked) by all. And he marveled in the knowledge that his name had been inscribed in gold plating at the great Table (magickally, with the help of the great Merlin, or so folk said). She knew she loved him when he could at least laugh at her comment that, on hearing of his forced arrangement, at least now a man in Christendom knew what it was like to be promised to another. She loved that laugh of his; it was really that of a boy.

The encounter with the Beast gave him something to work toward, a solid goal which fit perfectly into the royal scheme of quelling the land of all its ills. The unruly Garmani in Anglia would soon be crushed at the Battle of Badon Hill; that would remain about the only thing Arthur did to please the Cambrians, who were wary of eventual Garmani invasion.

That very next evening Pellinore arrived, unarmed and without his guards, at her parent's home. They were stunned by the gesture: the prince, self-defensively naked, riding around at night outside the protection of Caernarfon's walls. He asked her parents if she could accompany him on a moonlit ride, and they assented, perhaps too easily, perhaps just wanting to improve their station.

"So what else happened that night?" Dindraine said, allowing a smile. The pair of them offered few smiles to each other anymore. Dindraine was enraptured in the tale; she never knew any of this! And she still didn't know word one about her own father.

So the story continued.

Despite Dindraine's mother's anxiety and excitement on that evening years past, Pellinore had been a total gentleman. He said it was part of his commitment to a code or some new custom called chivalry. She asked him why he should follow such behavioral norms, to which he answered that it was a knight's way: to be brave, honest, and courteous. Apparently the young High Queen saw to it that all knights be taught about such virtues, and her personal champions and guardians, the Queen's Knights, were those who could demonstrate great skill in the gentler, non-combative arts. Pellinore wanted to try for such honor, but said his voice was not yet sweet enough, and his backgammon and literacy skills left much to be desired. He thought he could perhaps dance for the competition instead.

She encouraged him; he was, after all, a fine dancer. Tonight, so long afterwards, she could not quite remember much of what happened between that lovely first evening when he kissed her goodnight and when they married. His lips had tasted as sweet as honey, and she wanted to feel their supple moist warmth all night. The gentleman simply bid her good evening, and rode back to Caernarfon. For the next few weeks, he proudly ran through the city proclaiming his new-found love, and she never, back on the farm, had any shortage of fresh fragrant flowers or personal affection. It was her dream made real. It was months before she discovered the role he played in a final showdown with the native Britons who opposed the new rule, some time before Badon Hill, at a place she could no longer remember. They were already wed by then.

Mother did recall it had been during one of their afternoon rides. She always loved them as a girl and was not about to give them up, minor queen or no. Pelleham had quietly passed the previous winter, a lifetime of indulgence in that spiced wine finally catching up to him. The tribes people had said that a kingdom was only as strong and healthy as its king; that was why the kingdom was unstable and primed for revolt. His own wife, Pellinore's mother, died years before, while giving birth to a younger son, who had also run off to be knighted as soon as he could.

While she and Pellinore guided their horses along the coastline (his imported Andalusian charger and her native Camargue pony), he told her of his having killed another lesser king, Lot of Lothian, in the chaotic oblivion of battle.

Even so long afterwards she could not recall just why he had raised the topic. Maybe he was trying to protect her with his knowledge, maybe he was just feeling guilty about an action that had been justified by its sanctioned place in warfare. Lot was the commander of a battalion of northern warriors and knights, allied to the lesser rulers of Britain in their opposition to Arthur. Some thought Pellinore singled out Lot to eliminate a potential enemy (he had, in truth, been searching for a neighboring ruler on the battlefield, and found Lothian's instead). Whatever his intentions, the two of them had met in the thick of things, and Pellinore was simply younger and faster, case closed.

But as it turned out, the case definitely did not close. Lot had sons, who curiously sat at the Round Table. These children seemed to radically switch loyalties, against their kin no less, only to rediscover them after said kin was gone. The eldest, Gawaine, a boastful redhead and brutal fighter, was the King's own champion, and he vowed revenge, act of war or no. Pellinore did not expect any members of Lot's Orkney clan to actually come into Gwynedd, but he had a duty to periodically report his doings to Camelot. He sought his solace by returning to the hunt of the Barking Beast.

No one seemed to ever quite comprehend how Gawaine, and his hot-tempered younger brother Gaheris, could apparently change not just his mind but his heart also, after he had forsaken his father and supported Arthur.

Now, years later, perhaps that was why there was a new champion, the Queen's own, a stunning athlete and physically beautiful man from the Continent. She heard his name was Lancelot. She learned about it one night from Tathan during a private conversation in which she was trying to assess any potential danger to herself or her children, since she was the rogue ex-queen of a dead monarchy.

Dindraine watched her mother cringing, listened as she spoke. "Daughter, I cannot lose another child. I've lost so much family already, all to the power men wield like toys!"

"Was it worth it, then, to keep us in the dark for so long? How do you think my brother and I felt all these years, knowing everyone else must have thought us fools, all so you'd be safe?" *Careful. If this woman is ever going to share anymore of herself with you, it will probably be now.*

"At least I don't have to worry about losing you to all this brutish sword-waving, lady-courting nonsense."

"Am I to stay in Oerfa the rest of my life, then?"

Her mother did not answer, and instead insisted on finishing what she started. It felt relieving, to tell all of this. Maybe her ungrateful children could discuss it with each other someday.

Pellinore's mutilated body was found thirteen days after his final departure from Caernarfon to seek the Beast. Everyone was quick to say that, "the Beast got him, the Beast got him, the omen was correct," but she knew better; she could feel it in her soul. She wasted no tears just yet; they would have to wait. All she knew right then was that she had to leave. Gawaine had gotten to her husband, and it was only a matter of time before the tribespeople reclaimed their ancestral lands. She had no desire to be queen, especially alone, of a doomed kingdom.

She waited for nightfall, trying to remain calm while packing just enough to supply a single camp. That and her jewels. Pellinore had always been eager to lavish his chivalrous gifts upon her, even though she rarely wore them, for fear of the sin of vanity. She had an emerald brooch, the setting made of gold shaped into intertwining knots, two rings, one with a large deep sapphire and (she couldn't remember what the other one was like), and other pieces too numerous to count. She thought it humorously ironic that the jewelry she never cared for funded her anonymous resettlement. She silently swore to herself that night that she would never again lose someone close to her; she thought she would die of heartache if that happened again. She already felt that she would never see her elder son nor her parents as it was. So far she had been right. So many years later, her parents were likely dead.

No one even noticed her immediate departure. She had so wanted to bring her first born son, but he was already twelve and being educated as a knight by a tutor across the city. Leaving him behind was the most difficult choice she ever made; what would she say to him if she ever saw him again? She made no mention of his name to her daughter. That would reopen too many old wounds.

She knew she had to leave, to escape from the life she had wanted only because of Pellinore, and his damned knightly ways killed him and endangered her. She just hoped that no one would want her dead as well.

That, happily, turned out to be the case. She was already a few weeks pregnant with Perceval, and so decided against finding her first son that night (Lamorak, poor Lamorak, though she willed the name away, even when he was here, wounded and foreign to her). She would raise this second child in seclusion, and never allow him to hear any of her past. She had the money (the jewels, anyway) with which to start over, and she only wanted her child. In her haste, she barely considered her parents; she had not seen them since her older son's most recent birthday (they had given him a wooden sword and shield of all things, damn her father and his handicrafts!) She also had no idea about Pellam, Pellinore's brother, who also escaped into seclusion, or so she heard.

The native Cambrians had apparently forgiven her, or just lost track of her, or not even cared at all; their enemy was dispatched, and the tribes reestablished according to the ancient traditions. She had been safe in this part of the Severn Valley for many years, and she raised her children *her* way.

"And your way included making your son a moron?"

She slapped her insolent daughter, hard across the face. Dindraine did not flinch, feeling the heat rise. "He's not stupid!"

"No. He's brilliant, and a prince," Dindraine replied calmly. "Which makes it all the more tragic." Her mother could not face her, stung by the words.

Finally, frustrated beyond words, Dindraine stole down to the river branch with what felt like her only remaining friend, the other dog, Dannedd.

Unfortunately, the stream no longer seemed very special, and for her was now just a simple source of running water. The magick had gone from it; it held little aesthetic appeal for her. Besides, who could she talk to down here, other than her dog? Dannedd did appreciate her company, and for this she was thankful. He was a good watchdog and faithful friend, and would have been a good cure for the hole in her heart left by her brother's absence. Even if it were just to have one of their old arguments, she would have given anything to see him then.

It was already over a month since he had left, but to Dindraine it felt like years. Was he all right? Was he a knight yet? How did the people in Camelot respond to him? Did he miss her? She often asked Dannedd these questions, sometimes crying into his fur.

She sighed deeply. No one else paid much attention to her. Oerfa was a tiny settlement, with few children. The younger ones were either still in swaddling clothes, or too busy with their own apprenticeships to be with her (Nia was always too involved with her apprenticeship to spend much time with Dindraine). And what did she have to do? Nothing, it seemed. Her mother for the most part ignored her now, and she returned the favor, never forgetting how she acted before Perceval left.

Damn Nia anyway, she thought bitterly. Dindraine did not care any more how much her friend's father wanted her to learn the family tradition of brewing this and that. Nia was there that day, to watch Perceval leave, but afterwards had been virtually invisible to Dindraine. Nia was two years older than she, and they were the closest in age of any of Oerfa's children, but she now traveled a lot to help the family trade. Dindraine used to spend time with just about everyone, but now the villagers tended to ostracize her because of her more reclusive mother.

Mother. Damn her, too. Dindraine had just about enough of her for one lifetime. Their last discussion drove the wedge in between them that much deeper. Mother always seemed to be daydreaming, and had taken over the shepherding responsibilities, ignoring not just her daughter but her other tasks, like running a homestead. She wouldn't even impart the knowledge of Dindraine's own father. She and Perceval were only half-siblings, and she wondered if she was Beltaine-conceived. *God, Mother would fear for her soul if that was true!*

I should leave like Perceval. She knew it. Her mother was really off and gone now; Dindraine did not think she was reachable and she no longer felt willing to try to bridge the gap between them. The other villagers sometimes tried to talk to her mother, but she would just give them blank stares, and often start babbling about old, dead Pellinore and how life used to be before the Barking Beast and the Orkney clan came calling.

Dindraine screamed, just to release some of the tension, the frustration. Down by the stream she was sure that no one in the village could hear it. It surprised Dannedd, but he just accepted it. She would leave, too; she had to.

But where to go? And how could she get anywhere alone?

Dindraine bent over next to the water and cupped her hands in it. It was delightfully cool. She brought some up and splashed her face, as though the water could somehow cleanse away these bad feelings. Dannedd lapped up some himself in noisy gulps; at least he knew how to appreciate the stream.

They sat down, girl and dog, and just listened to the sounds: the birds chirping and squawking and gliding from tree to tree; the gentle flow of the water as it trickled south, heading all the way to the sea; Dannedd's open-mouthed breathing and occasional vocal yawns. It was peaceful here, but Oerfa was no place for a girl with dreams. Sometimes peacefulness was too stifling to bear.

More out of habit than decision, Dindraine finally stood to walk home, Dannedd joining her. She didn't want to go back, but what could she do right then, sleep next to the stream? In the woods? Out with the sheep? Lately the sheep would just remind her of the other villagers: boring, mundane, caught up only in their own routines.

She glanced at her surroundings. The woods.

She was a quarter mile from the cluster of trees that was the only forest she knew. Behind it stood another of the infinite hills. It was a lively-looking place, even with Perceval gone; they used to love exploring it together.

And up on the hill, a light, very faint, but a light nonetheless. Dindraine felt sure it was not a star; it was just past dusk, too early to really see stars. She knew about this hill, surely, but had never seen any sign of life atop it. Besides, the last time she had spied a light in the distance, her brother left.

Still, she was curious. This was the most exciting event for her all month.

The light came from where Kundry supposedly lived.

Who was she, anyway? Dindraine never heard much more than a word about her: "she's a witch or sorceress; avoid her; she's no good." Yet as Dindraine contemplated this, it occurred to her that these were odd sentiments coming from Pagans. Such comments sounded more like what her mother, the zealous Christian, would say. But the Pagans: they placed deep trust in their magicians and priests. Witches served as healers for villages; druids led religious ceremonies. What could be bad about this woman, anyway?

Dindraine realized she was leading Dannedd towards the light forest, and to the hill where lived the witch.

Or whoever she was. Anything had to be better than going back home. Dindraine was agonizingly bored, and that alone might have led her up the hill. Mixed with her curiosity, the urge became overwhelmingly pressing.

Uphill toward the light she climbed, Dannedd eagerly trotting at her side.

The people in Oerfa, including her mother, would not hear from her again, and for this she was always grateful.

* * *

Perceval awoke, groggy. From elsewhere in Jagent came the familiar bellow of his tutor. Gornymant was nothing if not a reliable alarm; Perceval awoke just before hearing the man's cries of, "Rise, you all!" and "How do you expect to learn anything if you stay in bed all morning?"

He looked across the small room. It was devoid of furniture other than the bed, and shaded only in gray. The feather bed was comfortable and there were plenty of wool blankets to keep him warm. Opposite the room in a tiny closet were his most prized possessions: a mail hauberk to cover his torso and arms, a pair of mail chausses to protect his legs and feet, both still giving the impression of redness with their clever painting at the joints; a long sword of exceptional construction; and a rosy-red shield some two feet wide at the top and three feet long. Naturally, the shield had three points to it: two at the top which curved down to meet at a third at the bottom.

Perceval knew he felt safer whenever he slipped his hand and arm through the twin leather straps on the shield's back. He felt more than protected; it was almost a sense of invulnerability that came over him when he tightened his hand into a fist over the second strap, the first one securing the shield to his arm. It was an active defense, one which he could move at his will, and if Llascoit should get by it, it was Perceval's own fault for not meeting the blow. The armor, which also felt secure but in a different manner, was a passive defense measure. He donned it, and then forgot about it. It was light enough to only restrict his movement by a slight extent, although he could not exactly run very fast in it, and he was never very pleased about the mittens which covered his hands. He knew he should try to keep every part of him protected, but the mittens bothered him because he could move only his thumbs freely in them; the other fingers had to move as a group. Still, he knew he had little to complain about; he had expensive armor, and the means to learn to use it to the fullest.

He turned again to the shield, ignoring Gornymant's hollering to get moving. Three points. Just like on the one in the dining hall, like so many other things. He tried to remember the triads from earlier. Three gods, three goddesses, three parts of the training. That was all he could recall right then. He would think of the others later. He had to get to work.

His breaking of the evening's fast during his training was simple and routine: each morning he and Llascoit would grab whatever leftover food they could find from the night before. Though the four of them usually plowed through their suppers, sometimes not even leaving any scraps for the keep's dog, Llio or the cooks would have fresh bread and some kind of meat jerky awaiting them. Chicken, beef, even pork and the occasional fish, were kept preserved in the pantry. The smell of the bread and the effort of chewing the toughened salty flesh always woke Perceval and his foster-brother right up.

Llascoit must already be outside, Perceval thought, realizing his tardiness. He tried to chew the meat as quickly as possible, washing it down, along with the bread, with some fast gulps of the morning wine. Water was difficult to keep fresh and clean once taken from its source; it was easier to keep wine on hand for thirst, although this necessitated caution on the part of the drinker to avoid excesses.

The meat was deliciously spiced, as always. Perceval wondered if it had come from one of the sheep he and Llascoit butchered. That had been one of Gornymant's early lessons: he said that a knight could not fully appreciate the awe and responsibility of killing another unless he had first killed some lesser creature. Perceval, of course, had already killed another, and no lesser creature at that. But he went to the slaughter, and was struck how he felt more sympathy for the lamb he decapitated than for the man from whose throat he had torn a chunk. The lamb hadn't known it was supposed to die; it looked innocent and afraid. The man, on the other hand, had spent a lifetime preparing to kill or to die while trying to kill, and was totally aware of the implications of his occupation.

Perceval had of course seen sheep slaughtered before; life at home prepared him for Gornymant's dictates. It was just the feeling this time. He never before considered the awesome power knights wielded over others: that of life and death itself. He silently prayed he would always know to make the proper decisions with this power. Killing and death were always part of life. He only felt remorse for the lamb because of its ignorance. It felt very different indeed from the incident with Meliagrant.

"You're late. Don't let it happen again," said Gornymant to the jogging errant as he emerged into the courtyard. Perceval would have to stop all these wandering thoughts of his! They were starting to interfere with his training.

"Back to the quintain today, lads. And this afternoon you're going to joust each other as well." Gornymant looked well-rested, as he constantly did. The man never seemed short of energy. Across the courtyard, Llascoit's wooden practice lance hit the circular target of the quintain squarely, and he ducked smoothly under the weighted leather bag which instantly circled around as the target was struck. He made it look easy; Perceval still had trouble getting past the bag. Maybe he was hitting the target too hard.

It was Perceval's turn. He must have been inspired that morning, for he found his mark and dodged the counter as well as Llascoit.

* * *

Uren had to clear his throat before continuing with the lesson. His voice had strengthened immeasurably since his arrival at Haughmond Abbey, but the full days of prayers and singing and talking to subordinates could become quite taxing for anyone's vocal chords.

He stood in front of his class, the nuns and the monks. Dyfed and Merin were absent, busying themselves with other duties. At the moment they were baking; a week's bread at a time could be created in the ovens within the abbey, in only a few hours. And they had many mouths to feed, not only the abbey's residents, but the commoners who frequented the countryside and relied on alms. The people of Haughmond were bound to give what they could to charity.

The room for classes was upstairs in the building adjacent to the chapel, just beyond the dormitory. Living space was a bit cramped for the monks. The nuns had their own room to share.

The room itself consisted of little more than two long benches, a podium from which Uren spoke to his assemblage, a cross above the heavy door, and a window on each of two opposite sides, permitting views of the cemetery through one and the progressively hillier countryside through the other.

Uren continued with the lesson. In slow, deliberate Latin that sounded straight from Rome itself, he said, "And so Joseph came to the vast misty shore, entrusted with the Holy Grail."

This confused one of the listeners. The young monk, Godfrey, asked, "With the holy blood, Abbot?" It was a legitimate question, although hinting at heresy; Uren dismissed it outright, aware of the problems of translations.

"No, my son. I refer not to the body of our Lord, but to the vessel containing His blood. You know the story already, now just listen to it in the older verse." The words for holy grail also meant, literally, holy blood. This same type of indiscretion had plagued the abbot just moments earlier: one of the nuns, Olennia, became equally confused over the ambiguity of another word. A 'drinking horn' could easily be mistaken for a 'body,' particularly a dead one. Such were the difficulties with lingual studies, and the topic was tricky, also.

No, decided Uren, *this is among the most sacred elements of our Faith, and they should be able to relate it in the ancient language.* His students simply had to resolve these difficulties for themselves, and continue with their studies.

Still, the vagueness remained. Why exactly would the Romans have chosen multiple meanings for the same ideas? Uren felt almost embarrassed; as his faith came through divine revelation, so must have come the language used by those who declared it their official religion.

Then why were the earlier Christians thrown to the lions, for the entertainment of Rome's population of sinners? And weren't they of course responsible for the execution of the Savior in the first place?

It occurred to Uren that perhaps the Carpenter would never have been realized as Savior without his crucifixion; it was better not to dwell on such sticky subjects, now or ever. He still had his class to contend with regardless.

And they sat there, motionless, all eyes upon him. Still awaiting the ancient verse proffered. *Ex fide fortis,* he reminded himself. *From faith comes strength.*

He cleared his throat again and continued, still in Latin, taking the time to enunciate perfectly. "Joseph was entrusted with the Grail, removing it from the Holy Land. At that time the Romans were still too numerous, and too restrictive, for the Grail to surface and fall into their hands." Uren left the 'Holy' description off this time, hoping to end the prior confusion. He was improvising the lesson; his own Latin was so excellent that he needed no text. Yet it was difficult to remain focused on the practice of the archaic tongue, given the day's subject.

Godfrey phrased his next comment in that same archaic tongue. "And he was eventually captured, but kept alive miraculously by the Grail?" Apparently Godfrey had only shared the latter of the mistranslations.

Uren nodded. Then Olennia spoke again. "Master, I am not sure I understand the point of the story." Her Latin was improving steadily, Uren noticed, and he admired her ability to speak her mind. A rare trait, in a nun.

"The point?" Uren queried. "The point is the lesson of sinning. Because Joseph eventually failed in his task, the Grail was taken from us. Forever. Recall how Jesus died so that we would all become aware of our basic sinful condition." Uren was an officer of the Church; he had an obligation to teach as the Church would teach. Sinners had to learn of their ignorance, or they could not be saved.

"Could it ever come back?" asked Olennia, a certain hope evident in the shine of her eyes, all but blotted by the habit and accompanying hood she wore.

Uren considered it, forgetting the practical approach to the day's lesson. Speaking now in Cymru, he answered, "Yes. So it is said. So it shall be."

The students murmured slightly at this revelation, and Uren silenced them. "But such is reserved for someone very special indeed. For he who is the best among we mortals."

He could see they wanted more of an answer. "In this time, centuries after Joseph collected the blessed drops from the Savior's wound, I suppose it would mean the best knight in the world. Someone who exemplifies Christian virtue, someone who can defend those who cannot defend themselves, and who marches into battle in the name of God, as in the example of the Just War. But it is not our task to question who this perfect soul might be."

Enraptured with the notion of another Savior-king coming to help humanity save itself (albeit this time more violently than the Carpenter!), Olennia asked Uren, "What will happen if such a saintly figure recovers the Grail?"

Uren was totally unprepared for such a question. All his fanciful daydreaming about questing knights and God's glory made real again on earth precluded his consideration of just what a person might do if he actually found the vessel. He gave the first answer that came to mind.

"Why, use it to heal, of course. Think back to the early part of today's lesson, child. 'Eat of this, it is my body; drink of this, it is my blood.' How else could Joseph have remained alive while imprisoned?"

He let the words soothe their way into his listener's ears. Then he added, "What on this earth could possibly contain more power than the healing ability of our Lord's own blood? Even if Joseph had not been in attendance at the Last Supper, surely one of the disciples would have told him about what transpired. I believe Joseph of Arimathea simply took the Lord's words to heart."

The monks and nuns could not take their eyes from him now; they had never prepared for any lesson like this! Why hadn't the Church taught more about such a clearly miraculous vessel?

A hand raised in the back of the room, slowly, uncertainly. It belonged to a young man from the city of Eburacum in the north, come this distance to try and infuse God's way into these rabble-rousing hill heathens.

Uren sighed, wondering if he could continue answering queries without succumbing to blasphemy. Or to the sin of lying. "Yes, Brother Godfrey?"

"Abbot," he began innocently, "you say this 'Grail' is capable of the utmost miracles. Can there truly be such a relic? That is to say, can miracles happen in the absence of the Angels or the Lord Himself?"

Uren considered the analogy to the Lord as the shepherd tending His flock; so it would be with himself and his class.

He responded as best he could, drawing on the numerous tomes and legends from which he took the story in the first place. "It can heal any disease, any wound. The Pagans I have talked to who have, somehow, heard of it, say it can go so far as to raise the dead. It can grant whatever one wishes, really; all one need do is ask. I gather it could even cause a rebirth of flower and tree where such had died. And he who looks upon it would likely be so filled with utter rapture that he might ascend straight into heaven. If he were so deserving, of course."

The nun, Olennia, looked at him quizzically. "Abbot, if the person who may recover it from its hiding place would be a knight, what is to stop him from falling victim to knightly excess and temptation?" All those present in the room knew Olennia had her suspicions about knights, and was not pleased with how the Church was beginning to consider their use for its own ends. There were even rumors of one day taking back the Holy Land itself from the infidels there.

Uren confessed. "I am unsure I follow you."

"What I mean is, what's to stop this knight from abusing the privilege that would come from such power?"

Uren shook his head. He never considered the possibility.

* * *

"*Dere ymlaen, Perceval! Mi ro'i ras iti!*"

Llio's beckoning shout took him off guard, but he urged Brownie into a gallop to try and match her horse's stride, offering her the race for which she shouted. Perceval had gone with her down to the lake two miles south of Jagent, where she was to teach him to swim. She and her brother were already virtual otters, learning to take the plunge with the help of their father, who swam growing up on the south Cambrian coast.

Llascoit and Gornymant were still at the castle, the son practicing at the harp. Perceval had little interest in the instrument, and Gornymant decided it was more important for him to learn to swim anyway, especially if, as a knight, he ever found himself fighting in or near water. Granted, chain armor would certainly inhibit a person's efforts to stay afloat; but Gornymant had seen knights drown, face-down, in mere inches of water, due to their inability to move around in it.

Llio loved teasing Perceval like this, still in the lead atop Fay; too often she got caught up in the household duties, and she craved time to spend with her family or their guest. He, too, had little time away from the more combative elements of his training, and this was an opportunity for them to get away from the routines of the castle.

Llio timed Fay's gallop just right; the mare pulled up ahead of Brownie and easily maintained that lead for the short distance remaining to the lake. Perceval rode up to find Llio giggling atop Fay, gesturing toward the water.

Llio dismounted, walking the horse over to a nearby tree and tethering her there. Perceval did the same, then walked toward the lake with the young woman.

It was more of a pond, really, not even big enough to have its own name. Llio and Llascoit just called it a lake to make it sound more impressive and exciting. Still, it was big enough to practice swimming. The river Cam opened up into the pond, and continued its way south, eventually leading down past Camelot itself. It was a narrow river, reminding Perceval of the Severn's tentacles which fed the area near his home.

A small boat, big enough only for two, was tied to a tree opposite the site where he and Llio tied their mounts. It looked old but seaworthy, gently rocking slightly back and forth to the casual rhythm of the passing river. He wondered who used the boat. It appeared useful only for fishing or idling by an afternoon.

Perceval was still admiring the surrounding scenery, sucking in the fresh air, when his breath became a gasp. Llio was removing her clothes!

"Llio! What are you doing?" He was stunned. This was far more like something from one of his dreams. The girl was almost naked already, down to her chemise and leg hose, her doublet cast aside onto the ground.

"Well, how did you expect to learn to swim, anyway? You can hardly do it fully clothed!" Perceval was even more shocked to note how she seemed to be *enjoying* teasing him like this. He had to think of something, and quickly.

"Maybe we could just wear our undergarments, or something."

Llio giggled again. "No, silly one. It's all or nothing out here. Now do you want to learn to swim or not?"

Wide-eyed and slack-jawed, Perceval watched as Llio removed the last of her garments. She was beyond mere comeliness; she was stunning. She had a lithe yet supple body without the slightest hint of flaw. She smiled gaily at Perceval, and her whole body seemed to greet him, beckoning to him, yearning for him. *I must be misguided,* he thought; why would Llio ever want him that way? Yet she was captivating to behold; her legs and arms strong but delicate and long, her hair waving lovingly in the gentle breeze, the curves of her face and breasts and hips just waiting for a sensual caress.

Perceval had to close his eyes just to attempt to regain clear thought. *No,* he considered immediately. He had already grown to adore this young woman, but she was off limits. This was Gornymant's daughter! Not some (what would his mother have called them?) whore or something. He was already feeling ashamed of the almost painful throbbing erection lurking beneath his own clothing.

"Llio, please. I-I'm –"

"Afraid? Nervous? Forget it." She did her best not to sound disappointed. She was as much virgin as Perceval, too shy to make any physical advances, though she did wonder about what it might be like with him (she did not consider nudity forward though, at least not for the present activity).

He is wonderful, she thought unabashedly. He was always courteous towards her, and quite attractive also. And obviously unlike him, she had never been taught to feel ashamed of her body. She wondered how much of the more rigid Christianity Perceval had in him, to be so obviously embarrassed. She went over to him, gently putting her arms around him.

"There, now is that so bad?" she asked soothingly. She honestly did not think she was coming onto him; she just wanted to help him relax. Their time together, always brief, was special to her.

Perceval was speechless, his lips quivering and most of the rest of his body wanting to follow their example. What does a young man say when embraced by a gorgeous young naked woman? His face felt like it was on fire. It seemed ridiculously hot out here by this pond. *Forget swimming!* He'd never be able to learn now. *Maybe the harp isn't such a bad idea.*

Gently, Llio helped Perceval disrobe, a single piece of clothing at a time. He resisted at first, then gave in to her touch. He was of little help; indeed, he felt rooted to the ground, immovable, although a bit more relaxed as her hands gathered up the articles.

At last they stood there together, naked before each other and the world, Perceval's erection still standing prominently in front of him. He was quite shy, but it had also felt dreamily wonderful to be touched by this person. He wondered how he could keep his hands off her.

So did she. But she led him to the pond, and began the lesson. At least the coolness of the water relieved Perceval's sense of overheating.

Perceval came to make sure this young headstrong woman was always close by. He grew to hate any time spent away from her. He ached for her, and she eventually hinted to him of her own desire, but also of how her father would forbid any carnal knowledge of his daughter without a proper marriage.

He had at least that much of the Christian. And, being practical, he knew Llio would have difficulty finding a husband later if her virginity was compromised.

Assuming, of course, that said husband was a man other than Perceval.

How could Perceval make himself worthy? This was the thought which kept him awake many a night. Llio needed someone equally strong and capable, and while his confidence and knowledge bloomed proudly since his arrival, he remained a squire, with little money or experience, no land or forthcoming inheritance.

And no title. He had sworn to not reveal what he knew about his past.

The pair of them became inseparable friends, though, sometimes stealing away down to the pond (both relished the swimming practices!) or just to walk along counting stars. Llascoit occasionally could be found with them, and other times when he knew enough to let them be, spent time with his father.

Perceval could tell Llio anything at all.

Except of his fear that they would somehow be separated once they left the security of Jagent for Camelot, and by the lives they each might lead.

* * *

The abomination could not be destroyed; at least, that was what Yvaine came close to believing about it. Any fun in pursuing it was over; now it became an issue of life and death.

They had miraculously kept on the Beast's trail for days, seeing it over there, hearing it right around here. But always, it lay just beyond reach, as though teasing them. Even the horrible barking sounds which pitched from its awful belly began to sound more like laughter than tortured dog souls; of that even Lamorak felt convinced. And he was more determined than ever now, once again fully mobile after his recuperation. It was slow healing in the wilds, but his squire's care and Dindraine's salves brought him back to strength.

So now he absolutely would not quit. The sight of the small but thoroughly ravished settlement, in the old style of a large wooden enclosure, only served to increase his resolve to find the thing and put an end to it. It seemed the creature had developed a taste for destruction. His father never mentioned that; always it had been described as merely offensive, a warning, to use the term of the natives.

But never as something deadly.

Yvaine would never forget the image of that destroyed *rath*. Nor the smell. He and Lamorak forbade the squires to go inside the palisaded wall; they thought it the only merciful act they could offer at the time.

The bodies became too numerous to count; counting was, after all, most difficult to accomplish when one busily worked to avoid retching on one's armor and tunic. Yet there was no sign at all of thievery. People's personal signs of wealth: brooches, rings, coin pouches, all remained intact and in place. No, whatever did this had been intent upon killing in and of itself, almost as though the act was purely pleasurable.

Yvaine knew his friend had no idea just what the Beast might be capable of, even if it intended physical harm to people. But Lamorak was quick to judge that day in the village: the creature was responsible for this senseless death, and it had to pay. He refused to consider even the remote chance that perhaps other people might have committed such a rampage. The residual personal effects were what convinced him; no war party left without its pillage, and the region was more peaceful since he left it as a boy anyway.

Of course, all that was before the two knights became separated, the squires both joining the eventual search for the missing Lamorak who had once again thrown his better judgment (which was never that good to begin with) over the cliffs of reason and relentlessly chased the monster again.

Or thought he had. When Lamorak's body was found there was no sign of any creature at all, faerie or otherwise. Indeed, the evidence at the scene consisted of horse tracks, at least two sets from mounts other than Lamorak's own. And no faerie creature could have put so many blade slices into a suit of mail. He was ruthlessly cut to pieces, almost literally, a wound at a time, as though whoever was responsible had wanted him to suffer horribly first. Yvaine knew what cold steel felt like when it lacerated skin.

But Gawaine was believed to be in Camelot. And no one knew of Yvaine's and Lamorak's exact whereabouts; they did not sleep more than one night in any single location, and spent enough evenings directly beneath the naked black sky that few people would have had any idea where they went next.

Maybe it was the monster after all. Maybe the tracks were another part of its mystery. Its legs looked like a stag's or hart's; maybe its hoof prints could mimic a horse's. There had been no horseshoe imprints; most of the tribespeople could not afford horseshoes.

And so Yvaine might have left the scene entirely, choosing to bury his friend right there and return his weapons and shield to Camelot for a more proper mourning. He was not thrilled by the prospect of a formal funeral, which would have insisted on a body; Lamorak's remains would be decomposed almost beyond recognition by the time Yvaine could return them to the city.

He was too busy thinking about the confusing scene to be angry just yet, especially since he was unsure who the recipient of said fury should be. And the squires were terrified. They had clearly enough of this nonsensical search which yielded only death. But the question remained.

And might have remained until Clydno, Vonnet assisting him with preparing the body for burial, inexplicably recoiled from his former master's remains, crossing himself while turning ghastly white on his knees.

"Clydno, boy, what is it?" Yvaine didn't need this behavior now.

When the squire refused to speak at first, Yvaine walked over to him, kneeling beside him. Gently, calmly, he repeated the question.

Clydno just pointed, his trembling finger indicating Lamorak's sword.

Yvaine was confused, and about to lose his temper, which happened rarely. "Yes, his sword. Your master looks like he gave whoever did this quite a battle before he died. Look how tightly his hand is wrapped around the hilt, even in death. And see the stains of blood in the ground." Indeed, Lamorak's slightly chilly extremity had stiffened around his weapon, as though to tell the world a knight never parted with his defenses. And the soil had several patches of caked, dry blood, presumably Lamorak's own.

But Yvaine stole another look at the blade, at what he thought had been obviously blood. The blood of a deadly enemy.

Yet this "blood" was purple, a rich imperial shade that reminded Yvaine of the King's own robes. Neither fresh red nor hardened black, but closer to violet. It clearly differed from the obvious clotted liquid which had seeped into the earth.

Clydno composed just enough of himself to utter a few more words. "Master Lamorak told me that when his father first fought the Beast, its blood was that color. I'm sorry, Sir, but I was afraid to touch it. What if it is cursed?"

Yvaine looked at it intensely, recalling the same story from his friend. He opted to try something. "Clydno, you're right. Turn around. Look away from it. Go on digging the grave. Vonnet, come here." Vonnet was right behind them, curiously watching the exchange, and the sword's quite subtle mysterious new coloring, evident only in a few flakes.

The latter squire knelt beside his master, himself a Pagan. Clydno was perhaps too devout to see what Yvaine intended. He whispered to Vonnet, ordering him to hold up the dead sword arm. With the blade now hanging in the air, Yvaine could see its other side. There was no such color on that side.

It couldn't be blood. Not even faerie blood. A cut or stab would have gotten life's fluid onto both sides of the offending weapon messily.

And there was more. Yvaine could scrape some of this color off with his fingernails, and when he did so it looked more like...

Paint, he though bitterly, *like the paint used to decorate a shield*. And he knew of scantily few knights who used the color: *purpure*, the term used by the heralds.

Vonnet lowered the unfeeling appendage, and the squires finished the burial.

* * *

The weeks turned into months, the months blossomed into seasons, the seasons stretched together in a blur. The training never ceased, regardless of the weather or people's moods (the former was often negligible, but the latter almost always were upbeat and eager for more practice). Every day Perceval felt more ready, and Llascoit felt the same way about himself. Both were eager to leave and set out on their adventures; Perceval, indeed, could hardly wait to return to Camelot. He wished to meet the King again, and to see his dog and Galienne.

He had grown to adore his foster family, allowing himself to forget any urgency, and still refused to return to Camelot until he felt prepared; the family spent some weeks there in the Spring, while he stayed behind. When they got back home,

Perceval learned the King eagerly anticipated the return of the man who avenged the Queen, a dog named Cabal had been adopted by the King after Galienne returned to her home some distance east (and quickly became known as Arthur's favorite for hunting), and Yvaine had ventured off, no one knowing exactly where. There was no sighting of Lamorak either, though Gornymant inquired. Partly from Yvaine's orders, and partly from fear of Gawaine, Clydno made sure the King only received news of the failed quest, mentioning no other knights involved.

Some months before receiving all this news, Gornymant began a different part of the young men's instruction, with Llio as well. Every night, Gornymant would help the three of them learn the old Latin alphabet. Then came letter combinations, very short at first, in both languages. He regretted he had no text in which a Cymru alphabet was found, had told them none such existed; the druids, centuries before, forbade any writing of the language, since words represented power over things. Still, Gornymant insisted on showing the youths similarities in language construction, even between two such different tongues.

They all knew this was the last part of the tutelage, especially the men. Maybe that was why it took them so long. They had already learned so much in the way of combat and knightly duties. Both had become quite proficient in jousting, dueling, and riding, and their practice matches were almost equally divided in terms of victors. Their saddles and their armor were second homes now, and they could swim and run, knew the rules of the tourneys, and could carry a tune when in the mood. Gornymant began singing some months earlier, and his students took to it quickly when he told them it was an excellent way to impress the ladies. Soon both were belting out their baritones as they rode at each other. Llio loved the attention from this, deliberately swooning at the sound of their voices, sometimes to encourage, and at other times because of Perceval's intonations.

The reading proved the most difficult, though. They all survived a translation of the dry poems of an old Roman named Cicero, and were fascinated with the excerpt from an unknown author whose hero went off to fight all manner of monsters and remained far from home for some twenty years before returning to reclaim his wife.

The other books in Gornymant's possession consisted of Plato's *Republic,* and also a Greek play about a king who was doomed because of a horrible prophecy about his parents (Perceval was particularly disgusted by the hero's relationship with his mother, and he finally realized how much time had passed since he left home; he had missed his deadline!) What would his mother think of him? He was so dedicated to his purpose that he refused to go home until Gornymant judged him ready. Besides, his mother had made no effort to get a message to him; it was not as though he was difficult to find. He was mere miles from Camelot, and some people there knew where it was he trained.

They read the story of Oedipus over a course of three weeks, Llio excitedly reading the parts of Iocaste and Antigone as dramatically as she could. Gornymant thought they would enjoy it all the more if they read it like the play it was, each person taking various parts. Then it became fun. The same approach made their study of the *Republic* that much more interesting as well. Perceval and Llascoit took turns reading for Socrates. Both the difficult words and the convoluted topics made it slow going, but they never failed to remember the introduction to the text they received during dinner one night, long ago now. Perceval took much interest in the story of the cave, and the heroic efforts of the individual to enlighten the unfortunate souls imprisoned within.

They all learned as much as Gornymant could impart to them. He regretted that Llio had to learn much of her craft from the kitchen staff; her mother died before teaching either husband or daughter much about running a house. Or a castle. Yet, he had one more piece of information he wanted to give them all before he turned them loose into the world, these two eager errants and capable young woman who dreamed of court life in Camelot.

It was cool that night when he summoned them all to the supper table, the kind of night in which the gentle wind soothes and refreshes, with just a hint of the warmth that would eventually follow it. It was the end of spring, late enough that the trees visible from Jagent's ramparts had their rich summer coloring, their leaves brilliantly clinging to the branches with the fresh life within them.

Gornymant walked slowly toward the dining hall, admiring the artistry of the building. He thought a castle was perhaps the greatest physical achievement people could manage, even a tiny one like this, and even if it could be a desolate, lonely place. He would continue to live here, riding, hunting, swimming, even reading until he too became like one of those leaves outside, clinging futilely onto the tree until it could no longer, then gently falling to the earth and returning to God's care. Maybe the King would send more trainees his way before that happened.

Perceval, Llascoit, and Llio virtually leapt to their feet as Gornymant walked into the room. All three stood motionless, paying their silent respects to the old veteran. Gornymant was unsure which of them began this little tradition, but he always loved when they did it. He walked over to the table, taking time to look at each of them, and they sat, the first course already on its way.

"My children, soon you will be leaving, each to seek your fortunes," Gornymant said. "I just wanted you to know, lest I somehow forget to tell you, that I love each of you dearly, and am very proud of you all."

Llio blinked back a number of tears. Llascoit and Perceval could feel their faces tingling as well. Gornymant did not want what might be their last meal as a group to be a spectacle of sobbing. He decided to give them their last test.

"Perceval, Llascoit," he began, the tightened sound of his voice a bit relieved, "I want you to compose something. I know your writing skills are basic, and that they are limited, as are mine, to the Latin tongue. I want you to compose something in native Cymru, memorize it as you go, and then recite it when I call for it. Start thinking about it; I'll ask for it soon enough."

"What exactly do you wish to hear from us?" asked Llascoit, puzzled.

"A poem, son. Simply a poem. It may be as long or as short as each of you wishes, but it must subscribe to this theme."

"Why doesn't Llio have to do this with us?" asked Perceval teasingly. He had grown so fond of his host's daughter during his stay here. They had never had as much time alone as they might have wished, except for the occasional ride or swim. Perceval was still both too timid and too considerate of his host's feelings to ever make any sort of advance toward her, but he noticed a number of times how she looked at him. No female ever gazed at him like that, as if she wanted him. Like the way she looked at him now, from across the table.

"Because she is to be the recipient of this poetry, dear boy," answered Gornymant, a wide grin growing on his face. "I want the two of you to think of a love poem and dedicate it to Llio. Now Llas, I of course realize she is your sister, but I want you to experience this anyway. Someday you'll undoubtedly find a fair woman who is a legitimate subject for your musings. *Si vis amari, ama.*"

Llio was thrilled. Poetry for her? No one had ever done anything like this before. And she savored her father's advice to the young men: "if you would be loved, you must love." She relished that both of the unpracticed bards blushed, almost glowed. She wondered how seriously Perceval would take this.

She loved him like the second brother he had essentially become to her. She had always longed to know him more physically, but that had been out of the question; it would have been a very great violation of the unwritten but rigidly followed rules of hospitality to bed the daughter of one's host. She savored their swims in the lake together; she had all but kept him from drowning while he was getting used to moving through the water, trying to coordinate arms and legs.

She remembered the talk they had later that first day, after they had retrieved both their clothes and their mares.

"So what do you want to do, or want to be, anyway?" Perceval had asked her, his shyness dissolved into his clothing, replaced by his usual candor.

"I don't know. Happy, I guess. I want to find a husband, and a family of my own. I'm going to Camelot, and I'll just see what happens there," she replied. She had yet to figure out just where all her own learning might lead her. She could weave, swim, cook, ride, manage a household, and speak Cymru and even a smattering of French. She also knew how to use a dagger, and had a lovely singing voice, sometimes accompanying Perceval and the often tone-deaf Llascoit as they sang whatever they could: carousing songs, mythical ballads, bardic tales.

She wondered then, as she did now, just what sort of life these experiences might reward her with. She had since added Latin, both reading and speaking, to her repertoire of skills, and sometimes kept practicing her voice while Llascoit played harp. But what would she do in Camelot? And where might Perceval go?

She thought now, as her brother and Perceval mumbled sentimental phrases to themselves, trying to decide which would be found most romantic, that she had more in common with Perceval than anyone else she knew. She, too, wanted nothing more than to leave home and go seeking... *something*. The difference was that she was unsure of what she sought. Would Perceval ever grow to love her? If not him, then who? And would she be happy as a result?

She didn't want to dwell on it. Something would happen in Camelot; of that she was sure. She just hoped it would be for the best. Besides, at the moment she already had two handsome young men composing poetry on her behalf. She was an incurable romantic at heart, and excitedly awaited the verses.

The supper table grew amusingly quiet; only Perceval's and Llascoit's murmurings could be heard. Gornymant looked at his daughter, another broad smile emerging from his lips. She grinned back. She knew her father was a wonderful man, yet he too had insisted she leave to seek her own fortune. He told her once that if she truly wished to leave, that he could not bear the knowledge of having kept her back if she stayed. She didn't think many men were quite as understanding, though he too had left home, to enter the service of a young king.

Llascoit cleared his throat. Perceval glared at him; how had he finished something so quickly? Perceval was fumbling with almost every word he thought, and felt a new respect for Tathan's skill as a rhymer and storyteller.

Llascoit had the full attention of Gornymant and Llio; Perceval was half paying attention to him, half thinking of what he could say when it was his turn.

"Blueness of her eyes flowing gently," began Llascoit, his own eyes closed so he could more easily remember the words, "like a spring stream."

Llio let out a slight hum of approval; she loved this!

"Meandering out towards my heart, capturing it. Lost in your gaze, I find only love. But that alone be enough to guide me evermore, for at long last am I happy, for I have found true love."

After a long pause, Llascoit simply added, "Sorry, but that's all I could think of in a few minutes."

Yet the others applauded him, Llio wearing a huge grin. Maybe her brother had some romantic in him after all! She noticed one of the younger female house servants staring at him after he finished it.

Perceval could feel his stomach swimming inside him; now it was his turn. The clapping subsided, and three inquisitive heads turned towards him. "Uh," he began, feeling ridiculous. He really had nothing to go with, and was just going to have to improvise as he went. That was how he usually dealt with life.

He felt the silence, so many times confounding, and now relished it, made it home, for from within the silence he alone would be heard. "And who is she, upon whom I stare admiringly, longingly, hoping for a return of my affections?" *So far, so good*, he thought. At least Llio was still smiling.

"She is woman, fairest and noblest of all creatures. She it is who lifts men up, loves men unto death, and is the true potency behind he who claims to be the strongest." He thought he sounded weak, but he had to keep going. Like Llascoit, he shut his eyes, but from fear in case the others started laughing.

"She is the sweetest song, the freshest wind, the warmest fire, and it is she I seek, with all my soul. For my life remains empty until I find her." The words fell gently, slowly, deliberately. And they soothed their listeners. Especially Llio.

He opened his eyes. The room was utterly silent again. Gods, had he said the wrong thing again?

The slow but steady and sincere clapping which followed suggested otherwise. Llio actually stood up, crossed over to him, and kissed him, for the first time, on the cheek.

Then Gornymant said, "You see? That wasn't so bad. And you both impressed a lovely young lady in the process. Knights of the heart, that's what you'll probably be." Perceval and Llio were still gazing at each other, their thoughts quite a distance from the dining hall.

"That reminds me," Gornymant said, "I told you I had one more lesson, and yes, it's something else that comes in a set of three."

The three younger people giggled at that. They were inundated with triads, and often made categorical jokes of things that could be grouped into sets of three.

"And what is this lesson, father?" Llascoit said.

"Chivalry. The ideal toward which every knight must aspire."

"I don't understand," said Perceval. Chivalry was a roughly defined notion that everyone knew of, but with some thought, Perceval realized he did not really know just what it was, beyond some vague hint of a knightly code of conduct.

"There are three types of chivalry," Gornymant went on, "but all share some traits in common, and honor and glory are the goal of each. What unifies them is the basic belief in how a knight should behave. For instance, no knight should ever harm or kill innocents, like children, or unarmed people, such as peasants, women, and weaponless knights. Do you see what I mean?"

They all nodded. Gornymant was largely embellishing; he knew of no place where chivalric code was written down and preserved, to serve as an example to others. The most known by most men was the saving of their own face, but he wanted them to understand what truly motivated knights.

"Good," he continued. "Now all knights are also sworn to their lords, and they all have the obligation to perform certain tasks for those lords. They see to the production of their lands, serve as troops, give counsel, and protect the lord's interests, such as his land and those who live on it."

"How do they differ, then?" inquired Llio. She, too, was curious; it would do her well to know how the mind of a knight worked.

"Well, daughter, I'm almost done with the similarities. All knights also must try to exhibit certain personal traits. They should all strive to be honest, brave, generous, and to be willing to grant mercy to anyone who asks it of them. The problem is that many knights live who care little for such civilized ideals."

"As to how they differ, well, there are three basic types of knights, as there are three types of chivalry to which they conform, more or less. The first are the warriors. Now I know that all knights are warriors, but what I mean here are those who give every ounce of their being over to the excitements of war and combat and tournament. These are the men who spend all their available time working to become more capable fighters, and spend little or no time learning anything else."

Once again, Gornymant could feel the total attention of the others as he held it during his lecture. *His* knights would be thinkers first, fighters second.

"The next type is the religious knight, who gives himself over entirely to his faith, be he Christian, Pagan, or Heathen. Such men are easily inspired by their spiritual convictions, and tend to see worldly matters in terms of their beliefs."

"Finally are the more romantic knights, a taste of whom I have hopefully given you tonight by asking for the poems. These are the men who see knighthood as an avenue to a woman's heart as they find their inspiration in dreaming of their true loves, and they often demonstrate their passions through poems, songs, and even dances and martial prowess. And that's about it. Chivalry is hard to define, but I believe I know it when I see it. And I think you will, too. Think of the Greek example of virtue, and follow it from there. That's the best place to start."

"Thank you, father," said Llascoit. The others thanked him as well.

Gornymant spoke again. "So the question, gentlemen, in my mind, is not whether you will be knights. I have not a doubt that you will be. The question is what kind of knights shall you be?"

* * *

With the Vernal Equinox offerings long given, and the Beltaine celebrations winding down as well, those folk who called the bleak hills north of The Wall home returned to their herding and light farming, though not much was left to do with the latter except wait for final harvest which would culminate in the spiritual awakenings of Samhain. This was Pagan land; no heavy agriculture would take place here, and certainly it would never involve the felling of trees. Entire tracts of forest remained up here, untouched by iron. It looked much like a counterpart of the hills of Cambria in which Perceval and Dindraine had grown, just a bit cooler, with more wooded areas.

The tribes occupying this region still bickered among themselves sometimes, as Cymru so often did, even drawing blood on occasion, in retribution for this cattle raid or that slanderous offense. But above these disputes which kept the people proud and prepared, sat the aging king Uriens and his powerful wife, Morgan of the Lake.

Morgan still felt drained, having personally overseen all the festivities of the recent days from the ruling couple's holding, a sizable *rath* made of lively promises and dead wood (which had nonetheless been consecrated by druidic tradition). From here Uriens heard disputes and dispensed justice, much in the manner of his counterpart Arthur to the far south. But here in the north affairs were far less formal and restrictive. Here women owned property and cattle, whole clans often migrated seasonally, and magick and the words of druids and witches held sway in people's attitudes, behavior, and beliefs.

This was not Pict land, though prejudice in the south still held that it was. The tattooed folk lived further north than even this, engaging only in their politics of survival and heathen

magick. The Pict clans did not worship deities in the traditional sense. They identified with totemic animal spirits, so clans
would be of the wolf, otter, or bear. Southerners thought them
barbaric: they did not embrace the cross, and the social hierar-
chies never took root with them.

Yet, like all of Caledonia, Gorre also was a holdout from
the more civilized lands of Logres. It was even more like Cambria in that regard. Indeed, there had been talk in freshly gone
years of uniting Gorre and Cambria, creating a Pagan stretch
from the colder reaches of the north to the milder and hilly
forested vastness of what the Garmani called Wales. But that
would not happen, surely no time soon. Several problems confounded such talk. First, Logres extended almost clear to the
wall of Hadrian, the extreme end of Roman conquest, so to try
and take such land was to effectively take from the Pendragon's
own dish. Second, not only the Garmani had invaded the great
Island. Irish raiders had landed and even settled in such places
as the Isle of Pomitain and the coast of Cumbria. The Picts,
too, took advantage of any opportunity to pillage, sometimes
daring to come as far south as the Wall itself. Finally, and this
was what really quieted the tribespeople: the wasted lands sat on
this peninsula, swelled now to the point at which they might just
override Cumbria. A number of smaller kingdoms just within
Logres had already been lost forever to the land-which-killed.

The queen may have felt worn out, but she determined
to make time for her son. He arrived late the night before, sleeping most of the day. He complained of having to skirt about the
Wall within Lothian while working his way westward, toward his
home, no longer so easy to find because of the wastes. He had
spent some months traveling alone with Vonnet, not wanting to
deal with Camelot, but not quite ready to come home, either.

Mother and son walked and chatted amiably, having
missed each other's company for some time now. "It hides us,
you know," Morgan told him.

They were in the absence of others, though hardly alone. Morgan could feel the spirits of the mighty pines and oaks about them, could almost talk to them and hear their replies. "What does, Mother?"

Morgan savored the formal address. Most folk who came from Camelot reserved far less endearing titles for her. "The bitter wastes. So many up here worry how these stretches will consume everything in their path, like hungry predators patrolling the forest. But as we grow stronger, Arthur's notice of us dwindles. His scouts cannot penetrate beyond the Wall." She trusted her son with the insight; blood was a stronger tie than homage.

Yvaine found the remark ironic, since Hadrian ordered the wall to keep those north of it out of the south lands, not the opposite. "That may be. But have you seen them? Or traveled through them?" Yvaine was terrified of venturing through the dead area again. The vision of a church gutted by fire still haunted him. His martial expertise told him that the many skeletons, arrows still protruding from many of them, were slain while trying to escape the blaze. What if the King or bishops ever found out? They might blame his mother's and Uriens' people.

And just who *was* responsible for that? Yvaine wondered, as he told it to his mother.

"The Christians might call such destruction a cleansing, akin to their Judgment Day, I gather. But you know that which it truly represents."

Yvaine knew. "Imbalance," he said meekly. Morgan nodded.

"I can't imagine what might set it to rights," he added.

"Like any disease, this calamity too has its cure. Its time has yet to come, though. Hopefully by the time a remedy is found, we shall be strong enough to resist whomever might venture this far north."

Yvaine had no wish to pursue the topic just then. He was too tired from his travels, and his mother sounded like her mind was still on the old rituals anyway. "Mother, I need some answers, and I came to you for anything you might offer me." His own boldness surprised him. Not many spoke so forwardly to the woman known simply as The Fay.

"Do you remember when I used to bring you near here as a boy? Over there," she pointed east, "Rogre Hill. Beltaine began there this year. The fires were taken all over Gorre, runners from each clan bringing them to their homes."

Yvaine nodded, recalling younger years spent in constant travel. Gorre, Lothian, Logres. That reminded him of his questions. "Why do they speak ill of you in Camelot?"

Morgan stared at him, studying the face which had grown from boy's to man's. Too soon, she decided. "I suspect most of them think me a witch. And I tried to steal Excalibur," she added calmly. "All I got was the scabbard."

"You what?!" Yvaine could hardly conceal his shock. And something else. A smile, perhaps, at his mother's audacity? Not even Dinadan would have ever dared a stunt like that.

"The witchy part you know about; you've my blood in your veins. As for the sword, it was decided he was no longer worthy of it. Though now I'm not so sure. Since I last left Avalon he's become not only more certain of himself, but of his cause and purpose also. It's like he feels as he did when he first had the sword, and his own dreams. And Merlin."

"Who decided? The enchantresses, or you?"

"The former. I'd not try something that chancy without Goddess' command as well as blessing, the King related by blood or no. Last I heard, the current tale is that I turned myself and my accomplices to stone while fleeing Arthur's wrath. Some think I can fly, others seem to reckon I can turn them into frogs or worms with my eyes." She smiled, but Yvaine saw a pain behind it. Some superstitions never quite died; fear could breathe new life into them.

"Maybe you should have Odgin head south and tell them some more legitimate verse. At least bards are still respected there." Yvaine remembered meeting the man who had so enchanted the enchantress. He was still a boy then, too; the only time Odgin left had been to see to the needs of another.

"If only we didn't need him so badly here. He even has a pair of students. Twins, a boy and a girl. They can sing like birds already, though their stringing leaves much wanted. And they've only just begun the memorizations." Yvaine had never wanted a bard apprenticeship; the thousands of verses with accompanying music they had to memorize, with absolute precision, still made him shudder.

The skin of the Earth Mother scuffed and crunched beneath their steps. Yvaine was taken by the area's solitude. It was the most peaceful place he had seen, or heard, in many months, at least since before he went adventuring with Lamorak.

"Mother, if you'll permit this boldness —" Yvaine began.

"You've not shied away from it yet," she said.

He swallowed. "What else is troubling you? So far as I know, you've always been at odds with the King. I remember how you felt when I entered his service."

"Do you? Tell me how I felt, then." Morgan's voice was rich and dark, with a measure of command to its tone even when it uttered simple requests.

"You were quite perturbed, to put it gently."

"I was scared for you, and you misinterpreted it. I was proud, though, and so was your father. We still are."

"Is it Uriens, then?" Yvaine tried to sound as confident as he could.

Morgan hesitated just a moment, then proffered her response. "Yes. I never could hide much from you. It was long before I married him; we came together at Beltaine. From boyhood you were always so intrigued with the latest talk of court, and you started with the sword when it was still longer than you."

Yvaine just nodded again. Nothing his mother ever told him carried much surprise. He had, after all, spent most of his life apart from her company. He spent his training years in the house of Lothian, knew Gaheris better than his own mother. His adventures took him to lands more distant than those seen by her, yet he still often felt intimidated by her presence. He could understand from where the rumors of her might be seeded and spread; she was a powerful figure, retaining the lithe grace and body of a woman half her age. Morgan carried herself with the regality and stature of the proudest lord, her speech was always measured and deliberate, and her face always looked full of the most complex thoughts, as though she was constantly formulating new ideas and solutions. It was a lovely but stormy face, dark eyes and full brows beneath flowing and luxurious hair. Yvaine had just been told who his own father was, and the main occupation of his mind now was how she told him. Such was Morgan's character.

Morgan, for her part, glanced at her son, and assumed he was still trying to digest what had just been told him. "You wished to know my troubles, and you mentioned that Arthur and I have been 'at odds' for a while. Yet you were misinformed of my sentiments concerning what you do with your life. You're a fine knight, son, and a symbol."

"Symbol?"

"You represent the life force which keeps Logres whole. How many Pagan knights sit at his side?"

"I could count them on a single hand. And they're all so proud. Trystan. Gaheris. Palomides. We've never worked as a unit."

"But don't you see? There are those who would have Arthur's table, his whole court, completely bathed in the waters of the cross. Britain cannot have that. She'd shrivel up and die. She's already started, although I still don't believe the wastes will come up here, nor into Cambria."

Yvaine wanted no talk of knights this time. "You're saying that Christianity is to blame for the wasted lands? Come, Mother, here you have an ear most sympathetic to your faith, and even I cannot believe that."

"That's not what I said. The wastes are a symptom, not the sickness."

"What is the sickness?" Yvaine celebrated the old feasts, worshipped outdoors to a whole family of deities, and yet he still had difficulty visualizing the land he had just ventured through (*and quickly, thank Mithras!*) as an illness. *Disease. She said it was a disease with a corresponding cure.*

"Disruption of sacred harmony. You already know that, though."

"I know that harmony is essential to all of us." Yvaine gestured to himself and his mother, as well as to the forest and some of its louder residents. "But if you're suggesting some actual illness, then I don't know what you mean."

"Which knight sits at the Siege Perilous, as I believe it's come to be known?"

"I-I-, no one. It sits empty symbolically. No one has tried since before I joined the Table. There was an accident, or something."

"No accident. Someone tried the coveted position who did not deserve it."

"I heard he was sorely burned." Yvaine had only heard fragments of the story. The knights had gotten used to the extra chair sitting empty, waiting for its rightful recipient. The golden name plates still were "magickally" engraved, so the tale went, and no one's name had appeared there yet. The likelier version, though not much less awe-inspiring, was that higher-ranking petitioners would make their pleas to Arthur from this seat; sitting next to a king was intimidating enough!

As a symbol, the chair was supposed to represent the one knight who not only had absolutely unfailing loyalty to king and cause, who would be willing to follow him anywhere, but who also possessed unshakable faith in the powers that reigned more supremely than could any earthly emperor. This knight had to be the epitome of faith, a walking incarnation of religious fervor.

Christian or Pagan fervor? wondered Yvaine. Though he guessed he already knew the answer.

"Did you know they blamed that one on me as well?" Morgan snickered. "I've heard how I apparently brought some magicked cloak to court, insisting Arthur try and wear it. Then some poor sod arose from the Perilous seat after making his case, and wore it instead, bursting into flame." She tried to laugh again, but failed. It might actually have been a bit humorous had it happened to someone else. "No one stopped to consider that someone would had to have been commanded to wear such a gift, even if I had brought it for him. And I can hardly start fires from a distance, yet folk were too eager to blame the evil Morgan le Fay. This from people who, when not in Camelot, beat their subjects to make them work harder, regularly violate their own sacred Commandments, and have come to fear the wilderness as though it were some foul creature." Yvaine had never heard this level of acidity in his mother's tongue.

I see now. So that latter prejudice has become real and whole. Yvaine thought of the wrecked church again. *No wonder they so fear the landscape.*

He was beginning to understand. "Is that why you've opposed him in the past? You feel betrayed?"

Morgan walked along with him in silence for a few lingering moments. "I suppose that's a large part of it." She rarely sounded less than certain of herself.

She looked at her son, the child she once had wished would become a druid, pride of Mona. She felt a love for him now complete enough that she would have been proud if he was a cattle herder or simple farmer. A knight of renown was no small achievement, either. She saw he sought more of an answer.

"Yvaine le Chevalier au Lion. That's what they call you now?"

"Because of my large friend and my Continental travels. It seems everyone in Camelot has to have some nickname. Part of the game of glory."

Morgan considered her own label, which only followed her to Camelot. She suddenly wished she *were* faerie-born; it might allow her to flee with Uriens into the hollow hills, only reappearing on the surface world to tease the humans. She savored the image.

Her son deserved the truth. How many years had he to wait just to learn of his father? No, he needed to hear it told. Morgan sighed, and began her tale.

"What do you know of the King's family, or his birth?" she said.

"Just what most folks know. A monastery has been constructed down in Dumnonia next to the old castle."

"Tintagel. I used to live there also."

"You, Mother?"

"Why are you so surprised? I am the King's sister."

"Half-sister," he corrected, then immediately regretted saying it.

"Yes. Half. Fortunately for me it is the half which reveres the Hallows over the Cross."

"I'm not sure I quite follow where you're leading me."
At least she's not angry about it. I think.

"Arthur and I share a mother in common. Though we have different fathers. Mine was a lord himself, the Duke of all Dumnonia."

"Old Gorlois!" Yvaine said.

"I see you've studied your history. Excellent. Yes, 'Old Gorlois.' He was kind and gentle, he only fought when he had to. I remember he used to tell me stories at night when I'd be afraid to shut my eyes against the darkness." Morgan could feel her eyes beginning to well up with tears then, but did not wish to be seen weeping like some bratty child. She took a few moments to compose herself.

"It was so long ago," she continued. "I've almost forgotten what he looked like. A young face, though his eyes seemed as though they were much older."

"I've only ever heard that he was slain in battle against Uther." Yvaine tried to soothe his mother's discomfort, knowing that speaking of her father's (*my grandfather's!*) death might be too difficult.

Morgan nodded quickly. "Is it any wonder to you that I came to hate that child? His father killed mine, and if that wasn't insult enough, our mother coddled him over us once he was born. Mother was so pious; she always wished for a son, and only Uther could give her one."

"Us?" inquired Yvaine. Again, he thought he already knew, but he wanted to hear it from her. He could not recall her ever being more talkative.

"Margawse and I," she said. "She was the elder, the more beautiful one. Even at fourteen, just before Father died, we had our share of suitors at Tintagel." She let out an amused exhalation. "Even Marcus was one."

"King Marcus? Trystan's uncle?" Yvaine hung on her every syllable, waiting for each new sentence as a mongrel awaited food scraps in the alleys of Eburacum and Londinium.

"One and the same. He was actually handsome then, and had the manners of a gentleman, no less. Too bad he soured later. I think he always expected women to fall into his lap like so many eager hounds."

"So 'aunt' Margawse rejected him outright?"

"Oh, she would have had him. Father was the one who said no."

Yvaine swore he could actually feel tiny wheels awhirl in his head right then, like the gears which enabled the war engineers to construct siege and assault engines. "So you sent me to the Queen of Lothian, my aunt, who would look after me as one of her own. And King Marcus allied himself to first Uther, then to Uther's son, because Gorlois refused him for his daughter. And you've tried to keep my origins locked up because you, and Margawse too, have become enemies of the crown."

"How quickly you've pieced all this together."

"I've had years to think it through. I just needed a little more information, that's all." Yvaine had clung to Arthur's side and his causes for so long because he never felt quite at home anywhere else. He supposed that he had, in a way, known this all along, but the suddenness with which the full realization then struck him was sobering. He loved being a glorious knight, loved the thrill of the missions which he undertook for prestige, including quelling the Garmani uprising with his friend, savoring the exhilaration and *fun* of it all, and he only felt out of place in Camelot during the old seasonal festivals.

The need he felt to celebrate and worship according to his customs sent him out of Camelot with Lamorak, although if it was looking for fun or peace he was no longer sure. So now he had returned to his ancient roots, following a drive and path he could neither quite define nor refuse. And now his mother, with a few words, explained it all to him.

He *was* a symbol. And proud to be one. "There's still something I wish to know."

Yvaine flushed again when Morgan reached over and took his hand, as the cool grasses continued to welcome their reaching feet. "What is that?"

"What happened between you and your sister?"

"Oh, Yvaine, sometimes I don't even know anymore."

"Were the two of you close once? You must have been, else it would not hurt so now, nor would you have sent me there."

"So you can see an old woman's pain?"

"I hardly need the Sight for that. I've never seen you so easy to read, if you'll forgive my saying so. And you're not old."

Morgan smiled briefly, thanking him for the compliment with her eyes. "Yes, we were close. There may be many seasons between us, but we were sisters. We used to climb around the rocks near the castle. Nobody knew that area better than Margawse. She showed me her secret cave down at the beach. I heard that Merlin made his way back there, and lives in seclusion there now. Can you imagine? The old codger would be bored to stone there."

"Did you ever leave the castle?"

"Oh, surely. Dumnonia was reasonably safe even then. The Garmani hadn't touched it; there's no good landing places anywhere near Tintagel. And my father made peace with Uther, for a time."

"I've heard Uther was too proud a man to wear a crown, too lustful for what wasn't his."

"Yes. It wasn't just our mother. Uther wanted everything in sight, except us. Margawse kept up the rebellious spirit we inherited from Gorlois, chasing off every other promising bachelor who came within sight of the fortress. By the time Uther would have condoned union with Marcus, seeing the practicality of having an ally through the marriage to his stepdaughter, she no longer wanted him. He wasn't available at that point anyway. I asked her what would be so bad about being married. She said that she alone would decide whom to marry, and no one else. I suppose that was when it really started."

"What started?"

"The fighting. Endless arguments, shouts uttered, threats made, items thrown and broken. We all took sides, and then even the sides started to crumble. We were all on our own: Mother awaiting the ripening wealth she carried in her, Uther actually yelling at her to produce a son, he was so tired of dealing with her 'impossible girls.' Even Margawse and I, once united, started to go at it with each other. And then Uther announced that Margawse was destined for the nunnery."

Yvaine almost gasped. "The *nunnery*?!" It was hardly an image that came to mind when he considered his aunt. His shock lessened a bit when he thought of how she might look in a habit, dressed almost entirely in black. Margawse bowed to no one, at least no man or god.

"It is a little funny now, to think about it. It always amuses me to think on how things might have been different, if only –" Morgan broke it off, letting the last two words float about, seeking purchase. Yvaine could fill in his own blanks. "But she ran off instead, leaving me to contend with the three of them. The arrival of the baby that Mother and Uther dawdled over was too much for Margawse, and almost as much for me. That was when we both realized there would never be any love lost between Uther and his stepdaughters."

"But then what of you and your sister afterwards? You said the pair of you began to fight even before she left."

"We did sometimes. Not as badly as we each fought with our mother and stepfather, though. She found the very idea of becoming a nun so abysmally disgraceful, oh, it's hard to describe just how much she loathed it. And Uther just kept pushing it. He had the vision to acknowledge that the future of his kingdom, even after he was gone, would revolve primarily around the cross. He wished her to start the family off right, in a way; having Margawse in a convent might have even given him higher stature within the church. I don't really quite understand how all the politics work; I know only the church also has its spiritual hierarchy."

"But more than anything, he just wanted her out of the house." Yvaine could see, for the first time, the source of hatred that came from Margawse. He was surprised, for the first time, that his mother had allowed him to even be housed with her. His aunt was kind enough to him, he recalled, but aloof. She never showed him the warmth she reserved for her own sons. Maybe, Yvaine tried to admit to himself, that was part of the distance which had grown between him and the brothers Orkney.

"For more reasons than you might imagine," Morgan said. She stopped walking, taking the time to breathe deeply of the cooling wind.

Yvaine knew she was trying to control unwanted emotions. "Mother, we don't have to continue this. Now or ever. You've already told me so much."

"If I don't finish all this now, then it may well be never." She cleared her throat. "There was another reason. Uther probably feared that Mother would believe her if she told. Though I certainly didn't."

Yvaine looked at his mother compassionately. He somehow knew that whatever she next said would speak volumes, like within the library at the college in Camelot.

"Told her what?" he asked, very gently.

Morgan's hand flew to her face; the tears came now, there was no more containing them. That was all right. She reminded herself that sometimes it took a flood to cleanse; even the Christians had a tale about that. "What Uther did to her. Bastard! I've always been glad he died slowly, of illness and pain, rather than on the battlefield which would have made him proud and welcoming of death."

Yvaine nodded, almost imperceptibly. He knew now.

Morgan continued. "He probably used the excuse of being drunk. He took much to our Dumnonia lager, and had gotten in the habit of using it to put himself to sleep. It was easier for him that way, it must have been. He had other dukes and kings to worry about, threatening to leave his side to protect their own homes. Or even an outright rebellion! And a wife who would not let him touch her. Mother wanted nothing to interfere with the birth of her son. She prayed for the coming babe with such conviction, you'd have thought we kept a priest right in the house. She was so pious by the time she birthed her last child."

"Mother, you're drifting." He eased her back into it.

"Sorry. It's difficult to talk about it. Whatever his pathetic excuse, Uther had his way with Margawse. He should have choked on his damned lager! And Yvaine," she started, then turned to him and pulled him close so she could bury her head in his shoulder, "I didn't believe her! My sister came to me and confided in me and I didn't believe her!" And Morgan sobbed. She felt like a little girl to Yvaine, not an imposing priestess of Avalon.

Yvaine was trying to think of something to say, but nothing came. How long she had carried this about! He wondered if Lady Viviane knew.

"I think that was why she really left, more than the threat of the convent. She couldn't count on me, she couldn't trust her stepfather, her own mother offered a deaf ear. And just after it happened came Mother's only son. Is it any wonder Margawse fled then? She's remained a mystery to me ever since."

Morgan slowly began to regain her strength and will. Then it happened faster; the years in Avalon had given her stamina and composure, and she was rarely in short supply of either.

When she was steady enough to pull herself from her son and stand there facing him, he asked her, "Was I an offering then? Of peace, perhaps?"

She took a hand from behind him and wiped her eyes. "I already told you why I sent you to them. I knew what you really wanted, and I was still so busy with my own learning. I could not have taken you to Mona unless you pledged to stay. That's exactly what Viviane told me when she came to Tintagel."

"She sought you out? I thought it was the other way round."

"I could hardly have found my way to the holy island alone, especially since I didn't know it was there! Only when Uther likewise threatened me with the nun's life did I really wish it. He was campaigning when Viviane came, I know not where, nor care. Mother was so busy with the baby by then, though I learned later only a few more days passed when Merlin arrived as well to claim him. Uther had made his own promises, you see."

"What did your mother think of Viviane?"

"She resisted, and of course knew nothing of Avalon itself, not really. There indeed is a monastery there, called Glastonbury." She saw Yvaine's puzzlement. "I'm not sure I could explain it any better than that; the holy island is so to all, it just depends on how you approach it."

"So then Viviane promised that I could at least return and visit periodically. That was more than she'd gotten from Margawse, and more from me had I been shut behind convent walls. But it still wasn't enough. I finally promised I would wait, though I didn't specify for how long. I think I had already seen her death, and considered that my presence might be one of the few joys she might retain. She somehow lingered on through a few more seasons, and then gave up completely."

Yvaine thought his mother looked similarly worn out right then. "So within a short time your mother loses her eldest daughter, has a son, learns she will lose her second daughter, loses the son, and then becomes a widow for the second time. I wonder that she even clung to a few seasons. Had I known such loss I don't think I'd have lasted another month. No wonder she prayed so much."

"I think that her faith was what kept her going at the end. We talked a lot, as well. We sewed and planted. I listened to her hopes of seeing Gorlois and even Uther again in the afterlife, though I never could quite tell her what I thought of this new religion. She was so enraptured with it that she actually willed the land to become a monastery upon her death. At least she had asked me if I wanted it first. But I told her no before she let me in on her whole purpose."

"So you stayed with her those last months, knowing what would become of your home?"

"Oh, they would have taken it anyway. By then the land was just chaos. The whole area, except for the lands your friend Trystan hails from, have embraced the cross. Only Marcus is a holdout now. And with no central king, no central land, not even a central faith, folk were snatching at whatever power they could. It made them feel safer. They just had to wait until a king came."

"Where were you when Arthur resurfaced?"

"I always knew Merlin would teach him something. That was quite a source of comfort, the realization that the King would be aware of his roots, even if I couldn't loose my own bias for him. I was still at Avalon, a priestess then, though just barely. We were permitted leave to witness the coronation. I never saw him draw the sword, though. I wish I could have. Viviane said it was marvelous. Maybe it would have saved some of the troubles since."

"Was Viviane involved with placing Excalibur in the stone?"

Morgan smiled impishly. "Either I cannot, or will not, tell you."

Yvaine nodded. He silently chided himself for asking such a question.

"Lot was powerful and brutish, but he always revered Margawse's strength. She really ruled him, despite any appearances to the contrary."

Yvaine thought about it. He had never known Lot; the proud Pagan warlord was killed before he went to Lothian. He remembered well how furious Gawaine was even then. Yvaine could never comprehend such hatred. Besides, Gawaine and Gaheris were only a few seasons shy of service under the Pendragon banner; they never seemed to care much else about what happened in the North.

Except Margawse. *She* cared. Maybe it was at her bidding that her sons make their way at the side of the new king all along. That would leave her largely alone in Lothian, free to judge as she saw fit, and keep her peace with the Picts. And that would give her a fighting force to be reckoned with, when added to the knights and warriors already in Orkney land.

Yvaine wanted to ask another question, but assumed his mother must have grown weary by now of hearing them. She answered it anyway, without his uttering a syllable.

"Margawse has no power, spiritually speaking. Perhaps that is why she so prefers intrigue and manipulation. She thrives on her reputation whereas mine has sometimes caused me to lose sleep. And if the superstitious lot east of here, so many Picts and those who willingly rally round her because she is a thorn in Arthur's side, if they believe her a witch, then to them she is such."

"So she doesn't know a thing of magick, then?"

"Do you? Do I, more than a few ancient talents? Son, the person able to truly wield magick is rare indeed. And what then of the magick itself? It is merely faith made real. When we project our beliefs into the natural world then that world becomes magickal. But belief comes first. Faith."

"Is that why you're on this path?"

"Goddess chose me, and accordingly saw fit to grant me certain abilities. That's all. This difference in my sister and I drove another wedge between us. I know not what she plans. I imagine you've heard the tale of an ill-begotten fifth son of hers. If I'd known just how far she had gone with her power-cravings, I'd never have sent you there."

She was looking at him inquisitively now. Once more, she was Morgan, indisputable Lady of the Lake and Queen of Gorre.

"I never saw her do anything fanciful, not like that," Yvaine said. "She used to talk to me sometimes, but it was always pleasant. And she never mentioned you. I felt as though I'd been forbidden to speak of you until I left her lands. And she always was hesitant to allow me near Mordred. I played with Gareth a bit, studied and practiced with Gawaine and Gaheris. Agrivaine and I didn't get along and used to fight and so we usually trained separately. But Mordred was alone much of the time."

"That hardly surprises me. Come, let's start heading back. Tonight we shall eat with Uriens. He's been wanting to hear the stories of your Continental travels for a while now."

"How should I address him? As king, or father?"

"I believe he'll be content with either, so I leave the choice for you. He knows also. I'm sorry that we've both been something other than typical parents."

"You never abused me or took advantage of me or sold me into slavery for Garmani gold. And how many knights can say they can trace their lineage to not just royalty but the priest-esshood as well?"

"Thank you, son. That's very kind of you to tell me."

"And I mean every word, Mother." They held hands again, and walked.

"Do you mind if I reverse our discussion, and ask you something?" Morgan said.

"Please. I can only guess what you might wish to know of me."

"What do you really intend to do about Gawaine? You neglected to mention him with the other Pagan knights."

Yvaine stopped. Even for having a mother with second Sight, who knew at least some detail of just about everything, hearing the question voiced jolted him.

He finally started walking again, his mother's hand and eyes never leaving him. "There must be justice for it, though maybe not in Camelot. Gawaine and I have barely spoken since I returned from the Continent, and I don't see any going back now. To return to the city means running the risk of finding him there. I'm afraid of what will happen whenever we meet again. But I need to seek an audience with the King, or if that doesn't work, then perhaps with the Bishop."

"Baudwin?"

"Yes. I've heard he'll listen to just about anyone, and I could use a fair ear. Either of them should be able to help settle all of this."

"The man's a virtual saint."

Yvaine was unsure if Morgan meant the comment as sarcastic, though it sounded sincere. "The King may not even be there. He's spending less and less time around the city. Maybe he finds it stifling after a while, like us."

"Perhaps he's off with Perceval, slayer of Meliagrant, the new red knight?"

"Even for you, Mother, such knowledge is amazing."

"You must be joking. The whole court knows about him. And I make it my business to know what the court knows."

Surely Morgan couldn't know what Yvaine chose to tell her next. "I met him once, many moons ago now. In Cambria, when I still traveled with Lamorak."

It was Morgan's turn for surprise. "I didn't know that. What was he like?"

"Oh, ignorant of the entire world. I've never seen anyone so awed in my life. He was with his sister, who's a bit of a
nursemaid. She helped Lamorak."

"I wonder what happened to his family?"

"I've no idea. I haven't actually seen him since we left.
Why do you ask?"

"Because I think it might serve you and him well to find
not just him but his family also. It might help prevent him from
wanting to follow the same destructive course you seem to have
selected for yourself."

"What do you mean?"

"I felt the way you clenched your hand when I mentioned Gawaine. I don't believe I've ever felt such contained
hostility before. And you know how sensitive I am to emotions,
especially when they're not intended to be shown. Even the
veins in your neck looked strained when I brought him up. It
scared me. You don't want war with the Orkneys. And I don't
say that for self-preservation or any fear of Margawse likewise
seeking vengeance upon me. I'm concerned for you."

"Well, don't be. It would be foolish to hunt him down,
and I'm not even sure I'd like to. We Cymru are so proud, we
take such offense sometimes."

Morgan laughed. The horizon of the hill they walked
along began to reveal the unmistakable shape of Uriens' modest
fortress. Its silhouette looked proud in front of the setting sun.
"We do, at that."

"What does Perceval have to do with this?"

"I can't tell you what I don't know myself, only what I
suspect. But I do think you should find him."

"I think he's back in Camelot by now. Perhaps a knight,
even."

"The Table needs all the unity it can get, Yvaine. The
instability of the brotherhood is that of the land."

Yvaine simply nodded.

"It's cooler than I expected." Yvaine crossed his arms, rubbing them.

"Yes. I'd hoped Beltaine would pass with more warmth. It's too late for it to get cold, with the few crops we do have." Morgan still tried to get used to the idea of regular planting, which she saw as a repetitive rape of the earth's sacred ground, but Uriens remained adamant that it was necessary for future survival. Britain had its share of immigrants, and had to be prodded to sustain all of them.

They walked onward to the *rath*. Uriens was waiting for them both with open arms.

* * *

Jacqueline of Quimper had seen the vast sea leading eastward to the Holy Land, the city of Paris, and the tremendous Cathedral of Chartres on the site where the druids worshipped before Vercengétorix surrendered to Caesar. Yet none of these wonders helped her overcome her giddiness at the knowledge that she would soon be in Camelot. She was going to see the great King!

All her life had been spent on the Continent, though she at least grew up with the advantage of successful parents willing to take her along on caravan trips. Sometimes, anyway. Her father was a prosperous man; it was his job to supervise the export of tin from Dumnonia on the Greater Isle, as it was brought inland to the port of Quimper in Armorica. Occasionally he had to make overland trips to keep the shipments heading further inland.

Quimper, too, had prospered since before Jacqueline was a gleam in her father's eye. She always enjoyed living on the coast, as she loved to walk down along the shore and watch the ships. She told her parents that the sea just *called* to her somehow, beckoning her forth. She loved feeling the sea's spray in her face.

The city's populace was of primarily Cymru stock, with residual Gaulish and Roman added to the mix. A duke oversaw the holding, one of King Marcus' vassals. The result was a proud merchant folk, who were all too eager to embrace the ways of the new Island King. He was, after all, one of them. Many of Quimper's own sons fought alongside the Pendragon banner as it marched through Gaul, and into the heart of the old Empire. The High King's power stretched well into the mainland. Knights like Yvaine sometimes visited, making the locals crave news of Greater Britain.

And Jacqueline had wanted to visit the Islands for years, weaned on tales of the King and his glorious Round Table. She especially liked the knights. And therein lay her dilemma.

Arthur's Queen, the lovely and visionary Guinevere, played quite an influential role in the formation of the Courts of Love, and all around Jacqueline sang the praises of the finer emotions, of the adored women and the gallants who tried to prove themselves worthy of their attention. Chivalry sprouted into full bloom across the Channel. Jacqueline wanted to feel that; she was quite handsome, her father turning away more than one persistent suitor in recent years. She had the nose and squared shoulders of a Roman, despite her blood. The gentle but firm curvature of her lightly-tanned body ensured no shortage of men for her father to consider, then ignore.

Except for one, and thus the problem. Jacqueline's arranged marriage to Girard, a young knight who watched her blossom into womanhood, proved disastrous, although she was the only one who seemed to think so. Her parents would not listen to her protests, and even when they came close to doing so, would remind her that it was for no good Christian woman to go loudly complaining about her nuptials. They were pleased with the arrangement; Girard was a comely man, with proven prowess at arms. Jacqueline was guaranteed a title and, eventually, the overseeing of Girard's modest lands, while Girard had been the recipient of a generous dowry, compliments of the tin trade.

So then why would the young woman be unhappy? Many wondered, though none would dare mention it to her husband, who proved to have quite a jealous streak to him. And that compounded the problem.

Girard had changed. Though Jacqueline initially tried to refuse her father's wishes, she finally conceded and thought she might grow to love this man after all. He was handsome, if a bit rough under the sheets (oh, how she had worried about giving her virginity to this man up to and including the day she wed him!)

She supposed she shouldn't complain too much, as she walked along the docks, alone with her thoughts. She took her sandals off to enjoy the cool breeze as it rounded her body and tickled her toes, tugged at her hair. Girard was an able enough provider (though his means of motivating those who worked his fields outside the city were violent at best; Jacqueline had already witnessed such sword-brandishing, and was just thankful to steal away to the city unnoticed).

She warred with herself, knowing that Girard grew more brutish and unforgiving all the time. She could not help but find some amusement in the irony that these very flaws resulted in him wanting to go to the Island as much as she.

News of the Pentecost Festival, and its accompanying tournament, traveled far. Girard wanted to show himself off to the knights, and so did Jacqueline. Divorce was simply out of the question. Only the Pope himself could perform such an act, and only then in the face of proven consanguinity. The young woman only wanted to have her own say, to live and love where she chose. She resented her father for the arrangement, and she had no interest in titles.

But the knights! Those heroic warriors, of whom the troubadours, the ancient bard's descendants, already sang. Jacqueline knew there would be different men among them; she could feel it deep within her breast.

She wanted no more of this lout she had unwillingly married. The only good she saw in her union with him was in that at least he had not forced her. Of course, she was always too afraid of him to put up much resistance. And she was tired of the soreness, tired of his drunken embarrassing behavior at festivals and even in the usually calm streets of Quimper, tired of waking up to the thick, scratchy beard and foul odors which permeated his entire body.

She looked out at the sea, wishing she had a boat. At least she would soon be en route to one of the larger British ports, and the closest to Camelot. From there it would just be a matter of a few days to the fabulous city.

And maybe, just maybe, an end to her sorry union as well.

PART THREE: THE KNIGHTS

T hey entered the forest again just several miles after their departure. Perceval all but forgot that the road linking Jagent Castle and Camelot ran through the Camelot Forest;
the land which contained Jagent, and the farmland which supported it, had all been cleared of these woods years earlier. Indeed, these were not the haunting trees of the Arroy which had
startled him. That memory seemed part of another life now.
He ignored the close proximity of these woods to the capital,
and how that alone essentially guaranteed the safety of travelers along its road. That, and regular patrols of the King's finest
warriors.

It was peaceful going now, after a difficult farewell from
Jagent and Gornymant. The man's children cried briefly, then
forced themselves to stop. They were excited to get going, but
had spent virtually their entire lives in a small, isolated vicinity,
like their recent foster brother. They had traveled to Camelot
before, just a few months earlier, but they felt a newness to it,
like Perceval on his first day there.

Gornymant, for his part, was perfectly content, and free
of the loneliness his children and student thought he might suffer. He was already busily planning his next activity. Before
he retired from active life completely, he wished to personally
sponsor his own marvelous tournament, one which would make
people and knights proud to attend. It was a suitable location:
close to Camelot, but isolated enough for folk to wander off
to their own private adventures. He already had Jagent's staff
involved with helping him plan it.

He received his inspiration in the knowledge that he
would soon receive more trainees. The messenger from Camelot
arrived discreetly, and Perceval and Llascoit knew nothing of
this, though Gornymant did share the news with Llio. She could

tell them later. He would personally show them off at the tourney; they could even help him plan it. He already felt giddy about being entrusted with the two new young men. Just after the departure of the others, he again studied the scroll which the Camelot messenger brought. It read:

Sir Gornymant of Jagent,

It is my hope this letter finds you well, and yet engaged in the noble pursuit of providing promising young men with the final steps of requisite training for becoming part of that great occupation of knighthood.

I fully realize our Lord the High King himself normally sends such talent in your direction, although on this particular occasion, I would ask you maintain these two fine and strong boys in secrecy. For now at least, I beseech you thus. They are my youngest sons, the oldest already members of Arthur's own court. It is my wish, Sir, that they receive the finest knightly education possible, but in the absence of any special considerations they might receive at Camelot, given their heritage. I regret my late husband cannot take them under his own tutelage himself. I believe the amount sent you shall be sufficient, both for your services and for the care of my sons. Kindly notify me if you find it otherwise.

Fare thee well, my lord. I know Gareth and Mordred shall profit immeasurably under your roof.

The Lady Margawse,
Queen of Lothian

He rolled the scroll up, feeling the excitement wash over him again. How many men had such opportunities! No sooner had his own children left, and now he would be blessed with the privilege of caring for two more. And the amount the queen sent him was more than adequate; it had to be a major noble's ransom! It could go towards making his own tourney that much more magnificent.

Gornymant prepared to receive his pair of new wards, and would instruct them there at Jagent for many moons.

* * *

Just a few miles away, Gornymant's children, along with Perceval, made their way northward. Despite their giddiness, none spoke. They had all packed up their most vital possessions, leaving behind more memories than personal effects. Llascoit carried the scroll case containing the fibrous sheet on which was written Gornymant's testimony as to the capabilities of these three persons. It was sealed with a black wax circle showing part of Gornymant's family arms: the sword from his shield design overlaying a heart. The heart was from his father's device.

Perceval carried only the bare essentials: extra clothes, his armor and weapons, Mother's cross, Gornymant's words. He took off the cross for his first bath in Jagent and had not worn it since, feeling that he would somehow have to earn it. He wore it now though, proudly.

He felt the cross, dangling to and fro next to his chest as he rode along, his faithful horse Brownie as eager as he to see the countryside again. He thought of the person who gave him that cross, knowing he had to see her soon! For now he looked ahead to the night-long vigil in church, perhaps the huge cathedral in Camelot, when he might prove his worth as a new knight in the eyes of God. Perceval had a difficult time picturing either Llio or Llascoit in a church, at least for the sake of worshipping; they felt more at home outside with family and friends.

He asked Llio about it once, during another of the delightful times they shared, walking beneath a black canopy pierced only by the stars.

"How can God or Goddess or whatever deities exist possibly care how anyone worships them, so long as they are basically good folk?" he demanded.

"Perceval, you're the sweetest, most caring person I've ever known. Why do you care what the gods or goddesses might think, when you've done nothing for which to be judged harshly?"

He thanked her for the compliment, not believing it. "But I don't know what religion I'm supposed to follow! How does anyone know?"

He had never raised his voice in front of her before. She looked at him nervously, seeing a face full of fear. *Fear of the unknown?* she wondered. *Fear for his soul?*

Her thoughts at the lake that day felt confirmed; she wondered if knowledge of the old, fire-and-brimstone god imported to Britain long ago had gotten hold of him, not on the surface, but down deep. Where the soul lived while occupying flesh. It must have been that mother of his. Llio had learned not to ask about her.

"Perceval," she said finally, "you have to find what is in your heart first, and then follow that. I believe that alone will take you toward God, in whatever form you find comforting. I see him as a kindly older man, like my father. The Pagans see him not as a him at all but as a her, a woman who takes various forms depending on the seasons and the traits folk display."

She thought about it a few moments longer, then added, "God is within you, Perceval. If you're going to go on some knightly quest to find Him, I think you'll doom yourself to a lifetime of depressing results."

He would always remember that talk, even though he tried not to think of it very often. He could just imagine his mother's response to his running around with the likes of these two, who claimed faith in the Christ but acted more on their own will than on the mandates of scripture.

No time to worry about Mother now, Perceval thought, even if she never tried to contact him. First he had to finish his quest, to become knighted. He looked over to Llio, the bubbly, smiling woman who had given him what was probably the best insight about religion he ever heard. She was beautiful, more so today than ever. *Maybe someday.*

Maybe what? he corrected himself. He still doubted Llio had much interest in him. Best not to dwell on that, either.

He rode with his companions for a little distance longer, and then the smell pummeled his nostrils.

Smoke. The thick, rank, black kind that feels heavy and is difficult to walk through. It was faint at first, but now the three travelers found themselves wading through a cloud of aerial stagnation.

Maybe there was a farm nearby, someone burning off crops, Perceval thought, just making ready for planting. That seemed a legitimate explanation, save that they were still in the midst of Camelot Forest: no farms. It was also a bit late in the year for that. Still, the smoke grew almost impossibly thick on the road; all of them could barely see the road beneath their horse's hooves.

Llio was the first to start coughing, and was unable to stop long enough even to talk. She looked frightened, and Perceval never heard such a deep throaty hack come from anyone. His and Llascoit's throats also expressed their disapproval, although much less violently than Llio's. They had to get her away.

Perceval rode up next to her, and announced that they should all turn back to find a healthier place to wait out whatever burning was taking place. Llascoit, too, expressed his concern for her safety.

Feeling like her chest would soon explode from the intake of all this smoke, Llio doubled over from the sheer force of her coughs, and struggled to remain in her saddle atop Fay. Nonetheless, she raised a defiant arm to her companions, pointing down the road. She wanted to go through. Her lungs were already abused, so what point was there retreating?

The two men looked at each other, dismayed. By late afternoon they could be in Camelot; maybe it would be best to just continue.

Still, not one of them had much idea as to just what generated this much pollution in the first place. Perceval thought again about farms; true, farmers often burned their fields as a way of purifying them for their next use, and sometimes also as an offering to Goddess for fertility. But it seemed too thick for that. So was the forest itself on fire?

Trying to remain calm, Perceval agreed with Llio. "Let's go on, then. It can't get worse than this."

Not wanting to stand around and bicker, Llascoit rode along one side of his sister, Perceval on the other, and they went as fast as they could manage given their murky view of the ground beneath them; it was the only way for them to navigate. Besides, had they seen what was within the smoke, they might well have been rooted in place by their fear, their mounts bolting away.

It seemed to go on for hours, yet the smoke never worsened. Llio kept on coughing, her stamina reducing with each violent heave. Llascoit and Perceval fared better, though their throats were already dry and felt like someone had scratched them with tree bark. Even the trees around them faded in and out of their blurred vision; only the hazy road kept them from becoming hopelessly lost.

Eventually the mysterious smoke began to recede, barely noticeable at first, then more obvious as Llio began to sound less like she was dying and more like she was just suffering a bad cold.

They never managed to see the source of the smoke. None of them glimpsed any fire anywhere. That did not reassure them. All wanted some justification of their suffering, and yet it seemed that the smoke had simply materialized in front of them. No one, however, was in the mood to investigate the source further. Especially Llio.

She looked blue. She had an arm around Llascoit, their horses walking close in a near embrace, and he felt that she was almost dead weight. They would have to rest. Unless the smoke came again in full force, Llio would have to give herself some time to recover from the abuse.

"If you want, I'll ride on to the city," announced Perceval, eager to do anything that might help. He felt as useful as a third wheel on a horse cart. "I can get someone to help there, and be back tomorrow. Even today," he said.

Llascoit looked at his sister, who nodded gently. She was in no shape to travel, having collapsed onto the back of Fay's neck. She could taste a bit of blood in her mouth, and just hoped it would go away. She did not wish to show the men her fear, and nodded her assent to Perceval's suggestion. She knew the forest surrounding Camelot should be the safest patch of woods in all Britain, and she had no fear of spending a night outside. Still, she did not wish to see Perceval leave. She hoped he would return right away.

"We shall be fine right here until you return, Perceval. Try to get a healer or a priest for my sister. But go, and God-speed." Llascoit sounded hopeful yet commanding, proud of safeguarding his sister.

Llio tried to say something to Perceval as he rode along, but her throat hurt too much. She missed him already, watching him trot along to Camelot.

* * *

Bishop Baudwin, the confessor of Camelot, could not remember the last time he had heard such emotion in someone, or felt as powerless as he did then. The young mother from Astolat had confided in him one of the darkest secrets he ever listened to, and now he could not even find her again!

There was simply too much needing his attention. Yes, that was it. The need to compose a suitable sermon to accompany the Mass for Pentecost was his primary thought; it had to be. He took comfort in keeping busy that way.

But he also had to hear confessionals. Never could he lag in that most important duty, of helping those in need of guidance realize both their errors and sins, as well as their potential and forgiveness through the lessons of Christ. And Elaine's confession left him wondering if he possessed the spiritual strength to hear any more of them.

The poor woman, he thought, sincerely hoping she was safe, and silently mouthing the prayer he had recited hundreds of times for God to hear so He might keep someone from harm. Elaine was always so unsure, but lately she seemed much more like her headstrong daughter. Galienne could prove so willful; a woman's place was home and hearth, and –

No, he admonished himself. *That's not the way to think. That won't help anyone now.* Baudwin sat alone in the rectory, in his large but undecorated chair, staring at the parchment on his desk. He of course was among the most literate and educated men in the land, but still debated whether he had overstepped a priest's place by writing down what he could remember of Elaine's visit.

"Forgive me, Father, but I have most grievously sinned, and for it I am to pay the price." He could still hear her initially calm voice in his head.

"Tell me of your sins, my child, and know that not only I but God listens." Baudwin invoked the holy name for inspiration and comfort, never knowing that some folk took it for intimidation or fear.

She didn't skip a heartbeat, however. Not this time. "I am in love with the greatest of devils, whom I thought was the greatest of men."

The bishop rolled his eyes. Why did so many think love was such a sin? But he didn't have a chance to answer.

"Father, my whole life has been dedicated to the singular pursuit of one I believed returned my affections. And there is a daughter born of our illicit union, but never did love exist for me from him. I am guilty of hatred, lust, fornication, and I have nothing left to offer this world which has made me the wretch you hear."

Baudwin knew the voice now: Elaine. The young woman from Astolat, who had such talent in her industrious hands. She had obviously rehearsed what she intended to tell him, not wanting interruptions until she finished.

For a few moments he could not think of what to say. "Who is this man, who would reject another who can think so clearly?" He at once regretted that; to this day he still had little idea how to relate to women. Galienne had actually helped him with that, and, *what was that of an illicit union?*

"It is none other than the Lord Lancelot, Father."

That was hardly new. Many women adored the Queen's most capable protector, and Baudwin knew Elaine always had feelings for him. "Well, Sir Lancelot is an extremely busy man, my child. Surely there is someone who –"

"And he is the father of my child," she added, interrupting him.

So that *was the illicit union!* He'd never known, assuming Galienne's father was back in Astolat, running the guild or some such.

He didn't have to wait for her to continue. "Father, I've made my decision, though it may mean the severest of punishments. I just wanted one person to know," and she started to sob. "One person to know how I felt, what I was going through. I can't even tell my daughter. She already distrusts her father so, and –" but she broke it off, taking belabored time to control the tears.

Calmly and gravely, Baudwin requested Elaine for more. He ran his hands over his bald head, his proud frame sagging and feeling all five of its decades. For a fleeting instant he was jealous of this woman nearby, with her youth, her rich bark-colored eyes and hair, her delicate skin and proud jaw. He sighed, knowing how fatigue could induce vanity.

She laid it all out for him, from mere childhood fascination to adolescent infatuation with the dashing knight, whose eyes were always on others. *One* other, she kept saying, but would not specify further. Baudwin tried to understand it. He had never been in love, at least not to such a destructive extreme. Elaine made Lancelot gifts with her own tired hands, devoted endless hours waiting for a chance to speak with him. She shut others, her own family, her friends in Astolat, out of her life and thoughts. She lived for the attention of one other.

And he barely knew she was alive. Not until one fateful evening. Baudwin learned that was what Elaine believed the heart of the sin: not her lustful feelings, nor even the blatant fornication, as she called it, but that she had dabbled in sorceries beyond her comprehension to ensnare the knight. For the pleasure of a single evening, she had jeopardized her soul. She kept reiterating to him that she could no longer live knowing it, and that her sins could hardly get any worse.

As with Lancelot's "other," Elaine would give no mention of whom she had bartered with in order to receive a charm to drive Lancelot into a lustful frenzy, nor what she had to trade to get it. It must have been that wicked queen Morgan; she had access to most persons at Court. Surely she could have manipulated Lancelot and Elaine for her own fiendish reasons.

But Baudwin still was unsure what comfort to offer this young woman. All he knew was that he must be handling it poorly. Elaine remained inconsolable.

And after the long dialogue, she felt her grim determination anew. "I must be off now, Father. Perhaps someday Lancelot will realize what he does."

He could hear her rising. "Wait!" he said, too quickly. "Wait, child, please. You've imparted such a story that I cannot help but think that perhaps talking to Lancelot —"

"I've done that!" she spat. "And it all comes to nothing! I'm a disgrace, and he cares not!" Baudwin heard the door open. Without thinking, he opened his own chamber door, and sped after her.

He caught up to her, halfway down the aisle, to the interest of the few persons in the pews, who raised penitent prayerful heads to wonder what was about.

Elaine whirled around and confronted him. "You would dare pursue me, priest? Have you forgotten your vow to secrecy?"

Baudwin was still unused to direct confrontation from a woman. "I have not, but there is so much at stake here, Elaine. Your daughter, members of the royal court, your parents."

"None of them care any more. I've closed the door on them all. Now leave me to my peace."

"That's what I fear the most." Gathering his composure, he lowered his voice, adding, "Taking one's own life is the most grievous of sins, above and beyond anything else you may have done. You've already confessed. Let me help you atone, and you may yet find your peace."

She actually considered it, for mere moments. Then she was out the cathedral doors, leaving Baudwin ignorant of how best to resolve the issue.

So now he reviewed his quickly written guilty notes. He wished to find the disturbed woman, and wondered how he might send word to her parents, all the while pondering if he had the right to make such an interference. Perhaps he should talk with Lancelot himself. He knew first-hand that knights often thought themselves beyond reproach. Elaine's confessional was now a day behind him, though it felt like months, such was his desire to find an answer.

And dimly, he prayed that whomever had proffered the love charm did not later offer a poison, for some infernal revenge.

* * *

Galienne still never told anyone of the visions, except for Bishop Baudwin. He always listened to her compassionately. She thought he was the only one who could understand; he was an appointee of God, and had known the one called Merlin personally.

She remembered her first vision as though it came to her yesterday, even though it was now three years hence. She awoke, embarrassed and ashamed. She could not tell her mother! What would Lady Elaine have thought of her faithful daughter, who glimpsed herself as an adult, walking down some cold, stone hall somewhere with two men at her side? And all of them naked, too! No, Mother would never learn of that image, not even if it ever happened. And Galienne hoped it would never actually come to pass; it had to be a sin to travel nude, much less with two men who, apparently, were neither husbands nor relatives! She blushed even now, these years later, just thinking about it.

Elaine had been good to her, though, sometimes bringing her to Camelot to see her father, who was rarely there. Even when nearby, he was always distracted and distant. Galienne had a vision once of her father sharing his bed, with the Queen of all people, and kept this image private also, even from Baudwin.

And now here she was, in the famous city again for the first time since that strange lad showed up with his delightful dog. Lupinia was with her that time, her eccentric friend who was fortunate enough to come to Camelot more often, who would likely become the wife of some rich lord. God knew she had the looks for it. She was jealous of Galienne being able to come while she couldn't.

Galienne remained in town just several more days last year following her crass reception by Sir Kay. That was when her mother whisked her back home to Astolat, along the River Wey, eastward towards Londinium. Elaine's own parents demanded she return home, and forbade her to chase after the man who fathered her child. It was bad enough, they told her, that her child, wonderful and faithful as she was, was a bastard and fathered through sin, but it was worse to follow that father around when he obviously showed no care for either of them. At any rate, Galienne's grandparents wished no part of any ill-sounding gossip about "Lancelot's folly," to say nothing of the worse titles Elaine could have been called. Galienne's grandparents were just that way, more concerned with outward appearances than with the utter shame and self-hatred their own daughter felt. But their granddaughter felt it. Every time Elaine wept or talked of Camelot in a soft, haunting voice, almost a whisper, the message remained the same: she felt used and abandoned, and had little ability anymore to lose herself in her work.

As far as Galienne herself was supposed to know, her mother had taken her home to resume work on her crafts. Then they could return to the city with their wares. Galienne still helped where she could, but felt like an errand-girl next to her mother. Elaine had such a gift in her hands! The work usually provided a good distraction from court intrigue, but Galienne knew what the source of her mother's private suffering was.

Thanks to the visions. So today she sought counsel with Bishop Baudwin to ask him about a topic which had bothered her for some time. Finally back in Camelot after too many months, everyone else would have to wait. Lupinia, her mother, her father the "great knight," the strange lad Perceval (if he was even here, as she hoped). It was time for her to sort out her own life, since her mother let hers become a virtual waste, all because of some ridiculous infatuation.

"Father, how truly harsh is the sin of illegitimacy?" she asked Baudwin. She loved her talks with him, even if done within the privacy of a confessional chamber. He was the only one who ever truly listened to what she had to say.

"Why do you ask, child?" came his neutral but compassionate response, still ringing in her ears now, hours later. She never realized how terrified he had been of her question, after his prior talk with Elaine.

"Because my mother is truly depressed this time. I fear what she may do, and my father continues to ignore her." She placed an undeniably facetious slur on the word *father*.

Baudwin was glad he could listen to this disturbed but bright girl once in a while, and he now knew of her illicit heritage. He still remembered the nervous child in Astolat who just wanted to learn to read. He regarded her a model Christian, who often asked him well-thought questions about the Bible and its implications and lessons. But now she was more worried than ever.

He thought he would try giving an example, albeit a bold one. He knew he could trust the girl not to spread juicy stories around the city; she hated gossip-mongering as much as he, considering it sinful for its accompanying vanity. "Child, sometimes one sin is surpassed, even canceled, by the goodness which may come of it. Do you know that any action, *every* action, has both good and evil results?"

"N-no, father. How can that be?"

"Why, just take our own great monarch, for example. Know you that he was the illegitimate son of King Uther and Queen Igraine?"

Galienne calmed from confusion. "What? Everyone knows that Uther and Igraine were properly married when the King was born."

"Aye, but they were not so when the King was actually conceived. I remember discussing the matter with Merlin after it took place. He told me he played a part in their... affair." Baudwin missed his talks with the long-gone Arch-Druid. Merlin may have been a Pagan, but he was sincere and usually compassionate, though it had saddened him that the druid fooled Igraine with his magicks, even if the purpose was to give Britain its greatest leader. The man was wise beyond Baudwin's imaginings, and had lent a caring ear to Baudwin more than once. The bishop knew of Merlin's reputation as the son of Satan himself, but Baudwin grew more tolerant in his dealings with the populace of Camelot over the years. He was a true religious diplomat.

Galienne, though, took several protracted seconds to frame a response. "So our own King is really a bastard himself?" She cringed a bit at the word. What would God think of her using that term in His church?

Baudwin paid the word no heed. "Aye. Now do you see what I mean? All actions produce good and evil results. We have our King because of a temporary evil better forgotten." He hoped she would not ask if Igraine had likewise forgotten Merlin's evil, having been fooled into bed with another.

Galienne mulled the words over, knowing she could return almost at her leisure to talk again with this man. "I really must go talk with my mother. She's been so morose lately, even worse than usual. Father Baudwin, thank you. I shall return and tell you what has happened." She felt better already; her mother had recently spoken of her fear of what awaited those who had not gained God's favor. Galienne once dreamt of her mother using some evil magick to bed Lancelot in the first place, just like Merlin had apparently done long ago. Maybe Lancelot was just responding to having been deceived that way. How was one to act who had been fooled into sex with a person other than the one anticipated?

She was far more concerned for her mother, though; Galienne just wanted her to be happy. She had not felt well for some time, and Galienne knew it had to do with her invisible father, whom she was trying not to despise. Why was Baudwin the only really trustworthy man she knew?

It was difficult: Lancelot was one for showing off or trying to bed with Guinevere. Galienne saw it herself, within her broadly seeing and knowing mind, and so did not doubt it. She kept trying to stop feeling ashamed about the visions.

Yet that did not make her any more eager to experience them. They were usually painful or confusing or both. That made her even more concerned about the image of nudity; she did not know the men in that sending whatsoever!

But the sendings themselves... maybe she could use them, somehow.

Whenever they came to Camelot, Elaine and Galienne lodged in a common hall used by anyone who needed a temporary bed. Not this time, however; the whole city was in the midst of preparations for the annual Pentecost festival. They had just missed it last year. Galienne was thrilled, even if it meant they slept outside the city in the family tent. She had heard of the wonderful festival, with its feasting and shopping and, oh yes, knights, the boastful elite.

Galienne came almost to the southwest city gate, which opened into the common area where hundreds of temporary homes stood erected. But now where was her mother? Galienne expected little difficulty in finding her. Perhaps she was with the crowd outside the gate.

She figured her mother, always eager for news of court and beyond, would most likely be mingling among the crowd, so she ran down to the gate. It occurred to Galienne that she had yet to see her mother this day; Elaine was an early riser, and Galienne figured she had just slept beyond her. What she found at the gate, though, was startling, and she all but forgot about wanting to find Elaine.

The crowd murmured cautiously but ceaselessly. Galienne could hear traces of something about a weapon or some such, down by the river Cam, one branch of which flowed close to Camelot. "Something miraculous," whispered one person. "We've not seen the likes of this since the King drew the sword from the stone," said another. Word was quickly circulating that some sword had been sighted in a stone down by the river.

Sure, right, thought Galienne. Then she overheard something else. A woman. Some woman had been seen down there as well.

Now Galienne was actually scared. Her mother was nowhere to be found, and she ran past the crowd, making her way past onlookers who walked or rode to or from the site. All had the same look on their faces, that which bespeaks some delectable tidbit of gossip, the kind to permeate the city by nightfall.

No one among the bystanders seemed to notice her; she weaved her way in and out of several peasants and traders, to the left of one knight, to the right of his squire. Anything to get her down to the river that much faster.

But why? All she had was a feeling, not an actual sending, or vision, or whatever she should call the messages about others. Still, the feeling persisted, and Galienne was not one to ignore instinctive feelings and reactions.

Visions also had a way of making one very spiritual, and Galienne had often wondered how many others, if any, shared her fate. Lately, the images shown to Galienne were more disturbing. The affair. The hellish magick her mother used to conceive her (*maybe the same magick had given her the visions?*) A hallway full of naked people. And now some sword. She felt she had to get to it.

She guessed, or hoped really, that she was about halfway finished with her run to the river. Trying to stay focused, she was all but run down by a knight whose horse galloped right past her. The creature was enormous! It probably could have jumped clear over Galienne. She could not recognize the armor, but had a feeling she would remember the appearance of the horse if she saw it again, even if she glimpsed its posterior.

Minutes later and closer to the river, the road became more crowded again. The knight stood there, amidst the trees and traffic. He was not alone, but next to one of his comrades, who was the only one on his knees, armed but unarmored. A group had assembled here, most of whom Galienne could not recall seeing before. *No, wait,* she thought; *the standing knight is Kay!* The one who had all but knocked her off the trail and threw girls into walls.

She had to get closer. This was actually easy; the others ignored her. She just wanted to get a closer look at whatever was prompting all this impending talk.

She stood next to the river's edge now, just another of many. The river flowed by peacefully, the gentle wind revealing its path in the ripples on the water's surface. It would otherwise be a pleasant scene, even a romantic sort of place to which the lovers came to look at each other's eyes, and the stars.

There were no stars out now. Only the body in an old fishing boat. And the sword embedded within the withered stump.

Galienne could just peer into the boat to see the source of the milky white arm that draped over its side. The clothing looked disturbingly familiar. She swallowed hard, and forced herself to look inside.

It was like looking at her own face, as reflected by the expensive hand mirror her grandmother once gave her for Christmas. Her mother lay in the boat, her eyes open but no longer seeing. She could not have been dead long.

No, Galienne corrected herself, the tears sliding from her cheeks, *Mother has been dead in heart for some time.* And all because of *him.*

Off to her right the knight still kneeled, whispering something to Kay. *Lancelot, it is you, you bastard!* cried Galienne silently, beginning to take a liking to the term which she feared using just earlier that day.

Her thoughts danced throughout her soul; she could feel them have their way with her, making her tense here, clench there. *Just like you had* your *way, false knight! And now all you even care remotely about is that stupid sword, damn you!* She had yet to consider the oddity of swords sprouting from dead trees.

In front of the two knights, the ancient oak stump stood, evidence of perhaps the only dead tree in the area. But whence came the sword? Surely someone would have noticed it, especially since it seemed planted there, waiting to be pulled, just like the one Arthur once wrested from a stone.

Galienne looked back at her departed mother. Where on earth did she get a boat? It could not have been far. But then, she recalled, horrified, she had not seen her mother since last night. Maybe she sneaked out of the lodging, and fled the city. It was not as though she would have had to get past the gate, since they slept beyond it. No matter now. She was dead. That *did* matter. And for what did she die? Infatuation. A false love affair with the best knight in the world.

Ha! exclaimed Galienne to herself. All her life her mother had told her story after story about how wonderful these men were, the one kneeling close by the greatest of the lot. "He wasn't worth it mother," she heard herself cry. She faced toward her father, the fury no longer to be denied.

"You were never worth it, false knight! You had the love of a good woman and you ignored it. Now look at what your manner has done to my mother!" Galienne screamed at Lancelot, who finally turned to her.

Kay looked nervous, Lancelot passive. The latter would not meet Galienne's eyes, only the direction of her voice, which infuriated her more. "Damn you, Lancelot! Damn you to hell! And damn anyone you ever love, because I know you never loved her!" She pointed to the corpse, almost touching the cool dead flesh of the draped arm.

"Or me!" she added, leaping to her feet, and running toward the sword just beyond the knights.

But Kay intercepted her. "No, lass. I wouldn't be going to get that, now. A pretty little thing like you would just hurt yourself with-*Yeeeoow!*"

The sound of Kay's scream pleased Galienne to no end. She bit him as hard as she could, on one of the callused hands that grabbed her, for the second time now. Instantly she was to the sword, the knight shaking his hand in pain.

Lancelot, for his part, was too numb from Galienne's insults and his own thoughts to manage catching Galienne himself, for he knew well who this dead woman was. But he froze, gasping, when she yanked the weapon from its stump.

The sword came out heavily but smoothly. Galienne had never grasped a weapon before, and she was trying to simply balance it as it came out, fitting into her small hands perfectly. It was an elegant long sword. The blade caught the sunlight and shone it around on the trees, where it danced gaily, like sprites.

The light also shone on the onlookers, who joined Lancelot in a furtive round of deep inhaling. Several crossed themselves.

A little boy among their number finally broke the silence. "The sword! The girl has drawn the sword!" He started to run, as fast as his young legs would carry him, back up the path towards Camelot.

Lancelot and Kay were the most dumbstruck of them all, save for Galienne herself. Lancelot had read the carvings in the stump, in Latin: "for the greatest knight in the world." He was considering what to do about it when the boat lazily bedded itself on the bank.

Galienne all but forgot her mother, and was scared, the blade jiggling in her nervous and sweaty grip, the spots of light increasing their rhythm to an utter spasm. What would she do now? She could hardly just strike him dead, although the thought crossed her mind.

Baudwin. She had to get back to the cathedral, and tell the bishop of what happened. She clumsily held the sword in her hands, fighting to control the shakes, carrying it at her mid-section, and ran after the noisy boy. Everyone who witnessed the drawing drew in their breath again as she passed.

She did not manage to beat the boy, who was still ex-citedly telling everyone at the city gate about what happened. There was no mistaking the source of his story as the "girl who drew the sword" scampered her way past them, refusing to meet their stares. She headed straight for the cathedral, and was cer-tain she would knock down anyone who tried to get in her way.

The murmuring continued, escalating rapidly into full-blown gossip, like a torch set to forest. Soon the whole city was abuzz with word of some girl who had pulled a sword, just like the King.

No one knew who could claim responsibility for placing the sword. The Pagans would come to talk of ancient glam-orous magicks, the Christians would liken the events to holy prophecy. Even the enchantresses would say it was one of the Hallows, a sacred prize reserved only for the worthiest of souls. They took pains to ensure that this girl would not have her claim challenged, and their resolve grew; the girl had proven herself! No one might know what magick there might be about it, although the sword itself had its own power, and was surely an excellently-wrought weapon. And no one would ever know what would have happened if someone else tried to free it first. Elaine's body distracted any takers.

And now Galienne had it. And folk would ever after say that the miraculous happened there that day, the day the girl freed the sword. Simple superstition was its own magick.

Even Lancelot, who came the closest, had been distracted by the oncoming deathly boat. He would never know now if he could have managed it; after all, the girl freed it easily, even if it felt awkward and heavy to her.

The girl was safely within the confines of the immense and cold walls of Saint Dubric's. The solid walls of a church felt comforting, not cool, to Galienne, as secure now as when she studied the Astolat Bible in a similar place, an escape from the taunts thrown her way for wanting so badly to read.

Her heavy breath echoed slightly in the chillier air. Several worshippers who sat in the pews turned to glare at her. She was ashamed at disturbing their prayers, and tried breathing through only her nose. That was louder! She had to go straight to the rectory.

Again, she had the feeling of other eyes monitoring her every move. It worried her deeply. Galienne had always known she was different, but what happened today was beyond even her own wild imaginings. *How did I ever get to the sword?* she wondered, still confused and afraid.

She had even dreamed of it once. *No, that's not true,* she thought; the sword had floated through many of her dreams. But only her dreams; they never figured into her waking visions, until today. She made for the chamber.

She thought she would faint dead away if he wasn't there. She ran toward the dais, shadowed by its gargantuan cross, and past the tabernacle. She had never before neglected to cross herself in front of a cross. She automatically reached for her own small personal reminder of Christ's gift to the world, fretting that she'd left it behind from being in such a hurry this morning. Now her comfort from the religious icon would have to wait.

Baudwin looked up from his age-blackened chair, where he sat reading. It looked little like a Bible to Galienne, but no matter. He could read whatever he pleased. Thank God he was here!

"Father, we must talk. Please, I beg of you." She started crying again, hoping the sound would not interfere with the worshipper's prayers.

Baudwin was nothing if not an excellent listener. Galienne was terrified, and all but convinced she was hell-bound for shaming her father and for running through the streets of Camelot brandishing a sword. She told him about the stump and its weapon, and was quite graphic in relaying the description of what befell her mother. She would not admit to it, thinking it a grievous sin, but Baudwin could hear the hatred of Lancelot in her voice.

Listening, Baudwin recalled a tale Merlin once imparted to him, about someone who would come and be the greatest knight in the world. And he would be known for having pulled an unpullable blade, just as a boy her same age did himself many years earlier. Surely this could not be that great knight sitting in front of him now! She was a child, and a scared one at that. Yet there was something about her appearance and demeanor that gave him pause.

Her eyes. *Yes, that's it.* Galienne's eyes looked completely confident. They were not the eyes Baudwin expected to see on one who had just lost her mother, and who might have dueled with the High Queen of Britain's own champion.

That was the other thought which stumped him. Everyone knew Lancelot was the best. Baudwin wondered if Gawaine begrudged the fellow knight his reputation, even though both served as royal champions. But if he really was the best, then why couldn't *he* have gotten the sword?

And Elaine. The poor woman. Somehow she had gotten to an archaic boat and just drifted downstream. Baudwin was unsure how someone could truly die of a broken heart, but could think of no other explanation.

Galienne went on, saying her mother looked physically all right, aside from being dead, but at least no one obviously killed her. There was no blood, no obvious injuries; even her clothing remained intact.

Baudwin's thoughts were interrupted by thick pounding coming from the door. Galienne jolted, almost screaming. Baudwin saw her wrap both hands around the sword's hilt. He hoped whoever was at the door would not upset her.

No such luck. The door swung open, revealing the King, with Lancelot.

Arthur spoke first. "Father Baudwin, could you help us?"

The bishop nodded, feeling no choice but to show them in, the child's feelings aside. Galienne did not see who it was at first, then recoiled and groaned at the sight of Lancelot, her fingers tightening even more round the sword's comfortable leather gripping.

The champion would still not meet her gaze, even now. *Good!* thought Galienne. *At least he has something resembling a conscience.*

"My lord," said Baudwin, "I do believe we have much to discuss."

"That we do," replied the King. "The citizens are awash with the latest intrigue. I would like to know what has happened. There are murmurs about some prophecy." He spoke gravely, never forgetting his own brush with the miraculous when he was the girl's age.

Remembering his manners, Baudwin said, "Please, my lord, be seated." The words were met with a hand gesture indicating that the King, and his knight, were content to stand. Baudwin liked that about him, and always had. The King was only formal when truly necessary, and was never presumptuous about taking someone else's place when he was in their territory.

"Bishop Baudwin," intoned Lancelot, Galienne intently focused on him, "perhaps this prophecy was real. The stump at the river had an inscription."

Galienne raised her brows. Inscription? She had not seen one, and she could read. Then again, she had only been searching for something with which to mutilate her father.

Baudwin's brows were equally high, the age-loosened skin on his forehead wrinkling to pull them upward. Lancelot continued, "It said that the sword was for the greatest knight in the world. It was just like the King's own miracle at the Tower of Londinium."

Baudwin was curious. "Sir Lancelot, did you yourself, or any other knights you may know of, actually attempt to free the sword at the river?"

"I –" he began, pausing to look, finally, at his virtually unknown daughter. For the first time, he was feeling sorry for not having accepted Elaine's advances more readily. She had been a passionate woman, full of life and wonder, but his own heart was already given away.

Best not to mention to whom, he thought, not in the present company anyway. He had been so infatuated with the Queen for so long that any other woman seemed, at best, like a sister. Or just another face in the crowd, like Elaine, suffering an infatuation of her own.

Now she was dead. Had he really been the cause of all this? Elaine never said much to him about the daughter born of their illicit and entrapped union. She had, after all, disguised herself like the Queen, right down to the rich rose perfume she wore, and met him in the shadows of a moonless night.

Back then Lancelot had not known Guinevere's touch, and was too impassioned to care. How could he have ever known it was really Elaine? At least there was never any public statement from her about the child.

It was not just Galie-*no, wait,* he thought. *Galian? Galleon?* Lord, he couldn't even remember her name!

"I-I myself tried the blade, sirs. It would not free itself for me." Lancelot hated lying; he wondered what kind of penance would be asked for lying to a bishop, if he ever bothered to confess it. Lying to Arthur was different; his heart had been lying to the King for years now. Another kind of lie, he supposed. Falsehoods did not have to be verbalized to remain false.

In the small dark room, none was more stunned by the answer than Galienne. *Is it really me then?* She couldn't even begin to believe that. Lancelot had to be lying! He was the best knight. *But,* she thought, *how good can a knight be if he lies?* Knights were supposed to be honest; it was part of their code.

Only Arthur came close to believing the implications of the strange events of the day. He too had been prophesied, and he knew all too well how dangerous the doubt of others could be; his first battles were waged against his own people, for their unwillingness to follow a boy who showed nothing of true kingship other than pulling a sword, and later being given another by a woman. But then, the drawing in Londinium was immediately followed with the brightening of what had been a dark, overcast sky, and many said that God was indeed shining His grace upon the new king.

But somehow, the sword drawing itself was enough, at least for him. The perfect sky and the personal instruction of the departed wizard helped the skeptics become believers, each in their own time, perhaps for no other reason the Arthur's success in uniting Britain. He wished Merlin was here now; he would know how to handle this. Baudwin was helpful, though, almost as wise.

"Lord Arthur, you and I both know that signs like this are hardly to be disputed. But surely Galienne is not to be a knight!" The idea was totally foreign to Baudwin. He could only imagine what his peers in the Church would say to this. But somehow he felt he was climbing into the pages of history, just being in this room. Besides, there had been famous women warriors before. Boudicca of the Iceni tribe. Teuta of Illyria. Hippolyta the Amazon. Of course, none had been Christians, and the Church considered them not just heretics, but devils. He glanced at the text he had been reading when Galienne burst in, a history of ancient heroes. And heroines. He forced himself not to smile at the irony.

"The greatest knight," said Galienne, surprised by her own sudden boldness. The sword was feeling better in her hands all the time.

"Galienne, would you come with us? There's something I want to show you." Arthur had his own method of testing this prophecy, whatever it was.

Then, from outside, a scream. "It's a sign! A sign sent from God!"

* * *

All four of them rushed to get back outside, where a huge swarm of the citizens of Camelot swelled around the cathedral. All wanted a glimpse of the "girl with the sword." And all were distracted by the sudden appearance of a pillar of smoke, crossed at the top by another, horizontal pillar, rising beyond the city.

"Is it a fire?" cried out one from amongst the throng.

"No, it's too thin a cloud for that. A fire would burn out of control. It's a sign, I tell you!" This from the woman who screamed the first time.

"It's a cross! Look at the shape!" Indeed, the two smoky lines were in a cross-like form, and several of those present followed with the appropriate hand-over-heart gesture. To others, including the King, it had more the appearance of a sword, rising skyward as though its point were embedded in the ground.

"It's a sign from the Almighty, I tell you!" It would be impossible later to recall who said what; the exclamations emanated from the group more than from distinct individuals, for all were caught up in the mystique of the shape.

"Look at the colors!" gasped several. And it *changed* somehow; there would be considerable discussion on this in the years to follow. For now the people were stunned by the several distinct green flashes within the pillar, like dying emerald leaves on a lifeless tree. Some would later say they saw faces of those they knew or loved in that cloud. None would ever recall being afraid of it, simply awed by it. The green tendrils snaked their way skyward, disappearing as they reached the summit, soon followed by others.

They watched, all of them, some thinking they were witnessing a dream. Many others crossed themselves, those who had already done so repeated the motion, still thinking they could see a cross shape in the cloud. Or a weapon. Several even came over to where Galienne stood, and knelt, asking to be healed.

Galienne watched the wretches in front of her, taking her curious gaze off the strange smoke. One wore a pus-soaked eye patch, another had a horrible limp. Were they actually turning to her for help? The likes of these poor souls were not among Camelot's native population; thousands had traveled to experience the festival, now all but forgotten, as they witnessed something even more impressive.

In the distance, the smoke pillar receded, quickly, until it was out of sight. No more smoke, nor steam, nor green cloudy fingers, nor anything, followed it. It came and went, with no warning for either.

And since some folk were now turning to gawk incredulously at the sword maiden, the smoke had served its purpose.

* * *

Nimue was thrilled, having forgotten the roe deer which lay at her feet, its life's blood now completely soaked into the ground, leaving only a rusty stain. She was exhausted physically, but remained seated where she had knelt for hours, in the Camelot Forest where she would not likely be disturbed. Beside the deer's body were the core remains of several green apples, plucked from the very trees of Avalon. Their skins and leaves and other ingredients which Nimue had sworn not to speak of were consumed for the sake of sending a message. Only the ceremonial dagger remained, forged in the shape of a miniature sword, though it too suffered the toll. Its once bright blade was rusted through, its rich velvety grip crumbled to near dust.

She had to be this far from the city to avoid detection; greater proximity would have been more impressive, granted, but this way no one would suspect her, not even the lone horseman who almost rode over her. The smoke must have so blinded him he did not see her. As for the dead creature, magick was a power which demanded sacrifice. The fruit was just as alive, and just as totally consumed, so that the effect could be worked by just a single practitioner. And the other elements, well…The druids themselves would have been hard pressed to come up with the necessary components of a pillar of smoke that shot into the air, dissipating after a few inspired minutes.

The rider was probably just like the majority, anyway. Nimue always regarded most others as far too easily impressed by such feats as a glamourous tower of smoke, even though it *was* quite taxing to perform. She tried not to be pessimistic about folk, often reminding herself that they were not all gullible, and those who could be easily fooled would only fall for it occasionally. Yet she knew she had really worked them this time; the people of Camelot demanded a sign, and she delivered.

Not that she knew this of the people first-hand, of course; but she knew that when folk encountered something

which not only suggested prophetic events, but which clearly
said something of prophecy (in *Latin*, no less, thereby lending a
sense of plausibility to the Christians), they would either take it
at face value, or, more likely, demand some further sign of au-
thenticity.

Such was the purpose of the smoke.

The people are confused and superstitious, Nimue mused to
herself, *more so now than in ages past. Spiritual ambiguity and paranoia
have left them vulnerable to anything bearing the slightest resemblance to the
supernatural. Such is the result when the folk bicker over whose deity is the
greatest.* That was the whole reason they needed signs: indisputable signs. Let them argue later whether this god or that goddess
was behind it. For now let them get used to a certain girl who
was bound for greatness.

Nimue was one of the select few herself, chosen by
Goddess, though she silently thanked the Mother for not having
made her a candidate for warrior training, as She had Galienne
and some of the young men who trained on Mona. Most of
Nimue's life had been spent safely tucked away in a magickal
place, an island hidden by both swamp and an almost ceaseless
cloud of protective fog. She was taught certain wondrous arts,
all the while waiting for her time when she would be called upon
to perform some sacred duty. Her own specialty, if it could be
called that, was the native Cymru magick of glamour: a temporary reality, a manifestation of the Other Side into This Side.

The enchantresses themselves, like the druids, worked
their almost extinct arts to alter the course of events in their
homelands. The magicians, be they enchantress or druid or bard,
knew that the time of kings and their old God would eventually
come to an end, and they wanted to ensure that there would be
places left unspoiled by the righteous civilizing tide of the Roman religion. Camelot was a Christian city in a Christian land,
even with Merlin's influence.

But Nimue would never sell out that way, not like Merlin, who was a peace-maker and advisor in the end. True, the druids wanted peace, but they much preferred the idea of sending the Christians far away than sharing their confining cities. Nimue would die before taking up residence in such a place, and she was proud of her intense feeling on the subject (never mind that this was the same mentality of the Christian martyrs whom she resented). The enchantresses worked subtlely for one sole purpose: to keep parts of this vast island safe from persecution.

Well, *usually* their work was subtle. Not so today! Nimue smiled, finally looking down at the animal sacrificed to produce what others would one day, long after her own bones turned to dust, call mere illusion. Blowing a tower of smoke into the air for all to see just so one young girl would be taken seriously was admittedly not exactly subtle, but it yielded the desired outcome. Nimue had never even laid eyes on Galienne, but the girl had been prophesied. Such was Nimue's conviction. The masses would believe whatever they chose.

Children born with the Sight did not go unnoticed for long. Not only that, but Galienne was Lancelot's own! Lancelot, forced to flee his homeland on the Continent as a child and taken for rearing on the sacred Island of Mona amongst the druids. Not even they expected him to become so tremendous a warrior as he had, even though this came at the cost of his former sentiments for the Old Ways. *That was what happened when one lost one's heart to a Christian*, much less a beautiful and powerful one like Guinevere.

Magick itself was weakest where civilization was strongest. And Galienne was desperately needed, to become a warrior like Lancelot, to show the followers of the God of sexism in Logres that a woman could not merely pick up a sword, but could use it as well. Boudicca's spirit would rest well this night!

Nimue found her memory wandering back to days spent among legendary apple trees and mists, in the company of others like herself. The invaders never managed to destroy either Avalon or its male island counterpart, which served only to strengthen the spirits of those who survived persecution (though they *had* ransacked parts of Mona). *The Mother works strangely*, she thought. Thanks to that sense of spiritual survival and necessity, the Pagans were now ironically coming out of hiding, much to the chagrin and prophecies of damnation of those who followed the newer religion.

But all the gods and goddesses are one. All of them. Your true task is to help folk see that. And that is why the warrior-girl is needed. Nimue could still hear the words of Morgan, her friend and mentor, now Queen of Gorre. Nimue could never quite understand how so many could so murderously disagree on spiritual matters. If Morgan's words were true, why did people die for and because of their beliefs? Morgan herself had once shared a terrifying vision of a time when the Christian knights would bathe whole kingdoms in blood for the sake of taking their own holy land.

The smoke took hours, and now she had to get to Camelot. Thank Goddess she would only need to be there until she had slumbered. It was risky, sleeping all day in such a place, but hopefully the citizenry would be so involved in the Pentecostal celebration they would not notice just another traveler. She would then find Galienne, which should prove little difficulty, and take her away to Avalon (how many of Camelot's children, especially girls, walked the streets with swords?) The girl's mother was dead anyway, and her father had forsaken the lessons of his childhood.

Yes, Galienne would be an enchantress. And much more. She would also be a warrior.

* * *

Outside the safety of Camelot's walls, the lone errant beamed. Perceval felt proud, despite his concern for Llio's throat. Didn't her mother die of something like that? He would certainly do whatever he could to help her. It did not really seem all that serious, but enough to make her weak for a little while.

Why am I suddenly thinking about my mother? he wondered. He supposed that whenever he considered anything that reminded him of home, he would inevitably think of her also. Why had he resisted thinking about her for so long?

Because he was late, he reminded himself. He missed his deadline, forsaking his sworn oath. A knight was only as good as his word! He had to get back. Maybe the King could just dub him a knight, have a feast, and then he could be on his way. After all, that was what knights did, wasn't it?

Brownie, also, acted as perky as Perceval had seen her since the day he killed the Red Knight. She was thrilled to be back on the road, although the strange smoke scared her almost to throwing off her master. Perceval wondered about that again as the walls of the city edged into view. Where had that smoke come from, anyway? It smelled oddly, like roasting meat and burning fruit and... something else. He could not place it.

Nor did he ever find the buildings he had thought lay through the smoke. It had, unsettlingly, simply receded, vanished.

Perceval continued, gently urging Brownie into a light gallop. He wanted to be back as soon as possible.

As Perceval drew closer, he could see a sizable crowd gathered for some reason just outside the city's twin-towered southeastern gate, and when he was close enough to notice details, he saw they were pointing at him. So far he was the only traveler to come down this road today. Perceval made no connection between himself and the mysterious smoke. He did not cause it, so why worry about it, other than its effect on Llio?

He thought the *smoke* was thick! The crowd was a mob, too bloated at the gate to grant him entrance. He was a lone rider in the company of humanity looking at him with a curious mix of suspicion and reverence. He could hear whisperings among them, about who this stranger must be, and if he knew the girl of the sword. This annoyed him more than scared him; he just wanted to get inside.

Those who greeted him were, for the most part, simple-looking farmers and peasants. They lacked the appearance of those persons he saw when he first arrived here so many feast days earlier. Had Camelot been overrun by this motley bunch in his absence? When Perceval first came here there was no sign of want in any face he saw, but some of these creatures seemed destitute.

Some of them spoke to him, asking unnerving questions. "Are you the messenger?" "Did you make the smoke?" "How?" "Who is this girl?"

Unknown to Perceval, the city's preparations for grand festivities had become annual pilgrimages of sorts for people all over the Island. The Pentecost Festival and Tournament brought every walk of life to the city, for a two-week celebration of Arthur's rule, which was certainly the kindest these folk had known. Nobles and peasants, rich and poor, sick and healthy, knights and ladies, merchants and entertainers; they were all here to partake of some small slice of the immense cultural pie which the Pax Brittanica enabled. There would be a grand tournament, a huge marketplace sporting the latest fashions, treats, and imported goods and creatures, with nearly constant feasting, carousing, and merry-making.

And in the midst of the preparations, some girl pulled *another* sword from *another* stone. Well, stump anyway. Stone, stump; what difference was a detail like that in the face of the seemingly miraculous? The people seemed to not notice this, nor to care. Arthur's own rule had been not only foretold by his drawing the sword in Londinium, but justified as well, through prophecy or conquest, it mattered not. The King's weapon was rumored to be a blade of immense, even divine power, capable of slicing through anything made by human hands. And now some *girl* had just done similarly? It was ludicrous! Girls did not go around waving swords like knights.

But then, neither did boys go around the same way, bastards acting like kings, and yet the masses had to consider all that Arthur had wrought since.

Galienne, for her part, was just glad the throng waiting for her outside the cathedral had all but left to flock toward the southeast gate. Only the three men still stood by her, making her nervous. She was tired now, not full of hatred for her father, nor of awe for the King, nor compassion for the bishop. Just tired. She wanted to sleep, to wake up from the nightmare of this eventful day. The visions told her of a sword, but she only half-believed them, for the same reason most folk now only half-believed the so-called prophecy; girls, especially apprentice seamstresses and weavers, were just not supposed to go out and ride the countryside meting justice.

Besides, her sendings, if that was truly what they were, gave no indication of her mother's untimely demise; why was the vision selective? She thought that the greatest curse about it, despite Baudwin's reassurances. If God had chosen her, and used the visions as a way of previewing her coming glory, then why were the holy messages not just partial but confusing and sad as well? If she had known the truth about her mother, she could have done something.

She remembered Baudwin's words to her once. *It is not for you, nor I, nor even the King himself to question God's intentions, child. He gives us signs sometimes, and we simply have to do the best we can to follow His bidding.*

So if this was the sign, was she now supposed to ride off, calling herself Sir Galienne or some such nonsense? She didn't even know how to wield the sword, although she had not released it from her grasp since she first drew it. It seemed *part* of her somehow. It felt like it *belonged* to her. Or she to it.

That was all she had time to think of when the traveler rode up to them, at a slight gallop. He looked dangerous; he wore glittering mail, even red in places, and Galienne at first thought he looked like the devil himself. The King and Lancelot did not flinch, but simply looked at this newcomer, expecting him to make the first remark or gesture.

Perceval urged Brownie on through, and it took several moments to navigate their way through the onlookers and gossipers. At a distance, he recognized the King almost immediately. Who better to talk to than the King himself? There was someone with him, as well: another knight, and someone who looked like a priest or a monk, like Uren. Surely he would have the healer's touch.

He rode up to them, feeling nervous and uncomfortable. What on earth would he say to them? Then he noticed someone else with them. A girl. A young woman, who held a sword at her side, grasping onto it for dear life, by the looks of it. Perceval thought she looked like Galienne, but then why would the girl be armed?

How would he act? He knew it was disrespectful to sit a horse in the presence of someone of a higher rank. He dismounted Brownie several yards from the group and led her over to where they stood.

"Perceval," said the King, not one to forget a face nor a name. In his line of work, forgetting could be very dangerous. Merlin taught him that.

Instantly following Arthur, Galienne whispered, "Perceval." Only Perceval himself did not ignore her. Wasn't he from far away? Hadn't he ridden off that day to go and learn the ways of knights? Would he take her with him? Right now, all she wanted to do was leave this place, this whole city.

"M-my lord," Perceval began, turning his attention back to the King, bowing. "I have been these seasons past in the company of Sir Gornymant and his family at Jagent Keep. I have returned, and wish to humbly ask that our Great King consider me for knighthood. As he can see, I have taken the arms of the traitor Meliagrant as my own." *Thank goodness for Gornymant's and Llio's speech training*, he thought.

All were silent for a few moments, waiting for Arthur to speak. Lancelot and Baudwin had only heard of this young man in passing before today, and both were so far impressed by him. For the second time in as many visits to Camelot, he managed to gain the King's attention. Baudwin thought in his reddish armor that he looked much like the image of the Holy Spirit come down at that first Pentecost.

"Perceval, I consider myself in your debt for ridding my kingdom of the usurper Meliagrant. I shall grant you your knighthood. This very evening may you partake of your vigil here within Saint Dubric's Cathedral. Your ceremony can be part of the ongoing festivities here at Camelot."

"Sire, I have seen that the entire city is making preparations for this festival. Might I ask, how long does it last?" Perceval was very anxious now. He wondered how much longer his mother could wait, even though the King would make him a knight!

"It continues for two weeks," answered Lancelot. "New knights are made then expected to participate to the conclusion."

Two more weeks! But what of his mother? Was she still waiting, all this time? Or had she forsaken him? And what of Dindraine? He missed his sister sorely. This girl in front of him; she reminded him of her for some reason. Maybe it was that they were close in age.

No! It is *Galienne!* This was the girl who kept his dog. Or so he hoped.

Talking to the King was no time to be worried about his dog. His mother, on the other hand –

"– over his vigil myself," said Baudwin, assumedly in reference to Perceval. He had been so lost he did not even hear how the comment began.

Galienne, to her surprise, was jealous. This person had returned, and now he was the center of attention? *What about me*, she thought, *who has just today been accused of performing the miraculous? No, sinner. That's vanity!*

"King Arthur," Perceval said, "this must be grossly out of my place to say, but m-may I make a request?" The last words came with difficulty.

Britain's sovereign seemed a towering figure now. Something about the way he simply stood commanded respect. His very presence lent a sense of awe to the air itself. Perceval's tongue was almost numb.

Arthur simply nodded, expecting a reply.

"It's my mother, Sire. She lives far from here, and because of my training, I've been unable to see her these past seasons. I believe she has been quite worried about me, and if the festival really lasts a fortnight, then, I, uh –" Now he was not just nervous, but frightened. He couldn't express what he wanted to say. Among the crowd, he thought he could pick out Sir Kay. Great.

Yet the King seemed to change the subject. "Perceval, come with me into the Cathedral. I should like to talk with you." He turned, and walked toward the immense stone building, with its colored windows and steeples that pointed straight up to the heavens. Perceval stood and followed, eager to leave the crowd.

Galienne watched them go, now standing with Lancelot and Baudwin, amidst the crowd full of anticipatory eyes. Baudwin looked unsure of what to do or say. Lancelot looked defenseless without his armor, almost like a boy trapped in an older man's body. A champion's. The champion's face looked defeated and tired, and he stole a quick glance at his daughter, the stranger, who would sooner take his head than talk to him.

The eyes he met were also distant, but more alive, even if frightened. He wished he could think of something, anything, to say to Galienne. Once again he thought of the Queen, considering that if he did not feel so passionately for her, he might well have loved Elaine. And their child. Now there was just an alienated girl. And a queen who would not or could not return his affection any longer. And the quest. Always the quest. The pursuit of glory was all Lancelot had to rid his mind of its torturing. He would soon make a request himself.

Galienne felt sure she would soon feel her bread and apple jam breakfast come shooting back up her, dumping itself in front of everyone. She had not asked for this! All she had wanted was a little parental attention, for God's sake. Now she just wanted to leave.

So what was keeping her here? She was not a prisoner in the city. Lancelot ignored her, and she felt justified in disobeying him even if he ordered her to stay. And for what was there to stay? This Pentecostal madness, the Lord's own holiday turned into so much carousing in the streets? Perceval wanted to leave, too. Maybe she could go with him, back to wherever he called home. *Where is he from?* she tried to remember. *Somewhere far.* Some place where the wagging tongues and wandering eyes of Camelot would not be upon her.

She walked right between Baudwin and Lancelot, and proceeded into the Cathedral. Neither bishop nor knight made any motion to stop her. She was unaware of the talking in the street as it increased, in quantity and volume, when she disappeared into the hall.

"– wait if need be, although I wish you would stay. I never even knew my mother, so perhaps I can empathize." The words reverberated off every wall and corner and pew in this place. Galienne had always been fascinated by the echoes in there; she thought it was God amplifying whatever was said in His house.

King and errant were near the dais, ignorant of Galienne's approach.

"Sire, please forgive me for what I ask. I know it is senseless and emotional, but I did not realize the guilt I carried until I arrived back in Camelot."

"There is nothing to forgive. Besides, as I have said, I owe you my thanks: for dispatching an enemy, and for such an amiable, excellent hunting dog."

"Cabal!" Perceval almost shouted. "He is in your care all this time? How is he?" Perceval briefly forgot his other concerns; at least his dog was all right.

"He's loyal and lovable as always. And his nose is already legendary around here. It's funny; the only person he ever growls around is Kay."

Perceval and Galienne both had to fight back a sudden urge to laugh. Maybe there was justice in this world yet.

Returning to the subject, Arthur continued, "Perceval, it sounds like your mother and sister may need you. Come back as soon as you are able; your ceremony will wait, and your lord will be there to dub you a knight personally."

Perceval drew in a gasp. So his dream would really become true! He would return with all haste, knowing he had the King's own word.

Galienne did not take time to consider what she said. "Take me with you! Please, Perceval. There is nothing here for me now." She ran up to where they both stood, emerging from the silent shadows.

"Galienne, you wish to go with him?" asked Arthur, a bit surprised, and annoyed that he was old enough to have trouble noticing when someone came sneaking up on him.

"Please, your majesty, I beg of you. You know my mother is dead this very day. Please see that she receives a proper Christian burial, but please let me get away from all these judging eyes and loose tongues!" She was crying again, missing her mother, but wanting so badly to leave she was willing to miss a funeral. Her mother would have understood, she told herself.

"I think that is more up to Perceval than to myself, child," said the King, always playing the diplomat.

Perceval was stunned into silence. He seemed to have a passenger. How could he say no? She was kind to him, that first day in the city.

"Have you a horse?" was all he could think to ask.

"I'll run at your side it I have to!"

"That won't be necessary. But I have one more thing to ask, and of the bishop this time. My lord." Perceval bowed as gracefully as he thought himself capable. When he rose again, he saw the face of a compassionate friendly man, not the stern expression of a battle veteran and politician. Arthur simply nodded, and they all left the cathedral, the King leading.

Outside, Perceval was pleased to find Lancelot tending Brownie. Perceval stopped briefly to ask Baudwin if he or one of his underlings would check on a certain pair of young travelers past the city, near the source of the mysterious smoke pillar. He added that they were the children of Gornymant, and were told they would be received by the King and Queen personally.

When she was sitting atop Brownie, Galienne clutched the sword with one hand, and wrapped the other around Perceval's waist for support. She was surprised to hear several cheers as they rode toward the northern gate.

* * *

"You haven't even returned home for this long?" Meant innocently, Galienne's words still tore into Perceval.

"No. It's been a long time. I've been meaning to get back, but my training…" He wanted to finish the sentence, but his thoughts just drifted off toward home. He wondered how tiny the village would seem; it appeared so the last time he returned, after meeting the knights. He hoped Lamorak was better.

"I'm sorry. It's just that I can't imagine being away from home for months at a time. My travels have been few and long between. I spent most my life back at Astolat." *If Lupinia could see me now!*

He held his anxious tongue. He wanted to get to know this girl better. She was his only companion now, save for Brownie anyway. Yet he felt almost crowded on the road with her. He had no one to answer to the first time.

"Galienne, tell me of yourself. What are you like? What do you want?"

Yet now she was strangely silenced. Then, "What do you mean?"

"Just what I said. I'm trying to learn something about you."

Galienne felt defensive about herself as ever. She would not admit that she inherited this from her father. Galienne had herself already judged and condemned him, but she refused to dwell on this, too.

"I am fifteen years old, sixteen come Christmas. I was born on Christmas Eve, you know. My mother said it was a great blessing."

Perceval could feel her ease her hold on him slightly. She all but molded herself to him when they left the city. "I can read, too," she added proudly.

"And I'm sure you can ride," said Perceval, interrupting her thoughts.

Suddenly embarrassed, Galienne tightened her embrace again, squeezing Perceval around the ribs. "I don't know, really. Mother never taught me. I've always ridden in carts or wagons."

"Anyone can do it. My own teacher helped me. Just last year I could barely ride, but I managed to get Brownie here all the way to Camelot. Isn't that right, girl?" He stroked the horse's thick damp neck. She grunted approvingly.

Perceval stopped Brownie on the road, already trying to dismount. It proved difficult, with Galienne all but wrapped around him.

"But, wait," she protested. "What if I fall off? It's a long way down there." She nervously glanced down toward the ground.

"You'll be fine. Brownie's wonderful. She wouldn't hurt anyone, especially someone who has been so kind to me."

The compliment had its desired effect; Galienne loosened up enough to let him off. He hopped down, then handed her the reins.

"It's easy. She understands commands. If you want her to turn, pull the reins in that direction. If you want her to go the other way, pull the reins in the opposite direction. She'll stop if you pull up toward you, and if you want her to go again, just give her a nudge with your heels here." Perceval pointed to the fleshy area of Brownie's midsection which responded most readily to gentle prods; he tried to keep contact from Meliagrant's spurs to a minimum.

"You mean kick her to get her to walk?" Galienne was aghast.

"You don't have to kick her. Just give her a push, with your heels." He grabbed her left foot, pushing it into Brownie's body, and the horse obediently started walking. She went deliberately slowly, sensing the novice atop her.

Galienne let out a short, startled but high yelp at the sudden motion. She was riding! And with no one else to control this huge creature. Perceval walked alongside them, refusing to take the reins back when Galienne tried to return them.

She had to confess though, it felt wonderful. There was something about being perched on a horse that made her feel... how? She considered it, smiling as she watched the fitted rocks

that made up the road pass under her, like the River Wey beneath
the Astolat Bridge, when she wished she could just follow it.

She thought of her adjective. *Free*. It felt free to be up
here. The breeze seemed sweeter and the scenery lovelier when
seen from Brownie's back. The mare, too, felt a bit freer; for a
while she could ride with only the weight of one person. And
Galienne was several dozen pounds lighter than Perceval.

He enjoyed seeing her smile. And it was good to walk
again. His back needed the stretch, after having her slumped
against it for a few hours.

"So now you can read *and* ride," he told her. She grinned
down at him.

Brownie then began to drift to the far right side of the
road. Perceval looked over, noticing Galienne manipulating the
reins as he had instructed.

"It works!" she cried, feeling triumphant. "She went
right where I told her to go!" Brownie snorted again.

Perceval laughed. So she wanted to show off, did she?
Fine. He followed Brownie over to the roadside, smiled up at
Galienne, and then slapped the horse on the rump.

"Hey!" shouted Galienne. "What was that for?" But
she was off, Perceval simply walking behind her now. The horse
took off at a good stride; to Galienne it seemed she was flying.

And out of control, too, even though Brownie was only
going straight up the road. After they went a good ninety yards,
Galienne remembered the instructions, and pulled the reins,
Brownie's neck and head rising slightly at the gesture, her teeth
putting another set of minuscule nicks in her bit.

The mare stopped as quickly as she started. Galienne
turned around, seeing Perceval nodding approvingly, still am-
bling his way towards them.

Not wanting to be outdone, Galienne pulled the reins
to the left, and kept pulling until she faced Perceval. Then she
immediately dug her heels into the muscled horse flesh beneath

them, and Brownie was charging him down. She got the horse to go even faster this time.

Perceval had to jump clear off the road to avoid them, hearing Galienne's giggle. By the time he was on his feet, she had turned around and ridden back.

"Excellent," he said, returning to the road. "I think you have a knight's blood, after all."

For the first time, Galienne felt proud to be mighty Lancelot's child.

* * *

Llio was finally starting to feel better now that the smoke had completely receded. She could sit upright again, at least, felt ready to continue and not devote a night to Nature's embrace. She was too glad about being this close to Camelot to consider how odd the smoke seemed; she was also too determined now to get to the city by nightfall. She worried about her throat, even as the pain began to fade; she tried not to think about how complications from a similar affliction ultimately killed her mother.

And now she was on her way again, riding alongside her brother. And the woman. Llio was glad neither of them objected to her still persistent coughing.

Nimue found these two along the road shortly after finishing her task. So shortly, actually, that she was initially worried they had seen her, like the rider (surely *he* saw her?) What would she say to visitors of Camelot who witnessed a sacrifice? *Oh, sorry. Don't mind the deer nor the spoiled fruit, really. It's just that I had to impress the likes of they who live behind those walls, and it's a beautiful day to perform some magick, wouldn't you say?*

She was comforted no such conversation took place. These two were even younger than herself. And so eager! They reminded her of when she first went to Avalon as a girl, so full of idealism and youthful energy. All she had wanted was to learn. She wanted to study and be taught the ways of magick.

She had sworn her life and soul to Goddess, who returned the favor by granting her the Gifts. She had the Sight, too. She helped the Lady to track down Galienne in the first place, with Morgan viewing the girl running to the river through the lens of the perfectly calm and pure water of the sacred well. No sacrifice was needed back there; the land itself seemed to want to explode from the power it contained. Nimue was very proud to say she came from the most magickal land in Britain.

And now she found a willing escort: some lad on his way to the city to become a knight. He was richly dressed, this Llascoit, although his appearance retained some signs of the old ways, she noticed pleasingly. His long hair had not been given up for the sake of Roman custom, and was braided in front into twin ropes. It helped emphasize his excited eyes, and easy smile. And the sword he carried: it was shorter, with a wider blade, than currently fashionable. It was a far cry from that which Galienne retrieved. Llio, too, wore a plaid, indigo and daisy-colored gown which would stand out proudly at Camelot. Her face was almost perfectly rounded, with the pronounced cheekbones Roman men would have adored. Her hair was just a shade darker than the golden apples of spring back at Avalon, and were it not for the rich bracelet and necklace she wore, Nimue would have thought her to look something like an enchantress herself.

"Who is he?" Llio asked her then, temporarily keeping the cough in check.

"What?" answered Nimue, blinking at her.

"The person you're going to meet at Camelot. Who is he? That is, if you do not mind my asking."

The question was innocent enough, its forward approach impressing Nimue.

"I travel to meet not with a him, but a her. A girl about your age." She wondered where this talk might lead. She did not want to have to lie to someone she just met.

"Oh. Is she family of yours?"

"Llio, what about me makes you this curious?"

"I just thought you might enjoy talking. You've been quiet since we started riding together. I was just wondering why you were on your way to Camelot, and alone, at that." She had to clear her throat again; at least the rusty taste of blood was no longer there. Her voice sounded strained, though.

"Well, what about yourself? I know your brother here is going to be a knight, but I wonder about you. Why do you travel this way with him?" *Damn your tongue*, Nimue cursed herself silently. She should know better than to speak prophetically. It was not her place to try and divine someone's life for them. She hoped no one would ever try to cheapen Goddess' gifts by dabbling in seemingly playful fortune-telling. Already scoundrels rightfully declared heretical by Pagan and Christian alike made fortunes claiming to show glimpses of what-would-be to the eager or gullible. And for what? Nimue thought foreknowledge more akin to curse than blessing; why would anyone want to know the future?

Llascoit just smiled back at this odd woman. "Thank you for your confidence, my Lady," he said. He fantasized about being knighted with Perceval. The thought of standing vigil in the grand church made the hairs on his arms stand almost straight.

Llio watched her brother, waiting for him to turn back to the road. He led the small party. Then Llio let Fay drop back a bit, slowing her so that she rode evenly with Nimue, hopefully out of Llascoit's hearing.

"Nimue," she said in a confessional tone, "I undertook this journey for two reasons. One, I love the King's capital. Two," she whispered this time, although she was a bit uncertain why she did not wish Llascoit to hear; he probably knew anyway, "is because of the man we were with until that strange fire or whatever it was overtook us. It's Perceval. I think I love him."

Why on earth am I telling this to an almost total stranger? Because, she insisted to herself, *no one else would really listen.* She wanted to be taken seriously, and not be told she was just having girlish whimsies. Besides, Nimue seemed so, well, trustworthy.

Nimue was amused. The girl was in love? Why had she not declared this to the object of her desire before? Whoever this Perceval was, he obviously had no idea about any of this, or else was too stupid to know to hang onto this young woman. Nimue saw the look in Llio's eyes before in the faces of others, respecting the longing that could define a person's whole manner.

"Llio, I don't know a thing about this man. But I do know this: if you truly love him, then eventually, Goddess willing, you shall have him as your own."

"You're teasing me."

"No, truly. Someday he'll realize the efforts you have made to be with him. You're really traveling for him, are you?"

"Yes, I believe so."

"Then, as with all things, time will tell."

It didn't help that Llio returned to her own questioning. "And what of you, then, Nimue? Is there some man somewhere who lays claim to your heart?"

No, never! she thought but did not say. Nimue wanted no one but the Lady to ever have sway over her decisions. Not some man; she could never live with that. The only man she ever really respected was Merlin himself, but he was gone now, and much of her respect with him. She did not know where, Sight or no.

"No, Llio. I am sworn to my own tasks, and have not the time nor inclination to pursue a husband." She had no intention of divulging any of her mission to this girl, wanted her to remain ignorant of just who and what she was.

"I don't know how I'll break the news to Llascoit, then," Llio teased. Up ahead of them, the errant turned around again, his look suggesting he wanted to know what they giggled about, but yet not really caring, either.

"Oh, stop it," Nimue said. She couldn't help but smile at Llascoit as he looked at her, perhaps suggestively.

Soon the taller edifices of Caer Cadbury, commonly known as Camelot, rose above the horizon, level with the trees they rode through. Nimue thought the place must be mighty indeed if the buildings already looked so big. They were still a mile away.

"Camelot!" cried Llascoit. "Sister, we are almost there!"

"Yes, I am not blind, thank you, brother."

Nimue's heart leaped to and fro within her chest. *The city. So this is Arthur's vision*, she thought. The end result of centuries of occupation, the Romans and their civilizing ways. *The magick is least where agriculture and walls are most.* She finally understood her apprehension, looking at this grand place; as an enchantress, her powers would be virtually non-existent within those walls, in that once sacred hill now modernized and overlaid with all manner of material. She had no protective talismans, dressed as a simple peasant woman to raise less suspicion.

"Where are you staying?" asked Llio.

"Oh, I'm not sure just yet. I understand space in the city will be limited." News of Pentecostal events did indeed reach far; Nimue was all the more skittish about being here during what had become the highlight of Christian debauchery.

"Well, why not stay with us? My brother's harmless, at least where women are concerned. And my father is still in the King's favor. As his children we have the right to one of the apartments inside the castle."

"A-apartments?" questioned Nimue. *Sleep indoors?* she wondered. She often slept in shelter, granted, but that consisted of huts, not these *apartments*.

"Sure. Private rooms. Locked doors. Privies. A place to cook a little. Storage space, though it's not like we own much.

I plan to stay there until I figure out what to do next. For now I just want to enjoy Camelot."

Such buildings were aptly named, Nimue thought begrudgingly: places *apart* from Nature. At least she would have a secure place to take her magickal slumber, dreamily performing her summoned labor in the Other Side in return for having invoked that Side into a manifestation for mortals to see.

* * *

It was the light-hearted attitude of the people thronging the city streets that finally helped put Nimue at ease. She had never seen so many having such fun. There was a bit of everything in this place! Knights, farmers, entertainers, laughing children, merchants and skilled workers; somehow every conceivable occupation seemed to have its representatives here (except magicians, though, of that she remained quite confident).

Nimue snorted amusingly when she walked by a "magician," a young lad performing parlor tricks, pulling Denarii from children's ears and throwing his voice around the courtyard without moving his lips. *So this is what magick is reduced to within the stronghold's walls*, she thought disdainfully. The lad made a move towards her as though wanting to inspect her head for coinage as well, and the glare she gave him stopped him in his tracks. She was delighted it took him several seconds to compose himself and keep performing for the audience.

That was the difficult part; there were so many folk here! She had gone with Llio and Llascoit to their "apartment," and entrusted them with the stabling of her horse. For the first afternoon, they parted ways, each going off to explore.

It was amazing how much was crammed into the space. Nimue felt like she had to fight even for air. She immediately longed for the peace of Avalon (and solitude; maybe a lack of candidates had its advantages). Still, she kept focused on her purpose. She had to find the girl.

Nimue made her way down to what was obviously the main castle in this place, wondering if she had any right to admire the handsome architecture of the King's home. *Perhaps the civilizers have magick of their own,* she mused. Then the voice startled her from behind, so entranced was she by the sight. She never thought to hear this one again.

"Lady Nimue. Well met. I never thought someone of your background to be interested in all this Christian merry-making."

She turned to face Lancelot. He was so much older now. "So, Queen's Champion. I, likewise, never thought to see someone of your background giving his life to all this Christian... place." She could not think how to phrase the awe this location inspired. It was a power she would respect, even if opposed to it.

"Lady, you know I have never broken my vows to the Old Ways. This is a Christian court. I worship as I please, not according to mandates of the bishops."

"And when, exactly, was the last time you saw the place of your teaching? Do you perform sacrifice or sacrament? You could have been Arch-Druid, Lancelot. Instead of arch-knight, or whatever they call you around here. You had the potential to be the next Merlin."

Lancelot was in no mood to be accused. "There will be a new Arch-Druid, or have you remained unable to see him with that confounded Sight of yours?"

"I have never seen the man of such destiny. My only hope is that he, unlike Merlin and yourself, will never cheat his religion, and the soul of Britain." *No, no,* she commanded herself; this was no good. Lancelot was not her enemy. She had only met him a few times before, most recently when he came near Avalon seeking the Lady's help in purging him of his love-lust for the Queen. But there was no help for him: no charm, no talisman, no ritual, no prayer, could cure one so smitten. She couldn't fight with the one person likely to know the where-abouts of his daughter.

She tried to defuse him before he erupted. "Forgive my hasty judgments, Lord Lancelot. I believe you still, in your heart if not your actions, cling as much to Old Ways as I." She reached and took his hand in hers, drawing a double-crescent on his palm, one of the signs of Goddess. Two crescents facing each other suggested phases of the feminine moon, and the birthing vagina of all life.

Lancelot had not seen nor felt that symbol in too long a time. He fought to keep from weeping; God knew what others might say if their hero was found bawling in public, and at the touch of a woman, no less!

"Come, Nimue. We have much to discuss. I know why you are here." And he led her down towards the gate through which she entered earlier that day. Leaving the city was the only way to get any privacy for the next two weeks.

They walked comfortably along, not wanting to arouse attention or suspicion, not that anyone would have noticed any-way, with all the merry-making, shopping, and gossiping about. From the gate they made their way towards the woods whence Nimue arrived. Few travelers were still coming this way, and were not in the habit of seeking intrigue amongst the trees.

Nimue listened, shocked, as the knight relayed what he knew, which was rather a lot. Perhaps she misjudged these knights. But no, Lancelot was raised according to much older traditions than those which fostered warfare for warfare's sake. Lancelot was a child of Mona, raised and instructed by druids.

He spoke of his daughter as though he spent far more time with her than he actually had. He was convinced that she was a Christian, more by inclination than conversion (the latter was the only manner in which Nimue believed *anyone* could buy into all this talk of guilt and sin and fiery pits).

"Did you know she all but taught herself to read? She would spend hours in front of the same Bible, in the same church, in the same town, just reading of the life of Jesus and his entourage. She has few friends. The only person she really talks to around here is Bishop Baudwin."

Nimue was trying to check her growing fury. "And all this while, you did *nothing*? You're her father, by Gwydion!" She dimly hoped the name of the druid-god would put its own sense of guilt in him; he deserved it. "The child could have been saved."

"Nimue, listen to how you speak. You use a Christian term, and talk of using methods you despise. What would you have had me do, force her into Avalon, a place she believes full of witches and faeries, which she also believes, on her own accord, to be things of hell?"

"Something must be done! She is needed with us; we have seen her greatness."

"Nimue, allow me to ask you this, though you may hate me for saying so. But have you ever considered that your Sight reveals its fortunes to you as it pleases, and not as you desire?" Lancelot remained calm through all this.

"Well, of course I have. The visions come straight from Goddess, and –" she stopped abruptly, bringing her hand to her mouth as though she might pull the words back inside it.

Lancelot knew he had her. "Do you see what I mean? It is not for you, nor I, nor anyone else, to decide the exact meaning, much less intent, of divine messages. Galienne has them herself, used to be deathly afraid of them. Baudwin told me, and only he could persuade her that they were sendings from God."

Nimue shrank in horror. What did the Christian God know of visions? Any sendings He might have given anyone could not even save his own Son!

"Nimue, Lady, could it be that the greatness you foresaw within Galienne will manifest itself along Christian lines? Not every young girl is destined for Avalon; you know that."

Nimue struggled for anything else to use as a defense. "But in the Island she will be safe! I don't even know where she is right now."

"She's gone. Fled the city this morning. I watched her depart." *And I'll have to catch up to her shortly, as per my lord's instructions.*

Lancelot actually had to move towards her, fearing she would collapse. She leaned instead against the steeple-high oak behind her, ignoring the feeling she usually adored, of bark, that natural armor, scratching her back soothingly, as though she were a she-bear.

The pink vanished from her face. Lancelot felt no tension at all in her shoulders when he gripped them.

She whispered. "You watched her go?! And you did nothing?" She looked far past him as she spoke.

"She is with someone who can take care of her, better than I ever could. Not that she'd even deign speak to me anyway. Surely your own vision would suggest her safety, whether she was in Avalon or elsewhere."

All Nimue could do was try and change the subject. "How know you so much?" she demanded, finding her voice again.

She felt the imposing man release his grip on her, although she had not even noticed his hands when they touched her in the first place. They then fell to his belt, to which were tied a couple of supple leather pouches. From one he removed a parchment.

"Read," he commanded, passing it to her.

It was in Latin, the court language (in all "civilized" lands, anyway, though Nimue too had learned Latin, all the better to deal with others who knew it).

She read:

To the poor soul who should find this, greetings...

Fear not the touch of my now dead body, for no disease has taken its ravishment of me. Nay, I have succumbed to that which the bards and poets call love, and of the most horrific kind.

Unrequited.

It is he, Queen's own man, upon whom I call to take over responsibility which I can no longer bear. I cannot live unloved by he who has my heart, nor with the constant reminder of one night of his touch. She is a brave one, far stronger than I, indeed than anyone I have ever met, but alas, I hold her back. Trapped in a place too stifling for one of her aspirations.

I do not do this for sympathy, but only for release. Curse him who has the love of one yet gives his heart to another!

I ask only for the proper rites. And pray my soul be kept as I have hoped, with Him above.

Elaine of Astolat, Seamstress.

Never before had Nimue felt so wretchedly sorry for a Christian. She looked at Lancelot. "Where?" she said.

"I found it on her body, before anyone else arrived. Kay almost found it before I." Lancelot again wondered how it had gotten there. Most women couldn't read or write, and Elaine hardly seemed any exception. But then, who? How might she have hired someone willing to take such a ghastly form of dictation?

"And, I assume, you are 'he who should be cursed.'"

Lancelot blinked back tears. "Of course it's me!" His voice emerged raspy from his throat. "I didn't even know it was her that night, had no way of knowing."

"Lancelot, it is no affair of mine whatever befell you 'that night,' but I ask one last time. Where is Galienne?"

He swallowed the salty drops in his mouth. "With Perceval. With a man who has already proven himself quite a capable warrior. Perhaps she'll be a warrior after all, just not quite according to your specifications." *But I doubt it.*

Perceval, Nimue thought, making a point to never forget the name. *The boy Llio told me she loved.* Even in the absence of the Sight, she had a feeling she would encounter him soon enough.

Unable to think of any other way to conclude the talk, Lancelot offered his arm to the enchantress. "May I escort you to the festivities, Lady?" The face betrayed nothing. Too long had this man worked to mask his feelings. He returned to his private hell.

Nimue was tired, and somehow the city seemed less imposing than it had hours ago. Besides, she would feel guilty if she just abandoned Llio and Llascoit, especially since she now had some idea where their friend was. She took the muscled arm, and they walked back into Camelot.

* * *

Perceval went over his vows in his head, and remembered his mother, sitting there that night, demanding his oath. What else might he have forgotten?

He remained anonymous, at least regarding his parentage; so far no one but Gornymant really knew who he was, beyond the "red knight." The warlord had interrogated him one night, insisting he receive some inclination as to exactly who he was devoting his time and efforts to train. Perceval begged Gornymant not to reveal the information to anyone. Not even Llio and Llascoit knew he was the son of an old king named Pellinore.

He missed them, felt guilty about leaving them behind in the city, but they would be well cared for. He hoped and believed they would understand the reasons for his sudden departure, in the face of all he felt. It did seem a hasty and chaotic decision to leave so abruptly (he did have a penchant now for such behavior), but he *did* have the King's own blessing, and all but a guarantee of his wish becoming realized upon his return. That made it easier.

But he had been gone from his home for too long, so long that he had trouble remembering his vows to a woman whose very face blurred in his mind.

Galienne quietly rode along next to him, as he walked. His legs were tired; they had already been gone for two days. The two of them had to snuggle closely together at night beneath his single blanket, since that was the only real bedding they had. Galienne softly wept at her mother's loss. And Perceval was intrigued by his lack of any appetite for this girl, despite their sleeping proximity. He figured it must have been his distracted thoughts, or that she reminded him a bit of Dindraine, or perhaps, no, better not to dwell on that. He forced himself to keep thinking that his affections for Llio were of the same type as his feelings for his own sister, or for the young woman now riding with him.

She took to the saddle quite well. He even imagined taking it upon himself to teach her more skills relevant to her chosen (or destined) path. Not growing up in the Roman-influenced centers of civilization like Camelot and Londinium, sexism was largely alien to Perceval. He had seen Melangell perform feats of raw strength and stamina that could shame most knights, and the women in his home went about and acted and loved as they chose.

Now he remembered, as plainly as he would always remember the sword at his side. He had almost met his vows, after all. Only one person knew his lineage, he had prayed when able (she had only asked him to pray when in a church, hadn't she?), he had gained not just the King's attention but his favor as well. Now he had even come to the aid of someone who needed it (*especially a maiden*, he could hear his mother say). Galienne had definitely needed someone. She looked relaxed and content riding Brownie; she was a natural rider. Of course, how could anyone from Lancelot's own seed not be?

So the only one remaining was the demanding of someone's hospitality. He had taken the blessings, invitations, and teachings of others. But he had never demanded.

"Perceval, do you see it? Look, straight ahead, on the road!" Galienne had finally broken the quiet of walking along this all but deserted road; it seemed everyone on the Island was already in Camelot.

Perceval followed her outstretched finger until he saw the brightly-colored tent adjacent to the road, maybe a half mile from them.

* * *

At least it was not some distant campfire this time. Perceval told Galienne to scoot herself way back as far as she could in the saddle, then climbed upon Brownie, taking control of the reins. The girl clung to him again, wondering who might be within the small pavilion ahead.

It looked deserted, save for a spotted beige riding horse tethered in the trees just outside it. As they rode closer, Perceval guessed the tent's owner could afford many of the finer comforts; the tent was woven from richly-dyed materials, an alternating vertically-striped pattern of deep sea blue and sunny yellow.

Galienne was at once intrigued. "Oh, look at how it was woven! It's beautiful! You see how they laced it up the side? That helps keep the rain and other nasty weather out." Perceval had little idea what she was talking about. He stopped Brownie, feeling a sudden urge to behave protectively.

"Gal," he started; he was starting to call her *Gal* as a nickname, "listen to me. When we get up next to this tent, I want you to let me do the talking. Whoever is in there may only be interested in talking to a knight."

"You're not a knight," she whispered playfully, tickling him in the ribs.

"Well, I'm closer to being one than you. Let's just see who's here, all right?"

Galienne continued to admire the tent's craftsmanship as they rode up to it, then dismounted. Still no one seemed to take any notice of them.

Perceval had to look around for an opening to this woven shelter, and started to walk its circumference to do so. Galienne caught him, pointed in the direction opposite from the one he walked, and he followed her finger (and her knowing smile) around the other side.

There was indeed an opening on that side, facing away from the road. Part of the tent was cut and the resulting flap attached to the tent's side to act as a door. Perceval and Galienne arrived there at the same time, looked around feeling slightly guilty, and then peered inside.

Whoever she was, she had obviously not noticed them yet. A woman, clearly older and taller than Galienne, with locks the color of the most fiery sunset, sat in front of them on a wooden stool. She was bent over at the waist and appeared to be working on something small with her hands, quite preoccupied.

Perceval looked at Galienne, as though suddenly changing his mind and seeking her advice. She smiled her same knowing grin, and then cleared her throat, loudly enough to be heard by many of the nearby forest creatures.

Not recognizing the surprisingly masculine sounding windpipe excavation, the woman shrieked and turned to face them simultaneously. She punctuated the double gesture with a gasp at the sight of not just a strange girl, but a *man* standing at the entrance to her sanctuary.

"I humbly apologize for startling you, Lady, but we are traveling these parts and stopped at your tent. You are the first fellow traveler we have seen this day." Perceval hoped he was sounding better with his speech all the time.

Still too shocked to speak, the redhead with the equally inflammatory body just sat staring at them. She forgot about her handiwork: her fingers were wrapped tightly around a jeweled ring and its polishing cloth. She couldn't let them see it, at least not until she had some inkling who they were.

"My Lady, I am Perceval, of Oerfa in the kingdom of Powys, and this is my, my —" he fumbled for the words. What *was* Galienne, in relation to him?

She saved him, trying not to laugh while doing so. "Sister. And my name is Galienne, Lady. May we ask upon whom we have called today?" She didn't consider it a lie, necessarily; knights spoke of brothers-in-arms, so couldn't she be Perceval's sister-in-arms?

The woman seemed to calm, sensing the obvious lack of threat from the likes of these two. "Jacqueline. My name is Jacqueline. And I am most recently from Lambor Castle, the holding of Sir Blamore of Ganis. Though it is on the Continent where I call my home." The words gently dripped from her mouth, like fresh pure honey. The accent with which she spoke was strange but discernible to Perceval, who felt the words roll gracefully through the tent, with softer consonants and longer vowels.

Perceval was expected to speak. "Is this Sir Blamore your lord, then?"

"Oh, no. He is lord of his own demesne, yes, and he is a distant kinsman of mine, but my own lord, Sir Girard, is away hunting. He insisted we arrive at Camelot in time for the festivities, but his love of the hunt is so great he could not resist the deer we saw this morning."

"How fortunate for him," added Galienne. "The King's forests are free and plentiful both."

Perceval continued to melt at the sound of the woman's voice, then thought *I know how your lord must feel.* He silently hoped this lord would be more successful than he had been that day.

Jacqueline continued to attempt cordiality. "So I've heard, young lass. Speaking of the hunt, may I offer you both my hospitality? I have some wine and some pastries stored in my chest, over there. You both look as though you could use some refreshment."

"Aye, Lady, that we could," spoke Galienne, who *was* hungry. They had not exactly had time to shop for rations before leaving the city.

Hospitality, thought Perceval, again running through the vows he made hastily one night. His mother would be impressed. Although he had not *demanded* it the way his mother insisted. "Thank you, Lady Jacqueline. That would be lovely," he said. He didn't have to demand anything.

The hostess rose, tucked the ring and cloth away, and went to the opposite side of the small tent where sat a heavy-looking metal chest. Perceval thought it could likely withstand a tremendous blow, but wondered why something as mundane as food and wine might be kept in it.

"Here, allow me," invited Galienne, moving over to help Jacqueline. She frowned at her "brother;" were not knights supposed to show more courtesy than to let a woman do her own lifting?

Jacqueline deftly opened the iron box, placing the ring and cloth within. Another chest, this one of the same birch wood as the stool, stood behind where the first one had rested. She was quite capable of moving this second sturdy chest, but allowed Galienne to help her carry it over to the stool, setting it down there.

Jacqueline betrayed a slight smile, finally pleased to have some company, never mind how her lord might respond. "I regret there is no space to sit other than the floor, but here are my offerings," she said as the two of them placed the wooden container near Perceval's feet. She then opened it with a pair of loud snapping sounds, letting the lid fall earthward on well-oiled ornamental hinges.

Inside there were a number of pieces of fresh fruit, apples and grapes, and some orange-colored spherical ones Perceval and Galienne did not recognize. Also were two pies, one of them half-eaten, made with meat that smelled like deer, and buttery pastry crusts. Jacqueline removed the pies, then quickly stole back to her stash of personal effects to retrieve a blue glass bottle of wine.

"Eat, please," she requested, making no move to partake of the food herself. She was pleased to have the company; her lord was not fond of visitors, and rarely let her out of his sight. Girard figured, almost rightly, that no one else would be on the roads today, and took his squire out for yet another hunt. Jacqueline did not look forward to his commanding her to clean and cook or salt another creature, especially if something the size of a deer was what they brought back.

Perceval and Galienne ate hungrily, not caring that they had to use their hands. Utensils seemed frivolous outside the centers of civilized life. Besides, those too belonged to Girard, and he guarded even them jealously.

Jacqueline felt content to watch her guests enjoy the ends of her labors. She all but forgot about the man who would be home soon.

"Do you mind if I continue with my work while you eat?" she said finally. They had already polished off the half-pie and started on the whole one.

Galienne and Perceval grunted their assent, not wishing to speak for fear of revealing Jacqueline's baking in a new, pastier oral guise. Jacqueline walked back to retrieve the ring she had been polishing, bringing it back to where the others were doing their best starving dog imitations.

The ring was a gift from *him*, of course. Girard purchased it with money he said came from a tournament ransom. She thought it more likely that he beat or forced a number of Blamore's peasants to come up with it; who would believe the word of some peasant against that of a knight anyway?

It *was* quite lovely, though, finely crafted with the painstaking touch only the truly dedicated and talented can develop. It consisted of inter-locking silver and gold bands, which wrapped around the finger. Jacqueline loved the ropy design, often imagining the bands to be intertwined lovers, forever joined and molded around each other. She never envisioned Girard as one of these, however; how had she ended up with him in the first place? Had she really allowed herself to be bedded by such a callous, gruff sot? Had her father been so blind?

No matter. It was done. And sooner or later Girard was likely to find someone who bested him. His image of himself was too grand to permit the refusal of any challenge, and it would probably get him killed someday.

Jacqueline hated when she thought like this. He wasn't *that* bad, surely. Was he? He had never beaten *her*; it was just that she did not like how he acted around anyone else, and her suspicions never diminished. He had challenged more than one other knight for having the audacity to *look* at her from across a room. Had she sexed someone in front of him, she might have understood, but a simple glance? No, she hated being thought of as property. He owned her as much as she owned the ring.

All had actually gone fairly well since their departure from Quimper just beyond a month past. He was relatively kind to her, too busy boasting to the ship's company of the riches and glory he would surely win at the King's grand tourney. At least it kept him largely away from her. Except at night, when he was his usual rough-and-tumble self again. She was almost continually sore in the mornings, learning to ignore most of the discomfort as each day developed.

But now she was here! In this wondrous land. The rich port of Gloucester would be dwarfed by Camelot, and it had still thrilled her and her husband. And then they began their journey inward, Girard flashing his wealth as he went. Although not many were around to appreciate such flaunting, since so many had already flocked to Camelot. Jacqueline could hardly wait to see it.

She kept polishing, unaware that her guests finished eating, chasing their food with thirsty gulps of wine. Had she noticed, she would have told them not to chug such a vintage; it came with her from the Continent, one of the last.

The stone stared up at her, like a watchful red eye. The ruby was an elegant touch to the silver and gold bands, but it looked out of place somehow, as though the jeweler tried to incorporate too much decoration in too little space. It was lovely, but now she urgently wanted to be rid of it.

What might Girard say about that? she wondered. Or do? She was unconcerned about it; let him say and do as he pleased. *Everyone should be able to do or say as he or she damn well pleases*, she thought.

"Galienne," she said, "I realize you are still young. Have you any man who has sworn himself to you?"

Galienne almost spat out the heady wine inside her cheeks. "No," she laughed, "of course not, Lady. I have much further ambition than that." She was slowly beginning to come to terms with all that happened to her recently. Her mother might be dead, but Galienne was becoming convinced that she could make her death meaningful by living out the "prophecy." Somehow.

"Well, whatever ambition you may cling to, perhaps this will help you realize it." Refusing to consider it further, Jacqueline reached for Galienne's hand, still greasy from the meat pie.

Galienne relaxed in the woman's grasp, allowing a ring larger than she had ever seen before to be slid down her finger. She gasped when she saw how valuable it must be.

Perceval interjected. "My Lady, please. We may be lonely travelers, but we are not so hard on our luck to need assistance, however thoughtful it may be."

"I understand, Perceval," Jacqueline said, "but I really wish her to have it, if it is all right with both of you." There. It was done. No going back now. She would just see how Girard reacted to this. The free spirit grew in her; it must have been their proximity to Camelot. She wondered if the folk of Logres tried to do things their own way like this.

Galienne beamed at her mentor. How could he refuse the look she gave him? He nodded, and the others smiled. Jacqueline immediately gave the cloth to the girl as well, explaining how to properly polish the ring to maintain its luster.

Perceval hated to feel rushed, and hated more being rude, but he was getting more anxious all the time. It was already to the point where he could barely do anything without thinking of his mother. During the trip he tried to help Galienne come to terms with her own mother; that just made him think of his own. Besides, there was not really enough extra space in this little pavilion for four. No, he corrected, five, counting this man Girard's squire. Galienne did not seem to mind sleeping outside, enjoyed it, actually. They should thus be on their way.

"Galienne, perhaps we will see the Lady again back in Camelot. You said you were headed there, yes?"

"I am, Perceval," Jacqueline said. "And I hope I will see you again there. Are you both staying the night here?" she asked, almost pleading. She did not particularly want to be alone with *him* again this evening. Tomorrow they might be in the city, and she could spend time away from Girard.

Galienne again looked at Perceval with her finest lovable puppy eyes. It was clear she wanted to stay. Perceval looked down, shaking his head, but not to say no. His head was shaking because of his amusement: not yet a knight himself, he had already taken on a pupil of his own, and she seemed to have more to say about what they did together than he did.

"We'll stay," he said. "But in the meantime, I'd like to get back outside, and just roam a bit. I shan't go far. Just yell if you need me." He added the last comment without any air of I'm-the-warrior-and-it's-my-job-to-protect-you like Girard surely would have. Jacqueline was pleased by that; even this young errant was more of a catch than the man she had. She wondered who might lay claim to his heart.

* * *

It was the scream which awoke Perceval and Galienne that night. Not a very loud one, nor particularly high or piercing. But *afraid*. The scream clearly came from someone in terror.

Perceval dimly recognized it as coming from inside the tent. Perceval and Galienne had bedded down for the night just outside, out of sight among the trees. They were so tired from traveling that they completely slept through Girard's arrival. Until now. A thundering, vengeful voice also came from the tent. Perceval was quick to his feet, not noticing a frightened Galienne laying at his side.

"*Who* is he?" the male voice pounded. "Deceitful bitch in heat, if you're going to take lovers at least have the decency to *hide* them from me!" This was punctuated with the unmistakable sound of a hard smack, followed by another short scream.

Inside, Jacqueline made no effort whatsoever to summon help. Clearly her guests would hear her being accused and beaten, and she was willing to take the chance that Perceval would come to her assistance on his own. No pleading from her; tonight she had learned what this beast knight was made of!

When slapped, she collapsed to the ground, impacting herself on her elbow. She had barely rolled around to face upward again when Girard was upon her, another violent blow coming from his outstretched hand. He held her arms when she put them up to try and block him, and then noticed something missing.

"And you gave him the *ring?* The very one I gave you? Whore! Is there anything of mine he *didn't* take?" He was already tearing at her clothes, despite her struggles. He was just too strong for her to move beneath him and his fury. "When I finish with you, I'm going to find him and slit his damned throat!"

Even in the face of impending rape, Jacqueline refused to call for help. She would prefer to have all manner of evil done to her than to beg. But no matter what else happened, as of this moment she was done with this bastard. Even if she had to die to be free of him.

"I took nothing other than what was freely offered, and that consisted solely of food and drink." Perceval stood at the entrance to the tent, making no motion toward the assault in progress on the ground.

"And as for my throat," he challenged, "you can see it is right here."

With that, he turned and walked out. Jacqueline was thrilled, the grip on her already loosened, then released. She would have to wait. And hope that Perceval was a better fighter.

"So it does, thief. Neddig, get your lazy self in here!" commanded Girard. A moment later the black-eyed squire came into the tent. *So,* Jacqueline thought, *I am not the only one to suffer the bastard's wrath recently.*

"Y-yes, master?" the squire said. Outside, Perceval heard the exchange. Did this wretch actually have those who called him master? Lamorak's and Yvaine's squires had far more respect from their "masters" than that.

He did not hear the rest, being assisted by Galienne, whose expression betrayed a mix of fear and excitement.

There was no time to armor himself, so Perceval simply grabbed his red shield and his sword from the wide-eyed girl, and stood in the road near the tent, awaiting his opponent.

Girard emerged in a rage, his pathetic-looking squire at his heels. He was all the more angry when he saw Perceval in the road.

"A *girl?* A bloody girl is your *squire?* For God's sake, man!" he thundered. Behind him, Jacqueline also emerged, looking as though she regained much of her composure. She wanted to see her husband get his due.

"Aye, braggart, and I'll soon be a better knight than you. For God's sake!" spat Galienne, crossing herself at the words with all the pride of Patricus himself. Perceval made no motion whatever to stop her; he had already decided he did not want some servant or squire waiting on him.

"In the name of the Lady Jacqueline, our gracious and kind hostess this day, I declare you, Sir Girard, unworthy of her. And I duel for the purpose of avenging your actions this night." Perceval could hardly remember ever being this *calm* before; he had trained well. His fear was under control, despite his having to fight this savage. It felt different from the time with Meliagrant.

"Then come and die, you miserable little bugger! Let's see if the 'Lady' still wants you after I leave you a bloody heap on this very patch of road!" The hateful words sputtered out, and with that, he came towards Perceval.

Girard had not time to fully equip himself, either, having just returned from the unsuccessful hunt which was the beginning of his mood; he had thought his spirits would lift by roughing up Neddig, but to no avail. No matter though; he would just run this pathetic sod through and be done with it. And God help his traitorous woman tonight!

His opponent looked unnervingly peaceful. Girard *hated* anyone who remained calm; it was part of what made him so easily angered in the first place. Jacqueline always could keep her cool as well, the betraying bitch. He did not yet see that she had come out to watch the ensuing duel.

He drew his blade from its protective scabbard quickly, so as not to be caught off guard by a sudden move from his opponent. But that same opponent removed his own sword slowly and deliberately, as though savoring the scraping sound of the sharp edge as it was drawn. The stranger then pointed his weapon at Girard's heart, keeping his shield at his side, and waited.

Damn this calm, Girard shouted to himself, and threw his sizable mass at his new enemy. He raised the sword above his head, grunting like a wild boar on the charge, and he was across the road to the other man instantly.

Perceval waited until Girard was almost on top of him, paying little attention to the outstretched sword, and instead focused on the man himself, on his exact position. When he was just about to run right into Perceval, the latter stepped quickly but effortlessly to the side, swinging his shield arm around to catch his attacker in the back.

The move caught Girard unaware; he was not prepared to keep charging, and the push of Perceval's arm kept his momentum going. Trying to stop proved futile. He ran two more steps, then stumbled and fell at the far side of the road. Jacqueline and Galienne watched admiringly; they never saw someone fight like this! Usually two knights just kept lunging at each other, hacking, swinging, and screaming their lusty battle cries until one was finally bleeding from a vital location. But this: Perceval imparted grace, more like he danced than fought.

Perceval could clearly remember his mentor's words. *Do not lose your temper, no matter the challenge. Most knights take fighting too personally, but there is no need to. Keep your wits about you and your opponent's own rage will be his undoing.* This was far better than the confused guesswork which defeated Meliagrant. He had thought that *all* fighting was personal; why else fight at all? But he also thought he was starting to understand the tutor's words. He never saw Gornymant angry, not once.

Perceval now turned to face where Girard had landed. The man rose quickly, muttering something about the evils which he would perform on Perceval when he returned to the fray. The man was beet-red in the face, even looking ashamedly at Jacqueline. He would not let her see him lose face!

He came at Perceval slowly this time, not wanting to have his own momentum take him down again. He kept the blade in front of his face, the shield covering most of his chest and waist. Then he began circling his enemy, looking for an opening, hoping for a decisive, agonizing one.

Perceval remained defensive; he doubted this man had the patience to keep circling indefinitely. It was too indecisive for a man of his manner. He merely rotated in place, slowly, matching Girard's larger circle, weapon raised similarly, waiting for the inevitable.

It came even sooner than Perceval thought it might. Girard kept his sword low this time, swinging it in a horizontal arc that sliced through the wind on the way to Perceval's midsection. He had only to adjust the position of his shield slightly to meet the blow. Girard was strong; the sheer force of the slash felt as though it would break his arm anyway. But the shield held, and Perceval instantly followed it with a similar swing of his own, as though to show Girard how futile an attack it was.

Girard blocked it as easily, then began the circular dance of death again. He thought a ploy of his own might catch this man unprepared. He centered his shield over as much of himself as possible, then charged again.

Girard was too close to sidestep this time, and Perceval caught the full force of the shield, being knocked back, Girard landing on top of him with a sneer on his face. Neither of them heard the gasps that escaped Galienne, Jacqueline, and Neddig.

All three wanted Perceval to win, and all three shuddered at the prospects of the opposite occurring. But no one ran, rooted by anticipation.

Perceval struggled, mainly to stay focused. The man's breath was overpowering, like an old vegetable that has begun its moldy decay into oblivion. The two of them rolled around on the ground, over and under each other like frantic lovers vying for the most satisfying position.

Girard managed to wrench a hand free, and brought it down into Perceval's cheekbone, instantly turning it red as it began to bleed internally. And again. He kept on punching him mercilessly.

Perceval was at first offended at the lack of knightly manners this man displayed, but then the pain in his face rapidly was becoming unbearable. Knights simply were not supposed to resort to the antics and brutishness of mere fisticuffs. They fought with style, not like peasants. He was finally starting to get angry.

Knowing he would have to be fast for it to work, Perceval released his grip of the man, lowering his hands to his midsection, and pushed away with all his strength. Girard was too busy looking for new areas to punch to notice what was happening, and he found himself thrown off his enemy.

Both of them knelt now, trying to concentrate on each other while simultaneously searching the surrounding area for lost weapons and shields. They both found their swords quickly, ignoring their shields, and rose. Girard lashed out with his, then slashed again, more as a scare tactic than an actual attack.

Perceval knew it would be difficult to get a blow in past all that hyper blade waving, so once again he waited. He had never thought much of tactics before arriving that day in Jagent, but he had focused on fighting defensively ever since; *let the other person make a mistake in his attack, then take advantage of that.*

Girard made it; he wrapped both hands around the grip of his sword, part of his left hand covering the pommel, as the grip was designed for one-handed use. Then he raised it again, slicing down at Perceval at an angle; he meant to cleave him in two at the shoulder.

But Perceval's shoulder was no longer there. No sooner did Girard raise the sword for its death-blow than Perceval raised his own, lunging in until the tip of the blade was pointed menacingly a mere inch from the flowing veins of Girard's throat. Girard froze his weapon mid-swing; if he so much as budged, Perceval could easily slice his breath pipe open.

Girard breathed heavily, and it was several deliberate moments before he dropped the sword at Perceval's feet. The younger man looked at him, with his swollen, bloody cheek. Not hateful, not vindictive. But the stare was alarming all the same. It was *knowing*, somehow, as though Girard's whole essence was visible to his opponent.

"You will kneel, *Sir* Girard," commanded Perceval finally, insultingly slurring the title. He did as he was told, still half-expecting Perceval to cleave his head off as punishment. He was unafraid, just spiteful. He never stopped looking for the opening in Perceval's defense that simply would not come.

"Since you are a knight, I command you to rediscover your loyalty to your vows." Perceval sounded winded himself, but took time to enunciate every syllable; he wanted no misunderstanding. "As the victor of this duel and as one honorable man to another, I hereby order you to escort this good Lady to Camelot. There you will tell King Arthur what fate has befallen you, of how abominably you treated this lovely woman, and ask him to render his own judgment upon you. Swear it, or I will kill you here and now!"

Girard, beaten and speechless at the forgiveness he received, gently grasped the business end of Perceval's sword, kissed it, and said, "I swear to do so, Perceval. On my honor as a knight." Jacqueline was incredulous.

"Neddig, come over here, please, and kneel next to your knight," Perceval said. He was pleased with how quickly his request was followed by the smiling squire. "I also hereby charge you, Neddig, as a future knight, to ensure that this man follows through with what he has sworn. You are to carry Sir Girard's sword until you all reach Camelot; only after his audience with the King may you return it, and then only with the King's permission."

Neddig swore his own allegiance, which was punctuated with a feminine voice asking, "Are you not coming with us, then?"

Perceval turned to Jacqueline, who was clearly frightened at the prospect of having to still travel with this man, even if only for a short time. "My Lady, forgive me, but I cannot. I have matters of my own which I must resolve. But I shall be back in Camelot soon. You may tell the King so, when you see him."

Jacqueline walked confidently over to Perceval, taking his hand in both of hers. She bent forward, kissing him on his uninjured cheek, then whispered, "You are the most honorable man I have ever met. Fare well, Perceval. I hope to see you again." Then she kissed him on the lips.

It was really just a peck, but Perceval swooned. No woman ever kissed him on the mouth before! Not even as a friendly gesture. He was glad his face was already red from the fight, so none could see him blush! Meliagrant had certainly not been known as the Red Knight for blushing.

Galienne then approached him, murmuring about how they all needed to get to bed, as they all had to travel come morning. She loved this man, and was also feeling a bit jealous. Some older woman had just kissed him! On the other hand, Jacqueline wasn't the one who got to sleep at his side.

Since when do devout Christian women have such feelings? she wondered.

* * *

By the time they made it back to Oerfa, Perceval and Galienne had become almost inseparable. They departed from Jacqueline and her men the next morning, both of them enjoying the look of utter shame in the eyes of Sir Girard (Galienne liked calling Girard and Neddig Jacqueline's "men," since, for a change, *she* got to command *them*). He appeared so humiliated that Perceval was confident he would prove good to his word; even if he did not, Neddig was acting as bodyguard.

Since it was many more days of travel to get back into the rugged slopes of Cambria, Perceval had the leisure to work more with Galienne, taking time to teach her more of the intricacies of riding and commanding a mount, and they even began fencing lessons. Galienne seemed a natural for the blade as well, although at first her main difficulty was simply getting used to its weight. Her arms strengthened themselves quite quickly this way, and when one arm grew fatigued from practice, Perceval had her switch arms, taking his shield in the tired one. This way she practiced longer, and learned to use her weapon ambidextrously.

They also sometimes broke into otherwise dull conversations in Latin, so both could practice the language of courts all over Europe, which kept the tongue as a last reminder of Rome's influence. This was one area in which Galienne surpassed Perceval; she had been at it a while, whereas he only began one winter earlier. Everything they did was for practice, Perceval kept reminding her, and to his delight his student did all that he asked of her. She never ran out of questions, and was clearly ecstatic about being in the wilds of Britain, the sorts of lands her mother had condemned as too dangerous and uncivilized. She loved the woods, and Perceval found he felt more at ease within them than he had the first time, staring into them blindly with Brownie and Cabal.

That dog. Perceval was glad the King had his dog. Who better a master than him? Cabal was undyingly loyal and extremely friendly (except to Kay, which amused him). Perceval missed him; even Brownie seemed to sometimes.

All the teaching and practicing helped to keep his thoughts from his mother and sister. All he could really do was hope they would forgive his long absence, and welcome him home. He guessed Galienne and Dindraine would get along as if they were sisters themselves. They were much alike, sharing the same lust for life itself, never tiring of learning and wondering. Perceval relished the mix; he hoped that whatever woman he found himself with one day would be similar to his two sisters, one by blood and one by association. *Lio*, he sometimes sighed to himself. He could hope. He thought he had known what it was to miss someone, and now the image of Gornymant's daughter was his favorite mental distraction.

Galienne, for her part, took very much to the efforts of this man teaching her to ride and fight as being the brother she sometimes wished for yet never had. Or the father, for that matter. She once heard her mother say that she never wanted another child. She claimed it was because Galienne was so wonderful, but Galienne suspected the truth: that her very existence was a reminder of Elaine's feelings for Lancelot, as the product of their illicit union. Besides, Elaine was dead, Galienne still coming to terms with the loss, and Perceval felt like the only family she had now. Her father certainly wasn't around! And would he have been so eager to teach her the way of the sword and the saddle?

They could cry together, too, with no one to pay them any bother or tease them. They'd had enough teasing; now came time for mourning and healing. "Why?" Galienne would sometimes sob, holding onto Perceval as though he were the last person alive.

Perceval felt glad he could support, physically and emotionally, but he always felt clumsy with the words. "I don't know, Gal. Why do we love anyone at all? I never knew your mother, so I can't say why all of this happened."

"But if it didn't, would we have ever met again?" she wondered, sniffing deeply and allowing her eyes to dry.

"I don't know that, either. Maybe fate, er, God, has a way of bringing people together when they need each other."

"Well, thanks be to God, then. I hope Mother's with Him."

"It sounds like she deserved to be. May she find peace at last, Galienne."

It was easy to lose track of time while roaming freely, although Perceval diligently counted the days, pleased it took the same amount of time to meet landmarks as it had when he came the opposite way. Wanting to make haste (and also because he did not wish to introduce his ward into certain areas or to certain individuals), he deliberately avoided Beacon Ring and Castle Rhun. Even Worcester, which Llio had said was the holding of her father's brother, would have to wait for later exploration. Besides, Perceval did not even know where it was. Just somewhere to the southeast of his home, he dimly recalled.

It was late in the day when they reached the tiny village. Galienne knew where they were by the way Perceval urged Brownie into a full gallop, carrying the two of them past the glistening vein of the Severn and into a place reminding Galienne of her mother's stories of the old Pagans, and their filthy rustic homes.

To her the *rath* did not look unpleasant, just different to what she was accustomed. The wall of tree posts had been erected with obvious precision, even if it would not withstand much abuse. Galienne did not feel threatened or out of place;

this was her foster brother's home, and according to the dictates of hospitality, it was now hers as well. She would be welcome. One of Oerfa's own sons had returned, and anyone with him would surely be given run of the place.

Wouldn't she?

If nothing else, the music was pleasing. Galienne could hear the faint but clear and sonorous strumming of a harp and an accompanying baritone voice come from the center of the village, even before they could see much of anyone. No one seemed to notice them yet.

Of course, she reminded herself; the people would listen with absolute attentiveness to their bards, no matter the spiritual bend of their courts. So Elaine had said; Galienne had never heard one before, only street musicians and church choirs. And she had not much thought of her own religion lately, being too caught up in her training to tend to her prayers as devoutly as before. She wondered guiltily if that was because her nagging mother was gone. And more, she noticed for the first time that Perceval was largely silent on matters religious. What did he believe?

Time to ask would come later. For now they rode quickly through an outer gate, into the shocking scene of devastation which awaited them. The place was almost deserted! And most of the homes had been destroyed outright! At least no bodies lay about, as was the case when Yvaine and Lamorak encountered a similarly stricken village. Here the survivors had taken time to bury their dead.

Tathan obviously remained, his musical story about a tremendously strong woman fighter who trained a great war hero on her mysterious shadow island was wasted on Perceval and Galienne.

They dismounted Brownie just inside the perimeter of the village, tethering her to one of the walls' support posts. Then they wandered cautiously within, Perceval wondering just who they might meet in the torn-up place. He looked about; the palisade itself still stood intact. Whoever did this had been let in the front gate, as it, too, still looked sturdy.

They rounded past a couple of the huts. At first there were only whispers, which then quickly grew, like fire out of control, into full shouts and smiles. "Perceval? Perceval! He has returned!"

Folk streamed towards them, far too few. Everyone wanted to touch him, smile at him, see he was real. Galienne was not the least bit jealous of her being ignored while others groped at him. Though she did feel a certain envy; when in her life had anyone ever fallen over themselves this way for her?

Perceval tried to navigate the eager bodies to look for his mother and sister, and found only Tathan at the end of them. Of course, Mother would likely be found at home further beyond anyway. Oerfa proper had simply been the first stop.

He looked over many of the old faces, all of which now looked more aged than he recalled. Gwyddnyn the brewer, Donngal the Irishman, still passing his stories on to Tathan, Melangell the smith, so generous to him when he left. The faces were there, all familiar but distant. He knew then he had been gone too long. He was welcome, but he no longer felt he belonged, even with the greeting.

And where was his family? And the other children with whom he had grown? Bradwen? Cadfannan? His sister's old friend Nia? Not even his other dog Dannedd was anywhere to be seen.

Tathan. Surely the bard would know. He stood facing him at last. As if reading his own thoughts, the older man said, "We must speak, Perceval. Much has happened these past seasons."

Instantly remembering the gentle but commanding authority of this person, Perceval nodded. "I see that." Then he went back to the front of the group, gesturing to Galienne when he reached her side.

He spoke quietly, uncertainly, wondering how he could help. He just felt he needed to say something. "I thank you all for welcoming me back here, after a long but, I assure, profitable absence. I have met the King personally, and he himself will grant me the honor of knighthood upon my return to his city. With me is my own pupil. No, not squire; I'm not a knight yet. She is the daughter of the Lady Elaine of Astolat, and is learning the warrior's ways herself." They cheered when he finished speaking, introducing themselves to Galienne. She was a shy step from thrilled; so the Pagans of old really did have warrior women! Why else would they smile rather than sneer at what Perceval told them? And he remembered not to include her father as part of her introduction.

She still disliked being referred to as *his* daughter. She also noticed how Perceval did not once refer to this place as home since they arrived.

After several minutes of back-patting and mead-swilling, Tathan led the two of them back into his own hut. Perceval had not seen its inside since he was barely old enough to remember. It was as sparse as any other hut in the village, save for a couple of possessions. A finely woven rug decorated the otherwise naked floor, a gift from a king who found entertainment many times in the tales spun and sung by this man. And a rich velvet draw-string bag lay on the straw bed, large enough to nest his sacred harp when not in use, which was rare. The three of them could be alone there, to talk. Tathan had much to say.

"Perceval," he said.

"Mother's dead, isn't she?" interrupted Perceval. "And Dindraine, too." He spoke as confidently as he could, his heart tightening from the premonition of impending bad news, visible in the older man's knowing eyes. Whatever happened had clearly claimed a number of lives.

"Well, yes. And no."

"How's that?" Perceval said. He let Galienne take his hand in hers.

"Your mother died. Shortly after your departure. She just became so morbid and so irritable. She found no joy in anything, and she felt, well —"

"Felt what?" Perceval demanded. Galienne was silent, thinking of her own mother.

"Abandoned, Purse. She felt abandoned. Your mother died of a broken heart, which no one could have ever hoped to mend." Perceval was never called "Purse" by anyone save Tathan. It was the bard's own personal nickname for him. When asked about it, he replied that a purse held all manner of riches, and he thought it appropriate for Perceval.

The boy, *now a man*, noted Tathan, sat on the ornate rug, his head in his free hand, his friend's other one gently rubbing the back of his neck. Tathan was not surprised the lad had found such a lively and comely girl; he wondered what their exact relationship was.

Finally, Perceval looked up at the bard. "What of Dindraine? What of the whole village?" He tried not to lose his temper; the bard was only trying to help.

"Your sister lives," Tathan said, confidently at first, but finishing the sentence with an air of mystery, "but I know not where. I saw her once, and do not think she saw me, heading up to Kundry's hut one evening. Even that was already a season after she disappeared."

"Disappeared?" Perceval was shocked. It was not like his sister to just up and vanish. She would have thought the matter through very carefully first.

"Perceval, I can only imagine how trying this must be for you. But your mother became unbearable, especially to her daughter. The whole village could sometimes hear your mother screaming at her, saying she was no true daughter, and why had she sent you off, and so on." Tathan had tried to talk with the woman more than once, and more than once been rebuffed with accusations of selling his soul to the Devil, or some such nonsense.

"Mother blamed Dindraine?" This was unbearable; it was never Dindraine's fault.

Tathan nodded, knowing the next question before it was asked.

"And what's this of Kundry? You saw them together?"

"Aye, lad. That I did. I think your sister has gone off and become a witch herself."

Perceval stood, mouthing some indecipherable syllable as he rose. Galienne gasped, half at the action, half at the mention of the word *witch*. Her own mother had told her something of witches, too. She crossed herself, a reflexive action.

"And you did nothing?" Perceval accused. "What has she become?"

Tathan remained motionless. "Purse, what know you of witches, anyway? Or you?" he said, turning the attention, for the first time, to Galienne.

Aware that he had reflexively gripped his sword at the hilt as he stood, Perceval relaxed his grasp, his mind searching for any tidbit it might find on the question. He was ashamed to find nothing at all. What the blazes *were* witches?

Answering before he could ask, Tathan explained. "The witches of old were tribal healers and diviners, Perceval," he said. "Some rare ones could talk to the animals, others could call weather of their choosing if the current sky disagreed with them. But they worked for the good of their homes, leading the seasonal festivals. I know these things because I studied them, back at Mona. The druids and witches used to work together, until the new religion came, and declared everything which it did not like, especially anything feminine, as evil." He slurred the last word, sounding every bit the fire-and-brimstone preacher, looking at Galienne as he did so.

Witches are *evil.* That was the only thing Galienne ever heard of them. She fought off the urge to cross herself again, recalling that her mother was no longer here to demean her with threats to her soul if she continued listening to this warped man who came from the druids. But he seemed so harmless; he had broken the awful news, and he clearly loved Perceval like a son.

But then, who was right about these demon women called witches? The bard? Or those who had influenced her while she grew? She kept listening.

"I confess to know little indeed of Kundry," continued Tathan. "She was a witch, a powerful one. But I heard once that something happened. She fell into some disease, or used some magick not meant for mortals, *something.* She became physically every bit the hag any sane soul fears. We all have our unique monsters to conquer. I'd say Kundry failed in her own quest."

Perceval didn't want to hear about monsters, real or figurative. "If Dindraine went to her then, it was a last resort?"

"Yes, Purse. And if Dindraine is gifted as I think, then she has become a healer herself. She will surely seek you out; you're the only family she still has."

Galienne shuddered at the thought of some *witch* coming to find them. But Perceval kept hope up, above all else. His sister was alive.

Tathan spoke again. "The younger ones, the ones who survived, all left, like you. Those who are older are in the midst of their own preparations to follow their children to more established settlements. What you see here is all that Oerfa will ever be, and when we are gone, so too the village."

"Who attacked Oerfa?" Perceval just stared at him, feeling no sorrow, no sadness, only emptiness. The *rath* was dying, its children gone to seek their fortunes where they chose. The few who remained did so from pride and familial duty, of which

Perceval shared little now. Home became something stifling when he learned his mother's secrets. And he was not of Oerfan blood anyway.

Tathan paused, having wanted and tried to avoid the issue the whole time. But the lad had a right to know. It was his home, too, even if he spent most of his life outside of it, isolated from his own. "We heard a sound one night, already a few months ago now. It was like the crying of a score of wolf-hounds. Some of us actually thought you were returning, bringing a flock of hunting dogs with you. You always did love those animals so."

The bard continued, his eyes glistening from having seen more than enough for one lifetime. "Did you see that scar on Donngal's head? He was the one who finally opened the gate. The thing was upon us before we even knew what it was."

Galienne could hear her mother again; *witches and demons and evil*, the voice wanted to cry out to her. She fought to keep it silent.

"It was an abomination. Your mother, had she still lived, would have called it such, a thing from hell itself. It was a monster; even my bardic tongue cannot do a description of it justice. It slaughtered and wrecked and then it was gone, just as we were gathering up weapons to try and stop it."

He paused. "It was like it *knew* we were ill-prepared to face it. And it fled once we armed ourselves. Like it was cautious, and knew when it could be hurt."

Perceval concentrated on the words, wishing Galienne would keep rubbing his neck. "Where did it go from here?"

The bard straightened. "That's the strange part. It went straight to your mother's farm, but could find nothing there. She had already passed away. We watched it go, and have not seen it since. But now everyone will have left this place within another few weeks."

"It's not safe here," Galienne said feebly, wanting to contribute something, trying to understand. She also had heard tales of monsters, told as warnings to scare children into bed. She still could not quite believe it.

Feeling suddenly practical, Perceval asked Tathan, "And what of the farm? Did Mother leave plans for it?"

"She did not. We sold the animals and divided the money amongst the clan, not being able to find you or your sister. I can raise what is rightfully yours from them before you leave." Tathan gestured to the outside; he wondered how much money these people might really have. Not much, he guessed.

"That won't be necessary. Knights in Arthur's service have little need for riches. I'm just glad I don't have to contend with the farm myself." Perceval wanted no hassles with a sheep farm. The others could use the sale's assets.

The bard remained silent for some moments, remembering his own training. He, too, had been immersed in triads to acquire vast knowledge, but his learning was sacred, and far more powerful. Mona was a place he was bound to not speak of, as it was the holy island of the ancients, where he memorized terrific amounts of poetry and song, and aspired to become the best bard in the land, bested finally by a younger man with even more promise. His knowledge was encyclopedic, and he often wished he could share more with the enchantresses, and vice versa. *But my own education is another story.*

Tathan stretched himself into a yawn, asked where they would be sleeping, and offered his own hut. Perceval thanked him but declined, determined to stay one last night in his mother's old place. He stood with Galienne, and led her outside, to travel the last bit of distance to the other hut, on the summit of the hill where sheep once grazed. It was plausible enough for the populace to leave; such a tiny community in an isolated place had numbered days. They stayed out of pride, but farming and commerce withered up anyway, to say nothing of the creature's effect. Plausible, maybe, but it was still hard for Perceval to believe.

How should he feel knowing that what was once his whole world would soon be so much rotting wood?

Perceval said his good evenings to the few who remained, maybe as many as a dozen including the bard. He untied Brownie and the trio ambled their way on to his mother's hill.

Once inside the old hut, already less than weatherproof, Galienne finally made a commentary of her own, speaking frankly but compassionately. "I'm so sorry, Perceval. Your mother's gone now, too, just like mine. This village is on its way, although I must say the residents have a remarkable spirit about them. Bishop Baudwin might say they have some of the Grail in them." She shrugged, thinking of the story she heard so often as a child, seeing her mother in her mind.

"The what?" Perceval said, barely hearing her. He turned to her, though; maybe a story would help ease his mind. And hers. They both had so much grief to work through.

"The Grail," Galienne said. "I was just thinking about it, that's all. I only meant that these people you grew up around have such life in them," she paused, then spoke lower. "The very life that was taken from our mothers." She wondered if some relic like she had heard about could truly have kept someone, someone important to her, alive. *But it is not our place to ask God's intents. When one's time is nigh, go they must.* She could hear the voices of her past remind her again.

Yet she still wanted to know why. Why did anyone die? Why didn't people just start in heaven? Or hell? And who deserved the hell Elaine so graphically and horribly described in the first place? Galienne crossed herself, her guilt still half-convincing her that even to think such things was itself sinful. But she was beginning to question. She continued.

Perceval had not felt ignorant now for some time. He met his oaths, he trained and studied, and now he felt again like the fool who left Oerfa to become a man. But there stood the question: what on earth was a *"grail"*?

"Gal," he said, hesitatingly, "what 'grail'? What is that? I thought I heard most legends from either that bard or from my tutor, but I have to admit this one escapes me." He was curious, though his voice still betrayed the doubt that he always had felt regarding the mythical and spiritual.

Galienne turned to face him, incredulously. "You mean you don't, er, you've never heard?" *Everyone* knew this story! They had to. She turned away. *Except this one*, she told herself. *This one who was raised next to this insignificant collection of rotting huts, knowing not a blessed thing about the rest of Creation.* It made no sense; he really didn't know, yet his mother had been a devout Christian. Some time she'd have to ask Perceval why his family had lived among Pagans.

In the meantime, she'd have to enlighten him. She cleared her throat. "The Grail, dear Perceval, is the Holy Chalice used by Christ at the Final Supper." She looked at the ceiling, as though she could peer through it at heaven itself, then sat. This might take a while.

Perceval sat opposite her, folding his legs in front of him like a little boy biding his time before committing his next mischief. *His mother must not have taught him much of the faith.* Galienne could not fully appreciate that, her own upbringing generously filled with churchly teachings.

"You mean Jesus, right?" he asked, unaware of how ridiculous the question was to Galienne.

"Yes, Jesus, the Savior. The Grail was that which he used during his last ceremony. Remember how part of the Mass includes Communion, where you partake of the Christ's blood through the chalice of wine. That comes from this ceremony. 'Drink of this, this is my blood.'"

"What do blood and wine have to do with this?"

This was going to take longer than she thought. She hadn't even mentioned the taking of the host, the flesh, of the Christ yet.

"Perceval, the wine becomes blood, His blood. And the chalice is now called the Grail. It still contains His blood, and with it anyone, anything, can be healed. If one believes truly." Maybe that would help him understand.

Perceval's face betrayed only the blank look of one who does not comprehend but wants to learn. Wanted it so badly that he never figured he might be making it unnecessarily difficult. Such was Galienne's impression, although she realized she did not know all of the story, only what she had been taught.

"You're saying this cup can just cure things. Like sickness?"

"Yes." Good. Maybe he was starting to get it.

"And it had Jesus' own blood, his very essence, in it?"

"Yes, quite."

"Then why didn't his followers, weren't some of them at this 'final supper,' just use the cup to heal him when he was on the cross?"

Galienne could feel her whole body heat at the sudden blasphemy. She could have reached over and slapped him, except...

Except that it was a good question. Why didn't the Apostles try to help? Had the cross remained under guard day and night? What happened back then? *Bishop Baudwin said the Bible has no reference to the Grail. Why is that?*

She faked her way through an answer, not realizing what she said until it left her mouth. "Jesus wouldn't have let them even if they tried. He let himself be crucified to make a point. He became the Martyr, taking all sin unto himself so that others might be saved. Besides, anyone would have done anything to receive the powers of the Grail itself, had the Apostles used it."

"Is that why he made this 'Grail' then? To help others who needed it, after he was gone?" Perceval hoped he wasn't asking too many questions, though with Galienne it felt different; talking to her, he felt he could ask and discuss anything.

Galienne considered Perceval's words while his mind wandered. She never considered it that way before. "Well, yes. That's why the Grail was kept around. Jesus' uncle, Joseph of Arimathea, understood the message of the Supper perfectly. He caught some of the holy blood in that very chalice, thereby keeping the Grail for the benefit of others, while Jesus himself rose up into heaven."

Perceval actually tried not to be offensive. He was simply curious, only half-believing this tale. Just like he only half-considered the worth of the stories Tathan used to tell. There could surely exist no such object! And not even the native tribes folk would deign to drink blood. "So now anyone who finds the Grail can drink this blood and be healed, is that it?"

"Yes, that's it!" Galienne had calmed after the earlier heresy, and was now getting excited again. "Joseph brought the Grail here, to this very Island. I think it's probably somewhere in Britain. Well, that is, if it hasn't left."

"How would it 'leave'?" Perceval was not about to verbalize the cartoonish image he had of this strange cup just hopping about on its own.

"One of Joseph's descendants. There's a story that someone of his blood line was guilty of some grievous sin. Joseph's line had become the Grail's keepers, but after this sin, it was taken, and we all judged unworthy." She crossed herself again, looking down at the ground floor.

"Who was it? What sin?"

"Perceval, I don't know!" Galienne snapped at him. "We're talking about something that happened a score of generations ago. How can anyone keep track of their family lines that long? All I ever heard was that it had something to do with fornication. Someone must have had some ill relations with someone else, oh, I don't know."

Perceval shrugged at his own lack of an answer. Maybe the bards would know; they studied for years to memorize the sacred traditions. But he had another question. "Gal, how did this Joseph get actual blood in the first place? Hadn't Jesus been strung up to this cross?"

"No, He was nailed to it." She was surprised to hear how casually she said it, as though it were routine for someone to have their extremities hammered into planks of wood, then raised to die a horrible, agonizing death, which came finally, mercifully, only after the weary lungs could no longer draw air. "But the blood didn't come from His hands. A centurion dog tortured Him with a spear."

A *spear*! Perceval's eyes were planning to burst right from his head. What had Tathan told him about a spear? And there was something else. Some other chalice. No, that wasn't it. Some other vessel. He would have to ask the bard.

"What are you thinking?" she said. She expected another of his endless questions. He had a habit of either remaining totally silent, or of asking to the point of growing tiresome.

"Hmm, oh. I was thinking what use a king might have for this chalice."

Galienne seemed not to notice the comment. She had her own thoughts.

"What about you?" he said.

"Perceval," she whispered, "there's something more. My mother once told me that my own father shares some of this ancient bloodline. I think that's maybe why she became so devout, after, after –" oh, she couldn't bring herself to think of that. She *despised* the way she was conceived, the product of hasty, sweaty, sinful lust. She tried to atone for that sin, as had her mother, but the shame never went away. Maybe that was why she grew lax in her faith lately.

Stop that rude talk! She still had her faith; she was simply busy with other things. Like traveling and learning. And trying to grieve for someone who let her feelings for another take precedence over her feelings for her own daughter.

They both sat there, gazing at each other knowingly, lovingly. They had grown to depend on each other in a short time. And their thoughts took them to countless places that night.

Finally, they rolled over, without changing into more comfortable night clothes, and went to sleep. It came soundly for both.

* * *

Some weeks earlier, Nimue was exhausted, then frustrated, then exhausted again, within the walls of Camelot.

The celebrations had actually been pleasant enough, not so full of pious prayer and pronouncement as she feared. Actually, the bishop at Camelot seemed quite an amiable fellow. She began to see why Merlin had taken a liking to him.

There was feasting, music, dancing, and exciting entertainments (Nimue especially enjoyed the knife-jugglers and sword-swallowers). She had even danced with a knight named Yvaine, who likewise was a devout follower of the ancient ways (his feline, alas, had to be kept in Guinevere's menagerie to prevent all hell from breaking loose; Nimue was amused by his use of the Christian reference).

Lancelot requested that the King not single her out for public identification, as was the norm for such functions; her wishes for anonymity were preserved. So far as she knew, only Lancelot and Yvaine knew who she really was.

So why had she been so nervous? Of course, it was the girl. And this Perceval. After the first night, Nimue returned to the quarters (the *apartment*) shared with Llio and Llascoit, and asked that girl more about this aspiring knight. After all, if she truly loved him, then she could provide some insight into his character.

When she reached the building, she had to wait a bit for her new roommates to show. Llascoit arrived quite thoroughly drunk, and promptly passed out, not quite reaching the bed on his way down to the floor. Llio looked rosy herself, but could still walk rather than stagger. *Good*, thought Nimue; *not so gone she'd be a babbling idiot, but with enough in her to loosen her tongue.*

After they both giggled at an unconscious Llascoit, Nimue spoke. "So, gracious hostess. Is there any sign of the man who has claimed your heart?"

"No, Nimue," Llio said, burping mildly, working clumsily to undress and make ready for bed. "So far I haven't seen him anywhere. Oh, and did you hear? There was a funeral earlier today. The festivities were held off until the ceremony finished. I heard the bishop himself did the duty."

"A woman, found in a boat down by the river?"

"Yes, that's right, or so I heard. How did you find out so much?"

"I just walked around, listening." That was certainly true. Nimue had already picked out all kinds of delicious gossip, merely by passing along the crowded streets. She knew of Lancelot, Galienne, and the Orkney brothers, whose mother was nowhere to be found in the city, or so it was said.

"Well, to answer your question, I haven't yet found Perceval. He said he was going to send someone out to check on me, but we arrived here pretty fast after all. With your help, that is." She coughed. "At least my throat problems have gone away, almost."

It was time to get some information. "Llio, I think I know where Perceval may be, but I need your help. What can you tell me about him?"

Llio felt apprehensive. How could this woman know where he was? Still, she did not mind talking about him, and that lovely vintage made her tongue move more easily. She had yet to put together the bits of gossip she overheard herself regarding the sword-maiden and the man who took her away.

"He's, well, he's so beautiful, Nimue. He has this adorable birthmark on his rear." She giggled. "And he's so kind, and generous. He once gave me several Denarii just for teaching him a song that we knew from our days in Cambria."

"So you're from Cambria?" asked Nimue, pretending to make small-talk.

"Yes. And Perceval, too, only he's from up in Powys somewhere. My family is further south. *Was* further south, in Deheubarth. I haven't been back there in years, but my uncle has a holding there."

Somewhere in Powys, Nimue mumbled to herself. Powys was a sizable chiefdom, and she wondered how difficult it would be to find him if that was where he had gone. She had a feeling. She could not utilize the Sight in the castle walls: too many prying eyes and ears, and too much interfering civilization. She had to perform magick to have the same benefits Galienne received just from walking around. Nimue was utterly exhausted, though. She had to get her rest in soon, or pay the consequences.

As if trying to validate Nimue's suspicions, Llio said, "Perceval was going to try and get home soon, to see his mother. He left more than a year ago, and hasn't been back, and his mother sounds like the temperamental type to me."

It made sense. He had incentive to return home, and Galienne would likely be safer in the far reaches of an old Pagan kingdom, where the idea of a woman wearing a sword was, if not fully acceptable, at least remotely plausible.

So, soon Nimue would go there, too. To do *what*, though? Steal the girl away? That would surely not help matters. Maybe just spy on them, make sure the girl was all right, make sure this Perceval would not have his way with her (although she had to admit Llio did not make him sound like such a man). She would keep track of them. And then report back to the Mother at Avalon.

"Are you going to try and find him, Llio?" she asked the girl, now fighting to keep her eyes open.

"Y-yes, I am. If he's gone back north, then I want to find him. I should stop in on that uncle of mine on the way. Besides, I know Llascoit wants to get out for some adventure." She looked at her brother, stroking his side as he lay snoring on the floor.

She continued. "I know I said I'd wait to see what happens in Camelot first, but this party will probably get old after a while. And I guess I need to know how Perceval really feels."

Nimue admired the independence this girl showed; she was either strong, or ignorant of more common ways, or both. Usually women were lucky to come out to their liking in arranged marriages. Perhaps that was part of Nimue's own rigorous devotion to her religion. Goddess was not a politician, forcing women and men alike into advantageous social and economic molds.

The enchantress guessed Llio and her brother would be gone soon. Good. Tomorrow she would ask Llio if she could stay in the apartment longer, if she and Llascoit were heading out of the city.

Nimue desperately needed her rest. She would start to prematurely and unnaturally age if she did not perform her labors on the Other Side, and she no longer had the energy to leave Camelot without resting.

* * *

What Llio heard about the brief funeral ceremony was largely accurate. The woman named Elaine of Astolat was laid in her final resting place just outside the city, in a public cemetery. The King's own mother was buried there, as were Round Table knights slain in duty. The King's father lay at the great stone circle to the east. No one knew if Merlin was buried, much less where.

Baudwin gave the last rites, blessing the cold but still pretty face, crossing her to release Elaine's soul to rise into eternity. Only a few persons came, and word was sent to Astolat to inform any family and friends of what happened. The ceremony was little more than a trusted man of God commending the woman's soul into immortal bliss, the few onlookers bowing their heads to pray with him.

Lancelot, perhaps from guilt, perhaps from a last effort to redeem himself, invoked the courage to read the letter taken from Elaine's body aloud to those present at the brief ceremony while still wondering who might have actually written it. No one said anything, though all in attendance could guess who was referred to in the note. Court gossip had it that these two had lain together, and murmurings were just beginning about their illegitimate daughter who roamed the countryside armed.

Guinevere did not attend the funeral, the excuse being her helping to manage the preparations for the upcoming feast. She had not wanted to see Lancelot that way, especially if he actually felt anything for the dead woman. Lancelot, for his part, felt only grief. He bitterly wondered if the meaning of the note could be stretched to mean the queen as well. After all, wasn't his love for her just as unrequited as Elaine's for him? It seemed so, although Guinevere's honest answer would have been more positive. At least he did not become suicidal over it.

Just closed. Nobody could get him to discuss any of it.

The King had, of course, heard much of the loose-lipped tactless discussions about his knight and his wife. He did his best to ignore it; if he displayed hostility about it, it would seem as though the gossip-mongers spoke the truth. Best just to forget about it. He knew Lancelot spent much of his time at the attention of Guinevere, yet also knew that his champion left the city whenever possible. Lancelot was only here now because the Pentecost signaled the annual meeting of the Round Table. Indeed, almost every member of the Table came this year, an excellent showing; manorial commitments often kept many afar.

The grief was still in the champion's eyes, almost palpable. Arthur could hardly remember the last time he had seen his wife's hero smile. He would have to grant Lancelot his leave soon, for the poor man's sanity if no other reason. Surely some vital quest could be conceived for the purpose.

As for the rest of the city, it seemed that the only sad souls that first day were Lancelot and the new helper in the kitchen, the boy Gareth. The latter was in tears earlier, so Guinevere had reported. Kay had a reputation of being hard on the kitchen staff, and Gareth was still young enough that he couldn't really protest. Besides, he also sought a knightly title, and saw little relevance in the manual labor found in a kitchen. He would soon be off to Jagent for training.

Only the King (and the lad's brethren, of course) knew his true parentage: he was the youngest son of King Lot, born shortly after Lot's death on the battlefield. And of Margawse. The harlot! Arthur wished he could be rid of her, half-sister or no. She was becoming far more of a nuisance than she was worth. It seemed a spring could barely pass without her sending her latest offspring to court. Gareth was different; he requested his own anonymity, not wanting any royal favors as the youngest of a family which served the King well.

Despite the emotional tugging to and fro, Arthur sighed contentedly. This time of year had grown into quite a spectacular event. Arthur chose Pentecost for three reasons: despite the influence of Merlin and Lancelot and the enchantresses, his was still, officially, a Christian court, though the time was close enough to Beltaine that folks could recall their roots. Second, this was the holiday on which the sword had come from the stone.

He didn't take time to brood over the third reason, even if Margawse was just on his thoughts. He breathed in the fresh breeze, smelling the season.

Late spring, going on summer. The time of rebirth, new life, a release from the cold bleakness of death. Arthur should be happy. His kingdom was extremely prosperous, beyond even the imaginings of Merlin. Never mind that his Queen could not produce him an heir (or was his own seed to blame?), or that his hero and friend was silent about what troubled him the most.

He should be happy. But he recognized that being a ruler was perhaps the loneliest job in the world. Who did he turn to when life seemed futile?

No matter. He would be king, the greatest he could possibly manage. The Fellowship was his proudest triumph, the beginning, he hoped, of a balance among ruler and subject. Everyone had equal say in that room with the Table, and Arthur was proud that his seat was no higher than those of his knights.

So who, then, would ever take the seat at his side, in the chair no knight would touch, the one from which many had offered their cases to their monarch's ears? The King stood at the cemetery, the last to return to the safety of Camelot's walls, alone with his thoughts and personal bodyguard; at the moment Agrivaine, Bedivere, and Lucan had that duty. Thoughts of a young girl. And her father.

* * *

Llio had wanted to leave immediately, but it took Llascoit another day and a half before his body fully forgave him for so abusing it.

She remembered, with almost full clarity, her talk with Nimue, who now lay spread on the bed next to her, as unaware of anything as her hungover brother. But she did not drink; what made her so tired?

They had both concluded that Perceval was heading home. Llio was concerned and furious both. What made him run off like that? He did not even bother saying good-bye to her and her brother! For that matter, he did not manage to send anyone back for them, either. She had no way to know Baudwin tried to send aid their way, but they had arrived in the city by then.

At least her throat cleared up, so there was no longer need for a healer, like there seemed earlier. The smoke had been frightful indeed, but it still looked normal. The people in Camelot were swearing up and down that it had been laced with green tendrils, tentacles, *something*. What in the hell would make them think that? Llio was there, and saw no green stuff.

She asked Nimue about the smoke as well. She answered that she was on her way to the city also, and had stopped when the smoke was about half a mile in front of her. Nimue, likewise, claimed no emerald glamour, just a thick cloud, like a small but heavy fire that managed to burn itself out quickly.

Whatever its cause or purpose, what mattered most to Llio was that it separated her from Perceval. She hoped the knighting ceremony would not last long; she wanted to get out of here quickly. What had the King announced to the masses? New candidates judged worthy would be dubbed soon?

Not soon enough, she thought, glancing at her still snoring brother. She could hardly travel without him, and she already agreed to let Nimue stay in the apartment after they left. "So become a knight and let's go," she mumbled to her incoherent roommates. To no avail. They would both be out for a while.

She decided to take a walk. Some air would do her good, help her clear her head. She had to think matters through. What exactly would she say to Perceval when she found him again? How would she be welcomed in her uncle's home along the way? She thought of her father's description of her uncle's stead: Worcester was an old motte-and-bailey overlooking a town (but no longer safeguarding it, such was its age), famous for its worked metal goods and ceramic creations. Oh, and gloves, too, she mused, rubbing her hands together in the slightly chilly morning air. If nothing else, she guessed she could earn her keep there by helping with the glove production. She was skilled enough with her hands, and gloves were difficult enough to be reserved for the most highly trained workers. Maybe Llascoit could help there, too; any place known for its metal products had to be carefully guarded. But why was she dwelling on this? She had no intention to stay there very long; it was just a stop on the way to find Perceval.

She stepped outside the apartment door, drawing as much of the fresh and aromatic air as her lungs could take. The smell of another day's feast in preparation hung in the air, smells of fruit pastries and roasting meats and brewers working to keep up with the demand of thousands.

She stood in the northwest section of the city, long rectangular apartment buildings surrounding her. These were the simple but reserved quarters for those with high status or impressive connections. Llio was just glad her father's own relation with the King ensured that they would be sleeping indoors, rather than with the mass camped outside the gates.

Directly behind her father's own building, she could see the unmistakable rise of Pendragon Castle, soaring up as though it would never tire of reaching for heaven. She smiled, wondering what it would be like to wake up in one of those proud strong towers, with servants to tend her every wish and need. She started walking, let the others awaken when they would.

Llio was surprised that the residents of Guinevere's menagerie had not awoken them all. Granted, Llascoit could have slept through a battle last night, but Nimue? Surely she should have woken. Llio now ambled along the dirt street, listening to the sounds of caged wildlife.

The menagerie consisted of a long strip of land, fenced
in on one side, with the city's invincible wall on another. Inside
were residents both domestic and imported, and all exotic as far
as Llio was concerned. There was a gigantic creature like a great
cat with a bushy mane about its neck in one area by itself, as
though it had special privileges. Other cats like it were here too,
in small groups, lazily lying about in the morning sun. Some of
the others were smaller. One group sported small black spots.
Llio briefly wondered if these were sick with something. In another set of cages lurked two beasts even larger than the great
cats, so big that they half scared Llio to death with their sudden
bellowing, which sounded like a high-pitched scream to wake
the dead. These things surely stood sixty hands high, she was
sure. They were gray with wrinkled skin and a lack of fur. Big
sheets of their skin flapped in the morning breeze; Llio figured
them to be ears, based on their location. And the most unusual
feature of all were the long noses (*were they truly noses?* she wondered) which hung clear to the ground. And they were picking
up straw from the ground with these noses. And guarding these
fabulous noses were the most humongous horns Llio could have
ever imagined. Part of her had to admit there was a certain loveliness to the horns; they were curved, and the color of alabaster.
Llio wondered how such creatures could have possibly been created; maybe Merlin and the bishop got drunk one night and cast
some bizarre magicks on field mice.

She was amused with that image, and kept walking. She
was still trying to relax; her mind still buzzed with images of
Perceval, and she tried to alter the mental pictures by imagining
what Worcester looked like.

Arriving at Gold Street, which led through the center
of town and linked the two main gates, Llio this time heard
the sounds of battle. Instantly nervous, yet too curious for her
own good, she jogged the few yards to the west gate to take a
look. Outside, hundreds of men were indeed dancing about as

though intent on stealing each other's blood, but Llio had seen her brother and, *ahh*, Perceval mock dueling enough times to know that the only spilled blood today would result from accidents. These knights practiced for the upcoming tournament.

She could see dozens of shields from her vantage point at the gate, which was notably absent of guards (some of whom were knights themselves and likely on the tourney field right then); what fool would attack a city, even one with its gate open, when so many capable fighters, the best in Britain, were just outside?

Most of the shields were painted brightly enough that Llio could make out certain emblems and designs. There was a purple field with a gold two-headed eagle on it, the unmistakable arms of the Orkney clan, adopted by Gawaine himself. Across from him Llio could see another similar shield, the same save for a bold red diagonal band through its middle. A brother of Gawaine's no doubt, using an acceptable inheritance model for his personal arms. *It must be Agrivaine*, she thought. Over there, almost hidden, was a hypnotic-looking shield with a black and white checkerboard painted on it. Llio could not recognize whose arms these were, but she thought of playing checkers, another famous civilized import from long ago. She had often played it with her brother, and even persuaded Perceval to give it a go several times. He usually lost to her, but was a good sport about it. Llascoit hated losing; he only dealt with his occasional mock duel losses to Perceval because he considered them knightly equals.

The clanging of metal and wood filled the air, probably rousing those within earshot to an awakening earlier than anticipated. Llio never really liked the sound, yet it reminded her of home, and of... She sighed. She would be there for Llascoit's knighting, but she would be impatient. Until she found *him* again. She hoped Perceval was safe, and thinking of her. She had a glimpse of herself rolling down one of Cambria's gentler slopes with him, laughing and playing like children. She never knew how fully she loved him until she missed him, even if she still had yet to forgive him for his sudden absence!

Llio walked back inside the gate, strolling down the dusty street, impatiently waiting for the vendors to start displaying their wares. She thought she might buy a special gift for someone.

* * *

Nimue was still quite unconscious when it came time for Llascoit's knighting. Llio was at first concerned; their guest had not awoken for days. Llascoit told her he had heard of people sometimes sleeping for days when they were utterly exhausted, as this woman clearly was. They had little idea of just where she truly was.

When she finally woke up almost two weeks later, after Llio and Llascoit had left the city for Cambria, she remembered dreaming of the faeries, both the *Seelie* and *Unseelie* Courts. But she would know that she had actually *been* among them, performing small tasks and works, until her debt was paid. Her glamour in the forest that day was not merely taxing; as a physical manifestation of the Other side into This side, the debt had to be repaid, the sacred balance maintained. Such was the price of dealing with magick.

The *Seelie* represented the faeries that folk cheered for because they were believed (and rightly so) to be beneficial. When the old Pagans and Heathens prayed and performed their rituals and sacrifices and ancient magick in hopes of yielding good crops for a season, the faeries sometimes came out to help. The *Seelie* were forever shy, keeping from human eyes. Their distance came from the knowledge that they were the Mighty Island's first inhabitants, older than time itself. The humans and their painful iron drove them north, or into hollow hills. Iron not only caused injury in the form of weapons, but was also extremely absorbent, or perhaps interferent, with magickal life force; perhaps that was why the likes of Merlin and Viviane were never seen strolling about in mail.

Perceval's horse was named for one of the *Seelie*. His mother would never have allowed that, except that she did not know any better, believing the name based on the mare's richly textured coloring. The other little people, elves and dwarves, were also among the *Seelie's* number. Even the Picts, the "diminutive savages," as the commoners of Logres liked to call them, were descended from them, the result of faerie and human mixing, or so it was told.

Nimue would later be glad she had not been summoned by the counterpart to the Otherworld, the *Unseelie*. She had heard of Pellinore's "barking beast," and knew of other abominations that found their way into This Side, by fortune or by intent of someone with a high degree of Talent. Giants that pillaged entire towns; great winged serpents like those that shook mountains in northern Cambria to their foundations, as discovered by Merlin; spirits disguised as huge animals that cursed lakes, like the loch north of even Caledonia; and nasty-tempered trolls and goblins all roamed This Side, not caring whose lives they took, and proud of the fear they inspired. Generations of human children grew up believing that if they were in the wrong place at the wrong time, the evil faeries would gobble them up.

No, fortunately for Nimue, she would remember blissful times spent in the company of those who served Gwydion, the god of the druids, the patron of glamour, the temporary reality of which Nimue partook for her own purpose. She would sleep, later recalling only images and sounds, but at least her magickal slumber would be peaceful.

* * *

On the eve of Pentecost, the squirely candidates were rounded up by their sponsors, be they knights or the lords that

the candidates would come to serve, or even their ladies (it was
a rare squire who had a lady, since his knight would likely swell
with jealousy, and distinguished ladies were not in the habit of
granting favors to non-knights anyway). Arthur was both astonished and delighted at the turnout; there would be more than
two dozen young men sworn to their lord's sides the next day.
The lord in question for some of these men was himself; the rest
were the vassals of powerful lords, and the King would knight
them both as a badge of great honor to the knight and lord, and
also as a means of further tying the bonds between himself and
the lords. After all, they, like everyone else in the land, were the
High King's own vassals.

The thirty of them who were assembled met, unarmed
and unarmored, dressed only in simple white clothing, in front
of Saint Dubric's. There they were told, Llascoit among them,
that their night-long vigil would commence within the hour.
It was only noon, and the candidates knew they would receive
no more food nor wine nor water until initiated. They needed
to stay awake the entire night, standing or kneeling penitently, thinking about the rights, privileges, and duties that awaited
them when Excalibur was laid upon their shoulders.

Llascoit was as quiet as the other candidates, all of whom
had been ordered to remain silent until called for the following
morning. Many of them received hopeful and excited looks and
cheers from the sizable mass of bodies assembled outside Saint
Dubric's Cathedral. Llio was there too; her bright eager face was
the last thing Llascoit saw before he turned and strolled into the
building.

The place almost burst with its holiness, the godly images and symbols silently screaming for attention. Yet the place
was remarkably solemn. The air was cool inside, kept that way
year round by the stone walls thick as several feet. Actual stained
glass had been imported from the Continent, mounted in the
windows of the cathedral for all to see.

The men spread out as they walked in, Llascoit wishing Perceval could have been with him, trying to understand his sense of obligation that made him run. As a knight he would lose the luxury of being able to travel wherever he pleased at a moment's notice.

Several of the men sat amongst the pews, clasping their hands and bowing their heads, offering whatever prayers they thought appropriate. Llascoit would pray also, but first he wanted to head to the front of this place. The large statue of Jesus was there, seemingly looking at him no matter where he happened to be in the cathedral, such was the workmanship. Or maybe it was miraculous. Baudwin never tired of pointing this feature out to the children each Son-Day, reminding them of God's eyes upon them.

Llascoit knelt at the dais, crossed himself, letting the awe of the place envelop and embrace him. He wanted to utter a prayer aloud, then remembered the order. God should be able to hear all their silent words anyway. He glanced around. In the corners stood a number of knights, all of whom he recognized by description or arms. They would wait the night here as well, offering physical encouragement to those who tired out. They also ensured silence would reign.

Glancing back to the dais, he thought his prayer. *Oh, Lord, hear my thoughts. It is my sincerest wish that Thou makest me a knight in your service, through your earthly representative the King.*

He raised his head. What else needed to be said?

And I pray for my brother-in-arms, Perceval of Powys. May he too prove worthy of this honor in Your eyes. Let us both be true and merciful and brave, and give us the strength to mete justice to all. By Your Grace, I pledge to protect the weak and the innocent with the might that You have placed within my breast and within my sword. Amen.

Llascoit liked how the words flowed through his head. When he opened his eyes he noticed some of the others gath-

ered near him. Behind them the rest were either humbly in the
pews or pacing to try and ward off inevitable fatigue.

It would be a long afternoon. And a longer night.

PART FOUR: THE LOVERS

Galienne and Perceval left Oerfa after just two days, the former not wanting to stay any longer, the latter not really caring about where they spent their time, so long as she could see her friend smiling again. Perceval had a rendezvous he wished to make, to find some old friends. At a place called Worcester.

They spent their first day just wandering the area closer to home, Perceval showing Galienne the river and the ancient bridge, the hill where he once hoped to bring down a huge deer, and where his sister had supposedly gone (though neither wished to venture up the witch's hill). Jokingly they looked for the lost javelin, Galienne making cracks about trying to find a seamstress' needle in a stack of hay.

The villagers had been courteous and warm, and Galienne was still trying to understand how Perceval came to regard them with a sense of distance, almost disdain. Maybe he was just trying to deal with the loss. A *double* loss at that, since no one, not even the bard, knew where his sister was. Galienne wondered how she might react to being back in Astolat, which she'd now not seen for roughly a month.

Galienne listened as avidly to the bard the two following nights as she had when they first arrived. His voice carried her off to realms of which she never dreamed, and her mother likely would have condemned. Yet there was no sense of evil to this man; he was compassionate as Baudwin, with a much better singing voice (the latter's often cracked while reaching the higher notes during the hymns of his own services). For Galienne's own pleasure exclusively, Tathan recounted as much of Arthur's own story as he could. She was enraptured: the mysterious birth in the old stony waterfront fortress of Tintagel, the education and teachings of Merlin (who began to seem far more like a wise old man and less like some devil's son), the drawing of the sword from a stone, and the ensuing battles both to unite the land and repel those who would take it. Nowhere in the bard's rendition came any mention of the pacts princes make to attain and keep their power. Indeed, few admitted to gossiping idly about the King's affairs, or the rumors of his past. What did that matter, if peace could be maintained?

"Do you ever want to be married?" Galienne said, riding solo on Brownie, Perceval walking at the mare's side.

"Me? I don't know. I'm not sure I've ever given it much thought." That was true enough. He was actually terrified of losing anybody else, now that he considered it.

"I don't want to. Any man foolish enough to marry me would have to get used to my being a knight, and I don't know of any such permissive soul. Except Bishop Baudwin." She thought the obvious. "And you."

Perceval looked up at her, wondering how serious she was, noting the smile which greeted him. He loved this girl, but not in that way. Besides, how could two knights travel together if they were also lovers? How could they fight together, being always so worried for the other's safety?

"Well, thank you," he said. "What makes you ask, anyway?"

"Because you keep mentioning this 'Llio' person, but never in detail. Who is she? Is she beautiful? Smart? Wealthy? Devout?" Galienne liked baiting him.

"She's, well, she's —" Perceval at once pictured Llio naked at the lake.

"You're blushing! She's *what?*" This was more fun with each question.

This was like having a talk with Dindraine. "She's very... *sweet.* And nice."

"That's hardly a description worth making yourself embarrassed for. I guess I'll have to wait until I meet her myself."

Galienne was pleased with her growing boldness and assertiveness. Errantry made one radiate confidence.

"Well, it's difficult to talk about. Yes, she's beautiful. Radiant, actually."

"Indeed. But smart, too? Please say yes. I'd hate to think you'd settle for someone dimwitted."

"That she is. She speaks Latin even better than you, and she has the skills to be a castellan."

Galienne loved that thought. "Perhaps she'll have us both as her knights."

"If she inherits her father's keep, maybe she'll do just that." After he said it, Galienne thought, *There, he's smiling again!*

Hopefully, Perceval pondered, the two women meeting would not be long in coming. They had been on the road for several days now, again bypassing features like Rhun, keeping to themselves. The road was still mostly empty of others.

He acquired some indication as to the whereabouts of Worcester from a number of Oerfans. So far he knew it lay in some flat plains land within the Dean Forest. It seemed they would only need to follow a different vein of the road.

Whatever else happened, travel to Worcester was certain to be interesting. To enter the Dean and locate it would necessitate following the main flow of the Severn, south of the Roman town of Viroconium. Perceval wondered if they would have to hire or buy a boat, hoping they could find one large enough for a horse.

"So will I get to meet her?"

"Hmm? Oh, yes, Gal. You'll definitely meet Llio. I just hope she's at Worcester. If nothing else this should be a shortcut back to Camelot."

"Why do you want to go back to Camelot?" She knew it was a ridiculous question to pose to him.

"Don't you want to go?"

"I'm not sure. I know I want to be a knight. I just don't feel ready. I mean, you're a wonderful teacher; I never would have made it this far without you. But –"

"Yes?" he prompted. She was right; she needed more training. Where better to receive it than Camelot? Or Jagent?

"But, Perceval, is Camelot *ready* for me? How do you deal with prophecy, anyway? And I –" she began, her face constricting.

He looked up at her, slowing Brownie with a pat to her head. "What is it?"

"N-nothing," she lied, sniffing.

"Your mother?" He had gotten to know her well.

Galienne nodded, brushing at her face with her hand, feeling her tears cool.

"I think I have some idea of how you feel," was his ever-simple answer.

She halted Brownie, all but jumped down, and fell into his arms sobbing. He couldn't help himself; he started bawling as well. Two motherless children, alone in the world. Suddenly their lives seemed puny, insignificant, as though what they were doing was pointless.

What *were* they doing, in the first place? This was the question running through Perceval's mind, like an annoying itch he couldn't reach.

We are errants, and we will become knights, he reminded himself, clutching her tighter, making her feel safe, comforted. And another thought came to him, more of the words of Oerfa's bard. *The truth against the world.* Individual truth different from world truth; truth relative to time and culture and person. He thought he was finally beginning to understand the bard.

To Camelot, he thought. "Galienne, I know you probably don't want to hear this right now, but have you considered talking to your father?"

She pulled herself from him, her face hot and damp. "And say what! He's made his choices. I don't want to hear how he never loved my mother; I already *know* that!"

Perceval sighed. He'd work more on that later. Eventually, she would have to try and make whatever amends might be possible with Lancelot. Wouldn't she?

"Look, I'm sorry. I'm just trying to help." *How do you comfort someone who has lost a parent?* Especially since the same had just happened to him?

Not *just* happened, his guilty, itchy mind said. It was some time ago, and he missed it. He was off doing exactly what she had not wanted him to.

He closed his eyes. There had never been any message from her, not even news of Dindraine's departure. Had she been that unforgiving? Now he was getting angry; at least it helped ward off the guilt.

"It's getting late. We should go," said Galienne, wiping her eyes with her sleeve and climbing back atop the mare. "How about we camp up on the hill top tonight?"

Perceval followed her point. It led to Beacon Ring.

* * *

Despite his initial apprehension at seeing the old hill again, sleep came easily and peacefully for both of them that night. He wondered if he should tell her about the dreams he once had up there.

It didn't matter. She told him the following morning.

Sure enough, they shared the dream depicting them together, although this time they were clothed, and not in some hall, but a palatial room. Perceval was surprised, though, at the ease with which she related the tale, especially the reference to the earlier version, in which nakedness and a strange third person abounded. She was quickly losing much of her childhood shyness.

"What can either of these dreams mean?" she said hope-fully.

He had to disappoint her. He didn't know. He could not understand where the stony cavernous hall was, or who the third person might be. Much less could he provide any answer to last night's version, much more vivid for her than him.

She filled in the details of what she regarded as her latest vision. She had recognized them both, although a bit older, and they sat at an ornate feast table, and an image came to all present, although later only a few could remember having seen anything.

There was a bright light above the table, so luminous it should have blinded all, but beckoned them instead. It was warm, and *knowing*, as though alive. Galienne had trouble describing that. What she did say, and what confused Perceval, was that from the light emerged a silky curtain, white as the freshest unspoiled snow, and perched on the curtain was an ornate chalice. Galienne awoke at that point.

Perceval listened to her as she passionately tried to convince him that she had seen the Grail itself, revealed not just to her but to anonymous others. She had felt the light on her the longest.

She relayed the tale casually, without the slightest hint of vanity. Indeed, she sounded more hopeful than anything else, for being part of some great chapter in the King's and Logres' life.

Yet Perceval remained skeptical. It wasn't just his usual reluctance for mention of things marvelous, nor was it Galienne's storytelling. It was something else, which he finally told her, when asked why he obviously didn't believe her.

"I was there, too, only I saw something else," he said.

"You mean you were there, but you saw something other than the Grail?" Galienne was dumbfounded. She had been given a symbolic message suggesting that the most Holy of relics might still be within the reach of sinful mortals, and her best friend couldn't even see it?!

"I saw something that looked kind of like a chalice or cup, yes. Only there was not quite so much light. And it looked more like, um, like –" he fumbled for the words.

"Like?" she said, imitating the manner he sometimes used with her.

"Like a big bowl. Maybe a wooden one. I don't know. I can't really remember it all." *But how did we have the same dream before?*

"Hmm," she said, "I wonder what it was." She was convinced of the validity of her own sending, questioning his. "Perceval, do you believe in God?"

He sighed. "Gal, if you're asking me if I believe in things and forces and, well, gods and goddesses, that are beyond us but affect us and help shape us, then, yes, I do. But beyond that, I'm not sure. I used to think Cambria was the whole world, and now I wonder who or what made all this around us." He turned in place, extending his hand toward the marvelous scenery. Something or someone had to surely be responsible for the majesty of these hills and rivers and forests and the creatures who called them home.

Galienne liked his answer, even though it was not what she expected. She was not used to talking with someone willing to consider a multiplicity of deities, or, what did he say? Forces. She learned that every object, every person, everything, was an extension of God Himself.

"I know you believe in God. Like my mother."

"Well, yes. Of course I do. My whole life I've tried to learn about God and the lessons left by His son. Don't you find it heroic that Jesus died for us?"

"He didn't have much choice, did he?"

"He –" Galienne started to say, but then couldn't finish. She did not want a debate they might later regret.

The cool hardness of his mother's cross still hung around Perceval's neck. He had never really considered the implications of wearing such a token.

"Here," he said, taking the cross off, holding it out so Galienne could reach it, "it makes more sense for you to carry this than me. I don't understand what it means. Besides, my faith doesn't grant me the privilege of wearing it."

She took it, passively, so much so that he had to wrap her fingers around it. She felt it in her tightened hand, convinced she could feel a power of its own. She missed her own cross, having fled Camelot so quickly she'd forgotten it, and felt hugely guilty for it, though that guilt was assuaged by Perceval's gift.

"Wasn't this —" she began, but he interrupted her.

"My mother's, yes. Now it's yours." He felt guilty for giving it away, but it might as well be kept by someone who loved it more than he. He did not need any more reminders of his late mother. She put it on at once, having left her old one in her mother's tent, the day she died.

They packed their gear, and two days later were in Viroconium.

* * *

The streets of Viroconium were lined with busy and haggling merchants, displaying wares from all around. With the events at Camelot having finally wound down, the people returned to their own corners of the Island. Viroconium was no exception.

It was clearly a trade town, one of the most important in all Cambria, and there was a noticeable lack of regular guards around the place. Either they relied on the High King's protection or they had their own means of safeguarding traders.

Perceval and Galienne led Brownie through the central avenue, and could not even begin to avoid the hecklers. "Good Sir, would you not care to buy some fine jewelry for your Lady.

Lovely pieces for a lovely woman." Or, "Trade in your horse! I've the finest steeds this side of the Great Forest!" Such were the sorts of pitches thrown at them, anything to make a sale. Much of the merchandise did look quite good, but Perceval and Galienne had other concerns.

They asked directions to the river from a cobbler who waved half a dozen pairs of leather sandals and short boots in their faces before he pointed them in the right way. Galienne enjoyed looking at the various wares, and Perceval bought her a new pair of shoes, which thrilled her. She had never shopped much before, other than to help keep Elaine's work supplied.

Neither had Perceval, but he just wanted to be on his way, and cleared his throat to get her attention whenever Galienne stopped to look at something. She was most pleased with the different horse traders. One had a charger the color of morning-fresh cream, with points the shade of boiled leather. She found herself wishing for the necessary money to buy such a superb mount. Perceval had plenty for travel expenses, but a warhorse, especially one of such a noble color, commanded a fortune.

The town showed its age, and the residents lacked the pride to keep it looking showy. It was a trade town, with one purpose, which was not attracting sightseers. The only children Galienne and Perceval saw were working, helping their parents or ferrying merchandise. The place buzzed with business, and the concern of most of the residents was making enough to pay the taxes and keep their families fed.

Taxes were high here; Viroconium enjoyed almost un-restricted trade through most of Cambria, and the local rulers made sure that the merchants paid for such privileged access. The iron for Melangell's forge came from here, although Per-ceval never knew, thanks to his mother.

Perceval kept plodding on, not wanting to even spend the night. It was only late morning; they could still get some miles in before sunset. And he knew when they found the river by the sound.

He had never seen the Severn so majestic before. At the southern edge of town, the veins leading to his home grew into the wide and deep murky fluid which would eventually flow clear to Gloucester, and into the sea. At once the water looked inviting, teasing Perceval and Galienne with its wet coolness. He wondered if she knew how to swim, and felt proud that he could teach her.

A dock stretched into the river, long and straight like an arrow. Tied to it were a number of boats, each one different, all utterly alien to Perceval.

Having grown up on a river town herself, Galienne knew her way around the various types of craft. She displayed her knowledge to Perceval, pointing to each and offering a brief description. Coracles bobbed slightly in the gentle current, but they were tiny fishing craft, useless to them. A ship unmistakably modeled after the Garmani longboats stood proudest, its eight oars and sculpted griffin's head declaring it the property of someone well to do. Two flat rafts swayed to and fro, long poles upon them for mobility and steering. Finally there was a larger trade ship, with enough deck space to carry a whole squadron of knights, with several men entering and exiting its cargo hold to unload whatever delivery its captain just made. It had an immense canvas sail, rolled up to prevent a glimpse of whatever design said captain had emblazoned on it. The mast holding it was tall enough to warrant a crow's nest, and there was a visible cabin on deck, in the aft section. No ships larger than this could make it so far up the river, and Perceval wondered if larger ships existed. It was almost the size of Oerfa!

The rafts, then, seemed the easiest (and cheapest) choice. And, as though perceiving their thoughts, a voice behind them piped up and asked in a slight drawl, "Be you needing river transport, the two of you?"

The pair turned, and faced a portly and short man, yet with arms more muscled than even Melangell the smith's.

"Yes, we do. Can you help us?" asked Galienne, not waiting for Perceval. She could tell this whole boat thing was just confusing him, and maybe she could help keep costs down if this burly man thought they knew something of boats.

"Aye, Missy, I can. Those rafts over there, they belong to me. You can have either one for six Denarii."

Galienne met the glance of the shifty dark eyes. "Three," she countered, "they look like they've seen some years, and we have far to go."

Perceval glared at Galienne. What on earth was the girl doing, haggling like some corrupt seller with inflated prices?

"Four, and it's yours, Missy. I'll even throw in the poles for free."

"How thoughtful of you." Galienne looked at Perceval, her eyes shifting from his face to the pouch at his belt. Her comment would have sounded sarcastic coming from anyone else.

Finally getting the hint, Perceval fingered around in the coins within his pouch, fishing out the silver coins. He put the coins into the man's outstretched paw, and was met with the response, "Happy to do business with you both. Good sailing."

Before turning away and leaving the two youths alone on the dock, save for the workers unloading the merchant vessel, the man bent toward Perceval, and whispered into his ear, "Lad, who in this family of yours wears the pantaloons, if you know what I'm saying?"

Perceval felt reasonably sure of what the man meant. He gestured to Galienne, who wore breeches bought in Oerfa, to make riding more comfortable. She and Perceval were both well soiled from travel.

"We both do," he said, and turned away.

* * *

The pole-oars took some getting used to, for both of them. They worked diligently to guide the raft over the shallower parts of the river; having a pole not reach the security of the soaked land beneath the water made them a bit edgy. Yet it was enjoyable, unless one could ask Brownie's opinion. The mare took no pleasure whatsoever in riding downstream on a bunch of dead trees fixed together, and had to have a strip of Galienne's precious extra fabric pulled and tied over her eyes to get on the raft at all.

The poles themselves measured a good nine or ten feet, and proved quite useful in getting the tiny craft away from Viroconium's dock. Perceval and Galienne contented themselves to paddling and navigating as best they could.

It was relatively smooth going; they both thanked the powers that be for the lazy current. At least they did not have to contend with rapids!

And by the time the sun cast its orange light upon the water, making it glow like the most brilliant of fires, they were within the vast confines of the forest.

Just where one forest ended and another began was more disputed and vague than even the boundaries existing between kingdoms. Neither Perceval nor Galienne felt quite sure if this was part of the Dean or Arroy, but it definitely had a gloom of its own. Maybe this was the Dean, then.

He could hear Tathan's warning again, and wondered what manner of beings might inhabit this place. He had not mentioned this to Galienne. What could attack them on the river? Then again, they couldn't just drift all night; who knew what surprises the river itself might hold?

The Dean was enchanted, the bard had told him.

"With what?" Perceval asked. With his experience, he found the forest inviting, almost home, free with the creatures who lived within.

"With all manner of things. Dear boy, recall what I said of the monsters we all carry with us, our fears and inadequacies made whole and real." Perceval still was not fond of being called anyone's *boy*, but Tathan had looked serious.

They would have to pull to shore, and make camp for the night, just like they had many times already. But the apprehension persisted; they never traversed such unfamiliar terrain before. Galienne did inform Perceval that she could swim, however. Well, paddle like a dog anyway, compliments of time in Astolat's baths.

They drifted on a little longer, almost due south, the river never changing course more than slightly, until a bank appeared which provided an easy mooring. Galienne led Brownie onto dry land, removing the blinders, while Perceval tied the raft to one of the thicker trees. A good bank it may have been, but the forest here was impassable, especially for Brownie. Everywhere there were trees widened to several feet with age, others fallen which, at best, could be climbed over (provided the climber was limited to two legs). And there were rocks and boulders all about, some so grown with moss that they became camouflaged, and dangerously slick. No, there would be no walking out of this place. Perceval checked his knots on the raft line, and had Galienne do the same.

That night they listened to an entire chorus of bewitching sounds, some familiar, though Galienne was less accustomed to the sounds of the likes of owls and bats. Other sounds proved eerie and unsettling. A screeching noise, growing from a dull wailing, scared Galienne into wrapping herself around Perceval.

Brownie was no fan of the nocturnal noises either, and stayed close enough to the human's blanket bedding that they could smell her grainy breath. The occasional shriek of god-knew-what prevented them from getting a well-deserved sleep. Indeed, the realm of dreams came to them only intermittently.

Galienne and her brother-in-arms both had a sense of other, baleful eyes watching them. They knew they were not alone, and hoped the forest consisted solely of birds, rodents and game creatures. In the distance, though, there came periodic howling, as if from some immense wolf or dog. A bit closer was the disturbing sound of heavy breathing, almost grunting. They had no desire for a run-in with something hungry, and hoped these sounds were really just their own exaggeration of the mare's breath.

Even the tiniest creatures plagued them. Insects buzzed in and out of earshot, and Brownie shook her head to be free of them, while Galienne and Perceval swatted their faces red, more annoyed at missing the bugs than at causing themselves brief moments of pain.

Perceval had the most trouble of all sleeping. Galienne still clung to him, even in her unconscious state, as though to let go would mean certain doom. She did not mind how sweaty they both became from their mutual warmth. And Brownie, nervous and twitchy at first, settled her head down at last.

The sweat and animalistic echoings did nothing to help Perceval's sudden longing for Galienne. He smacked himself again, hoping Galienne would think he was merely swatting at more flying bugs. Her closeness, her traveled but soothing scent, and the feeling of her arms around his chest brought an unexpected and unwanted erection. He fought to clear his head of the lustful thoughts.

Hearing the internal voice of his departed mother helped keep his arousal in check. Soon he forgot about both of them, transferring his sexual speculations onto Llio. Where was she? Did she ache for him at night as he did for her? Was she all right? He hoped she was not also in some part of this dismal forest.

And to touch her! To feel her sweaty form molded to his, their tongues as entwined as their bodies. And to think he had already seen her glorious body, as available to him as the air he was rapidly breathing!

Behind him, Galienne exhaled deeply, rolling around to face the other way. For Perceval, sleep would come only occasionally and partially.

The other reason Perceval stayed awake much of the time was because he considered it his duty to guard the camp. Not that there was much real threat, but he considered it his obligation as a knight. Well, no, perhaps as the ranking errant or squire. No, errant. That was it.

Galienne looked so peaceful, snuggled against him, her breath flowing deeply and easily. Perceval really had to think about what kind of future awaited them. They were certainly two of most unusual candidates ever: he, with his questionable, if nonetheless noble birth. And she, daughter of the man considered the greatest fighter of them all, who sought admission to a club regarded as men's only. She really was starting to believe in the "prophecy."

Somehow they would make it. Maybe.

Morning came as the color of the surrounding flora brightened, from virtual blackness to an inky shade and finally to the green of Galienne's eyes. The water's soothing sound gently prompted all to waking, save those creatures which were most active during the night. Already the sun reflected off the river.

The raft knots held. Perceval thanked God, whether there was a God to care or not.

Brownie was hesitant to board the raft, not wishing more river travel. It was not until she tried climbing her way through the impossible density of the forest's growth, with Perceval giving her free roam so she could learn her own lesson, that she conceded, and begrudgingly boarded the flat craft, again with her soft temporary blinders.

It was several miles further downstream by the time they found the old man and his escort fishing.

* * *

Ah, the city! It was more than Jacqueline could have ever hoped for, and beyond all imaginings of anyone back in Quimper.

And such an occasion. She was delighted to be free of Girard for the festival, abandoning him at his tent outside with the others to frolic about. Neddig, brave boy, insisted on going with her. He said it was for her own safety, and she didn't mind. She could have filled his words with holes; what place was safer than Camelot, and besides, did not he also wish to partake of the newness and wonder of the place himself?

Everything felt free and fresh. The light breeze, the delicious odors, the endless incoherent buzz of thousands talking at once. It was glorious.

They strode in through the southeast gate. Neddig licked his lips when he asked about the sign over one odd little building: the Unicorn's Horn, a busy alehouse. They'd both have to have a drink in there later.

They were still enjoying the sight of the tavern when Jacqueline, her attention diverted by the immense cluster of buildings and trying to guess what each might be, bumped into someone coming the other way.

"Oh! I am sorry," she said automatically, turning to see the victim of her slight clumsiness. And she saw a man standing there, looking hurried.

"No, good lady, no need to apologize now. It's hard enough to avoid walking into people this time of year."

He was a handsome fellow, though not in the way Jacqueline normally fancied. His face was the shape of her own, and he looked almost short despite the link armor engulfing him, as though he had to swim his way out of it each night. The hazel eyes darted about frantically; this knight clearly had trouble with eye contact. And his scarred cheeks were mostly covered by a thick, bushy beard.

He wanted to continue on. The woman stopped him, more from eagerness than rudeness. "I can appreciate that. I've only just arrived myself. Lady Jacqueline of Quimper." Curtsying, she almost forgot. "This is my, er, brother, Neddig." Neddig offered his own bow.

"In Armorica, on the Continent?" asked the man, brightening, but still scanning the area for something unknown.

"Is there another?"

"Hardly. I am Bors, my Lady. Of the clan Ganis, also on the Continent."

Neddig looked about to soil his breeches, and Jacqueline's surprise was just as great. "Ganis clan?" the squire said. "Does that mean, well, please excuse my asking, but does that make any relation to Lord Lancelot?"

"I am a kinsman of the Queen's champion, yes lad. Though I assure you, the relation is distant." It was now obvious Bors tried to hide something, as if mention of Lancelot by name was too difficult.

"I don't understand, though. I thought Sir Lancelot was raised by the, oh, the —" Jacqueline hated stammering. "The Lady. The Lady of the Lake." News of Avalon was slow to reach Continental lands, especially when all Jacqueline heard of it came purely through conjecture. And Ganis. That made Bors somehow related to her! How distant could relations become before no longer mattering?

"He was," Bors said directly, as though that should be enough.

But with this woman's curiosity, it wasn't. "Then how can the pair of you share blood ties, even if distant ones?" The stories were told of Lancelot on the Continent, but what he was actually like in person remained a mystery. He left all familial ties behind.

Bors looked at the ground. Jacqueline immediately apologized.

"No, please don't," offered Bors. "My lady, might I have your permission to escort you and your brother on a stroll of the city, during which I will be pleased to take whatever time you both wish in answering your questions?"

"What makes you think we're so new to the city?" Jacqueline said playfully.

"Because you both looked at this tavern as though you never saw it before, and you clearly didn't know that this is, shall we say, a seedier locale within these fair walls?"

Seedy, is it? Jacqueline would remember. "Lead on, Sir Bors," and she took his arm and followed where he led, with Neddig bumbling on behind them, giddy as a puppy to be shown the sights with a knight as guide.

And they walked on, having to keep a healthy pace just to keep out of the way of so many others. Bors showed them his favorite spots, the half dozen foot bridges which crossed the irrigated branches of the river Cam, the King's stables, home to every breed of equine imaginable, clean enough to not offend even the daintiest of noses, and then the tourney field. Neddig was particularly pleased with the field, imagining himself out there, defending some lady's honor in feats of arms.

Along the way, Bors' guests learned that Lancelot had been sent away for fostering once it was learned what gifts he possessed. Bors enjoyed the response his listeners gave when they heard the Queen's champion was once destined for druidry! Jacqueline could imagine him singing like a bard, but not performing old rites among the oaks.

Jacqueline was stunned by Bors' mention that he had not spoken to his kinsman in some years. "How can cousins not speak?" she pleaded.

"Sometimes relatives just have to go their separate ways," the knight said, letting it go. Jacqueline thought of her own husband, hoping this trip would be the last time she had to speak to him.

As they inspected the stables, Neddig noticed what Jacqueline did not. As they approached another knight, unrecognizable in face as well as arms, Bors subtly sidetracked them all, leading them away from this second knight.

The only part Jacqueline evidenced of that was when she looked back while they left the area, commenting on what a handsome knight the stranger was. She said it as innocently as possible, not wanting to be labeled forward.

"He is indeed," Bors muttered. *Yes, he is, and I know it too well. Perhaps in another time, Sir Trystan, perhaps in another life.* Bors could ill afford to have others spreading rumor about what Lancelot already knew, and he feared that talking to Trystan would lead him to reveal too much. An inappropriate word or gesture could set mouths to flapping. The lips of strangers had too much to reveal already: many folks seemed to be aware of Trystan's love for his uncle's wife. There was even a tale of the pair of them falling mad with love from consuming a magickal potion; else, why take such a risk? Trystan sat at the Round Table, and King Marcus was a necessary royal ally in Dumnonia.

And Trystan had been drunk. Yes, that was it. Certainly drunk with love at any rate, which as all knights were aware, was at least as intoxicating as any wine, even the common vintages which caused headaches and regret come morning. All he had spoken of that night had been *her*, his *"Beale Isolde,"* and that he could never have her, but he was already poisoned with love. Bors had no right to take advantage. But he was so comely, and had it not been for Lancelot's arrival...

No. What was done had to be relegated to the past. Bors couldn't change it now. What would he have even said to Trystan? Or Lancelot? Two of the greatest knights in the realm. Guinevere's own love court decreed that passion was purest and truest when illicit, since so many married for politics or holdings. If the affairs were true, they could rip apart…

"– other knights?"

Bors stopped, missing most of Jacqueline's question. "I'm sorry, Madame, but it proves difficult to hear amidst all this bustling."

"I just asked how well you knew the other knights. And their ladies. Do you know the King and Queen?" Jacqueline felt more gay than she had felt since before her marriage. Did Camelot have this effect on everyone? Neddig, too, wandered in delight, never fearing if his purse would be stolen or if he'd be run down by some heedless knight or merchant wagon.

Bors almost laughed, welcoming the relief from his pre-occupations. "Yes, dear Lady, I know the royal couple person-ally. I have sat at the Round Table for some years now."

Neddig's eyes almost burst from his head like twin firing catapults. "You, Sir Bors? You're a knight of the Round Table?"

"Since before my kinsman Lancelot, but after two other kinsmen, one of them Sir Blamore."

Jacqueline mentally stammered. *He has to be ten winters old-er than I took him for. And Blamore is family, lord to Girard!* It would be rude to ask his age. "Surely you must be landed somewhere back home, with a wife, children to carry the Ganis name?"

"No, Lady Jacqueline. I retain my bachelorhood. That's the term folk used to call we knights, you know. Bachelors. Un-wed, unlanded servants of our lords. Now it just indicates how successful we are in bed." Bors winced at his own words, still bitterly remembering a night long since faded.

"The King must keep his elite knights busy," Jacqueline probed.

"Aye, he does indeed. I was there when we took Rome, was next to Gawaine when he, uh, interceded with the Imperial messengers, and rode with Lancelot on his journey to his keep of Joyous Garde up north. It's enough challenge just making it back here for each annual meeting of the Table." Bors smiled at this memory. He had been terrified at first when Gawaine decapitated Lucius' delegate, but hindsight told him there would have been no peace between the Islands and Rome without resolving Lucius' Roman claims to the purple. The ensuing battle was glorious. Bors had felt quite taken with Gawaine's lusty battle-thirst, with his immense white form accented by the fiery locks.

Jacqueline spoke again. "Sir Bors, is it a safe assumption that you will be competing with the others in this tournament?"

"In both the joust and the melee, my Lady. Be sure to get there early if you wish to see it all; good vantage points get snatched up quickly." Neddig nodded his eager assent, ready to rise before the sun if it would allow him to see the glittering knights make ready for their mock war and lance duels.

"Then would you consider wearing this on my behalf? It isn't every day a girl might have a knight fight with her charms." She betrayed not the slightest hint of presumptuousness, not having given such a token to any man before save Girard, who would never touch her belongings again. She would have liked to give him a certain ring, but that was on the hand of another now, and she hoped Galienne would always cherish it.

Before Bors could answer, Jacqueline unwrapped her *ferronniere* from about her forehead. It was certainly not quite as spectacular as her ring or other similar headbands were, but it was special. Her father gave it to her when she reached the marriageable age of sixteen.

Bors slowly accepted the piece. The thin ornate silver chain had a round white stone mounted in it. It was a larger pearl than Bors thought possible. "Thank you," he said softly. "I shall be proud to wear it."

"The least I can do for my relation," she smiled.

"What? What do you mean?"

"Sir Bors, I have not heard your name before, but you said Blamore was a kinsman of yours. He is also the lord of my, my former lover." She gritted her teeth over the final bit of the answer.

"This lover would have to be your lawful husband, would he not?"

Jacqueline flushed. "Yes, but it should not be! He was bested by someone who made him swear to forsake me, and it has become my hope that King Arthur will overrule this false marriage. I want no more of him!" The memory of Girard made it easy to speak of her dangerous relationship with him.

Bors was too overcome to fret over the endless rules governing who was related to whom, and how or why. He had grown weary of family ties and obligations, which in his mind just led back to some version of the lord-vassal arrangement anyway. "I am nonetheless honored you think of me thus," he said. "And I'll mention your situation to the King myself."

She beamed. "Oh, thank you! Thank you, Sir Bors. May every lady rejoice at the mention of your fair name!" Neddig listened, entranced.

"I do beg the pardon of both of you," added Bors, "but I must be on my way. I was heading for the pavilions when we met, and some of the other knights still await certain news from me."

"Of course," Jacqueline said, then offered him her most graceful curtsy. Neddig also bowed, wishing the man the best of luck with the upcoming tourney.

As Bors strolled off, he thought to himself, *Aye, lad. So far luck is the only lady I have ever intimately known.*

* * *

"Well, all the Saints be praised, if you don't look like the Holy Spirit come at Pentecost himself! Or is it itself?" guffawed the old man in the tiny craft. The younger man seated opposite him in the boat sat motionless and silent, at first out of view of Perceval and Galienne.

"Well, just look at you two, three if you count that fine mare of yours. So, you would surely be the Red Knight of Cameliard then, eh?"

Perceval remembered his armor, and of whom it might remind those who saw him wearing it. He was not nervous about wearing the armor on the river, since he could swim, and remove it quickly if necessary. Yet the river remained calm; only Brownie's periodic nervous jostling of the raft suggested otherwise. Perceval and Galienne had barely worked at maneuvering it all morning, content to let the water take them where it would. Brownie finally seemed to overcome her anxiety, and relaxed in the soothing embrace of the flow. She even occasionally dipped her head over the side to lap up some of the unspoiled crystal liquid, only to be reprimanded by Perceval for almost tipping them over as her weight shifted. As for the fisherman, he must have traveled to know of Meliagrant; Cameliard was yet many miles to the east, further than it looked like this person could likely travel.

He looked at Galienne, who was as surprised by the appearance of these two as himself. "I am Perceval of –"

But he was instantly cut off by the gruff, confident tone of his elder. "– of Oerfa, resting snugly among Goddess' bosoms, er, the hills of Powys, if memory serves."

"How is it you know so much, Sir –"? Galienne carefully dragged out the last syllable, hoping for a response. She and Perceval shared a nervous glare.

"Pellam, young Lady. I am Pellam, a retired knight, and now just a meager landholder." The man sounded pleased with having to introduce himself. His tone took on a sudden gravity, laced with an air of certainty. "And you: you are the Chosen One, judging by that which hangs at your side."

She hadn't thought of the sword all morning; it rested comfortably next to her leg, and she felt accustomed to its presence, as though it were yet another part of her which she would not notice unless she needed it or couldn't find it. With practice, the weapon becoming another extremity, an extension of her.

But now she stood, face to face, with some codger who knew more about them than he should, or could. His companion, though, remained still and expressionless. And both men had yet to stand. They probably didn't want to tip over their small coracle, either.

Yet the coracle took on a life of its own, suddenly rocking to and fro, sending the water rippling in every direction in perfect circles.

Before anyone could utter anything else, the old man laughed triumphantly. "Ha, ha!" he bellowed, adjusting his weight and pulling with all the strength he still retained, which now seemed remarkable. "I've got one!" He instantly forgot the two youngsters.

Pellam's confused visitors barely noticed the long oaken pole with its drooping line until now, the wood bending as the retired knight wrestled with what must surely be a very heavy or very strong fish. The servant's face still betrayed nothing, patiently waiting for his master to reel in his catch. He sat adjacent to Pellam, grasping a net large enough to hold a hunting dog.

Pellam never lost his smile; this was turning into a wonderful day! He felt young again, free of his penance, as he gave the rod a final yank which catapulted a salmon of some twenty pounds into the air. His aide caught it expertly in the net, and it thrashed there, refusing to give up its struggle.

Perceval finally collected his thoughts as best he could, though they stretched out from him in too many directions to track, like the water ripples. "Lord Pellam," he said, thinking the addition of the title would impress the man, "since you seem to know something of us, then could you tell us of your lands, or how far we are from the town of Worcester? We seek someone there."

Still admiring the day's prize, Pellam said, "There always is time for questions, lad. And answers, too. But come, please, let us paddle on to my castle. It's just a bit further on. It's called Bridgnorth. And this is my servant, Clellus. He'll take care of you when we all arrive. Now, how is that for a start, eh?" Talking to the youngsters was the most pleasing activity he'd had in weeks. It almost let him ignore the pain for a change.

"Sir, I do apologize if I have offended you. I was only trying to determine how much travel we might have left before us."

"Oh, dear boy, you haven't offended anybody. Besides, the two of you look as though you're about to fall right off that raft from exhaustion. When did you last sleep inside, anyway? And if you'll pardon my saying so, you both smell more like a dung-heap and less like the knight and lady you are. I can smell you clear over here." Raft and coracle were still a good many yards apart. Galienne anxiously sniffed at her shoulders, wondering how offensive she and Perceval might have become to the noses of others.

Ah, but there's where you're finally wrong, sir, Perceval thought, keeping his internal voice to himself. He was still not a knight, and at his side stood one who would likely never wish to be called Lady.

But, like Merlin reading thoughts, he added, "Oh, I am sorry, daughter of Lancelot. I know you think of yourself as a knight too; it's just that I've never seen the likes of you before." Galienne finished her nasal self-inspection, concluding that they really should bathe soon. Mention of her father roused her.

What *hadn't* Pellam seen? Perceval wondered nervously.

"H-how?" Galienne began, in a virtual whisper. It was all she could get out. Could there be someone else who shared her gift? She had heard of others like her, never mind that her mother had branded them all as demonic soul-sellers.

Perceval turned to his friend. She looked tired, the travel seeming to catch up all at once. He, too, felt the weight of their journey from Oerfa. He suddenly felt like reclining and snoozing right on the raft. The flow of the water had a way of absorbing energy.

"Galienne," he waved his hand in front of her face. She closed her mouth, swallowing so that her dry throat could moisten again.

"Gal, maybe we should accept his hospitality. We could use the rest."

She turned to him, her eyes seeing more than he knew. "Besides," he said in a quieter tone, "hopefully we can get some more answers at this man's home."

So far, it seemed Tathan's warning had been appropriate.

* * *

Bridgnorth Castle seemed unnecessarily large, given its number of inhabitants. It lay just over a mile southward of where Galienne and Perceval met their unusual hosts, whom they beat there by a few minutes. Clellus had to row by himself, whereas the two younger persons, despite their fatigue and Brownie's added weight, could outrun him.

Bridgnorth's most immediate feature was its round symmetry. Three towers spiraled their way skyward, each capped with a pointed rust-colored tile roof. The walls linking these towers and providing the outer shell of defense curved like the moon in waxing and waning stages. The castle resembled a circle, with the bulges of the towers the form's only interruptions.

The locale's other principal feature was its namesake bridge spanning the Severn, still under construction, although

Perceval and Galienne could see no evidence of workers. They left behind signs of their previous labors however; the bridge, laying just south of the tiny dock near the castle, still had attached scaffoldings, picks, yokes, and stacks of the materials of construction. The laborers must have already gone home for the day. The bridge stretched clear across the broad Severn, yet still had gaps.

The place was silent, castle, bridge, and landing, all but hidden among the verdant depth of the surrounding forest. No one called out to Perceval and Galienne. No one opened the well-polished gate in the closest tower.

Not until Pellam and his retainer arrived.

Clellus was busily tying the coracle to a tiny dock along the east bank of the river. Perceval and Galienne had already left the raft there, also tied safely. All were glad to be on solid ground again.

Yet Pellam refused to get out of the tiny craft, and it seemed Clellus was deliberately ignoring his master, wanting to get to other tasks first, and he walked over to where Galienne and Perceval stood.

Using no more communication than an outstretched arm, Clellus gestured to the castle, then followed his guests as they walked slowly toward the gate, looking at every detail as they went. Clellus took Brownie by the reins and led her. She snorted her disapproval at first, and only began to walk at Galienne's beckoning.

Perceval turned completely around as he walked, observing the depth of the forest, considering that without the raft and the safety of the castle's walls, he and Galienne would become hopelessly lost. He really was not the best navigator; he just followed obvious paths, like rivers and roads. He wished they both could find their way about with the help of the stars. Perceval only knew the basic directions, depending on the sun's location.

There appeared to be no road to this place, not even a path. And the ground leading to the castle looked like it received little foot traffic, and none at all from anything heavier, such as horses or wagons. Galienne noticed this too; Perceval could feel her tension in her grip on his hand.

The castle remained silent, although the gate did open as the party approached. Who was responsible for the action remained hidden, likely in the tower containing the wrought-iron security. Perceval stole one last glance toward the river landing. Pellam still sat in his fishing boat, looking out upon the river. Perceval wondered how cozy anyone could be in this place, this vast forest, this strange castle, with someone who seemed to know as much about him as did Galienne. Maybe the place *was* enchanted; was this the Other Side?

He passed through the gate, thinking he likely would not know something enchanted if it came up and bit him on his posterior. He quickly looked behind him to see if anything might be trying just that. To his rear, there was only the servant leading his horse.

Again he wished he'd paid the old bard more attention, or at least been less cynical in his response to the old tales. Creatures who could make themselves invisible or breathe fire, distressed damsels who were really witches, deities who walked among the mortals; Perceval heard stories of them all, and never believed in them. He wondered what sort of magicks might exist in this forest.

And this old man, Pellam: he *knew* about them, traveling towards his castle, as though he could smell them coming. Perceval wished Tathan was with them.

The inside of Bridgnorth displayed an empty stable and a long, roughly oval keep, spacious enough to contain living quarters and a sizable hall. The keep rose a good thirty feet, and it was painted brilliantly all about.

The incomplete painting was a collage, the individual representations whirling together as though the most unforgiving winter wind had blown them about. Galienne instantly found a depiction of Jesus on the crucifix, an armored Roman horrendously poking at his midsection with a spear. The centurion's armor looked strange: it only covered the man's chest and shins, and he wore an oddly shaped helmet, with some kind of hairy brush protruding from the top.

Perceval noticed what must be the Round Table; a huge circle was shown, with armored and proud-looking knights gathered about it. The seat next to the King stood empty as the other knights gawked at it. They were good likenesses. Galienne frowned, noticing the image of her father at the King's side.

But that was only the beginning. Clellus let them be, mesmerized by the work, and saw to Brownie's needs in the stable which had not sheltered any creatures, two-legged or four-, in some time. Then he entered the keep near the image of Christ, unobserved by Perceval and Galienne.

The two youths circled the surprisingly large keep independently. Galienne was surprised to find, in addition to the previous themes, pictures of faeries, none of which seemed as terrifying as her mother had depicted. Some even looked attractive. One was a handsome thin man, with the pointy ears of an elf or devil, holding a long spear in one hand while tipping his cap with the other. His skin was very dark, making it look like this individual would hide well in the forest; his spear and cap were both colored crimson, like blood.

Perceval next found a lovely scene of some tiny islands, with one rising above the others. It had a church or similar building on top of it, and all the islands were mostly hidden by misty fog. A minuscule boat with several persons on board paddled towards this island that was half in and half out of the mist.

Some of the images were life-size, others so small they had to be looked at up close to determine what was what. All were quite well done, looking like the product of the same artist. How long could this work have taken? And how did someone manage to paint the two dragons clear at the keep's top? One was red, the other white, and they were trying to kill each other. A ruined castle lay next to them. Perceval looked around the courtyard, small as it was. There was nothing he could see that would enable a person to get that high, except...

The stable. There was a wooden frame of some kind next to the stable. It appeared sturdy enough to support someone, and had a ladder on one side of it. He indicated these to Galienne, who deduced their purpose. They wondered if they would get to meet the artist.

They separated again, looking about. Then Perceval circled back whence he came, searching for Galienne, and he almost bumped right into her. She busily inspected a picture of an immense creature, looking like a huge cat, except that it was golden brown in color, and had some darker colored hair around its neck. It was fighting with something long and slender, with a hideous forked tongue. Perceval recognized the serpent, although he still did not know its name. Near the struggling creatures, some other cats, more normal-sized and looking like the big ones' offspring, were hidden behind a boulder. Perceval thought the long forked-tongue thing would get to them if it finished off the big cat.

"Perceval, where in heaven's name have we arrived?" whispered Galienne.

He could only shrug. He had no idea. He wanted some answers, and he wanted to get to Worcester. If only they weren't so tired.

Mysterious or not, Perceval decided, their host would grant hospitality, at least for the evening. He and Galienne could get fed, some decent sleep, and maybe even some fresh supplies.

"Won't you join us?" came the voice behind them. Galienne let out a yelp. Perceval's heart tried to jump from his chest. Both turned to the voice's source.

Clellus stood there, impassive as ever. At least he had not taken a vow of silence like Merin.

"Join who?" Galienne said, greatly annoyed at being surprised. She disliked surprises, especially when she knew the man had sneaked up on them silently enough to have killed them, had he wished it.

"Why, Lord Pellam, Maiden Galienne. He has bade me invite both of you to his supper this evening. You will stay, yes?"

The question was innocent enough. "Has your lord come up from the river, then?" Perceval asked, thinking the question a bit rude. But he was really curious; what did Pellam do, just sit in the boat all day?

"Yes, Sir, he has. And we will be serving up the most scrumptious food momentarily. If you please, I'll show you to your quarters. The servants have left some fresh water out for you both to freshen up with." Clellus again gestured with his long sinewy arm. He was dressed in a pleasant blue tunic with matching breeches, with a tabard over the tunic, showing a pattern of alternating red and white squares. His voice was raspy, as though he did not talk often, yet his diction was flawless, the syllables all receiving their proper enunciation. He was a full half foot taller than Perceval, yet had the bearing of a true gentleman.

Perceval and Galienne allowed him to lead them inside.

* * *

The knight was just glad to be heading home, along with his brother. Camelot had grown too crowded in recent weeks, and besides, he needed to check on the status of his kingdom.

Gawaine of Lothian, eldest and probably proudest member of the family named Orkney, presented a daunting enough figure since he almost appeared to stand in the stirrups when he rode. Even his towering destrier became visibly nervous whenever his master was in a foul mood, and such horses as these were known to keep their wits about themselves, even in battle.

Gawaine himself had a braided mop of hair so red it glowed, radiating the midmorning sun. His eyes matched the nearby sea in both color and severity, and yet this virtual giant had a reputation for compassion, which he had carefully cultured. His nickname at court was "Silver-tongued," as he could use his voice sweetly and persuasively as any bard. Arthur sought his counsel on more than one occasion as an ambassador, even though Gawaine's temper got the best of him on the Continent some years back.

His prowess and courage remained legendary. He was the only one who accepted the Green Knight's challenge, dutifully following a prescribed quest, then learning that the other knight only wanted to test him. Gawaine had great belief in justice ever since.

But that was long past, and now they were returning, at their mother's request. Gaheris rode with him. Agrivaine was in Camelot, young Gareth sent into tutelage.

And Mordred. Gawaine sighed. He wondered how long the child might have lived had Lot survived. Not very, he surmised. Lot could be quite jealous, never mind the women other than his wife that he bedded. And there were rumors of the High King having something to do with that child in the first place.

That bothered Gawaine, for several reasons. First, Gawaine had already been named regent of Logres, in the absence of an heir. He understood that if the royal couple could produce a child of their own, such a position would be relinquished. Second, the brat Mordred could prove quite worrisome if word of his lineage (even if only rumored) got out. It might be the first spark that would engulf the whole Island in an inferno of rebellion, just because the child could never be acknowledged. Guinevere would not have it, nor would the court.

But Mordred, for his sake, wasn't all bad, Gawaine admitted. Just spoiled. Hopefully the hard work required to transform him into a knight would temper his unruly manners. Gawaine was almost sorry he missed those first embarrassing times when the boy fell from his horse while mastering riding.

He sighed again, suddenly wishing for the early days, when he was sole champion, when the Round Table had scarcely any members at all, before the arrival of that troublesome Lancelot.

Gaheris noticed him. "What are you thinking about, brother?"

Gawaine looked at his younger sibling, darker of hair and eyes, every inch of him Lot's son; Gawaine more closely resembled their mother. "I was just thinking of the old times. Life at Camelot used to be so, so –"

"Simple?" his brother said. Gaheris often finished sentences for others. It was an annoying habit, one which kept anyone from getting very close to him.

This time Gawaine found no annoyance in it, though. "Yes. It used to be that things were easier in Camelot. The people didn't talk so much, and no one questioned the king's ways."

"Are they being questioned now?"

"Gaheris, look. I had no doubt in Arthur at all, not even when he made Lancelot the Queen's champion, and started perhaps more gossip than he should have. I'm sure that the Queen was quite influential in that decision. But now, with what we've just done, he just expects all of us to –"

"Get along with each other, no matter what?"

Gawaine considered it. "Right. He has to realize that with so many men at his table, from so many backgrounds, there will be conflicts. Now I can understand not acting these feuds out in the royal hall, or even in Camelot. But to forbid his knights from settling their grievances absolutely? I think not. And then there are the other problems."

"Brother, what kind of talk is it for a man to so openly disagree with his liege?" Gaheris was a proud and devoted servant of the crown, a Round Table member himself. In his eyes Arthur could do no wrong.

Gawaine stopped his mount, then looked at his brother sternly. "You know I would give my life and soul for that man. I am proud to have fought at his side. Gaheris, I know you're almost too young to remember, but I even fought against our own father for him!"

"Exactly. So how is it you can question him now?"

Gawaine had no immediate answer, just nagging, vague concerns. They both continued riding.

Gawaine had never felt love for his father, and, family loyalty or no, never felt much guilt either for supporting the boy king, who was almost his same age. Gawaine would never forget the beatings, nor the scars that he had said on more than one occasion came from the battlefield. He grew to hate his father. Lot was obsessed with turning his kingdom further and further away from the example set by the Romans, and it did not help matters for Gawaine as a child to hear his mother talk about their "Roman son."

Lot had always prattled on about how Rome should have done this, shouldn't have done that, and his answer to the factionalism that crept into Britain was to build a big wall around his own home and kill anyone who might try to cross it. Gawaine knew it was ridiculous; who would attack an isolated, cold, barren kingdom like Lothian? No one besides the Picts, who were too poorly armed and organized to be much more than an occasional nuisance.

Lot wanted a Pagan kingdom, and was ecstatic when he managed to wed an appropriate woman. A sorceress, no less, or so it was said! He just hadn't known of her blood-tie, even if distant, to the new king. He kept his desire to get rid of her to himself, for fear of her transmogrifying him into some lowly creature (who could kill a sorceress?) But he never stopped fathering children on her, and she never stopped caring about him. Lot was just another of their children to her.

So the people of Lothian regressed to the Old Ways. Not much of a step for them, since the place lay far north of the Wall. Most wanted no part of Arthur's rule, which was why Gawaine chose to remain a figurehead. Officially he was king there, but decided it best if his mother ran its affairs. She craved the power.

Gawaine wanted decisions like these to be easy again. It was simple to oppose the father he already hated, who beat him mercilessly in the ignorance of his mother. "Don't worry, wife," he would say, "those cuts and bruises are part of becoming a warrior". It was just as simple to allow Margawse to single-handedly govern a wild kingdom of Pagans and Heathens. And it was simple to hate a man like Lamorak.

That was the part which always confused Gawaine, his hatred of that man. Perhaps he felt some of Lot's own jealousy; what man would be good enough for his mother? Especially if that same man was the offspring of the man responsible for Lot's death in the first place? Perhaps it was the ancient code that the Christians adopted for themselves, calling it "an eye for an eye," or some such. The debt was settled, the balance restored.

And yet Lamorak had done nothing to Gawaine personally. He was just another knight trying to find his place. It wasn't love for his father that drove Gawaine to hunt Lamorak; it was that his mother deserved better, should have taken better. She wasn't thinking clearly, that much was certain. How wise was it to take into one's bed the son of the slayer of one's spouse?

That, and Margawse had tossed out certain allegations, made sure Gawaine heard them. When those in the know questioned Gawaine's ability to switch loyalties, what they did not realize was that he saw it as two-fold vengeance. He'd kill the offspring of the man who took his father, but more importantly, he would also kill the thief and rapist.

Only her own sons knew of Margawse's empty accusations, which sealed the fate of a man of whom she had simply grown weary, not needing him any longer. And Lamorak hadn't wished to leave when told.

"Well?" prompted Gaheris, tired of being ignored.

"Oh, nothing. I was just thinking again. I wonder what our mother has planned for us this time. She surely summoned us in a hurry."

"She probably just misses us, now that the others have left."

Gawaine considered that, too. He began to wonder why Margawse was so insistent that all her sons become great knights. What might she be planning now?

"You're probably right," he said noncommittally. And they rode north.

* * *

Finally, there were some people present. And attractive ones, no less. Perceval and Galienne were greeted by a round of warm smiles, coming from some of the most beautiful human faces they ever saw. Two young men stood near one corner of the room long enough to gaze curiously at Galienne, then went on with their task of setting for a grand feast. Three girls, one with shining blonde hair like Galienne's, another with rich onyx hair, the third a flaming redhead, paused near the young men, and all three cast their eyes on Perceval. They, too, were otherwise engaged, each carrying pitchers and goblets toward the table.

Clellus let them all be for a few moments, allowing the guests to get a feel for the atmosphere of the place. The entry and feast hall were magnificent, with no expense spared to make it grand enough to rival any keep in the realm. The wall behind the table had more art work on it, and although more scenic, it was just as captivating to observe. The likeness of Camelot was painted on this wall, in all its radiance, towers and buttresses all rising proudly into the endless sky, the city's inhabitants mere colored specks lining the streets and poking out of windows.

There was no visible coat of arms present; Pellam said he retired, but wouldn't he still keep his shield device displayed in here? Perceval would have to ask him about that; he just hoped his host would not be offended by the question.

The candelabra illuminating the place were brilliant. Three golden pieces, each holding a trio of brightly burning candles, stood on the table (round, Perceval noticed). Another half dozen similar pieces lined the other, unpainted walls. What lord would not be proud to boast of such a room?

Wanting to offer them a chance to freshen themselves, Clellus led Galienne and Perceval toward the stairs, leading them up to the second floor. This level consisted of a short hall flanked by several doors, with another set of stairs at the hall's end, again leading upward.

Clellus stopped in front of one of the doors, a heavy oaken piece carved to resemble the depths of the forest. It was well enough done that Perceval could identify several of the trees in the carving. An oak, an ash, and a fir were easily recognizable.

The door swung open noiselessly, Clellus having to make little effort at it, and within the small room was a bed just wide enough for one, looking soft enough to cause total relaxation in seconds. Near it stood a small end table, with a bowl of water on top of it. A window overlooked the courtyard, offering a view of the stable below. Brownie was contentedly munching on some grain within.

"This shall be your room, Perceval," Clellus said, the words sounding like a command.

Perceval and Galienne quickly exchanged glances; they were no longer used to sleeping apart from each other, and relished the comfortable sense of security that lying next to a warm, friendly body offered. Galienne no longer thought it the least bit sinful. They had no carnal knowledge of each other, and might as well have been related by blood anyway, they had grown that close.

"Where is Galienne to sleep, then?" Perceval asked shyly.

"Ah. Maiden Galienne shall be right behind us, across the hall." Clellus gestured, and the guests turned about to see another wonderfully carved door, this one showing various religious depictions. Galienne thought the cross and chalice of the Mass quite lovely; both were ornamentally detailed. Twin roses entwined the cross, while spiral-like knotting appeared on the chalice.

The door also featured an image with which Galienne was unfamiliar, although Perceval recognized it, or thought he did. The wood showed its carvings of four items, or relics; Perceval was unsure. He knew he could remember Tathan speaking at length about things like these, but now he had trouble remembering. There was a sword, looking as though flying, a stone lying on the ground nearby, a spear with flames surrounding it, and a bowl filled with some liquid.

Clellus opened this door as well, revealing a room decorated identically to Perceval's. He told them these were the guest quarters, and that the residents of the keep made their homes higher up, within the third floor. "You understand," he added, "that it is only proper for you each to sleep privately. The Master would only allow otherwise if you were married."

Galienne blushed a bit at the mention of marriage. She had been taught this way, after all, and supposed she would just have to content herself with a night alone, like the nights of her childhood.

Perceval wanted to ask him how often these quarters were used, but changed his mind. He'd wait until later, or else not ask at all.

Clellus left them there after announcing he would go to the river to fetch their precious few things from the raft. They had completely forgotten them, and were surprised by how much Clellus noticed. No one here seemed to miss much.

Until he returned, each guest checked out their quarters. Both rooms were a bit barren, but cozy. Galienne's window looked out upon the courtyard and the castle gate through which they entered. She saw Clellus walking quickly down to the river. The incomplete bridge lay slightly within her view, beyond the walls.

Both washed their hands and faces with the cool water which smelled of fresh roses. Perceval could swear it had a slightly bitter aftertaste as he drank just a few meager sips, and Galienne said it was probably just a difference in the quality of the well.

"But this place is so regal," protested Perceval. "Why would everything be perfect other than the water? It really tasted funny."

"Oh, would you just relax! You're starting to sound like my mother." At the unconscious mention of the recently deceased, Galienne crossed herself, looking up, as though her mother were staring down from on high at her.

I'm starting to sound like my *mother*, Perceval thought. He wanted to utter some witty retort, but Clellus was back, holding the blanket and its contents: spare clothes and the few meager rations they still had. He was quick.

"I was unsure of what to bring, so I brought it all," said Clellus, sounding more light-hearted than before, like a child who has just done something good to please the parents.

"Thank you. We'll get it organized ourselves," answered Perceval, still trying to decide whether to trust this man.

"The evening dinner will be starting soon. Please come down as soon as you're ready." With that, Clellus disappeared back downstairs.

Perceval took the bundle into his room, Galienne following. He dropped the contents out onto his bed, and they both rummaged around, locating their fresher clothes. Perceval knew it would take some extra time to get out of his armor, and he asked Galienne to help. Expertly she unclasped the buckles on the leather straps which held it all together as one piece of protection. Then she helped him pull the chain chausses off his legs. They always stuck a bit uncomfortably at the ankles, and it took a little twisting and turning to wrest off the lower part of the armor. Perceval stood there in his undergarments, having long ago lost his embarrassment at being seen this way, at least in the company of Galienne. The mittens came next, and finally the hauberk. There were no separate boots to this ensemble; the bottoms of the chain feet were metal reinforced with hard leather soles, to protect from not just injury, but also from simply walking along the ground. The armor would need cleaning soon to prevent rust, and Perceval wondered how Meliagrant had cared for it; mail normally was shaken in a bag of vinegar and sand, if they could find any.

Perceval stacked the armor next to the end table, the redness of the protective joint plates dulled somewhat by the dusky sky beyond the window, then fished through the extra clothes. He put on his brown and stained soft cloth breeches and a white tunic (well, mostly white, anyway, this too being a bit soiled) with ruffled cuffs at the ends of the sleeves. He pulled his short boots up over his aching feet, ran his fingers through his matted hair, and felt himself as ready as he would get. He splashed some more of the rose water on his face, and thirst compelled another swallow, although he was still curious about the aftertaste.

Galienne, too, made herself more presentable. Her undergarments were slightly fresher, not having been soaked with the sweat that armor encouraged. She still had a lovely midnight blue dress with her, unworn since she left Camelot. She scooped up a couple handfuls of the water, wetting her long hair and her face. It felt soothing, and it tickled as it ran down her neck, between her shoulders and breasts. She had not felt any urge to make herself attractive since before Elaine's death (which was vanity anyway, she could almost hear her departed mother say). It felt good to be attending the sort of function which would have made her mother envious, vanity or no. She also put on the new shoes Perceval bought for her in Viroconium.

They met outside their respective rooms, closing the silent doors behind them. Arm in arm, they walked downstairs to the feast hall.

Already the scents wafting up their noses were divine, meeting them while they were still halfway up the stairs. They had trouble identifying the individual food odors; many delicious aromas swirled together to form the enticing, inviting smell which beckoned them further. Galienne and Perceval could feel their mouths moistening, and had to lick their lips to keep from drooling.

They arrived downstairs. The table was trimmed well enough to receive the noblest visitors. Several individuals stood behind their chairs, waiting for Pellam's entrance, which would signal the beginning of the feast. The table itself was draped in a silky sheet of material that reflected the light from the expensive and rare candles. Dinner bowls of hard rosewood accompanied every heavy ornate chair, along with spoons and knives of polished silver which reflected as well as any mirror. Several bouquets of flowers stood proudly on the table, nested within glass vases which sent colors dancing in all directions.

Truly it was an appetizer of heaven, Galienne thought, already feeling the rapture of this strange old man's company. How wealthy must this Pellam be to afford such brilliance? He had clearly been quite a successful knight; she wondered to whom it was he swore his allegiance. *Someone* had to have been this man's lord; mercenary knights and errants were known for their struggles against destitution.

They had just reached the bottom of the smoothened stone stairs when Clellus arrived, as usual, to show them where to go next. He led them both to the far curve of the table, standing them together amongst the other diners.

Everyone was silent now, simply awaiting the arrival of their host. Clellus departed the room, presumably to escort the older man.

Is this a good time to make idle talk? Perceval wondered. Galienne seemed too preoccupied with the appearance of the table and the room, her eyes shifting over everything in sight, drinking it all up into memory.

Clellus had made no introductions; Perceval and Galienne did not even know if these others standing with them were fellow guests, or more inhabitants of Bridgnorth. Three of them stood there: an older woman, perhaps a grandmother, staring at Perceval with, compassion? Admiration? Perceval was unsure. At any rate, the years had been less than kind; she was a shriveled and ugly vision of what might have once been a more attractive self. She had to be ancient! Another woman stood there as well; if not for Llio's racking, painful reaction to some smoke one day, Perceval might have recognized this woman. She gazed excitedly at both the younger guests. She wore a forest green robe over the same-colored gown. No ornamentation was visible.

And there was a man, barely older than Perceval, with long wild native hair tied back in braids. He was thin yet stood with more confidence than the others. Like Perceval once had, and which Galienne now did, this man wore a cross at his neck. Yet its base was shorter, making it seem more square, and it was adorned with spiral knotting similar to those carved into Galienne's door. His eyes looked gentle but knowing, and he frequently peered behind him, checking on something of which only he knew.

Again the urge to start speaking overtook Perceval. Would that be considered rude? He wanted to know more about these people. They all seemed so official. The older woman still stared at him, with her ambiguously emotional glare which was the only part to shine through her scarred and wrinkled ugliness. What might she know? Already there was at least one person here who knew too much, the lord of this house himself. Perceval felt unwelcome at this gathering.

The anxiety drifted away as Pellam entered, although he had some help with his arrival.

An additional chair was carried in, with Pellam perched upon it. Clellus carried one side, while the other was manned by a house servant, previously glimpsed preparing for the meal. The latter appeared to be truly struggling to keep his master airborne. Clellus was far stronger than his manner and look suggested, having no trouble with the task at all.

The two men carried Pellam up to the table, setting his chair gently to the floor, the younger in a light sweat. He looked glad the job was over, for now. He then immediately turned and left for the kitchen. His outfit was interesting: black trousers, white shirt, and a red and white checked tabard over that, something like Clellus.' Another servant, lurking in the kitchen, was dressed identically. Perceval thought the squares of alternating shades might be connected to Pellam's shield, now retired, somewhere. He would like to see that sometime.

Pellam was dressed in a rich robe, of some elegant fur. Silver fox, perhaps, or wolf. He looked weary, though his eyes bespoke an unusual energy for one who lived largely alone, who was getting older faster than he wished to. And who was often in agony. But he could not openly discuss that, not with just anyone.

Clellus remained, and spoke.

"Honored guests, on behalf of my lord, Sir Pellam of Gwynedd, I bid you all welcome to Bridgnorth Keep. May your stay be a pleasant one. First, however, I have been requested by his lordship to make certain introductions."

Clellus circled the table slowly, reciting each guest's name and home in turn. He included no titles for anyone, and began with the two youngest.

"Perceval of Oerfa." He strolled next to Galienne, while Perceval was greeted with nods of recognition from everyone else present.

"Galienne of Astolat," Clellus continued. Then he proceeded to the older woman. Galienne smiled feebly at the mention of her name, unsure of how to act and feel in the presence of the others.

"Kunneware of Gwynedd," he said, from behind the older woman.

Next was "Nimue of Avalon," said from behind the other woman, who rarely took her eyes off Galienne. She looked kind and eager, but perhaps demanding and impatient.

"Taliesin of Carmarthen" completed the introductions. And the feast only became stranger from there.

* * *

Lancelot had arrived late, but that could not be helped. It had proven difficult enough to keep up with the unlikely pair; they possessed a drive and an energy he had not seen in some time. It was the same ambition and purpose that Nimue exhibited when he spoke with her in Camelot.

Arthur had personally asked him to follow his daughter and the errant Perceval, partly to ensure their safety, and partly to spy on them (Lancelot was impressed how his help had been unnecessary back at the pavilion; the lad dispatched the boisterous knight Girard gracefully). This was the first time the champion ever made a concentrated effort to see about his daughter. He disliked doing so from behind the scenes, but some view of her was better than nothing.

How she had grown! Had it been so many years since Lancelot had unwittingly lain with Elaine? For the first time, he felt some sense of pride in what transpired from that evening. He and the late "Lady of Astolat," as they were already referring to her back in the City, produced a marvelous child. A willful, intelligent, and yes, attractive girl. Lancelot was as much impressed by Perceval's restraint around her, especially since they slept side by side; another must have claimed his heart.

Lancelot tried to ignore the aching throb of his own heart while he rode. He located the barest remnant of a trail which led him straight to this strange small castle called Bridgnorth. If he was correct, then he stood within a lost chiefdom, with an unknown ruler, within an endless expanse of purportedly enchanted woods. That meant he was still, hopefully, within the confines of manorial land, but it was small comfort. He had no desire to be caught alone in tribal Cambrian territory, since the tribes had not been properly administered, perhaps not ever. The whole place was too remote and too wild to be tamed. That had been tried already, and Arthur was content to leave these folk to their own affairs. Besides, some of his own knights were from there. And it was just like Lancelot to consider political boundaries, seeing Britain as a collection of domains first, a magickal, hilly, forested island second.

Anything to keep my mind from her, he thought. He was constantly distracted by thinking about the woman who had enchanted him more surely than these woods ever could. Her heart and mind were more labyrinthine than the almost invisible footpath which led him here.

Lancelot had too much on his mind: how to follow the trail downstream; whether to stay completely out of Perceval's and Galienne's way, and report their doings to the king later; to get away from Camelot itself, not wanting any part of the celebrity that had all but overtaken him. Men at the Pentecost festival promised him their daughters, women promised him things which would make him no longer want or need said daughters, and children begged to be taken for just one ride, or to see his sword and lance up close. A number of souls had camped as close to his pavilion as possible, and in his frustration he packed up and went back inside the city, to stay for the duration in his reserved quarters in the main castle.

That, of course, was when he ran into *her*. He wished he could be free of the Queen, but, God save him, he found it almost impossible to tear himself from her even now.

Now that they both knew they had to reject each other. It became too risky; theirs were the most scrutinized lives in the Island. He wondered if they really could, though. And he could remember every word of their most recent talk.

"Lance, what are you doing back in here? For goodness' sake, man, the Queen's Champion should be at the tourney grounds already!" He never got used to that title; it was a weight more burdensome than the heaviest of armors, like the mail with reinforced metal plates which had become fashionable lately for those rare few who could afford it.

"I do apologize, M'Lady." He often slurred the pronunciation this way; the possessive pronoun was too painful to utter properly. "It's just that too many people seem concerned with seeing the great Lancelot before he withers up, no longer able to please them so at such events."

She walked several steps closer to him. No one else appeared present in the hall of the grand keep that day; the weather insisted everyone frolic about outside like children running ribbons around the May Tree. He could smell her on the gentle breeze which flowed through the hall from the open archways on the exterior side. He had long since addicted himself to her fragrance.

"Lancelot, the people adore you. You're every child's hero, and the unofficial leader of the Table; most knights would die for your honor alone."

He snorted. "Would they? And what about you?"

She turned from him, to look out over the courtyard, the city which looked like it would continue clear to the horizon. She could see her delightful garden from here; it was crammed nearly full of couples, young and old, lost in their own affections. "I would die for the man behind the honor."

She turned to face him, suddenly angry at the happy couples below her perch. "Damn it, Lance! It's difficult for me too!" Guinevere, with all the wild emotions she had felt in the presence of this man, was now overwhelmed with the only one which remained: pity. Not remorse, nor even guilt so much any more. She simply pitied this man who had made her his life's ambition. Just like the way Trystan loved Isolde; because she was not only beautiful but unobtainable.

Lancelot wanted to hold her, just to comfort her. Even that was out of the question. One never knew when the next passerby might decide to walk through the hall, and the rumors of the two of them already floated freely, like a fog which settles in and won't leave, all but blinding those within.

"Those same people you say adore me so talk behind my back. I can't stay here anymore. I can't even make camp outside with the other knights, they mob me so. I was going to tell you I'm leaving again."

She looked at him again. She rolled her eyes. "Where to this time?" She hated this arrangement. She had a wonderful man, but he was a king. And kings had more pressing concerns than romance to occupy their thoughts. Arthur was sovereign first, lover second. Guinevere loved him, truly she did. But her heart yearned sometimes, even now. Before her stood a hopeless romantic, a lover and adventurer, who embodied all she once believed her husband did. But it was difficult for a king to find time for a wife and time for adventure.

That, and the royal couple had been unable to produce an heir, a prince to one day wield the great sword. That came between them, followed them to their hearts, though neither intended nor wanted it to do so. The queen's barrenness, or a king who couldn't produce seed. How to reconcile the problem when they couldn't even be certain whose fault it was? They both wanted to blame someone, something; more was at stake than the joy of a family. Who would tend Camelot when they no longer could?

"On Arthur's own command, I am to follow two children through the countryside. No one is sure exactly where they're headed, and I'm to provide them with a largely invisible sense of security."

Guinevere raised her thick eyebrows, unaware even now of how seductive Lancelot found the gesture. "Who?"

"Haven't you heard? It's gotten around by now, surely." The Queen looked puzzled.

Lancelot explained the tale of how his own daughter became involved in part of a prophecy of a measure similar to the King's own, making it sound ludicrous. Guinevere listened empathically; she too had been destined for greatness, promised to a king at a quite tender age. Such was the cost of being another king's daughter. The famous Round Table was her dowry.

This was the first she heard of the miraculous "girl of the sword," however. Not that she was ever inclined to hear of anything concerning Elaine, although she lowered her head when Lancelot told of how he found her at the river. She sniffled, a number of crystalline tears falling onto the folds of her bright gown. Lancelot thought her even lovelier then. Perhaps it was her looking like a scared girl more than a queen. Something about the tears didn't quite fit her; perhaps that was what Lancelot found so attractive, a sign of frailty among all her strengths.

But he had a child, wanted or no, the only thing ever denied Guinevere. For a fleeting instant she despised him, just for being a parent. It felt like whole lifetimes had passed since the Queen's kidnapping by Meliagrant's own men, since Lancelot's mad rescue of her before she could be raped into anonymity, since their eager and sweaty consummation, since her fervent praying to both have and not have a child by him. She must be barren, she concluded, barely listening to the man now; she had known more than one lover, but knew nothing of birth pains.

He finished the tale, looking dreamily at this woman who amazed the Island's populace. Here was the flirtatious girl grown into a capable diplomat and castellan, completely running the King's affairs during the Continental and Badon campaigns. She single-handedly created Camelot's famed Court of Love, toiled on her own hands and knees to make her dream garden a reality, personally oversaw the care of the creatures inhabiting the menagerie. She only wished she still had time to cook, the skill she learned earliest and loved most. She could sing even the most brusque knights into laughter or tears, and her smile could warm the coldest heart. She did not smile now. If Guinevere had any weakness it was envy, envy of her husband's lack of time for her, since it carried with it a certain freedom, and envy of a man she so often wanted to be with, who had a daughter whom he barely knew.

She deserves better than you. She deserves the man she first loved, not the fool who follows her like a puppy. Lancelot could not force the words out. He just knew it was time to leave.

"Guin, I have to go after them. They have already left the city. This upstart spoke of wanting to return home, and apparently it lies in Cambria somewhere."

"Cambria!" Guinevere gasped. No one civil came from those heathen hills. She composed herself instantly, from years of practice. No one could read her emotions if she did not wish them to do so. "Do be careful," she wished him flatly.

"I shall, my Queen."

She blew him a kiss before he walked down the hall. Then she left herself, becoming wrapped up in the gaiety of the festival.

And now here he was, leading his horse down what passed for a trail, but it was too overgrown for him to ride through. Either the stallion would have injured himself, or the man would have been knocked off by one of the low branches.

Two aspects of Bridgnorth surprised Lancelot: it smelled delicious, and its gate stood wide open.

Lancelot, like his offspring, had no love of surprises. He continued on foot up to the inviting gate, noticing neither the unfinished bridge nor the rapids which began just downstream from it. He wondered how close he could get to the keep without being noticed. He decided to tie up the horse outside, for quiet. He hoped it didn't notice the mare tethered within the tiny stable just off the keep.

The dinner guests all seated themselves, all looking each other over carefully, scrutinizing. Perceval and Galienne felt they received more of this attention than anyone else, however. Galienne stared at her place setting to avoid the looks of others, which only made her edgier. Her mother would have been terrified; the spoon was facing upward. She was raised, and had taught her daughter, that evil could be kept at bay by keeping those utensils face down until used. It was unsettling; Galienne hoped, as did her friend, that the others did not know as much as their host.

Everyone remained silent, taking in the atmosphere of the feast hall and observing each other, until the first dinner course arrived, brought out on a silver platter which shone throughout the hall: a reddish fish, poached in butter and slivered almonds. Perceval did not recognize it, and felt embarrassed to apparently be the only one who did not. Everyone else immediately set about devouring it, even Galienne. Not wanting to be the first to speak, nor to ask about anything so trivial as a fish, he started to eat also.

It was quite savory, and his stomach pressed him for more. Too long had it been since he and Galienne truly feasted themselves. Even at Oerfa, the pickings were slim, but of course most of the residents had left the village.

As the dinner party began to partake of the salmon, the servants brought out a heady, strong-smelling wine, pouring liberal amounts into the fine goblets adjacent to everyone's supper bowls. Galienne's nose twitched at the bouquet; she could smell it in her cup even when she sat upright and away from it.

The eager young woman opposite her decided to speak, just after washing down a mouthful of fish with a gulp of the wine. "Lord Pellam, truly you honor us by inviting us all here for what promises to be a wondrous feast. Who would have thought such a gathering of different souls possible?" She said it with the slightest hint of knowing to her voice, like she was toying with her host.

Pellam acknowledged the compliment, then offered a toast. "My friends, let us drink to something worthy. Please forgive my not standing properly for such a dedication, but the old wound will not permit me so." Perceval and Galienne wondered what the old wound was.

He raised his goblet triumphantly. "Let us drink to the healing of archaic injuries, and to the restoration of matters gone askew." All raised their cups, drinking the rich vintage. Perceval knew it must have been a good year somewhere, to make such a concoction as this. The wine warmed his mouth, then his throat, next his stomach, and from there the rest of his body as it went down. He swore he could feel it tingle in his fingertips and toes.

When he set the goblet down, he was vaguely aware of all eyes in the hall upon him, all but Galienne's. It must have been the wine; Perceval never consumed much alcohol before.

Neither had Galienne, who had the same impression as her friend. Again she felt scrutinized, like when she recovered the sword. She felt isolated and less safe without it. It was in her room, as Perceval's was in his.

The other man at the table wanted to keep things light-hearted; such was his way, although he was curious. "Lord Pellam, I see the years have been prosperous. From where does one get the resources to erect such a magnificent holding as this?" Taliesin's voice was as warm and soothing as the wine. Galienne remembered hearing about him; he was a poet of some kind. Already he had a wide repute, and he looked barely into his third decade.

The older woman interceded. "Oh, Taliesin, leave the poor man alone. He has to stay cooped up here like some chicken in its pen, so what's wrong with him spending his wealth on the finer accoutrements?" Her voice had an interrogating tone to it, like Perceval's mother.

Before the bard could respond, Nimue jumped in. "But, Lady Kunneware, who is to say where he spends his time? He clearly devotes many an hour to reeling in these excellent salmon." Indeed, Nimue continued munching contentedly on the flaky, tender fish.

Perceval and Galienne looked at each other and shrugged. They thought all present were strangers to one another, yet here they were, carrying on like old friends reunited after a long separation. Almost like family, really.

"All I wished to know was the story of how he had such obvious success in his earlier career," Taliesin said, aiming the statement at both the women.

"But don't you think it's rude to ask such things of one's host?" Nimue said. *But,* she thought, *not so rude as using this occasion to try and know that girl sitting across from me.*

Pellam raised his hand, signaling silence. Taliesin could not resist one more question. He had traveled widely, studied the ways of the bards and druids, and could befriend just about any living thing which walked the earth. But he did not know the answer to his query. "My lord, why pray tell have you brought us all here to begin with?" His words fell into the air, hanging onto nothingness.

Behind him, Pellam's servants were waiting to bring the next course, a sweet-smelling spiced apple bread. It would have to wait for Pellam to finish first.

The host himself waited until he had everyone's attention. "I have brought you all here because each of you has a tremendous gift to offer, and because I wished to be able to say I knew you each personally." Pellam had gone to considerable lengths to bring this ensemble together. Clellus had dutifully taken down dictated letters, in his flowing penmanship, then sent them to where Taliesin and Nimue happened to be.

They were in Camelot at the time. And as for Perceval and Galienne, Pellam had some aid in knowing where they were. And where they would be.

A number of eyes glanced around the room, wondering what "gifts" the others possessed. Pellam continued.

"Think of it! Here in my very feast hall I have," he gestured to each person in turn, "a priestess, a healer, a bard." He paused when he got to the last two. "And two warriors." He was careful not to use descriptions like "enchantress," "witch," or "druid."

Perceval was pleased to see that now everyone except Pellam looked a bit confused. No, the old hag-like woman looked pretty content herself. Indeed, he half thought this was the hag that he had in mind when he used to insult Dindraine.

"But to refer again to your gifts, consider this. A wise teacher named Pelagius once spoke of the importance of the human will, and the need to use it. It represents utter freedom of action and discourse, and I have willed it that I should have guests this evening, as you have the will to exercise your talents."

"But weren't Pelagius' teachings declared heretical by the Church?" asked Taliesin. "Augustine suggested that the human will be subservient to the will of God."

"What is important about the Bishop of Hippo's own words is that the will must remain free. Freedom is what I am talking about. The freedom to pursue one's heart's desire, to work toward one's dreams and aspirations. And most importantly, the freedom to make choices and take responsibility for the results. The responsibility is reinforced through faith; I think that was what Augustine meant."

"I see," the bard said. "So while it may not always be rational, the will is the source of power, manifested in choice and responsibility."

"Precisely." Pellam could see he and the bard were the only ones interested in a philosophical discussion, but hopefully their words would not be wasted. If the others could see through these words, they might be able to work wonders.

The kind of wonders Pellam desperately craved, but no longer possessed the freedom to attain himself.

"If nothing more, I am simply pleased to have you all in my house. You are my guests, and as your host, it is my duty and privilege to provide you with food, lodging, and, if possible, entertainment." He stared at Taliesin, who in turn stole another glance behind him, where his beloved instrument lay wrapped up, safely tucked away from all others.

The bard knew the next question before Pellam asked it. "Taliesin, might you consider honoring us with your exquisite verse? I promise there will be no shortage of food." The parties of lords and ladies occasionally ate up the offerings before

an entertaining bard could get to them. That would never have
been tolerated by the tribes, but newer days and customs were
upon the land.

The request was simple enough, and Taliesin knew that,
as a bard, it was likewise his own duty to provide such entertainments for his hosts, whomever they might be. He did not like
that he knew little about his current host; Pellam was certainly an
odd sort. But he had heard of Nimue. She was the bright star
of Avalon in the eyes of those who taught him (*no, who allowed me
the chance to find my own voice*, he thought, seeing the blessed Mona
in his mind's eye). He had little idea about the others.

Dutifully, he rose from his seat. The servants brought
in the sweet, fruity bread, offering generous slices to all at the
table. Taliesin retrieved his faithful harp, the name of which was
reserved for him alone.

He carried the beautiful carved pine instrument back to
the table, fondling and caressing it as suggestively as any lover.
It *was* his lover, the most faithful woman he would ever know.
Perceval was at once intrigued; such an instrument was much
grander than Tathan's.

The diners ate the bread, chasing it, too, with wine, and
Taliesin began to play. He had little idea what he would play and
sing of until the music simply took him, like it always did. To
the listeners he seemed a master of the harp; he knew his mistress was truly in charge. And she sang for them.

Nimue smiled at the bard warmly as he sang of apple
trees in the misty spring, and of the ladies who made their home
in a place no man's eyes could ever see. The harp's strumming
sounded like Nimue's own cries as she committed her sacrifice,
pouring her glamour skyward for all to see, yet he bespoke nothing of what transpired that day.

Next Taliesin took his listeners to Camelot itself, into
the meeting room of the greatest knights on earth. The harp
told of proud Gawaine; of the heart-wrenched lover Trystan

and his ill-fated partner, finding their own forbidden love; of Yvaine rescuing his starving lion from a trap far away; of Dinadan the prankster, who once mooned Lancelot after being unhorsed by him at a tourney. Even Galienne laughed at what her father must have thought right then.

The bread was delectable, the apple chunks melting inside the mouths of the diners. And it sweetened the music. The man from Carmarthen who taught a young Trystan the harp teased their feelings, made his emotions theirs. And he sang, his lovingly callused fingers summoning the melody from his lady's strings.

Then Taliesin's tale turned melancholy, and the music echoed of a barren place in the northern reaches of the realm, so remote that most knights barely knew of it. It became the source of all manner of fell creatures, and Taliesin sang of how it must have come to be. Voice and harp told of adulterous love, of brothers fighting and slaying one another anonymously, of a seat which allowed no one to claim it, and of grievous wounds which were unforgiving. And unhealing.

During the sonorous story-telling, Kunneware did not take her eyes from Perceval, which only made him more apprehensive. Galienne, also, felt nervous among these odd folk, but was beginning to calm and even enjoy herself. The food was marvelous, the entertainment lovely, even during the gloomier parts. Whenever Perceval looked at her she was chewing eagerly, ears attuned to the young bard.

Perceval was unsure what was expected of him. Sir Pellam talked about their gifts, but Perceval did not know what he really had to offer anyone. Maybe he could ask after the music ended. Then again, like Nimue indicated, it was often rude to interrogate one's host, who was, after all, both gracious and charming. He wondered how well Pellam knew the others. They all seemed to know him.

Perceval idly nibbled at his bread, barely noticing its wafting aroma. Across the table, Kunneware leaned over and whispered something into Nimue's ear. Both women then glanced towards him. His chewing slowed, self-consciously. He really did not like this feeling, but did not think it his place to ask what they might be saying. Besides, what were they? A priestess? A healer? He had no desire to antagonize a representative of practiced faith, nor a chirurgeon.

Galienne, for her part, was more concerned with enjoying herself to share Perceval's reservations. The food and hospitality were both outstanding here, not that she had much with which to compare it, not in her short experience. This was exactly the sort of activity Elaine told her about in Astolat: that knights feasted and were entertained with their ladies, and everyone waited on them. Galienne never had anyone wait on her before, growing into independence early. Her mother provided for her, certainly, but most of what the girl knew she came by on her own. It had been difficult for Elaine to speak of courtly life.

But this wonderful feast! Galienne could hardly contain her excitement. The bread and wine went down easily and quickly, and already Galienne reached the early stage of feeling a bit tipsy. Unfamiliar with liquor courage, she spoke, trying not to drown out the bard too much.

"Lady Nimue, if you will pardon my asking, you look at me as though we know each other. Do we?"

Nimue was both startled and pleased at the girl's directness. Neither of them noticed Perceval shoot Galienne a look which suggested she keep her mouth shut. Gornymant had told him it was sometimes wiser to hold one's tongue.

"Not exactly. Although I am acquainted with your father. He really is a good man, you know."

Galienne, to her own surprise, was for once not immediately hostile to mention of the man. Maybe she was beginning to forgive his absence, maybe it was just the soothing effects of the wine.

"You know the Queen's Champion?" she said. "Tell me, please, what is he truly like? I have never had the chance to find out for myself."

Taliesin automatically softened his voice and his strumming so that the speakers could hear themselves. He was not used to being interrupted, but on the other hand, according to ancient tradition, Nimue outranked him. Bards had their origins as apprentice druids, and a priestess was of the same standing as a druid. He was finishing the story anyway. And he was curious; everyone would want to hear a musical tale about the mighty Lancelot. Was this really his daughter?

"Well, despite his bearing and his reputation, he's actually quite soft-spoken. And caring, feeling."

Galienne shrugged. "Ha! That's a good one! I've never had the impression he cared much about anyone. How compassionate could he be?"

"But, Galienne, he stayed away because he felt he had to. And he did not know he conceived a child that night, had no way to know. He lacks the Sight."

Galienne's eyes brightened. "The what?" she said, ignoring any sense of formality.

Nimue, a priestess of the sacred Isle, a woman with a natural gift for magick far more impressive than mere vision, did not falter easily. Right then proved an exception. She knew she said too much. Kunneware glared at her. Perceval sat back in his hard chair, arms folded, listening to the exchange.

Instantly, the enchantress improvised. "Galienne, recall how Lord Pellam spoke earlier of the gifts each of us possesses. Some of us have what could be called second Sight." She would not give anything more away.

Galienne pressed. "I'm not sure I understand. Second Sight of what?" She felt Perceval put a half-silencing, half-reassuring hand on her arm.

Taliesin stopped, straining to hear. Only Pellam even noticed him.

Nimue cleared her throat and continued, hesitantly. "Galienne, do you ever have visions of things which come to pass?"

Galienne recoiled as if smacked across the face. "H-how do you... how can you know that?" Galienne had largely learned to live with her own sendings, but was not prepared for the possibility of anyone else sharing such a power. Had this woman across the table seen her somehow? If she had, it was surely no sending of God, because she didn't worship Him. Pellam called her priestess, but there were no women ministers of any kind in Britain. Baudwin had told her so.

The priestess began to utter some bit of response, but was interrupted by the arrival of the next course, which differed for everyone.

* * *

Lancelot managed to keep his steed silent after retrieving some of the freshest hay he ever saw from the stable inside Bridgnorth. He could smell it, too, from inside the open gate. And within the stable lurked Perceval's own horse. Lancelot was not one to forget someone, whether someone was human or equine.

He was quite taken by the artwork surrounding the keep. He recognized a number of the faces painted thereupon, and smiled when he saw the depiction of the Round Table. Of all his accomplishments, all the vanquished foes, the tourney awards, he remained proudest of his status as a member of that group.

He had come so far from his birth on the Continent in the kingdom of Ganis, raised on the island of the druids after being abandoned on the Island of the Mighty, showing far more aptitude with the sword than the sickle, journeying in search of a king worthy of his talents. And becoming champion to his wife and friend to both. Lancelot was, in truth, a simple man. He did not ride his ego as did Gawaine, preferring solitude or the company of close friends than gaping throngs. He had one love, and one obsession. At least the second was available to him.

Lancelot held his status as a knight with all the fierce pride of the most zealous religious fanatic, yet even here he remained simplistic. His arms bore the banner of the kingdom of Ganis, the diagonal alternating red and white stripes showing his allegiance and his place at the head of what was regarded far and wide as the Ganis clan. Like the Orkneys from the northern reaches, the Continental clan produced its own great knights: Lionel, Blamore, Lancelot himself. And Bors, although no one took Bors very seriously because of his, *oh, don't think of that now,* Lancelot ordered himself.

The sounds from within the keep were likely audible for miles, and Lancelot, rather than enjoy the festive and colorful singing and merry-making, worried that someone, somewhere, would hear the sounds and come barging into this poorly defended place.

So he fed his destrier, left him tied to the inside of the gate, then closed the gate and walked back to the keep. He hoped his armor would not reveal his location, but the sounds from within were likely far too loud to allow anyone else to hear iron bending and pressing.

Lancelot stole up to the main door, walking as quietly as he could. It, too, stood slightly ajar, perhaps for ventilation.

He arrived just moments before the music slowed, and the topic somehow became *him.* He listened attentively, wondering how invasive it would be to just rush in unannounced. He had to admit it would be amusing to see the expressions.

Lancelot pressed against the heavy door, which was oiled into silence, and was shocked to hear Nimue's voice. It sounded like she was talking to his daughter.

And the two of them spoke about him? He was flabbergasted. Hadn't he all but convinced Nimue that Galienne would have to find her own destiny?

Then it grew silent, inexplicably. He strained to get a glimpse inside, but could not. The door led into an entryway, and then turned to open into the hall itself, so he would risk revealing himself in order to see what was happening. Then he heard the gasps of all those in attendance.

* * *

The three serving girls entered, carrying a large serving bowl. It smelled heavenly, although none of the diners could see what was in it. The girls carried it at chest level, above the seated diners. Taliesin immediately set about returning his beloved to her leather holding and rejoining his host's table.

Galienne was served first. She noticed how everyone smiled while the blonde and the redhead brought the bowl over near her, and the brunette spooned out her dinner.

It was exactly what Galienne had hoped for, although she had only half been thinking of it. She missed her mother's cooking, though she knew her own way around a kitchen. It was her favorite; Elaine herself could have hardly made the dish better, when she used to prepare it occasionally for Galienne's benefit. It was an entree of Continental flavor: *agredouncy*. Chicken flesh had been sliced, glazed with honey and mustard, and rolled in rosemary and pine nuts. It smelled divine; Galienne had not had any since before she and Elaine left home.

Wanting to keep her manners, she waited until the others were served to begin eating.

Perceval was next. It was also exactly what he envisioned: venison. Ever since one warm fateful day when he lost his spear, he had wanted to try the succulent meat. It was lightly coated with a sauce made of apples.

The maidens continued serving everyone this way, and no one commented about how none present could ever quite see into the bowl. After the girls reached Taliesin, dishing him up an assortment of steamy buns filled with what smelled like ham and which had little "x" or cross shapes baked onto them, Galienne leaned over to Perceval and whispered.

"Isn't it the most beautiful thing you've ever laid your eyes upon?"

Perceval followed her glance; she stared at the serving bowl. "The big dish?" he whispered back.

"That's all you can say about it? It's the most spectacular piece I've ever seen. It must be worth a fortune!"

Perceval looked back at it, where it was now near the women. He could not identify what Kunneware was about to eat; it looked like a heap of slimy noodles, in some kind of thick puree. The bowl was just a piece of wood, ornamental and aesthetically pleasing to behold perhaps, but still just a wooden bowl.

"Gal, why are you so excited about it? It's only a serving dish."

Galienne ignored him, wondering how he could possibly not be equally enraptured with the beauteous object that almost floated from one guest to another. She watched eagerly as Nimue was served, and finally Pellam himself. Everyone began eating their own courses, each person enjoying something different.

Any residual discussion was completely superseded by the sounds of contented dining. The maidens took the large dish back into the kitchen and reemerged with more goblets, for some exquisitely fresh water. Only Nimue had seen clearer water, of a well named for the greatest artifact known. And Perceval was pleased it did not have the funny rosy taste the water in his and Galienne's quarters had. It was a pleasant alternative to the wine.

The room fell silent. Perceval burped slightly, his stomach well-filled. Galienne relaxed in her chair. Nimue still did not take her eyes off her.

Then the maidens returned, each carrying a candle the color of her hair. They walked out from the kitchen, one at a time, changing course just behind Pellam's own chair and proceeding moon-wise around the table.

Pellam was silent, taking the time to look at each of his guest's faces. He was starting to feel apprehensive, and the pain returned to his thighs. He had waited a long time; he hoped this would truly be the grand occasion he desired.

The maidens stopped, spaced out around the table, their candle flames flickering impatiently. Then the men appeared.

The first, the one who had helped Pellam to be seated, brought out a silver platter. It shone like the sun making its morning rise to light up the world, every candle flame in the hall magnified a dozen-fold in its reflection. It made the light dance, much as Taliesin could make the people dance, and everyone gasped, marveling at the glimmering white spots that jumped about the walls.

The second lad brought out the spear, and the second round of gasps was chilling. It was a rather nondescript weapon, really. It was an unknown hardwood, long darkened with use and age, shaped into a strong pole, thick enough to require a full hand grasp yet light enough to be hurled a short distance.

Except for one particular feature. The polished steel tip, which might have otherwise illuminated the hall like the platter preceding it, was bleeding.

Well, covered with blood anyway. That was Perceval's immediate conclusion. Lances didn't bleed; no weapon did!

Only something alive could shed blood. They must have just used the spear to butcher something but forgotten to clean it. But knives were the normal tools for such a task, not something as big and requiring of combat skill as a great spear. And Pellam kept an immaculate home; surely the blade would have received proper cleaning.

Pellam looked about again, scanning faces. Kunneware looked at Perceval, Nimue at Galienne. Taliesin watched and memorized; he envisioned this becoming part of some future story. He could not say why exactly; it was just a feeling of this being far more than an ordinary feast. Why did the old man really get them all together? Such individuals were unlikely to meet otherwise.

Not one of them would ever be able to say they noticed a change in Pellam's demeanor. While his pleasing face did not contort nor reveal the slightest emotion, his heart was breaking. He supposed he would just have to wait for someone else, with even more promise than these souls offered. If such existed.

Pellam had already offered everything to his guests that he could. If none of them could possibly take what he thought sufficient cue, then it seemed hopeless after all. An enchantress. A bard. A promising knight. And a girl who wanted to become the same. Yet none understood the significance.

Kunneware, though, was another story. She knew Pellam from long before any of this. She looked disappointed, but none of the others noticed that, either.

Perceval tried desperately to remember whatever Tathan might have told him about a spear. It came after one of Perceval's hunts. Only the stag had ever eluded him, his aim with the cast javelin was that good, and the spear now in front of him was little different. If he could just recall...

The servant carried the spear around the table, in the same direction the maidens had come, although rather than stopping like they had he continued with the weapon straight back into the kitchen. All eyes watched him proceed.

Perceval just glimpsed, from the corner of his vision, Galienne instinctively crossing herself. Years of conditioning were not about to leave her now.

Yet he still could not see what was so memorable about what happened here. Some infirm old man invited them to a rather odd dinner. But what had the priestess said? Second Sight? What was that about? Did Pellam have this Sight?

Perceval sat helpless before his volatile thoughts. He barely saw the next part of the unusual procession: Clellus brought out what looked like the very same serving bowl from before, and set it in the middle of the table. In it was more of the perfect crystalline water that filled the diner's second drinking vessels.

Second Sight? Can the future be seen? Was it the future I dreamt of on that hill when I first set out? What does it mean to dream of Mother, of Llio, of Dindraine and Galienne? How does Pellam know so much? Why does the "healer" keep looking at me like that? Who are they who inhabit those dreams? The boy, the man, the persons in the hall...

The others listened, engrossed, as the maidens remaining at the tableside began to sing, beautifully standing in their pristine gowns of colors to match their hair. Even Taliesin was impressed by the strength and harmonious beauty of their combined and practiced voices. It was a ballad; they sang of the coming of various peoples to the Great Island, the Picts and Cymru and Romans and Garmani, each one proud, yet each chased back by the next. They made it sound both sad and inevitable. But promising somehow. As though all the people could live more harmoniously than they did.

Poor Perceval. *Tathan spoke of an enchanted forest and we found one! And why is it everyone here seems to know some potent magick but me? I wish someone else was here. What can I say or do? What can I even ask this man?*

Pellam looked at him, puzzled. The lad looked as if he wanted to ask something.

Only the lad misinterpreted. To him, Pellam seemed hostile, staring at him as if to keep him quiet while the girls sang. He again decided it would be better to hold his tongue. *Wait until the feast is over. I can talk about some of this with Galienne tonight, and ask the others about it all come morning.* His decision actually helped him relax.

Perceval looked at his dear friend. She seemed content. *No,* he thought, *enraptured is more like it. Her eyes never stray from the water bowl.* She was far too moved by the whole ceremony to say anything herself. And Perceval had the same impression of all others present. Still, the ugly old woman kept glaring at him from time to time, making him more self-conscious each instance.

And right as the tune finished and the maidens walked back to the kitchen in the same manner as they came, Lancelot at last made his presence known.

* * *

He definitely did not intend to be discovered like that. But in straining to hear and, better still, see what transpired in this hall, he peered just slightly around a corner to steal a peek at this strange dinner and its procession.

Once Lancelot had his first taste of view, he couldn't resist. He peered more and more around the corner, as the maidens were finishing their fantastic song, until he stood completely in view of those assembled at the table. He stood oblivious there until all the servants filed out. Then, Pellam noticing the intruder at once, Lancelot was aghast that he had been so careless.

"I say, Lord Lancelot, won't you please join us?" The old man's words forced the knight into a fully erect position. He could not, would not, just turn and flee. He was honor-bound to stay, having just been invited. And Pellam was suddenly elated; maybe *this* was the person he should have really brought!

All heads turned at once to follow Pellam's voice. Nimue smiled. Kunneware's eyes widened. Taliesin studied the man's face. Perceval felt humbled. And Galienne looked horrified. What was *he* doing here?

Pellam actually identified the knight, not by his face nor his aggressive, athletic build, nor even his imposing manner (although he looked more like a child caught with his hands on the honey cake before supper). Instead, Pellam could tell who stood in front of him by his tunic. Pellam had devoted untold years to the study of heraldry, and he knew the stripes of Ganis instantly.

"My lord, I thank you. Please accept my meager apology for intruding upon your supper. But I found your own gate standing wide open, and thought —"

"Now, lad, we'll have none of that. I appreciate your concern for our well-being, but I assure you, we are quite safe here. I imagine you yourself had no small trouble finding my home, eh?"

Lancelot nodded. He quickly scanned the people present. He of course knew the enchantress. The scrawny old woman was a mystery, as was the tall inquisitive looking man next to her. And then there was his daughter. And the man she had ridden off with, making Lancelot feel largely useless as protector.

"Clellus!" barked Pellam. "Bring an extra chair at once. We are honored with another guest!" Immediately the servant produced the requested furniture, placing it between Perceval and Taliesin. Lancelot shyly approached the chair, locking his eyes with those of his daughter at every step.

Perceval watched in awe as the man approached. Here was the best of the best, right in front of him, for the second time! Pellam was also delighted; here was another outstanding adventurer, come to grace his home. Perhaps Lancelot could make sense of a ceremony in which the others became muddled.

"Lancelot, may I ask how long you were eavesdropping on our meal?" Pellam said. The procession would not be repeated, could not be. These few present would have to take what they knew and spread what word they would.

"You may ask, of course. It is your roof beneath which I sit. And I noticed, I believe, just about everything which transpired since the bard started singing." Lancelot sat rigidly, still feeling Galienne's glare. "And if I may ask in return, what was the purpose of that procession, other than to hear those lovely maidens sing?" He heard a girlish giggle come from the kitchen, but ignored it.

Pellam brightened. "It was only to show my guests a few of the additional things which are in my, uh, possession."

"I'm afraid I may have missed the objects of which you speak." Clellus came back into the hall just then, carrying a final dish which he placed in front of the knight. Lancelot inhaled the savory smell deeply, remembering he had just been thinking how satisfying a serving of roasted lamb chops served with sweet potatoes would be; now they sat enticingly in front of him. God, he was hungry!

"And since I don't wish to further interrupt anyone's supper, I'll have to content myself to asking more about them after everyone is finished."

So close, Pellam thought, trying not to be bitter, failing.

Taliesin watched the newcomer eat, as the others, all but Galienne, set about finishing whatever remnants of dinner remained in their bowls. *So here is the great knight. And he doesn't even know who I am. The druids lost all contact with him, and now here he is, sitting right next to me.* Taliesin could already hear his muse working inside him, in the creative region he never spoke of except to his masters. *Lancelot of Ganis, come across the sea. Grown on Mona, student druid. Your heart always on the blade, not the lute.* Taliesin would have to work out the exact phrasing later; but he could already feel a ballad swelling in his mind. Hardly a bard ever had a more exciting and dramatic subject!

"You came to spy on me, didn't you?" demanded Galienne. Perceval sat between them, calm before the storm. The girl finally forgot about the bowl sitting at the table's center.

Lancelot had to pause between juicy bites of lamb. Then he turned to her. "The King himself sent me."

"That sounds convenient. But why do you suddenly seem to want me in your life? You were never around before. Do you finally feel guilty?"

Perceval could take little more of this. "Hush, Gal, please!" he cajoled.

"No, Purse, I will not hush! I want to know." Taliesin's future epic grew more intriguing all the time.

"Galienne, I want you to know something about me," Lancelot began deliberately. "It will never be possible for me to make amends for what I have done to you. All I can do is apologize, and hope that someday, perhaps you might find it in your heart to forgive me. I never had the chance to apologize to your mother, and now it's too late. The only thing of which I can be glad is that you could be here to hear me now."

Galienne listened, almost interrupting at one point but letting him finish. He sounded sincere. She wanted to believe it. But the spite in her insisted that he had merely cornered her; part of her faith was based on forgiveness, and he called on that responsibility. But had he done so intentionally?

She glared at him. As softly as she could, she said, "I know that wasn't easy to say. Thank you for offering your peace."

Lancelot forgot about his food. He didn't even want it any more. His stomach was starting to burn again. It burned a lot lately. He remembered the old cure, but tying sprigs of mint around his wrist only made him feel foolish. No wonder he turned his back on the druids.

A few uncertain moments passed quietly. They all grew tired, and all present already thought of what they would do when the meal ended.

Pellam, as though once again reading them, glanced behind him, and nodded to Clellus. In a few more moments, one of the serving boys came into the hall, carrying a long, slender instrument. From a distance it looked slightly like the spear which paraded through before. The boy began to play the shawms; its piercing, oboe-like wailing signaled the end of the feast and that the guests were welcome to adjourn.

* * *

Galienne remembered her father's words about Bridgnorth laying open and vulnerable. She took advantage of that knowledge, and headed directly for the open gate. She wanted to be alone. No father. Not even Perceval, who silenced her. She would forgive her friend easily enough, but was still upset.

The night was peaceful and perfect, a welcome alternative to her mood. The moon had chosen to wax just shy of its full face, granting shadowy double life to all it illuminated. The river sparkled beneath it, following its own course. The trees and shrubs gently swung their limbs to and fro, as though waving or trying to embrace the night air. The wildlife made their nocturnal noises, signaling to each other or going about their hunting or mating. Everything felt *alive*.

How can the Church say this is all evil? Galienne wondered. Her mother had always cautioned her about going out of doors, especially in the dead of night. Those were her exact words: *dead of night*. Yet there was only life outside Bridgnorth's doors.

Her faith made a point of damning darkness and what it said it symbolized: uncertainty, falsehood, an absence of good and of God's love. Galienne never gave any thought to how powerful that message was. Yet she never feared the literal dark. She sighed. This was no time for her to question her faith, though she grieved for her mother. She was beginning to accept the loss, and tried not to think of how her life was simpler and happier since Elaine's passing.

Nimue found her, having noticed where everyone ventured off to after the boy concluded with his shawms. She walked up next to the girl, silently as always. She was so used to maintaining her quiet approach, but did not want to upset this girl, especially after the exchange with her father.

"Am I interrupting you?" came the maternal voice next to Galienne.

Galienne turned to look at the woman, little older than herself. Then she turned her gaze to Mother Moon. "No. I mean, not really. I just wanted some fresh air."

"I can empathize with that. I've lived in the freshest air my whole life."

"Where?" Galienne said, not feeling any of the usual anxiety for posing a question. She was not Perceval; he worried too much about what people would think of this or that. What harm was there to a question?

"Oh, quite a special place, really. I think you'd like it there yourself. The apple trees bloom and bear fruit year round. It's peaceful and private. No wandering eyes ever reach it."

Galienne was interested. Could such a place exist? She never felt much at home anywhere in her life. Except with Perceval, out in the wilds.

"So where is this wonderful place, Nimue? Could Perceval come too?"

Nimue knew that if she was caught in a lie, she would definitely lose this child. She had to be honest, and hope the lack of men would not set Galienne back too much. "It's south of here, not far from the Dumnonia border. And I'm afraid your friend, as close as you clearly are, would not be allowed."

Galienne looked at her incredulously. "But what sort of place keeps out men?" She was used to the opposite: no women warriors, no women priests in the churches, education devoted to boys rather than girls.

Nimue said the name slowly and passionately, the very magick of the word flowing out of her, riding her breath. "Avalon. I speak of the Island of Avalon."

"*Avalon?*" demanded Galienne. "But that place is haunted! Full of witches. And no one knows where it really is anyway." Unconscious of the action, she reflexively pulled away from the enchantress, as though to touch her would invite certain doom.

"Galienne, please listen to me. It is true that I am a priestess of the island. Your own faith has its priests and priestesses; surely you recognize the need to have those who minister and keep the faith."

The younger woman, still a girl, to judge by her sudden squeaky emotional sound, was aghast. "There are no women priests! The Church forbids it."

"But your own church allows women the freedom to oversee the Christian rituals, just not here. They do across the sea, in Armorica and Eire-land."

Galienne had heard of "Eire-land" also; the lost souls lived there, with their evil giants and human sacrifices. "No! Women officiating is blasphemous. I could never become a priest."

Nimue recognized too late that contesting this girl on matters of faith was doomed to fail, and would only serve to antagonize. But she couldn't help it; she was too proud of her own faith, too critical of Galienne's. Yet the latter's was strong, despite her roaming with the spiritually-confused Perceval. She could hardly be expected to abandon it just like that. "All I mean

is that, like Lord Pellam said, each of us has a gift. You and I
share that gift, Galienne. And Avalon is a place where your talent can be nurtured and developed, not shunned. How many
know of your visions?"

Still reeling, Galienne offered her answer. "Only Bishop
Baudwin. In Camelot. He knows about them, and said they
were a gift from God."

"Bishop Baudwin is very wise. Did you know he was
friends with Merlin? And do you know that I am trying to be
friends with you? Surely I am not some demon or evil witch."
She held her arms out in supplication, feeling the Mother's cool
evening breath flow around her.

Nimue let her words dangle about, swirling freely, soothing enough to comfort, strong enough to persuade. Time was
vital; the future would not wait.

"Do you know that your own Joseph of Arimathea was
a tin merchant, with connections right south of us in Dumnonia? Or that he planted a miraculous thorn bush on Avalon
itself, which blooms during the Yule time?" Nimue savored
the knowledge of how, depending on direction and belief, one
would find either a matriarchal sanctuary with small huts and
a circle of potent stones or a holy place left behind before the
coming of the Romans, transformed into a monastery by the
Saint called Patricus.

Nimue continued, making her point. "And as for wom-
en, King Coel's daughter granted refuge to the Christians fleeing
imperial persecution, and she was the first in these islands to see
the Holy Land." Nimue had studied the ways of those of other
faiths. It was the History, the Law; she guessed she might know
more about Galienne's religion than the girl herself.

Galienne stood motionless, thinking about what the
woman said to her. She clearly wasn't any demon. *But mother
would have said demons can disguise themselves to appear like anyone. No,
no! If she were so evil how could she speak so kindly, and appear so beauti-*

ful? Her mother's demanding voice rang inside her. She warred with it, trying to see the reason in what Nimue said.

Hoping to get close enough to wrap a soothing arm around her, Nimue stepped toward Galienne. The girl recoiled at once, keeping her eyes down.

"Galienne, please. I don't make my request for selfish reasons. Avalon needs you, and it could be your home, for as long as you like. Forever, even." Again, Nimue realized her verbal mistake too late. She had a flickering image of those who slept for untold eons, as in the labyrinth beneath Avalon, awaiting the time when they were summoned again to this life. But Galienne was a believer in redemption, not in cyclical renewal of the spirit in new bodies.

"The only place I wish to spend forever is in heaven," the girl whispered, finally looking up. She knelt down on the cool ground, glancing her eyes to the endless sky. "I'm sorry, Nimue. I do not belong with you or your kind."

Nimue had never seen the victor as the one who kneeled. She knew she had lost the girl. *For now, at least*, she thought. *But this does not mean I shan't be keeping my eyes upon you. The Ladies will have their new priestess someday!* And she turned from the girl and headed back to the castle. She had to make ready at once to return to Avalon and report what had transpired to Viviane.

Curse Lancelot and his improper guidance!

* * *

Lancelot took advantage of the dispersing of the party to tend to his destrier, and he too wished to be alone, wondering if his estranged daughter despised him.

He untied Grymus. The dignified stallion was the impressive offspring of a warhorse from Frisia, in northern Germanic lands, and a lithe, fast mare of Persian stock. The stallion had waited patiently for his rider's return, devouring the hay offered earlier. He itched to get a closer look at the mare inside the keep.

Lancelot knew his horse could easily tear that stable into splinters, given the proper arousal, so he carefully led Grymus inside, over near the stable, tying him again but this time to a horse ring mounted within the stone wall. Urge or no, the horse could hardly bring down the side of a castle. And it was while he stood beside his mount, expertly securing a Centurion knot which would take the strength of several of the ancient chariots to break, that Taliesin found him.

"May we talk?" came the innocent-enough question, but Lancelot instantly wheeled at the sudden sound, his hand sliding reflexively to his weapon's hilt.

"Relax, knight. I assure you I've no wish to provoke your skill with the blade. It's Germanic steel, isn't it?"

Lancelot felt the frayed leather wrappings of the hilt, his callused and worn hand telling him it was time to replace the fitting. The metal of the sword was indeed a fine alloy of Jutish origin. "Yes, it is. You know your weapons."

"Among other things," he said mysteriously. "You should realize that."

Lancelot stared at the man, relaxing his grip.

"Lord Lancelot, your training. I refer to your tutelage, not with that heavy piece of life-taker at your side, but your true learning. Have you forgotten?"

The knight did not like where this was heading. "I am not one to forget much, bard. Why not tell me something of yourself, so I'll have the pleasure of recalling it later, when I might need it?"

They warned me he had all the subtlety of a catapult, Taliesin thought. "Surely," he said. "I was wondering if you might tell me your impressions of what happened in there this evening. You plainly wished to know in what we were engaged at the dining table."

"I really don't know what you mean." Lancelot turned away, pretending to secure the knot. He did not like looking at druids, not any more.

"I mean, I want your input regarding the odd things we saw. How much did you see or hear, exactly? Only you had the foresight to even ask of it."

"I also had the foresight not to interrogate my host. It was bad enough I stumbled in like that."

"But you obviously thought about the procession, as you called it?"

"And as I said further, I missed most of it. I only heard the singing. I would have noticed more had I been seated earlier, with the rest of you."

"What were your impressions, then, since you clearly became curious?"

"I heard everyone talking either excitedly or not at all. I heard people draw in breath as though it would be their last. And I enjoyed the finest serving of lamb I ever tasted, and then lost my appetite." He turned back to the bard, forcing himself to make eye contact. Taliesin felt like he was such a lamb, the fox Lancelot staring him down.

But he was not moved, not for an instant. Taliesin had yet to meet the person who could make him afraid. "And you were not puzzled by the manner in which we all came to be here this evening?"

"No, not really. I'm only here myself because I was sent." This was irritating. Lancelot never felt kinship with the bards; they always fretted about how their verse sounded, or how to satirize a sovereign who crossed them. Maybe a rather powerful one had grown irate with Pellam; it might explain his infirmities.

"I received a most curious letter. It was after I arrived in Camelot for the Festival. It seemed only proper that a bard should attend, to record for immortality who might have won the joust or melee, and who fell in love with whom." He did not mention any sword, nor a dead woman in a boat.

You better not be talking about myself and the Queen, Lancelot fumed silently, trying not to give any emotion to his face. Bards were excellent at reading others, if little else.

"So you got a letter. What has this to do with me?"

"Pellam said it himself. A bard. A knight. An enchantress. Whoever 'Kunneware' may have been, though I suspect she is some tribe's witch. Why would the man cultivate such a group?"

"I really don't know," Lancelot said, shrugging indifferently. He actually felt a bit jealous, wondering if he was the only one who did not receive an invitation.

"I ask only because of that serving bowl. It resembled the cauldrons of which I had been told since boyhood."

"I know this story. Cerridwen or the nine maidens in Annwn keep the cauldron which restores life, or wisdom, or whatever people want."

The bard cut him off. "That is only part of it! And would you, a child of the Sacred Isle, blaspheme this way, as though the stories were just tall tales to speak of for amusement?"

"I didn't say that. I just remember the stories; who could forget something like that?"

"No one must forget it. It is certain doom to forget sacred knowledge. You should know." Lancelot did not like the tone in the other man's voice.

Rather than drop hints of his own internal demons, Lancelot changed tactics. He wanted to see what answers the bard had of his own. "What are you saying then, that we just saw that very same cauldron in there, and that Pellam went to part of the Otherworld to retrieve it? Don't be daft, man!"

"I did not suggest that. But I cannot rid the feeling that we saw something marvelous in there this eve, and now none of us knows what to do about it."

"Have you any questions?" the knight queried, feigning interest.

"Well, to begin with, I thought that Pellam was much more than a knight. A king, to be frank, and of lands far and gone from the Cambrian borders."

Lancelot was still not quite intrigued, his mind constantly on either of two women, both of whom he wished to love, neither of whom would accept him any more. "That would explain his wealth. God, he really flaunted it in there. I haven't seen the likes of it since Arthur's own halls."

"Lancelot, please. Now Pellam, if memory serves, is from somewhere near here, though I cannot recall exactly now." Taliesin's memory was trained to notice subtleties most others missed. Years of practice ensured he rarely forgot any detail to cross his ears. He indeed knew something of Pellam. He was from Cambria, was known for hunting men and beasts which scared most others into better judgment, and acquired fortunes from these great hunts. Rewards, perhaps. Or ransom or sale of captive goods. But his kingship was largely inconsequential: a comparatively small land just southwest of the old emperor's wall, attained by unknown means. Taliesin could remember nothing of the man's kinship.

"Why does it matter where he happens to be from?" Lancelot said. "Obviously he can afford other holdings just about wherever he wishes."

"But it's his kingdom I'm curious about. It's Listeneisse."

"Listeneisse?" Lancelot searched the depths of his own excellent memory. Of course. "In the dead lands?"

The bard nodded gravely. "Listeneisse is the land of waste, a place of death and stagnation. The people within are dying or mad, or ghosts wanting revenge on the living. A breeding ground for the *Unseelie*."

Lancelot looked puzzled, his attention finally somewhere other than women. "How can Pellam be so overloaded with riches if his own kingdom is such a disaster?" Lancelot loathed so-called rulers who let their subjects and lands wither and die. That was why he devoted his life to an idealistic king, younger than himself. How could the old man have let it happen? Of course, Lancelot wasn't sure he trusted the bard, either.

Taliesin only could shrug, the slung harp gently mimicking the rising movement of his shoulders. He didn't even notice that sensation anymore; he only noticed if the harp was not there, so much was it part of his essence. "From what I know, this land is increasing. Already has it begun to overtake neighboring kingdoms. The Red Lands. Cambenet. Rheged. All have started feeling the effects of this desolation."

"Are you proposing that this land is somehow *growing*, as though it were some living thing wanting to be fed?"

"Come, Lancelot. Being from the Continent, surely you know something of how a plague takes root and spreads in all directions. Or, for that matter, a fire in precious woods such as these in which we stand." Taliesin thought the knight would not accept the literal answer that he proposed, but perhaps that was the best way to understand it. Something alive. Something which could grow and kill.

The Continent had certainly confronted its share of plagues and wildfires. Lancelot had heard of entire cities, even whole kingdoms, laid to waste. And the plagues and fires were alive, too; they moved, breathed, hated, killed.

The wasteland.

It was like Perceval's image of the end of the world, where all went to die.

"What can be done about it?" Ever the gallant errant, Lancelot asked the question automatically.

The bard looked into his dark eyes. "I do not know. I do not even know why Pellam told us nothing of this."

* * *

The woman considered rather hideous by those few who ever saw her sat at the table, now alone except for the man in the chair at the table's head. She gazed at Pellam for many minutes after the others departed.

The knight or king or cripple or fisherman simply sat, his breath coming regularly but with a raspiness Kunneware would have guessed could be attributable to too much time spent within the confines of castle walls. She could prescribe some remedy for him, but knew he would not accept it. She had known this man for years, and only had an inkling as to why he would refuse her. And from what she knew, it would prove fruitless anyway.

"What do you think of this bunch?" he said finally, making no movement other than that required for speech.

"At least we found them all. They all came, even Lancelot." The woman's own voice was quite scratchy, and she knew that no cure would help her, either.

"Aye, thanks to you. We found them. But not one of them bothered to ask the right questions. Nothing!" Pellam was disgusted. He had spent so many years in this perpetual state of infirm; nothing brought joy now other than fishing. Oh, he could still read. And paint, to be sure. But he was an outdoorsman. A knight. Having to remain bedridden, or damn near it, was too much of a drain. And then tonight, to come so close. It was more than he could bear.

"At least Lancelot asked of the procession," she said. Kunneware had barely a rough idea of what should have been discussed during the feast, but knew that Pellam was under strict obligation not to discuss it unless someone else approached the topic first. Someone with the right frame of mind, who asked for the right reasons. Such a person was difficult to find, to express it with extreme understatement.

She could not reach him, Pellam hated herself for that. She had known him years prior, quite intimately. But that was part of another lifetime now. She barely recognized the shell of a once proud man who currently sat in front of her. "I still think the girl and the boy are our best hope. It may not be too late for them." It was all she could think to offer.

Pellam's ancient and exhausted eyes glared at her, struggling mightily to do so. "Everyone in this room was our best hope, and all failed." He looked past her at Clellus, who dutifully stood near the keep's only door. Pellam could not permit anyone else to hear this conversation.

"But what were they supposed to do, just instinctively know how to act, what to say?"

Pellam ignored her, though he at least began to sound vaguely hopeful. "No, I fear I may be finished with all of them. What about your student?"

Kunneware sighed. "She was meant for something else. You know that. I've taught her to be more responsible than myself, and not some doting errant poking her head into everything."

"Kundry, we may need her." Pellam was groping at anything, anyone, who gave any indication whatsoever of possessing the ability to cure. An unconventional cure, surely, but a cure nonetheless. They only had to exhibit the proper will. Pelagius, the old philosopher, would have been proud.

"Even if that's true, what of her brother? How can we trust their next encounter, if there is even to be one? We've already seen what happens when we attempt to mix blood ties."

Pellam didn't answer. He felt so tired, as though he himself performed the rituals which took place just minutes before. He could feel his eyes growing leaden. It always happened that way. Too little activity leading to too much rest and recovery. He wondered if it would ever end.

"I took liberties to ensure that the younger ones would be able to see things in a new way. That alone should help them to realize what is at stake." *And just what is at stake, you frightened old man? Why can't you tell me?*

"Always the potion-brewer, aren't you?" Pellam smirked just slightly. "They must have their own will to do what is right. No one can be made to do otherwise." He looked carefully at this woman, who once brought him so much joy. But now she looked like the doomed seeker of the alchemic formulae.

"Galienne might call that notion heresy. She knows Pelagius' conception of human will was combated by Augustine. The Church says his views are outlawed now." Pellam had no answer to that.

But he had another suggestion. "What of the other knights?" He thought he already knew the answer.

Kunneware's laughter confirmed his suspicions. "The Round Table members? Surely not! Gawaine is a materialist. Bedivere is Arthur's dog. Trystan's too in love with music and his woman. We don't have many choices."

"At least you're laughing about something."

"Pellam, never underestimate the power of laughter. It's perhaps the strongest magick I know."

They sat there, silently, both lost in their private thoughts and worlds. They were totally oblivious to all the curious talk which the feast, while unproductive and disappointing in Pellam's estimation, created nonetheless.

* * *

It took Perceval some time to find Galienne. She bolted for the door at the sound of the shawms. He tried to take the time to dismiss himself more properly, but likewise wanted to be gone from this strange place.

He found her down by the river. The pretty woman, Nimue, was with her. They talked, beyond earshot. Then Galienne got to her knees, and Nimue finally walked away.

The priestess went off to her own affairs, not seeing Perceval emerge. He had remained in the woods, listening to the animal conversations and activities, so lively and mysterious. Like the feast, he gathered, so full of energy, and so confusing. He wanted to talk to Galienne about what happened.

Only his vision came in slight blurs, which he had not noticed until the maidens began their singing. It took him several moments to distinguish Galienne from Nimue in the first place; both were virtual silhouettes against the shadows of trees and the flowing blue crystal of the river. Yet it was unmistakable; when he held his hands to his face, they looked not like his own but like someone else's. He did not know whose. At one point he even thought they looked more like an animal's paws, even a bird's feet.

But that was ridiculous. The feast was strange enough, and his mother warned him of the hazards of eating the wrong things; maybe it was the food.

Yet the food was scrumptious! How would his mother have explained that? He would seek his answer from Galienne instead.

He approached her cautiously. She looked truly penitent.

When he reached her, she was praying silently, though her lips moved to the voiceless words. He felt like he was intruding again, like he had felt ever since they arrived in this stretch of forest. It really was enchanted; he'd have to tell Tathan the whole story whenever he saw him again.

"We were just offered a vision of the miraculous, and none of us did anything." Galienne's voice was cold.

Perceval was twice surprised: that she heard him coming, and by what she said. "How do you mean?" *Maybe miracles are just strange.*

"What did you notice during that whole procession, Perceval?"

"Just an odd man, who knew us too well, as though –"

"As though he had 'second sight,' like Lady Nimue mentioned?"

He had not considered that. "Well, yes. Maybe. I don't know. But he really did know too much of us. All of us, not just you and me."

"It's like he knew we were all coming. Even my father, and the bard. I liked the bard."

"His voice was lovely. It was the greatest singing I've ever heard." He wanted to avoid this small talk. "Why did you ask me what I noticed?"

She stood, brushing dirt, leaves, and grass from her clothing. Even out in the middle of the woods, she strove to keep herself as clean as she could. "Because I think we just saw the Grail."

"What? The *Grail*? *Your* Grail? You mean the cup of Jesus that you told me about?" *No way*, thought Perceval. *It's gone. She said so herself.*

Still, there was the nagging doubt. How had the old man known so much? And why put on such a show for such a carefully selected audience? And why was he even chosen to comprise part of it?

"What did you see when they brought out our food? What did the serving dish look like?"

Perceval remembered Galienne's virtual rapture at the sight of the thing. "Like a big, wooden bowl. Well-carved, sure, but just a bowl."

It was Galienne's turn to look incredulous. "No, it wasn't! It was the most ornate, wonderful, beautiful, sparkling piece of work ever seen." She stuttered through her adjectives. Mere words could hardly describe the sight of it.

Perceval was no help. "Describe it," he demanded.

"It was silver, with gold trim. Jewels were laid about it, diamonds, garnets, sapphires. There were crosses made from the stones, three I think." Perceval closed his eyes, trying to picture such a rich piece; such a work of art would have certainly funded Pellam's lifestyle!

"And it shone candlelight all around the room. I tell you, Perceval, I could feel the presence of the angels when we were brought that food! I swear it."

So why did Galienne see it this way? No one else responded with the same fervent look she did. "Gal, then why do you think we saw it differently? It was a bowl. Truly. My own village had artisans who could carve as well as that. And there was no silver or gold or those stones you mentioned." Perceval did not know what diamonds, garments, or those other things were.

"No, it wasn't! Don't you believe me?" She backed a step from him, just as she had done with Nimue.

"I –" he started, fumbling, groping at whatever words would come. "I don't know! I thought it looked so different. Maybe I was wrong. Maybe you. I just don't know. It was like those weird dreams."

She stood staring at him. She loved him, but they would never share the most fundamental faith. Galienne sought the Christ; Perceval had the most convoluted spirit she ever encountered. "Perceval, I don't want to say this, but maybe you didn't see it in all its magnificence because you don't believe in it." Galienne thought it sinful to speak in a tone suggesting pride. Was she somehow *worthy* of receiving such a sight?

She was probably right, he had to admit. What *did* he believe? He had so long ignored Tathan's stories and his mother's usually silent Christianity.

Wait! Tathan. That's it! The old bard and the three crosses on the cup that Gal saw. He closed his eyes again, trying to imagine what it was he could remember about Tathan's stories. *The spear.*

And the shield with three points. Three crosses. Three singing maidens. A whole intermingled collection of half-forgotten tidbits of information flashed across his eyelids, each craving notice.

"Perceval, are you all right? You look a bit faint." But he did not hear Galienne's words. She thought he looked much like she did during the feast.

The spear of Lugh. The spear of Longinus. The swords drawn from divinely earthen scabbards. The Hallows. The Innocent crucified with two thieves on three crosses. Gornymant's words came clearly back, and led him into other regions. He was right; the three points served as a powerful tool for remembering. *Never forget,* he said. *It is doom to forget the essential lessons.*

Now he heard Galienne's voice again, relating again the tale of Longinus, the Legionnaire who tortured a crucified Jesus with his spear, but at the same time released the precious Blood which imbued the Grail with its potency. And Joseph. He braved so many miles to bring the holy vessel to this island.

But could that same chalice be so richly made and adorned as Galienne suggested? *No, insisted was more like it.* Surely it would have been fought bitterly over, stolen, lost. But Perceval managed to suppress that doubt.

The other spear was that of Lugh, the perfect warrior of the ancient Cymru, who later became revered and deified, even playing foster-father to the mighty Irish hero Cu Chulain. His spear would grant wounds that would not heal (*what did the old man say about a wound which would never leave?*) Lugh had helped those who settled in Eire-land to overcome the beastly beings who lived there before.

And he took the place of the old, infirm king, judged unfit to rule. The old stories, ignored and displaced for so long, came back to Perceval. Tathan was such a storyteller that his words could hardly be forgotten. And Donngal, Oerfa's Irish butcher with his own stories! Perceval smiled. He had never missed them so much.

Until now. But why was the king judged unworthy? *What was his name? Oh, yes. Nuada. The maimed king who received a silver hand after the first great battle to take the land.*

A silver hand? Perceval never thought much about that. And Galienne spoke of the precious metal used in the creation of the serving bowl, even though he still swore it was made of hardwood. Oak, perhaps.

The oak! Tathan said the tree was sacred to the druids. Perceval vowed silently to seek the counsel of a druid as soon as he could. *Was Taliesin one?*

Nuada Silver Arm. The Cymru would not let him continue to rule because he was infirm. Because his kingdom was an extension of his own health. And Lugh took over the battle, won the day for them all.

The Cymru. His own heritage, and he barely even realized it. For all his mother's ranting and raving over Pagan indecencies, she was tied to the same stock. She was of Roman culture, surely, but the blood tie was there: to Cymru land and people.

And a Cymru lord. One who lacked the strength to even lift himself from his chair, spending most of his time on the river hauling in salmon.

From where had the people come, these Cymru, that the Garmani called Welsh or Irish, and the Greeks and Romans labeled Celt? To which other figures did they pay their respect and reverence? How were these two spears related, the Roman Christian one and the Cymru Pagan one, if at all?

And the cauldron. Of course. The cauldron. Like the spear, it was another of the sacred Hallows, with its Christian counterpart too, Perceval supposed. And the two swords, and...

The Grail. Surely not the Grail.

It was too much. Perceval wanted some answers and he wanted them yesterday. He opened his eyes. Galienne stood in front of him still. She looked at him compassionately, like she understood something herself.

"We need to talk with this old fisherman," he said.

Galienne nodded, and walked at his side back to Bridgnorth castle.

* * *

Lancelot, for his part, had no wish at all to spend a night under this roof. He had completed his mission, and learned more than he wanted to know anyway. And he wished no more thought of Mona; it was painful enough to confront his daughter, not that she was much more willing to speak with him.

But she did speak, more to him tonight than ever before.

Maybe he would just spend the night in the stable next to Perceval's horse. He would be out of everyone's way, and could keep Grymus and his primal urges in check as well.

Oh, sure, and while you're at it maybe you could just bring Elaine back from the dead, too. Lancelot found it increasingly more difficult to refrain from cynicism; he had loved too passionately, become too great in his profession. He excelled beyond anything that had ever been expected of him. But he still felt morose and unapproachable. Someone tried talking to him this evening, and once again he had made matters unnecessarily taxing. Taliesin had only tried to help.

Lancelot needed something, another quest perhaps. That had always come so naturally, being out in the wilderness, taming the land, fighting foes. He fought creatures not of this realm, recognizable to him because of his unusual upbringing. He knew exactly what the redcap was, the malicious elf Galienne noticed in Bridgnorth's exterior artwork. And he would need more horses if he wanted to carry his laurels and awards and ransomed booty, all prizes from the tournaments he won.

So what was left for a knight beginning to show his age, who felt at home away from civilized society? That part of his druidical heritage never left Lancelot; he never found much comfort in urban areas, and the feeling increased exponentially with his growing fame. What did a man do with no discernible family except a daughter who wanted nothing to do with him, and a lover who abandoned him?

The Grail? Chase after the impossible?

Was it the cup of the Mass or the Cauldron of rebirth? The path to salvation or the cycle of renewal? Whichever, it would be a marvelous prize for the King.

Lancelot knew this goal was inherently selfish; Arthur himself had never discussed such an artifact. Oh, he believed in its existence, but felt there was more power in the stories behind it than in the cup or bowl or cauldron itself. How would the achiever of the Grail be rewarded by a ruler?

Lancelot was tired, so emotionally drained that rational thought was leaving him for the day. He was not about to go after any Grail, if it even existed. He just wanted to find enough to keep him occupied.

He stroked Grymus' neck affectionately. His best friend was probably this stallion. And he was superbly trained; Lancelot really only had to tell him once (albeit with a good smack) to calm down about the mare in the stable next to him.

He turned, thinking he heard Nimue's voice. He had not seen her since they all left the keep.

It was his daughter, his little girl. And Perceval. They made for the keep's door. Galienne looked at him in passing, then quickly aimed her eyes forward.

It looked like Lancelot would be better off sleeping outside after all.

* * *

It was unlike the Orkney brethren to ever become lost, but there was no other explanation. They simply could not find their way any longer.

The road led north from Camelot, past several towns, through several distinct forests, past flatlands, grazing lands, occasional hills, even twice right along the western coastline. It was easier to follow than the scent of a luscious woman, like the one Gawaine met in Camelot prior to their departure, so how on earth could he and Gaheris lose the damned road?

Yet they managed exactly that. The road could no longer be seen, even though both brothers knew it had to be there. They had made the trek from Lothian to Camelot and back again many times. They could time the lengthy trip down to within a couple of hours. Gawaine was an expert tracker. How else did he always manage to find his quarry?

They estimated the range to the Wall at a day and a half of riding. The road had been going smoothly enough, but once they crossed into the Cumbrian hills south of Gorre, the road just disappeared, like it never existed at all. And the surrounding countryside was barren, devoid of anything. Gawaine the expert tracker had noticed no animal spoor for almost two days now.

They continued to ride silently, having spoken little for some time. What pleasantries could be exchanged in the face of a strange, dead place?

The quiet was the worst part. The brothers rode for hours on end and heard nothing other than the pounding of hooves and the creaking of saddles and stirrups.

Despair was likely around the next bend, except for the sudden sound.

Both knights stopped their mounts. "What was that?" asked Gawaine.

Gaheris shook his head. "It sounded like, almost like a festival of some kind." Who on earth could be celebrating in this bleakness?

"I think we should —"

"Find out," answered Gaheris. "I agree. The noise comes from beyond that hill to the west."

Further west meant closer to the coast. Maybe they could navigate again along the shoreline, even if it lacked any significant roads.

They rode on, the faint smells of a bonfire penetrating their nostrils. A woman's voice shouted out. "She sounds like that lass you met during the Pentecostal," said Gaheris, trying to lighten the mood.

As the knights made for the scent of the bonfire, Gawaine allowed himself to recall that last night in Camelot. He could not help smiling. Now there had been a real woman! Shimmering eyes and a strong, healthy body ready for bedding. Or so he had thought, back in The Unicorn's Horn.

The tavern itself lay on High Street, near the southeastern gate of the city. It was sometimes a very calm place; in other words, the King's security tried to ensure no one got into fights there, or they were sobered up in the royal dungeons. Then again, when the rabble-rousers were Round Table knights themselves, who would stop them? Gawaine was a regular there.

He and Gaheris had gone to Camelot to join everyone else, and to clean their consciences. The mead and wine were in no short demand; indeed, people had lined up outside the establishment just to get their hands and lips on fine and heady drinks. The brothers Orkney took their usual seats near the bar table. No one was about to try and take a seat from Round Table knights, except maybe others of their order, none of whom were present that evening.

And then she walked in, a breath of heaven itself. She looked confident, radiant, and eager, all traits Gawaine looked for in the women he won. She approached the bar directly, leaving behind the scrawny boy who entered with her.

Gawaine turned his hulking self in the stool. "Those horns are real, you know," he said, indicating to fine white vessels which hung above the huge wooden kegs behind the counter.

She was not shy, whoever she was. "You mean some-one actually went out and killed those adorable unicorns, only to fashion drinking horns?"

The unicorn story had worked with others. Gawaine would have to watch his step. "Well, no, not exactly. Though they are made of ivory."

"I see. So I'm supposed to be impressed by someone having slaughtered even rarer creatures, like those in the Queen's menagerie." The woman was in a playful mood; even this brag-gart, who clearly had only mead and sex on his mind would hardly prove disparaging. She felt alive again!

"You certainly have a soft spot in your heart for big dumb creatures." How could such a strong-looking woman be so faint of heart regarding mere animals?

"Some of them. If what you said was unequivocally true, then I'd likely already be in bed at your side. Two mugs of your finest, please," she said, looking at the bartender while delighting in Gawaine's pained facial response as she spoke.

Now what? Gawaine could hear Gaheris snickering be-hind him, found solace in his mug. At least no one else could hear the wench; the place was overflowing with people and the combined sour odors of wine, beer, and sweat. "Have I given you cause to insult me, pretty lady?"

"The last person to call me that I was stupid enough to marry, but I'll soon be free of him. He just lost a significant amount of face, and to a young man barely older than Neddig over there." She pointed behind her to the scrawny fellow. He looked attentive and nervous all at once, like a squire.

"Who was your husband? And if I may ask, where did you acquire that sweet accent?"

"He is a man of no consequence. And I am from Ar-morica, here in glorious Camelot for the very first time."

Unlike many men who shared his station, Gawaine was not the least turned off by someone who had already relinquished her virginity. Actually, he preferred it; how could he enjoy an unpracticed virgin? "Was he a knight, like me?"

"He was. And as proud of himself, too." She smiled again, baiting him. Jacqueline had enough of boisterous men like this one.

"If it pleases you, I am Gawaine of Orkney, and I sit in a rather prominent position at the King's own table."

"A knight of the Round Table? Now I admit I am impressed." Gawaine glowed. "But I'm more taken with he who came to my rescue."

Who could need to rescue a woman like this? "And who was he?"

"His name is Perceval," Jacqueline said. "I only wish there were more like him."

The conversation had dwindled shortly afterwards, Gawaine's ego finally giving out, and he watched as the woman soon left with the unknown knight's squire. Her appearance had gotten her in past so many of the other waiting patrons. Gawaine grinned. Hopefully there were more like *her* also.

"Aye, she does," Gawaine told his brother, alerting back to their present situation. The voice did indeed sound like that comely lady whose name Gawaine had almost but not quite received, despite using some of his best opening lines. "But I doubt it's her; at least I hope not." *Any lady deserves better than this place.*

They climbed past the crest of the hill, then slowed, riding into the scene which awaited them below. Nothing in the experience of either veteran could have readied them for what they saw.

The few buildings in the villa had fallen into a state of perpetual decay, completely beyond repair at this point (which town was this anyway, since neither brother could remember it being here?) Even an edifice that had once been a church, noticeable as such only by its broken and splintered cross pointing up from its roof, was gutted and burned.

Finding the source of the sounds was no problem: the local residents were carousing. An impressive bonfire stood in the center of the open village, with about twenty persons dancing merrily around it. Gawaine and Gaheris might have thought it pleasant under different circumstances. The town was dead.

But the people were completely naked, the red sheen of fresh blood smeared all about them. Some of the wretches could be seen coupling off to the side in front of the former church; others danced to the point of what should have been exhaustion, yet kept going. All of them laughed as though privy to the most hysterical of jokes.

Then there was the bonfire itself. Whatever they were cooking sent tall smoky emanations into the sky, and the smell was impossible to identify. Gawaine thought the scent ghastly.

The knights rode closer, picking up the details as they proceeded. The skeletal remains of horses and cattle lay piled behind one of the huts. Crows flew about, hoping for whatever morsels they might find. There was no visible source of water, no trees. Only the humans and their falling structures.

"How did we happen to come upon hell?" Gaheris asked, half-jokingly, half-scared to wanting to turn and flee.

Gawaine would have offered some response, but was taken by that of the people. As soon as his brother spoke, the dancing, the mad intercourse, the laughing, all stopped.

Dead silence. Only the crackle of the fire could be heard. The brothers now had to wrestle their reins to keep their horses under control.

All the maddened eyes were upon them, having forgotten about the bonfire fueled by their former friends and deceased families. Only now could the knights see the roasting limbs and whole bodies carelessly thrown into the blaze. They each wondered about the circumstances regarding the woman's scream. Had it been one of the merry-makers, or –

No time to ponder it. The group ran towards the knights, surprisingly fast. But then, they had neither clothing nor armor to slow them.

Gawaine and Gaheris wasted no time in turning their horses and urging welcome charges. They would be all too happy to search for the road elsewhere!

They broke the crest of the hill passed just minutes before, not noticing its dead soil, and kept riding until they were certain their pursuers had fallen back.

* * *

The woman who had so intrigued Gawaine was still in Camelot, having persuaded the Queen herself to let her work in the main kitchens with her industrious talent. She had already been in the city for many days, and the kitchen work was a productive way to see the knights and to try and establish contact with the tin merchants. Dumnonia lay not so far from Camelot, and attempts to make connections with other dealers and miners would help please her father, whom she thought likely to lose heart when he heard that his little girl had lost her husband, her future title, her money.

But she found her freedom, and in Camelot no less. Jacqueline and Neddig had so enjoyed their stay. The squire was busily engaged in the massive stable work which resulted from having hundreds of knights, each with several horses, stay in or adjacent to the city. The boy enjoyed the work though, and it was a good way to earn some coins before returning to Quimper.

Jacqueline was just unsure of when such a return might take place. And she was enjoying herself too much to care. Even boisterous Gawaine proved amusing; such behavior would have once disturbed her, and resulted in a feud with Girard.

Girard. She could say the name without wincing. What a sight that had been. Perceval was right; no sooner had the trio arrived in Camelot than the defeated knight had undertaken the heroic task of seeking an audience with the King, during the busiest time of year! He wanted it over with, that was certain.

It was during the helm show, one of the preludes of the grand tourney, that Girard got his attention. Arthur and his closest knights took their time strolling about the collection of armor put on by the warriors who registered for the tourney. The officials were busily matching up two great teams for the huge melee, and trying to pair up all of the first round of the joust so that no clansmen nor blood foes would be against each other. The games would be kept clean and fair.

Girard had loudly uttered the King's name, then knelt in the most humble gesture Jacqueline ever saw him perform; she did not think him capable of bowing to anyone. Of course, this was Arthur! And he noticed the man quickly enough. People even cleared a path towards the knight, murmuring amongst themselves.

The helm show temporarily paused. The King bade the man speak.

"I am Girard of Quimper in Armorica, my lord. And I come to ask your pardon. Another knight left me with strict instructions to come here, after he had," Girard swallowed the words before uttering them. "Beaten me," he added.

The crowd grew quiet, all wanting to hear. Girard hated that, but he knew he must continue. To have not come would have been cowardly, and there were two witnesses to what happened, both of whom stood behind him and before the King. He supposed he could have killed the bitch and the annoyingly dutiful squire, but then he would have had to explain to those back home how he had been unable to defend his own woman against her assailants. He stood to lose a lot if he reported killing his wife and servant out of jealous rage. Either way, to back out would have meant sacrificing some significant measure of manliness. Girard's pride would not allow that.

"Who was this knight?" asked the King. "I thought all great knights were already in attendance here."

Girard looked up, saw the bold and strong face, mixed with caring eyes. The eyes were a contrast to the man's physique; Arthur was as large and naturally intimidating as Gawaine, but he had the eyes of a wise priest or an eager puppy. Girard could not quite tell which. "It was a young knight named Perceval. I know not from where he hails."

"The Red Knight!" someone exclaimed. "The one who took the sword maiden from the city!" declared another. No one dared speak when the King replied, however. He held up a hand, silencing everyone immediately.

"And where has Perceval gone to now?"

"I know not to where he heads, only that he and his companion went northward from Camelot."

"I see. I thank you for your report, Girard. What is your relationship to the lovely woman who stands behind you?"

Jacqueline beamed, feeling the warmth of so many eyes upon her. "She is my wife, Jacqueline, my lord. And the boy is my squire, Neddig."

"Do you know why she looks so pleased, that her husband has been defeated and made to acknowledge it publicly?"

Damn that wench! This is hard enough without her and her sultry looks! "It is because she wished to be rid of me, sire." They were the most difficult words he ever spoke.

"Is this true?"

Jacqueline gaped, unprepared for being addressed by the King. "Your Majesty," she said while offering her finest curtsy. "I fear that it is. Sir Girard and I are less than ideally suited. It is in both our interests." That small saving grace was all she would offer the kneeling man, now and ever.

"Then Girard, this is my offer. You are hereby pardoned on the condition that you consider yourself divorced from your lady."

This King is so confident he would overrule Rome! But then, what power can the Church have in so remote a place, which has a sovereign so respected he can silence a city with a flick of his wrist? Girard was stunned, but not about to question the decision. It was most politic to have phrased it like an "offer;" everyone knew the King just handed down final judgment on the matter.

"Yes, my lord."

And Jacqueline had been dancing on the wind ever since. Girard sulkingly returned to the Continent, after performing in a most mediocre fashion at the tourney. And the Queen proved most gracious, even seeking Jacqueline out herself when she heard of her situation.

And while she cooked and served, impressing the knights and other folk with her demeanor and her appearance, she remained unaware that Arthur had determined to find young Perceval as soon as possible. He wanted to knight the lad himself, more so now than ever.

* * *

No one was even within the feast hall in Bridgnorth when Perceval and Galienne reentered it. The only sign of prior occupation was the silently burning candles, nestled within their holders along the table and the walls.

"Where is everyone?" Galienne whispered, feeling she should talk quietly.

"I wish I knew," Perceval said. He still hated silence.

They skulked about the hall like a pair of thieves, even peering into the kitchen to see if they could locate any trace of the others. The kitchen stood mostly empty. It boasted four large cooking areas: two ovens set into the walls with fireplaces beneath, and two fire pits with cauldrons for boiling near them, plus shelves filled with an assortment of jars and baked clay vessels for food storage, and stacks of wooden barrels for wine and mead containment. No persons were within, though, nor the devices which paraded through the hall earlier. The skulkers wished another look at the mysterious serving piece.

They walked the length of the warmly lit hall, throwing their shadows to dance along the walls. Still no one else entered, and there was nothing audible from upstairs. Maybe the residents just chose to bed down for the night. It was getting late, after all. Perceval and Galienne both began to wish to do the same.

Perceval made a quick mental checklist. He saw Nimue come back towards the keep. Had she entered the gate again? He could not recall for sure. Lancelot was last seen at the stable tending his horse. That was all. He could not remember seeing any of the others since leaving the hall.

He exchanged a befuddled look with Galienne, then suggested, "Maybe we should just get some sleep. We can always talk to them come morning."

Galienne wanted her answers immediately, but admitted she was getting quite tired. She nodded to Perceval, then they both walked upstairs.

They noticed how the walls leading up the stairwell had also been illuminated by a series of candelabra mounted within the walls. The flickering glow extended all the way up, past the level which housed their rooms, to the third floor, where Clellus had said the master's chambers were. It all would have felt welcoming, except that both grew a bit tense from their inability to find the others. Apparently no one wanted to stay up and discuss any of what happened.

They reached the ornate doors of their rooms, both simultaneously opening them and walking in slowly. Both rooms were just as they had been left. But the tension started to build into anxiety.

Galienne really wanted to sleep with Perceval again, more now than ever before. She had gotten used to his warmth and found comfort and security in it. But the host had indicated his rules; they would have to sleep in separate quarters. They would both likely rise quite early, as always, and see each other right away. Until then, they would just have to content themselves with whatever sleep would come; neither thought the evening's close would prove very restful.

Still standing in the doorway, Perceval turned to Galienne, who had entered her room, left the door open. "Gal?"

She stopped pulling back the blanket on the comfortable bed. "Yes?"

"Do you really believe what you saw?"

She considered it, for just a moment. "Yes, I do. What about you?"

"I'm not sure what to believe. I just wish we could talk to our host again."

Galienne nodded. "I wish we could be together tonight. You'll seem miles apart when you're only across the hall."

"If you need me, please remember that I am right here. Right at your side."

"Always. I love you, Perceval." She could count the number of persons she had ever said that to on one hand.

He smiled. "I love you, also. Good eve, Galienne."

"Rest easy."

They closed their doors.

Alone, Galienne thought inside her quarters. *This is all too much! How do I sort it all out?* She once again found herself wishing for the comforting tone of Baudwin's voice. She wanted to talk with Lupinia, too, and her mother.

Mother. She felt the tears welling up again, feeling misguided. Galienne and Perceval had devoted so many hours during their travels together to simple grieving. It came upon them with no rhyme or reason, but just happened: Gal suddenly crying into her evening stew while they camped in the hills, Purse taking a break from his swordplay with her to weep, falling to his knees. She was so glad to have him with her, and felt alone again to not be at his side.

There is no sin in sharing a bed with this man, she thought defiantly. Neither of them had yet to give their virginity away, like some commodity, and she had listened to him talk of that sometimes. Anxious and guilty for her curiosity at first, then finally getting comfortable with the idea. They were close, but not that close. Galienne thought the single bed looked very isolated.

But that's not the main reason for your fear, now, is it? You lost the visions when you lost your mother, and now someone new claims to be able to harness that power. Was it power, then? She questioned that so often, but received no more sendings. Could Nimue rectify that? It felt like toying with God Himself. And Galienne was disgusted with herself for even considering what it might take to have that ability back.

But why? All it had brought her was painful imagery. She didn't want to see her father's adultery, which always reminded her of her own bastardized birth. She didn't want to see anyone else die, like the people back in Oerfa, who never knew what came for them.

She missed it because it was familiar. Terrifying more often than not, it was nonetheless something she was used to experiencing, and talking with the bishop made it easier. Learning that Nimue knew something of it, too, carried its own strange comfort, but she would not admit such to that Pagan. God, what did those women sacrifice for their gifts?

It just strengthened Galienne's faith. The sword, the departure of her sendings. She was unsure of her exact course, but still believed fervently that God had chosen her for something. He substituted the shield of the visions for the steel of the sword she now carried. Galienne just hoped she'd be able to use the latter better than she had ever managed with the former.

And Perceval. They shared a dream once, that was all, but it was strong all the same. What in God's name were they doing with another man in a hallway? Naked, with only their faith to lead them.

Where? Where would it lead them?

Perceval went over to his window, touching and admiring the hard and clear glass which spread throughout the frame. It felt cool and pleasant; he wondered what other marvels Pellam might have in store. Down below, he could just make out the tiny stable. Lancelot was nowhere to be seen, but Perceval thought he could see the silhouette of his warhorse. Brownie was under the shelter itself, so he could not see her. There was no sign of the scaffold, either.

Sleep would not come for some time. He finally relaxed when his mind brought him the image of Llio. He tried to devote less time to thinking about her lately, there had been so much else to do, so much else to occupy his thoughts. He wished she could have been to see Oerfa with him; he felt certain he would never see it again himself, so how could Llio ever lay her own eyes on it? He wanted her to be safe, to be before him again, longing and vulnerable.

What he felt for her was different from that which he felt towards the girl in the room across the hall. Galienne had come so far, undertaken the same journey he had, against even greater odds. How could he help but love her? Yet it wasn't the same love. Maybe there were three kinds of love, too. He smiled, picturing old Gornymant, sitting beneath his shield in his own hall. He remembered the words after all: the trio of students at Jagent, learning trios themselves.

Three images of the dish, then?

Love of Galienne, who was like a sister? God, where was Dindraine! Love of his mother, even after she had gone. Love of Llio. He missed the others. He had spent so much of his time around women, knowing fewer men. What was it like to have these feelings for a man? Like Yvaine and Lamorak, or the King? He supposed it would feel like the love of Galienne or Dindraine.

Part of his armor was red, the color of love. Also the color of anger and hatred; Perceval supposed its prior owner chose it for the more violent symbolism. Love was the stronger. Was that why he won against Meliagrant?

On and on. Perceval felt hopelessly romantically entranced when he finally drifted into sleep. His dreams about Llio would have embarrassed him into another shade of red had he been awake. It was wonderful and beautiful and she called to him and he was there, in her arms.

He didn't like being woken up by the knocking on the door.

The noise was heavy and thick, the wood of the door trying to muffle the sound. But it kept coming, more diligently each time.

Perceval's eyes tried to unglue, looking up at the ceiling as they finally broke their way open, like a hatchling struggling to break free of the egg. Daylight poured into the room, filtered through the window panes. It was already late morning, judging by the sun's angled intensity.

Again the knocking. Someone really wanted to interrupt his rolling around with Llio. He was twice frustrated; the assorted kissing and caressing had been the product of dreamland, and the knock proved irritating quickly.

Finally he tuned his ears to the other sound beyond the door. Galienne.

"Perceval, wake up! Oh, would you please get up out of bed!" She wasn't normally so demanding.

Grumbling, Perceval got to his feet, plodding the tiny distance to the door that felt like miles. He grasped the iron opener and lifted. Locked. He couldn't remember locking it last night. No matter. He fumbled with the dead bolt until it slid back into its housing, then lifted the handle again, and in fell Galienne.

She had been leaning on the door, listening, suddenly afraid Perceval would never awaken. What if he just lay there all day? Oh, she hated sleeping alone now, she let herself get all irrational. Her discovery had not at all helped.

"What is it? And what time is it out there?"

"I'm not sure, but it's late. We slept in today; it's not very like us."

He nodded his assent. "What are you so excited about?"

Rather than offer a verbal response, Galienne threw her arms around his chest and squeezed, hugged until he had to struggle for breath, until she felt her arms begin to strain from the exertion.

"What happened?" She clenched him tighter, then released him.

"Please tell me." He was always interested in her thoughts.

She sat on the bed beside him. "I just got scared, that's all. I thought I had another dream last night, but now can't remember any of it. And Perceval, the castle is empty!"

"What?!" He stood at once, wanting to see their host.

"I'm serious. There's no one about. I scared myself awake, and thought I'd just take a peek about the place, but I can't find anyone."

Perceval didn't like the sound of that at all. "Let's get dressed, and we'll head down together. Are you all right?"

"I'm always better after talking with you." She smiled slightly. "It's late, Perceval. Shall we make our own haste getting back on the road? After all, the sooner we leave the sooner we can get you back to Camelot. I can't wait to see you made a knight by the King himself." Perceval himself wondered about Llascoit.

His pile of armor and accompanying clothes of less vibrant hues sat in the corner where he left them the night before. He stole a glance beyond the windows of his room while beginning to dress. In the stable stood Brownie, looking as eager as Perceval felt. He'd let Galienne take the first ride today. There was no sign of Lancelot's stallion, however, nor of the knight himself.

Not worrying about it, he readied himself as much as he could. It was quite difficult for him to reach some of the straps of his armor, and he called Galienne back into the room to help him with them. She had the proficiency of any squire.

"Perceval, when will I get armor of my own? I already have a fine sword."

As soon as you kill someone and take theirs, he considered, then was glad he did not voice it. Bitter sarcasm was unlike him. "Once you've the skill with which to wield it," he said instead. Galienne grinned at him, fastening the straps behind his calves. It hurt a bit to bend over to get them himself, when the hauberk already covered his torso. It otherwise did not restrict his movement.

"You've been in the hallway at least," he began. "Is anyone else about?"

"Not a soul. Seems the whole place has either slept in like us, or they've already gotten up and about and are just waiting for us."

"Then let's get moving. I'd still like to talk with Sir Pellam before we leave. Maybe ask him about that cauldron."

"Chalice," Galienne corrected, and they walked out, clutching their few belongings as they strode downstairs.

The feast hall indeed stood empty, all signs of the prior dinner removed. It was spotless, yet no one could be heard moving about. There was little light, the candles long extinguished.

They arrived outside. It looked like it could be a beautiful day, so long as the gray cloud line from the north didn't creep in on them. It looked dark and mean, ready to drench the ill-prepared. Already a gusty wind blew.

No one was in the courtyard, either. They found it most disconcerting, likely having to leave without a proper sendoff or the chance to give thanks for the hospitality. Where had everyone gone?

Near the stable, Brownie gnawed on her breakfast of fresh hay, Perceval wondering what he and Galienne might share for their own morning meal as he untied her. Did Lancelot leave that hay for the mare?

"Still no one?" he asked when he reached the gate, where Galienne stood impatiently circling, making sure she looked into every bit of the surrounding area, in case they missed noticing someone.

"No," she said, clearly disappointed. It was inhospitable to abandon one's guests, even if they slept late, and Pellam was not one to go very far regardless. Maybe he was already on the river fishing.

The mural circling the keep looked even better in the morning sun. Perceval marveled again at the detail, savoring one last look at the King and his company. Galienne was uninterested, wanting answers, not aesthetic pleasure.

They decided to be off, Perceval offering Galienne the reins as she smoothly and effortlessly swung herself up atop the mare. It was a short distance to the landing where they left the raft, since they never found any other way to or from

Bridgnorth. Besides, the raft could take them further downriver, to Worcester, maybe even clear to Camelot itself.

They had covered a little over half the distance between castle and landing, and could see the bridge, which still lacked the requisite artisans to finish the project. Then they heard the voice.

A woman's voice, unknown. "You goose!" it cried accusingly.

Galienne and Perceval turned toward the castle instantly. The sound clearly came from there, or nearby. But nobody appeared among the battlements, nor along the keep. "Who's there?" yelled Perceval in return. The voice had a familiar ring to it.

"That didn't sound like anyone we've met lately," Galienne said.

"One of the maidens?"

She shook her head. "I don't think so. That voice sounded deeper."

Perceval was in no mood for games, nor anything else from this place, especially when he considered of whom the voice reminded him. "How about if I put our things on the raft, and you ride back to the castle and see if anyone's there. If there is, just yell, and I'll come right back."

"Very well." Galienne was glad to be entrusted with the task, feeling proud and important trying to solve a mystery. She prompted Brownie into a gallop and in moments was back at the castle, while Perceval finished the walk to the landing, unloading their spartan possessions and admiring the handiwork of the bridge. Under other circumstances, he might suggest trying to cross it to explore the other side.

Still there was no one visible in the castle. Galienne rode up to its front and was astonished to find the gate closed.

So who shut it? Galienne swung her leg over Brownie's back, hopping to the ground. She tried the gate manually, finding it locked from within.

"Lord Pellam?" she shouted to no one. "Lady Nimue?" also to no avail. Frustrated and nervous, she climbed back onto Brownie, deciding on a lap around the rounded castle walls. Maybe someone was just playing a joke on her.

The woods went on forever in all directions. She still could find no evidence of any way to this place other than the river, and questioned how anyone could have brought the tons of quarried rock here to build a castle at all.

A sound jumped from the woods, near the trail Lancelot had found, the pathway invisible to Galienne's untrained eyes. A sound of leaves crackling, the noise they make when walked upon. She gasped, drew her sword, and demanded, "Who's there? Show yourself!" *Father. You're supposed to be following us.*

She waited a few moments, finally deciding it was probably nothing. The mare showed no signs of fright. It was just Galienne's own anxiety. Had to be.

Then, from near the river, another shout. Perceval's.

"Gal! Come quickly! Galienne!"

From where could such a thing come? It was hypnotically beautiful, breathtaking in its perfect glory. Perceval never imagined anything which even remotely fit its description.

A stag stood across the bridge, shyly walking almost up to the gap in the construction. It had not seemed to notice Perceval until he noticed it.

Except this stag was flawless. Its coat was white as the snow in which he and Dindraine played as children.

Dindraine. Why did the voice from Bridgnorth sound so much like hers? He thought never to recognize it again, not hearing it for so many moons now.

But surely it couldn't be her. *Not unless witches can throw their voices.* Even if that were possible, wouldn't it mean Dindraine had to be close?

He'd deal with the voice later. For now, only the stag mattered.

Unblemished, radiant white, pure, virginal. The stag seemed more curious than afraid. It must have seen Perceval by now; its senses were better than his.

Then why would it just stand there, almost daring him to come closer to it?

Perceval instinctively but dumbly groped for his javelin, remembering it was packed onto Brownie. Then he wondered why he would even consider killing such a wondrous creature, and he rarely carried the light throwing lance at the ready anymore regardless.

The stag moseyed clear up to where the bridge gapped. The unfinished space between the extensions was perhaps fifteen feet, a moderately difficult jump for a running Perceval. He wouldn't move that fast, though, unless the stag did first.

He didn't bother to consider how much more he weighed in his mail.

Perceval walked slowly, cautiously, onto the bridge, looking down at the interlocking cut stones, admiring how they were assembled so they would not just collapse into a pile of rubble.

Closer now, closer. Perceval looked up, locking his gaze with the stag's. They studied each other for several seconds, neither wanting to make any sudden motion, both too curious about each other to care about confronting the unknown.

Perceval glanced down again. He was not about to step on any loose pieces of dead wood or anything else that would make a sudden unwanted noise. He had learned to be stealthier since the last time he stood this close to a large deer.

Almost to the gap in the bridge now, just a few yards to go. Then Perceval could jump or climb across the scaffolding which, while only capable of supporting the weight of several laborers, nonetheless linked the two bridge sections.

He studied the stag's face again, seeing the scenery and his own image reflected in the bright brown eyes. Perceval thought those eyes shielded their own special wisdom, of what it was to be a stag, facing an armed human and showing no fear nor hesitation. What did the animal feel? Perceval felt himself growing entranced with that white face.

He could look down now and see the river flowing by beneath the bridge, finally noticing how its current sped up considerably to his left, where the water ran south on its endless trail. At least he knew how to swim.

But when he looked back up, the face had turned away from him, like it was having second thoughts about this whole encounter. Maybe Perceval had gotten too close. Then, without any other warning, the stag turned its massive but perfectly muscled body about, and trotted back whence it came.

Into the woods, perhaps never to be seen by inquisitive errants again.

Perceval had already foolishly decided he could perhaps tame the creature somehow, or at least feed or even pet it, if he could only get close enough. Not stopping to rationalize, he backed up from the gap several yards to get a running start. Then, remembering that Galienne might want to know his intentions, he shouted to her. He looked back quickly at Bridgnorth. He could see no sign of her yet; she was probably back inside talking to someone by now.

She could wait. He raced for the gap, his metal skin clinking each time a foot hit the stones. And he jumped, his legs straining to hurl him ever forward, not wanting to give in, and bending back up beneath him as he flew through the gentle clean air, ready to take the impact of landing on the other side.

Only he misjudged, his legs denied the opportunity. Instead, he arrived at the edge, his chest having to absorb the shock, the wind leaving him as he thudded into the masonry. He clung to the edge, just hanging on. Below him the river paid him no heed, not slowing to wonder if he would fall.

And across the bridge, the stag stopped and turned, deciding it had run far enough for the moment. It looked at Perceval, baiting him.

"Purse?" Galienne shouted, receiving no response. She hoped he was in no danger. She immediately urged Brownie on, finishing the circumference of Bridgnorth, shouting his name again as the river came once more into view. She never did find the tracks left by her father when he departed the previous evening, not wanting to take shelter with people whom he felt did not trust him nor even want him around.

She could see the bridge, and a horse on the far side, running for the trees.

And Perceval, that dolt, charged after it! Galienne had studied the bridge a bit herself, when they pulled the raft up yesterday. She wondered if even Brownie could make that leap.

But there was Perceval, trying to clear that gap himself, and failing miserably. Galienne winced as she saw him crash into the opposite side. She dug her heels into Brownie's flank muscles, prodding her into a full run. They arrived at Perceval's launching location in moments.

"What are trying to do, get yourself killed?" Unlike the young man, the young woman had little experience with the open water. She could wade, but did not want any part of the river where it started turning violently white.

"No," he grunted, frustrated. He held on, never taking his eyes from the stag. "Do you see it?" he said, trying to summon the strength to hoist himself up. Even then he did not quite realize he had made himself too heavy.

Galienne looked across the bridge, awe-struck by the sight. That was no horse. It was a stag. He was gorgeous! Big, too, and perfectly white. She drew in breath sharply, reaching for the cross at her chest, a gift of the dangling hunter.

It was no use. Perceval's arms were quickly tiring, and he could neither pull himself straight up, nor swing up a leg. The armor made him too clumsy and heavy. It was foolish to try the jump, would have been so even without the mail. But he wanted so badly to see the stag up close.

Haven't you ever chased after anything you couldn't catch, not even for just the excitement of it? His own words rang through him, one of the last things he told his sister before leaving home, relaying another failed pursuit. "Gal, could you help please?" He tried not to sound pathetic, failing as much with that as he had with the leap.

"W-what?" She barely heard him. "Oh," she said, jumping off Brownie. The only way she could see to assist was to work her way across the scaffolding. That shouldn't be too difficult. Then she could pull him up, and they could both cross again and get back to the raft. Still, she too had trouble averting her gaze from the creature across from her.

She held onto one beam to brace herself, stood on another to walk across. One nervous foot went in front of the other. "Gal, hurry please. I can't hold on."

Perceval still looked at the white stag, angry for letting it tease him. He was still determined, but was slipping, losing ground and grip.

Galienne was just stepping onto the other side when he fell.

"Perceval!" she screamed, so loud the water below might have moved from the force of the utterance. She dove for the far edge, sticking out her arms in front of her, as if she could still get to him if she was fast enough.

There was no way she could be. She peered over the edge just in time to see the splash. Brownie whinnied. Galienne screamed again. He was wearing too much armor! And he needed her help to get it off.

The coolness instantly penetrated armor and clothing, jolting the flesh beneath. Perceval looked up, seeing the blurry image of the bridge far above him. He wondered how far it really had been to the river; he seemed to reach it instantly.

He should have just floated back to the surface with little trouble. The mail! He was still fully armored, the panic hitting him like the water's chill, making him flail about. He had to get air soon.

The current was already moving him downstream, and he tried to use its force to help fight back to the surface, back to precious air, back to Galienne.

He had worked so hard for it that when he finally managed to breach the current helped left him. "Galienne!" he shouted, seeing her numbly looking down from the bridge.

Back underwater. He had to get out of his armor, or else get to a shallow enough spot so he could stand. The second scenario did not seem likely, and he was already wrestling with the straps which kept his iron skin fastened to him. He did not care about losing it; he would replace it somehow.

The mittens were already off; they slid from his hands and lower arms easily. Now the hauberk. Perceval fumbled with the leather lacing at his sides, undoing one side, then the other, his brain demanding another dose of air before it rebelled against him and gave in to fate. He worked his way to the surface again, shaking off the torso protection as he did so.

He had drifted more while working off the armor. Galienne was easily thirty yards upstream. "Gal! Get to the raft. Meet me downstream!" he sputtered. And he was under again, the current picking up more speed, more aggression.

She heard him, and obeyed. Back on the mare, she made for the raft, no longer caring if anyone was still around this place. She had to get to Perceval. There was no other way out

besides the river. Except for the bridge which led deeper into
the woods, and maybe a trail or even a road as well. She looked
across. The stag had fled.

She got to the raft, all but shoving a still cautious Brownie onto it, finally remembering the now filthy fabric used to cover the mare's eyes. Perceval had left their gear on board to get
closer to the bridge.

Both poles were there, Pellam's fishing boat nowhere to
be seen. Galienne grunted, heaved, and finally pushed the tiny
raft into the current.

Perceval had at least begun to control the panic; some
base part of him realized that if he lost his nerve, he would lose
his life. Underwater again, he bent himself over as tightly as he
could, his abdomen protesting being crunched into the armor.
It was the only way to reach the leg straps to release the chausses.
They were the last part of the armor remaining. He hoped he
would not have to sacrifice the weight of the sword at his side.

Galienne plunged the pole into the river again, and again,
still close enough to shore to find grounding for it, but it frequently slid along the bottom anyway, affording little in the way
of locomotion. Brownie's bulk was no help, but there would be
no heading back upriver; she had to come along.

For the first time, Galienne sincerely wished her father
were with her. She needed his strength, fearing she would not
make it to Perceval in time.

He threw himself above the surface again, gasping and
spitting water. Reaching the buckles was an ongoing process.
He could not hold onto them for long before needing more air,
and when he reached them he had to strain not to exhale what
precious reserves he took while above the surface; his stomach
demanded he let that breath out when he curled up into a ball.

Under again. There. He loosened one! He started to kick the legging off.

But it snagged. The branches and roots of trees which lived uncomfortably close to the water grew into it here and there; Perceval's armor latched onto one of these, immediately pulling him below. For the last time, he could already tell. He hunched over again, not ready to give up yet.

He dimly thought he could hear Galienne's screaming further upstream, hoping she would not actually come out this far. The current grew ever more powerful and mindful the further it flowed, and navigating a raft with a horse aboard through it would prove treacherous at best.

His head was growing light, brightening. He wondered how it would feel to just let himself go, to just suck the water into his lungs, to stay affixed to the tree for how long... forever? The peace of death might be a welcome change to the roar of the current flooding his ears.

Yet he still grappled with the soggy leather, slippery to work with now, cold fingers unconsciously prodding. He could feel it come undone, but not all the way, and he slid an inch, feeling the strap tighten it again.

With a final effort he pried at the buckle until he thought he had worked his fingers bloody with the effort. Some dismal part of his mind stopped to admire the handiwork of Meliagrant's armorer; the product certainly held together well!

The buckle released; Perceval was free, bobbing to the surface.

He tried to stay above, and scan for Galienne at the same time. He could not see her yet. Again he thought he heard the shouts, but the water muted all which tried to sound more impressive than it, like a jealous lover. Besides being far from the bridge, he also found himself near the shore, the same side of the river where Bridgnorth lay. He supposed, if need be, he might be able to slowly work his way back there, climbing from one tree to the next.

But why return? After their reception this morning, or lack thereof, he almost preferred the river's chill. At least the season was warm, or Perceval might have numbed over with it and died anyway. But he was alive, blissfully alive!

Alone, on a river leading to a destination he knew not. And out of sight of his companion.

Galienne saw Perceval riding the rapids just before she entered them herself, Brownie neighing her protest. For the first time it dawned on her that traversing such an angry part of the river might not be wise; she just knew she had to reach him. But now it was too late; the white water engulfed them.

The raft bobbed up and down, waves lapping over its sides. Galienne had to not only try and navigate, but keep the mare calm as well. Neither was easy alone, and together they became truly formidable.

She quickly lost sight of Perceval, having to pull Brownie back to the raft's center by the reins, lest the mare fall off and spill the whole raft in the process. Galienne guessed they both could swim if need be, but their gear was on board, and she certainly didn't want to lose the raft.

She yelled his name, hoping it would carry over the loud crashes of the water. She was distraught that they had both so misjudged the river; it would not take commands from any mortals foolish enough to brave it unprepared.

It was several minutes before Galienne could maneuver again, the water's power finally beginning to wear down, the ride becoming gradually easier. Brownie's eyes were wide brown balls. She looked ready to try a jump even more impressive than Perceval's ill-fated attempt. They were on the far side now, stopped at the bank for the moment, and there would be no going back to Bridgnorth.

Perceval was nowhere in sight. The only sounds were the heavy breathing of girl and horse, superseded by the onrush of the never-stopping river.

Perceval saw her go by, of course, but despite his cries was unable to get her attention. Not that she could have managed to get to him, though. He stood in a pool of sorts, recessed from the river and protected by the rocks and trees. It would have been a lovely place to bathe, had he the time and inclination. He was waist-deep in the water, not yet wanting to try climbing out. The forest still stood impassably thick; he could either try to squeeze his way through the trees, taking untold amounts of time to get anywhere at all and perhaps starving or preventing some larger creature from doing the same in the process.

Or he could face the river again. He was a strong swimmer, his armor was off him, and the river became calmer further down, that he could see.

His armor. Whatever would he do about that? And the raft? How far did Galienne go? He had not seen it tip, thank goodness. He yelled again. Still nothing. Perceval could hear no response, no call coming from her. She *must* be all right. He felt sure he would know if something happened to her.

Galienne still had no inkling as to Perceval's whereabouts, and grew more concerned by the minute. She had to find him. Or he had to find her. How long could she wait for him? What if he had drifted further downstream? Surely the current would have carried him beyond the point she reached.

She took time to soothe and comfort Brownie, recognizing that attention offered the mare helped relax and reassure Galienne as well. The horse was in no mood to board the raft again, but apparently had learned her lesson from two nights prior. She made no effort to run, and responded readily to Galienne's touch and voice.

Back to the water. When Galienne looked at it again it seemed less the formidable and impassable river powered with a mind and attitude of its own and more the gentle river with its sudden rough spots. She felt sure Perceval had survived it. After a few more minutes, she decided that he simply had to have passed the point where she and Brownie stopped. With some prodding and coercing, she got the mare back onto the raft, and cast off from the thickly wooded banks. She would look for him southward, following the current until she found him.

Perceval could not see Galienne, either. He was wary of trying the river again, having given up on any chance of navigating the trees, at least if he wanted to be beyond the woods in this lifetime. But when the morning breeze wanted to chill him to his bones in his soaked clothes, he plunged back in.

The inlet's calm allowed him time to get used to the water again. He still had some whitecaps to pass. Galienne had gone by already, so he would just have to try and catch up to her. He summoned his courage, made sure that his sword was still snugly strapped about him, along with his coin purse, and eased back into the current. The water snatched him at once, pulling him downstream.

* * *

Previously, Llio of Jagent Castle, formerly of Carmarthen in southern Cambria, truly enjoyed her own travels, which took her and her brother through regions and settlements not seen since infancy, and thus lost from memory. The time since Perceval's departure brought enough events to keep Llio's mind fully occupied, even if they did not quite compare to the wonder and strangeness that Perceval encountered (God, she was still furious at his leaving the city!) Still, she carried the fresh images of recent happenings with her.

The swearing ceremony was accompanied by all the flash and spectacle that Llio and Llascoit had anticipated, even more. The group of new knights-to-be assembled at sunrise following their night-long vigil and were led outside the city walls to the immense tournament grounds (Llascoit proudly stayed awake all evening, even if not always on his feet, occasionally seeking a few moments of refuge on a pew). Those souls who already had the privilege of calling themselves knights awaited them, donned in their polished armor, tunics and shields brightly displaying their colors of arms, showing this family crest or that mythical beast. The new knights would have just until after the breaking of the fast on that Pentecost to ready themselves for the tourney. That automatically put them at a disadvantage, since the older knights were better rested (those who had not spent the night carousing, anyway).

"He better get back to see what he's missed," Llio quipped to Llascoit.

He thought she only referred to the ceremony, and not also to herself. "He'll make it here, sister. He couldn't wait any longer, right?"

"But he never talked about home. Not to me. Did he ever speak of it to you? And why go now, in the mist of all this pageantry?"

Llascoit was exhausted from the vigil, running on pure reserve energy to get through the ceremony. "No," he said, half-thinking, half-asleep. "Are you jealous?"

She informed him that she would not even dignify that with a response.

The city poured bodies forth that day in a seemingly endless belching stream, all wanting to witness such a grand occasion. Some were admittedly more opportunistic: merchants selling smaller, easily-carried wares to haggle over, and shrewd, deft pickpockets numbered among the masses. Yet the overall mood remained one of wonder and awe. Tournaments in lesser kingdoms could be riotous, frenzied affairs, but this was Camelot. The men honored with new rank and status represented the safety and security of all that Arthur had wrought.

Llio left Nimue in their apartment and became just another part of the curious assembly (the latter was *still* sleeping; she must have had quite a time). She could only hear part of the ceremonial speech. "…and to each of you…fealty…rightful liege…" The King's voice was loud and commanding, reminding Llio a bit of her father during one of his lessons. Yet the wind was enough on that cool morning, the dew still wet beneath thousands of eager feet, to keep the King's words limited to the ears of just the closest few hundred.

Llio could tell when the ceremony reached its zenith. The tired young men simultaneously knelt, gaining applause from the crowd. It would take some time to dub each of them, but Arthur did, repeating the sacred vows of acceptance and obedience to each, out of hearing of the rest. The individual lords of each knight stood behind the men as Excalibur touched strong shoulders and reflected light onto brave necks.

Llascoit's sister found it trying to focus all her attention upon the details of the large ceremony. Indeed, Llio grew more interested in the colorful, heraldic tents and gay merchant pavilions strewn about and near the field, and in the remarkable assortment of important persons present. No, she told herself, she would not be jealous, though she confessed a certain envy; she knew of no one else who felt so free to venture off.

The Queen stood off near the grandstand, a huge timber construction, shielded from rain by rich blue draping (though inclement weather seemed unlikely, for the sky remained brilliant and clear, as it had since Llio's arrival). She had to admire how the Queen stood aside, yet still largely without guards. Only two knights stood close by, one of whom was recognizable to most full-time Camelotians: Sir Kay.

Llio also picked out the members of the famed Orkney clan. The large one had to be Gawaine, with his curly, red hair and perfect, strong posture. They all had variations of the same shield design, with Gawaine leading the way as the eldest brother: a violet field with a flying creature on it looking much like an eagle, albeit with two heads. One brother had the same design with a red stripe across it, while the other had the same pattern surrounded by a white band filled with…Oh, it was difficult to see from where Llio stood. Blood droplets, perhaps?

Bishop Baudwin was there, too. Llio had met none of these souls in person, but could overhear the comments from the crowd as so-and-so could be seen over there. The bishop followed the King from candidate to candidate, officiating the entire ritual to sanctify it in the name and under the eyes of God.

It still felt funny not to really know anyone here. There was Llascoit, of course, but he remained preoccupied for a while. And Nimue proved a likable sort, if a bit too easily fatigued. She showed a genuine interest in Llio's affections; the latter was struck by the talkative nature of the former.

And there was the other chatty person she met here. Lupinia, she was called. She had introduced herself when Llio, out of curiosity, stole down to the river from the other side of town to see the stump which once housed a sword. The boat and its deceased cargo were gone, and the tree remains betrayed no indication of having been penetrated by the blade. Even the supposed inscription was gone, perhaps faded away so that it only existed in collective memory.

If it was ever there at all. Some had their doubts.

Few others were down there at that point; the funereal services for Elaine were already past and, mystery or no, most folks had too much else to interest them for the event- and intrigue-filled days.

"I knew her, you know," the clear voice near her had said.

Llio turned to face the amber-haired young woman with the round, intelligent face and kind but excitable eyes. She was dressed in some of the finest leather clothing Llio ever saw.

"I beg your pardon? Knew who?"

"Galienne. She and I were good friends." *Galienne! Thought Llio. So why aren't you still good friends?*

"Oh. I heard she's run off." *And with the man I love, no less!*

The girl, probably Llio's own age, give or take a few seasons, looked at her. "What might you do if you learned you might become something you never thought of, something you weren't even allowed to be?"

Llio gestured helplessly. "I-I don't know. How could anyone know?"

"I'm sorry. It's just that I was so looking forward to seeing her again. Then I heard her mother died. And then I heard she almost took her old man's own head clean off his shoulders."

Llio had not known that detail yet. It would be interesting to know someone who knew the girl with whom Perceval disappeared.

"By the way, I'm Lupinia," the young woman said, complimenting the words with the appropriate curtsy. "I live in Astolat, but I come to Camelot often."

"My name is Llio. I live, or used to live, in Jagent, to the southwest."

"Cambrian name. It sounds like you're trying to hiss. Where now?"

This person had even less shyness about her than Nimue. But she sounded honest enough. And knowledgeable, if she could place a name like that. Llio had only images of what Cambria was even like.

"Oh, I suppose I'm trying to find my niche." *Maybe you should try the honest approach also.* "And I happen to know the person whom she ran off with, although I have never actually met your friend."

That lit up those eyes in a hurry. And so they talked by the ancient tree stump, sharing stories and laughing like two old friends. Lupinia was wonderful company. Her father was working in the city as both a tanner and dealer; she showed off the exquisite boots that she had helped him to fashion, though she admitted hating the stench of working with leather, using dog urine to soften it. "I'm his apprentice," Lupinia said proudly. She loved city life, knowing little of what it meant to sleep beyond the royal guard, and sounded delighted to follow in her father's footsteps, maybe marrying into a bit more wealth and prestige someday. She already had her share of suitors.

Which was why she shouted so loudly now, seeing the new knights. All of them were cheered on by someone, some more loudly than others. One of them had made his own rebuffed advances towards Lupinia already; she cheered him on regardless, feeling too good about the day to fret about who would win her.

And then there was Agrivaine. She liked him about the best, and pointed him out to Llio, enabling them both to look the Orkney brothers over. "Gawaine? Nah. Too many muscles, and I hear he's pretty rough in the sack. Gaheris? No, him neither. He's too much like his mother, too remote. But Agrivaine? Just look at him. How could you not find anything but pleasure with a body like his?" Llio was amused, hoping Lupy would keep her voice down.

"Like they can hear us, with this many people," came the reply. Lupinia was quite a character; Llio could get used to hanging around with the likes of her.

It seemed like the whole ceremony would never end. Most folks there were excited about one of two things, or both: the start of the tourney, which consisted of the helm show followed immediately by the joust competition, and the start of the market. Goods and foods and services not found anywhere else in the Isles could be located here, during this time. Imported wares such as Iberian steel for weapons and tools, pottery from the Greek lands, horses from the Continent and beyond, even silk from lands far to the east that no one seemed to really know anything about, could all be had if the coinage was good. Arthur's imperially-influenced currency was accepted across the Islands, as well as in Armorica, Gaul, and the remnants of the western Imperial lands. The merchants were itching to start their pitches, the warriors similarly thrilled by the prospect of dramatic and exciting mayhem lying just around the corner.

Llio thought she could make out Llascoit when it came time for his dubbing. She and Lupinia cheered together, making sure their voices carried beyond the furtive excitable sounds of the throngs. People jostled and poked their heads and extremities about, vying for the best vantage points, or so they could shout some piece of folk wisdom without deafening their neighbors. The scene remained quite a spectacle. Llascoit rose slowly on tired knees after he felt Excalibur's chilly metal. He joined the others knighted before him, all having received the liege pledges from a man wielding a blade said not to be of this earth.

"Come on, we have to try and get decent seats," ordered Lupinia, taking Llio's hand and dragging her through the crowd. The Queen and the Seneschal would not permit anyone to take their places in the grandstand until they had been seated themselves, and then certain key nobles and lesser visiting monarchs, and finally, in a mad, chaotic dash, everyone else who would fit. The lumber would creak and moan under all that flesh, and people would scamper for as high a seat as possible, all the better from which to see the tourney field.

"Are you certain that was him? That was Llascoit, right?" Llio wanted to be sure she could say she had seen her own brother receive his spurs.

"He's your brother, isn't he? Wouldn't you know better than I? But yes, even though I've met him just once, I'm sure that was him. Now come on!" They had met just a single time thus far; Llascoit had all but fallen in love with Lupinia from the moment he saw her, forgetting at once about the bewitching woman who still, assumedly, lay dormant in their temporary home.

"I just want to be sure. Our father's going to want to hear all about it."

They almost lost each other twice, their clasped hands becoming undone by the mass of gaping humanity. "What does he do? You never told me," shouted Lupinia, trying to keep Llio moving while talking about pleasantries.

"Oh, he's best described as a teacher, I think." Llio worried about her father. Gornymant would be virtually alone back in Jagent, though she knew of his upcoming tutoring of young Gareth and Mordred. Her father had asked her to check on what remained of their family back in Cambria; she would have to leave the city soon to go with Llascoit to Worcester.

But not until the tournament and the festival were memories. It was a time to have fun, to just thrill in new experiences! Gornymant's brother could wait just a while longer.

Lupinia had to repeat her question; it was difficult to carry on a conversation, much more so when moving. "What does he teach?"

They reached the clearing separating crowd from field and stands, and stopped. Only a few others waited there, preparing for their own pseudo-knightly charge for good seats. "He teaches young men to be knights."

Lupinia beamed. "What did you do all those years then?"

"I studied myself."

"To be a knight?" Lupinia said. She still could not believe all the talk surrounding her friend, run off to the wilds with this girl's romantic interest.

"No, silly. To be a steward. I know enough to be a castellan." Llio let the pride in her voice emerge.

Lupinia laughed. "Maybe you could teach me a thing or two."

"First you'll have to find yourself that wonderful husband. Look, they're almost done."

They both stared at the scene adjacent to the field. Only a few young men still knelt. Those standing had to try and remain at attention, admired by onlookers and their lords alike. The lords gained their own glory just for the honor of having the High King knight their vassals. Those who had already been knights for a while cheered and shouted louder and louder, overcoming the rest of those in attendance, never mind that the commoners outnumbered the knights by over a hundred to one.

Llio thought to look back at the Queen, now much closer than before. Guinevere looked pleased enough. But there was something about her face. Llio could not determine what lurked behind it. What did a queen feel and think? Llio had never aspired to anything so high and important as that. The Queen looked troubled, as if she had just received some bit of unfortunate news.

It shouldn't matter to Llio. She would never know the Queen personally, so why worry about it?

Lupinia started to hoot again. "They're finished! Look, Llio. They've all been knighted!"

Sure enough, all those who had spent the previous evening considering their new honor, privileges, responsibilities, and relationship to God, now stood as a unit. Not Round Table knights, not members of the same clan or hailing from the same homelands, some not even speaking Cymru as their native tongue, they were nonetheless bound as one. Bound by ritual, by duty, by the right to bear and use arms, and bound to their lords. The lords, in turn, had their bonds to Arthur himself, who strengthened his position by this public display, the largest single knighting that anyone had ever heard of. The festivities were officially in full bloom now, a triumphant start to the Pentecost celebration.

And during it all, Llio could think of little other than two things: Perceval, and the pressing need to get to Cambria.

She did consider one of her later talks with her father, though, just before leaving home. "I want you both to go to Worcester," he simply indicated.

"Worcester? In Cambria? Father, why would we go back there? I cannot even remember it now."

"I know, daughter. But we do still have family there. I've not seen my brother for some time. It's actually quite far east of Carmarthen, where you were born, and where I met your mother."

"But I thought we were the last of the family. Didn't you and mother leave to avoid the trouble starting there?"

Gornymant let out an even but frustrated breath. He had never had this talk with either of his children. They needed to know more about their roots. "It is true that the land I once called home may revert completely to the Old Ways. The hills people have never taken well to outside influence, and some are no friends of the High King."

"Father, is that why you support him so? Because you sought to secure a stable position beyond the boundaries of the old country?"

Llio's shrewdness often caught him off guard, but it always made him proud. She had so much of her mother within her. "Uh, yes, that about covers it. Jagent is certainly a secure place to live, deep within this kingdom. And my soul does belong to God, so it was proper I should raise my family in a Christian land."

"But I thought Cambria was likewise bound by the cross?" Llio said.

"Parts of it, yes. But the hills are full of tribespeople, proud ones who would take death over the conversion. Their tradition is strong." Gornymant had no love of heathen ways, but he had to admire the strength of their convictions.

"What about the abbeys? And the monks and nuns who live out there?" Llio was waxing disbelief; she certainly was not of the orthodox faith which Rome proclaimed, but she still believed in the holy trinity, the virgin mother, the resurrection and ascension and the hope of salvation.

"They try their best. One of them, I don't recall his name, even went all the way across the sea to the Eire-land. His faith defeated that of the druids. But they hold on to their own heritage, as we hold onto ours." Indeed, only a little more than a century had passed since Patricus had begun converting the Irish. He had even founded a monastery at Glastonbury, near the misty marshes where the first Christian church had lain.

Llio considered it. "Father, what will it mean to the King's court to have Pagans living just beyond the woods?"

"Oh, the King is strong enough to keep them out, if that's what you suggest. I suppose those who cross into Logres will just have to adapt, like Merlin did."

"Merlin? A Christian!" The waxing completed.

"No, no. That's not what I said. I mean he assimilated his life and his beliefs so that he would be accepted into a court which followed another path." Gornymant could see Llio did not follow this. "Llio, I think it's just a matter of being tolerant, and practicing what you preach."

"How do you mean?"

"I mean that the Christian manner is not the only way to come into contact with the divine. We call that divine God, represented to us in the form of a man who died for our sins. But others call it by different names. Gods. Earth Mother. The

Other Side. What difference does it make how someone choos-
es to believe in the powers that lie beyond these walls?"

Llio remained silent. Then, no longer wanting to pursue
religious topics, she asked, "Could you tell me more of Worcester?"

"Of course. You should know this. My brother and
I used to be close, but he remained determined to stay in the
town. There's all kinds of business there: porcelain, worked
metal products, stitched goods. Its only protection, though, is
the old motte-and-bailey that's stood there for years."

"So you were worried that those old Pagans would get
excited by the lure of easy money, and just take the town?"

"Something like that. Worcester is no one's vassal.
They owe no taxes that I know of, living off their own devices."

"Sound like quite an unusual place. Why exactly do you
want us to go?"

"I just want to know how my family is doing. My brother
was married with his own children, and used to negotiate some
big deals for all that trade. After you and Llascoit, they're the
only family I still have. And it's been years. I'd really like to go
myself, but —"

"Hmm?" Llio smiled at her father. She knew him well.
"You've received new pupils?"

"Not yet, clearly. But I will. And I'll be paid handsomely
for it. I'm not sure how many winters I have left, and I want to
teach as many as I can. Besides, the money will eventually fall to
you and your brother."

Llio cared little about the money, knew that under the
law most would go to Llascoit anyway. She had never known
much want, and so gave little attention to financial concerns,
always assuming someone would be there to provide for her. If
nothing else, she could earn a good living by managing somebody's household.

She did care about her father, though, and could see he had already made his decision.

They spoke a little more, embraced warmly, and three days later, she and Llascoit and Perceval were on their way to the city.

She was still thinking of the need to get to Worcester quickly as the heralds announced the end of the helm show. Llio had not noticed the smaller crowd that gathered near the King as a man named Girard swore his obedience, nor the woman and squire who stood near him while he did so. She was in her revelry, ignoring the swarming of the grandstand, until she and Lupinia got their seats (close enough to the top to be able to turn around periodically and gawk at the nobles), and the heralds announced the first pairing of the joust.

* * *

Perceval's efforts exhausted him, bringing him once into what he swore must have been shouting distance from Galienne. Yet she remained too far ahead of him to hear. Though the current had dulled considerably, the Severn still sounded its potent rushing.

If he would ever return to Bridgnorth, it would have to wait. He spent the entire day trying to catch up to Galienne, who maintained a speed impossible to match. The raft rode the water much more smoothly than the lumbering Perceval, who had a rougher go at swimming while clothed, sword at his side.

Galienne, for her part, grew more and more disheartened. She desperately wanted to see Perceval, to know he was all right. She did not know where this river led, was not from this land. Twice she thought she saw someone darting among the forest, once on each side of the river. Then they were gone, and she had to focus on steering the raft again. The thought of a bunch of bandits or heathens running about chilled her; such folk would likely want a good strong breeding mare. Or, for that matter, a strong, young, breeding woman.

She was not about to land again. She'd wait for nightfall first, stopping only when she could no longer see what the water did before her.

It was no use. Perceval would never reach her until she stopped completely, which it seemed she would not do. He realized she was searching for him while he simultaneously sought her, but she looked in the wrong places, and he just couldn't get to her and tell her not to worry.

Now what? he wondered, dog-paddling to the west bank and climbing out to rest. He stared downriver, looked as long and far as he could. No raft.

The gray sky left him alone until late that afternoon, and then decided to pounce upon him like a cat. The clouds twitched and shimmied, then charged, felinesque, southward. Perceval soon found himself in a downpour. He questioned when he might feel the dryness of fresh clean clothes again.

He failed her. That was all there was to it. The last time he was so thick-headed and single-minded about some damned deer he had separated himself from Dindraine. Now he had parted from Galienne. He could only guess where Llio was at this point, hopefully in Worcester, which was hopefully really south of where he sat moping in the downpour.

How had he managed to so befuddle his relations with the women in his life? His mother, his sister, his friend, and the woman he longed to hold and to wake up beside. He disappeared on all of them. Always was there something more pressing, something more adventurous and exciting. He even put off his own knighthood, he was that weak-minded and easily distracted.

He felt for the cross. *Of course.* It, too, was long gone, likewise because he chose to be rid of it, given to someone worthier than himself.

Perceval knew full well that the closest church could be days away, and even then he could only guess in which direction. To the east, most likely. He had prayed so little. Doubted so much. Questioned.

What was he shown? Was Galienne right? Surely they did not see the Grail last night!

But then why did they see it so differently? Galienne swore, almost on that same cross of his, that she had seen the most magnificent piece of ornate and rich jewelry imaginable.

He saw a bowl, and a dull one at that.

He breathed in deeply, taking in the scent of the forest as its fragrances were mixed about and lifted into the air by the buffeting of the rain. It smelled of life, and energy, and freedom. Only the sound of the river came to him now, and the pelting sound of raindrops landing on the leaves and branches. How far did they fall from the great sky?

The water. And the scent. Why was the water scented? It smelled like fresh flowers. And why did we sleep so late? We never do that!

Perceval had no experience with herbalism. He could not imagine the idea of using philters and plant reagents to cause changes in another. A druid might have told him that such feats as strange visions and inexplicable drowsiness could come from such mixtures, assuming the skill of someone versed with their natures.

No, he thought of other matters. Pellam had remained so quiet when his servants paraded through the hall. Perceval remembered how his host looked right at him, totally ignoring the ceremony. It felt like Pellam singled him out, gazing at him with fierce determination, almost mentally willing him to do…

What, exactly? If Pellam had wanted Perceval, or any of the other diners, to do something, why not just ask? Why the procession? It was his own household.

Perceval should have just said something. He was confused and alone. And he was furious with himself for all the grief he brought so many women.

Now he wanted to distract himself; his travels did not need the added misery of contemplating those he had let down.

Why was there blood on the spear?

He felt afraid to mention it at the time, but it looked... no, that was impossible.

The spear itself bled!

He stood up, getting angrier all the time. He had too much hostile energy to work out. Without thinking about it, he plunged back into the water. He wasn't getting any drier on the bank, and he wanted to be on his way again.

* * *

Galienne made excellent time. Perhaps too good. Still there was no sign of her beloved friend.

The Severn eased up and became quite serene and peaceful after the initial few miles of more turbulent travel. Even Brownie relaxed at last, seeming to enjoy herself, though she too had a look about her that suggested concern.

Seeing this, Galienne commented, "We'll find him. Won't we, Brownie?" She watched as an infinity of trees passed them, waving their branches and leaves and going about whatever tasks with which they concerned themselves. Amidst the quiet and the forest depths, she added, "I swear we will. I swear it."

* * *

Sir Clamadeus of Salisbury was used to having his own way with matters. But matters had gone awry, and he was furious. That bitch in heat holed up in Worcester's motte-and-bailey was proving irksome at best; he'd show her how he usually dealt with women when the siege broke. And it *would* break, that much he promised himself almost a fortnight before, when he first decided to take over certain interests.

Worcester was his, damn it all, and he was not about to be put off by some pompous girl and her lame brother.

It was bad enough learning that his friend and ally, Sir Meliagrant of Cameliard, had met his maker at the hands of some whelp, some infernal half-crippled gelding of a boy who must have had the help of the faeries. But now to return to his premiere source of wealth and be met by this girl, a Cambrian hick no less, who all but threw not just her brother's but her uncle's gauntlets at his feet, mocking him! It was more than he was willing to bear.

Thus the siege. If Padern was willing to let this niece of his speak for him and nephew fight for him, then let them all starve in their lair, just another bunch of rats for Clamadeus to run down. He already savored the impending moment of victory, when he would hear Padern's pathetic pleas for mercy and justice, answered only by the cold sharp slide of Clamadeus' dagger along his throat.

The dagger-wielder walked outside his campaign tent, considering his options. He carried a sword, too, a huge two-hander, almost six feet long.

The engines lay in place: a mangonel, the huge powerful catapult, which would be able to knock the old wood fort to sawdust in hours (Clamadeus would save that, for now; it would probably just kill everyone inside, denying him a more personal opportunity for his lethal satisfaction). There also stood a menacing pair of ballistae, over-sized crossbows firing man-sized bolts, aimed at the gate. Clamadeus' wealth was impressive even by the standards of kings and queens; he had access to the latest military hardware, but chose not to use it. Yet.

He debated: how much time would he let pass before he just laid waste to this irksome establishment?

Clamadeus had worked hard to set up his power structure. A landless mercenary knight, son of a man killed in service to those who opposed King Arthur in his youth, Clamadeus wanted the kind of strength and support that the young king managed to secure. Arthur had been just a boy; so what if he had been given one of the Hallows in some cheap theatrical stunt engineered by that doddering old fool Merlin?

Clamadeus was barely older than a boy then, and he dreamed. And planned. And bided his time.

The first ambush of a wagon loaded down with too much jewelry and weapons and too few guards to wield them was planned and executed by Clamadeus and Meliagrant, whom he met as a young knight at the wedding of the latter's supposed sister to the High King himself. He was delighted by one with whom he shared much in common. Both sought their own domains, their own spheres of influence, money, power. There was much to fight for, so much worth having, and this damned king wanted to consolidate it all for himself!

Whereas Meliagrant despised Arthur and would do anything to harm him or those he loved (Clamadeus even now wondered about the accuracy of his dead friend's claim to Guinevere's lands), Clamadeus wanted to eventually meet Arthur as an equal. As another sovereign monarch, as a fellow knight. He didn't just want what Arthur had, he wanted to take it from him and then rub it in his face, showing the king that he deserved the right to rule more.

Ah, to dream and connive. Clamadeus loved that at least as much as impaling opponents and watching them twitch their final moments away uncontrollably and in agony. The image he had when he thought of that wench inside the shoddy excuse of a defense that was formerly all of Worcester.

He had to save his position in this town, whatever the cost. Bringing in heavy equipment was not easy and far from subtle, but even that would have its merit, in time. He had taken the liberty of liberating the gear, all constructed within Cameliard, from Meliagrant's own holding, a tiny castle on the Cambrian border of Cameliard. Clamadeus was now beyond the King's jurisdiction, or so he thought. Besides, the Round Table knights could hardly get there in time, even if they knew what was happening. And if they could, they would still have to pass through some inhospitable terrain, and risk encounters with hostile local residents.

Geographically and politically, Worcester lay in a vast opening space in the endless group of forests in this region that could have been called a "no-man's-land," to use an expression popular with the long-dead centurions. To the north and west lay the tribal lands and trackless hills; to the east and south lay Logres. But the forests...Within them, anyone pretty much could do what they wished. Meliagrant had taught that lesson to Clamadeus quite well.

The attacks on merchants with what few men could be found to help, a few knights and mostly peasants and hill folk, enabled the "influencing" of those who ran the affairs of productive Worcester, with its artisans and craftspeople. Clamadeus had a disdain for artistry itself, thinking those with a flair for aesthetics were mad at worst, aloof and removed from society at best. But their products sometimes proved valuable. He wondered if they knew that someone was indirectly robbing this isolated community blind and on top of that, using the collected money to take over the town itself.

That was the plan: steal first, then buy the source and watch the wealth grow. And make sure no one stole from them in return. It had gone well enough, with Padern and the other members of the impotent town council bought or coerced into silence, until Meliagrant once again fomented his claim to other lands. Damn fool. It got him killed, and little had gone right since.

It was vital to keep things controlled. No one in the nowhere town had ever resisted him, and Clamadeus couldn't let some pseudo-rebellion poison his work. He still had much to do and strive for, and it required money and obedience. He would make an example of Padern and his nephew and niece.

He decided to try a cheap insult. It wouldn't work, but it always made him feel more in control. He strutted back to the gate, eyeing the ballistae.

"Hey, barnyard heifer, are you ready to give up? You can't stay in that shit-hole your whole life! Hasn't that worthless crippled brother of yours healed yet? I will graciously kill him in honorable single combat and let the others go. You hear that, you others in there?" Clamadeus' men and knightly followers laughed. Until a response was offered.

A woman, shouting back from within the elder wooden palisade. "Heifer I may be, but it would take far more bull than you to render me otherwise. As for this hole, it smells cleaner than any on your own useless body. And finally, my brother possesses more strength in his manhood than you have in your entire vile form. Now be gone, and let honest working folk alone!"

The knight was enraged, his subordinates scurrying out of the way of his wrath as he clomped right up to the gate. "Vile bitch!" he spat into the splinters. "All your insults and empty boasts will count for precious little when I slice your family to ribbons, sparing them just enough life to let them watch as I take you into submission. I *will* have this town!" Clamadeus wheeled around, marching back to the ranks of his men. There was no other response from the walls yet.

Llio felt elated, ignoring the threats she had already been hearing for days. Putting down a pig like Clamadeus reinforced her own confidence. She had a brother to nurse back to health, an uncle who had aged from sick worry before his rightful time, and she wondered how much longer her fortune might yet last. More than ever she wished Perceval were at her side, but she was further than ever from forgiving him for leaving them behind.

If only Llascoit hadn't been injured at the tourney. *No, perhaps that was for the best. It would take someone more skilled than my dear brother to defeat the likes of that bastard maggot's offspring outside.*

So much for her wonderful trip to see old family. *Father would have known what to do, and he would never have allowed himself to be battered into a corner like his weak-willed brother.* Llio turned away from the gate, walking back to the nearly rotted fort domiciles that sheltered the few of them these past days, since they fled the vindictive wrath of the man claiming to be the sole arbiter of events in Worcester.

Llascoit had begun the tourney quite impressively, all things considered. He had been paired for the first joust round close to the beginning; the better known knights would have at each other later on, to get the crowd eager and anxious to see them perform. Besides, the new knights might have fallen asleep if they had to wait the couple of hours it took just to finish the first round.

He bested a stout and agile Gaulish knight who could not get past Llascoit's shield. The other knight's lance splintered on impact, sending him sprawling.

Llascoit achieved his second wind with that blow; he had looked forward to whomever might come next for him.

After the first round, the winners were paired with other winners (half of the entrants who had begun, their numbers cut in half again with each consecutive round; there were so many knights it would take nine full rounds to reach a final match). No one knew who would receive their match with whom, but soon the heralds began to shout the names. The knights looked at each other inquisitively; *would it be* him, *or will* he *be as easy to topple as the first?* They all asked their own minds. Only the veterans betrayed no anxiety or hopefulness, their faces solemn masks, or occasionally smiling visages of confidence. Few of the new initiates made it that far.

Llascoit was to joust opposite one of the Orkney's own, the man for whom Lupinia had shown a growing fondness: Sir Agrivaine.

The handsome red-haired fellow immediately set about learning who this "waste of my time" was, and sneered when the latter announced himself. Agrivaine looked him over from head to toe, snorting and chortling lightly as he sized up his competition. He shoved his shoulder into Llascoit as he passed him, barking orders to his squire to bring up his favorite charger.

Llascoit felt ready for the pressure. Even if he lost, there was no shame in being bested by one of these famed knights; all the Orkneys were well-known, and were expected to win over non-members of their fraternity. Only three things mattered now: the lance, his strong steed, and the man facing him.

Llio and Lupinia had watched entranced from the grandstand, straining to hear the herald's call and the bellow of the signal trumpets.

The match was given its start. Llascoit and Agrivaine sped furiously at one another, clashing so hard that the onlookers gasped, watching as the pair of broken lances spat slivers of wood at squires, other knights, officials. Agrivaine teetered in his saddle, at once turning his mount around to see the result.

Behind him, struggling to stand up from the cool and surprisingly hard earth, sat Llascoit, already having forgotten the other man. He was too busy trying to get up on legs that wanted to remain planted.

"Get up, boy!" commanded the arrogant other knight, slowly urging his horse closer. "Let's finish this!"

Llascoit was stunned. This was just a joust, and he already lost. What was left to finish?

He raised his hand feebly to Agrivaine, then strained his way into a standing position, his heart charging like his horse and his vision too bright. His left side felt like it burned with the fires of hell itself.

"That's it! Boy, no one's ever hit me that hard in a joust. Now what, pray tell, have you against me?" Agrivaine's tone had all the soothing warmth of a snake's hiss.

"N-nothing, Sir Agrivaine. It's just that –"

"Oh, and since when do you presume to use my given Christian name? I'll have you know, beggar, I've bested far better than you. As God is my witness, I should run you through just for such an insult alone, to say nothing of how you deliberately tried to impale me!"

Llascoit didn't know what this man was talking about. He had tried to win, nothing more. And the left side of his torso screamed to be let alone, for him to lay down and not even breathe.

He gasped through his retort. "On the contrary, Sir. It seems, ugh, that you tried to do just that to me." Llascoit winced with the words. He was in too much pain to care whom he addressed.

"You would dare –?" gaped Agrivaine, disbelieving but glad to be able and justify what he next had in mind. He reached for his sword hilt, but a commanding voice froze his hand in place.

"Come now, Agrivaine. Injuries occur at tournament all the time. You've already won. Why not be the bigger man and concern yourself with your next opponent?"

Just when he thought he had enough of the Orkneys, Llas was delighted to see and hear older, wiser Gawaine, still master of his family, at least when they were in Camelot. Then Agrivaine looked more like a pouting child than an armored warrior thirsty for blood. He rode off sullenly, shouting, "We shall meet again, virgin. On that much you can surely count."

Gawaine, for all his family pride and brusqueness and womanizing, was not called the silver-tongued for nothing (how else could he keep potential feuds from festering, or coerce so many women into his bed?) He even helped personally with Llascoit, giving a cursory look at what was clearly an evil bruise.

"Best get the chirurgeons to look that over, lad," he said, though to Llascoit it sounded more like a direct command.

"Aye, I will. Thank you, Sir Gawaine."

Gawaine feigned ignorance. "You know of me?"

"Doesn't the whole world? It's not every day I get to meet a king's champion."

"Ah, that was another day, when I defended Arthur's life and limb. He has his own bodyguards, and I've more personal matters to fuss over now. A body can only bash so many heads in a single lifetime."

How could someone like this, who rumor said could hurl boulders like a giant, still have a kind face and an even disposition? Llascoit had heard of the one who once challenged this knight; maybe the green man humbled him somehow.

Right. Humble the red-headed walking arsenal in front of him. Llas couldn't picture it.

"Can you walk, then? The King's hospital awaits."

Llas nodded, then limped his way to the beds laid out specifically for the occasion. Several dozen others would need to have the prices of their manliness and boasting examined before the day was through.

And in the grandstand, Llio and Lupinia had stood to make their way down to him. They would have to stay in Camelot long enough for the injury to lessen.

But presently, Llio still worried about the wound to Llas' port-side ribs and the delicate lung they shielded. He had been so insistent about leaving, about her and Lupy not seeing him "all dolled up like some fussy whining girl." And so they left the city just days later, the festivities winding down for another year, the people returning to their old haunts and labors.

Llascoit was now simply in no shape at all to meet Clamadeus as the champion of free Worcester, or what was left thereof.

But they couldn't stay in here forever. Granted, Clamadeus had no such thing as an army beyond the motley bunch surrounding just a few persons tired of having the fruits of their dedicated labors hoarded or used for ill purposes. He had maybe a quadruplet of knights, and about two dozen mercenaries, she supposed.

She checked on her sleeping brother. The journey out of Camelot went without trouble, though Lupinia remained behind. Llascoit said nothing to her of the treatment he received at the hands of the object of her infatuation. He did not wish her to think he thought poorly of the man because he wanted her himself; Lupinia would have to make her own decisions, and so brother and sister left the city alone. Even Nimue had left without saying good-bye. It seemed the entire visit to Camelot was just one disappointment after another, save for Llascoit's knighting. Llio wondered what they would do next, and remained confident enough to picture her life beyond this episode with Clamadeus.

What would she do then?

* * *

The forest grew more maddening each day, even each mile. Every step wanted an answer, and Perceval had to confess that he had no solutions.

The labyrinth would never end. That was merely one of the thoughts preoccupying him. Yet he never stopped unless eating, sleeping, or relieving; he just kept on, hoping for his salvation from the shady green depth. He even moved while eating, foraging as Gornymant had taught.

He still found no sign of Galienne's passing. No raft, no horse, no friend. He actually took some heart in the lack of evidence; had the river swallowed the life from them, it could not also have kept the remains beneath its surface indefinitely. Bodies and rafts washed ashore, that was just the way of things, one of the countless lessons Perceval learned since leaving Oerfa the first time.

How many others had he learned? Forgotten? He felt ashamed for not arriving at the right question, the right tidbit to say, at the dinner fed him by Pellam and his servants. There had to have been more to it than what he saw! He could feel it, like a knot in his heart, throbbing to remind him of tasks undone.

What did all the ceremony mean? Was that Pellam's own dish or bowl, or did he find it or take it from another? Why did Galienne and I swear the same thing was two different objects? And damn it, why do I keep failing women?

He occasionally apologized to the trees, wondering if Tathan was correct, if the trees actually listened to foolish humans whom they outlived. They remained silent save for their whispering breezes; Perceval took it as some small sign of confidence that they usually blew at his back, and less frequently in his face.

He tried to persuade himself rationally, often speaking his arguments and points aloud. He first thought that someone must have placed some herb or something into his cleansing water at Bridgnorth, and in Galienne's as well. Something smelling as sweetly as a flower impregnated by spring. But then he could not decide how he and his dear friend had such visual disagreement.

As for the ceremony, he figured it was a Pagan fertility rite or some such; the old man was a virtual cripple, so maybe the singing and the good food helped him feel better about his infirmity. But then Pellam hardly smiled during that part of the evening; he frowned, looking not much at all like the playful coot who reeled in a salmon with excited ease.

The bowl itself? *It had to be a bowl, no matter what she said.* Perceval figured a man as well-traveled as Pellam might have just, well, just *found* it somewhere. Who knew? It could have come from anywhere.

From the Holy Land, or even beyond, he could hear Galienne's declarative voice speak in his mind.

So long as Perceval followed the river, he headed south, and eventually would arrive at the old town of Worcester. The difficulty lay in keeping the Severn in view. The forest was thick and entangling, and the minimal passages through it often led Perceval away from the water flow. At times he got so off track he could not hear the river, either. Those were the most disheartening occasions; once he had to backtrack for what felt like miles, and then seek another almost non-existent pathway back into the woods.

It was this haphazard navigating, traveling mostly by sound and feel, that became responsible for Perceval's completely missing a certain geographical feature, one he knew nothing about. Roche Sanguin, like Bridgnorth, lay nestled securely out of view of most; it could only be seen (and barely, at that) from the Severn itself. It sat upon a stretch of earth just inside the magnificent Dean woods, offering refuge only to a certain type of person. Perceval was so engrossed in his thoughts, direction, and purpose (the last of which was becoming more blurred all the time) that he devoted no time in looking for any refuge from the wilderness other than that promised further south.

And despite his bleary brain and weary body, he soon found an opportunity to do something for a woman besides let her down.

* * *

"I've told you before, children, whomever I choose to love or bed or anything else is my own decision, and no one else's!"

Margawse was livid. How dare her eldest sons take matters into their own hands! It didn't matter that she all but ordered their actions; she was not about to voice that she would have preferred to resolve the issue herself. Margawse knew something of blood sacrifice.

"And what's this business about a bunch of madmen chasing after you? I'd say the only lunatics around these parts were the two standing before me now!" In her lap, she stroked her favorite cat, an ebony-colored tom with emerald eyes.

The queen's bodyguards cleared their throats, not daring to snicker for fear of retribution at the hands of the queen's sons. Their faith in her strengths paled in comparison to their knowledge of what Gawaine and Gaheris were capable of when angry.

The two brothers had escaped a rather inhospitable portion of the great wastes. They even found the road taking them back into beloved Lothian, the stretch of which had never before felt so welcome. And, as their mother requested, they sought her out at once, wondering what all the to-do was about. Her message sounded urgent in Camelot. Her wrath suggested that was the case.

The ruling family of Lothian possessed a large concentric stone castle built by the vision of Lot and the money he took in from the surrounding landscape. Such funding mostly came easily; Lot had been no fan of Arthur's, and the people north of the Wall guarded their traditions and lifestyles jealously. They would have no part of a Christian kingdom.

Margawse felt more sheltered and safer out of doors than in the drafty, chilly hall within her keep, but the fortress had become a symbol of pride in the northern regions, and she chose to rule from within it. She left the piled stones as often as possible, however; she was a creature not of the hall but the heath.

So here she sat in the reception room, sparsely lit and cold, having listened to her sons' report of their travels. Her cat made her feel warmer.

"Dear boys," she began, speaking with an ambiguous tongue, "Lamorak was no comparison to your sire, surely, but he was good at keeping a lonely bed warm. You did not have to cool it again by slaying him."

Gawaine and Gaheris knew their mother well enough to realize they should not bother questioning how she came about that knowledge; the woman had her ways, which were not discussed among them at all. Not ever. And even so, did she not all but accuse the man of rape in their presence?

"Mother," Gawaine said, "would you have us forgo our duty to our father by finishing the debt of blood? Our family honor is restored." As fearless as Lancelot, perhaps more so, Gawaine spoke calmly to the purported sorceress. His brother reined control over his own apprehension; their mother would not see him tremble at the sight of her.

"That may be, but at what cost? Lamorak, too, sat at Arthur's side. What will the King say of his knights who kill each other off in their spare time? The people of Logres will be either terrified or as vindictive as you; they will pray to their king for deliverance from such events either way." Margawse was secretly delighted by this part: all the more disunity to the fabled Round Table.

Margawse, in truth, knew nothing at all of witchery, sorcery, nor any other supernatural talent. She received potions from her women subjects on occasion, as payment for favors better left unmentioned. The ones she used with that fool Elaine were just experiments: first the love charm, then a test of lethal poison. Margawse could sacrifice to further her own ends, and that was the end of her perverse interpretation of magick.

She was so informed because of her network of messengers and knights, all hand-chosen and of Pictish blood. She had grown to despise her sister because she *did* have Talent, and doubly because she wasted it, in Margawse's opinion. Avalon was dead, that was plain enough. What life was it when one had to hide not only one's nature, but one's very home, from the encroachment of invaders, be they zealous Christians or axe-toting Garmani?

No, Margawse could not allow herself to live that way. She knew, could just tell, that the time would soon come when the entire island would fall under the cross, or else be decimated by the hairy and odoriferous Germanics. So it became her self-professed duty to ensure that her lands would remain both unspoiled and free, free to follow the ways of their ancient ancestors. She could not hide the lands within some musky fog like her sister and her ilk, but she could ensure the continued safety by her own devising. Maybe even win the crown herself. Arthur's indecision would cost them all dearly, and she had initially thought these eldest two of her brood would fall next into Britain's kingship, but their loyalties were too strong. Gawaine might have ignored Lamorak otherwise.

But there were others. Agrivaine, Gareth. And Mordred. Arthur's own blood. Margawse had her own ideas about how best to use her boys to help with the thorn in her side, especially her three youngest. The time would have to come soon, though; the younger sons could not be polluted by these lecherous ways!

And now her eldest two, her proud flesh and blood. She always knew she could rely on their loyalty; their bodies might show up in church sometimes, but their hearts and souls followed the same path she did. Margawse could tell. She just didn't know their sense of justice and family honor was strong enough to smite down a fellow knight in his prime. Had it been retribution in Lot's name, or jealousy for any man whom she chose to bed? She no longer remembered that she shamed Lamorak's name in front of her eldest sons, ensuring her justification in having the man dead at last. She knew Gawaine had a violent temper, but she had her own reasons for ridding herself of Lamorak. If nothing else, he was actually an unsatisfying lover.

"They will not know, mother," Gawaine said. "No one will. We covered our tracks too well. The knight he traveled with was completely out of sight, and is by now likely so convinced of the truth of that Beast tale that he'll believe the creature responsible, not us. Arthur will hear only of how his knight bravely fought, but lost, against the monster of the hollow hills." Gawaine had gotten careless; he didn't even know the other knight was a kinsman.

The tempestuous man's words had their merit, Margawse supposed. "You're sure of this, then?" The two men nodded. "And the King doesn't even know of your additional brothers –"

"– who study with Gornymant in the south?" interjected Gaheris. Margawse hated when he finished her sentences. But their nod to her second question was likewise answered by nods. The men thought their younger siblings were training with the old battle lord to keep their upbringing anonymous so they would receive no special treatment or favors, from Gornymant or anyone else; Margawse went along with that belief. She had other schemes for her youngest.

"Then, aside from your vindictive streaks, you have both done quite well. Come, let us ready for a welcoming feast." She clapped her hands, instantly summoning servants to her side. They listened to her commands, bowing when dismissed. The tomcat jumped from her lap, eager to seek its own affairs.

Gawaine and Gaheris were bound to this woman by blood and a sense of loyalty which grew hazier every time they stood in her presence. They certainly had no love of Lamorak, but they felt a slight pang at their mother's refraining from shedding so much as a single tear over the loss. She would find another lover soon enough, and she would have to take care not to flaunt him about the way she did with Lamorak. The strings tied to her eldest two were starting to fray.

* * *

Perceval wondered how he would ever get into the fort beyond the rich little town; there were far too many knights and soldiers surrounding the place, and he grew nervous indeed at the stories he heard since arriving the previous night.

At first he believed it could not possibly have been Worcester he stumbled into. It was so easy to find! All he had to do was follow the river. Keeping the water close by was the tough part. And yet the labyrinthine forest thinned, then became barely a cluster, and finally all but disappeared, while the mighty Severn continued on south. For about two dozen miles, if Perceval's estimate regarding the last two days was accurate. His wanderings had already occupied close to a fortnight. And then the town just came into view, like a wonderful dream longed for during the deepest, securest of sleep.

The tentacles of the forests surrounded the entire region, which Perceval learned was a rough oval-shaped patch of flat grazing land, occupied only by the residents of Worcester, and a few minuscule settlements dotting the landscape. He surmised the reason for the town's defensibility as well as relative anonymity was solely those woods. If they were anything like the groping mass of trunks and branches which toyed with him for the last days, then surely no army or brigands could ever reach this town, much less plunder it.

Except for the occupational forces. Perceval spent his first night unnoticed by those of a more military bent; he had neither horse nor armor, after all, and even thieves were known to carry swords from time to time. He had slipped into a farmer's yard, knocking at the door and humbly requesting hospitality, which he refused to take outright like some braggart; he was still not a knight.

The farmer and his wife and children accepted him graciously enough, even allowing him to sleep in their barn with several heads of cattle after they fed him and gave him enough water to bathe. He scrubbed his clothes as best he could, enjoying both the cleanness of the water and the absence of any noticeable scent within it. He was surprised that the family could afford cattle, but then every building in the town bespoke a level of wealth which, while not regal, would nonetheless all but guarantee endless pillaging were the town more topographically accessible.

So he lay there that night, missing his old blanket and the warm body which usually slept next to him. He had seen no sign nor sound of Llio, though the farmer suggested she might be holed up in the rustic dwelling, along with Padern and whomever might still be left of the town council. Perceval was not looking forward to any confrontation with those who apparently claimed the town as theirs, but if the farmer's suspicions contained any accuracy, he resolved to stop at nothing to gain entrance and ensure Llio's safety.

And where was Llascoit during all of this?

No matter, Perceval thought, closing his eyes to embrace slumber, if not a body other than his own, *on the morrow I'll just have to find a way in.*

* * *

It was not the farmer's rooster which awoke Perceval the next morning, but the loud baying of commands, met with guttural responses. Men were ordered to watch the tower for archers, or prepare siege equipment. It sounded clearly enough to Perceval that Worcester was about to be stormed.

Perceval quickly scanned the barn: nothing but him and the cattle. His sword lay sheathed next to his belt and coin purse; ever since becoming separated from Galienne, he had traveled on the bare essentials alone. His leather leggings and woven tunic were beginning to stink clear up to the clouds, not that he could notice. He had just his wits, his steel, and his coins.

He stood, quickly donning the belt from which hung all his current worldly belongings and security, not bothering to consider what these men might think if someone looking much the thief tried to sneak past them. On his way out of the barn, he took a denarius from the purse, leaving it on an obvious spot on one of the stable cross-beams. It was more than the cost of a decent night's sleep, even in more civilized quarters, and the people of Worcester hardly seemed in need of more coinage. But hospitality had been freely offered him; non-knights had to pay their way. He winced at the thought.

Was that why we couldn't find anyone at Bridgnorth that morning? Because we did not offer any sort of payment for such a gracious welcoming? He shoved the thought aside; Pellam had no need for further riches, and seemed far more interested in esoteric topics anyway.

A slight mist pervaded the town. None of the villagers appeared in its quiet, infrequently traversed pathways; indeed, the dwellings seemed secured against any outside interlopers. Perceval would find no help today; he would have to deal with the situation himself. *Or get some aid from within the old fort,* he hoped.

It was a quick walk to what was now a monument to history. Worcester could have repelled, at best, maybe a dozen men-at-arms. The forest, with its reputation (*God, why didn't I listen better to that bard?*), kept it not only secure, but in some regions of the Isles, completely unknown.

Clamadeus and his men paid no heed to the tall, confident but shabbily dressed individual who strolled right up to just behind their pavilions. The one closest to Perceval reminded the young man of Meliagrant, but he wasn't sure why. The other men present busied themselves with what would obviously be an early morning invasion, an easy effort at breaching the gate leading to the souls trapped beyond. The errant thought he could break through that gate with either his sword or a good strong kick, it looked so old and brittle. Not even termites would waste their time here anymore.

Perceval tried to reach the gate unobserved (or at least without anyone caring), stealthily gliding from the pavilion to a large tree, from there to a prone position within a ditch dug before time, and across to crouch behind a large wheeled machine of some kind. Perceval had never seen a catapult before. It seemed a bit excessive for just an old fort. He also noticed the gigantic crossbows aimed at the gate. He was glad they weren't loaded, for nearby stood the ammunition for them: the bolts were as long as himself!

So far, so good. None of the men paid him any heed. And that was when he heard the voice.

A shaky, sickly sounding voice, but familiar. Llascoit sounded like he was as close to death's door as Perceval was to what was once known as the gate of Worcester. "P-Perceval! Up here!" He started to hack in the tower where he sat, perched like some observant bird.

Some murmuring from inside the gate, where awaited… whom? Llio? Perceval prayed she was here, his prayer directed to no one in particular.

"Get him! Detain him, you dolts!" Perceval whirled around to see the brawny knight shouting at his peons. That had to be Clamadeus, he surmised. He had no wish to tangle with the knight now, alone, unarmored. The farmer gave him the name the night before.

Three men-at-arms, arrayed in cheap leather breastplates beneath a more protective covering of iron scale mail, were the closest, and all brandished their massive pole arms, hoping for an easy capture. Or kill.

"Llascoit! Open the gate. Let me inside! I'll help you defend this place. Is Llio in there?" Perceval's frantic shouts went unanswered. Llascoit had deserted his post.

"If you live long enough, boy," muttered Clamadeus, inaudible to all save two of his brethren knights, who had their own swords drawn, and advanced to the gate. The siege equipment was for now forgotten; if Padern and his whore were stupid enough to allow this lad in…

There was still no answer from the rotting door. The footsoldiers were close enough now to smell the disheveled Perceval. He faced them, continuing to pound on the gate for any response with his left hand.

His right, of course, fell to the cold, hard comfort of Meliagrant's old hilt.

"Look, it's just a beggar," said one of the infantrymen, chortling at Perceval's expense.

"No, I tell you it's a thief. Where'd you get such a fine sword then, hey?" Perceval could not place the accent on this second man. Behind them, the knights edged ever closer. They did not appear in a prisoner-taking mood, and the heavy equipment suggested a massacre in the making. He'd have to prove himself worth taking seriously, or else be finished here, so close to his goal, hacked to bits by the likes of these arrogant sods.

"Back off, loud-mouths, or I'll send your hands home to your loved ones, assuming the existence of anyone desperate enough to love you three."

The soldiers braced their weapons, couching them steadily and pointing them at Perceval's midsection. They could reach him with single well-aimed thrusts now. The one who thought himself an expert at identifying law-breakers said, "You talk smart, boy. Where might you be from? Or shall we just run you through and ask questions later?" His two companions giggled.

Perceval had quite enough of being called "boy" by anyone. He backed up one more step, feeling the gate resting snugly against his back, and simultaneously unsheathed his sword with an alacrity Gornymant would have truly admired.

He decided to exaggerate, if not outright lie. *All right, so I'm lying, technically. But it's better than facing these kinds of odds.* "You're in no position to ask anything of Sir Perceval of Powys, and I warn you, this is your last chance." These men deserved no better than a lie. They were prepared to kill innocents just for monetary pay and the added chance at booty.

The most talkative of the trio lunged at Perceval, shouting, "Liar!" as he did so. Perceval parried the eight-foot halberd with his blade, and continued to spin in place, completing the circle with an overhead slice that instantly cleaved the man's leather helm, then skull, then brain. He collapsed with barely a groan, and another came at him.

The last of the three, content to laugh with the other's jests but offering none of his own, drew back. He never felt so comforted as when he turned to see Sir Clamadeus and the other knights just behind him. They stopped for the moment, watching the fight. For now.

"My lord," panted the soldier. "This 'Perceval.' It is he who defeated my good Sir Meliagrant. I swear it. Now he comes to kill us all!" The man hadn't intended to sound so pathetic, but he would never forget how Perceval so easily and surprisingly smote his former master. Only a few of Meliagrant's men actually entered Camelot that day; the others, fearing retribution but not trusting the King's justice either, had to seek some kind of employ. The man had numbered among Clamadeus' squires for several months.

"Oh, do shut up, you squirming little boy in man's clothing. Look at him! He may have learned something of how to swing a sword, but I've had whores who could best him! Now go back and help, and let me worry about how to deal with this fool."

"But Sir!" pleaded the man. He had no desire for another of Clamadeus' reprimands; scars were left from the last one. Seeing no choice, he turned, just in time to see his fellow soldier crumple beneath a horrible blow to the shoulder. The thief, or knight, or whomever he might be, had gotten inside the range of the halberd, and taken full advantage.

Perceval felt proud that he was not even breathing heavily, but the feeling was countered by the knowledge that he had killed two men. He tripled his number of slayings in mere seconds. He willed the thought away; a knight's job was often ugly and brutal.

"You fight well, for a thief," Clamadeus said, walking slowly up to the gate and the fallen bodies. The caw of nearby crows could already be heard.

Perceval had just about enough insults for one day. "I told them I was no robber, and see the result. I am Perceval of Powys."

"But I thought I heard you identify yourself as *Sir* Perceval. And Powys? Why, only the heathen hill scum come from there." Clamadeus won more than one duel by setting his opponent to anger; hostility made one careless, tense, and slow. He would enjoy claiming this false knight's head.

Perceval quickly weighed his options, disliking them all. He was doomed if he fought this knight here, among his fellows, minus even a shield. He kept facing his enemies, unmoving, until another voice interrupted.

It came from behind the rotten door and its brown hinges. "Perceval! It truly is you. Get yourself in here at once!" A woman's voice.

Perceval dared not turn and show his back to the men who would all too happily kill him. "Llio?" he asked the air, hoping for too much.

"Of course, silly! You already saw Llas. And we saw you take on these two. Now get yourself inside before the others have their way with you!" Her words were followed by the subtle noise of a large wooden bolt being lifted from its securing within the door. They were opening the gate.

Perceval could scarcely believe it. The others were so close they could easily charge on foot and reach the inside of the fort before the gate could be shut again. He had to think of something.

The code. Gornymant's sacred code; it mattered not what type of knight heard it. Whatever the sort, all were supposedly bound by chivalry's mandates. He hoped the same applied to Clamadeus.

"Sir, are you noble enough to face me come dawn, alone? And if I am still shy of armor, would you then meet me likewise? Or do you just talk threateningly, taking your safety from those at your side?" If the code of honor didn't work, maybe an insult would.

The knights stood incredulously. Only the footsoldier with them looked serious, and afraid. "You challenge me to single combat? For *this*?" He gestured broadly at the small hill-fort.

"Are your ears as full of shit as the breeches of that coward hiding behind you? You want the fort, the town, you kill me for them."

"Perceval, no! I won't let you! I've seen him fight —" but Llio's words were silenced with a hand wave from Perceval. Behind him, the gate stood partially open.

"That I will do, lad. But how do I, in turn, know that you're not what my men think you are? Some cheap villain unworthy of neither my considerations nor time? If you are that, I will watch you try to take back your insults even while I bleed you." The words came coolly, smoothly. Clamadeus was fascinated by the young man's resolve.

He had a point. Without the proper trappings of a knight, and looking and reeking as he did, Perceval supposed he appeared far more the thief than the questing errant. *Questing for what?* he mused.

Without another thought, he tossed his sword to Clamadeus, who caught it cross-wise. The knight's eyes widened. "I'll expect that back come morning." And Perceval turned and slipped inside.

* * *

"Are you mad?" exclaimed Llio. "You just threw your personal treasure away to that bastard? What do you plan to use to fight him tomorrow?"

"The very same sword. Bastard or no, he'll return it." Perceval beheld that exquisite face. How long since he had seen it?

Her manner was not quite so inviting. Llio held him at arm's length. "And where in God's name did you just run off to? How dare you abandon me in Camelot!"

He knew he deserved the reprimand. "But, Llio, I —"

"No, you don't get to talk yet. You know your foster brother's already a knight. He outranks you. The High King himself dubbed him, while you were out and about with someone else, no doubt taking part in some heathen sacrifice in those hills you call home!" Perceval glanced about the keep, listening and studying at the same time. This old wooden shell wouldn't last ten minutes of onslaught from Clamadeus' men.

"And what about me?" Llio continued. "No word back from you to see how I was doing!" She coughed once, violently, and Perceval wasn't sure if she was having him on, or if it was a lingering effect of the bad smoke. He looked right at her, helpless and concerned. "Llio, I'm sorry. So sorry. It was selfish, but I needed to go."

Llio was equally disarmed by his vulnerable honesty. This was the lad she taught to swim. The tiny band within the keep had gathered by this point, watching their visitor berate their rescuer, unsure how to react. "You mean it?" she demanded. "You really understand how you made me feel that day?"

He nodded. "I won't leave your side again."

She could no longer help herself, having missed him so. She fell into his arms, squeezing him and feeling the power of his chest as it tried to engulf her in return. At last. The man she loved was back with her, just when she needed him most. She had prayed for just this, and she never wanted to release him.

"Perceval!" A limping but smiling Llascoit came at them with his best speed, given his condition. He never slowed, not even when he threw his arms around the both of them. "Welcome back, brother," he said. It was enough.

Perceval let the seconds crawl by, not wanting to release either of them. He closed his eyes, blotting sight, relying instead on warmth and closeness. He would defend these two with his last breath if they needed it.

He opened his eyes. The others were present, all smiling, some murmuring amongst themselves. He tried to place Padern. One of the men was older, with Gornymant's exaggerated cheekbones and knowing eyes.

Llio took him by the hand, her smile shining up at him. "Let me show you what little we have here. And there are some who want to meet you; they've heard a lot about you, Perceval."

"All bad, I suppose," he said.

She elbowed him playfully in the ribs. "Yeah, right," said Llascoit. "You're about all she talks about."

"Well, she's about all I've thought of lately," he added. *You, and three other women, the whereabouts of the two who still live totally unknown to me.*

He would find Galienne and Dindraine another day; for now, he was content to have Llio at his side.

Did she never stop smiling these days? For the moment, Clamadeus might as well have been leagues away. "Perceval, this is my uncle, Padern. You shall never find a better potter in all the realm." The older man accepted the compliment graciously, offering Perceval a bow befitting a knight. He returned with a suitable bow himself, thanking the man for allowing him inside.

"It's the least we could do for someone come to rescue us," said Padern. "You showed true courage out there."

"Now I just have to make it through tomorrow in one piece. I don't suppose I could trouble any of you for a decent covering of mail, now could I?" The others laughed a bit, not wanting to show their fear.

"Afraid not, lad," replied Padern. "All you have to do is hope that goat's true to his word. We watched you fight; you were quite impressive." Not wanting to leave out his nephew, he added, "Although under better circumstances, I'm sure Llascoit could have whipped his ugly hide into submission. Couldn't you, Llas?"

Llascoit grinned, still looking the warrior's part despite his relying on a walking stick for balance and mobility. Perceval hated to see him like that. It reminded him of Pellam.

Llio, keeping her arm locked in Perceval's, escorted him about the motte-and-bailey, pointing out certain features she thought interesting. She always had been intrigued by history, and showed him the old-style stable, lacking stall dividers and using just a swing-gate to keep the animals enclosed. Then came the secondary fort, slightly further uphill, connected to the primary enclosure by only a narrow walkway. He admired the woodwork, painstakingly done with primitive tools, to yield a perimeter fencing which, at the time it was constructed, made for a very defensible position, with the few animals they managed to get inside after Clamadeus and his men arrived. Llio showed it all off, as though the features in this fort were the greatest treasures known.

Perceval asked about the others staying inside. Llio happily told him. They numbered just over three dozen in all, including herself, her brother, and her uncle. They were the members of the now defunct town council, a collection of artisans and farmers who managed the loose political and economic affairs of Worcester in their spare time. To Perceval the place began to seem utopian; it was just a group living and working together (and quite profitably, at that) with no one to bother them. Until now. He did not look forward to the next morning.

Still, he wished to know. They strolled alone into the secondary enclosure, useless for defense now since the wood was more decayed there, even in the long dead chieftain's house. "Llio, what happened to Llas? Why is he limping?"

She had gotten used to it enough in the past weeks that she barely noticed anymore. "Oh, he got that compliments of Sir Agrivaine, at the tourney you missed in Camelot." Perceval could detect the note of regret in her voice.

"I've never heard of him. Was it an accident, then?"

"I guess so. I watched it happen. It was dreadful. Agrivaine's important, one of Gawaine's own brothers. He seems like just another loudmouth to me. Llas had done well up to that point, too. It was like Agrivaine taunted him. But we couldn't hear what was going on."

"We?" Perceval's eyebrows raised slightly. He felt some guilt at being automatically envious of whomever else Llio might have spent time with. *But you left her there, didn't you? Outside the city, ready to spit up.*

"Oh, a girl I met down at the river. She said she knew you. Lupinia?"

"Lupy? God, yes! I had all but forgotten about her."

Llio's eyes turned inquisitive. "How did you meet her?"

"She and her friend were the first two people I met in Camelot. The other one –" But he broke it off, still seeing Galienne riding the river, trying to keep herself and Brownie from drowning.

She had never seen him look this saddened before. "Tell me. Please? Tell me about her. She's obviously important to you." Llio wanted so much from this man; she would not put her heart on the line unless she knew exactly how he felt about her in return. And how he felt about the "girl with the sword."

"Sh-she's a dear friend. And a good fighter. She fancies herself qualified for candidacy." Perceval sighed.

"Then she really did draw that sword? Like the King claimed Excalibur when no one else could?"

"Yes, I guess so. Galienne's quite remarkable. She's like a sister to me. But we became separated, back up the Severn."

Sister? thought Llio. "What led you two to the Severn?"

And so he told her. He spoke animatedly, as they walked relaxingly back to the main compound, about their departure from the great city and what they found along the way. Llio was pleased, though still anxious about his feelings for her; his caring and compassion for this other girl were tremendous. She was amazed how quickly her anger at him dissipated. She also felt delighted to be privy to his deepest thoughts. Her father used to tell her knights were great, proud warriors, but not very good thinkers. And to speak of their passions? Ha! Knights usually considered that unmanly. They only thought it good to speak of their feelings when they were in the mood to bed the objects of their desires.

But not this one. Perceval was the truest knight she had met thus far, and he hadn't even been properly dubbed and sworn.

Llio listened eagerly, craving his stories. She apologized, feeling empty, at the news of his mother's death. She thought of her own mother whose melodic voice could soothe the tension from anyone. And she became wholly engrossed in the tale of the fate of Oerfa. He never mentioned much of it when they still lived at Jagent. Indeed, now that she thought over it, he had never been so loose with the facets of his personal life in front of her before. She loved it.

But he stopped suddenly, as they meandered about in the front courtyard, the others preparing an evening meal carved from scant leftover supplies. Their champion's presence made them more at ease. He had just gotten into telling of his and Galienne's raft travels, and he began to chew on his lip furtively when he got to a loose description of an old man and his servant fishing.

"Perceval? What is it?" Llio took his hand, massaging it gently. She did not want to pry, but did wish to know what troubled him. His eyes looked sad.

"Llio? We're getting ready here. Could we get some help with the rest of supper?" It was Padern. A sizable hunk of recently slaughtered cow sat roasting atop a sizzling fire. It was almost all the meat left. The smell of meat and mead and the beginning of nighttime hung loosely in the air, pleasant and refreshing.

"Yes, of course, uncle," she said dutifully, sounding like the castellan Perceval and her father always knew she could be. Would be, fortune permitting.

She leaned to Perceval's ear. "Tell me after supper. I'll listen all night, if that's what it takes." And she kissed him on the cheek.

Perceval instantly felt his face, just moistened with Llio's affection. It was warm, and he stood there a few minutes longer, thinking of the only three other persons who ever kissed him like that.

* * *

The first residents of Worcester hillfort in untold decades enjoyed their succulent beef and onions with slightly stale local bread with a sense of peace. Whatever the morrow might bring, at least the siege would be lifted.

They just hoped they could safely get back to their interrupted lives. If Perceval lost, then what might Clamadeus be inclined to do? Would he act on them all from vengeance? How unmercifully was he likely to tax them?

There was nothing to do about it tonight. Most of them decided it was in God's hands now. Some of them prayed accordingly.

Perceval ate hungrily along with the rest of them, pulled from his revelry by Llascoit's words, "Get your out-of-shape rear over here and eat."

Llio and her brother exchanged a silent dialogue while the only sounds were the crackle of the cooking fire and the contented slurping and masticating of the diners. They each glanced at Perceval, who noticed their looks not at all, and their eyes concluded with each other that they were in good hands. The best here, certainly. Llascoit was surely not up to the challenge.

Damn that knight and his taunts anyway, Llas thought angrily, wishing Agrivaine were in front of him right then, no matter his heritage or what other connections he might have. Llascoit was growing concerned that the injury he sustained at the tournament might continue to plague him for longer than he and the Camelot chirurgeons had thought. At least Agrivaine got his trouncing later that day; Bedivere unhorsed him and made it look like child splay, and went on to win the whole joust. In the curious absence of Lancelot, Bedivere's victory surprised very few, though it was Trystan he overthrew to win.

Perceval had not eaten such fine food since Bridgnorth. The steak almost melted in his mouth! What was that wonderful sauce Padern roasted it with? Of course, Perceval had reached the point, all but hopelessly lost in the woods, when any small animals and even insects tasted just fine. At least he didn't starve. Tathan once taught him a bit of the art of judging round-topped fungi and other odd-looking herbal life so as to find those which could be safely eaten. After a sampling of some of the softer plants, he had thought the taste bitter and unsatisfying, but recalled that the clarity of his thought greatly increased afterwards, and he had an easier time remembering the discrepancies between his and Galienne's visions of what transpired at Pellam's feast.

They all sat back for a while after that, content to look up at the moon in all her luminescent glory. She was almost full to bursting, and Perceval thought he could almost see her wink at him. Back in his home, all but his mother would have thought that a good omen.

Several of the others began talking quietly amongst themselves, not wanting to bother their guest, who would need all the rest he could get before morning. They felt badly that they could not produce more than a cuirboillic breastplate for him, but it would help keep Clamadeus' blade away from the vital things within Perceval's chest.

Llascoit stood at last, slowly, taking the time to stretch the leg muscles which had tightened so since Camelot. Llio followed his lead, and finally Perceval, the others watching the trio wander away.

"Do you feel like talking about the rest?" Llio said gently. "I'm sure Llascoit would love to hear of your adventures also."

Llascoit did indeed look longingly at Perceval, hoping to hear his news. He had much to share with his foster-brother himself.

"Um, well, after we got to where this old fisherman sat in his boat," he began, and kept talking for two hours after that.

* * *

Perceval was already tired when the group decided rest could no longer wait, and broke from the fire, returning to the sleeping arrangements they made for themselves under the pressure of having to take refuge in the place. The ramshackle tiny abodes inside the building remnants, out of doors on the ground, proved quite humbling to persons used to greater degrees of comfort.

Padern's position ensured that Llascoit would sleep near the beck and call of those who aided his recovery. Llio enjoyed the privacy of an enclosed room (as much as could be enclosed, at any rate, given the general wear of the place), and she felt guilty about that. She was a stranger here, and made to feel welcome, though she occasionally felt the eyes of the others upon her, perhaps envious or spiteful for Padern's special treatment.

But tonight the guilt vanished with the final gasping glow of the embers; tonight Perceval was here at last.

Hand in hand, they walked back to Llio's "room," once the haven of a chief's second or possibly first wife. Llio had found shards of pottery and tarnished jewelry scattered about the floor, just beneath the dirt, suggesting that Worcester's ancient dwellers left in quite a hurry. She kept them displayed in one corner of the room, across from where she kept her traveling gear. She showed the trinkets to Perceval; he already had seen her other things.

"Llas' wound seems to be healing improperly. Did you notice?" Perceval courteously waited until Llio had revealed what might be the last items she would ever own to him.

"Of course," she said, "and I don't have it in me to tell him so. I'm no nurse, but I'd say there's a bit of infection in him."

"So he can't very well walk, much less run or sit a horse. Did the wound close cleanly?"

"So far as I could tell. The chirurgeons at Camelot themselves examined him, and couldn't find anything else wrong. A young nurse proved the most helpful, and we'll just have to get him back to see her soon. They promised he'd be on his feet and ready to sprint with the best of them in a fortnight." Llio held back tears. Too much had happened, too quickly. There had been no time between incidents, all unexpected: the smoke, her brother's injury, Padern and Clamadeus. She sometimes wished to be back in the safety of Jagent.

"Perceval, I still don't understand why you left us at Camelot. Who really is this person who has become so special to you?"

He didn't answer at first, squinting the images from his eyes. "Did you know she's Lancelot's own?" He saw Llio look at him curiously. "It's true. I imagine the whole city's been full of stories about what happened that day. The smoke never much affected me, as I could ride right through it. I thought I saw someone in it, thought I saw a farm off the road. But nothing else appeared, not until I reached the gate. Some of the people thought *I* started the fire."

"So it was a fire?"

He shrugged helplessly. "Not in the sense that we'd understand it, no. I mean, it was like a fire, but something controlled it, shaped it somehow." He saw her look skeptical. "How else could the sword pattern have appeared?"

"I heard it looked more like a cross. You still haven't answered my question."

Perceval almost laughed. Galienne would have admired Llio's candor; they at least had that in common. "Galienne needed help. When I first reached Camelot myself, she was the first person I met. And probably the nicest, too. She and her friend looked after Brownie and Cabal while I tried to find the King."

Llio found a delicious satisfaction in being able to recite the other name. "Lupinia."

"Yes. She's quite a character." He glared at her, basking in the knowing grin and nod which met his eyes.

She had him. He might as well get it over with. Hopefully she would be forgiving. "Llio, I never meant to leave. Especially since I didn't say good-bye or even find out if you would be all right. I asked the bishop himself to check on you and

Llascoit. But Galienne was so terrified, and she probably would have left the city on her own. With so many people gathered I worried about her safety. A young girl, alone with nothing but a sword."

Llio was more amused than insulted by the sexist innuendo, and interrupted. "Some women are quite capable of taking care of themselves."

"I know they are. It turned out that I had to work to keep up with her." She could ride so easily. And she could almost outduel him now, even with his own skill increasing steadily. She never grew tired of practicing or learning.

"Perceval, if this young woman is so important to you, why not ask for her hand? Can you just imagine the kind of dowry you might receive from Lancelot?"

"Lancelot hardly claims her. At least, she wants nothing to do with him."

"Answer the question, bush-beater!"

"Because she reminds me of the time I used to spend with Dindraine. God, why have I so destroyed my relations with women?"

"What in heaven's name are you rambling about?"

And he told her, his voice constricting, as he spoke of the women who had become so central a part of his life, only to be torn from him. Llio started to see it as circumstances taking them elsewhere. But Perceval tried his hardest to convince her it was his fault: leaving his mother, abandoning his sister, falling in a river and losing all track of his friend.

Llio soothed as best she could; she had done so much of that lately, and grew frustrated by the feeling that so many expected women to wait on them and take care of them, while they just went about their own affairs.

But with Perceval, she finally received her second breath. With him, it felt not like playing nursemaid or mother, but friend consoling friend. God knew they both needed it right then.

Maybe they could have more, also. Llio took him to the floor, holding him against her while he wept and let his wounds show. She cried gently too, wishing she could know these other women who so affected him.

Perhaps that was the greatest part: Perceval adored these individuals. His mother was gone, but Llio could tell he would gladly die for the others. And for Llas as well. She finally saw the dimension to him she always suspected was there, the side he so often hid out of embarrassment. Perceval was the most compassionate soul she ever met.

It allowed her to almost forget what lurked around the corner, the events that would be heralded by the coming dawn.

"Perceval, I don't want anything to happen to you tomorrow. Clamadeus is worse than even Agrivaine; he won't stop at just an injury like with Llas."

Somehow he could be confident when discussing his dealings with men. "The only thing which will happen will be Clamadeus kneeling before me and surrendering his sword."

"But, damn it, he won't settle for that! To him it's either succeed or die. I don't think failure is a choice for him."

He didn't have an answer for that. Perceval didn't think it much of an option to have to take someone's life. Meliagrant's death was accidental. He preferred to think that might always be the case, but he also had to face the hard truth: knights killed and got killed. It was just the way of things.

"Llio, look, with all that's happened recently, I don't know whether I should pray for success come morning nor to whom I would even pray in the first place. I don't know who listens to prayers, or what becomes of them once spoken. What I do know is that I've seen Clamadeus' kind before. I also know that I'm a good swordsman. I'm going to be a good knight, too."

She gazed into the dark eyes, seeing the source of his confidence. "I believe you. And I think I know who listens to prayers. I certainly know what becomes of them." She smiled at him.

"What?" he asked, willing to grope at any answer. Agnosticism could be terrifying.

"If they're honest and sincere, then they get answered."

"What makes you so certain?" His voice this time betrayed a hint of sarcastic doubt.

"You're here, aren't you? Mine was answered." And she gently but decisively pulled him closer, settling his lips to hers.

She found a confidence of her own, surprising herself. They took their time, two nervous but eager virgins, their lips warming and getting used to each other's. Among Llio's earliest memories was walking in on her parents; she had seen them engage in all sorts of intriguing activities before being discovered and sent out. She playfully sought Perceval's tongue with her own.

It startled him at first. He always thought that affectionately wet kissing looked painful, but never lost his curiosity, either. Llio's mouth was sweet and inviting. He closed his eyes, as she had already, and lost himself. Her mouth grew hot and receptive; he ran his tongue along her teeth, the top of her mouth, on the outside of her lips.

They let their own rhythm guide them now. Each took their turn exploring the neck and ears and face of the other, kissing and tasting as they went. Each wore a faint smell of sweat and desire, known to the other for some time yet never acknowledged before. Perceval swooned, collapsing to the floor completely, as Llio teased his face and neck with her mouth, sometimes playfully biting, which surprised her as much as him.

They continued on for as long as they could keep a rein on their potentially explosive urges, made all the more tense by the uncertainty of who should be first to remove pieces of clothing. Llio drew her fingers through Perceval's lengthening hair, touching his stubbly face, stroking his ears, curving down the back of his head. Perceval ran his hands up and down Llio's back, excited by the way she arched to his motion. He wanted to touch so much. He hardly knew where to start!

The fire beneath his breeches yearned, his desire matched by the heat within his face. He didn't know how to please a woman! How could he know? His initial instinct was for general roughness and fondling rather than stroking, but he determined to keep his wits about him. He wanted them both to remember this night fondly in the future. He wanted no regrets.

What to say at such a time? He was almost relieved that the deep mouth exploration came to a lull, allowing both parties to regroup. They rolled about in Llio's room, ignoring both the excited but rather hushed sounds they made and the straw which passed for bedding in the absence of wealthier furnishings.

Perceval panted as much as Cabal would on a hot day in the hills; he'd no idea this experience could generate sweat the way it was beginning to. "Llio, I-I," he said, having to catch his breath first. He collected what composure he could.

"What is it?" she asked, a bit calmer than he sounded, though she too was anxious about what could happen during the night, and what might happen come morning, and beyond.

His breathing slowed a bit, and he beheld the priceless sapphires looking back at him tenderly. "I love you, Llio."

Silence. Perceval's anxiety grew exponentially with each second. Had he fouled up again, with yet another woman who cared about him? He didn't dare take his eyes from her; she deserved his openness and vulnerability, which she had already offered to him. The answer would come.

She smiled! Just enough to bare a flash of glistening teeth, but it was enough to lighten the constriction of his heart at once. Llio smiled at him, and all his travels, his being lost in the woods, his uncertainty about Dindraine and Galienne and knights and weird bowls were blown out of him with his next breath. "I love you also, Perceval," she said.

He pulled her to him, or rather himself to her, and just held. Neither ever felt so secure from the feel of another person. Llio kissed his cheek. "My knight. My lord. I've wanted this day to come for longer than you can know." And she giggled playfully, at ease with her feelings at last.

He withdrew just far enough to look at her. "'Longer than I can know?' You mean – ?"

"Yes, silly," she replied, pecking him once, then twice. "You were the brightest thing to ever set foot in that drafty old keep of my father's. Did you ever know that he wanted us together?"

What?! "No. No, he never said anything of it. Not to me, anyway."

"I think it's because he saw greatness in you from the start. Remember how he lit up when you told us all of how you bested Meliagrant? But he also realized it would be more respectful of him to hold his tongue, and give you your own option. 'A great teacher is not one who forces things upon his students.'"

Perceval chuckled at her imitation of her father's voice, recalling his tutor's words. "I've never felt forced around you at all, Llio. Except maybe that first time you taught me to swim!"

They giggled some more at the memory of their wet and chilly nakedness that day. Then with another thought, Llio began to wax serious. "Perceval, I don't want to think about anything tonight. Not about tomorrow, not about the future, not about anything except you and me, here alone. The way I've wanted us for so long." She slid back down into the straw, pulling him gently but insistently atop her, at once adoring his weight on her body.

"Tomorrow will work itself out," he mumbled, welcoming her mouth back to his again.

The love they made and shared was part joining, part release. The anxiety left them, only returning with the pain of a first intercourse. Initially both were unsure how it should feel, and the slight trace of blood from Llio was at first embarrassing, then forgotten. They lost themselves in each other, letting time crawl to a stop, as they became the only people alive. Both had to stifle laughs during what would have otherwise been a pair of noisy if mild climaxes, and they felt that much closer for being able to let go and enjoy themselves, content in knowing they would never be ashamed in each other's arms. They slept peacefully, soundly.

Only the morning call of the town's roosters informed them that the world still waited outside the sanctity of the tiny room. Llio at once roused Perceval from sleep, dreading what might still come with the new day.

* * *

Perceval was used to sleeping inside more garments than he currently wore. He was surprised that the straw beneath the blanket had not bothered him more; but then he could hardly recollect a deeper slumber. Bleary-eyed he stretched, stood, and fumbled his way back into his clothes. He inhaled as he drew each article on; they would either have to be washed or else haunt the fort by walking about on their own volition.

Llio. She was his first sight, sitting over him in the morning light. How he loved her! He silently thanked the powers that be for his union with her, and embraced her again when he had finished dressing.

"Clamadeus will fall. Your knight and lover has spoken." He grinned at her, barely even thinking about the duel.

"Aye, my lover has spoken. Beat this bully into submission, and the bards will speak of he who defeated this villainous knight before even being himself dubbed." Llio thought she hid her terror quite well.

"That's true. The part about the dubbing, I mean. Llio,

will you return to Camelot with me?"

"Of course, love." She kissed him on the cheek, her stomach already rebelling inside her with trepidations of doom; she dared not let herself think of what would happen to Perceval if he lost, of what would happen to them all.

Outside the rotting edifice the townsfolk had gathered, all smiling as their champion emerged. Llascoit led them in a cheer, simple enough to be memorized by the few children present. Perceval was unprepared to have others relying on him so; fighting was one thing, but having a fight's outcome affect others was a situation he never gave much thought.

Perceval thanked them for rising early to see him on his way, his words met by shouts of how they wouldn't miss this duel for anything. Then Padern carried over the one contribution he could afford to make for the occasion: a circular shield, devoid of any heraldic devices, but sturdy enough. "I hope this shall help you against him," he said.

Perceval took the shield graciously, thankful more for the gesture than the item, which looked old and incapable of warding off the strikes Clamadeus was likely to send at him. "I've had it since childhood, when my father used to take myself and your teacher out in the woods on the hunt. Oh, I know it's not exactly a knight's pride, but it can still block with the best of them, believe you me."

"Thank you," Perceval offered sheepishly. "Now let's see if the leader of this feeble siege remains true to his word." His confident words fed those who heard them; the people had begun to question whether shacking up in the fort was really their best option. Perceval's tone helped them remember that it was: better to flee and lose the town altogether than to let some pompous fool whose only skill lay in killing dictate their lives and their works.

Llascoit had already hobbled over to the excuse for a gate, wanting to be the one who opened and closed it for his friend. "I wish it were me," he said quietly.

Perceval put his hand on Llascoit's shoulder. "It will be you again, Sir Llas. Stay in here and heal yourself." Then, under his breath, he said, "And take care of her, no matter what happens."

Llio stayed a bit back from the crowd, not wanting to be a handicap to what was surprisingly good morale, given the circumstances. She felt a longing thrill as Perceval sought her out for one last glance before leaving the fort. He mouthed the words to her, and she said aloud, "I love you, too."

The bolt slid into place behind him. Perceval now stood in the open, a number of knights and soldiers already rushing up to him. He recognized his opponent at once.

"I keep my bargain," Clamadeus boasted, walking to within ten feet and calmly laying Perceval's sword and scabbard in front of him.

"Just half. You can see I wear only the protection offered by mere clothing, and a single leather breastplate." Clamadeus was arrayed in his mail, freshly polished to the point of reflecting the sun.

"Yes. Surely you didn't expect me to come out here armed like some peasant. It's beneath a knight's station not to wear his armor at the appropriate times, and a personal combat seems quite appropriate."

Perceval hated the man for his contempt. He gripped the archaic shield, releasing the anger into the wood that was cut into a circle before he was born. *Never fight angry.* "I see your point, but still you contradict yourself." He knelt and picked up his sword, girding the scabbard to his belt and then drawing the blade. The worn grip felt comforting and natural in the hand it had callused.

"How can my words mean anything whatsoever to one who soon shall never hear them again?" Clamadeus approached, walking slowly and deliberately.

"Hold, Sir. If you ignore one promise, then what binds you to another? Recall that we had an agreement." Perceval had to get him to swear his oath.

To his surprise, it was easier than he thought. Clamadeus never considered Perceval any real threat, and stopped, shouting his words so that his men, the town, and the folk under siege would hear. "Hear me, then, all those who would witness this duel. Should I, Sir Clamadeus of Eburacum, actually fall beneath the blade of this young fool who has not the right even to bear arms in the first place, then shall all those within Worcester be free!" His men laughed, all except for one who had seen Perceval before yesterday; the soldier who had once given his services to Meliagrant cowered behind the others, wanting to cross himself for fear.

Shouting over the silence, Perceval added, "All who can hear thus know the proclamation of Sir Clamadeus. You are all witnesses!"

"Enough talk, boy," he snarled. "Talk is for lovers and bards. Let us fight like men." He again walked towards Perceval, unsheathing his sword.

Perceval had never seen the likes of such a weapon. It must have weighed two stone, all told! Clamadeus strained to position it with just a single hand; it took two to properly balance and wield it. He used no shield. The blade looked slow, and Perceval estimated how much faster he would need to be when it swung.

Clamadeus raised the great sword over his head and stampeded at Perceval, cleaving down with the blade with all his strength. Perceval had no trouble side-stepping the move, but was impressed and dismayed alike with the speed and strength of his enemy. Clamadeus never over-extended nor lost balance with the mighty cut, and managed to follow Perceval's motion to instantly face him again.

"Scared, boy? Have you ever seen a man cut with a sword like mine?"

Perceval warily ignored the taunt he had so come to hate. He had to stay out of the way of the sword; Padern's shield would be useless against it.

He had to use it anyway. Clamadeus chopped down again, so fast that all Perceval had time for was to block. The force of the blow was absorbed partly by shield, partly by stiff arm, and was sufficient to send the younger man to his knees.

"Ha! You thought you could best me?" Clamadeus leered at him.

The pain in his arm screamed at Perceval, and he thought he would drop the sword along with his weight. He hoped it hadn't broken; Clamadeus would slaughter him if he had to face the heavier sword with only one arm and no shield. Perceval lacked the strength to continually block the weapon with his own.

He fought for clarity. "This isn't over," he grunted, swinging his sword at Clamadeus' legs. The latter parried the strike effortlessly, even pivoting a full circle in place as a follow-up.

Perceval could not hear the gasps and shouts of the on-lookers, both warriors and townsfolk alike; he took advantage of the delay from Clamadeus' showmanship to back up several feet, regaining his stature as he did so. His arm continued to burn, as the shield fell meekly to his side.

He thought himself ready enough to meet another on-slaught, except Clamadeus insisted on talking yet again. "You're finished, boy. I don't know what sorcery you used to defeat Meliagrant, but I am twice the fighter he was."

Meliagrant? How could he know about that? The ruse worked; Clamadeus seized the opportunity offered by Perceval's bewildered look, and came from the side this time. He swung his full strength at Perceval's ribs, smiling at the feeble effort the younger man made to bring sword and shield into a defensive position. The sheer force of the attack would probably do it.

Perceval went sprawling. He met the swing head-on; it was powerful enough to carve a chunk from the shield, push the blocking sword against his chest, and send him to the ground, rolling over several times. He tried at once to stand, or at least crouch, but too much dirt had entered his mouth. He coughed and heaved violently, fearing he would retch just in time to be killed.

"Perceval, Perceval," Clamadeus said, the sarcasm in his tone obvious, as he strode over to claim victory. "You're not even a knight. Still, your bravery is impressive, though some would call it stupidity. I know it to be the first." He crouched down, just feet from Perceval, sword at his side. "I'd say you've earned a quick and painless death, rather than the one I initially had in store for you."

Perceval groaned, saving his strength, which was sapped in an instant. He tried to forget his useless but fortunately un-broken left arm, the feeling of blood on his chest, spilling into the earth like a druidic sacrifice. He rolled over, his vision still slightly blurred. He could make out the man hunched over him, and the fort behind. The other troops milled about, jeering and cajoling, and Perceval could see people lining the wall of Worcester fort. He tried for a moment to make out what anyone said, but it was all convoluted noise, like angry bees buzzing.

"Give it up, boy," Clamadeus commanded, rising to stand. "It's over."

Perceval could only groan again, then speak, barely a whisper. "Three points," he said noncommittally.

"What's that?" his enemy said, changing stance to cock an ear closer.

Perceval noticed his own sword lying uselessly away from him. Clamadeus could slice him in two before he could even stand, much less reach it. "Your shield. Had you bothered to use it, you would have noticed it has three points."

"What in blazes are you chattering about? Talking in verse like some damned poet?" Still, Clamadeus found curiosity outweighing his urge to kill.

"Reason. That's what I try to cling to. But you, you're too emotional, too unrestrained." Perceval could hear Gornymant's words ring true: *stay calm, lad, and the answers will work themselves out. But you must keep your head in a tight spot, else someone will lob it off.* He steadied himself as much as possible on his left hand, shaking throughout the chest from the pain in his arm. He had to roll over and get to a crouching position.

"Why, you insolent, fatherless heathen! I'll take you one limb at a time then!" He raised his sword for a death-blow, not caring that Perceval had shifted himself onto his knees, facing him. He was about to kill when he himself was interrupted.

"Clamadeus!" It was working. Perceval's shout gave him just enough of a delay. He pawed as much dirt and pebbles into his hand as he could, like he did as a boy when sifting the earth just to see what it looked like, to see what might live in it or walk on it. He and Dindraine.

And he tossed the mineral mix into Clamadeus' face, harder than he had ever thrown anything. Harder than he threw his javelin, harder than the folk in Oerfa had thrown hops about the fire during the blessing of the lands, harder than he thought possible. And as he lunged from mother earth, throwing his head and both arms into his enemy's chest, he remembered. *Three points. Three kinds of knights, and the three weapons they carry, sword, lance, and dagger.*

Perceval grappled with Clamadeus, forcing him to the ground amidst cursing and the pain of having one's eyes invaded with foreign matter; the knight went down quickly, landing hard beneath Perceval's weight. The sword bounced out of his grasp, clanging as it hit a nearby rock. Perceval ignored it; he only cared about the other weapon, the third of a knight's essentials. While Clamadeus rubbed his eyes again and again, reddening them, Perceval reached for and unsheathed the thick-bladed dagger attached to the bull hide belt around Clamadeus' waist. He then raised it until it rested against the man's throat, exposed and unprotected by the mail.

He waited until Clamadeus stopped wrenching at his eyes, attention given to the new sensation at his neck. "Yield, Sir, or die here, a liar's death."

"What's this?" the knight demanded. "You lack any display of true chivalry; it is cowardice to best a man with trickery and child splay."

Perceval was no longer to be intimidated nor silenced by this man's words. "You're wrong!" he shouted, "On two counts. First, as you so enjoy pointing out to the world, I am not yet a knight. No lord claims me his, though it's what I've always wished." Perceval was beginning to seethe, starting to stray from his own example. It finally sunk in just how close to death he had come from this man's hand. "And second," he spat, "had *you* any claim to chivalry's lessons, you'd have never sacked this town at all. You're a villain knight, just like your friend Meliagrant, and I say again, surrender yourself to my custody, or feel your life's blood spill with the help of your own dagger."

The others began to circle about them now, first the knights, then infantry, then even the townspeople themselves, who threw caution to the breeze and came flurrying from the fort. Llio and Padern led them.

The hatred in Clamadeus grew, festering. He would know no forgiveness, and silently vowed to be Perceval's undoing. "Very well," he said darkly. "The others are free."

"Louder, so all can hear you. You had no problem shouting for miles when you thought you'd win. And you'll also swear to make straight for Camelot. There you will present yourself and an accurate telling of your actions to King Arthur. He will then decide what is to be done with you."

Clamadeus set Perceval ablaze with his eyes, the vow reinforced. Speaking quickly, he recited the oath demanded, and only then did his enemy get off him.

The knight stood quickly, shoving some of his men out of his way, annoyed by everyone. He groped for his sword, sheathing it, promising it blood someday.

By the time Clamadeus and his entourage of fighters rode from the town some while later, the engines of destruction slowly tugged by a score of horses, the entire populace, small as it was, had turned out to greet their rescuer. Llio approached Perceval, taking his arm and hand in hers, leading him to her uncle's home. There would be much celebration in Worcester come sunset!

* * *

Margawse rode alone, the sole sign of life among the slopes of her homeland, which the more "civilized" folk to the south called bleak and barren. She had spent most of her life here, a blend of Pictish and Cymru blood flushing through her. She had her own agenda to pursue, and needed some time alone.

Her sons. How long could she keep them at her side, doing her bidding? Lamorak had been a lackluster lover, but served his purpose well, another brick removed from the supposed indestructibility of the wall that was Arthur's table. He had disagreed with her ultimate plan, to rid Logres of its king. She would have killed him herself, but her two eldest sons beat her to it, remembering her false accusation against him. Thinking about it now, she was glad Gawaine smote him; Lamorak reached Camelot, but could not get time with the King, as Gawaine was constantly by his side. So he fled, on his empty quest after that creature, with her sons at his heels.

And her two youngest, Gareth and Mordred... They would not be polluted by Camelot until they were ready for dubbing, and by then they would possess minds of their own, minds which would be more readily influenced by their mother than by a Romanized king. Her sons!

The highland pony she rode was perfectly bred for this sort of terrain: short but strong, agile enough to negotiate some of the roughest landscape Margawse's land could offer. No knight would be caught dead riding such an animal; they looked like miniature chargers, with longer hair to help protect against the harsher northern winters. But few knights ever came this far north. And Margawse looked with utter contempt upon anyone who did not like the cold, as though getting chilled were to insult her home, her family, her pride.

She had learned from Lot, oh yes. Learned that the Roman ways could infect in a manner far more subtle than the overt invasions which landed them on the Island. And yet he shared with them the one piece of knowledge that was ingrained in the Cymru spirit: share your land and abundance with your own, but be ever wary of those who would take it. And her pathetic pseudo-brother had taken far too much already. He was losing in the western hills even now, he had to realize that.

Those Romans: they never learned the one thing that might have saved them. Too spread out with too few capable administrators to manage the provinces. No wonder the Pope became just a titular head, and even a lowly king like Arthur could claim the imperial robe.

She tried not to hate him, had tried for so long. Arthur was a just and compassionate man. His rule was based on a sincere desire to ensure a fair share of the prosperous land for everyone who called it home. She had to grant him that much: he unified people in a manner not done since the Romans had centuries before, when the Empire was in its prime. And even then, that way was forced. Their villas filled with right angles and plaster and statues of strange gods (who were often stolen, Margawse recalled, from other cultures and given Imperial stature). How could anyone follow such manners? Arthur had a unity under him of which the ancient Cymru would have been proud, and could never attain due to rivalry among clans and tribes.

She rode on. It was getting cooler than she had anticipated, but she loved the feeling of the cold winds rushing into her face, sweeping her hair behind her. She was almost to the cliffs. Her favorite place was at the cliffs, where she could just look at the space that guarded Britain from all invaders. The water was always inky and fearsome, the whitecaps of the waves suggesting loyalty to the Isles through a willingness to capsize the small boats the bearded Garmani used. No wonder they always had to make their landings so far south. Too many of them, as well.

Margawse hated thinking of her sons as tools. She wanted to love them for the warriors they were, or would become, but ultimately they were pawns. She often preferred to think of them as spies. Unknowing perhaps, but agents nonetheless. The eldest had reported home regularly their whole careers, supplying the aspiring Queen of Caledonia with pieces of her much-needed intrigue. That was the only way to work, after all: behind the scenes. The necessities of remaining home proved a good excuse to avoid Camelot, and she had all the information she needed.

Ah, sister Morgan, what shall become of us? The cross is forever planted upon the Mother's breast, so why don't we just accept it and adapt our ways for the good of all?

No. That wasn't their way. Margawse and her sister retained their ancient heritage, lost in Arthur. It must have been the blood. Yes, that was it. Uther's mixing with their mother produced an impure child, with poison blood and bad seed. No wonder his Queen had gone so long with an unswollen belly; it was likely not her fault at all. No wonder she took her solace in another bed.

Yet ironically Guinevere needed an excuse. Too often had knights returned with news of how Margawse or Morgan (but strangely, never the two together) had plotted such and such, or been guilty of this and that. Tales for eager listeners grew from such intrigue: Morgan's entourage turning to stone, Margawse imprisoning maidens in scalding baths which tortured without killing. It was so ridiculous! Most people made up stories for what they didn't understand or just adopted the Christian explanation of the miraculous. Like with that girl recently, Gal-something. Rumor held she possessed the Sight. Margawse wondered what became of her in the interim.

She slowed the pony, letting it trot its way to within sight of the magnificent coastline. She let out a deep breath, surprised by how much she suddenly missed Lot. He was abrasive, to be sure, but he had loved her, and the boys. He was devastated when they began to show an interest in the ways of the boy king.

The southern crown had to fall to ensure the safety of her home. If the Pendragon remained in power, then magick would fade and the Christians would forever dominate the land. It was easier to repel the Romans; they fought with iron, not ideology. Margawse would not allow herself to flee into the hills, like the faeries. Morgan agreed with her in spirit, even if hesitant about Margawse's conclusions: rebellion could be fostered here and there, individual sparks which could meet and grow into the very hell-fires the Christians feared so much.

Such meetings were treasonous, to be sure. But the pincers were in place. Agrivaine would lead from the north, Marcus from the southwest. Logres lay in the middle. She remembered her first meeting with Marcus as though it was yesterday.

It was at Arthur's coronation. Lot introduced them, recognizing in Marcus an ally, a man who supported the new king purely from necessity. "Lord Marcus, my wife," he had intoned, towering over both of them.

By then the revelers were too drunk to care. Only Merlin seemed to notice them, the doddering old fool. "Charmed, my lord," she said, savoring the sound of Marcus' Roman name. "How fares the kingdom of Dumnonia now that the Garmani pose no threat?"

Marcus bristled at that, Lot amused by his wife's candor. "My peace is made with our new king, Lady. My people are safe now." The anger in his voice had been obvious.

"Yes, but how much of Logres did you have your eyes on before? Dumnonia is small, I should know. My father always wanted to secure a greater share for himself, and was held back by Uther." Margawse spat the name.

"Lady, such a topic would hardly be welcome in the present company. Our good lord Arthur has just determined his own borders, and has the power to repel anyone who might oppose him. Besides, I support him to keep the Germanics away." Marcus was somewhere between intrigued and fearful of her forwardness.

"But how many of us could he repel at once?" Lot muttered.

How many indeed? Margawse wondered presently. Thus, the Round Table. Arthur made them all swear, by cross or by cozier, that while serving him they were bound as one, as equals. They could only resolve their own differences amongst themselves when out of Logres, and only if the results did not deter the strength of the vast armies the High King could summon.

Lot got drunk that night and made his way through several of the womanly courtiers, somehow without eliciting suspicion or violence. And Margawse stole away to Marcus' quarters to persuade him of the merit of her husband's words in a manner that Lot would not do. She grinned impishly; no man ever fully recovered his judgment after tasting her mouth, her breasts, the treasure between her thighs.

Not even the King. If the cross-bearers were right, Margawse was due in hell.

Hell was just another story, too, Margawse believed. She would do all she could to use their own weapon of fear against them. What would happen to Logres in the absence of its sovereign?

The Mother will return. She must. Hear me, Lady, hear my prayer, feel my spirit, touch my heart. The land must be free again. The misogyny of these invaders must be lifted from your sacred shores.

Arthur was a capable and extremely difficult antagonist. To anger him would have no recourse other than solution; either he or those who opposed him would perish. Margawse was proud of the finality of that. Lot would have been too, had he lived to see her plans to fruition.

Margawse watched the ocean for hours before turning towards home.

* * *

She had lost track, now, of the last time she received a sending. And it had already been many days since she saw Perceval.

Or were they visions? Galienne was unsure how to even categorize the experiences anymore. What was the last one? The hallway? Perceval's dubbing? Which of them came true and which remained mysteries?

She had little time now to concern herself with such matters. Galienne stood overlooking the Severn river, straining to see the point at which she last saw Perceval. She thought she could still see the place, miles upstream, where she and a greatly unnerved Brownie took refuge from the water's drive for a few minutes before forcing themselves to continue.

She gripped the sword at her side, her sweat and pride forever part of the hilt, the cover of which was showing its first signs of fraying. The women had honed her skills, surprised by how much she already knew about swordplay.

The small keep of Roche Sanguin, the "bloody rock" most heard of only at bedtime as another ripple along a fruitful stream of faerie tales, stood securely and very real among the hidden network of forest dividing the Cambrian wilds from Logres. Cautionary words such as those of Tathan helped retain the place's mystery; virtually no one knew of the matriarchal fortress built on the Severn in the time before the coming of the Legions.

This "kingdom" was unnamed, and most stayed at its hypothetical borders because of the forest's thickness. Or from fear of mass assault by the wild hills people, still now sometimes charging into battle naked save for jewelry, weapons, and adrenaline, or maybe due to no one knowing who this land's sovereign truly was. No one saw him; no one in civilized lands knew his name.

Partly because he was a she, and she preferred her anonymity. Lady Ygerne had stayed here virtually her entire life, born within Roche Sanguin's palisade. The motte-and-bailey was her true home, and she wished no outside contact unless absolutely necessary and unavoidable. The enclosure housed her family: thirty-one women who knew little other than self-reliance and independence from the ways of men.

Having traversed closer to the western side of the river while futilely chasing Perceval, Galienne had seen the small fort at once, though she also noticed that a person would have to be in just the right position, either on the river or across it, to view the place. She and Brownie were eager enough to leave the raft behind; Galienne exhausted herself trying to keep both her and the mare alive. She had promised to resume pursuit come morning.

Yet she was met at the bank by six women dressed in leather armor and carrying spears. Since she was in need of hospitality for a night, these gruff-looking souls had to suffice.

They all spoke with a thick accent reminding Galienne of Oerfa and the dialect of the hills. After helping her secure the raft, they led her and Brownie into the fort itself. The mare was quite pleased to receive such loving attention: she was fully groomed, watered, fed, and talked to before taking what she considered a very well-deserved rest. No other horses were present.

Galienne could still recall times, not recently passed, in which she would have felt dreadfully afraid of these heathens. Travels with Perceval, and the events of turbulent weeks, had their effect. She offered the woman in charge her finest bow, and formally requested shelter and food for the evening.

Ygerne had beamed, delighted at being able to house such a person and also amused by the formality of the girl, who carried a sword with the same defensive pride most women displayed carrying children. Ygerne was tall, Galienne guessed her at six feet, and wore an elegant deep green robe and no ornamentation except a pair of earrings, silver maybe. Galienne could not tell without closer inspection.

"And who would attempt the Severn alone?" Ygerne said. Galienne related the entire story, needing someone, anyone, who would listen.

Ygerne did just that, compassionately. The other women emerged while Galienne stood there orating, sometimes murmuring amongst themselves. The release of tension made time speed up for Galienne; she did not think an hour could have passed while she told them her adventures. And she thought nothing of telling them in the first place. Ygerne seemed matronly, and besides, a hostess had the right to expect a guest to speak of what kept them busy. "You have traveled far indeed, and have more than earned a portion of our offerings."

By dark the women were hungrily devouring an assortment of rabbits, chickens, and wild berries, all of which were plentiful around the fort. The hens they raised within. Ygerne asked about Galienne's personal decorations.

"Oh," she said, clutching the cross tightly, "my friend gave me this."

"The one who dined with you last night?" Ygerne was careful not to refer to describe Perceval as the one who floated downstream, not to be seen again.

Was it just last night? "Yes, Lady. He said he didn't need it anymore."

"Oh, bah! Everyone needs something to remind them of their calling."

Maybe these aren't the savages my mother would have called them, and probably to their faces, too. "Wearing the cross next to my heart is comforting."

Galienne was quite surprised when every other woman at the feast, eaten outside the dwellings and without the refinements of tables and accouterments, only Mother Earth beneath them, reached for their own symbols of what mattered to them. She looked around the circle. One woman wore a ring with a stone the color of Ygerne's robe set in it. Another carried a simple collar-like embroidered *gorget*. Still another had a pair of leather gloves tucked inside her clothing.

"Galienne, those seated about you are survivors and outcasts, and they cling to what reminders they can of better times, times that may come yet again."

"I'm sorry, Lady, but I fear I don't quite follow you."

"I have lived here for almost more years than I can count." Some of the women laughed, one even jested with the term "crone." "Roche Sanguin is a haven to some, a permanent home to others, and I am quite confident that no one male knows it even exists."

"But I've heard of it before. I think. It was part of a faerie story, like the women at Avalon." Galienne just spoke with Nimue last night; she felt gratitude for Ygerne making no advancements toward her staying indefinitely.

"There is an Avalonian refugee among us tonight, one who has what the ladies call 'talent' but who lacked the conviction needed to become a priestess. And as for your friend, we saw him pass right by us."

"You saw Perceval!" She forgot her manners. "But why didn't you, couldn't you –"

Ygerne was patient. "First, we have no boats here. To cross the river is to head towards the eastern lands of the patriarchy. And second, I hear how dear this 'Perceval' is to you, but we have here sworn to proclaim the nonexistence of this place with regard to all men."

"But I don't see why."

"The forest here is protective and inhospitable to travel. We ourselves have to venture out occasionally to secure rations, and that can take weeks, mainly because we must cover our tracks. Look at this fort. Doesn't your training tell you that any man would be envious of such an advantageous position, one which could be reinforced so that nothing could get by this river uncontrolled, no creature or bush taken for food from the woods without a lord's knowledge of it?"

Some of the other women continued eating, others sat as engrossed as Galienne, eager to hear justification for what was, according to society, renegade at best and criminal at worst.

Ygerne continued. "There are people here who have survived rape at the hands of their own lords, rich landholders and knights. Others have no homes, driven from what land was rightfully theirs, but being widows were told the land reverted to the eldest male heir, in one case a nearby duke. Still others, myself among them, are simply tired to death of kingdoms and land-rape and knights' warfare and taxes sitting in rich male coffers while poor women's babies starve in their arms outside. A time is coming, Galienne. Perhaps sooner, maybe later, but a time when women will have their say, even their way. This fort is a haven until that time arrives."

Galienne waxed nervous; this sounded more and more like Avalon, less the magick, but maybe they did that, too. Wasn't one of them from the foggy island? She had to know, or she'd never sleep here! "Lady Ygerne, please tell me. What manner of faith have you here?" Her cross had been welcomed, but…

"Perhaps these will offer some indication." Ygerne, all eyes upon her now, deftly removed the two earrings from her lobes, and passed them to the woman next to her. She then passed them to the woman at her side, and so on, until the last hand opened over Galienne's, and the two ornaments fell into her palm.

An ornate cross, lined with Cymru symbols and swirls. And a crescent, the shape of the moon when just new or fading into memory.

"Oh, there are no sacrifices, to be sure, at least nothing that would resemble the harshness of those who came before us. Aside from that, there is mingling here, if you will, a blend of certain faithful elements."

"How do you mean?" Galienne said, looking over the earrings, then passing them back.

"What type of Christian be you, then? Answer me that first."

"I-I believe in the one true God, and the divine message sent through His mortal son, and; wait, I still don't see… There's just one type of Christian!"

"So sure, are you? Do you see any place for a Goddess in the faith with which you were raised?"

Galienne, her exasperation starting to show, took a moment to consider before asking. "No. I do not see how."

Around them both, the others had mostly finished eating, and stretched out to listen now, content under the stars.

"Whence came God's human-born son? Surely he just didn't materialize, although that certainly would have been miraculous."

Galienne ignored the blasphemy. "He was born of the Blessed Virgin, of course. From Mary."

"Then Mary was Jesus' earthly mother?"

"Well, yes." Galienne had never been taught to think of Mary and Joseph as parents. So much emphasis was placed upon the virgin, clean birth.

"A woman birthing a god? Now we really are getting miraculous!" Some of the women chortled. "Galienne, I don't mean to speak heretically, but I find it easier to discuss difficult and emotional subjects if I can find the humor within them. Now then, I ask you, is it possible to look at the Virgin Mary as an incarnation, or even a symbol, of Goddess?"

What would Bishop Baudwin say to all of this? "Maybe. But even so, why have I never heard of this before? I used to read the Bible myself." Numerous eyes flashed over Galienne; most folk couldn't read, and most who could were men.

"If you've studied it first-hand, then you already know that womanly symbols, especially those pertaining to Goddess, are passed by, mentioned only when unavoidable. What would the church fathers have done in the absence of Mary, the person able to bring Jesus into his earthly, mortal form? Why did the Romans insist not only that men were inherently superior to women, but made a point to subjugate them wherever they went? Do you know what life was like for women in Rome and its conquests? Do you know why Queen Boudicca rebelled against the invaders?" Ygerne was getting carried away. Galienne would have to confront the nature of her faith in her own time and way.

"Galienne, I've simply seen too much hurt towards women. They are made to pay for men's mistakes and fears. But there truly is room in the Bible for the feminine in life, the life-giving power itself. What could be more miraculous? That is why other women retreat to Avalon, and why it is next to impossible to succeed once there, for the priestesses are trying nothing less than the summoning and use of feminine powers. Earth magicks. And until the church influence dwindles, this sanctuary will remain likewise, shielded from the eyes of men."

"Look at yourself," said another woman. "You carry that sword because you wish acceptance in a man's discipline."

"Sexburh could surely help you with that." came a different voice, with an accent that Galienne knew came from close to her home.

"Yea, that I could do, if she's willing. Are you then, girl?"

Galienne turned to the last sound. "Sexburh," if that was truly this woman's unfortunate name, was the largest female Galienne had ever seen. She leaned back, away from the fire, on meaty stumps of arms, and a chest strong-looking enough to wrestle down an armored knight. Galienne felt suddenly lucky to be half the woman's size. "Y-yes, I am. I am! Perceval already taught me a thing or two about using the sword. If I can just find some armor, and a lord to dub me... Oh, who am I trying to fool? No lord will do anything save mock me! A woman, wanting to be a knight." *Like her father before her.*

"Even a recluse like myself knows there are mercenary knights, those without masters. Or mistresses." Ygerne was the picture of calm reason.

"People won't take you seriously with a feminine-sounding name like Galee, Galyen... How do you say it?" This from she who had recommended Sexburh's aid.

"Galienne," she said slowly.

"What kind of name is that?" one of the women said.

"What my mother saw fit to give me."

"Sounds foreign."

"It is. My late mother told me it comes from the Continent."

"Galienne, I did not realize your mother had passed away. She must have been young." The maternal voice of the unofficial leader soothed.

"It's a long story, I fear."

"Maybe you'll speak of it sometime." Galienne nodded.

"How about a more masculine name?" one of the women cried.

"Yes! That's it. What about 'Kay'?"

"'Kay' is the King's brother's name, you ninny."

"Well, I'm just making suggestions, now, aren't I?"

"I'm not sure how changing my name will do any –"

"Maybe something closer to your name as it is, just more manly."

"Oh, sure, turn a good woman's name into something fitting a man. Didn't you just hear Lady Ygerne?"

"I'm only trying to help. That's why we're all here, right?"

"Galahad."

"Yes, but what of the name of one of the other knights? Maybe someone's 'kicked it' recently, and there's a name made available."

"Don't be vulgar, Sexburh."

The woman said it again. "Galahad."

"What's that?" Galienne asked the last to speak. It was a woman bundled up beside herself, normally the quietest of the group, a recent arrival.

"Galahad." The eyes which had aged much too quickly looked up at Galienne, offering what brightness they could. "It fits you." She smiled faintly.

"Galienne, all know the value of a good omen. That's the first thing she has spoken in weeks." Ygerne was pleased to hear the poor woman's usually frail voice again.

"What happened to you?" Galienne did not know how to phrase it without making it seem a spectacle. She caught Ygerne from the corner of her vision, signaling that the young woman was better left alone.

"Thank you," Galienne then added feebly. "I like it. It's a good name." Then, to the others, "But do I call myself Lady or Sir Galahad?"

They laughed aloud at that. The consensus was unanimously "Lady."

Sexburh proved a feisty, skilled warrior, who began by defeating Galienne's moves one after another. Their work commenced the following morning, after some more talking and showing off of mementos. They all enjoyed Galienne's ring, the one Jacqueline gave her.

Sexburh, it turned out, was a Saxon, so Galienne could understand her bias against the name; Astolat lay adjacent to Garmani holdings, and she grew up with the sentiment that the only good Garmani was a dead one. The folk of Astolat often worried about what they considered an inevitable onslaught, no matter how far back the rout at Badon sent them. Sexburh's own husband was killed at the historic hilltop, and she fled. Being trained by her late lover in weapons but not in navigation, she wandered west instead of east, and somehow eventually found her way into the woods in which men dared not tread.

But now Galienne was very glad this woman was a live, and not a dead, Saxon, though she pretended her most earnest to make her otherwise.

"No, you're over-extending again. That takes you off balance every time, and unless you're a tumbler, you'll wind up dead for it." Sexburh enjoyed the exercise. She was the only resident who knew anything of the sword and axe, the Saxon's preferred weapon.

"But you're so big! How can I compensate?"

The tutor laughed. "I'm the size of any knight! Get used to it! Your advantage is speed and your own size. That makes you a more difficult target."

"But how can I get past those tree trunks you call arms?" Galienne had yet to get her weapon inside any of Sexburh's superior blocks and parries.

"By finding where I'm weak, and aiming there." Galienne swung at her legs, and the move was again blocked. But barely.

"See? That's better. Now let's try another move. And then I'll pull out a battleaxe, and we'll see how you fare with that."

And on it had went. Galienne felt at home among these women, even in the knowledge that she could not stay. *Could not or would not?* She questioned herself. It had to be the former. Too much lay beyond this place, too much to do and see. She missed Perceval deeply, praying every vespers for a full hour for his salvation, either from the river or in the hereafter. She asked God and Mother Mary both to look after him.

She actually missed her father, too. And Lupinia, crazy girl, perhaps betrothed by now and maybe even expecting her own little miracle. Fewer faces than perhaps most people knew, and for that very reason more special to remember, each one. Yes, she would leave this place soon enough; Sexburh was already impressed with her progress. With Galienne's help, they even designed a crude version of the quintain so she could practice at the lance. Sexburh knew nothing of this weapon, only having heard that a formation of men carrying them on horseback was indestructible. Galienne insisted on working at it. She still had Perceval's javelin, which would have to do.

Returning her thoughts to the present, she continued looking, admiring the lovely flow of the river, peaceful now when one wasn't in it struggling. The denizens of the woods could be heard emerging for another night's activity. The breeze was crisp, scented by heather and the fragrances of a million trees.

Galienne wondered if Nimue's Avalon could possibly smell as sweet and pure. She would never trust the witchy woman, that was certain. If she and her "Ladies" knew about the prophecy, perhaps knew even of Elaine's death, then why had they done nothing to prevent it?

Elaine might have lived that way. Of course, Galienne had to admit that she surely would not be here in this place now, if events transpired otherwise. And what of the prophecy itself? How could Avalon have known, if Galienne herself was so devoutly Christian?

Could there be two prophecies? Or was her pulling the sword foretold by Christian and Pagan alike?

She would have to continue her thoughts later. The reassuring voice from behind her called. "Galahad! Time to continue with the fencing lesson!"

* * *

Yvaine had long since missed the tournament, but that was hardly his chief concern. He wanted to learn if Gawaine or any of his ilk were still in the city.

It was easy enough divining knowledge of Gawaine. Even without his fame, he would have proven easily recognizable from his appearance, the northern blood flushing his face even when he wasn't roused to battle-frenzy. And it wasn't like Yvaine to miss a tourney. Especially when the chance to go up against the best presented itself. The melee teams were huge, he heard, even larger than the previous year; he was sorry he missed it.

Even sorrier was he that he missed his cousin. Yvaine had hoped to put him on the spot with the King and the other Round Table members present, or at least close by. Facing Gawaine in the open was nothing Yvaine wished to chance, for he had already witnessed the knight's tactics when things didn't go his way.

No, fool, you witnessed nothing. All you had was a body! And these accusations could get you killed.

Lamorak's body was no longer even in evidence. Yvaine decided to wait until he had the King's own attention before revealing what happened, and would have to gauge the time to add the part of his suspicions.

He had sent Vonnet to find out what he might about Gawaine's whereabouts, and Clydno, who remained in the city since the tourney, was dispatched to seek any next of kin. Yvaine didn't think Lamorak had any anymore, but wanted to be sure. So far no results had yielded.

Since Yvaine was fairly well-known himself, he figured he might as well retrieve Chat du Soleil. At least with the cat he was likely to remain perfectly safe.

Cat, ha! He almost forgot just how large his pet was! Guinevere's staff took excellent care of him, especially considering how much meat he could swallow. The Queen regularly sent extra hunters from Camelot just to keep up.

Yvaine had approached slowly, wanting to give the feline ample time to sniff at what walked towards it. It at once recognized its friend and jumped right onto Yvaine, licking him as a lord's hound would. People nearby gasped and gaped, even shrieking at the thought of seeing a knight gruesomely devoured right within the Queen's menagerie.

No such feast took place. Yvaine and his most trusted companion walked gaily through streets which were much quieter now that spring was rolling on into summer. He enjoyed people's startled expressions and the alacrity with which they sidestepped the knight and lion as they passed.

His mother certainly questioned the wisdom of keeping such a creature, but then Morgan had heard how he came about finding it in the first place, and later decided it was a healthy sign. He would have to return to Gorre sometime soon again and visit, as far as he could get, anyway. Or might she be back in Avalon? He could not keep track of the enchantress' schedules (Nimue was a delightful dancing partner, but would not speak of the whereabouts of her sisters). He'd see them again soon enough.

After he resolved certain affairs, of course.

He missed Lamorak, more than he guessed he might. Yvaine always felt like an outsider, but also surmised it was part of his condition, something he also enhanced. What other knight wandered with a lion? How many could say their mothers were priestesses, especially in a Christian kingdom? And very few could boast of knowing of the Old Ways, as well as those of sword and lance.

Lancelot. He knew something of the old customs. Yvaine would have to speak with him. He had always found the champion a bit unapproachable, but never considered the common thread between them. Yvaine could always use another friend. Or an ally. There wasn't exactly an abundance of Pagan knights in Logres, much less at Arthur's table. Himself. Trystan, who was so love-struck that he rarely showed himself around court anymore. The wild Saracen, come from so far to prove himself. Another, also well traveled, somewhere from the eastern Continent, where it was said the mountains reached clear to the sky. Not many of them, indeed. And the lives of all steeped in some mystery, making them appear that much more suspicious to those who followed the cross.

Yvaine made a point to not become too engrossed in religious squabbles or political uncertainties. The Pagans, at least the Picts and Cymru who so populated the main Island, had never possessed the Christian's unity, not against any invaders. Only Arthur could do that, although Yvaine always suspected the man's true loyalty to lie in something other than the anthropomorphic deity to which the Christians bowed.

The tribes could only stay as united as their appetites and greed would allow. Britons they sometimes called themselves as a whole, but when they left Logres, they spoke of being from other tribes. Even Vercengétorix, for all his charisma and leadership, still was too late to resist Caesar. Yvaine learned that from his mother, had learned all about the figures from the old ways: the coming of various folk to Eire-land, Queen Boudicca's revolt, the deities and observances. Yvaine had laughed with his mother at the stories of the Christians bringing whole trees into their homes for Jesus' birthday, quite an extension, literally, of the simpler yule logs used still on the heaths. Jesus had been no druid, even if he spent time being educated by them, only to head home and face the Romans himself.

The Romans, always the Romans! They had so intermingled with this place and then abandoned it completely, like a lover, forsaking his mistress over sudden guilt regarding the wife who awaited him at home. The lover could only weep, put on her shoddy clothes again, and continue.

Yvaine always surprised himself with his introspective moments. He often found it difficult to focus on a single task, wanting instead to move on to the next activity, particularly if it was something fun. Like racing his horse with another knight. Or trying the latest in physical humor. Dinadan was the only one who ever beat him there, not surprising given the man's own sense of utter foolishness; Kay certainly had not appreciated the bucket of water in the Round Table chamber which came crashing down upon him from the slightly open door. Yvaine wondered what would have happened if Arthur stepped through just then instead.

Fun would have to wait. He was still walking through the center of town. The streets were busied with merchants and artisans, nobles and children, but less so than during the festival. Saint Dubric's Cathedral loomed ahead of him.

Yvaine wanted to talk with the King. Or Lancelot, or his mother. He did not know how to find any of them.

He stared transfixed at the gigantic cross atop the steeple. *The bishop, then?* He never sought Baudwin's counsel before, but perhaps this was an appropriate time to start, like he'd suggested to his mother. One thing Yvaine had learned about the priests, at least those who held any real power: they were sworn on their very souls to keep discussions confidential. Yvaine took his pet back to the menagerie, and headed for the cathedral.

Baudwin seemed trustworthy enough, at first appearance, anyway. And provocative as well.

"And where again did this all take place?"

"Up northwest. The Cambrian hills, removed from any major settlements." *And the ones we did find were ravaged by someone. Or some*thing.

"And your evidence is just the shield?"

Yvaine lurched forward in the chair opposite the Bishop of Camelot. He had so convinced himself, he didn't think much of convincing anyone else.

"Sir Yvaine, consider the King's perspective on all of this. You say Gawaine is responsible. Perhaps he is. But your evidence is limited to some marks on the late knight's shield. You yourself said the creature's blood is similarly colored. What do you think might happen if news of this got out?"

"But, Bishop," Yvaine was uncomfortable with calling this man *father* in the manner expected, "I'm trying to stand up for what's right. If Gawaine is innocent, then let him come forth and face his accuser. Even if the King had trouble weighing the evidence, I'm sure he would permit trial by combat."

"To prove what?"

This was infuriating. Combat trials, the *trus dei*... They were the hallmark of this Christian chivalry; Baudwin knew damn well *what*. "Why, to prove whether Gawaine did this! Your own faith says that in such a duel, he with the wicked heart shall fail. And what of Lamorak? What of his memory, of his contributions to the brotherhood?"

"And what of them? I know you don't want to hear this, but ultimately, your friend was expendable. Knights die fighting all the time, Yvaine."

"What?! You bastard, do you know who you're talking to? And knights often die young, yes, but they should not fall to treachery!" Yvaine threw back the chair as he rose, letting it crash into the wall behind him. He wondered if the other man knew knights sometimes killed for lesser insults, not considering that most of Camelot's residents feared too much for their souls to speak so to the bishop.

But Baudwin stood, his height equal to Yvaine's. "And do you know to whom you talk, you brash heathen? Arthur shall hear of this!"

"But what will he hear of Lamorak's death? That he died fighting something most people don't realize or even believe exists?" Despite his earlier taunts toward his friend, the knight believed in the Barking Beast, seeing too much death. Others would believe, too; they lived in superstitious, fearful times.

"Anything which exists out there on the heaths I have no doubt is due to foul sorcery and evil headhunting. The goblins, trolls, giants... oh, yes, I know of them all, and there would be no such things if folk would live right!"

"'Right' meaning by your Book? Something almost no one can read? How can anyone be certain of what you say if they can't verify it for themselves?"

"Enough! I will not be drawn into a theological debate with you! Now go."

There was no way past this. Yvaine believed the man incapable of rational argument. He made for the door, only to be interrupted by Baudwin's voice.

"Sir Yvaine, do you want me to mention these events to His Majesty?"

He had to trust someone. But not this man. "No. Forget I even came."

Watching the knight storm from his sanctuary, Baudwin was immediately regretful. Had his talks with Merlin been for naught, then? He considered the matter, then decided that Yvaine could hardly be accountable for whatever vile deeds brought monsters and evil out of the depths of hell.

Or from That Side to This Side, he could hear Merlin say, the venerable teacher who lived in Baudwin's memory now.

He handled it poorly. He would have to make amends with the man, though he could not forget his heritage. Yvaine was *her* son, the lesser queen about whom the stories never ceased. She stole Excalibur's scabbard, which was purported to keep him from receiving wounds. Or tried to poison him. Or subvert the throne. Or kidnap hapless knights through her charms.

Lord knew who Yvaine's father was. Old Uriens, perhaps.

Baudwin grew tired of these debates more quickly nowadays, especially when he had them with only himself. Why would the royal family be at odds? Granted, some of the blood relation was only half, but still...

Baudwin sighed, returning to his duties. He had more confessionals than he cared to count still to hear. How could one man absolve so many of so much?

* * *

It was no use. The man had no gift for divination. The stones etched with Ogham runic symbols told him nothing, and he began to despair.

Of course, in ages past, had Taliesin possessed the nerve to even inscribe the stones with the symbols, he would likely have had his heart torn from him and fed to the ravens. The druids never allowed their sacred knowledge to be contained in written form.

But Taliesin was a bard, a branch of the druidical tree. He justified the stones with the need to know, but now, he had to confess, he felt ignorant.

Nimue had welcomed him as he caught up with her after Pellam's strange hospitality. They rode clear south to Avalon, and Taliesin was proud to call himself one of the few men allowed to see the sacred place. Although that did not prevent Nimue from commanding him to keep his eyes closed during the gentle boat ride over to the island through the impenetrable fog. As a bard, his word was both his most sacred possession and most trusted gift, even more than his precious harp. He was curious, but Nimue knew he would not open his eyes. Taliesin knew better than to ask how to reach their destination.

Along the way he did ask other questions. "What do you think happened back there?" he divined of her, during a peaceful ride close to Logres' capital.

"I know that I failed my mission. And I learned how troubled Lancelot is. He should come back to us." Bards, druids, enchantresses; they often spoke as if members of the same family. In a vital, real sense, they were.

"I'm not so sure he ever really left. If it weren't for his infatuation —"

"Good point. Guinevere's as pious as anyone in court. Maybe she does it out of guilt."

"Guilt?"

"Yes. I mean, guilt over her feelings for Lancelot."

"I was unaware his feelings were at all reciprocated. That must make it even more difficult for him." Taliesin truly lacked the Sight; the Ladies always knew more than he, and he was the one who had devoted a lifetime to learning how to know others!

"I suppose." Nimue wanted to change the subject. "What of Galienne?"

"She reminds me of her father, though I'm not sure I'd say it to her face. She and Perceval were never apart. That kind of loyalty will help them both."

"Were you aware of why I attended the feast?" Nimue wanted Taliesin's input about the girl, and saw no harm in divulging her own mission. Though she would not tell him of how she received a messenger, like they all had she supposed, specifically inviting her to Bridgnorth. She did not like how Pellam knew so much, right down to where people could be reached.

"I thought about it, and wanted to ask. I am curious."

"To bring Galienne back to Avalon."

"The Mother thinks she'd be an asset, then?" Nimue nodded.

Then she stopped. "Taliesin, we need all the help we can get."

"To accomplish what? This is a Christian land, now. Christian kings will continue to inherit it. If we hadn't won at Badon, we'd all be up to our ears in foul-smelling Garmani who worship no deities unassociated with destruction."

She almost reached across the horses to slap him. "Don't try that 'lesser of two evils' logic with me. And how can you say that about the Christians? You sound as though you want them here!"

"Nimue, almost more than even music itself do I know history. I'm sure the Picts used to have the same discussions about us, who came to break their bronze with our iron. First the Picts, to drive the Faeries into the hollow hills, then we, the Cymru. Now Romans, Garmani, Irish. Who will be next, Nimue? How will you handle the next wave? The Islands are the richest place on this earth, and everyone is going to want a share of Goddess' wealth. There's more at stake here than religious differences."

"You'd fit well within Arthur's court. Quite the diplomat, for a bard."

"Five years ago I might have taken that for an insult. Now I thank you for the compliment. Arthur's table is a start, Nimue. Yes, only men sit at it, while Camelot's women make their supper and tend the gardens. The important part is that others do sit at it. There's a Saracen, two Picts, some Irish, many Cymru, the grandsons of Roman citizens, and those who represent the Christian, Pagan, and even Wotanic faiths. Arthur sits at the same level they do, and these men would die for him. Have you ever seen them, Nimue? Other than Lancelot, I mean?"

She shook her head. She hated it when he made sense. Bards were more tolerable when singing.

"No one has ever had people come together like that! Even our ancestors once preferred to lop each other's heads off than meet with others of their own kind, much less with so many foreigners. This British peace is about more than justice. There have been just kings and queens before. It goes beyond that. He's trying to represent everyone."

"Then why are there no women present?"

"As I said, it's a start. I'd probably be more hostile towards that part of it, too, were I a woman."

The "hmmph!" which came from Nimue at that made Taliesin decide to drop the subject for now. They still had to reach Avalon. And the sooner the better, to Taliesin's thinking.

He remembered his original question. "Nimue, what do you think we saw in Pellam's keep?"

"How do you mean?"

"I mean the procession. The spear, the dish, the meal itself. What did you think of all that?"

"I thought it was a delightful meal. Taliesin, what are you driving at?"

Sometimes sight can blind, too. "Did you notice how we all received to eat whatever we wished? As though Pellam's servants knew exactly what we would be hoping for?"

Nimue frowned at him. "How do you know this?"

"I spoke with whomever I could after the feast. We all ate our heart's content."

"I still don't see what you —"

Taliesin cut her off. "You have the Sight, Priestess, you tell me. How could Pellam divine our appetites? Knowledge of future is one matter, and reading the waters or entrails might reveal much. But hunger? And for specific courses?"

Her answer was what he expected but hardly reassuring. "He could not have known. That's impossible. When the Sight comes, it is shadowy at best, at least for me. It's rare to make out exact faces and locations in the vision."

"Could Pellam be so gifted to have surpassed anyone else who possesses such talent?"

"I don't see how. He was a knight, yes? Knights and lords devote their time to hunting and fighting and making future knights. When would he have had time to hone such a skill, especially in the absence of someone to guide him?" *The way I wanted to guide Galienne.*

"What about Kunneware? I was unable to speak with her again."

"She did just sit there most of the time, didn't she?"

"Yes, and did you notice how she looked at Pellam sometimes?"

"Or the way Pellam glanced at Perceval, like he expected something."

Good. She did pay attention to more than the girl. "Right. What do you know of Perceval?"

"I think he may have ridden right past me outside Camelot some time ago."

"I mean, do you know of anything useful? Where is he from, who's his family, his lord?"

"He's not a knight. Though he wants to be. Maybe that's why Galienne travels with him."

"Not a knight?" Taliesin was unprepared for that insight. "Then why was he even there? Or Galienne, on that note?" All the other guests, even tardy Lancelot, were already known in the land, and regarded as the best representatives of their respective talents. Why *had* the younger two been there?

"They must have been invited as well. Taliesin, what do you think? You keep asking me what I thought about it all, and I've tried to tell you."

They continued riding for a long silence while the bard worked out his response. "First, I believe the whole occasion was too strange and wondrous to result from mere coincidence." Nimue agreed with a determined nod. "Second, Pellam has a kingdom up north, or at least, he's supposed to. I want to know why he was this far south, and how he knew where to find us all and get us together."

"Anything else?" *So he suspects that messengers found us all.*

"Yes. Lastly I wish to know how Perceval and Galienne fit into all of this."

They both thought about it, and were still no closer to any answers by the time they crossed the marshes to the sacred Isle of the Ladies.

* * *

"Spear of fire, sword of air, stone of earth, cauldron of water. You know this already, bard."

Viviane's voice was calm and wise, though curious. She agreed to meet with Taliesin at once, Nimue having pressed the matter of his urgency. Besides, men were not often at Avalon, and the Mother wished to see to his needs.

"Yes, Lady, although I infrequently think of them as a group. Some try to mix them together amongst the Thirteen Treasures."

"And it would prove easier to set them straight had Merlin not selfishly tried to keep them." Not even Viviane could divine what became of the old arch-druid, nor of the Thirteen Treasures, the relics of the British people, last entrusted to his safe keeping. Now no one knew where they were.

That they existed, Viviane and Taliesin had every faith. A significant part of druidry was based on them and the legends surrounding each: the magnificent talismans bestowing legendary potencies to the worthy.

Taliesin wanted more answers. "Mother, is it conceivable that all could have manifested somehow at once? In the same location?"

"No. The Hallows must remain separate. Too much power resides in them, and they can corrupt as well as save."

Taliesin had to stifle exclamatory laughter. "Your words sound like Son-day sermon."

"From where do you think they got their wisdom? The Hallows are not mine, not even part of my tradition. They are timeless, universal. The Christians adapted them for their own needs."

Taliesin looked behind him, across the crone's sparse quarters at Nimue, still standing in the doorway obediently. She had not yet been dismissed, and this time was quite glad of it. There was much to hear.

Not deigning to speak, she mouthed "what?" to the bard, hoping Viviane would not notice, but of course she did. She said nothing, however.

"The spear. Nimue, you saw it. The spear that bled, as though freshly having found its target. Spears cannot, of course, bleed on their own, and yet that one did." To him, it had looked that way, and he was in the habit of voicing his conclusions and observations with certainty.

Viviane looked at Nimue expectantly, granting her, with a glance, permission to offer her opinions. "Yes. It did. I forgot until you mentioned it. How could it bleed of its own accord?"

Taliesin, excited and as on the trail as any hunting hound, turned back to Viviane. "Mother, the spear used against Jesus: what became of it?"

Nimue frowned. *No spear killed the Christ; he was crucified.*

"It is said it came here, after what his followers call the Ascension."

"Here?! That's it, then! And the chalice, that used by Jesus at his last meal?"

"Here as well. Both brought by someone brave enough to be the friend of a condemned man."

"But they must be kept separate, as you indicated?"

"From each other, yes. Though one person could, I gather, keep more than one, so long as care was taken to ensure they never contacted each other."

"Do you know anything of their appearance?"

"Just how Christian do you think me?"

"My apologies, Lady, I accuse you of no cross-worship. The Hallows. What did they look like?"

"That's just it, bard. It is not for us to choose their precise form, though they will always be recognizable as the four relics. When Arthur recovered Caliburn, it had the form of a much longer weapon, heavy and for slashing, not short like Caesar's swords." Arthur had not exactly "found" the blade now known through the land as Excalibur, and Viviane would not divulge the role she played in his acquiring it. She had simply known that it was destined only for he who possessed the sacred and inherited right to rule. The bards and minstrels could tell what tales they would. In a Christian court, it was probably better that way.

"Could the cauldron have seemed like a cheap bowl? Or the spear seem to bleed on its own?"

The silence that fell over the wattle and daub hut was deafening.

Nimue, just beginning to sense what Taliesin drove at, spoke again. "But it did bleed. And the serving dish. It was more like, like, a platter."

"Of wood?" pressed the bard.

"No. Metal. Like silver. It shone."

Again the silence, seeming to bathe them all in its own coolness, like the first chill wind of autumn sending the leaves into their death-dance.

Viviane spoke this time. "You're saying Pellam possesses the Hallows? Or, at least, two of them?"

"No, Lady, I am not. Not yet. Even if he had them, the larger question remains, one that bothers me even more than the possibility of one man laying claim to that which is not divinely his."

"And?" Nimue said. She had never felt so blind and clumsy.

"Why? Why does he have them, if that is what they truly are, and why would he go to such lengths to ensure we see them?"

"Maybe to show them off? He is quite wealthy, you know." Nimue had instinctively not taken to trusting the man, whatever his credentials.

"Then why not invite kings? Why not invite Arthur, Lady Viviane, Bishop Baudwin, and all the rulers of these lands? Why not seek the ultimate in prestige, so as to compensate for his infirmities?"

"How was he wounded?" Viviane said suddenly.

Taliesin's excitement and wonder vanished in a wisp of obstructive thought. "I don't know."

"Nor I," added Nimue. The old fisherman spoke nothing of his injuries, even going out of his way to pretend they did not exist, though it appeared they could have caused him great suffering. Perhaps they still did, beneath the lavish suppers and warm smiles.

"I shall have to find out, I suppose," Taliesin said, barely audible. He was not about to ask the Ladies for divinations. The Well was sacred also, and he would not profane it merely to play the spy. It might be better to go back and ask the old man, anyway. Yes. That was what the bard resolved to do. He suddenly wished to leave Avalon at once, but it was dark, and he was honor-bound to provide the Ladies and their students and charges with his finest entertainment. He would sing the evening away for them, and be off in the morning.

* * *

Perceval grew anxious and giddy both. The time with Llio and in Worcester proved more delightful than he could have imagined, though now his thoughts turned to the task left unfinished.

The folk had gotten back with their lives, the interruption of Clamadeus and his men now something merely to discuss in memory. The artisans resumed their endless work, and Perceval never lost his amazement for what they could produce, and in such a seemingly effortless fashion. The metal goods included ornamentations crafted in gold and silver, as well as solid but flexible blades for daggers and swords. The weaponsmith also formed iron painstakingly into lance and arrow tips, axe blades, even the heavier heads found on the busy ends of maces and morning stars. It took some time for the metal to be forged; the people knew of the more advanced techniques of molding metal directly, but shunned them in favor of a more personalized approach to the art.

Pottery and an assortment of specialized linens, such as gloves and more aesthetic adornments, were also hallmarks of the town. Perceval enjoyed watching the spinning of the potter's wheels, and how their endlessly dirty hands lovingly worked wet earth into perfectly round vessels. The people likewise enjoyed having him around and showing him how they lived and worked; they all knew they would not have savored such livelihood again without him coming.

And Llio. Being still a stranger to chivalry's woman-worshipping, Perceval contented himself to becoming the best partner to his lover he could. He was surprised by how much it felt like old times back in Jagent, the pair of them laughing and talking the hours away. Now there was also the added intimacy.

How he loved that. The feel and smell of her sent his head reeling, and her smile or just a kind look could warm him and make his legs feel shaky. They lived and loved there for as long as both patience and the situation would allow.

For Perceval grew to missing Camelot, or at least what it represented to him. So much remained unresolved.

The fire in his loins had been quenched, for now; it would heat again soon enough. It was enough of a comfort for the time being to simply dream of having Llio again. That first time was a bit painful for both, but they were each comfortable enough with each other (and with their own bodies, a lesson at the pond not lost on Perceval), to learn trust while learning love.

And Dindraine and Galienne. He had to look for them, even if they were forever hidden or even passed from their lives into the next. And the King. Perceval had a duty (so he kept saying) to report back on his whereabouts and doings, and he was hungry for the knighthood which had eluded him so long. As for the others, they had to get on with their lives, too. Llio had her own obligation to stay on for a time to help her uncle manage the town, at least until it had its own small government restored. Clamadeus killed two council members before the siege, and all were concerned with ensuring that nothing like that would happen again. Obviously more knew how to find the tiny settlement than they had thought. Besides, Llascoit still needed some rehabilitation, even if he refused to admit it, and Llio was the only one who had the time for him. His wound had to finish healing, else his own knighthood would be one of the shortest ever.

Sitting and discussing the inevitable separation one afternoon before mealtime, Perceval helped Llascoit with the painting of a new shield. It was more properly a knight's defense than that lent to Perceval for his duel.

Perceval laughed. "I can just hear your father again."

Llascoit had just completed the background field. He had something other than his father's arms in mind for the rest. "Me, too. I wonder how he's doing."

"Probably tutoring some new kids who have no clue what they're in for."

"'Kids?' So, are you saying you're such an adult now?" Llascoit teased. "So mature, that's Perceval!"

"All right, all right, so we're still immature. Did we get any wiser?"

"I doubt it." He laughed. "Knights are dumb. Don't you know that?"

"You know, if you weren't such a damned inconvenience, I'd teach you something."

"Come back to kick my tail, huh? Are you forgetting I'm the knight here, and I therefore outrank you?"

"Like you could have beaten him." Perceval clapped Llascoit on the back.

"Hey, careful, this is serious work."

"At least you've had time to think about this. Personal heraldry has hardly crossed my mind. What are you putting on it?"

"Two things," Llascoit said. "The first, here, is a wolf's head. The wolf means strength, family loyalty, and I've heard they mate for life."

Perceval chortled. "What's so damn funny?" demanded Llascoit.

"You. That looks like no wolf I've ever seen. And why are you concerned with mating for life? You haven't even mated at all!"

Wouldn't you just like to know? "How would you know, anyway, Sir World Traveler? Do you mean you're just going to run from my sister, and hop from bed to bed like most of our kind?"

Llascoit had not expected the wounded look he received. He smiled at Perceval, half-expecting a response, eager to get back to the painting.

"No, of course not! I'd never do that, not to Llio. She means too much, I love her so much, and, and why I am spilling my heart to you?"

Llascoit shrugged. "Who else would you tell?"

"Good point. Llas, do you think your father would want me to ask his permission before I ask her to marry me?"

"Marry? You want to marry Llio? How do you plan to support her? When was the last time you earned a denarius by performing labor?"

"That's what lords are for." Perceval felt instant guilt for saying so. Cymru provided for themselves, even their rulers. Servants were only for true luxuries.

"You're not a knight! Sorry, not *yet*."

Perceval hadn't told his foster-brother about his encounter with the High King. "Llas, trust me, when I get back to Camelot... what are you smiling at?"

Llascoit kept his mouth shut, almost choking on laughter.

"Very well, I accept, since you cannot even turn round long enough to notice me," said the voice from behind Perceval. Llascoit had watched Llio walk up to observe their male banter.

Perceval wheeled in place, stirring up the dirt inside the fort's walls, where the three of them had come to enjoy staying, even in the absence of amenities. Llio stood there, smiling down at him.

"It makes perfect sense," she said. "You're already down there on one knee. Is this to be your proposal, then?"

Perceval opened his mouth and no vocal sound escaped, only a strangled breath like the sound of a fish forcibly pulled from the sea. She looked so confident to him, smiling brightly and lovingly, her eyes teasing him with their wide liveliness.

"I am a grown woman, Perceval. I need no father's permission to wed whom I choose."

"Then whom would you choose, if you could have anyone at all?"

"The King, of course. Although I think something would have to be done about that queen of his."

Llascoit ignored his task, bemusedly watching Perceval almost collapse, his arms seeming like they would buckle beneath him. "You would, you'd –"

"What do you think, silly?" she said. Then, "You have my answer. Now what about you?"

"Well, you. No one else makes me feel like you do, Llio. How could I ever be happy with anyone else?"

"Are you hastily composing another love poem on my behalf?"

"Not yet, but if you give me more time, you'll have it."

"It would be you. Poem or no, I should hope you know that by now. Besides, don't knights seek precious virgins? They're unspoiled, stupid, giddy."

"Llio, please, how many people do you wish to know about –"

"About us? How many in Worcester *don't* know? Especially with those sounds you made last night?"

"You asked about the wolf's head, Perceval. Was that actual howling I heard in the darkness?" Llascoit was enjoying this almost too much.

"You-, oh, do shut up, both of you!" They laughed at him.

"Shall I be off to plan our nuptials, then?" Llio said.

"But I haven't even asked you yet."

"Better hurry, the King awaits," she teased again, and ran off, giggling. Some of the women from the settlement had come with her, remaining at the fort's gate during the discourse. They all left together, chattering like children.

"I think the wolf's head means more to you. I should have chosen another device." Llascoit resumed his artwork.

Perceval shook his head, more from a vague frustration than humor. "No, you keep it. Someday you'll be as hopelessly in love as I."

"I hope so," Llascoit said, with a tone of sudden seriousness.

"What else is going on it?" asked Perceval.

"Hmm? Oh, it's also going to have a ram. A symbol of determination and purpose, something that can survive in difficult times and lands."

"A what?"

"A ram. Don't they have rams back in Cambria?"

"I wouldn't know."

"They're kind of like sheep, except more noble. The males grow these enormous horns, and they curl as they grow, and, what?"

"Some new mystical creature perhaps? Why not just use a brownie, or some other elf?"

"But they really exist! The rams, I mean. I know nothing of brownies or elves. There are rams on the Continent, and people admire them because they have a lot in common with normal sheep, but they're strong, and no one can contain them or herd them."

"I see. And that's why you want these two animals on your shield?"

Llascoit nodded. "The wolf and ram. They'll look good together, especially since they're usually enemies."

"So these two natures of yours you wish to represent, are they enemies as well?"

Llascoit thought about it. "I'm not sure. I don't think so, and I hope not. I want neither to win out over the other."

"Then I wish you good fortune, Sir Llascoit of Jagent."

Seeing the shield made Perceval want the noble status that much more. He had no time to plan a wedding, had no idea what even went into the planning of one. And where would they have it? Not in Worcester, surely. But then where? Camelot? Jagent? And he had not even asked her yet, for mercy's sake!

While watching and talking with Llascoit that afternoon Perceval resolved how he would pursue the matter: he would give Llio her proposal in the form of that poem she wished for. And after receiving her response, he would be off to Camelot. He understood it was normal for the betrothed to be out of one another's presence during the preparation anyway, and Llio had already made it clear she needed to stay, at least for now. He was welcome to use the family accommodations in Camelot, she had told him the previous night, when they made more of their sweet yet tentative sensuous love and Perceval had apparently woken up even the dead themselves. He remembered that part differently.

But would leaving be turning his back on her? He couldn't live with that, and she told him repeatedly that she would wait for him enthusiastically, and never claim any save him, however long it took to actually wed. Yet Perceval felt that his knighting ceremony would just take him from another person, *no, another woman who trusted me*, he warned himself, who needed him.

On the other hand, maybe someone in Camelot could help him with what else he wished: knowledge. He wanted to speak with anyone who might tell him something of Pellam, or who knew anything about Galienne's Grail. Maybe the bishop would know of it, the man whose name escaped Perceval.

Maybe the other knights would know something. What was Pellam really up to? And what did all the items and events they saw at Bridgnorth mean?

He thus decided his next course. First, a lovely evening with Llio, complete with poetic declarations. Then, to Camelot, which he firmly resolved not to leave again until he had both his title and the legal right to bear the weapon at his side, and some answers or leads to the thoughts which were never far from him.

And perhaps he could find new mail, too.

"– fairest and evermore, may she lead me to the dish of plenty within. *Dim ond drosot ti, 'nghariad i.*" *Only for you, my love.*

The sung words hung in the air, savored only by the two of them, until Llio spoke. "That was beautiful. Oh, Perceval, I loved it. Your poetry has improved since last I heard it. You must have practiced with Galienne."

"Only the sword and my Latin. And I've told you before, there's no need for jealousy." He hoped he wasn't as tone-deaf as he thought.

"Not jealousy of her, but envy for the time she had with you, roaming the land. And you better mean the iron sword, and not that of flesh."

"Of course, love. May I proceed now, or must I first submit to more of your accusatory jests?"

"Oh, by all means, my dear. Proceed at once."

Perceval remained on his knees, feeling much more penitent than he ever had at Haughmond Abbey. He took Llio's offered hands, squeezing their warmth. "I love you. Now and always." It was enough.

"And I you. Through this life and that which follows."

Perceval rose, bringing her towards him. They embraced tenderly, more relaxed than during their animal releases of numerous inquisitive and sweaty nights, letting their feelings engulf and bind them. Perceval swore he would ask Gornymant's permission anyway, to which she assented, though not without another reminder of her autonomy. They would work out the details later.

For now, for a moment of love a lifetime in the making and after patient waiting, neither knowing for what exactly, they felt at peace, needed, cared for.

Neither wished to end it, but they pulled apart enough to see each other. "Tomorrow," said Perceval.

Llio nodded, wrapping her arms about him again, and let herself be eased down into bed with her lover. She sighed contentedly; most women were assigned lovers, but not her.

* * *

"You haven't considered searching for them?"

King Arthur sat upright in his cavernous bed, large enough to hold an orgy. Sometimes he woke up during the night and literally had to look for his queen. He rubbed his eyes, shaking off sound slumber. "Of course I've thought of it. But it might be construed negatively. What of a king who has to search for his knights?"

"But he needs you to dub him. He has no other potential lord." Guinevere still lay among the soft woven bedding, partly wrapped up in a magnificent quilt depicting Camelot from the outside, the King and Queen perched upon the southeastern tower, looking toward the Continent.

"Yes, sweet, but he must return on his own. If he does not, then might he not seem irresponsible? Hardly an admirable trait for a knight."

Guinevere was more awake than her king, but didn't feel much like rising to face the day. "Suppose he's lost. And besides, people are talking about the girl. Are you jealous that she experienced the same miracle you did?" Guinevere enjoyed chiding him.

"What miracle? Lancelot found the blade. It must have been left there."

"Suppose it was. That doesn't explain what happened outside the city. Can't you appreciate the miraculous when it happens?" Arthur sometimes forgot how devout his Queen was, her faith ingrained from birth. Cameliard had always been dangerous; faith gave folk strength to survive.

The King also recognized the reason behind Guinevere's new-found penitence. But he was her husband, not her priest, and so never asked for an explanation. Of that she would always be glad; she had her life and her relationship to rebuild. She prayed fervently that she and her champion would never be discovered.

To her knowledge, they had not. Lancelot was gone, again, just the way she had so often thought Arthur was, when the King was actually right here at her side, much more often than not. The campaigns were ended, Arthur did not have to leave the city for battle anymore. And Guinevere was largely coming to the conclusion that her feelings for the other knight were based on her exasperation of playing the sovereign one day followed by the despairing boredom of it the next. Romantic ideals, encouraged by her own romantic courts. The man's obvious passion, his equally obvious ability to conceive (though the Queen still suspected her king had bad seed; it was more palatable a thought than the notion of her own barrenness). It was hardly natural for a queen to go bed-hopping, especially since discovery would be interpreted as treason. Perhaps the risk was part of the appeal.

No. When she considered it, that wasn't really the case. Lancelot embodied all she had seen in Arthur when they first met. But it became too easy to bring diplomacy and authority into bed. A monarch's problems didn't go away in the darkness. Now that they could enjoy a life of peace in the aftermath of fabled victories, with business as usual reduced mostly to petty bickering and grievances, their relationship strengthened again.

But there was more. They still had no heir, and not for lack of trying, even though she was likely too old now. Guinevere had reached the point at which she almost would consider the ancient remedies for barrenness, but they still couldn't be sure of just who was to blame. And the rumor of an actual son, which they could not speak of, just added fuel to the blaze. More than just family joy was at stake; who would see to Camelot when they were gone? That was what divided them, for a time. Indeed, all these criteria could be sufficient to lead a queen astray, even if only briefly.

Arthur was here, flesh and whole, at her side. They made love last night, the most peaceful and delicious it had been for them since, how long? She could not recall.

"Miracle or no, what would you have me do? Make her a knight also?" the King said.

Guinevere rolled over to face him, stroking his back, feeling the lengthy scar there which almost took him from her at Badon. He never discussed it with her, and she had always mistrusted the curious silence of men. Even Lancelot was more of a talker. "Is that the real reason for your hesitancy, then?"

He paused, taking her other hand, massaging it between both of his. "You can read me better than even Merlin. Will the Brotherhood accept a woman?"

"What if she can take the seat? At your side? She's already done more than anyone thought possible. You were there;

you saw the cross. Of what other miracles might this girl be capable?"

"I know nothing of miracles, Guin, you know that." The King paid little heed to Baudwin's sermons or his queen's musings. He recognized the power of all faith in his land, and for that reason could never allow himself to take up arms for religious reasons. Arthur was a dreamer and a soldier, not a theologian.

"But suppose she could?" Guinevere listened to the tales of the Siege Perilous. Had Merlin engineered it? Had Baudwin or even the archbishop from Rome consecrated it especially? She knew not. But the knights, the whole superstitious lot of them, firmly believed that one chair was enchantedly reserved for one exclusive member; the only ones who did sit in it were not knights. Some fool had years ago vowed he could sit anywhere at the Table once Arthur made his invitation, and had begun to spontaneously combust. No one knew whence the flames came. The man survived, fled from the room, and was not heard of again in Logres. Since then the seat on Arthur's flank became known as the Perilous Seat, both for the flames, and the anxiety of the lucky petitioners granted royal audiences on feast or holy days. The seat's name was certainly an understatement.

Maybe a woman could tame the fires in a way no man could...

Maybe. Still, the King had to make up his mind. "I gave my word that I would knight Perceval. I owe that much for how he handled Meliagrant." Guinevere shuddered at mention of the Red Knight's name, the man related to her by blood who nonetheless almost raped her once and had certainly attempted to steal other things that were not his. Yes, Cameliard was too close to the heathens; the Queen was glad to have an excuse not to return there, entrusting it to stewards.

"Then why not seek him out? He must have seen to his home by now. And Galienne has no home anymore; she must grow weary of running about the wilds."

Envy. That's what Guinevere felt for Lancelot. He had a child, and a rather special one at that. And the selfish champion could hardly be bothered with her. She wondered if that was why she had turned from a second lover back to her first, back to her king. Had she been able to conceive, she would have treated her child with all the reverence Baudwin proffered Jesus. The royal child would have been adored by all Camelot, all Logres, and the Queen would have been endlessly proud and loving of such child-wealth.

She was glad she still faced Arthur's back; she wished him not to see the anger flushing her face. "That's it, then," he said. "I'll need to find him, call him back to court, give him what he rightly deserves. I'll take Kay, and Bedivere."

"Gawaine and Lancelot are still gone?"

"Yes. Lancelot has been seeing to the safety of his daughter and a future knight. And Gawaine is not yet returned from Lothian." Arthur carried his own demons; he could ill-afford to inform his wife of a score and four years that before they even met, he had affairs. Men were expected to do such, of course, particularly those destined for matrimonial ties, but the surprisingly Christian guilt which had its own hold on the man would not allow him to speak of who the affair was with.

Margawse must have magicked him somehow. Arthur could believe that, did believe it, sometimes. He was too drunk with battle-energy, too intoxicated by knowledge and acceptance of power and the growing wisdom proffered by Merlin, too blasted on army wine, to care. Now the Picts and northern Cymru circulated some tale of an illegitimate son, one who wished access to certain claims.

Arthur considered himself wholly justified for how he had attempted his revenge for that incident, even though others might disagree. He reminded himself the decision about the newborn sons of Lothian had been political.

"What did you say?" Guinevere said, Arthur once again becoming aware of her touch on his back.

"Oh, nothing." He knew not what he said, could only vaguely recall some mumbling about "the queen."

Guinevere didn't need to know he spoke of another queen. One he would rather forget, but who would not permit him to do so.

"Let me go with you," Guinevere said.

"What?"

"Let me accompany the search party. Galienne will want to speak with a woman, after all. Sword or no, I doubt she's quite prepared for all your mysterious bonding rituals."

Arthur laughed. He loved Guinevere's ability to assert herself, a gift perhaps not in accordance with her faith, at least not for a woman. "Very well, you're officially invited. It will be like old times, Guin."

He looked at her, the wife who stood with him during the painful building of his Pax Brittanica, and listened to all his worries. "Old times? So now you're calling me old?" She hit him with one of the feather-down pillows.

"I just meant, it will feel free."

She sighed. "Free." The greatest word there was, other than "saved." No rules, no castles, no duties. Just the peace of the outdoors, in which Guinevere felt much safer since the King had cleared it of bandits and other evil-doers. She could remember being taught to hate it, fear it; who knew what lurked in the forests and hills? Now it was her place of refuge, away from the walls.

She credited that sentiment with the safety offered by a just Christian king, rather than admit her own faith's role in subjugating and trying to control the wilderness. She loved the wind in her hair as much as any Pagan, but was pious enough to not allow inconsistencies to creep into her view of the realm. A just rule was a sign from God.

And the ability of someone to sit in a certain location would likewise be a signal of God's acceptance and Love. The King and Queen began making their preparations at once.

* * *

"You're wearing the sash again?" Gaheris had not seen his brother pull out that particular accessory for many seasons.

Gawaine was securing the evergreen makeshift belt about his waist. "It's a reminder. Remember how I wanted –"

"The other knights to each wear one? Yes, I remember."

"Brother, you really should stop that."

"Stop what?"

"Finishing other people's –"

"Sentences?"

Gawaine sighed. "Yes." The lengthy sash was a gift from the only man who ever bested Gawaine. The Green Knight had come to offer his challenge to the finest knights of Logres.

Gawaine and the others knew not whom was responsible for the glamour which obviously accompanied the man; how else could Bertilak's head have been seen to topple at Gawaine's decisive axe stroke? And Gawaine took it as a source of immense personal pride that he alone possessed the courage to take the challenge, as even the other Pagans were terrified.

The Green Man thought the Table in disharmony then; if he returned to court and saw it now! Matters were so much simpler then. We all followed and cherished the Cause, now we are torn apart by infighting. Gawaine's pride would not permit him to assign some of the blame to himself for that discord. He was unaware his own cousin sought him in earnest.

The challenge had been simple enough: the Green Knight dared anyone to have the courage to take his head. Gawaine all but jumped at the chance. Magick or intimidating knight had weaknesses.

The axe sliced clean through. Gawaine could remember the sound of skin and bone splitting, could still sometimes smell the blood; at first he thought it real enough, given the different, potent sensations.

The man left, head in his arms, Gawaine honor-bound to meet him a year hence for a return cut. Gawaine arrived on time, barely, sidetracked by the knight's wife attempting her own potent but failed seduction. But he survived; Gawaine hoped his challenger returned home to tell of the courage he had evidenced in Camelot. The sash was a parting gift.

Gaheris knew his elder brother well enough to realize that he only wore the green garment now when he felt afraid. "What is it? What are you thinking?"

Gawaine finished tying it. It looked quite handsome, amidst the iron outer skin. "The region we traversed. We may have to go through it again."

Gaheris recalled the screaming mad folk all too vividly. "Yes. You would think Mother would know of it. I wonder why she didn't speak about it."

It was part question, too. "I couldn't say. But I do know our visits with her keep me longing for Camelot again."

The pair of them had discussed their mother's strange and sometimes disturbing ways often enough, something of which their younger siblings were not yet privy, but they suspected Agrivaine knew. Though he probably didn't care, bitter Agrivaine, wanting to hate his brothers for not taking the throne in Lothian but unable to himself, and actually needing them to bail him out of trouble since the time he could first walk.

Gawaine and Gaheris suspected their mother dabbled in arts better left unvoiced further south. They knew nothing of her plans nor of her involvement in any number of otherwise inexplicable happenings: captive knights and maidens, sacrifices those of the newer religion would call damning and unholy; they only had suspicion of her greed and lust. Power and paramours, those were the food which sated their mother's appetite. Gawaine often wondered how she could have birthed not just one but several sons who were, as a whole, viewed as chivalry and romantic idealism in the flesh. He supposed it was due to their own greed, for their own power and prestige; their celebrity and adaptability gave them a second home, one they now found more pleasant than the one in which they grew.

It doesn't matter, Gawaine concluded. Their mother would not change, and neither would they. For kinship's sake he would keep the formal relations going, never mind that he was beginning to fear the woman.

"You're right," Gaheris said. "It will be good to get back. Maybe the King will have some new quest for the undertaking."

"A good war would suit me just fine," Gawaine said, who truly missed the energy-charged chaos of a bloody field.

"We could find some new enemies of the King," Gaheris said. "You're good at that!"

Gawaine chuckled with his brother. "Yes. Do you remember Bors' eyes when I took out Lucius' diplomat?"

"They practically shot out like arrows!" Gaheris laughed harder.

"Ah, how I miss that day." They continued on, knowing the laughter good for them. The Old Ones said laughter was full of powerful magick. Anything would be welcomed by them as they rode forth, and in two days found themselves back in the great wastes.

Once again the veteran had to admit he was lost. Gaheris proved of little help. Gawaine kept thinking he recognized certain landmarks, even some of those they witnessed on their way north. Yet he couldn't be certain which marks had ever actually been viewed by either of them. They resolved to keep to the roads as best they could; nothing else seemed to keep them on track.

Gawaine despised the feeling of traversing in circles, being a more linear-minded sort. There were times that both knights felt they could identify places they passed the previous day, even the prior hour. Gaheris was starting to despair; Gawaine just got more frustrated. He would never admit defeat until he was already dead. Or so he swore.

At least there were no naked and bloody tribes folk gone over the last cliffs of reason, plunging into the mental void which enabled them to attack fully armed knights without fear. Gawaine and Gaheris had seen true battle-rage, beyond what even they could muster through inspired and rallying cries; the berserker frenzies of the bearded Garmani swinging their heavy axes almost turned affairs around at Badon Hill.

They camped in dusty oblivion, chilly for the season, and it felt more like dead winter through their field tents and wool blankets. During each night, they were awoken several times by the unwanted invasion of wind-driven dirt in their tents, doing nothing to improve their fraying nerves.

It was approaching evening a few days later, a point at which they both felt they should have been in the Cumbrian lands, that Gaheris saw something else. Or so he thought.

"A castle! Gawaine, do you see it?" He gesticulated determinedly southwest.

"You and your habits. There's no castle near here!"

"But the areas we used to know have changed, and I'm telling you, there's a castle yonder!" Gaheris pointed again.

Gawaine looked, just to humor him. But unless he was either hallucinating or someone had spelled more glamour their way, there truly was a castle, perhaps a mere three miles distant.

They would have to leave the road to get there, Gawaine noticed, looking what he thought was southward from where they stood.

But any castle had to be better than spending another night in the open, leaving them vulnerable to things they dared not give voice to. So the castle won, road or no.

They arrived in several minutes, urging their mounts into gallops, but not so fast they might cripple themselves stumbling into the many holes which dotted the land, like the tart cheeses imported from the Continent for grand feasts. The stronghold was multi-towered, though they couldn't be sure of details without getting inside. The fog which so often covered this area later in the day had crept in once again, so that no identifying marks could be gleaned from the fortress: no arms, no banners.

Only the plaintive women above. "Help us!" cried a female voice. "Release us, please!" begged another.

Gawaine and Gaheris looked up at the ramparts. A number of women, they knew not how many, looked down at them from the many windows and archways. "Who the devil are they?" Gawaine said, actually hoping for a useful answer.

None came, not surprisingly, only guesses. "Prisoners. Captive maidens?" Gaheris, too, tried to comprehend how these women got here.

Ever the woman's defender, Gawaine resolved, "No matter who they be. The villain who imprisoned them will pay. Come, brother. If we're to have shelter from the wasteland, it seems we must first liberate this place."

They rode around the perimeter, and soon located the main gate, a solid-looking iron lattice-work, quite a barrier except for one detail.

It was open, hoisted into the gate tower, leaving only the bottom teeth protruding.

The brothers eased closer. Likewise, the interior doors, heavy oak capable of taking many hours of battering rams, lay open and beckoning. And not a soul manning the battlements. No challenge sounded, no welcoming horns blew; indeed, there was no sign of occupation at all.

Save the women. And they were out of earshot now. Gawaine was half-tempted to ride back to where they saw them just to verify their existence. He had lost patience with illusory magicks long ago.

"Should we?" Gaheris said, vainly trying to keep the apprehension out of his voice.

"Gaheris, we have a duty as Arthur's knights. Besides, look behind you." His brother obeyed. "Would you prefer to spend another night out there?"

Out where? Gaheris could only see fog, thick as the beefy chowder his father Lot used to adore, when Gaheris was just a baby. The hollow hills lay behind them.

So they dismounted, escorting their horses inside the gate. The gate promptly slammed shut behind them. Gaheris refused to jump, but his nerves still craved release, and flooded his body with the warrior's potion, that which made men fight or flee.

"Who's there?" Gawaine demanded, the shout echoing off the walls of the gate tower.

No answer. Just heavy breathing. The brothers couldn't tell if the breath came from them or their mounts.

"Sir Gaheris and Sir Gawaine of clan Orkney of Lothian," Gaheris said.

The doors still stood wide open. Gawaine headed inward.

"Gawaine, wait. Shouldn't we –"

"Do what?" his elder said, adopting the younger brother's habit. "We may be the heirs of Lothian, but do you think we can lift that gate?" Gawaine maneuvered his horse so that he was just past the doors.

And that was when they, too, swung closed, cutting Gawaine off from his brother, before he could even mutter a response.

* * *

Perceval had managed good time thus far. Padern saw that he received the finest mount the residents of Worcester had to offer: a stallion named Styfnig, a proud horse who chose its riders, rather than the opposite. He stood fully eighteen hands tall, a challenge just to climb into the saddle, and lived up to the stubbornness that was his namesake. Perceval was glad to have the help of the strange foot-rings to help with that basic task.

"Stirrups, those are, lad," Padern said to him, while he introduced stallion to errant. "They help keep you in the saddle, and they're sturdier than the four-posts you're probably used to." Perceval had seen what they referred to back home: the native saddles with four grips, two each in front and in back of a rider's thighs, virtually locking the rider in place. These "stirrups" were supposed to be better. Padern said they were part of what made Arthur's cavalry so formidable.

The goodbye to Llio was quick, both of them wanting it that way. Perceval rode just a few yards before turning to watch his beloved head back to the fort, readying herself for another day of therapy with her brother. Llascoit could now keep up a jog, and had even ridden a few times, but on horses smaller and less intimidating than the veritable monster the errant led towards Camelot. It was unlike riding Brownie, who was tranquil or slightly edgy most of the time. Styfnig gave every impression that he was in charge, and whoever was gutsy or stupid enough to swing his legs up had just better enjoy the ride.

The deeper shades of summer would soon arrive. It would be months before the woodland inhabitants readied themselves busily with vital food storage and the securing of domiciles, though Perceval noticed some such creatures curiously engaged with that work already. It made for a peaceful ride back. He spent a few days mostly uneventfully, passing a merchant caravan heading northward. He traded with the owners for a new javelin, carefully counting the few coins which somehow still remained from the purse his mother gave him. He also bought some better food. Llio gave him plenty, but he already finished it. And Padern was of little help, insisting that hard tack, biscuits more suited for house-building than consumption, and water taken from the cold hill streams, would "toughen you up like the white bull of the druids!" Perceval didn't even bother asking; it was another question better suited for Tathan or Taliesin.

So it went, the travel opening into the broad heaths laying between the forests, until he spotted someone familiar.

Daylight did nothing to improve Kunneware's looks. Had Gawaine been with Perceval right then, he would have thought her to look something like his own once cursed woman, given her second chance at beauty through an act of compassion. Perceval enjoyed the sight of someone he met before, as he saw his share of strangers. But that did nothing to help ease him of the dread which coiled its way into his bowels. He still didn't like the way she looked at him.

Kunneware bravely rode alone, though there was another horse with her. She looked out of place on the dun palfrey, her aged weight slowing it. She and the horses had been mere ants crawling on the horizon, as she and Perceval continued toward each other. He wondered where she might be headed.

"Do you feel yourself satisfied, then?" she said to him when they were close enough to notice each other's facial distinctions.

Perceval thought first of Llio. Of *course* he was satisfied! Galienne's reasoning would consign him to some years in purgatory for how he spent his nights just a short time earlier. The hag awaited an answer, though. "Generally, I believe so, lady. Is there reason for me not to be?"

Her eyes vexed him murderously. The anger made him fearful. "Hear you, false knight. You know nothing of the harm you have caused?"

Perceval really could think of none, shaking his head.

"Pellam is gone once more. Even I cannot find him now. And the question was so obvious, man! None of you thought of it!"

"What question?" Perceval resisted the urge to grasp the comforting pommel.

"It would have taken no more than a simple act of kindness, and you mussed it up! You and that other knight. Knights cause so much harm, but they never know how to heal what they've done." Kunneware was livid. Since her talk with Pellam he had disappeared, and her only recourse now was to blame the handiest person. Perceval was quite handy right then.

"But I did nothing," Perceval said.

"When good folk do nothing, it is the same as doing ill."

What in Annwn is this old hag talking about? He could have sworn she heard his mind utter the thought. "Lady Kunneware, please accept my sworn apology. I know not to what you refer."

"Then there is no cure. Not from you." The old woman made to leave.

"But, I protest my innocence! How would I defend myself when I don't even know of what I stand accused?"

But she rode past, yelling back, "To Camelot, boy! Your title awaits."

Perceval remained there, numbed. He could feel himself grow heavier, not that Styfnig noticed. Why did so many want so much of him? There was too much to know, too much to do. He could never finish so much, never find so many answers. He didn't even have a chance to ask the woman why she rode one horse while leading another. And where was she going? To find Pellam? She said she couldn't. But then, where else?

He half-considered riding after her, but to what avail? She wished nothing more to do with him. And she was heading away from Camelot.

He was so tired of the delays with his knighting, of not knowing all that others expected of him. Knighthood had to be easier than this! As a knight he would take his orders from the King, no one else. He could live as he chose, he could take Llio for wife. He liked the bustle of the city; why not settle?

His resolve partially back in place, he urged Styfnig forward, never turning to see Kunneware staring back at him, trying desperately not to give up hope, anger preventing her from any other course.

* * *

While Perceval rode in melancholy and the king and queen left Camelot with an entourage, Gawaine and Gaheris still lingered much further north. They would not all meet for days yet, and the latter men found themselves rather busy in the meantime.

Gawaine could hear only muffled shouts from his brother, now trapped between the outer gate and inner doors. He dismounted at once, setting to banging at the heavy oak with his mailed fists. "Gaheris! Gaheris, can you hear me?"

Behind the doors Gaheris heard dull pounding and could vaguely understand what his brother said. They would not be able to communicate more effectively until the doors were reopened.

"Try to get the doors back open!" pleaded Gaheris, not wanting to be let alone in the small space. His mount already showed signs of fear, its usually proud eyes widening into comprehension, almost as if it could smell Gaheris' fraying nerves, like a dog. The thick fog had returned, and would soon envelop the whole castle. Gaheris would be lucky to see his own horse once the density of the mist took hold in the tower, much less anything which might lie outside, waiting.

"I can't. They're too heavy. Gaheris! I'm going to try and find a way to open them. There has to be a key or latch somewhere."

"Wait, Gawaine!" Gaheris' shout became almost a whine. "Do you have to leave?"

"Oh, please. I'll return for you, fear not." And the elder brother left his horse at the doors, searching for a way into the main castle.

It was not long in finding. Gawaine went from the gate house to another large set of doors, shut but not barred, and pushed them inward. They opened into a sizable courtyard. He thought a castle this large had to belong to at least a duke or some other important noble. There were not many like this, not in all the realm.

But it looked deserted.

Lavishly decorated, yes, but devoid of life. He sensed no castle-sounds, no smells of food or horses or offal. And the women seen in the walls earlier had grown silent, giving no indication of their whereabouts.

He passed through the courtyard, noticing the stable, granary, and walls.

Whoever owned the place took pains to ensure it would remain a daunting conquest. The walls were enriched by battlements, arrow-slits, even murder holes, all for catching the unwary invader in lethal crossfire, and the stone itself had to be many feet thick.

One wall in particular caught Gawaine's eye. He instinctively drew his long sword, calling out his identity without receiving any response other than chilly silence. He walked slowly to the wall detail, taking time to study it as he went: a rich mosaic, painted with both excellent skill and patience. Gawaine had never tried his hand at the more artistic form of personal expression, though he felt respect for the time and study it must have taken to produce the work.

It was easy to recognize the infamous "Green Knight" who provoked him those years past, when the King's champion took up the challenge at once, even though the man all but dwarfed him. Gawaine still recalled the immense battleaxe the man carried into court; the likeness was uncanny.

It is said Lancelot himself once fell prey to one of the witches and became accustomed to painting. Perhaps a brother knight is here awaiting rescue. How a knight could reach the courtyard and create all this remained a mystery, though.

Hadrian's Wall had been reproduced as well, showing the end of Roman expansion. Knights, elegant ladies, a harper, a druid, some praying monks (or were they writing?) all occupied the broad scene, refusing to be limited to a single episode. Gawaine would have to compliment the artist, and request hospitality.

If the lord could be found. Gawaine hailed again. Nothing.

The fog surrounded the castle, invading it with misty tendrils and fingers. Soon the knight would have to be just feet from the artwork to see it. He continued. He could just make out a tall keep past the courtyard.

The keep was just as empty. The sword remained at the ready. Starting with the main hall, Gawaine systematically searched about the keep, entering every room and chamber he could find. He never refrained from calling to whomever might lie just past a door, just in case; it was a serious breach of hospitality's protocol to enter anyone's chambers uninvited or worse, unannounced.

He could just hear his former love Ragnell chastising him for this behavior, barging into a castle while leaving his brother alone at the entrance. She taught him a thing or two, then left from his life, and he never knew where.

"Who is sovereign?" he could hear her ask from years earlier. The voice from the past had been another challenge, only months after his final encounter with the Green Knight. But this new challenge did not use weapons, which set Gawaine to confusion even more. Again the knights at the table had set to philosophizing, which was their wont after talk of battles and glory died down. "What do women truly want?" they said, many of them befuddled by lovers who idolized them from afar or by wives who hated them for having been made to marry.

The riddle was thus set. Gawaine wanted an answer himself. He had lain more pipe than the builders of the old aqueducts, but still had nary a clue what women desired in return. It must have been *something*. That was right when the Crone appeared.

Upstairs now. The keep had three levels, each consisting of lengthy hallways mostly unadorned, yet with numerous rooms, lavishly decorated. Each displayed its own unique character, clearly the doing of different persons. Probably none were done by the painter. One was lined with furs of creatures Gawaine had seen rarely or not at all. Another had all manner of weaponry and armor, though it was rusting or in disrepair. He kept searching, remembering the Crone, recalling the lesson of sovereignty. *Who was sovereign here?* he asked himself. *Who could possibly afford this locality but not live here?*

Ragnell had been so loathsome just to behold those years back, emerging from God-knew-what haunt to proffer the riddle. Gawaine thought her just some cantankerous sot not long for this life, but she promised great rewards for he who could answer the riddle. She also dared Gawaine to kiss her.

He did so, not without distaste, and heckling from some of the other knights. She complimented his courage. "And I shall meet you in the Queen's garden this eve," she said sweetly. The voice was deceptively warm and promising.

He arrived promptly at the designated place, outside the Garden of Love in Camelot, wanting answers, not kisses. Gawaine often thought the Queen added only more ambiguity as to the nature of women's hearts with her courts of love and romantic chivalry. But she arrived just after him. "You came." She was elated.

She had to first convince him she was the same person. She was gorgeous! Dressed in an exquisite cream gown, hair shining and billowy in the moonlit breeze, she offered him a proposition.

"Stay with me, and you will have a marvelous choice. At your bidding, I may remain this way day or night, though not both."

Gawaine had been smitten at once; he longed to be able to hold such a woman each night, would give so much... but *he* had to make the terms? To keep her the picture of divinity at night would give him no small amount of pleasure, but she would be treated no better than a leprous mongrel come morning. To leave her hideous at night would leave him feeling...he didn't dwell on it.

So he wisely chose to turn the decision back to her, if she was capable of making it. *Surely she must be*, he had thought, else why bother with all the glamour and games at all? He could think of no other explanation. Between the Green Knight and his own mother's reputation, it was little wonder Gawaine preferred a life of materialism. Having seen the workings of faerie before, he assumed Ragnell to be some petty magician come to win a knight's heart.

Instead, he received his answer, which he announced at the next Round Table meeting. Women wanted sovereignty over themselves. That was all. The meeting remained silent for some time after he said it. And then his lady disappeared from his life, and he missed her sometimes. Like now. He had never become very good with these riddles. He never knew if Ragnell was a true magician, or an actress.

Back in the present, Gawaine stood in the main chambers now, the biggest he had seen outside Camelot. The master and his lady surely slept away the cold northern nights here. Gawaine could only guess what the fineries might be worth.

An elaborately ornamented table and chairs stood in one corner, appearing as though they only saw use during certain occasions. The inlay of the board alternated gold and silver in a chess-board pattern. Gawaine had played chess, but never proficiently (Guinevere's hand-picked knights sometimes opted for games of skill as a way to test their non-military virtue; others danced or sang or composed elaborate love sonnets). Gawaine preferred the older game of *gwyddbwyll*, which he and his brethren played while growing. Lot and his sons had enjoyed seeing a wooden world, moving the pieces about and trying to conquer one another. Gaheris usually won.

Near the table was a window, the frame portraying a floral design in wrought iron. Gawaine stole a quick glance beyond; it looked out upon the courtyard, barely visible now in the fog, and past it the gate where his brother still awaited his salvation.

A large mirror, reflecting Gawaine's menacing stare, stood adjacent to the bed. Gawaine had little experience with his own likeness, thinking it too rough, else the mirror lied like the women who should have been in this keep, somewhere.

Gawaine thought perhaps the bed could have supported the better part of a Legionary cohort at one excited time, such was its spaciousness. A canopy soared above it, supported by fine cherry beams, while billowy sheets of silk took their gentle time floating down to the mattress. It looked too comfortable to pass by.

Gawaine gritted his teeth, thinking, and sighed exasperatedly. He sat down, eyeing the goose-down mattress, eager to take some of the weight from his weary bones, even if just for a moment.

But it wasn't there any longer. Gawaine's rump hit the solid floor the bed had just occupied. He was at once enraged, throwing himself into a standing position. He became further incensed by the floor; it was adorned with rich rugs, and all black. He hadn't noticed it before.

The bed lurked just out of reach, teasing him. *No, Sir, it's not mocking me. It just had a trip-release trigger, like those which activate gates and mill-wheels. But who released it?* Gawaine glanced about, ears twitching, though no evidence was gleaned by his battle-sharpened senses. Perhaps someone beyond the room?

The door stood open still, as he left it. He would have heard someone in the hall, even in the other rooms. He would try the bed again.

It made no further motion. He approached it again. This time he put away his sword, then charged the bed, lunging through the still air at it.

It moved away again, right under him while he was still airborne. He crashed behind it, while it resumed its original position whence he had found it. Gawaine shouted several obscenities at it and rose once more. He was tempted to take a slice of it, then decided it wasn't worth the effort.

He stood there, studying the scene again, when he finally heard the clicking noise. Gawaine hated the weapon to which the sound corresponded, considering it the tool of cowards and peasants, both of whom deserved to die painfully for raising such against a knight. He raised his sword once more, turning and rolling to face his attacker and dodge any errant bolts.

The crossbows fired, though several seconds would pass before Gawaine could identify the source. A lethal storm of bolts sailed past and at him, and he could only dodge them, though he managed to block one with his sword. He cursed the moment he had elected to leave his shield downstairs with his horse. The bolts kept coming, from within a closet at the far side of the room, several that become close calls, two which scraped at his mail-enclosed legs, and one which managed to find its mark.

Gawaine felt his hot precious blood at once, ebbing down his shoulder. He swore right then to have the head of whomever shot him, host or no. He lost track of all his scars and injuries, now only recalling those which had hurt the most: the broken leg at Badon Hill, an axe wound from Cerdic's own weapon. The bolt would be remembered as well; it pierced tunic, mail, skin, and muscle, and now lay painfully at rest in his upper left arm.

He got to his feet from the crouch and charged the closet, throwing back the curtain which screened his attackers. But only the machines were there.

Gawaine stood in mute shock at the set of mechanized warriors. A number of heavy posts had been planted into the floor, each supporting a crossbow with an additional set of gears which kept reloading and firing the weapons. The knight peered at the contraptions: small metal boxes rested above each bow, and must have contained the load of ammunition. Rage and fear mixed together to create a foul brew in Gawaine's blood and he hacked the machines to bits, the hilt of his sword vibrating painfully at the onslaught. He ignored it, and kept chopping until the weapons lay in a pile of so much trash and firewood. Then he reached for the bolt, remembering dimly that at least crossbow bolts weren't barbed, and wrenched it from him. He allowed himself one quick scream, more of a shout, as he had learned to deal with pain as a boy, and then turned to storm from the room.

It's just a big trap. Whoever lives here has taken his entire entourage and gone on bloody holiday somewhere, and these are traps to kill off anyone who enters the place with a mind to steal. But then why the women? And why leave the damned front door wide open?

He'd have to attempt his answer later. A lion had poised itself menacingly at the door, looking to Gawaine like it wanted supper. *Where in blazes did* that *come from?* He had not heard it approach.

Had his cousin followed him? "Yvaine?" he shouted, refusing to let panic into his voice. No answer. The lion growled at him, pacing back and forth by the door and eager for killing. *Kinsman or no, it's the beast or me.* Gawaine closed quarters with it, ready for blood himself. It would have to be quick; he began to feel a bit dizzy from rage and the throbbing meat in his arm.

The lion continued its pace. Gawaine waited for it, deciding he would have to fight it defensively. He'd no idea how a lion might attack, how it would move: not like a man, and that was what Gawaine knew how to kill.

It sat, right in front of the door. It licked its chops, then brushed a huge paw through the shaggy brown mane. *Why, it looks like any cat. Just bigger.*

Then it stiffened, turning an inquisitive ear to the door, but not taking its eyes from its quarry. After a few more agonizing seconds, it rose, sniffed the air once, then departed out into the hall.

Gawaine was too struck to follow it. Was it just playing with him? If it was truly a large cat, maybe it played with its prey before killing it. He remembered young Mordred playing with the kittens at home. His mother adored cats, and always kept several around. Kay once had fought a beast of this stature, a monster of a cat plaguing the lands near Mona. He told the Table it lashed like any other cat, and he took advantage of it by playing possum until it was ready to ignore, finally delivering a death blow. But Kay said nothing of a mane. How many of these things were there?

He finally found strength to go after it, or at least to leave the room. He couldn't stay there, and would have to find a dressing for his wound. Keeping his sword in a slashing position, he entered the hall.

No sound, no sign of prior passage by anyone. Or anything. Gawaine had already given cursory searches of the other rooms, so he made for the lower level. He hoped to find something to serve as a bandage, but if need be he could always use extra clothing from his saddlebags.

Still no lion. It had approached him with the grace and silence of a *boucca* spirit, and now he could find no sign of its whereabouts. Gawaine, who could track deer through downpours, could not locate it.

He worked himself into virtual exhaustion getting back to his horse, taking pains to dress his arm. After several minutes he stopped the bleeding by crudely stitching himself back together with needle and thread borrowed from his mother years ago. He had seen enough wounds, had enough himself, to know how important it was to seal them, after cleansing them of course. Almost as many men were lost fighting Lucius outside Rome and Cerdic at Badon Hill from disease and infection than violent slaying. Gawaine considered the former no honorable way for a warrior to die.

The painful sewing finished, he placed his removed mail tunic on the horse, and estimated what it would take to patch the armor up back in Camelot. No smiths lived in his homeland. Margawse said no iron would be allowed in her house save the gear of her sons. This done also, Gawaine turned toward the keep again. It was invisible now, lost in the fog thick as cream.

He pounded on the doors. "Gaheris! You still there, brother?"

From behind came nothing at first, then more muffled replies. "Can't you open this cursed thing? It's bloody freezing out here!"

"What's the matter, Gaheris, afraid the faeries'll get you?" Gawaine couldn't resist. Besides, it helped him deal with his own growing fear.

"No! I mean, this place is bad. It smells wrong. Something unnatural's happened here."

Aye to that, brother. Gawaine began searching for some way of opening the inner doors. The owner could clearly afford expensive engineering, so there would have to be a latching mechanism somewhere.

He kept looking. It was about to become a long night.

* * *

The High King of Britain loved the early summer. He had spent too long indoors at court, his Pax Britannica not requiring him to campaign, when what he adored was the wilderness, uncivilized, unforgiving, and deliciously untamed. This was the sort of day which let him feel his Cymru blood rush about him, bringing new energy to every muscle and limb.

This warrior was always on someone's tongue, the topic of some bard's song. His vassals had surprisingly open access to him, able to plead their cases from the admittedly intimidating Siege Perilous or inquire about the nature of his policies. He and the Queen listened attentively during set hearing times to the voices of those whose lives they governed, always eager for improvements, alert to possible threats or dangers in their land. The residents of Logres considered the King the most just sovereign they ever had.

For all that, though, very few knew anything of the man, the emotional and strong figure who looked oddly out of place on the few occasions he chose to wear any finery of his station. Arthur hated the actual crown, thinking it ostentatious in the extreme as well as the cause of too many headaches, but he kept it out of respect; Leondegrance had given him that, along with the Table. And the robes? Arthur only liked the imperial purple since it was his favorite color growing up, and preferred hunting leathers as much as anything. Even these articles retained their basic simplicity, lacking adornments. The robe sat in his closet, largely untouched.

And so this king rode now, refusing to let him or his wife be escorted about in some carriage. They each saw the landscape from the raised vantage point of two magnificent steeds, the king's a British great horse, a specially bred destrier from over the sea, the queen's a sleek local courser. Horses and royal faces shone with the energy imbued simply from riding along the land they would gladly die for. They officially were taking part in a search, although they grasped hungrily at any opportunity to live as they had in years past.

The impeccably-kept road led north towards the famed city of Aquae Sulis, source of the fabulous hot springs which could return anyone to a state of wellness with a single good soak. They would stop there for the second night out, enjoying their first beneath the naked stars. Arthur and Guinevere had managed to get mostly used to the constant presence and occasional interference of those who traveled with and protected them. Kay was along, as was the beauteous Isolde of Eire-land. Bedivere came as well, Arthur's boyhood friend, the only person he'd known as long as his foster-brother Kay. Various other guards and attendants rode with them, including the keeper of the royal mews, who looked forward to seeing his king use a freshly trained eagle to hunt.

Too many rules, too much court intrigue and loose tongues, thought Arthur. *Let them say what they wish, I cannot stop them. But let them remember who we were and what we accomplished. This is the greatest peace this land has known since the Empire, and even then peace was grudgingly enforced by men too far from home earning too little pay, on people who despised their presence. No, this is not Roman land. It is Cymru land.* Arthur felt the pride ride like a wave through his spirit, the crest crashing through him with the excitement of a squire allowed to grasp his master's sword and shield for the first time.

Everyone had a place in Arthur's realm, which was blissfully not Roman. He regarded that as the primary, perhaps the sole, reason for the fall of imperial power. Arthur had been careful not to expand too far, stretch his army and resources too thin. He had seen the Continent once, for a mere five seasons, and wanted never to return. He had only deemed it necessary to go to repel an invasion before it reached the shores of his home.

Arthur actually desired kingship very little, viewed it largely as a job rather than a right, and never told anyone save Merlin and Bedivere and Guinevere. He had come to believe himself destined for it, and tried his most earnest to prove himself worthy of it, but there was nothing a ruler could do which would possibly surpass how magnificent he had felt lately.

"What gives me the right, or anyone else, to rule, to send others to die and impose hardship on the survivors?" he asked Merlin, so long ago now.

"You were born to be king. Kingship carries great power and great price alike, and it sometimes brings necessary cruelties." Arthur had once thought his kingship based on the simple act of drawing a sword, but came to recognize there was infinitely more to it than that. Excalibur was a token, a symbol of old faith blended with the image of the cross, as the metals in its perfect blade were likewise mixed in the forging. And he had used it well. His right was revealed in his blood and talent; the land and its people needed a peacemaker. Or a god, as Merlin used to tell him. The simpler folk saw their ruler as just that, an image of the divine, the imposition of the divine right to rule, the unearthly intervention of sovereignty. Arthur always tried to forget what else Merlin had said about deities.

The Table is just a start. Dreams take hold, single candles can signal the coming of infernos, a mere stone cast into a pond sends its ripples to every edge. So long as people recall us in the memories of tomorrow, I will have succeeded beyond my wildest hopes. Then may I be sacrificed as Merlin proclaimed.

Arthur had instigated equitable forms of taxations, taking like portions from all, and giving back where he could, in the building of whole new towns, churches, farms, manors, mills. He delegated authority regionally, learning of goings-on throughout the land by holding Table meetings. His knights were his dutiful subordinates, and they enjoyed no small power and wealth of their own, managing their holdings and giving fealty and service to the King. He was a brilliant orator; Merlin had given him all the skill of the ancient Greeks, whose texts told him so much of rulership.

In theory. In actual practice, Arthur found he had to almost constantly improvise, often making up new rules on the spot. In order to avoid hypocrisy, he ordered these codified, and a set of Logres laws grew detailed enough to require specialists to record and keep it all. He would prefer things to remain simple, but his people were more complex: so many tribes and families and faiths.

The other part of true kingly practice was the wars, which Arthur missed but was careful not to say so to many. Those who had opposed him were met with inspired cavalry, line after line of armored men wielding lances, indestructible waves of knights who could move faster than even the legendary speed of Caesar's legions. The masses had put their faith in that strength and mobility. "We need Arthur," they would cry. "Send us the King!" That was the cause: folk could be unified when their common land was threatened, and he had kept a multitude of foreigners in check for many years, then inviting those of their number who would come in peace to Britain's fertile shores.

Arthur breathed in the clean air, letting it fill every bit of his soul and the body housing it. *Let Lucan stay behind for once; this is my journey. I should have made it years ago.* His knight indeed remained back at Camelot, castellan for the whole city while the King was away.

If Arthur had any weakness, it perhaps was a certain narrowness of vision. Certainly, he permitted any faith to be worshipped in his realm, so long as no living thing was sacrificed and no destruction done to land or edifice. It was easy to build more churches in such a setting. What he didn't know, or wouldn't accept, was that such a state was almost, but not quite, good enough for all. He knew of potentially combustible situations beyond his borders, but remained determined to permit local law and custom hold sway there as much as possible, refusing to tyrannize with his own (*didn't the Romans make everything theirs, razing whole cultures in doing so?*) He realized the Garmani lands were still occupied, their laws fed to them by a duke who had served him so well during the Wars of Unification. Said duke was a tyrant who ruled with iron sword and fist, keeping his subjects, numerically far in the majority, in a state of constant near-rebellion. But to remove the duke from power would jeopardize other relations, and Arthur wanted no Garmani ruler there, either. Cerdic came from there, almost beating him at Badon.

There were other disputes, too. What should be done with Cambria? Or Caledonia? His officers often discussed that. His answer was, and remained, that even the Romans could not keep the wild hills subjugated, and destroyed the Pagan centers at Mona more from anger than anything else. Arthur refused to fight what might escalate into a genocidal war with folk who shared his own blood. It was the Imperial diplomat in him which kept the royal army out of such regions.

And the wastes? Arthur had difficulty gleaning much useful information about them. Merlin warned him of growing disease in the land. "In which land?" the naive boy-king said.

"In the land itself. Folk only deserve the land and its bountiful gifts if they live properly. Balance in all, remember.

If you adopt a Christian court, then you must still give outlets for those of other beliefs, like myself." Arthur did just that, but tales of growing discontent still abounded. Rogue knights and fell creatures still haunted some areas, especially the thick forests. He did his best, so what else did people want?

"There will always be those who never find satisfaction, Arthur. And every king, no matter how beneficent or evil in ways, must be sacrificed for what and who comes next. It is the way, the Law. Your task is to offer your people something beyond the mere transitory life you now lead. But remember that everything, everyone, has its opposite, its counter, and there will never come a day which is short of those who insist they have a better way."

Arthur missed the poetic druid. No one knew where Merlin had gone, and it was years since his passing. Some said the enchantresses were responsible, supposedly even imprisoning him in a tree. The King doubted it; he knew of their power, and knew they and the old teacher clung to the same path. Others claimed he wandered the land still, though unrecognizable now, as if to watch life unfold rather than tinker with its course as he had for so long. Whichever, it was a frightening day for the young king to no longer have his mentor at his side.

That actually marked the beginning of the times of troubles, as Arthur had come to speak of them. Months passed, with the King growing melancholy and unsure of himself, the knights questioning some of his decisions, after the old mentor and intriguer disappeared. Arthur and Guinevere began to quarrel between themselves, sometimes about aspects of power, more often about their inability to give Logres an heir, a son to carry Excalibur or a daughter to be named regent. They never truly blamed each other, but their frustration led to more personal infighting; the King could not even be sure of who to blame, since no conception ever occurred. Arthur did most of his growing up then; always there had been Merlin to ask questions of, Merlin to seek inspiration from, and then he was gone. Vanished with no trace to follow, like one of the old spirits beneath the hills.

Those years proved difficult enough, but at least the central concerns found answers. The invaders were quelled. The carnage at Badon sent the message far and wide: Logres was secure under Arthur. That was what made the lack of a child so painful for both him and his queen: not only no family, but no heir, no continued protection for the land. The other chief worry then was internal: the people demanded problem-solvers and fair lives to lead, and Arthur was fortunate enough to have his own personal legion to attend to such matters.

The King retained enough strength during those years to avoid falling into the alcoholic deluge which his knight Sir Trystan found. His sworn lady Isolde rode with him now, in need of some healing of her own. No, Arthur spent a time staying out of public view, often alone in his chambers with his books. Cabal proved a welcome change; not since boyhood had he seen the likes of that dog, and the hunts resumed recently. He owed Perceval a knighting for that, if nothing else.

The Queen, however, did look elsewhere for solace, and found it. Arthur wondered if she realized he knew about her affair. Occasionally she spoke in her deepest sleep, and he had never known her to tell any falsehood while she did so. It started as rumor, and Arthur was once tempted to forbid certain expressions, then thought better of it; he did not believe a person could be fairly blamed for what they thought. He wanted all to be able to find their own voices, even though some of his advisors wondered where such freedom might lead.

Finding it within his monarchical soul to forgive his queen, to not even bring up the topic at all, was perhaps his greatest challenge. He had built so much, and he hoped dimly that maybe his name would still survive. No good would be served by exposing the queen, especially since he would have to punish regal adultery quite severely. He loved her still, and often blamed himself for not being worthy enough of her love. It would be difficult enough, without an heir, never mind the malicious rumors that he already had one.

Arthur treated the matter of this supposed claimant as he treated some of the regions connected to his own demesne: his concern was with Logres, and beyond that he would deal with others compassionately but diplomatically. And diplomacy often called for restraint. He tried a more unrestrained approach to that problem once, and it cost dearly. He would waste no time or energy searching for one who claimed to have a hold on the throne. If true, the claimant would come to him one day anyway.

Such was the acute need for an heir, an officially recognized and sanctioned one. The High King would die before seeing his reign usurped by some bastard. He found it ironically humorous that a kingdom's dependency upon someone to take it over made it easier to forgive Guinevere and Lancelot. He could still love them both, even these years later, and he would have welcomed any child born of their union. The needs of Logres outweighed the shame of any betrayal.

Of course, Guinevere never bore a baby to anyone. There was still no youngster waiting to wield Excalibur.

So much to think about. I truly have spent too much time shacked up like some prisoner. Camelot is grown beauteous, but like any settlement, waxes stuffy and confining after a spell. A king has his best thoughts when nature inspires them, and even the hunts no longer are enticing enough. So here then rode the King, glorious Arthur of the British, of all the combined tribes who called themselves Cymru or Britons, feeling he was once more on campaign. He never should have stopped. *Idleness breeds no good, Merlin and Baudwin both taught me that, and it's taken so long to learn the lesson.*

Guinevere glowed with the rapture that was in her heart the day he first laid eyes upon her. They rode near the front of the entourage, only Kay and Bedivere ahead of them. "What do you see, my Queen?" Arthur said to her, watching her bob up and down slightly on the gray courser, refusing to ride side-saddle.

"We're close, Arthur. Close to home. Do you know how long?"

He laughed. "I no longer care to guess, lover. Since the day Gawaine rode to escort you?"

The comment took her back, he could see it. They had reached a point at which her birthright of Cameliard lay just another day or two further. It was close to Camelot, surely, but like a king, a queen busies herself. Day in, day out, listening to the demands of others with no time for herself, much less a husband who could prove equally taxing. Too much time devoted to laws, entertainments, diplomatic sessions, war councils; Guinevere just wanted to be the young girl who ran about in these lands.

"Gawaine sounded so proud that day," she said. "He was the lapdog who would follow you into hell and then ask to do it again. He organized the entire move." No small feat, that: the Round Table was at first just a feast table of her father's, who had let it tarnish, chip, and become infested with termites. By the time it got to Camelot in was inlaid with precious metals and looked as though carved with the patience and precision of the druids and their sickles.

Arthur smiled at the man who should have been a sworn enemy, but could envision the future as well as Merlin. Gawaine recognized sovereignty, pledging himself to service and claiming his late father to have been misinformed. The warlords had been greedy, he told the King later, and just hadn't wanted to bend knee to anyone. Besides, Arthur was family. Gawaine's mother was careful to point that out to him, to all her boys, but always had sounded on the verge of wrath while doing so. Blood was crucial, the rest could only be friends and lovers at best, though that didn't mean one had to like one's relations. Blood ties to the throne were more powerful still.

"You never told me why you made two champions," Guinevere said.

Perhaps just another hasty decision by a king who would have rather idled the years by reading instead of ruling. "They all loved Lancelot, Guin. As do you and I." He pretended not to see the Queen blush. "And no one would I ever trust more to guard your life than him. Besides," he jested with her, knowing intimate talk of Lancelot was dangerous ground, "at each Pentecost tourney they've been the natural leaders of each melee team. As for Gawaine, I love him as well, though he can be a bit heavy-handed sometimes."

"You forget how much he learned. Remember the Green Man?"

Arthur did indeed. The strange knight's appearance served as a wake-up call for every knight in the realm who had grown soft with peace, including the King. "Yet that was after Lancelot became your champion. Lance was just gone then."

"Still, I think it must have been hard for him, to perhaps feel usurped that way. He took a great chance serving you. Had you been like his own father you might have killed him just because of whose blood was in him."

Kill Gawaine? the King thought briefly. *Far simpler to drop a charging bull.* "Gawaine still sits at the Table, and has other concerns now. His brothers, his lands back home. With the wars done, I think he'd prefer to roam the land finishing all manner of quest." Arthur had no inkling his knight was trying just that, many leagues north.

"I'm sorry to raise the issue, love. I just worry about the men sometimes."

"Men of action grow sleepy in the absence of enemies. They have to seek other reasons to keep their swords and skills sharp."

"Is that why you make no move to settle the problems in the land? Is it better to have the knights do it, gaining their own glory while enhancing yours?"

I am a king surrounded by those with clearer sight than that gained by my own aging eyes. "Yes. I hear the tales of the faeries turned evil, the bandit raid here, the treasure to be sought there."

"Do you believe the tales?"

She put Arthur on thin ice with that one. Guinevere believed the Gospels more verbatim than interpretive. So he'd offer an answer which she could understand. "Yes, Guin, I do. I believe there can be all manner of evil. I know not, for example, if there exist actual beasts which look like men but stand twenty feet in height, or elves lurking in old burial mounds seeking vengeance on the living. I think evil can be manifested in different ways, though, and my knights have sworn to undertake those tasks which will eliminate the manifestations. The thieves and mercenary knights are real enough. It seems little stretch to imagine magick old and new alike creating monstrosities."

"Magick. I've never grown accustomed to that term. It is supposed to be evil itself."

"Guin, there's as much magick in the prayers of Bishop Baudwin as there was in the divinations of Merlin. They call upon different powers, or perhaps just give different names to the same power. But that power is real, be it miraculous or glamourous."

"It is said, also, that all the gods are but one. That likewise seems heresy from what I learned." Guinevere had difficulty respecting views not her own. The queenship came with its own education, however. She was more willing to discuss other possibilities of spiritual truth than she had been when Arthur met her.

"I think the Greeks and Romans anthropomorphized the deities, old and new alike."

Guinevere chuckled. "Anthro-what?"

"I don't see God as a wise old man, Guin. I see Him and all gods, remember that they're all one, as just –" He could have left it at that, but his last word hung in the air, no longer an adjective.

"Just what?" She was quite curious.

"Just power. Life beyond what we can know. Answers to questions we often dare not ask. Any wise old man in my life was Merlin, and he was as far removed from God as any mortal can get."

"If he *was* mortal." Guinevere laughed again. Despite how she distrusted the gray-haired druid at first, with his solemn look and his constant manner of dress in his white robes and green cape, he was always kind to her, pleasant to talk with, and had been one of the Queen's few companions while the knights campaigned. He told her he was incapable as a military strategist, preferring to advise on other matters.

"Aye, good point. Who can really say about him?"

They both felt refreshed, traveling with only a couple dozen attendants and knights. A bodyguard seemed hardly necessary so close to Camelot, but Arthur and Guinevere were not taking chances, no matter how tired they might grow of always having others about.

The first lady of Camelot looked at her husband. "I love you, King Arthur."

"I shall love you now and always, my Queen of Cameliard."

She leaned over, kissed him sweetly on the lips (it took quite a lean on her part to accomplish this, though he helped by leaning towards her), and said, "I'm falling back to talk with Isolde."

"She could use a good ear. I think I'll take the lead of this train away from Bedivere and Kay."

* * *

Many miles away and still displaced, Gawaine awoke to Gaheris' shriek. Gawaine dismissed it at first, having fallen asleep inside the courtyard at last. He maintained a vigil against the possible return of the lion, but it never came. Maybe he dreamt it all. But he hadn't dreamt the wound; his shoulder throbbed alarmingly when he tried to move his arm. At least the bleeding stopped. It hadn't grown, either, so Gawaine was confident it would heal without infection, if he could keep it clean. He had seen field chirurgeons remove gangrenous limbs before, and did not relish the idea of asking his brother to take his arm before it died and took him with it.

Gaheris shouted again. Gawaine stirred, tired and aching. He couldn't have gotten more than two hours of sleep, between standing guard and hearing his brother in terror. "What? What the hell's wrong?" Gawaine shouted back, not getting up from the spot of earth he had warmed.

"S-sorry, brother. The fog's still out here. It's starting to clear, but I kept having dreams."

"What about?" Gawaine rubbed his eyes, getting used to what passed for sunrise around here. Light came down, but was muffled by the receding fog and perpetual haze lurking about the area. The air smelled wrong, polluted by something dead. The odor had traveled with them every time they got lost.

"Those people. Dear God, Gawaine, what happened to those wretches?"

If we're lucky, they finished each other off by now. "You've seen what blight will do to folks. They had nowhere to go and their land was dead. What would you have done?"

"But the blood. It was everywhere." Gaheris tried to speak calmly, talking nervously on almost no sleep at all. He had finally begun to relax, but he spent the entire night with the feeling that *something* watched him through the fog. He felt unarmored, unmanned; the gate could only keep out so much.

The doors still kept their voices partly muffled to each other. "We still need to get out of here," Gawaine said. "You're not the only one stuck." Gawaine surveyed the interior of the castle in what light there was. He had never found any other gates or links to the outside. Gaheris was a good whiner; Gawaine was twice trapped whereas his brother was imprisoned only by the gate.

"How's your horse?" Gawaine thought to ask, searching for topics Gaheris would not find upsetting.

"He's well. It's just a little snug in here. I haven't slept this close to a beast since Badon."

"I have, though I can't remember any of the wench's names." He could hear Gaheris chuckle at that. *Good. Laughter can get a body out of anything.* Gawaine plowed his sword into the ground, using it to lift himself to his feet. His charger immediately rose to follow his master's lead. *Now, to find a way out.*

He found no levers or pulleys, nothing that would open the doors or raise the gate. He supposed the door might be forced, with both horses working on it, one pulling and the other pushing. That still left the gate, though. Gawaine feebly searched about for anything metal protruding from the walls. He decided to climb up within the gate tower and look there.

The tower itself was accessible through either of two other heavy oaken doors, both of which opened easily. Gawaine was surprised to find neither of them locked, although they creaked slightly as he pulled on them. For all the wealth of the place, he thought the master would keep his hinges better oiled, especially in the northern cold.

Then the thought hit him in the face like a frigid gust of the deadened air. *Shit, we're abandoned here. The bastard who owns this place no longer cares about it. He's fled. He saw the wastes coming to his door and packed up so fast he never bothered to disarm his traps or feed his pets.*

Fighting panic, which would serve no purpose and render his arm useless with its numbing effect, Gawaine considered the one flaw with his hypothesis. If what he said was completely true, the lion should have starved to death by now. Yet it looked strong, with enough of its wits intact to choose to ignore Gawaine. Ravenous, it would have attacked him, sword or no.

The rest sounded plausible, though. Gawaine knew enough of stewardship to know he wanted no part of it, and for a lord who had people like *them* at his doorstep, feeling fearful certainly didn't seem dishonorable.

He stood at the top of the tower now. He could jump out, though likely shatter his legs in the process. It was a good two-score feet down. And that would do nothing for his brother.

Being at that height proffered another insight, however. He could see the wastes, from a unique vantage point. They went on forever. As far as Gawaine could see, they had already swallowed the earth. He swallowed himself, his throat dry and itchy. He could not even see exactly how it was they found the place; all evidence of their route had been consumed. They never should have left the road. "By Jesus and Mithras both, we've got to get out of here." He said it softly, Gaheris not hearing.

"Find anything yet?"

"What? Oh no, not exactly. But I've decided something. You're coming out of there and into here." It was all he could hope for now. Horses could force doors, but served no use against a gate which had to be pushed back up into its housing. Once inside, Gaheris could help him look for another way out.

If there was one.

Gawaine shimmied down the steps, barking orders to his brother while he got his own steed ready. "Get set to push in on the doors with everything you've got, the both of you."

That was the only way; to push the doors outward might just crush Gaheris. They were designed to open inward regardless. Gawaine busily worked the ropes he always kept with his saddlebags, thanking a plethora of deities for the wisdom of having brought them again, though the knights had opted to travel without their squires, not wanting them to be exposed to Margawse. His horse was the stronger, and would take most of the weight.

"Are you ready yet?" he shouted.

"Yes. Just give me your signal." Gaheris positioned his own horse so that its rump rubbed against the door, and then found a solid part on which he could push himself. It was going to be difficult, but the knight swore silently he would not spend a second night trapped beneath the tower.

Gawaine's rope was secure. He was no good himself, and if he pulled at all he'd rip his shoulder back open. So he'd have to coach and coax. And yell.

"Now!" he shouted, slapping his horse on the rear and watching it obediently dig its hooves into the earth and strain against the door. "Come, on, brother. You can do it! Keep pushing. I can see the doors moving. God damn it, these doors are going to crack, just keep moving!"

Behind the doors, Gaheris heaved, the veins in his face and neck surging, as he pushed on the doors with his shoulders and kept his hands free to coerce his own mount into shoving. The horse did so willingly, seeming to understand what was at stake.

"A little more!" screamed Gawaine, his powerful lungs booming across the dead landscape. "Almost there. Keep pushing!" He smacked his horse's flank again, and it lowered itself a little more and exerted the kind of force which made most folk deathly afraid of a knight's charger.

The doors gave way so fast and suddenly it was almost amusing. Only Gawaine's horse still stood when they broke inward, dragging them behind it. Gawaine, Gaheris, and the second mount came crashing earthward, the former having to roll out of the way of the broken wooden remains as he ordered the horse to stop.

They all rose quickly, their shouts and neighs giving way to thankfulness. Gaheris was free, though they still had their problems.

"You're hurt. What happened to you?" Gaheris said, surprised to see Gawaine out of his hauberk and then noticing the blackened blood stain.

"Last night. I'll explain as we go. Come on."

"To where?"

"We still need to find a way out of this place."

"You mean there isn't one?" Gaheris' momentary joy dissipated like a snowball thrown into a Beltaine fire.

"There's one. We just have to find it. You don't think someone who could afford a spread like this would have just one door, do you?"

"No. You're right." A little of the snowball survived.

They started toward the keep, considering it the most likely place to begin looking. "Keep your blade at the ready," Gawaine said. "The horses can take care of themselves."

Gaheris stopped. "Why?"

"Oh, no reason. There's just a lion. You might wish to grab your shield, too. It was a cross bolt that struck me."

Gawaine almost laughed at his brother's expression, but decided it would not exactly help morale. Gaheris obligingly fetched his shield, drawing his sword as he ran to his horse, and ordered both mounts to "stay," as though they were lapdogs.

On they went into the keep, Gawaine pointing out features as they went, advising full caution by the time they entered the master bedroom again. If there were any clues in the keep, the most logical place was in there. Gawaine indicated the felled mechanical archers. "I hacked them –"

"– to bits," Gaheris said. Gawaine was glad of that habit now; it meant Gaheris had rediscovered his courage.

They rustled through closets, fumbled about furnishings, overturned anything which would move to try and find a secret entrance, or lever, or *something*. Gaheris just stared at his brother for several long seconds when he ordered him to stay away from the master bed.

Their search took them through every room in the keep. They cared not at all whom they might offend with their sloppiness; a lord's hospitality could only be breached if he still called his home a home, and not a memory. Back down on the main floor, they rummaged through shelves and cupboards, even turning the kitchen into a shambles. Gawaine heard a number of metallic bounces on the floor as Gaheris liberated the contents of a table back in the main hall. "What's all that?" he shouted towards his brother.

"Well, would you look at that?" Gaheris said, noting the shining piece of wealth he had discovered.

Gawaine emerged from the kitchen. "What did you find?" he said hopefully.

"This." He showed Gawaine the goblet. It was finely-wrought copper.

"We should keep it. It might fetch a lot back at the Camelot jeweler's guild. Or at the least, it would be a souvenir of this place."

"If it's such a prize, why didn't the owner take it? It's small enough to put into any saddlebag, so why did it remain behind?"

"I'll keep it, it's mine. We'll take it back."

"No. I don't want any tangible reminders of this place. Leave it."

"But Gawaine –"

"That's an order, Sir Knight! There's something wrong with it. It's like everything else around here. It'll probably stink like death once we get home." Gaheris learned two things from Gawaine's otherwise incomprehensible mandate: he was confident of their chances, but was terrified of staying there any longer.

Gaheris tossed the goblet aside, and they kept looking.

The light in the wastelands was such that the searching knights did not even notice the sun trace its arc through the heavens, counting off the hours as it went. It was noon by the time they found anything useful.

Their haphazard investigation yielded no lion, no other traps, no eager maidens, and led them outside the keep, and into all corners of the castle. The object of their quest lay behind the stable; Gawaine found it by tripping over it.

His mood had grown short indeed, tired from the wound and knowing he needed to rest it. He swore as he came crashing earthward, but he successfully pulled the rusty bar forward several inches.

Gaheris came running, alerted by profanities extreme even for Gawaine. "What is it?" he said, pulling up beside his brother.

Gawaine would not be helped to his feet, but Gaheris knew he appreciated the offer anyway. "This damned pole. What do you think it is?"

Gaheris surveyed the derelict piece of metal which looked like a buried smith's hammer. He found it moved back and forth, and required some strength to send it from one position to the next.

Gawaine heard the light clicking sound as it switched positions. "I'll be damned. I think I know. Come on." He first returned the lever to the position he had knocked it to with his clumsiness.

"Where? What does it do?"

Gawaine knew his brother was lackadaisical when it came to mechanics more advanced than the straps which kept his armor on his back. But Gawaine had seen all manner of technical marvels, mostly at Camelot. Arthur's engineers learned well from their predecessors, who had brought the fabulous plumbing and irrigation techniques, organized streets called blocks, ornate glass windows. And they took matters further, developing mills which could run as long as the rivers kept flowing. They could make steering mechanisms for merchant wagons, fashion siege engines which could bypass any defender's walls, and adding machines with which to keep track of the royal coffers (Gawaine always had a particular fascination with the abacus, coming from a heritage which did not distinguish between one, ten, and many). So surely they could come up with an elaborate trap door; Gawaine's shoulder already paid the price of their mechanized infantry.

He didn't care that he had only witnessed such things in Camelot itself; Arthur kept the most skilled artisans at his beck and call, and there seemed no reason for any to venture this far north.

They searched the courtyard eagerly. "Gawaine, look. There's a door!"

Gawaine wheezed his way to where his brother was all but jumping up and down. As sure as the endless heat in his arm, there stood a door in the west wall where none had been before. They had thought solid rock lay behind the wall. Gaheris moved to the black entrance and peered into it.

"Can't see a thing. We could get torches, lead the horses through. It looks wide enough."

Gawaine inspected it for himself. The portal was a good six feet wide, enough for even the largest steeds. But where did it lead?

"We're going in first. We'll see where it goes, and if it takes us outside then we can return for the horses." He let out a deep breath. "Find some kindling, cloth, anything that burns. We need to make those torches."

Gawaine eased himself onto the grass, his breathing quick and shallow. Gaheris knew he had to move fast, and get his brother back to safety.

They were already lost, and probably could not find their way back to Lothian and Margawse. Besides, they figured they had already come more than half the way through the wastes. Or hoped they had. Gaheris decided as he ran into the kitchen that it would be easier to try for Camelot. The best chirurgeons in the world were there, all the better for Gawaine's injury.

He returned soon with the makings for several torches, having grabbed candles, scraps of firewood, strips of cloth liberated from the upper chambers, and the flint which always accompanied any competent knight's gear.

While Gaheris made the lights and explored the tunnel himself, Gawaine sat, eyes closed. Calming himself, he reopened them, and could still see the dancing shadows cast by his brother in the cave, growing anxious when he could no longer see him. He had never felt more thrilled than when he heard Gaheris shout, "It leads outside, Gawaine. We're free!"

Working the horses at almost twice their normal capacity, the Orkneymen kept an excellent pace getting south. As Gaheris had hoped and Gawaine prayed, the wastes indeed ended, opening once again into the lush landscape they knew and never loved so much as when they saw it this latest time. In the absence of squires, Gaheris saw to grooming and rubbing the horses personally, letting his brother rest, and treating them to whatever morsels could be found. Fruit was relatively easy to come by, and the proud mounts showed no shortness of delight when it could be obtained for them.

Gawaine's shoulder actually began to improve, and they had left the north a few days before the King and Queen made their sojourn. He could almost lift his shield again, and never felt more grateful for his brother, who ventured into the blackness which so scared them both as children. Lot laughed at that at first, then forced the boys to sleep outdoors on moonless nights, determined to get them past their fear. Gawaine hated the old man's abuse, and that particular method had worked on all but him.

They managed to pick up the road again, refusing to ponder the consequences of not finding it while they searched. It indeed led south, and within another day's ride they arrived in the land no cavalry ever tamed.

Thus it was that they determined not to stop for anything before reaching Camelot. Gawaine had to have his arm mended, though it seemed to be doing all right on its own, and they both had to report their findings to the King.

If their count was accurate, it took them an additional day to travel through the wasted region than before, and little time separated the two trips.

* * *

Perceval was slowed by the snow which arrived way too late for his taste. He was still enjoying the lush countryside when it fell. It started while he still rode to Camelot, as he was just within the forest. At least he would not get much of the white blanket on him while still shielded by trees which had most of their growth already. But the chill was inescapable; he was glad for the extra blankets Llio insisted he take.

Styfnig seemed not to mind the cold as they made camp once again, and likewise had no objection when Perceval took one of the blankets from his stash of three and laid it over him. They slept close enough to share at least a little heat that night, both glad for the other's company.

Perceval awoke to Styfnig's contented munching of half-frozen grass. The snow had mercifully not found them. Perceval rubbed his eyes and sat up. The squirrels and other wildlife continued to be especially busy this morning, slaving away to ensure their own stocks of food in their warm trees.

The errant arose, breathing the morning chill into the reaches of body and spirit. He would have to hurry to make it back to Camelot before he froze. Hopefully the snow was just a fluke, and it would warm again within a day or two. He remembered snows like that from childhood; the Severn valley often would get extremely cold, only to have the whiteness thaw to crystal liquid within the week. The slushy water would trickle its way down the hills to be swallowed by the mighty river, sounding like endless laughter on its path.

Only a few more days. Soon I'll be back in the capital. I want to see the look on Kay's face when the King dubs me.

Perceval would actually receive the opportunity to see Kay's face even sooner than that.

* * *

Gawaine and Gaheris reached Arthur's party on the road, near the forest outside Gloucester. They had never been so relieved to see the Pendragon banner flying proudly at the head of the party, held aloft by Bedivere. Arthur's friend would drop his own wife before dropping that banner, such was his loyalty.

Kay and Bedivere were startled indeed to see two knights charge their way suddenly, and readied their weapons instinctively. Only when they saw the Orkney crest on Gaheris' shield, customized for him by the surrounding band of white with drops of imaginary blood, did they ease their guard.

"My lord!" Bedivere said. "Sir Gaheris approaches, though I know not with whom he rides."

Arthur at once cantered up alongside the man who had been his virtual right arm since he could first ride a horse. Bedivere had lived near Arthur's foster family, the two getting into all manner of mischief with Kay all too often telling on them.

Bedivere almost went down, banner and all, at Badon Hill, and was always there to serve as a most trusted advisor and friend. He knew the King as well as Merlin had, and had been jealous of the time spent with the old druid.

"See that hair? It's Gawaine," said the King. He'd recognize one of his leading men even in glamourous disguise.

"Why does he not wear his armor?" wondered Kay aloud, always alert to any indiscretion upon which he could pounce. Kay longed to tease; it helped him deal with his own impotency, which of course, no one else in court knew about.

"Arthur, he's hurt. Look how he hangs in the saddle. He should be riding loud and proud as ever."

"Bedivere, ride with me," commanded the King, and he broke the ranks of the small party to see to the well-being of his friend, a nephew if Margawse's relation to the King was considered. This part of the forest was safe; crimes committed upon it were crimes against the King himself, punishable by death of no small pains. Yet Arthur abandoned safety in numbers for the safety of one. Guinevere beamed; *it was typical of him.*

Kay obediently stayed behind, staring about at the nearby woods and almost daring anyone to come and proffer assault. One's sword, like one's manhood he supposed, grew flaccid and dull with infrequent use.

Gawaine raised his good arm to offer salute, despite his feeling so drained. Gaheris at once took the reins of conversation, informing the King and Bedivere of all which befell them since leaving Camelot.

"So you were trapped in this place all night?" Arthur said afterwards. He also had been tricked into places he would prefer not to speak of, some as dark as the tunnel Gaheris described.

"Yes, my lord. We were separated by these doors all the while. Gawaine had to deal with archers aplenty, and a lion! Can you imagine? I really could have helped in there, but I was trapped."

Gawaine would have taken lashings over hearing his brother's endless prattle; he already listened all the way south, and all he wanted was a night of uninterrupted, painless sleep. "The archers were just devices, Uncle. Though I can hardly guess why their maker wished them pointed at his bed."

"I suppose that's one way to keep undesirables out of your own sheets," mused Arthur, still pondering past lovers, mostly mistakes when seen by hindsight.

Bedivere took the cue of Arthur's sideways glance to ride back with Gaheris, filling the spaces between excited sentences with, "oh, really?" and "how odd." He had never seen the man this excited before, though Gaheris' ability to keep talking to mask apprehension was known. The fear of the wastes had etched itself into the lines on Gaheris' face, the same fear Bedivere unconsciously showed when recalling his near-killing during the unification battles.

Watching Bedivere and Gaheris ride back to the others, Arthur pressed Gawaine. "How are you truly doing? I'm no chirurgeon, God knows, but it looks like you'll need one right away."

"No, it'll be fine. Some rest and real food will have me going again in a few days. The bolt came out clean."

"Bolt? They used crossbows?"

"Easier to make one fire on its own than one of those absurd bending bows from across the Channel or in the hills. Damn shame, weapon like that. I thought siege gear was inhuman enough." Gawaine, like most of his class, despised "dishonorable" weapons, such as the bows used by Picts and wild hill folk in Cambria and Caledonia; it was regarded as braver and more knightly to close quarters with an opponent and duel.

The choice of words was curious. Gawaine was used to spitting his enemies like so many rabbits headed for roasting or the stew pot, so where did humanity come into it? Arthur agreed with the premise, though: killing was always personal, at least when it came to humans.

"I tell you, Arthur, if people start using equipment like those foul machines, honor will leave the battlefield and courage will flee men's souls."

"Well spoken, especially for a northern barbarian."

Gawaine laughed. "Better than an inbred horse's behind like yourself. My lord." One detail of Arthur's closest knights: they could usually laugh at jests thrown at them by each other that they would have happily drawn swords for had they come from other mouths.

Arthur loved the man, found it difficult to think of him as nephew. Lancelot was actually heir-apparent (Arthur always hoped that decision would not rankle Gawaine too much, who could still claim kingship of his own in Lothian). Kings didn't live forever, having to eventually surrender to history.

"Come on. Let's go back. Guinevere will likely want to tend you herself. Isolde's with us also."

"Isolde?" Gawaine said, who knew the power of intrigue but hated what it did to some. "And Trystan?"

"Don't even mention his name around them. He's gone, I saw to it. I can't very well keep Marcus as an ally if I flaunt his nephew before his eyes."

"Then what's his wife doing here?"

I always admired your candor. "She grows tired of court life down near the sea. Dumnonia can be pretty boring if you lack the right kind of company. I should know. She's here to spend time with the Queen. She has quite a way with the animals, and has all but taken over Guin's menagerie."

"I see. So Trystan the harper is once again working for a living, eh?"

"I gather he must be." Arthur laughed, picturing the other knight strumming some of the finest poetics in Logres to whoever would offer him lodging for the night. Trystan had shown some jealousy to his musical tutor, Taliesin, who was clearly the recipient of Brigid's embrace. Or was it Arianhrod? Arthur had trouble remembering now; his half-sisters would be shocked to know how many of Baudwin's sermons he had attended, confusing the names of antiquated deities in the process.

"How is it you and I managed to avoid the uncle-nephew relation Trystan shares with the old man?"

"Do I seem as old?"

"Only in your hair, oh graying one."

"Because I'm hopefully not the bastard Marcus is. And because we both knew we needed each other."

Gawaine was taken aback now by the other man's frankness, a rare and dangerous trait for a ruler. Arthur never told him that before.

"It's true and you know it," the King said as they began to trot slowly through the premature snowfall. "I needed a hero, someone who held sway with the north. Bedivere would have suited fine, but he's from Dumnonia just as me, and he's as Roman, as you say. I wish what happened with your father could have worked differently."

There, he's doing it again, Gawaine thought. "Lot was a great warrior, no one will fault him that. But the simple truth was it became an issue of whether to ally yourself to you or be at war with you; Britain's king can have no peace with the Picts without a buffer, and we all know how unsuccessful the walls were. I just never thought we'd become friends as well."

Arthur knew all this, though was glad to hear it voiced so coolly. He changed the subject, hoping Gawaine's jovial mood would continue. It seemed a good time for honesty. "I chose Lancelot because he represents the future. He has no ties to any tribe or family, no lands to keep, no peasants besetting him with their grievances."

"Arthur. Uncle. You don't need to tell me this. As my liege it is yours alone to make these decisions. Besides, I could take him, bum shoulder and all."

"I'll bet you could," Arthur said, laughing. "He's always so serious."

"Thank you for answering my question. I lose no envy on Trystan. Or that bastard who gets the most beautiful woman in the land."

Arthur shot a half-amused, half-challenged look his way. "Except for the most exquisite Queen Guinevere of course!" Gawaine laughed himself now.

"What is it?" the King said, sensing a change of expression. If Gawaine had any more insights, they'd have to come now. Their talks were not the privy of many among those who patiently waited for the King and his hero, listening to Gaheris tell them of how he rescued them both through the tunnel out of a cold and foreboding castle.

"A womanizer and bed-pirate I may be, my uncle, but never with another's wife. I think that's the reason for Trystan's sorrow."

Arthur had no comment for that. *If I had kept Gawaine in the most honored position, maybe Lancelot and the Queen would never have happened. He is the Queen's Champion, after all.*

* * *

Perceval was pleasantly surprised by how joyous it could be to ride in the snow. Back home he had loved the snow, but navigating his mother's occasionally obedient sheep through it was trying at best. They only managed to break past the fencing during the winter. Mother always said the fence was only good for a year at a time, needing replacement with the spring.

He guided Styfnig along the road, easy to see even beneath the few inches of freeze caked onto it. He tried to estimate his travel time again, finding it confounding. He counted on his nippy fingers once more, and kept trying since at least the flexing of the joints helped keep them warm.

Perceval was surprised once more by the sound of the birds. He recognized the honking overhead at once. He looked up to see the swarm of geese, shouting among themselves and clearly irritating Styfnig. Weren't geese supposed to be returning from warmer places? He didn't know where they were headed.

But then the snow came unexpectedly. The poor birds sounded like they were just trying to find some food and a place to rest.

They headed in the approximate direction of the road, then chose a more easterly course. *To go where the birds go...*

They could lead him to a watering hole, if nothing else. There might be food nearby, and he'd have to stock up more if he wanted to get to Camelot. Also, the thought of spending more money didn't sit well with him, and he grew weary of asking others for hospitality.

Perceval urged Styfnig into a light gallop, guiding him towards the gaggle. He just wanted to see where it went. He still never tired of trying to keep up with the birds, and now that he had a warhorse, he figured he might just track one down. How else did the falconers obtain their new hatchlings, ready to train?

Why was he thinking of Galienne again? There was no reason to; he could hardly do anything for her right then.

The voice. He heard it again, inside him. *You goose,* it said, taunting him. Like Dindraine's voice, when he was still with Galienne back at Bridgnorth.

The geese proved easy enough to follow, especially as they made an instant course change, bringing the whole flock back near Perceval, heading north. He could see their alternating patterns of black and white against the cloudy sky.

Why would they do that? What do they see?

Then the falcon sped by, obviously having sighted the geese. Perceval had seen the lightning-quick grace with which falcons normally struck; this bird must have been half-starved to risk confrontation with dozens of prey at once. Perceval pushed Styfnig to go faster still, curious to see if all the geese would outmaneuver their natural enemy.

The open terrain blurred as Styfnig worked up to a full canter, almost charging. Perceval guided the warhorse with pressure from his knees, keeping his eyes on the birds alone. The falcon was having difficulty keeping up with its quarry, since the geese remained in formation, traveling as a group.

Safety in numbers. Perceval tried not to think of Galienne. She was so innocent, he wanted her to be safe. *Her virtue is as white as the frozen earth.*

The birds continued. The falcon's erratic darting divided the gaggle into two more or less equal groups, one staying northward, the other turning for the south. The falcon opted to pursue the second. So did Perceval.

Styfnig did not even begin to show signs of exertion. *This is not the time to dwell on Galienne or anyone else. Not Llio. Not Dindraine. No, stop it! Stop thinking about them and follow the birds. This is what you always wanted.*

The falcon soared above the flock, taking its time and making its final bid for supper. It then dove, driving earthward almost faster than Perceval's eyes could track the motion. The geese honked and screamed, and then one of their voices shrieked above the others. It faded at once, echoing across the land. Perceval thought the whole world must have heard that goose's death scream.

He had fallen behind. Fast as Styfnig ran, he could hardly be expected to keep up with birds, especially panicked ones flying for their lives. Perceval kept him on course to where he saw the falcon fly straight into the flock. He thought he determined where the falcon came down, bringing its needed food with it.

Perceval knew he had arrived at the spot by the blood. He squeezed his legs, bringing Styfnig to a quick stop.

I'm surprised I even found it. There's barely any. The falcon had indeed made a clean kill, shedding only several drops of the goose's blood as it plunged its claws into the larger but weaker bird, killing it quickly.

The blood held his gaze. *So innocent, but it had to die. We all have to die so that others may live. Why do we feed on death?*

He focused on as many splotches of blood as he could see. There were three of them. *Why am I getting so worked up about it? It's just blood, the cycle of life and death. Gods, where do I get these thoughts?*

Perceval remained so transfixed he didn't notice the sizable band no more than a mile distant, approaching north on the road. They had escaped the cold themselves by spending the night in warm Aquae Sulis.

* * *

"So where is this lad supposed to be?" Gawaine said, his shoulder feeling better all the time just being in the presence of the others. Even Kay made him glad to be back. He and his brother had already received the news of Bedivere's shining during the grand tourney. Guinevere said nothing. She presented him with the laurel afterwards, wishing, still, that it was Lancelot; she was surprised how some feelings never quite died.

"Still further on. Up in the hills."

"Surely we're not going into Cambria itself?" Images of projectile weapons still danced across Gawaine's mind.

"No, Gawaine," Bedivere said. "Perceval was supposed to head home, then turn around and come back to Camelot. He's just been gone a while. That, or Arthur's just getting restless."

"I haven't seen the old man this pleased in a while." Gawaine was proud to be the only one save Bedivere who could get away with calling the King that.

"Nor I. He looks as though the Queen has put the smile back in his face."

"The march back into his stride."

"The height back into his stance."

"Which stance?" Gawaine said. Bedivere laughed. They led the party now. Kay and Gaheris always got along famously, and this gave both of them the chance to brag about their recent doings. Bedivere and Gawaine shunned that. Whether it was knight's humility or not wanting to gossip, they preferred to keep most of their activities reserved for family and Round Table meetings, and even then certain details might get left out.

Bedivere was still chuckling. He had difficulty picturing his friend and Guinevere making love, in the same way he could never quite imagine his parents doing so. So long as they were happy.

"Stop," Gawaine said, raising his fist to signal the others.

"What?" Bedivere looked at Gawaine, whose face instantly froze into granite, his other hand slowly falling naturally to his sword hilt. He no longer noticed any pain from moving his shoulder to signal. Bedivere traced the man's gaze, searching for whatever he saw.

"Shhh. Bandits."

"Where?" Gawaine pointed. Some distance off, there appeared to be another knight, just sitting there. Only a knight would ride such a huge horse.

"Any idea who it is? Or how many?"

"So far, it's just the one. But he's probably a decoy."

The other men had ridden up behind them. "What's the verdict, Gawaine?" Arthur trusted his nephew's judgment completely. He swore Gawaine had better outdoor sense, nose and all, than even Cabal and the other hounds.

Gawaine indicated what he had noticed. "Your decision, my lord?"

"Our banner's visible for over two miles. Whoever would be here will recognize it. Gaheris, go. You have a lot of energy to burn since you got back."

"Me, Sire?" He regained his nerve quickly. It was just one man. "Of course, my liege. Is there any specific message, or shall I just identify him?"

"Only that I want to know why he's seen fit to just sit there blocking the road, like a challenge knight." Arthur smiled at the memory. "I thought those who spent long times in the same place taking on all comers were a thing of the past."

Gaheris bowed slightly to Arthur, then sped off toward the knight.

* * *

This is no time to be thinking of God, either. Blood and God aren't supposed to go together. It's just a goose's blood. So red. Shiny, like mine, like Dindraine's her first time. Balls, that terrified me. I thought she was dying.

Perceval lost track of the falcon and its kill. The geese were just an echo now, ignored by buzzing ears.

He couldn't close his eyes. He had seen blood before, shed it himself and caused it to flow from others. *So why now? Is it because the goose was innocent?*

No one is innocent, he heard Galienne say, from nowhere and everywhere. *Gal, stop. You're innocent. You're so easy to be with because you're clean. Look at me. I wore Meliagrant's bloody-hued armor, thinking myself so vital and eager. I couldn't even keep you from danger. All from desire, all from what my mother said was bad.*

Did you want this or need this, Perceval? He couldn't tell whose voice he heard now. Sometimes it sounded like Galienne. Other times his mother. Llio. Dindraine.

Where are they all? He looked up at the sky, the geese mere specks moving ever further. The two groups had rejoined into one, the image reminding him of proud deities, passing judgment upon those they looked down on from the heavens. *If you want me to believe in you, in* any *of you, then show me why I should!* He could not form the actual words with his tongue, afraid to address the geese like deities flying back to Heaven, the Other Side, Valhalla, Tír na nÓg. The part of him in which his mother still resided kept its fear of being struck dead, or worse, for such blasphemy.

He gazed down at the blood again. He had just about enough of this faith-talk for one lifetime. If the druids were right, he'd have another chance to sort matters out in his next incarnation. *Where is Mother, then? In Heaven, or a newborn babe?*

Sir Gaheris rode purposefully, oblivious to considerations for stealth. He guided the horse urgently, more from fear of ambush than any sense of alacrity. He was unused to playing the diplomat.

Gaheris slowed when he came to within a bowshot of the stranger. The man just sat there. Staring at the ground, like he had lost all his hopes in it and sought a way to unearth them again, let them grow. He looked not hostile at all. Still, Gaheris was not about to take chances; whoever the man was, he carried a sword and lance close by.

He eased slowly closer. *That's no lance. It's a javelin. Who on earth uses those things anymore?* Gaheris had heard of the old folk, faeries or such, who threw envenomed javelins. He hated thrown weapons, thinking them the product of the same cowardice his brother so despised; the Garmani carried small axes and threw them, so why wouldn't some hill-heathen such as this try the same stunt?

"Hail from his Lordship King Arthur!" Gaheris said, trying to sound enthusiastic. "I am Sir Gaheris of Orkney, in the

King's own guard for twelve years now. Who, pray tell, might you be?"

The peasant made no movement, uttered no response. Even his horse was still. *The bugger must be plain deaf! And that horse. He had to have stolen one trained such as that.*

"I say, boy, who exactly are you? We can't very well have the likes of you filling up valuable road when the King himself wishes to pass, now can we?"

Still no response. Gaheris slowly pulled his sword from its housing, keeping it at his side, and rode still closer, blade out of view.

Someone calling me "boy" again. When will they leave me alone? I'm a man, damn it. And a tired one. Galienne, Dindraine, Llio. Can you hear me? Why does the blood remind me of you all? Blood is death, does that mean you're... No! Only shed blood is death. You're all alive. I can feel you. When I look at this, I can feel you, so close. Close enough to touch, to embrace. Ah, women-folk, I'm sorry. I am unworthy, I can't even protect any of you. Perceval closed his eyes, half-thinking he heard the familiar sound of an unsheathing sword.

"If you won't tell me who you are and what business you have, then you will have to leave this area. This is the High King's road, and you'll not be joining arms with anyone in his entourage." Gaheris was now close enough to strike, part of him still hoping not to have to, another part just wanting it done. Besides, he could use a fine steed like this one. It made his own charger look quite the nag.

The glare the peasant shot Gaheris could have melted the snow around them. Gawaine's younger brother had never seen a look such as that, the look of a madman, surely.

He was not about to fall to some heathen and his evil eye. Gaheris raised the sword to striking position; one lunge, and all would be resolved.

Gaheris projected his movements to Perceval, who watched not just the knight's face, but his entire body, even his horse. He could not reach his own sword in time, and the javelin was useless at this proximity. Unconscious of the motion, Perceval mirrored the cutting arc, coming up under the arm and blocking its further movement towards him. He found his target in the knight's forearm near the wrist, grabbing it once the initial force of the blow was redirected.

Gaheris was shocked. This heathen had just defended himself against an armored knight, showing not the least trace of fear. The knight was so caught off guard by the subtle motion that the peasant was able to keep pulling him, using the force of the swing for momentum, until Gaheris looked down and saw the ground himself, beckoning to him.

No! No, I won't be sacrificed to the earth, not by this heathen trash! he thought dimly. But then his shoulder landed squarely on the hard ground, the snow absorbing nary a portion of his weight.

Reeling and panicked, Gaheris rolled over his side to right himself up. He had gotten no further to a vertical position than on his knees when he saw the other sword. He had not even heard it drawn.

Perceval sat atop the statuesque Styfnig, merely pointing the tip of his blade at the part of the knight's throat his mother had said was the remnant of Adam's fall from grace, forever stuck in the neck of unworthy men like himself. *Stop this!*

Gaheris knelt in the snow, looked piteously at the man who would surely kill him just for being a knight. At least he knew Gawaine would avenge him. Gawaine would always avenge blood.

Except the dirty man made no killing slice. He just waved the sword, indicating to Gaheris to leave him be. *He'll throw the javelin through me when I turn my back. That's how they must do it.*

The sword waved again, the glare intensified. Gaheris cautiously stood, his sword limp at his side. He climbed his mount and backed up, not turning away until he was sure he'd prove a difficult shot for any thrown weapons. Then he turned and shouted his horse into full speed, charging back to Arthur.

Idiot. He almost got himself killed, and for what? At least he's still alive, more than I can say of some.

Like myself. Dead inside. Too dead to even recognize Galienne's grail when it stood before my grasp. Perceval sheathed the sword, brought his palms to his face, and rubbed them firmly, too firmly, up the sides of his face. Frustrated. Spent. Unworthy of Llio's love. Maybe she just wanted to be rid of him; Gornymant could find a more suitable suitor, one with a name, rank, land.

Stop this! You're not unworthy. Whose voice is that? Mine? It comes so familiar, feminine.

It's not mine, why listen to it? Perceval pulled on some tufts of his hair, grown longer and chaotic during his travels, uncut since his first trip to Camelot. He stared again at the blood, blood from the goose. *That's what the voice called me. A goose. So purposeless, so easy to kill. All it wanted was to keep traveling, look for food and a comfortable place. Its wishes were so simple.*

God, it's so red. I never noticed how dark blood is. The boldest of the primary colors, it looks almost proud against the snow. Three primary colors! You always think of the training and so little else... Perceval shook his head, never taking his eyes from the stains, which would shortly be reclaimed by Mother Earth, then nurtured by Father Sun into some other living thing, reaching for light.

He looked up at last, the image too painful. The blood of a mere bird already reminded him of too much. Blood was cyclical, the source of life, and he was shocked at how it reminded him of so many women. People who painfully shed their blood had to, to go on with life or create new life entirely. What was he? Just the sword. The sword to penetrate a woman's cup of life, then claim it his.

He missed Llio terribly. His peripheral vision caught someone else approaching him. He turned, seeing a group behind the lone rider, united under a banner darting about in the chilly wind. It looked like the same sort of creature seen in his dreams, that slithery, skinny little thing. Except this one was larger, and had wings. It could fly. *And of course, it's red. Red against white, like the blood in the snow.*

"That pathetic little motherless son of a shit goddamned
—"

"Kay, hold your tongue. There are ladies present, in case you'd forgotten." Arthur remained passive during what took place in the distance. They were still too far off to recognize Perceval. Arthur himself could identify any horse he ever laid eyes on, but he had never seen the proud one the stranger rode; the King could have placed Brownie easily.

The party all made their appropriate sounds while events had unfolded, the women oohing and the men grunting and wanting to cheer, but no victory shouts escaped them as they saw one of their own flung into the ground. They watched Gaheris ride back quickly, turning his head often to see if anything followed him.

Gawaine said nothing to Kay, knew he had referred to the other man, the confident fighter who stood clearly larger than the tribespeople in these parts. He raised his brawny brows at his brother, spoke volumes with his accusing glance.

Gaheris would have none of it. "He surprised me! The little whelp charmed me right off my horse."

The women had to rein in chuckles at that. The other men were too intrigued by the stranger to laugh. "He fights oddly," Arthur said. "He grapples as if by choice. I haven't seen the likes of that since –" and he let it trail off. The hell of Badon had come down to him and Cerdic grappling for a dagger.

"Well, he's certainly armed, my lord," Gaheris said. "A sword and javelin. Nothing else to identify him, though, save that stolen horse. And he's so far gone he never even drew till I was on the ground."

"Yes, we saw that," replied the King. "How did that happen?"

Cheeks flushed, Gaheris retorted, "He's bewitched, my king. What man stares at the ground and ignores another who would have easily taken his life?"

"Yet could you have so easily snuffed him out like some candle? It seems his fire burns much hotter than that."

Gaheris flinched, beaten. He was not about to argue with the man who was his liege first, distant blood second.

"Let me go," Kay said. "Bedivere is your personal guard, and Gawaine injured. That leaves me." He was just itching for the chance, not having taken part in a good fight outside of Camelot's taverns in a number of years.

"Very well," Arthur considered quickly. "Have a word with this supposed horse thief. Give him one chance to return with you or else surrender the road. Otherwise, I trust your judgment."

Gods, winced Gawaine, his shoulder suddenly aching again, *that's like trusting the ripest of virgins around me.*

Kay rode off, sword already drawn.

Perceval watched the rider close with him. He looked familiar for some reason, maybe the man from his dreams? *No, this one's uglier. And he's come ready for a fight. Why does he want one with me?*

Kay stopped a horse length from the stranger. He inspected the raggedy-looking younger man. *He's just a whelp! He can't be any older than that lad "Beaumains" who was sent off to Gorny-*

mant recently. Kay had enjoyed hazing the pretty Gareth, whom he nicknamed white-hands; then the King sent him away, thinking him full of some potential which clearly did not reside in him.

"State your business, heathen, or leave." Perceval saw the man was near to lunging; the first knight at least attempted to sound diplomatic. And the knight still looked so familiar; if it weren't for the mail covering so much of his head…

Of course, he demanded a response. "Be off with you. The High King of Britain lets all those who come in peace to use his roads."

Kay would have exploded, except he was struck by the unwashed longhair's expression. "Where'd you learn to talk like that, boy?"

Boy, again. All everyone does is call me their damned stinking boy. I'm a blooded man! Perceval could not help but steal another quick glance at the stains, now blurry and of a different shape in the snow. *Not the blood again.*

"You'd better give a bloody answer, or I'll run you through here and now and return that steed to its proper owners!" Kay inched closer, just a couple of feet beyond range of a sword cut.

Now I'm a thief, too? When do the insults cease? Perceval looked skyward this time, hoping for some answer from above himself. *Is this the plight of those without faith? No answers, only jests?*

"God's not going to answer for you. You're just another hill-heathen, a faerie-fucker. God has no time for you."

Perceval turned on him now, with the same glare which disarmed Gaheris even before he was toppled from his horse. "I learned to speak so well from your own mother, you conniving sod. Do you care to ask what she taught me first?" *We men take our mothers so seriously.* Perceval almost laughed while saying it.

"You, you, filth! You –" Kay said, stammering, so furious proper annunciation left him. Perceval took full advantage of the opening. He immediately jumped off Styfnig, leading the horse out of the way by the reins, then redrew his sword.

"Come down here, then. Fight me toe to toe. Your rage has you so unbalanced you'll likely kill your poor horse. Or *mine*." He was careful to sneer as he uttered the last word, showing proper ownership, or at least a challenge to have the issue proven otherwise.

Kay was dumbstruck. What foolishness was this? Long seconds passed, the bumpkin awaiting him on the ground. Finally, the words came. Slowly. "You would sacrifice your only advantage?"

"If knight you be, fight me on foot. The code won't permit a man of chivalry to face another when only the one has a mount."

Kay regained his composure. "You're not even a knight."

"Then jump down and prove it." *Wait. I do know this maniac. Kay! It's one of Arthur's own men.* He looked past Kay for a moment, seeing the dragon banner still dancing in the breeze. *How did I not notice it before? I've never been so lost in my mind before.* That made Perceval edgy. He could have been caught off guard by either of these men and gutted before they bothered identifying him.

Much to Perceval's astonishment, Kay obliged him, clutching his sword and shield like a child holding his favorite toys, not to be put away even when parents announced bedtime. The shield was just as Perceval remembered: the blue field, with the trio of keys symbolizing Kay's access to so much in the city. How much would a man with that kind of trust abuse the power which came with it?

"Come at me then, if you've any more balls than whatever fathered you," Kay said.

It was Perceval's turn to oblige, and he did so with full force and fury. He'd identify himself later; Kay didn't deserve that much, and Perceval could always claim he hadn't recognized him.

They clashed and clanged, swords meeting each other again and again like two lovers divided repeatedly who could only meet with aching passion. The symbolism was not lost on Isolde, who several hundred yards away, refused to watch any of what happened.

The dancers spun, counterspun, slashed and sliced, blocked and parried. Kay regarded each notch in his weapon's blade, created from force such as this; he viewed them as conquests of the sword, much like the notches in his bedpost. Well, the notches in his bedpost *would* have represented other sword-like conquests, only Kay had to find his hardness elsewhere.

Neither fighter gave an inch, both seeking openings. Kay was pleased to have such a worthy opponent, even if hill-trash. Perceval was impressed that the old boy could still wave the weapon at all; he looked too heavy in his armor.

Finally, Perceval decided it was time to finish. He had gotten his daily exercise, and he didn't want Kay feeling overly proud of his performance. He feinted, made to go to the left, as though looking to get under Kay's shield.

Kay went with the movement, lowering his shield to block, keeping the sword cocked behind him for a final overhead swing which would brain this young fool once and for all.

He never got the chance. Perceval timed the motion smoothly as ever, bringing his sword down hard against Kay's shield arm, giving the sword an instant half-spin at the last moment.

Kay screamed, knowing at once the arm was broken, sword and shield both dropping uselessly to the ground. He also knew that the scraggly stranger could have easily taken the arm off, rather than just fracture the bone; the slice was strong enough to cut through armor, skin, and joint all at once.

"Now get lost. I'm finished talking to you." Perceval stood over the kneeling, whimpering Kay, who slowly gathered his weapons and returned them to his horse. He had to make two trips, his left arm useless. But he mounted and rode back to the King.

Why can I not receive the attention of the King himself? He promised to make me knight.

Then the realization hit him with the same force as his blow, the kind which made him recall Kay, after it was too late to bargain with him. He felt his beard, looked at his new horse, lack of armor and shield.

They don't recognize me. Horrified, he remounted Styfnig and watched the party from his safe distance. He wanted desperately to know what would happen next. He foolishly never identified himself, as the code demanded. He had been too lost in his own wanderings to mind what happened around him. *Focus on yourself first, then your surroundings,* he could hear Gornymant command.

What if Kay still didn't recognize him? Would knights keep coming until Perceval was slain? What if the King himself came to kill him? He hardly looked like the errant arriving in Camelot that day. His hair was longer, but his beard had itched into a stubbly forest and he lacked what identified him before.

The armor. Meliagrant's armor. Some have talked of the Red Knight.

Red as the blood in the snow, he thought dimly, and looked down at it yet again, awaiting his fate the way the residents of Haughmond Abbey waited for judgment from the office of Uren.

Kay had yet to bother with a sling for his useless arm, retaking his position among the party and giving his report. He was livid; the pain in his arm gave him an excuse to growl and sneer menacingly at no one in particular. It would be his only release for the anger right then.

"Two for two," Arthur said. "Do I have any other volunteers, or I shall I go myself?" The knights knew that tone. It meant the King was growing quite irate, wondering how many besides the group and the single mystery man might have seen the stranger dispatch two Round Table members.

Bedivere and Gawaine spoke in unison. "Let me go." Then they stared at each other, wondering who would be chosen.

The decision came at once. "Gawaine, they don't call you the most glib tongue in Camelot without cause. It's your turn. Bring him in peacefully. No more fighting." Bedivere could be courteous when he saw the need, but he preferred duel to diplomacy like most of them. Gawaine was already tired, hurt; hopefully the lad would see that and not take advantage. It was clear to the King that he fought with the highest degree of integrity.

"Arthur," Kay said. "I think I recognize him." He winced as he spoke, preparing a sling from extra material in his saddlebag.

"Hold, Gawaine. Who?" Arthur said. "Where could you have possibly seen this man before?"

"In our own Camelot, brother. I believe it's the same fool who took on Meliagrant." Kay's pride would not let him admit that the same fool killed Meliagrant, giving the Queen no small peace of mind.

"Perceval? You're saying that's him on the road?"

"Looked and sounded like him." Kay finished wrapping the cloth around himself, holding arm to chest supported by neck.

Arthur turned to his weary nephew. "Gawaine, you've never met the man, never seen him. Find out if it's him and then see why he can't seem to identify the dragon standard. But get him back here. If we all go, we may scare him off. I want to talk to him, if it really is him."

Gawaine saluted with his healthier arm, and cantered away.

Perceval wished for the lost armor in the face of the giant who came towards him now, slowly, methodically, as though sizing up prey. *This knight must stand near fully seven feet out of the saddle,* he thought dimly. He was tired of fighting. Maybe this man would allow him an audience with the King.

Gawaine stopped just feet from the younger man, close enough that their horses could look each other over and nod and snort their own greetings. "Well met. Perceval, is it?"

Perceval gawked at the man. How could one so large speak so well? He seemed more the sort to drag his knuckles along the ground like a goblin. "Yes, Sir. I am Perceval from Oerfa, a tiny village of no consequence which likely appears on no map you have ever seen."

Gawaine was amused. "From the way you handled Kay and my brother, I figured you would speak with more confidence."

Perceval stammered. "Your brother?" *That's it. I'm going to spit teeth for this one.* "Sir, I'd no idea he was your kinsman. I do apologize, and sincerely hope he received no grievous injury at my hands."

"Only to his pride, and that's probably the strongest thing about him. Perceval, I am Sir Gawaine of clan Orkney of Lothian, so far north of here that you might think it at the ends of the earth. And on behalf of the King, I am at your service." *Just like sweet-talking a comely lass into the bed.*

"Gawaine? *The* Sir Gawaine?" Perceval bowed as deeply as he could without falling from the saddle. "Your presence is service enough. I thought never to meet someone of your stature." *Please don't let him take that as a comment about his build.*

Gawaine ignored the praise. He was sometimes as tired of it as Lancelot. "The King awaits. He's been searching for you for some time now."

"Surely that band of folks beneath the banner can't be for me." Perceval thought they looked more like a hunting party, out to follow the hounds as they treed the fox, or whatever Arthur was used to chasing.

"Aye, they are. The King has plans for you."

Perceval swallowed the lump growing in his throat. "For me, you say?"

Gawaine smiled. He loved hazing freshmen knights. He'd have to make sure he helped Perceval receive his second baptism, in the near icy water which awaited all new knights made in Camelot, like Llascoit and many others recently.

Of course, that was a privilege pertaining to the Christian knights. Gawaine's own cousin had refused that part of the ceremony, never letting go his Pagan ways. Just like some of the others.

"Of course, for you. The Queen is there also. I believe she has something to tell you herself."

"T-the Queen as well?" *How badly can I muck this all up? I hardly need to disappoint more women.*

Gawaine loved this. "Oh, and you might wish to stay out of Kay's sight for the first few days. He's not known for his kind and forgiving nature, like me."

Perceval's second swallow was audible. His voice cracked as he spoke. "Shall we be off to them, then?" he said uncertainly.

"At once."

"Sir Gawaine, before we reach them and I make a complete horse's posterior of myself, could you tell me what creature fills the King's banner? I recall seeing it now above the great castle on my first visit to Camelot."

Gawaine glared at him, surprised. "A dragon, of course. The Pendragon, chief dragon of our fair and blessed Island."

"Of course." *You moron! You should have learned all this months ago.*

They turned towards the party, guiding chargers with their knees, holding the reins as an afterthought. "Perceval, what happened there? In the snow?"

"Oh, I saw a falcon make a kill there. It just got me to thinking."

What could you have been thinking about to enable you to over-throw two of the best knights in Logres? Gawaine wondered.

"Would you answer me a question?" Perceval said. Gawaine nodded.

"What happened to your arm?"

"I chanced upon another fierce creature, at a place far from here. If you make it as far as I think you will, you'll hear about it sometime."

Perceval wondered what he meant, as they arrived back at the waiting party.

He was wholly unprepared for King Arthur to personally ride out to be the first to greet him. "Perceval! It's been longer than we'd hoped. Have your travels been successful?"

Perceval looked quickly at Gawaine, who seemed to know what he would have liked to ask. But Gawaine was one to learn by doing, to teach by example. He bowed surreptitiously to the King.

Perceval copied the bow as best he could. "They have, your majesty. My foster brother, a loyal knight in your service as of Pentecost, sends his regrets that he could not return."

"Is he all right?" the King said, with all the compassion Perceval imagined his own father might have shown him, had he lived.

"Oh, yes. My, uh, my," *Llio's not my wife, and I don't think I can speak of having a fiancée to the man who has yet to make me knight.*

What if he arranges a marriage for me? "My friend, Lady Llio of Jagent, is taking care of her brother as we speak. He took a wound fighting a knight named Clamadeus." *No, wait, that's wrong! It was from Agrivaine. Perceval, you clod, stop acting so nervous and tell the truth. And stop stammering.*

"I know this villain. He's a robber knight up near Cameliard, or thereabouts."

"He was, Sire."

"Then Llascoit dispatched him?" Arthur was gleeful, relishing any story of good knightly combat against any enemies of the crown. Clamadeus had committed thievery on the King's own roads.

His memory's better than I ever imagined. I suppose that's necessary of one who would be king. "Uh, no, Sire. I did." Perceval looked at the ground again, almost wishing he had the bloodstain to focus on still. Now there was just dirty snow, already showing signs of melting for having arrived too late.

King and knight stared at the lad wide-eyed. "You did?"

"Yes, King. Please accept my sincere apology for not giving you the opportunity to –"

"Oh, nonsense, lad! First you resolve a conflict with the Queen's enemy, and now you take care of my own. That's twice I am in your debt, Perceval."

"You in my debt, your majesty? Impossible. If anything, it is I who owe you." It was difficult to look this man in the face, yet Arthur commanded something intangible from Perceval. From all those who saw him. Perceval wondered what it was. Respect? Awe? Trust?

"Perceval, knighthood is about mutual responsibility. So we owe each other. From you I have received the most excellent knightly service, and from me you shall have your title, as promised."

Gawaine beamed at Perceval, swung his good arm to clap him on the back. It stung Perceval, who still needed some new armor.

"You mean it? I mean, King Arthur, I could think of no greater honor." *If Mother could see me this moment... And the others... How long have I wished for this?* The blood and its linking thoughts were hastily put away for now.

"We shall attend to it at once. That is, after we reach Camelot. But first come with me. There are those I wish you to meet personally." Arthur nodded and smiled at Gawaine. *The Silver-Tongue of Lothian.* Gawaine felt better than he had since he left Camelot for home.

*   *   *

The young woman had not seen an arm this mangled since the Pentecost tournament, when one of the competitors insisted on keeping his shield locked in front of an incoming blow, no matter how much damage it might do. She worked as an apprentice healer, a nurse, as the people in Camelot liked to talk of her. She liked it when people spoke to or about her. It made her feel welcome.

The owner of the broken arm was one of Arthur's senior officers, Sir Kay, and he did not take to the salve well. The woman was painstakingly careful with the preparation, and she was determined to ensure that he kept it in place. It was quite an honor, to mix a very particular blend of herbs into a healing poultice. It was the first time Bishop Baudwin let her do that all on her own; she was supervised previously. He told her Kay would never know the difference, who was always one to bemoan the healing arts anyway, so it was a good opportunity to show the bishop how much she knew.

It had not been easy for her. Her family was all gone, and her home had a bleak future at best. So she went elsewhere. To Camelot. Every profession, every skill, every talent: all could find work in the capital. She loved it from the moment she saw it. It was like something from a dream, like the stories her mother used to tell her as a girl.

The nurse was highborn, though she had no inkling to speak of the royal blood in her veins. It might be contested anyway, since she doubted many remembered her mother, and not even she knew who her father had been.

She leaned over Kay's arm now. They were together in the royal hospital, a long stone building kept warm by continual fires and well-lit through the many windows the Queen insisted be placed to promote a sense of wellness in those who had to be brought here. Not many souls wandered it this day.

The arm looked good, the knight still dozing from the strong boozy potion the young woman gave him earlier. Kay had, for once, taken it without fuss. The yarrow root had been applied at once, to soothe the pain and help prevent any infection, while the heady broth inspired warmth and relaxation. Now the woman gently checked the wood anemone mixture coating Kay's arm. It looked comfortable and secure, and the knight would just have to try and keep patient so the bone could set and fully heal.

She was alone in the room with Kay and the other patient, delighted to have the trust of Baudwin, who apparently spoke quite highly of her to the King and Queen. The bishop knew of her teacher, and of that person's reputation, and simply told the royal couple that, "the girl comes to us from a great healer known in lands to the north and west of here."

The young woman smiled, easing her way from Kay's still body over to a nearby bed, this one containing the form of Sir Gaheris, apparently wounded by the same person. No one knew she heralded from the same general area as the "barbarian" who whipped both of these knights. But she knew; the Queen and Isolde had been careful to point out their own bias against those who came from the timeless hills and forests. The newcomer tried to put it out of her mind.

She felt at once fascinated with the stunning Isolde, the innocent eyes out of place in the body which inspired the most lecherous and possessive of thoughts from the men who beheld it. Since she and Guinevere had already been talking to this nurse, the nurse learned a bit about them, and their relations to the knights who adored them (each woman had *two* knights who would gladly destroy themselves or anyone else to be with them!) The young woman grew more accustomed to the Queen's presence, forceful and aloof at first, but then warming to anyone she found intriguing. And she had indeed been intrigued by the newcomer.

"Oh, does she come from Eire?" the Queen had asked, curious of anyone who had been further west of her home of Cameliard, and wanting to know if this young woman could be trusted inside the keeps and towers of Camelot. That was the day Baudwin explained the new immigrant to the royal couple.

"Oh, no, My Lady," the bishop said. "But from Cambria. She comes to us orphaned." The young woman smiled again, now enjoying her solitude save for the knights in her charge, remembering what Baudwin told her, after the excitable days of the festival died down.

And the work proved steady. Bishop Baudwin oversaw the healers, splint-makers, chirurgeons, brewers, and herbalists who practiced their respective talents in the hospital. They were at once amazed by how this person could do all of these things, and do them with a smile and a kind word. People came to her often now, and she had only been in Camelot a few weeks. Those with the sniffing chill, those who had cuts or breaks or even minor scratches, they who needed burning fevers broken, or those who suffered from whatever affliction, they all came to her, seeking the graceful youth of whom many had heard, but no one really knew.

Baudwin helped see to that; he had been at once bedazzled with her performance following the tourney, recommending just the right treatments for the wounds inflicted upon the knights, even conjuring up some the bishop himself was unfamiliar with. He could tell at once she would be an asset to this place, and took her aside during one of the few calm moments he had during the spectacle.

It was the day after Baudwin spoke with another frightened girl, who held a sword and whom others had come to from a sense of destiny and need. He would remember that day forever.

As would the nurse, nearing Gaheris, who also slept. He was not as handsome as Kay, yet she admired his brusque northern features: fairer skin, lighter eyes, the lines etched upon his face from the unforgiving northern chill. He appeared to be doing quite well. The young woman was glad; there had been such a commotion when these two arrived, returning with the King and someone looking very much the part of the hill folk of which she had been warned as a girl.

"Your first time to our fair city, then, is it?" Baudwin had asked her back then.

She was nervous, unsure what to say. "Yes, Father. My mistress sends her regards. She thought this the best place for me to practice the healing arts."

"And who might this teacher be? Clearly she knows of me."

"Yes, she said she knew you when you both were much younger. She is Dame Kunneware from the central hills of Powys."

That stopped Baudwin cold. All he could do was stare vacantly at her. For her part, she grew more anxious still, unsure of how to behave in such a sprawling community. And her mother, rest her soul, might have flown into some fit at how she spoke casually to the bishop.

Then again, the person who taught her this "magick" would have scared the girl's mother to death. "Did she also know Merlin?" was the bishop's only response.

The young woman hadn't seen the relevance of that. "Yes. She did, and spoke of him sometimes. She missed having him around. I've never met him."

"There's no way you would have, he's been gone since before your birth," Baudwin said back, barely audible. She had heard more than one story of the venerable arch-druid. "And a number of us miss him."

"You also, Father? That seems strange."

"You'd be surprised at how much I learned from that old codger. Then again, considering your teacher, you might have some idea."

The young woman wanted to know exactly where she stood with this man; she was not one to chase around the bush, as her mother used to say. "Father, is there a problem regarding my mistress? If so, then may I suggest —"

"Oh, there's no problem. None at all. I was just surprised." Baudwin was rarely surprised anymore. He had seen enough wonder to last two full lifetimes.

"Then could you stand to benefit from my services?"

Baudwin was taken by her forwardness. She reminded him a bit of Galienne, only shy when terrified, which was seldom. "Yes, child. You have the Lord's own blessing in those hands."

"Goddess enables me to work with the skill I have," she said, allowing the bishop to see the faintest of smiles.

So she's Pagan, of course, Baudwin considered. *All right, then. We have plenty of use for her in the city. More and more folk come to us with their ills, like a blight on the land. Even Camelot is no longer a total refuge from our growing malaise.* Baudwin fretted much of those days over the number of patients in the hospital, and not those who had earned places there from their own bragging and gallantry on the field. It was the others, those sick and wretched creatures, who came from all around the land, hoping to be healed. Like those poor souls who turned to Galienne when they were so easily convinced of the sign within the odd smoke pillar. He had spoken not a word of this to the woman, though; he needed skilled healers, not cynical bureaucrats like himself.

Presently, Gaheris stirred, rolling to and fro slightly in his bed. The young woman felt his forehead, dabbing the sweat with a clean cloth as she did so. He had come down with a bit of fever. His brother, the indomitable Gawaine, told her she must take care with him. He witnessed quite a lot in his most recent travels.

"And that arm?" she said to Gawaine. "What of that, then, Sir? You look as though you could benefit from some of the art yourself." The woman kept her forwardness, even in the face of a man who had two feet and seven stone on her. And she always referred to her skill as *art*. Only the very foolish or the very faithful considered healing otherwise. Kunneware taught her that.

"This?" Gawaine said casually, as though it was nothing beyond a cat's scratch. "This will be fine in days. I rode clear from Listeniese with it thus." It was as honest as he could be; Gawaine was a quick healer, and not one to receive the medical attention of a woman, especially one young enough to be his daughter. And he thought they had ridden from Listeniese. It was his closest estimate.

He had walked out then, leaving the woman with her patients.

Gaheris' motion became more restless. He began to mumble, still unconscious. "Dark... can't see. Gawaine, where are you? I don't want to leave the cup, it's worth... Who might you be, then, barbarian? No! Falling, falling –"

He convulsed once, his weight thrown downward into the feather mattress. The mattresses also resulted from Guinevere's attentions, as she wanted people to be comfortable here. Britain's peasants generally considered hospitals as either holy sanctuaries or places where folk were bled and amputated in the name of medicine.

Gaheris opened his eyes instantly, blinking several times. He looked at the healer. Then at the large room, full of beds. He did not seem to recognize Kay in the nearby one.

"Who are you?" he demanded. "Why am I here?"

"You don't remember, then," she said. "You're here because you have a fever and have acted a bit deliriously."

"But I remember things well enough. Except for who you are. Answer the question."

The woman appreciated knightly courtesy and custom when it was compassionate, not when it insisted. And she was not in the habit of freely giving her name out; she had learned not to, fearing she might somehow be connected to the destruction which reached her home. There was no going back there now, never would be. "I am your nurse, Sir Gaheris of clan Orkney. And I will be here until you feel well enough to leave this hall."

"No, actually, _I_ am Sir Gaheris of Orkney," he said, laughing, and coughing as he did so. At least he had his humor.

"Yes, of course, Sir knight." She didn't want to discuss herself with this stranger.

"This is the King's new hospital, then, is it? I'd not seen it inside before."

"You've already been in it for a few days. Is it to your liking? I mean, is there anything I might do to help you feel better?" She asked mainly out of courtesy; she had in mind a specific course of remedy for this man and she intended to follow it precisely.

Gaheris was still groggy, but immediately considered just how he would answer the question; with a body like hers, she was quite desirable. He guessed she couldn't be older than her teens, the ripest age for a woman according to him.

Yet there was something about her which precluded his normal forwardness. He tried to put his finger on it. Innocence, perhaps? Or a genuine kindness, of the sort he never knew from his parents? He wasn't sure exactly. "I'll be fine right here, so long as I get out soon. And if I have the pleasure of seeing your comely face staring down at me, so much the better."

The nurse, for all her knowledge and frankness, was unused to receiving flattery from men. She had not known many men; she did not let on how nervous she had been treating the participants after the tourney. "It'll be soon enough, I'm quite certain. And thank you for the —"

"Compliment?" he finished. She nodded. She thought she sounded like a feeble child saying it.

"Why is there such a rush, anyway?" she said, hoping she wasn't overstepping her bounds. She couldn't help it. Gaheris made her blush, even though she felt not the slightest attraction to him.

"I assume you've already heard about the 'encounter' Kay and I had some distance west of here." It was more a question than a comment. She nodded.

He continued. "The man Kay and I fought with is someone for whom our King feels a remarkable amount of kinship, for reasons I am not altogether familiar with." He was careful not to say The Man Who Bested Kay And I.

"Why? Is he some relative of the King's?"

"Oh no, thank God, although Arthur wants to knight him. Personally, in just another day or so, if I remember properly. He wanted to give the heathen some time to get used to Camelot again, and change his appearance." Gaheris winced, obviously disgusted by the prospect. "He reeked worse than his horse."

The nurse checked the bindings on the knights' wounds, ignoring the crack about heathens. "You say he's actually been here before? That's strange."

"I was elsewhere when it happened, but talk has it that this is the same fool who somehow killed Sir Meliagrant some seasons back."

She asked about Meliagrant. Gaheris had to confess he knew nothing beyond his having been a villain knight wanting some ill with the Queen. Then she asked him, "Do you know who this man is?"

"What does it matter?" he said, his tone suggesting that it was time for him to rest some more. Fevers did that.

Without another word, Gaheris drifted off into dreamland once more. The fever broke within hours.

* * *

Perceval did not think he could possibly remain patient even a few days longer, and ask the King for yet another delay. He assumed, correctly, that Arthur would grow perturbed with such a request. No, he could not wait, not even for Llio and Llascoit.

Fortunately, he did not have to do so. They arrived by the time Kay and Gaheris were back on their proud feet. They informed Arthur that they certainly felt less than enthused by the prospect of some common trash meeting them on equal footing, but the King would not be deterred. Even the Queen, so Perceval heard later, personally chided the two knights for being too quick to judge and too slow to forgive. At any rate, she felt a deep obligation to Perceval. With Meliagrant gone, she remained free to administer her homelands from afar, remaining in the capital with her husband.

Knights who were not on specific errands or duties for the King returned to their own homes, where they became lords in their own rights. Merchants busied the roads, lovers uttered their vows and pursued one another with the zest of youth. The time felt so peaceful; Perceval almost thought he could smell it in the morning air. A tranquil sensation not felt since childhood, it was lined, perhaps, with just the slightest whiff of something sour or going rotten. He ignored the sense which suggested this to him; for the moment he had greater glory awaiting him.

It proved achingly difficult to stay obligingly out of the one private room in Gornymant's apartment, where Llio was staying. It would not be proper, taking his daughter in his tutor's own housing! Perceval was about to be dubbed knight! He would not tarnish the image he had never lost of the ideal, despite his encounters with those who fell short of meeting the measure.

"At least I won't have to listen to you grunting and howling this night," Llascoit said, sitting and grinning at the table in their apartment.

Perceval laid back on the large mattress nearby, a sort of massive seat by day and a comfortable bed during evening, the place where Llio and her brother almost thought Nimue had died, she had lain there so long. "At least I'm loving," he said.

"Oh, you don't get off that easily. Come, tell me. What's it like?"

Perceval thought of the old poetry. Llio was in the next room preparing for bed, and might hear him. "Like you're dreaming. It feels like you just lose yourself, forgetting all else."

Llascoit chuckled. "No, no, man. I mean, how does it *feel?* To be atop someone, to taste another person's flesh? How does a woman taste? And forget about the poetry for once."

Perceval stole a glance at the other room. No sign of life from there; maybe Llio already fell asleep. She had grown quite tired during the journey back to Camelot. Perceval guessed she had more of her mother in her than they all had previously thought.

"Delicious," he started. "So divine you'll never think of any other food or drink, never *want* any other."

Llascoit perked right up at that, straightening in his chair. It was actually good for him; he had grown lazy of late with his posture, owing to the injury. Yet it healed most satisfactorily. "That's better. This is what I really need to know."

"Didn't your father tell you about this?"

Llascoit had some idea of how a woman felt, but wanted to hear his friend describe it, since he had never felt the love. "Had there been any good women around Jagent in so many dull years he might have shown me. Why do you think I spent so much time riding a horse? I had to ride something."

"Llas, that's vulgar."

"You're the one who's lost his virtue, as it's said. Now go on."

"You could go find one of Gawaine's rejects and save yourself the time of listening to me. What better way to wait for me to spend my vigil?"

"Because I want to know this first, before I'm with someone else. It might save myself some embarrassment later." *What I need is more bloody* practice.

Perceval could empathize with that, at least. He had surely lit up the night from the heated glowing of his face, and an erection which grew painful from his uncertainty. Llio, too, had been as nervous. *No, that's selfish. She was calm and patient. The first time was surprisingly sweet.*

"Well, you already know what it's like to sweat."

Llascoit nodded, almost drooling. His eyes were those of the wolf he had emblazoned on his shield.

"But when you taste this sweat, love-sweat, it's completely different. You ignore the heat, ignore your muscles that protest being made to fit positions other than what they're used to. You can feel yourself glistening with that sweat."

Perceval looked about again to make sure Llio was no-where nearby. This talk was doing nothing to help him deal with his own urges! He wanted to be with her, with the woman he sought to marry.

Still, the talk excited him. That was the reason he kept talking. "Have you kissed a woman yet? Really kissed one?"

That caught him off guard. "Not really," Llascoit said defiantly.

"You can barely imagine it until you've done it, then. First, your lips just make contact, softly, warmly."

"Perceval, what does this have to do with fucking?"

Perceval sat there dumbly. "What? How can you say that?"

"Kissing is something you do with family and pets. I asked what it was like to be with a real woman. One you're not related to, I mean."

Perceval still could not speak. Was Llascoit this naive? Gornymant was always so careful, but he admittedly could hardly have given his son much genuine learning in the art of love, and he hadn't known of his son's own bumbling experimenting with the younger house servants. Was the creature in his breeches a lurking conqueror or a part of him that could be used to express affection? Perceval wondered how many other men saw the acts of love in such a shallow context.

Then Llio came storming through the doorway dividing the rooms, to stand rigidly near her brother, though just a bit closer to Perceval. Perceval thought she looked quite the formidable erection herself.

"Why, you loathsome, contemptible pig. You're hardly fit to be a man, much less my brother."

All Perceval could think at first was how incensed she'd be with him next. She obviously heard them. He dimly recalled that women were not supposed to like having their intimate experiences shared, especially with aroused young men.

"But Llio, I'm only trying to understand it."

"That's the problem, dolt. This isn't something to understand and write little theories about like the plays and philosophies we used to study. The only thing you can write about it is either a poem or a song, because both of those speak from the heart. There happens to be a difference between what you call 'fucking' and sharing love."

Llascoit was honestly confused, perhaps the only acceptable defense for an otherwise pig. "But that's the way the animals do it. Don't you remember how at Father's farm we'd see them?"

"But we're not talking about Father's farm, you braggart! Honestly, will the ignorance of men never cease? We women don't go around sniffing posteriors like Father's dogs. They don't get to look at each other while they're doing it. We look for romance, and music, and excitement. The sweaty part, if there's to be any sweaty part," Perceval was unsure if he liked the glance she shot him, "that comes later. *If* both parties are willing to take that step, and *if* they care about each other."

She was breathing heavily. Normally Perceval found that attractive. Right then he was inclined to keep his male mouth shut, but he spoke anyway. "Llio, I'm sorry. I was just trying to help him understand what it's like."

"Then tell him what it *means*. Every beast on earth knows what it's like. But I'm not upset with you." She leaned toward him, planting a kiss on his lips which only hinted at the warm wetness of her mouth. She was close enough to smell. It would be a long vigil. Perceval supposed the perpetual aching in his groin would at least help keep him awake.

"Then what does it mean, sister?" Llascoit said, watching their every motion from across the room. "And why is it that women routinely find themselves in marriages based on property and titles and not love?"

Llio drew away from Perceval, hoping he would not see the furious expression which crossed her face as she did so. "Because men arrange them that way!" she spat. "Women are treated like so much cattle, traded and used for the benefit of men only."

"But our parents were arranged. Father adored her, and still does. He's never had eyes for anyone else since she died, and he could have had many."

"Numbers don't make the man, brother. I may not speak to you again if I hear of marks in your bedpost someday, like so many coins kept in a chest."

"Well then, what of the King and Queen? They've found joy with each other. Explain that to me, if these relationships are all preordained."

Llio had heard gossip regarding the Queen, and decided Llascoit was still ignorant of it. At any rate, to speak ill of her was to risk committing a heinous crime, treason against the crown. Llio thus opted for what she could say safely, and still get her point across.

"You're right, Llas. Those marriages were arranged, and despite what I said they worked out to everyone's satisfaction. But how would you feel if you were the expectant bride, waiting for your first glimpse of a man you wouldn't likely meet until the day he took your hand." Llio resisted the urge to use the term "shackled" instead. "A man who might easily be twice your age. Can you imagine your terror? Especially if you were a virgin, like marriageable women are somehow supposed to be, and knew not how it felt, nor what it meant?"

Llascoit was unconvinced. "But that time passes when the affianced meet."

"But don't you see? The women aren't given any say. Mother and the Queen were both very fortunate, but I would ask you to please keep in mind that they were the exceptions, not the rule."

Llascoit could tell he was losing. He tried another tactic. "But isn't virginity a virtue when one is wed?"

"For women! Men, the hypocrites, are expected to have their fill of sexual awakening by the time they 'settle down' with the right woman. But women are expected to refrain. God, what can any virgin possibly know of love and marriage? And then to not even have a voice in matters later!" Llio had not even realized the pent-up hostility she carried within her. She wondered what spurned it on. Maybe her wanting to marry a man regardless of anyone else's consent. Would Father allow that? He loved Perceval, had told her as much, but marriage? She wished she could speak with her mother about it; she was partly angry for never having had that chance.

"I agree with the last part. That's why I want to know." Llascoit sounded less chauvinistic and more simply curious with each sentence.

"Then don't you think whomever your lifelong partner turns out to be deserves to know also?"

He sat there just thinking it over. He had clearly not considered it before. After a few moments he returned to his earlier question.

"So it's rare for it to work out, at least in the manner you would prefer?"

God, he can be thick-skulled sometimes. "That's right." She thought about what Lupinia had told her of Trystan's love, an immeasurably comely woman, thoughtful, kind, even learned to some extent. And promised to another. She made it seem like Trystan and his uncle would inevitably come to duel over the matter, neither one caring so much any more for what Isolde felt. Lupinia sounded like Sir Bors' heart had broken because of it all; that was the only part Llio could not quite understand herself. It was sad, but in the end, someone else's problem. The person she truly felt for was Isolde herself. Caught in the middle, others warring over her like two bears fighting over a salmon.

Llascoit stared at her uncomprehendingly. Llio felt exasperated. "Llascoit, just tell me one thing."

"What?"

"Will you respect your additional lovers? Or will they just be the ones who initiate you into the wonders of a woman's body, and left to their own recourses afterwards?"

"How could I not respect them?" *How did she know?*

Llio sighed, finally smiling again. Maybe he wouldn't muck it up after all. He sounded much like their father when he said it. She took Perceval's hand, who still looked sheepish.

"Stop worrying," she said to him. "It's all right, with Llas. Just don't let me hear of you talking about us to the likes of Kay and Gawaine." Perceval nodded, feeling the warm suppleness of her hand in his. There was strength there also; both of them could feel it.

She leaned toward him again. "I love you, and I wish to be with you. I know you'll fare well at the vigil."

"I love you, Llio."

"And Llas," she said, turning to face him. "If you ever get a woman to say the same to you, count your blessings as Father taught us."

* * *

Gawaine was right on time to meet Perceval at the apartment. The latter bade Llio good eve and Llascoit stayed up to wish Perceval well and tell him, "It's not so bad if you can just keep your mind occupied." Gawaine then led the initiate out of the building and down High Street toward Saint Dubric's Cathedral.

Along the way, Perceval tried frantically to remember all he had learned of this time, the night before one is to become a knight. He felt troubled at once.

"Sir Gawaine, what shall I do about my lack of armor? All I have is my sword and mount." The one was carried by

Gawaine, Perceval surrendering it to him previously. The other was biding his time in the royal stables where he ate and mated freely and let no one other than Perceval upon his back. The stable master was only tolerant of the vast food consumption and sexual romping because Arthur decreed it to be a special horse indeed. The lad had a way with beasts; had he not already given the King the finest hunting dog he ever saw in Cabal?

"Ah, don't fret about it, lad. The only thing you need to worry about this night is your stay in the church."

That worried Perceval more. He had yet to find the words he thought God might prefer to hear. Maybe the bishop would be there to help. "I'm anxious about sitting penitently in church all night. Something about it seems wrong."

Gawaine was amused. "What's the problem? Are you a Pagan, then?"

Perceval found it challenging to keep up with Gawaine's stride, the man's legs were so long and powerful. "I, that is, well, I –"

Gawaine helped him, snickering as he did so. "Perceval, I'm more Pagan than Christian myself. It's all right. I doubt old Baudwin will mind either way. He and Merlin go back some time, and while there may be a cross and steeple on this place, it's open to all whose hearts are good."

Perceval was struck by the last word. He would have expected "pure" or "faithful." Something holier, perhaps; he wasn't sure.

"Do you know how this tradition started? It's been around since before the best warriors were called knights. Back then we might have spent whole days and nights fasting or hunting, as part of the initiation into manhood."

"I thought the idea was to pray to God, and emerge next morning reborn."

"I only care to be born once per lifetime, lad. What about the soaking? Where do you suppose that came from?"

Gawaine only ever had this talk with his brothers: Gaheris, Gareth, Agrivaine, even Mordred.

Perceval considered the ritualistic bath in bitter cold water that would wait patiently for him until morning. It represented a second baptism, that of boy into man, squire into knight. "I don't know." He never served as a squire, either.

They could see the tall steeple now. The streets and alleys of Camelot, arranged in their Roman grid and order, lay fairly silent. The festive sounds and smells of eating and drinking came from several buildings. The other businesses were closed up for the day, some of their owners and workers likely found in the sources of noise. Here and there pairs of knights strolled by, a visible security force which, while largely unnecessary in the city, was maintained by Kay. A few couples strolled freely. Perceval thought he could heard some unusual pipes played by someone trying to win either a lady's heart or some extra coins. Perhaps both.

"Part of the warrior code before all this chivalry came about was the teaching of the skills needed to become a great warrior. One of these included fishing. They used to fish by diving underwater with spears, no matter the time of year. The Church, wanting to preserve its own traditions in the name of knighthood, borrowed that tradition and called it their own second baptism. Like that which awaits a babe to cleanse it of its supposed original sin."

"I had no idea." Perceval had not heard of original sin in a long time. How could the creation of an innocent new life be sinful (even when certain parties described it as mere fucking)? It confused him, but Gawaine continued.

"When the Romans came and brought their new religion with them, they were smart enough to tell that the only way it could really take root here was to introduce it through traditional channels. Like Yule time. I remember celebrating that with my father. My mother used to go out with him to gather the perfect log, and a sprig of mistletoe for people's affections, especially theirs. She's a proud one." Gawaine sighed. "Now it's Christmas and Jesus' birthday, and some have begun hauling entire trees indoors for the season. It seems a blasphemy to me. Can you imagine what the druids might have thought at the notion of killing a tree for the purpose of decorating a room?"

Gawaine made it sound like druids were something of the past. Why would he do so? Even Perceval knew otherwise. He wished Tathan was with him now. The musician playing a street or so over made him miss the old bard even more. Perceval recognized the tune: a sharp melody Tathan had sung more than once, about loves' pains and the agony of separation. The pipes were piercing and joyous all at once, showing genuine emotion.

The knight awaited an answer. "Uh, I'm sure they would have been incensed," Perceval said finally.

"To put it lightly, at that. Now the druids move underground, living like moles. But that may be the only way to preserve the past."

Perceval took a dare, based in part on the sorrowful tone Gawaine used. "Sir, I suffer not from lack of faith or spirit. I just have trouble telling which way it leads me. May I inquire about yourself?"

Gawaine did not mind a bit, even though the door to the cathedral was within shouting range. "Perceval, your beliefs are your affair. I believe that the most. My uncle has his reasons for keeping the cross to overlook his city, but I'll die before anyone tells me whom to follow, and whether I should make sacrament or sacrifice. In my mind there's little difference in approach, only in teaching. But behind the teaching is an element of control. I will bow to this cross if that is truly the sign of things to come, but will not allow it to otherwise control me."

Perceval thought it a great deal to ingest right then, though he would have all night to think it over.

Gawaine clapped him about the shoulders. "Listen, lad. You've more to worry about than God. So what if you're going into a church? It's the only building in town sure to remain quiet for the evening. And solitude is what's important for the warrior to realize himself. Good blessing on you, Perceval."

It seemed an odd thing for the large man to say, but Perceval was touched by the sentiment. He had not forgotten his deep melancholic state when this knight found him and snapped him out of it. *Melancholy? Fool, you were* morbid. "Thank you, Sir Gawaine. Maybe I'll make it to Arthur's table yet."

Gawaine smiled, though Perceval mistook the reason. He was amused by the younger man's directness, absent-minded but sincere. He didn't mind the way Perceval used the King's name, either.

Perceval turned and looked up at the steeple. Bishop Baudwin stood in the doorway, waiting for him.

Yes, it would be a long night.

* * *

Galienne decided it was time to leave as soon as she had grown to feel truly at home in Roche Sanguin. She was welcome all along, from the moment the raft ran aground and she had her initial glimpse of the residents.

It was not a bitter sentiment she felt now, surely. Indeed, she knew she would miss those who lived within the obscured tiny keep, not even knowing when, or if, she would lay eyes upon them again. No, it was more a sense of purpose; she might have called it duty but then remained confused at how best to explain it further. *Duty to what?* others might ask. *To myself, mainly. But also to some vague prophecy I know almost nothing of, and have begun to doubt of late.*

That was as close to an answer as she likely would come, and it bothered her. Ygerne and Sexburh and the others asked her about what would come next for her. Ygerne fervently

hoped she would not return to men and their ways, while Sexburh relished a good fight, even deciding to leave herself and
head for home once Galienne did. The girl's strength and direction inspired them all.

The only part of the alleged prophecy Galienne was
comfortable with now was the pseudonym. She delighted in
the sound of "Galahad," savoring the way it rolled off the lips.
It sounded powerful, even masculine. She supposed adding the
title "Sir" to the front of it would boost that impression further,
more than "Lady" at any rate. Either way, however, a title was
something she lacked. She was Galienne, daughter of that-old-
hero, now preferring Galahad-of-Roche-Sanguin.

That was part of the drive. She still felt she had so much
to prove. She could hardly keep Perceval out of trouble if she
was leagues away, either. But she could not shake her ghostly
thoughts off any longer, and must be on her way.

The prophecy made no sense. Her visions left her!
Gone were the images of others, the voices and motions of
people she knew and others who remained strangers. No more
vivid dreams. No more reflections proffered by God for her
benefit. They so often scared her before, but she had not been
prepared for how much she missed them. She had used them
to try and comprehend. God's wisdom presented itself in mysterious ways, so the Great Book proclaimed. Baudwin himself
helped her try and come to terms with that. Of *course* it could
be frightening; divine wisdom could hardly be otherwise.

Galienne felt much more comfortable now that she had
time to think it through, the idea of remaining a symbol of sorts.
Had God chosen her for something? To heal, perhaps the likes
of those poor souls who beseeched her for just that in Camelot?
Of this she could not be sure, having been so terrified at the
time. But then was she to be a prophet or teacher? She doubted
this. What good was any prophet without the proper sendings?

Even God needed a messenger, but if that person could no longer receive the message, then what good was she?

She didn't even notice the blasphemy of that thought, of God "needing" anything at all. She now believed that part of the holy mystery was working God's plan on earth, and in that sense, surely He could use all the help He could get. She concluded there'd be no need of preachers, teachers, or healers otherwise.

This much remained clear: she had to *find* her purpose, whatever shape it might take. Since she no longer had the sendings nor the words of an educated bishop to guide her, she would have to follow her own course, until such time as she became convinced of her own destiny. Her mother would have liked that; Galienne realized destiny put her in that fateful boat as much as her own bereaved heart. Her father would have favored her conclusion also; she smiled at the image of Lancelot praising and cursing destiny all at once, for having him first lay eyes upon Guinevere. Galienne's parents had been so smitten from their initial glances of what they desired. Perhaps that was part of why Galienne sought no love. Well, no lover, anyway. What man would want her, since she had reached a level of skill which would enable her to overcome many manly opponents? Men could not often bear shame as well as women.

So, back to Camelot, then. Back to a King who, if he would not knight her, should at least treat her with respect, perhaps even finding tasks for her to do. Where else could she go? Astolat held nothing for her; she could not legally inherit her mother's home, and had no interest in the family trade, such as it was. The most exciting part of her childhood was learning to read, and she grew weary of the taunts thrown at a literate girl. She could only imagine the taunts they'd offer now. The Cambrian wilds? No. She loved seeing Perceval's old haunts, but she did not share them. Besides, in case he truly was dead, she would be forever reminded of her failure to reach him on the river were she to return to his homeland.

The only other place Galienne had seen other than those was the fort of the Bloody Rock, with its displaced, diseased, and disgusted women. Some would remain, others would sally forth on their own to make it in a man's world, usually going to new lands and even changing their names. The one thing the women behind Roche Sanguin's walls truly had in common was this: they were comfortable and unashamed to be women, and they wanted something better than what the past had offered them. Beyond that, they had more diversity as the men who sat at the Round Table.

Galienne most missed Perceval now because he taught her to love all this, the fabulous wilderness stretching forever in all directions. He showed her how to identify oak from elm from alder, which shrubs and berries could be eaten, and how to make sure the water she took from stream or lake was safe to drink. That alone made his friendship worth everything; she would have learned none of this otherwise, growing gray at her mother's spinning wheel.

So now that she was finally, willingly outside again, where was he?

Galahad sat next to the mare that had once been his. Brownie, too, had felt a bit cramped in the small fort, never apart from the attention lavished upon her by a number of the residents. Horse and rider left just two days before.

Ygerne asked if she was sure, as she was more concerned with Galienne's safety than with trying to keep another person within Roche Sanguin. There was always the danger, the older woman believed, that whenever a woman left the security of the rock its location might eventually be betrayed if that woman grew careless. She did not have that anxiety about Galienne, though; she just wished she would find some rest for her yearning, curious soul.

Sexburh and some of the others questioned her also. "What's Camelot like?" they said. "Do you know the King?" "Are the knights really chivalrous like it's said?" "What will you do there?" Galienne listened to all the questions patiently, aware she did not know the answers to some of them.

She had stayed with them, slept next to them, planted and brewed and slaughtered with them, and enjoyed the fruits of such labors around their fires, leading more than one prayer with them. It was quite a busy time; the devil would never think her hands idle.

Yet she would only miss a couple of the women.

Oh, they were good people. Galienne firmly believed that now. But the spirits of some were irreparably damaged. Not even her most fervent prayers could seem to rekindle the woman-fire which should have heated their bellies.

Galienne smiled now, at Brownie, who grazed almost silently beside her, the pair of them beneath the shelter of a bracken of rowan trees. *Would Baudwin call these thoughts heretical?* She wondered. She thought not. To speak of woman's spirit and fire was to speak of the energy imbued by her holy soul, a sacred gift from God, immortal and hopeful. She merely chose a more Pagan way of phrasing the thought. And she felt secure in the idea of leaning against the gnarled old tree.

It felt like a chair of God's own, not some dark, foreboding, cold thing that should be cut down to make room for more buildings or churches.

Her faith had changed her and she had changed it. Never would Galienne forget the Holy Trinity and the teachings of Christ, but she acknowledged that while the Lord may work in strange ways, so might the faith which brought one closer to Him.

She spun the ring Jacqueline gave her around her finger a few times, always enjoying the smooth sensation of the worked jewelry. Then she reached for the cross which rested comfortably between her breasts, grown to their full maturity now. She closed her eyes, clutching the cross with the intensity of one saying a final Hail Mary before facing that event which takes one right to one's maker. *Perceval, dear friend. Hear me. Hear my prayers for you and for us. Be well. Wherever God has seen fit to lead you, please be well. And Lord, keep him safe. This I ask you as your humble servant.*

Galienne fell asleep less than five minutes later.

* * *

It was proving difficult to stay awake after all, despite how much Perceval had on his inquisitive mind.

Baudwin left him alone in the cathedral, returning to his own work in his chambers. Perceval had little inkling of what such work might entail; he was still uncertain of just what to say or how to behave in a house of God.

The feeling that eyes were upon him remained with him since he departed Gawaine's company and gone inside. Now, hours later, the pews, the stained glass, the decorations, the podium with its immense, illustrated Bible, all sat achingly silent, as though awaiting Perceval's next word or motion.

Yet nothing came. He sat there equally silent, no more confident of himself than he'd been at Haughmond Abbey. At least the monks and nuns were not watching him now.

It felt as though they were, though. Maybe it was the shadows. Without direct sunlight, the colorful glass mosaics behind the lectern could not glow, their images reduced to mere dream-like wisps of dark blues, reds, yellows. The only other source of light came from the rows of candles criss-crossing the pews. Perceval thought Melangell the smith would have been quite impressed by the huge holders they had; they looked like giant iron candlesticks to him, taller than himself.

Perhaps that was it, then; this place felt mightier, more important than he did himself. Maybe it was that he was the only one having a vigil this night. Perceval guessed that it had

been a bit easier for the mass of candidates present when Llascoit stayed the night here. They could not speak either, but just
the sight of others in the room must have helped them stay
awake. *And how would anyone know if I dozed off?* he wondered.
That made him edgy as well. Might Baudwin come storming
back into the room if he heard snoring? Or someone stationed
outside? Perceval knew a rotating shift of knights would man
the cathedral's entrance during the night, peeking in periodically
to make sure that whomever wished to join their numbers remained conscious.

His growing fatigue played games with him. Perceval's
mind decided it would be fun to show him image after image
of his life. And so he struggled to stay on his feet, never sitting
for more than a few minutes at a time, watching his mental the-
ater performing the past. Running deer, quiescent sheep, finely
forged weapons, dozens of names and faces, places within deep
woods, high atop hillsides, paths linking all. The barrage of
scenes combined with his fatigue made linear thought extremely
difficult; it became circular instead, jumping from one to the
next with no particular semblance of order.

All along he continued to question his worthiness. Was
all the training enough? Did he deserve to wear spurs and mail,
carry sword and shield? Could he possess the right to do justice
and make decisions affecting the lives of others? He hoped so.

Amidst his thoughts, he dimly heard the sound of a large
door opening. At first he was too tired to care.

But then other sounds followed the first. Noises far off,
yet still perceivable. Talking, perhaps some singing. The clank-
ing of mail as its wearer walked. Was it the city guards, or his
watch changing hands?

So why did the door stand open, letting in such sounds
in the first place?

Perceval remained sitting for a brief time in one of the pews. Then he stood, and walked toward the main doors. The right one was open just enough to let in a single person, along with the noises, which were significantly fewer and quieter than when he and Gawaine walked together. Perceval hoped this meant much time had passed; he wasn't sure how many more hours his stamina could last. He never spent an entire night awake before, not even in the woods.

"How goes the vigil?" the whisper said.

Perceval wanted to shout a response, just to make more noise. Then he remembered the rules. He followed the voice. It was quiet enough to prevent his ascertaining so much as the gender of the speaker. Curiosity alone could keep one on one's toes, so he tried to get as close to the voice as he could.

"I know you can't reply," whisper came again, "so I'll be brief and then on my way. It's almost dawn, and I have the bishop's own permission to bring you something. You can't drink it till it gets light, though."

Perceval inched his way ever nearer, trying to guess just who this person was, and why he or she would bring him anything. He could just make out a figure, a mere shadow. The shadow held something in one hand.

Perceval shrugged, hoping the meaning would be conveyed.

"It's an elixir of sorts. It might remind you of home. Back in Cambria we used to break our fasts with this."

He took the small clay vessel, bowing just slightly to show his thanks. His intent was understood. "You're most welcome," the shade said. Still no facial detail could be made out, but Perceval noticed that the voice was correct: outside, the slightest glowing tinge of what would grow into a pleasant day rolled its way through the darkness. He was almost finished.

Without another word, the shadow disappeared out the door. Perceval watched it leave, noticing a discreetly feminine hint to the walk. The person was shorter than him, as well, suggesting a woman or somebody younger than him.

It was likely his imagination playing tricks again; the guards had no reason to let in a woman.

Sure enough, a knight peered around the door, checking on the man within. Perceval recognized the face after a moment: Sir Gaheris, the knight he fought with just a few days previously. He hoped there would be no grudge about that.

Perceval took the vessel inside, and returned to his still warm pew. Before setting it on the floor, he sniffed at it once. The scent was immediate and identifiable: apple juice, laced with cinnamon. He hadn't tasted any since he first left Oerfa. Apple juice by itself, yes; it was common enough all through the land. But the added spice he only knew at home.

It was silent then, too, when he told his mother of his ambitions.

He sat down again, confident in his sneak preview of the coming morning that he would not fall asleep now. So there was someone else from Cambria in Camelot, so what? Camelot had residents from lands far more distant and even completely foreign. He remained there, losing track of time and thought.

He could not take his eyes from the earthen goblet. He sat transfixed by it until the doors opened again, Baudwin leading the way into the church.

Perceval's first thought was of where the other door outside might be. Yet this was quickly extinguished by the sight of how many people were outside. Where did they all come from? And where did the intervening time go?

He stood at once, nodding to the bishop as he strode up alongside him. "You did it! I wondered if you might myself, but you really did it. Few can stay up a whole night shrouded in darkness. Come, Perceval. Your king awaits."

Perceval could still feel the blood after it rushed up to his brain. The fatigue was upon him, and now he had to face King

Arthur, and look good doing so. He ran his hands through his hair, feeling the inches added to it in recent seasons.

It was a pointless gesture. Gawaine and Llascoit were upon him, literally lifting him by the shoulders and carting him outside. The sunlight hurt his unready eyes at once. "Wait!" he shouted. "My drink." He vainly reached behind him.

"I'll fetch it," Baudwin said, and Perceval was brought fully into the awaiting audience.

It was like nothing he envisioned. A hundred souls, at least, had to be there, all looking at him. He tried to recognize someone, anyone. Had they all come to see him knighted?

Was that Lupinia? Where's Llio, since her brother's obviously gotten up in time? What of the King and Queen? He was giddy and terrified all at once.

Lucan was there. It took Perceval a moment to recognize the voice. "– from the realm of Powys to the northwest, to be made knight by His Majesty King Arthur, on this day in the year of our Lord –" Perceval tried to hear the rest, but already Lucan was drowned out by the cheers of those assembled.

"And you already survived this! No wonder you wanted to be here this early," Perceval said to Llascoit.

"Oh, you've yet to experience the best part," Llascoit answered. Perceval decided he didn't trust the tone, and looked to Gawaine. Arthur's nephew's expression had too many grinning teeth in it to make him any more at ease.

"To the bath with him!" shouted Gawaine, and they all but dragged him back into the cathedral.

It was darker again, his eyes protesting. "Wait! There's no bath in here. And where's my cup?"

"Following you," Baudwin said. "We did consider your privacy, as we do that of all new knights, and those who receive baptism, on that account."

"And I'm surprised at you," Gawaine said. "We talked of the plunge last night on our way here."

"Yes, but where? Not in front of all those people!" Perceval hardly wanted his ceremony to be a public display of what Llio called his "naughty parts."

"In here, lad," Baudwin said. Now it was just the few of them, though muffled rambunctious talk filtered through the doors from outside.

Baudwin led them to a door out of sight from the main part of the church, behind the dais where worshippers gathered to sing God's praises. He opened the door, and it swung gently inward, leading to a dimly lit stairway of perfectly fitted stones. Perceval wanted to ask when the torches along the wall had been lit, but feared the bishop's reprimand for what might have been God's own work. The candidate didn't realize that monks had to live somewhere, too, and that some of them rose very early from their short slumbers in the cathedral's basement.

At the entrance to the stairway, the odd trio halted, Llascoit already on the first step. "Well, come on," he said, not wanting to waste any time. At least he was behaving more gently than some of the knights who had roused him and the others during the mass knighting in which he took part.

Gawaine hesitated at the top of the stairs. "We'll get him there right enough. The old arm still hurts a bit sometimes." He would never publicly admit to the fear he felt when Gaheris ventured forth into the escape route from the strange haunted castle in the wastes; what if that passage had led nowhere? That same trepidation came upon him now.

Gawaine shrugged aside the image of his dying out in the middle of nowhere in particular of a stupid crossbow wound, and positioned himself on the stairwell, his brawny arms wrapped around Perceval. Clumsily they made their way down, Gawaine chuckling to himself at the image: he thought the top-heavy trio maneuvered with all the unified grace of fornicating cattle.

The four of them made it to the bottom hallway after much panting and crass comment-making (as much as Baudwin would tolerate in what he considered "his" church). There, the hall continued on past several empty cells, the monks nowhere in sight. Baudwin had instructed them to see to their affairs until after this was finished. They had readied the tub, then left. At any rate, the bishop did not want them soaked in the ordeal; it was all too easy to catch a bad chill down here.

After the cells, the hall led into a circular room, which Baudwin explained was for song practice or transcription. The monks sheltered themselves from the world here, preserving and recopying priceless texts which would otherwise not likely survive. Aristotle's *Poetics*. Plato's *Symposium* and *Phaedrus*. Manifestos detailing expenditures of the Empire when it was still at its peak (the Romans recorded everything, it seemed). The Gospels, some copies with lovely illustrations by recent converts in regions like Eire-land. The epics of Homer. The poems of Horace and Ovid. The histories of Herodotus and Thucydides and Ptolemy.   Even a smattering of notes recorded of a sermon supposedly given by Jesus himself, not far from Dumnonia. Baudwin refused to let go of that piece, even though the Papacy would declare it heretical, along with Pelagius' notion of the human will and even the tales of the Grail. Rome sought religious relics, but the Grail had too many Pagan sentiments for them to take seriously, and it also bordered on idolatry.

And it appealed to women; clearly it had to be stamped out.

Now the signs of the monks' work lay aside, within their rooms. It was too much of a chance for them to get wet.

Perceval almost laughed when he saw the tub. It was just a converted barrel, probably once full of wine, standing upright. Baudwin insisted the monks in his charge live in the poverty preached by Christ, and so they bathed, rarely, within the old barrel. Perceval briefly wondered what became of the wine itself.

"Good thing he's not in armor," Llascoit said.

"Aye to that, lad. Let's get him in, before we have to listen to any more of his protests." Gawaine loved this moment; he relished seeing candidates at their most vulnerable, willing to listen to any words of wisdom the knights had to offer.

"Recall what we talked of last night," he said simply. "And remember. The King once told me that evil is the only result for those who forget what's important."

"Yes, Perceval, note the words of Sir Gawaine. You'd do well to remember something for once." Llascoit's tone was far too full of humor for Perceval's taste.

"This coming from you, of course," answered Perceval, trying to ignore that he was being dragged ever closer to the barrel. He could see the water, almost up to the rim, looking colder than the pond in which Llio taught him to swim.

"So, Perceval," Gawaine said, "shall we rip the clothing from you like you were some tasty whore, or shall you peacefully disrobe yourself?" Baudwin ignored the comment, still thinking of the Church and how it decided which relics and artifacts were genuine holy treasures and which were false icons. What might it say of Excalibur?

"Since you put it that way, if you'll let me down, I'll oblige you."

Gawaine and Llascoit helped him to stand again, having carried him by each pair of limbs thus far. Then they both walked to the front of the hallway.

"Oh, come off it, gentlemen. Wherever would I run, especially naked?"

"You never know," Llascoit said, grinning his playful toothy expression.

Baudwin recalled himself, and took over the ceremony, such as it was, while Perceval quickly took off the few articles he was wearing. The floor was quite chilly, and he wanted to get this part of it over with.

"Perceval, on behalf of His Majesty King Arthur, I have been instructed to tell you the following."

The two knights picked him up again and now held him next to the waiting barrel of rainwater. "Yes, Your Grace?" Anything delaying his soak might be worth hearing, despite his nudity.

"Are you prepared to accept the responsibility laid upon you, as you take the high honor of knighthood?"

Perceval relaxed somewhat, his squirming forgotten for the moment. Llascoit and Gawaine eased their grips on him, just supporting him now.

A flurry of images ran through his mind. The stags. Eager chases. The women he had known and loved, each in a different way. It was still so easy to question his worth.

It was no time for insecurity. He'd waited so long for this! "I am, Bishop Baudwin. I take responsibility as the King's own man."

"Then let this bath cleanse your former life from you, and wash away your boyhood. When you come from it, you will be a man."

Does that mean no one will call me "boy" *anymore?* It was the last thought Perceval had before every inch of his skin met a chill going to the core of his bones.

Llascoit and Gawaine grinned menacingly at one another, holding Perceval beneath the water's surface. The barrel was narrow enough to prevent his loosing their grip and coming up on his own.

Perceval opened his eyes, as Llio taught him he could do underwater. He had been terrified to do so then, thinking the water would hurt. It did, but just for a moment. Now he did it as second nature, watching the bubbles from his nose float upward. The four hands gripping his shoulders were strong but yielding, and he felt confident that they would let him surface at his leisure.

His body already began to fight off the water's cool edge, letting him take actual pleasure in being held in a vat of it. It did feel oddly cleansing, and not only from the perspective of bathing. *A man*, Baudwin said. Perceval had once been made man by the blood of the hunt. A second occasion of manhood was his first time in the arms of a woman. He hoped that really was her in the crowd. Llio wouldn't miss this!

And now the third time, in an old wine barrel, the strangest of them all, yet that which would be taken most seriously because of the station which awaited him once he left it. Armor and spurs. A title and the King's tasks. No one would question him any more. He would be a knight, valiant and true.

A volume of bubbles large enough to tickle his nose as they left rose up now, as Perceval chuckled.

The third time. Gornymant and his three points. And he grasped the hands on his shoulders, letting them hoist him from the purifying bath water.

It was like reemerging from the womb. Perceval was sure he could suddenly recall that triumphant escape, covered with sticky blood and coming forth to the cries of a pained but then relieved and thankful mother, mingled with his own terrified yowls of receiving the first glimpse of an uncertain world.

Perceval found the image so oddly tranquil that Gawaine and Llascoit had to help him fully out of the barrel, easing him back onto the floor.

"You didn't fall asleep in there, did you?" Gawaine said.

Perceval opened his eyes, focusing on the other men and the small cluster of rooms lit faintly by the ensconced candles. He saw there were no hour-lines on those candles; the monks passed untold hours down here without counting them, at peace with their work. "No. Of course not."

Baudwin was struck most by the young man's calm, as though this all came so naturally to him. Often, candidates were visibly edgy about their initiations, having listened too well to stories about how they might be treated.

But Arthur, as lord, was different. He took this process very seriously.

"Get you dressed, then," Baudwin told Perceval softly. "They're waiting."

Near the barrel stood an unadorned wooden bureau, in which the monks kept the pieces for basic purposes: tools for the cutting of tonsures, extra rope for their robes, a store of expensive paper and leather binding for books. For this day, it also held a white robe. Baudwin removed it and held it out for Perceval.

"I'm to wear this?" he asked.

"White is pure and true, what every knight should be. It's the same fabric we clothe babies in for their baptisms."

Instead of protesting or showing his usual concern for his lack of Christian faith, Perceval took the simple garment and slipped it around him, securing it with the length of hemp cord Baudwin proffered.

"Cheers," Llascoit said triumphantly.

"Let's be off with you then," added Gawaine, who sounded vaguely disappointed that Perceval had not offered them more resistance.

The four of them remounted the stairs and made for the cathedral's exit.

* * *

Camelot's young nursemaid told herself she was just coming to make sure that the men in her care were still doing all right by themselves. But she had to admit her own curiosity. Despite what her mother told her about knights, this was quite a spectacle. The King and Queen were bedecked in their fineries. Some other knights brought their retainers. Banners of the King and his courtiers whipped proudly in the morning wind, and several women giggled and gossiped about the "handsome new lad come to be made knight by Arthur's own hand."

One of the women stood out, however. The healer decided she could not possibly be much more than sixteen, if that. And she was trying, rather poorly, to conceal what she carried at her side: a long sword, looking both quite lethal and expensive. She was clearly attempting to draw little attention to herself.

It was impossible to catch all of the talk, but here and there clear snippets came to her. "He vanquished Meliagrant! Don't you remember how he threatened the Queen?" "Wasn't he with the sword maiden?" "Look! Even Lancelot has shown this day." "Why is Kay's arm slung?"

The nurse followed the reference to Kay, and she once again concerned herself with his wellness. He looked quite recovered, and she was certain his arm would heal much quicker than his pride. The healer watched and waited with the others, of whom she knew almost none at all. Then she decided it would really be worthwhile to learn the name of this young man.

After all, she had brought him a sampling of her finest juice not an hour earlier, having heard of his homeland.

* * *

Perceval thought he'd go blind, more by the spectacle of so many than the bright sunlight warming the city. And again he met the cheers unprepared. Did all knights confront this?

The thought that this was all for him made him nervous. What would his mother have ascribed this to? Vanity? One of the deadly sins. But he did not ask these people to attend his ceremony. And after all, the swearing of a man was seen as cause for celebration and intrigue; Perceval didn't much care for the way a number of the men, in addition to a variety of women, eyed him as he was gently but firmly brought out of Saint Dubric's.

He decided to try and pick out as many familiar faces as he could. Bedivere was easy, standing off to one side with his arms folded, his face bright and excited at the anticipation of a new brother-in-arms. So too was Kay, his arm hanging uselessly in front of him, supported by a fabric sling.

Was that Lupinia? No, too large. Lupinia would probably go mad if ever she put on the weight of age. Where's Llio? There are so many of them winking at me! Who's that lord, you'd think he wanted me for his own. And, no, it couldn't be... There's the Queen. And Lancelot, never quite far from her side, looking morose as ever. I must ask him of his daughter soon. Wait, I think...

He missed the signal which politely informed the throng that silence was now in order, and strained to hear what the herald read from the outstretched scroll, standing next to the King. Perceval could only think of how much he wished right then to ask Arthur if he had heard from Galienne. By now he supposed it might be a foolish gesture, and might not rate highly with Llio, for that matter. She all but figured the girl for dead. So, like that night in Bridgnorth, he held his tongue. One's knighting was certainly no time for a flippant lip.

Perceval focused on the herald, a young man draped in ornate robes of sky blue. He continued reading the scroll, of which Perceval picked up bits and pieces. "– to which our sovereign, King Arthur, lord of Logres, chief Dragon of Britain, unifier of the Great Tribes, is rightfully minded to raise –"

Perceval lost it then for a few seconds, then was surprised to find attention once more in his direction. Some applauded.

"– of Powys, in the heartland of our sovereign neighbor to the West –" At mention of Perceval's name, a woman's shout, almost a scream akin to those released by Llio during the times Llascoit complained of being kept awake, came from the far side of the crowd. Some turned to look at this woman, but Perceval could still not see her, as she was to the rear, one of those who would be first to walk to the tournament field where the actual knighting would take place.

"– on this blessed day receive the honor which is rightly his." Perceval still had his doubts; could all this really be for him?

"That's our cue," Gawaine said, who grasped his arm again and began to lead him westward, to the applause of the onlookers.

"Why are there so many of them?" Perceval said sheepishly, letting his arms go slack while the two knights escorted him.

"There can't be more than a few dozen, and they're curious. People in this city like to do and see things, no matter if it's a new knight or a recent shipment of spices and dyes from the East. They like to be informed, and to know what goes on in their kingdom. No other king has fostered that like my uncle. And don't let it go to your head; thousands of others are busy with other matters today." Gawaine sounded proud to be part of it all, to have achieved no small status in a realm much different than any preceding it, different now than even ten years before.

"Look at it this way: when else in your life do you think you might have this much attention?"

"At least you got the advantage of safety in numbers, Llas. Who says I want this much attention?"

"Perceval! Perceval!" The cheers became repetitive shouts. Was this the reward for getting lucky with one javelin blow at a man so unbalanced by rage that he became an easy foe?

"Stop doubting yourself. You've earned this." Llascoit's comment caught him unaware; he forgot sometimes how well Gornymant's son could read him. Llio, too. He wished his teacher could have seen this day, but Llio said he kept busy with new students.

"And did I earn all this attention? Why is everyone so interested in me?"

Gawaine's grip on Perceval's arm slackened slightly, due to his surprise. "What's wrong with the attention? For the next few days, you're going to be all these folk talk about. Enjoy it while it lasts." Gawaine was not always opposed to it like Lancelot was.

"Why couldn't this ceremony be smaller?"

"Your foster brother here was involved in a ceremony many times this size."

"And how many men were sworn that day, Sir Gawaine? A hundred?"

"Hardly," Llas said. "And there were other events going on as well."

"Exactly. So why should I be paraded in front of so many now?"

"Because knights are so damned important, Perceval!" Gawaine retorted in a more gruff tone. "Because we're the ones who made life so good for these people. We protect them, defend them, give them lands to work and the right to their share of the rewards. We keep the peace so everyone else can prosper."

Perceval dimly recalled the classical philosophy Gornymant made him read. Plato called them the *Guardians*, the central structure of his three-tiered society. Protectors, a security force, even an offensive army: they were charged with all these duties. And that was precisely what Arthur's knights did. The tasks and quests he assigned to them were rarely of a military nature now, but his men were respected, if not outright feared, across the land. How many treasures had they brought back from faraway lands? How many disputes had they judged, sparing the bloodshed often resulting in the absence of such rulings? How many times had the Pendragon banner rallied people of different tribes, opposed cultures, even conflicting faiths, to the single cause of defending Britain and allowing its continued growth? Britons, they now called themselves, throughout Logres.

"But leading me off like this is so embarrassing."

"Did you learn nothing during your training? Of course, you hardly could have, it was so rushed. That's part of what fascinates people about you: you slew Meliagrant at a time in your life when most young men are lucky to be squires."

"What about that, then? Who will be my squire?" Perceval didn't want anyone else to look after. The only person who ever felt like a squire to him was Galienne; he wanted no one else to fill such a role.

"Stop worrying about it," Gawaine said. "And you studied, with no one but Llascoit and his father, and in just a few seasons, you're back roaming the countryside, doing the King's work without realizing it. Did you know he's had some of us try and hunt down Clamadeus before? And you're the one who pulled it off."

The trio led the curious throng. Arthur and his Queen led those who followed. The whole affair seemed just another bright day in Camelot; the world's problems could wait, for within this city life felt different. Purposeful. Tranquil.

It seemed only Perceval fretted over it. "Don't these folk know my successes are due more to luck than anything else?"

"Damn it, Perceval, when are you going to start thanking fate for what it's brought you? No matter your faith and station, I think we all come out evenly in the end. Knights have privileges and rights, more than most others. You have the gifts to be a great knight. You're already one hell of a warrior."

"So how do we come out evenly?"

Llascoit jumped in. "We do tend to die young. But better to live short and accomplish much than live long and die in obscurity."

"Exactly," pronounced Gawaine. "That's why we lead you west, to the melee field. In the old days, west was the direction of wisdom and knowledge. So keep in mind what you've learned."

"I'll try."

* * *

Galienne actually was glad to hear the other woman shriek, whoever she was. It would help keep attention focused away from her, which was precisely what she wished now. Her father was here, and would recognize her at once, but she wanted to remain hidden longer.

She watched her father, and those who fluttered around him, mostly young boys and older girls. Before such people adopted a more mature object of faith, she supposed he *was* their god. The eternal hero, flawless. Worship only ceased when imperfections revealed themselves.

And to Galienne he looked as wretched as ever. Not evil or malicious, nor the gallant example of male perfection so many saw in him. She began to think that his handling of her mother's love was simple ignorance. Lancelot, for all his glory and achievement, really had no idea how to deal with women.

And what of the other woman? Was that Llio? She didn't look like Perceval's description. She was shorter, and dressed in the clothes of someone just getting by. And why would she yell like that?

Whatever the case, it was irrelevant now. Galienne had made it here, at last! She would greet Perceval as soon as he was dubbed, perhaps locate Lupinia, maybe talk to the King and the bishop...

She kept shrugging her left shoulder back occasionally, still thinking it would help hide the sword she had drawn from a withered tree. If she bumped into Kay, she could only imagine what punishment he'd find her worthy of for carrying a concealed weapon in the presence of the King.

She heard a gasp nearby. Was that the same woman who sounded so faint of heart earlier? Curiously, Galienne turned toward the sound, then was greeted by a familiar voice.

"Good Lord! Is that you?" The commentary went unnoticed by most, who still paraded toward the field.

Galienne turned and looked into the face of her old friend, somehow even lovelier than the last time they'd seen each other. "Lupinia," she said quietly.

The taller woman rushed forward and embraced her childhood friend warmly and tightly. Galienne could smell the perfume she wore, like heather on a spring morning. "Where have you been for so long? I've worried so about you."

"Busy," was all she could think to say, pulling herself away, not wanting to miss the ceremony. "We'll have to talk about it all soon."

"Damn right," interjected Lupinia, resorting to her old callous talk, the kind she knew she could only get away with in front of certain persons. Galienne had never minded it, despite her piety. Lupinia attended mass fairly often, even the occasional confessional. "You've come to see all of this, then?" Lupy said. "Isn't that the boy we met when we took care of his dog and horse?"

"The same."

"And you've been traveling with him all this time? Galienne, I never would have thought you, of all people –"

"Stop it," Galienne said coolly. "It's not like that at all." She knew too well the sorts of thoughts Lupinia would have of any young man and woman running about the countryside together, and she would not have her intimate times with Perceval perverted into so much gossipy lust.

"Oh, far be it from me to judge," Lupinia said.

Galienne wanted to be apart from her old friend now. Suddenly Lupinia seemed shallow, restrictive. She hadn't changed, just become more of a prize in the eyes of who-knew-how-many suitors. "Lupy, what about you? Haven't you found that rich husband yet?"

"The richest are all spoken for, not to say I haven't tried. Though there are so many which might prove worth my efforts." She paused, grinning. "Perhaps I should try Lancelot on for size. After all, didn't we always say a girl should know what it is she shops for before settling on a price?"

Lord, Lupy, you cheapen it so. And you *always said that, not* we. "Then I wish you luck." She was about to move on, guilty for how she felt about the woman who showed her the wonders of Camelot, but she had to reach Perceval.

She had a sudden thought, seeing the people begin to form a more or less organized curve around the center of the field. "Lupinia, did you hear that woman who shouted when Perceval's name was mentioned?"

"Yes, how could I miss it? She's that one over there, see? Wearing the blue gown, there," she pointed. Lupinia was not one to forget a face or a body.

"Do you know who she is?" Galienne found herself once again counting on her friend's ability to know who was who in this vast urbanity.

"I haven't heard her name, but I saw her doting on Kay and Gawaine. Oh, and Gaheris, too."

That wasn't what she wanted to hear; she didn't need Lupinia's assessment of the woman's flirting skill.

Hearing her sigh, Lupinia said, "To use your words, 'it's not like that at all.' She's a healer. Every time she's spoken to the knights, she's sought Baudwin out, and he oversees the hospital."

How does one acquire such skill in knowing some useful bit of nothing about everyone? "Thanks. I need to catch up."

"You go right ahead, Galienne. Whatever it *is* like, that Perceval is turning out to be quite a man, even if he still looks like a peasant farmer. In the meantime, I'll be talking to Lancelot."

Galienne started to jog towards the crowd, taking care that the sword didn't make noise or become too visible. Then she turned. "Oh, Lupy?"

"Yes, love?"

"Call me Galahad."

She went on to see the knighting, never turning to see the bewildered look on the other woman's face.

* * *

Perceval was about ready to pee his britches, except he had none, just a smock of white cloth which he thought left little to the onlooker's imagination. Gawaine and Llascoit held him firm, though there was no need. King Arthur and his entourage had arrived and taken their places. They formed as though attending a tournament, the crowd filling into the seats overlooking the field, the royal party assembling into the main pavilion. The eyes of many had to strain to catch any view of what would happen next, for the activity was restricted to the pavilion and immediate area in front, where knight's chargers brought them to clash against one another in the jousts.

Not today, though. Arthur waited until everyone had a chance to seat themselves, and grinned just slightly as he saw Perceval begin to shiver. At least there was no indication in the sky of further chilly weather. Indeed, the day had already shown promise of being quite pleasant, even warm.

When the Queen and various famous knights retired to their appropriate places within the pavilion for a full view of what would transpire, Arthur waved his herald aside, and addressed the onlookers himself. His voice commanded instant silence, and carried the undeniable tone of authority and purpose.

"Fellow citizens of Camelot," he said, "on this excellent day am I, Arthur, King of all Britain, of the mind to initiate this latest candidate to the station and title of knight." Several seconds of deafening cheer immediately followed this. Arthur waited for them to calm down, watching Perceval.

The candidate never stopped scanning the crowd, looking hopeful but uncertain. Arthur wondered who he might be looking for. Perceval said that Galienne had disappeared, and Lancelot confirmed this, giving up the search for her himself after many days. Perceval also mentioned that he had no family he knew of anymore, at least no one who would attend his knighting. The King suspected a young love somewhere in the stands.

Llio watched her lover intently, looking almost wretched in his white robe and serious expression. She silently thanked her brother for his assistance with the brush, as she held the gift she had purchased for Perceval at her feet. She carried it this far draped over her shoulder in a leather pack. It grew cumbersome that way, and she was glad to have it off her back and on the sturdy wooden beams of the stands. She listened as the ceremony progressed.

"Some of you have seen this man before today, and I have little doubt you've all heard of him by now," Arthur continued. "But today it is my personal pleasure to introduce to the citizens of Camelot, Perceval of Powys, vanquisher of my own enemies Sirs Meliagrant and Clamadeus, a young man who has already proven his worth to me on more than a single occasion. He hails from the hills of Cambria, and it was due to his chance encounter with members of the Round Table that the sacred order of knighthood became his true calling. With my thanks to God do I most proudly proceed with proclaiming Perceval knight."

More cheers ensued, including those from three women who had never met, who all had their own feelings for the man in front of them. Galienne wanted to rush right up to the royal pavilion; she could scarcely believe that no one other than Lupinia recognized her. Lancelot was also there, though, and she still had little inkling just what to say to him. And Llio, looking around the people herself, as Perceval continued to do, searched for any other recognizable faces. She picked out Lupinia among them. Then finally the woman in blue, whose gaze shifted from Perceval to Kay to Gawaine to Gaheris, then back again. Like the other two, she could barely contain her budding excitement.

All of this was lost on the man at the center of the attention. Perceval had finally overcome most of his apprehension at feeling put on display, and now felt the joy he had hoped would reach him when this day finally arrived. And now it was here. He would be knighted! And later he could find Llio, and celebrate with his new brother knights; oh, how glorious he felt! Never mind his unresolved relationships, and the evils he'd heard about through the land, and the meaning of Pellam's dinner party; he would be knight now, at last! Perceval's eyes began to moisten, and he blinked rapidly to ward off happy tears.

"Perceval, kneel before me," commanded the King. Perceval strode up to his future liege, climbing the steps to the front of the pavilion. He knelt, smiling even as he watched the wooden floor in anticipation. Gawaine and Llascoit remained at the front of the audience, also kneeling in the presence of the King, who faced the crowd. Perceval's back was to them.

"Perceval, do you swear to acknowledge me as your sole and rightful liege?"

"I do, my lord," came the proud response, audible to all in attendance.

"And do you further swear to uphold the good name of knighthood, knowing that in her name shall you be required to mete justice at any time, in any place, throughout my kingdom?"

"I do so swear."

"I would remind you, Perceval, that the path of knight-hood is one of continual trial and hardship. Knights know he-roic deeds, great riches, and special privileges, but these do not come without cost. I make only those men knights who dis-play loyalty, bravery, leadership, fairness, and, above all, honesty. Truth is most important. Tell me why."

Perceval looked up at him, suddenly flushed. "W-why, sire?"

"Yes."

Perceval considered it a few moments, feeling the intan-gible weight of so many curious eyes upon him. This was like Gornymant requesting poetry. "Well?"

"Without truth, not only the law but life itself is be-trayed and doomed. A person must be true first to self, then to liege, and finally," he paused, uncomfortable now. Baudwin sat in the pavilion, awaiting the obvious response.

"Finally to whom, Perceval?" Arthur queried.

"To Creation," he said. He thought it the most honest, least offensive answer he could offer.

"Very well. In turn, I, as your liege, do swear upon this most precious artifact," he drew Excalibur, its metallic singing in echoes across the field as it left the scabbard, "to protect you, honor you, and reward you, as befits a knight. Be true then, knight, ever valorous and vigilant."

Arthur brought the sword close to Perceval, resting it just above his shoulder. He then began his favorite incantation, planting the flat edge of the sword on the candidate's shoulders, shifting from left to right with each mention of a holy name. Arthur's voice could be heard by some of those still in the city, such was the command and volume to his tone. "In the name of God, Sovereignty, Saint Michael, and Saint George, I dub you knight and grant you the power and right to wear armor and spurs, wield sword and lance, and in the name of truth and goodness, bring justice and compassion to all those you encounter while in my service." The blade came to rest on Perceval's right shoulder, having arced over his head three times. Murmurs and encouraging gasps emitted from the crowd.

"Arise, Sir Perceval, and take your place as a knight of the realm of Logres." With that, the crowd got to its feet in an explosion of excited sound and fanfare. Perceval's own legs felt like they would never rise again, but he hoisted himself up to look into the face of the man for whom he knew he would gladly die. He could see so much in that face: kindness, trust, pride, determination. A slight weariness. Arthur had been at this since before Perceval's own birth. "Thank you, my liege and king," he said. Arthur smiled at him. It was enough.

Already the crowd was filing down from the stands, most of them heading back to Camelot with another excuse to either work hard that day or spend it carousing. Arthur saw some of the others heading for the pavilion, and while he still had Perceval to himself, he wished to do one more thing. "Perceval, thank you. You've been of immeasurable help already. Because you've earned the title not just once, but really twice, in your handling of some of this kingdom's laundry, I have a surprise for you. Gawaine," he signaled, and the eldest son of Lothian went up the pavilion with Llascoit.

"My lord, what is it?" But the King would only smile at him again.

Perceval stared at where the two other knights went, rummaging behind the curtains of the pavilion. He hadn't realized there was a storage area back there. Nor did he quite comprehend what Arthur meant by "laundry," not knowing what the cleaning of clothes had to do with running a kingdom.

But when Gawaine and Llascoit emerged they carried the brightest manifestation of chain-link armor Perceval had yet seen, complete with spurs and a sword belt.

The new knight was awe-struck. He wanted to hug the King for thinking this highly of him. "F-for me?" he said quietly.

"Who else? Lancelot told me of your misfortune at the river, and I had the armorers produce it. Did you think your lady friend took your measurements solely for new clothes?" He grinned yet again, savoring every minute.

Perceval shook his head. "I should have known, Sire. About Llio, I mean."

The King gestured behind them. "Yes, you should have," said the amused voice. They both turned to see Llio, still holding a bundle of her own. "And when you finish donning your new armor, perhaps you might find space for these?"

She curtsied gracefully to the King. "My Lord," she added, setting the parcel down and extracting a crimson surcoat, stitched by her own hands. Perceval reached over to her and felt the material; it was smooth and inviting, like Llio's skin. "Llio, I don't know what to say." He was again on the verge of weeping.

"Say 'thank you,' but it's not over yet." She then playfully fumbled about in the sack some more. As she pulled out the shield, she motioned to her brother, who held the armor with Gawaine. "You can thank Llas' artistry for this," she said. The shield was of the standard kite design, a wooden frame reinforced with iron around the edges, with strong leather hand grips inside. Its field was painted to match the shade of the surcoat, and within the field was the likeness of a single rose. Its petals stood in colorful contrast to the background: white, with the stem and a few thorns in the appropriate shade of green.

"The rose was my idea," Llio said. "You mentioned Meliagrant's shield was the color of one, but I chose white for the flower for purity."

"I should've referred to the loveliness of such a flower in that poem your father had me compose for you. Dare I ask what the thorns mean, or do they appear just for accuracy?"

"I'm glad you asked. The white is for purity of spirit, while the thorns are the trials you meet as a knight. I suppose our good King considers two of those thorns removed. My lord," she said, and offered another bow.

"Lady Llio," the King answered. Then to Perceval, "Don't lose her, sir knight; she's as rare a find as the flower she commissioned for your shield."

Perceval knew the only way to keep from wailing like some hungry infant was to rush forth and embrace Llio. "Thank you," he muttered, mostly into her hair. "I love you."

"I'm so proud of you," she answered, kissing him. "Maybe you can talk to Father soon," she said, teasing with her eyes as much as her lips.

With those who remained at the scene so involved, the tone one of joy and triumph, the healer decided it was time to make her appearance. She trepidatiously walked over to behind Perceval and the woman he clearly adored, and as calmly as possible said, "On the matter of roses, Perceval, do you remember the one Tathan showed us as children? You thought it so beautiful and precious, and I was just curious if you could still imagine it now?"

Perceval turned to the speaker, and Llio at once felt his arms sagging behind her, their energy dissipated. "Dindraine?" he intoned, very sheepishly.

There were tears in the healer's eyes. *Yes,* she nodded.

Perceval opened his mouth to say something and couldn't; it dried up somehow. "Sister?" he finally managed.

"Yes, bone-head. And it's a good thing these people care enough about you to outfit you properly, since you've never been able to take care of your gear."

Perceval, feeling suddenly proper, waited until Llio had also turned towards Dindraine. "Llio, this is my sister. Dindraine." It was all he could manage before running to her.

Llio was in the midst of saying "how do you do" but it all turned to laughter as she watched Perceval wrap his whole body around his sister and wrestle her to the ground, the pair of them giggling like children of crawling age.

"So now, witch, will you turn me into a toad for tackling you?"

"I'm not a witch, I'm a healer. And besides, the damage is done, for toad you are. And you didn't even thank me for your refreshment early this morning."

"That was you?"

"Of course, silly, though I thought you were just another lost soul from Cambria." And she laughed with him, rolling on the ground with not a care in the world for dignity, and pecking him on the nose like she used to. "Come, Perceval, is this really how a new knight is expected to behave in front of his liege?"

Perceval's expressions waxed serious instantly, so quickly that Dindraine found humor in that as well. "No," he said, then stood, bringing her upright with him. He turned toward the King, Queen, and assembled dignitaries. "My lord, I apologize, it's been quite a busy day."

"Pay it no heed, lad," said the King. "You should have seen the way I went about when I earned my own title."

"Thank you, sire. May my judgment approach the compassion of your own." He watched as Arthur turned and strode back to his escort, and his Queen.

Dindraine giggled at him. "If Mother could have heard you say that. Such the knightly diction!"

"I had a good teacher."

"As did I."

"That reminds me. I've been wanting to ask you of that for a while. Do you know what Tathan told me about that?"

Dindraine only shrugged, teasing him.

"Come," Llio said. "Let's all retire to my father's place within the city. There's much celebration to take care of."

"Your father has a holding here?" Dindraine said.

"It's a long tale," Llascoit added, walking off the pavilion with Perceval's armor. "But we've plenty of time, for once. Here," he said, piling the mail into Perceval's suddenly outstretched arms. "It's yours. You carry it."

"Perhaps I should reconsider the issue of a squire."

They laughed at that, even the King and Queen, whose entourage was already heading back to the city. The excitement of the moment enraptured each, reminding them of what it was to be part of Logres. So often did these people feel caught up, swept away, by the revolutions of time's unforgiving wheels, that they relished the chance to simply enjoy the morning and the happiness that it brought to a single man. Arthur was perhaps most pleased of all. His wife stood proudly at his side, and he found great satisfaction in the knowledge that those who entrusted him to lead and govern them could still find the comfort to laugh and play in his presence like children at a father's feet.

Galienne watched all of this, still trying to sort it all out for herself. Perceval, his lover, even his sister, they were all here. *Dindraine hardly seems like the witch my mother would have described*, she thought. Actually, Perceval's sister was short, and didn't look as strong as even Galienne herself. No, she decided, watching the scene unfold, she would wait until later to present herself. It was Perceval's moment, and she didn't want to get in the way. She silently thanked God for his safe deliverance unto Camelot, and then meandered behind the pavilion so she could seek an audience with Baudwin.

The young group wanted to be away; there were many stories to tell. Perceval never felt so at home. He hoped his mother felt proud of him, wherever she was. Her children turned out all right after all. He faced the King once more.

"Your Majesty, with your permission, we shall retire to the city. I fear my exhaustion from these past hours is finally getting hold of me."

"Be off with you then, lad, though don't stay bedridden too long. Soon I'll have to find some assignment for you both," he said, indicating Llascoit as well. "Until then, get some rest."

Perceval, Llascoit, Llio, and Dindraine all acknowledged their thanks and offered bows and curtsies, then laughed their way back into Camelot.

"Father," said the voice, the possessor of which had waited until Kay and Lucan escorted Arthur and Guinevere back towards the city, for the sake of a more intimate conversation.

Only Baudwin and Lancelot remained, each finding it difficult to talk to the other, but both wanting to do so nonetheless. They turned, both facing Galienne. Neither was sure to whom she had referred.

For her part, she wasn't that sure herself. She'd never used the pronoun in front of the man who sired her. Yet they both looked at her incredulously.

"You're all right, child!" Baudwin said. "I'd been so concerned for your well-being." He shot a glance at the knight. "I'd heard your whereabouts were unknown."

"Perceval and I became separated after we left his home. I'm just thankful he's made it back safely."

"But why aren't you with him? Today of all days, Galienne?"

"Please, Father," she said to the bishop. "Today he's with family. I'd feel out of place. And at any rate, I returned myself to seek your counsel." She looked at Lancelot. "Yours, too, I suppose."

"Mine, Galienne?" Lancelot probed, feebly. He did not believe he could use the more appropriate pronoun for her, either. He still felt shocked; he all but gave her up for dead weeks earlier! He'd no idea how to go about grieving for her.

"Indeed. I'll be direct. How would you each respond if I told you I wish to be called Lady Galahad, and that I want to be every bit the knight Perceval has become?"

Lancelot bit his lip to avoid saying something he'd later regret. Baudwin stared at her incomprehensibly. "A knight, Galienne?" he said finally.

"Yes, and please, Father, it's Galahad now. Galienne was a wistful girl with little mind to the future."

"Why do you wish this?" inquired Lancelot.

"Why did you wish it? Why did Perceval, or any of the others? Why did our bishop here become who and what he is? This is a calling. I'm not sure I even see it so much as a choice, but rather something I should do, like my 'prophecy' suggested. Can you both understand that?"

Lancelot and Baudwin actually nodded. Galienne was surprised; perhaps her work might be easier than she'd anticipated.

Neither of them wished to voice the obvious objection, but Baudwin decided he must. He told himself it was for her own safety. He was not about to risk losing Galienne the way he still blamed himself for losing her mother, Elaine. "With respect, Galie, er, Galahad, you're a woman."

"Thank you for noticing. At least you no longer consider me the girl who used to come to you terrified." Ygerne and Sexburh gave her confidence, and she had some training to back it up. She enjoyed seeing Lancelot wince as she spoke.

"You're missing the point," interjected Lancelot, hoping she would not view the line as the distasteful sort of pun on her gender that his brethren knights would. "There are no women knights!"

"Then it's high time a new tradition started. I'd consider it an honor to represent my gender on the road to martial equality."

Lancelot and Baudwin glanced at one another nervously. Neither of them had ever seen or heard this person so full of fire before. Then Lancelot reconsidered, wondering if Baudwin knew how she almost took his head off once.

With that sword, he reminded himself. A sign that folk across the land still spoke of in wonder, guessing what her purpose might be.

"But, Galahad, who would look out for your welfare?" Baudwin said. *At least she's not so morbid, but hopeful, unlike her late mother.*

"'With respect,' as you put it, don't you think I already know the dangers? I saw Perceval almost die. Twice. And I don't claim to know what will eventually befall him." She briefly wondered if Lancelot had any way of knowing of her now departed visions. "But he understands the risks. And his preferred way of meeting his maker will be in following his sacred duty. I don't ask to be kept safe. I ask for the chance to serve Arthur and the greater glory of God."

Baudwin replied at once. "But think. Do you truly wish to further Arthur's name and spread the Word, or is it your own glory you seek?"

The answer came just as quickly. "All three," she said.

Lancelot vocalized his remaining objections. "Who will make you a knight? Who do you think will risk reputation and ridicule by girding arms on a woman? Have you thought of what some might say?"

"Since you weren't there to know," she all but spat in return, "I don't imagine it would be any worse than the ridicule I endured by learning to read, especially since I largely taught myself."

The champion never raised his voice in front of his daughter before, but he supposed there would have to be a first time. "What about my other questions?"

"Since when does the girding on of weapons diminish a lord's manliness? And what of the embarrassment knights have been known to cause their lords? What, with their debauchery and occasional thievery; how pleasing did certain lords find the actions of men like Meliagrant and Clamadeus?"

"Galahad," Baudwin interrupted, trying to keep remembering the new name, "this isn't the way. Insulting those already in the order to which you wish membership is hardly the best manner to impress anyone."

She turned on him now, too, for the first time feeling utterly confident in the face of the man who had been her sympathetic ear, her confessor, almost her father in Lancelot's absence. "Then pray tell me, Father, what is the way, for someone with no other options? I've no home, no source of wealth, no functional means of income like Perceval's sister or lover. I'm terrified of meeting them both, for they may respond to my wishes in the way you do. That's why I didn't approach Perceval in his time of glory. What, then, is the way for me?"

"I know your faith. I think it likelier you'd make it as a minister than a fighter."

"My time in monastic settings is done. Between my mother's embroidery room and my childhood hours in the church of Astolat, I'll have no more bother with closed off rooms designed as places of sanctuary."

"You just implied you had a valuable skill. I still have some of your mother's stitching," Lancelot countered, though he had to admit he'd not seen such energy in someone's soul since, when? She must have gotten it from her mother, or from the residual passion which he had forced down into his bowels, not allowing it to surface else it get him in more trouble.

"Mother taught me something of the trade, yes. But I want no part of it. You should know how that feels." The look she drove into him reminded him of the same paths Tathan had walked to arrive at the most sacred places in druidry. Only

Taliesin ever dared confront him with that. And how did she know?

Baudwin looked at him quizzically. He elected to try a reversal tactic. "What if you prove your worth as a knight, like Perceval did? Like Lord Lancelot himself has done, time and time again?"

This was getting nowhere fast, and Galahad knew it. As if she wasn't hesitant enough just to initiate her own reunion with Perceval! She needed to stall, gather her thoughts; she was getting too worked up about it. But she had the passion. Knights were nothing if not passionate!

"What did you have in mind, exactly?" she said.

That caught Baudwin off guard. "Oh, I hadn't given it much thought, really. Perhaps you can be given a task –"

"To do what?" Lancelot chided. "Run errands for the Queen, or survive Kay's abuse as one of the kitchen staff?"

"Whence comes this bitterness of yours?" she demanded.

"Maybe from having a child who hates me!"

"I'm not a child! I'm a grown woman with wits and training to use them."

"People, please," Baudwin said to no avail. He looked around quickly to see if they were alone. They were; everyone else had made it within the city walls by now, although the tower guards might notice them.

Baudwin went ignored. "Training? What training? In all the times I've seen you, you could barely pick up a sword, or you were so enraptured with Perceval you both got into situations you were lucky to escape from."

"You would dare!" She would not have her relationship with Perceval so cheapened, putting it on a level more in line with Lancelot's or Gawaine's own liaisons. "That does it! I drew a sword on you once before and I'll chance it again." And to the complete shock of both men, she threw back her cloak and expertly unsheathed her weapon.

"What's this?" Lancelot said. "I'll not fight you. I have no wish to kill family, however sour our relationship is."

"We have no relationship!" she spat acidly, and swung the sword close enough to his face that he could feel the thrust of wind against his cheek. Too close. And it was a good attack.

"So be it," he said, drawing his own blade. "I only hope you don't fight so clumsily that you get yourself killed."

Baudwin was frantic. "So help me, you'll both be saying hails to the Virgin until hell holds Mass for this! Aside put your weapons. Now!"

"Judge not lest you be judged, Baudwin," Lancelot said. And he lunged at his daughter, intending to show her the error of her ways with a single aimed maneuver. He closed the gap between them, and batted her sword away, as the blow's force landed her on her posterior.

"Now then," he said, looking down at her, the sword hanging at his side.

"A good knight never lowers his defenses," she replied, coming to her knees while simultaneously aiming at his unprotected side.

Lancelot had to back up for the blow to miss. With the extra space and time that allotted, Galahad rose to her feet, eliminating his advantage.

Baudwin tried again. "Do either of you have any inkling whatsoever as to the shame and guilt you'll feel if one or the other takes a wound because of this? Or worse?"

Galahad wondered if by "worse" the bishop referred to enhanced physical injury or potential peril for her soul. *Both*, she decided, and was proud to have opted to take the chance. Hopefully God was as forgiving as her faith proclaimed.

Lancelot considered the words also, circling slightly around with his daughter. *His daughter!* What would the King say if word got out he'd dueled with her, or hurt her? What would the Queen think?

Intimidation often worked for him in the field. "This is pointless, Galienne. Put up your sword and I'll put up mine, and let us talk."

"It was our talk which led us to this," she said, and as she came at him added, "and I've told you before: it's 'Galahad!'"

Lancelot parried the overhead lunge easily, though he was impressed how she retained her balance and strength throughout. Someone had indeed taught her something of the steel. Perceval?

They faced each other once more. Baudwin cried out, "Yes! That's it. Stop, and we can all go back to the rectory and talk our differences through."

That actually sounded good to Galahad, though she would not confess to it. She was dueling with the greatest warrior in Logres!

It was Lancelot's additional reply of, "Not until I teach her a lesson," which kept her facing off with him.

She knew he'd take her straight to the ground again if she didn't think of something fast. Maybe she should quit…

Then she rethought her tactics. She backed up two paces to see if he'd follow. When he chose not to, she lowered the sword at her side. Maybe she could surprise him with a timed fake.

Only he wasn't closing the space this time. Lancelot had fought against innumerable foes, who used different tactics. No doubt he was sizing her up; she was flattered that he at least considered her a threat.

Baudwin, not even realizing it, evened the odds. He took advantage of the gap and moved to stand right between them.

"Father, kindly move aside. This is not your fight," warned Lancelot.

He turned to him. "It is always my fight, when folk become involved with what they cannot resolve. Especially when family are concerned."

"I thought you just asked her why she wished a title, and now it would seem I hear some of that same vanity in you. Let it be, Father."

Now came Galahad's turn at taking advantage. With Baudwin all but blocking Lancelot from sight, she stepped up until she stood right behind the bishop, almost bumping into him. Lancelot instinctively tried to push him aside.

"What are you doing, bumpkin?" demanded the bishop, never receiving such treatment from anyone before. Was no one safe from knightly abuse?

Lancelot said nothing, realized at once that trying to move the priest was the wrong approach. He decided to try moving around, in the direction opposite that to which he had tried to shove Baudwin.

When he got to the bishop's flank, Galahad's sword was there waiting for him. All she had to do was raise its tip to his throat and await his recognition that she had him. He had not even seen her as she bobbed to and fro behind the priest, being shorter and thinner than the older man.

As Baudwin sensed that all activity had ceased, he finally moved aside, on his own. When he looked at the daughter holding a blade to her father's neck, he froze. *Dear God, Galie, er, Galahad! In all holiness, don't do this! You'll be banished or imprisoned!* But either fear or shock overrode his tongue; he could not vocalize the words.

He didn't need to. The pair of adversaries just stood, looking at one another, neither flinching nor even blinking, so far as Baudwin could tell. And then Lancelot dropped his sword to the earth, its sharp heaviness piercing the soil to leave an upright steel cross at their feet.

Battle-lust subsiding, years of frustrating anonymity released through violence, Lancelot and Galahad both felt tears of sorrow and longing well up in their eyes.

"Why did we do this?" Galahad said faintly, brushing her eyes with her free hand.

"We brought this on ourselves," was the reply of a man used to inner suffering.

"Do you so despise yourself that way? Or am I as much to blame?"

Lancelot could only look at her. *Still a stranger to me. Yet she's clearly got my blood in her.* "Does it matter?"

"Then answer me this. Will we ever be family? Or are we to remain enemies?" Galahad could feel her tear ducts heating again.

"You're clever, and lovely, and you're the only person who's ever gotten a weapon that close to something vital. I would be proud to call you daughter."

"Thank you, Sir Lancelot." She spun on her heels, ready to retreat to the city. *Will there ever be a man besides Perceval who understands me?*

"Galahad, wait," Baudwin said. "Whatever shall I tell the King of you?"

"Just tell him Perceval's soul-friend has returned, and will follow in his footsteps or die trying."

Lancelot and Baudwin glanced at each other, then watched as Galahad strode away.

* * *

"And to think I could have just stayed in here all the while, safe and snug with you!"

"Yes, Perceval, if only you hadn't been in such a rush that day. You just damn well better be thankful that my throat got better! Imagine how my death would have played on your conscience."

"Llio, don't, please. It's bad enough Galienne didn't make it to see this."

Llascoit and Dindraine were also in attendance at Gornymant's apartment. Llas opted to change the grim subject. "Would any other woman carry a sword to your knighting, Perceval?"

"What do you mean?" he said, half-listening. He strolled about the place, noticing the heavy eating table and chairs, the cooking pot with water buckets in one corner, the collection of Llio's trinkets and treasures taken from Worcester, the two plush beds, furnished with down mattresses and pillows! It was quite a welcoming for someone used to sleeping beneath trees.

"I mean, there was a young woman there, quite comely, but who I thought looked ill at ease, almost weighed down by something. And she kept covering up her left side. I could have sworn I saw a scabbard there."

"Oh, Llas, don't be foolish. No one is allowed to carry weapons about like that other than the knights." Llio was glad Perceval obviously liked this home; she always felt like the dutiful hostess.

"But I saw her as well, Llio," Dindraine commented, still trying to regain her confidence in her brother's presence. What a family they'd all become.

"See such a woman you may have," Perceval said, "but it couldn't have been Galienne."

"Well, I disagree, but who am I to argue with you on your day of fame? Now let's be off. I've a place in mind to celebrate this occasion properly." Llascoit was eager to go. He had heard of a tavern which sounded entertaining enough: the Unicorn's Horn. Lupinia knew it well, and flirtatiously shared this knowledge with Llascoit. He hoped she might be there that night.

Although the present company was sensational to behold; Dindraine hardly seemed the rosy-cheeked girl of Perceval's stories. She'd grown up quite quickly.

Stop that, Llascoit commanded himself, the memory of last night's berating from his own sister still fresh in his mind.

Though she was several years his junior, she had learned to carry herself with the dignified grace of a lady of class and distinction.

Perceval thought of her as well, albeit in a different fashion. "Fine, but I've barely had a chance to talk with my own sister. There's so much we have to catch up on." *And I want to know about Kundry.*

"Well, this will give us all a place to visit and socialize. Besides, it's customary for new knights to buy older knights their first few drinks."

They all glared at him. "Trust me," Llascoit said, and they made ready to leave the apartment for an evening of life on the town. Perceval had never known it well, and Dindraine had much she wished to show him.

* * *

Galahad roamed the streets until she noticed the band leading eastward. She followed at a distance, trying to keep out of sight as much as possible. The chief traffic in Camelot at this time of day was from tired workers and artisans heading home, or in for a stop at one of the city's evening establishments.

She passed house after house, shop after shop, again marveling at how regal each seemed in comparison to those in Astolat. Here was the bakery from which Lupinia used to liberate buns flavored with raisins. There was the weaver's guild, which bored Galienne to no end as a child; Elaine always wanted to go in there to hear the latest news or pick up additional supplies for her own work.

But now Galahad felt out of place. This was never her home, exactly, yet she had always felt welcome here, content to take in the sights and sounds. Now it seemed stifling, as though every building wanted to chastise her: "there's no place here for a woman knight," or, "why can't you be more like...?" She filled in the blanks herself. Always like someone else, that was the game. People living in a mass enclosure like this sought conformity; creativity and freshness allowed a city to exist, but were also targeted as unwanted in order that so many might live together in relative harmony.

Galahad sighed, watching Perceval and the others enter a large tavern. They laughed and walked arm in arm along the way, and she could not hear what they said. That was harmony, what she wished to be part of. Not the false civilizing influence which praised law and justice but which still somehow encouraged Lupinia to steal. Or her mother to kill herself for attention. Or she and her father to duel in plain view. She wondered how many felt as she did. Camelot had lost its magick; it seemed like a giant cave now for so many lost souls.

She would not be one of them, that she vowed. If Perceval would not welcome her back, into his fold of family and friends, then she would leave and travel until she found a place and people which would accept her for what she was, and what she strove to become.

They were inside now. Galahad had never seen the interior of the sort of place her mother would have publicly condemned but privately remained curious about. Hopefully the newness of it would help her overcome the anxiety.

The smells were the first feature, impossible not to notice. Pungent wafts of ales and lagers, more fragrant scents of heady wines, and the odors of roasted meat or fresh bread for those who thought to eat in such a place, met her nose at once, all struggling with one another to be the most prominent and enticing.

The place also was fully impregnated with people. Some drinking, some talking, others who had done too much of both needing to pass out, throw up, or be carried home by comrades.

Galahad loved it at once. It was a veritable den of iniquity, but not a single eye seemed intent on judging her met her as she walked inside. Here, folk were equal and themselves, the mood relaxed. She did not know that Round Table knights and city watchmen regularly had to break up fights here.

She considered how much money she had, and how best to guard it against thievery. It was secured at her waist in a belt pouch, and she would have difficulty reaching it without drawing attention to her sword, clumsily concealed by her large robe. She didn't have much cash. Ygerne gave her some, and she would have to soon see about getting more. Maybe she could work as a guide; Perceval and the women at Roche Sanguin taught her how to live with the land.

She made her way to the bar, with as much grace and speed as the cluster of bodies would permit. Behind it hung a poor fake of a unicorn horn, some deer's antler, most likely. There were also barrels of assorted relaxation-promoting beverages stacked behind it, with an assortment of clay drinking mugs and goblets. A door led off this area, leading presumably to the keeper's own home.

A number of persons were seated at the bar, on a bench leading clear around it. They were all men, looking a bit down despite the jovial overall atmosphere of the place. Galienne had to wait several minutes before being able to talk with the keeper, during which she managed to pick out Perceval and the others with him. They continued to laugh, especially Perceval, who seemed to not quite know how to deal with a heavy mug of ale.

Galahad mentally placed the others, too. The man he trained with, surely. Llascoit. And the one with her arm draped over him must be Llio, the one whose name he'd called out on more than one occasion when Perceval and Galienne had slept

outside. And the other, his sister. She tried to recall what she
had learned of witches. Despite what Elaine told her as a child,
there was not a single facial blemish to this woman, the result, so
it was claimed, of pacting one's soul with the Fiends. Dindraine
was actually quite comely, onyx hair draped elegantly behind her,
and animated cheek bones suggesting a warm smile. Her mouth
looked honest but reserved, her eyes remained upon whomever
she spoke to, and she didn't look much like Perceval.

The keeper finally found time for her. She ordered a
round of ale to be delivered to "that table near the window," and
he started to pour while summoning a buxom serving woman
who looked tired but eager to serve drinks to someone so enthusiastically receptive as Perceval and his companions.

The keeper finished pouring. "Trying to charm young
Perceval, then? Well, you'd best be quick about it. Looks like
he's fairly well off already."

Galahad didn't notice the man at the bar stir from his
apparent stupor and glance first at her, then towards the referred
table.

"Are you always this direct with your patrons, good
man?" she inquired.

"No, not always. But a tavern-keeper prides himself on
being well-informed, and news of a fresh knight spreads quickly
anyway."

Galahad had already fished coins from her purse while
working her way to the bar, so as not to show any sign of the
weapon which never left her side. She thanked the barkeeper,
filling his hand with the minted silver.

"You know Sir Perceval, then?"

She looked at the other man, who smelled as though
he'd been occupying that part of the bench for too long. "Of
him, yes," she offered cautiously.

"I've never seen you here before," he said. Galahad considered if all the men in here shared this forwardness.

"Nor I you," she said. She watched as the serving woman navigated the flow of persons to bring the drinks to the table. "To whom might I have the pleasure of conversing?" she asked, feigning interest.

"Someone who knows of Perceval as well." When she quickly looked his way, he extended a hand in greeting and added, "Sir Yvaine, from Gorre."

"Who did you say ordered these?" inquired Llascoit.

The serving woman pointed, knowing from years of experience that yelling the answer over the noise would have little effect other than rendering her hoarse.

The four of them followed her outstretched hand, looking at two attractive young people who appeared to be together. They were busily talking.

Then the woman at the bar stopped and looked their way.

"Oh, my lord!" gasped Perceval. "It's Galienne!"

"Are you sure?" Llascoit said. "I thought Lancelot had reported her as, um, I'm sorry, Perceval." Llascoit realized how fresh that wound must still be.

Only his friend didn't notice. "Of course, I'm sure. I'd know that determined face of hers anywhere." He started at once to rise, then bent to kiss Llio before charging through the throng. She saw tears in his eyes.

"This is the best day of my life," he whispered to her. She clenched his hand tightly as he strode away. "May we both live long enough together to enjoy more moments like these," she said, and he beamed at her.

Galahad laughed at the slightly clumsy way in which Perceval waded in front of and behind bodies. Knighthood hadn't increased his gracefulness. When he was close enough to hear her she shouted, "Moves like that were what separated us in the first place!"

He fell into her arms, laughing. "And what of you? Do you know how to swim any better yet?"

She released him, running a callused hand through his hair. "That, and more. I saw the ceremony. You looked marvelous, though your hair could use a trim."

"Llio says the same thing, and you're both wrong. Come on over. The least I can do for someone who buys me a drink is invite her over to my table."

"I'll be right there, Purse."

He looked into her gaze. She was the only one besides Dindraine who knew Tathan's private name for him. "I missed you."

"And I, you. Now be off, and I'll be right there."

"Right," Perceval said, quickly eyeing the man next to her. He looked familiar. He was halfway back to the table when he considered it, and looked again. *Not the man from my dreams, the one who slices malicious boys open...*

No, it probably wasn't him. Still, Perceval tried to think why the man should matter; a name or face was another form of knowledge potentially hazardous to forget.

"Sir Yvaine," Galahad said, "I'm off to be with an old friend. Can I trust you to stay out of trouble, or shall you be needing an arm home later?" She, like Perceval, found the face familiar. It was later that she recalled his face from one of her old visions, when Lupinia told her of the knights who repelled the Garmani uprising near her home.

Yvaine was too far into his drinks to care about the woman's forwardness, surprised she had given him her name. "I'm fine, thank you. Lady Galahad."

Galahad enjoyed the scrutiny of the four persons at the far table. She wondered what Perceval had told the others about her. Llio's face suggested warmth with just the slightest hint of something else: jealousy, perhaps? When Galahad arrived, she

Dreamers of the Grail

was surprised when everyone except Perceval rose to greet her. She felt well received at once.

Perceval flushed, then stood as well. He fumbled for proper introductions, but Llascoit already beat him to it. "Lady Galienne, it is my humble pleasure," he said, bowing in a manner suggesting the Queen stood before him.

Perceval took it from there. "My foster-brother, Llascoit of Jagent." Llascoit shot him an irksome grin. "And his sister, Llio." Llio leaned forward and embraced Galahad like an old friend.

"And my own sister, Dindraine." Dindraine felt quite pleased when Galahad, who had to be within just months of her own age, came forward and offered the same embrace she'd just received from Llio. Perceval's sister was a bit confused; he'd told her of their belief in her being a witch, and that Galahad was very devout in Christian faith, but here she was willing to interact with them. They all sat, Galahad remarking, "I'm glad to see you're still such a charmer, Perceval."

"You make it sound as though we've not seen one another in years."

"Sometimes a day can feel like a year, though," said Llio, Perceval's earlier comment still fresh in her mind.

"Well, before we get all teary-eyed," Llascoit said, "or just too plain wasted to care, permit me to make a toast."

They all raised their cups, Galahad having brought hers from the bar.

"To friends and family who should never part ways, and who should never stray from that path which binds them." They all drank. Galahad thought the liquid too bitter to truly enjoy, but chugged it anyway.

She mused, "You're quite the poet, Llascoit. Have you much practice in turning a woman's heart afire?"

Llascoit stuttered for an answer. "Well, no, Lady. I mean, not yet." Llio and Perceval tried with some success to stifle laughs.

Perceval, not having listened attentively to Tathan's tales or his mother's lectures, noticed really for the first time how a good story could distract to the point at which other impressions got filtered out. Maybe the ale was helping him relax, but he found he concentrated on every word that each person spoke, whether it was just to offer a witty line of comment or expound upon some event. It was a time to learn of each other, and Perceval felt the most pride, out of that entire wondrous day of his life, of the simple detail that he was the reason for the five of them coming together.

And the talk never slowed. They each took turns listening to Llio speak of future plans, wanting Perceval at her side, of Llascoit and Perceval and their knightly duties, of Dindraine's long months spent in self-isolation from home, still close enough to hear Tathan's harp, but intently studying to become a healer just before their mother passed. Dannedd was older than Cabal and died peacefully, while she was a student.

Despite Perceval's sureness, Dindraine steadfastly denied having ever even seen the remote keep of Bridgnorth, leaving him to wonder just whose voice he heard that strange morning, mocking him for waterfowl. And Galienne, who grew comfortable enough in the other's presence to share her new name with them, if not her purpose, and delighting in that none of them found any reason to doubt her the way Lancelot and Baudwin had. It was likely that many others would someday.

The ale was as smooth as divinely silky samite. Tongues were loosened by it, yet trust abounded at the table, so it didn't really matter.

Yvaine watched them all the while from his perch on the bench. They never seemed to notice his scrutiny. He didn't care about talking to people after he had too much. Yet he hadn't drunk so much, not yet. He knew he'd still recall all of this clearly the next day. It was just that the ale and wine had become too easy lately. Other Round Table members were famed for the strength of their ability to imbibe and still did all right. It was just all too much to deal with as of late. Yvaine had heard enough in the past weeks to last the rest of his years. And it just wasn't fun anymore; thus, the ever-full cup.

Rumors of Margawse's plotting. His lack of a clear plan of how to deal with Gawaine (they were both family, which just added fuel to the fire). The growing desolation up north. Banditry and outlaws at Logres' borders. The old ghosts his mother had dug up when he went to Gorre.

And he had heard of Lamorak. He knew something of the late knight's lineage now, and traveled widely to confirm it. Nimue and Taliesin helped, whether they'd realized it or not. And the research kept Yvaine largely from Camelot.

His eyes wandered back to his mug. The thick heady lager had a slightly bitter smell, grainy. He calmly drained it and then resumed his eavesdropping.

"Another toast!" cried Llascoit, who had made too many of them already. Yvaine was getting tired; the rambunctious quintet had shouted more than enough justifications to imbibe additional intoxicants. They had reached the stage at which a toast to toasting itself sounded good to them.

"To honorable Sir Perceval, and his victories over villainous knights near and far," and they all raised their never-quite-emptying cups. The women giggled like children. Perceval and Llascoit got to laughing just by looking at each other. Yvaine, for his part, saw his cue and pounced upon it.

He stood, and shouted over the noise of the place, which over the past few hours of carousing had dwindled considerably. Only the dedicated remained now. "To the slayer of the Barking Beast!"

More heads than five looked at him; most assumed it was the alcohol talking. Galahad tried to recall whether she had shared the man's name with the others. She noticed, however, that Perceval and Dindraine looked horrified.

"Yvaine," the Cambrian siblings muttered under their breath. He met both their glances and raised his mug to them. Perceval finally managed to recognize the stranger despite his tiredness. And it wasn't the man of his dream.

Perceval rose and walked over to the bar. Once again, his curiosity got the better of him. The others decided to wait until he returned to badger him with questions. They were all almost exhausted anyway, to say nothing of being at various degrees of physical numbness.

"So you do remember me," Yvaine said. "That's good. We have to talk, Perceval, and now that you're a knight it would seem the best time."

Perceval was unsure whether he was glad to see the man or not. "Where's Sir Lamorak? I thought you two were all but inseparable."

Yvaine motioned to the keeper to refill the mug, his speech remaining surprisingly unslurred. "That's part of what we shall discuss. And know now that whatever you decide tonight, tomorrow my sword will gladly be at your side."

PART FIVE: QUESTS

P erceval never lessened in his amazement at how
time moved quickest when its captives were most satisfied with
their lives. Years never passed fast enough when he was bored
and curious in the hills, but as a grown man and a knight, days
and months flew fast like so many geese.

The Barking Beast remained elusive at first, traceable
only through either its occasional mark of devastation in the
ruin of a small settlement, or as folk had begun to say by then,
its supernatural ability to only be conquered by one of Pellinore's line. Whatever the case, Perceval, traveling with Galahad,
Yvaine, Llascoit, Dindraine, and Llio, caught up to it after several
weeks back in Cambria. Apparently it had never left those wilds,
and indeed a number of souls in Gwynedd reported seeing it,
often to face accusations of drunken observations.

But it had been there, for how long at that point no one
could say. Perceval and Llascoit were the ones to finally chase it
down, almost killing their mounts just to keep pace and follow
the thing.

They almost felt sorry for it as they sent it back whence
it came.

It surprised them as much as they it. It led them further
into the depths of the wooded hills, in which it could take advantage of those two dominant types of terrain. It had almost
reached Mount Snowdon when they cornered it.

It seemed tired but eager to fight, or eager to return to
the Other Side, despite the agonizing death it would have to
endure on This Side to achieve that end. Perhaps, as some folk
later said, it was because it knew that the last of Pellinore's blood
had returned, and it all but licked its grisly chops in anticipation.

Llascoit led the charge, while Perceval traversed to its
flank in an effort to get position behind it. Despite the speeding
lance, it ignored Llascoit almost completely, merely kicking out

at him with its hind legs in an effort to dislodge him from his charger as he attacked. It focused instead on Perceval, almost exclusively, never refusing to face him.

Llascoit's lance hit home, bringing the horrible sounds of the creature to their deafening climax. The two knights would always later swear that dozens of hounds had to have been close by to make such noise; the beast must have eaten them but kept their canine souls in painful limbo until its own quest was met, or so the tale would be told. Llas backed up his steed, seeing and feeling its terror, and jumped off before such panic would do him more harm than help. Perceval had dismounted as well, and the two horses charged away together for mutual protection, ready to climb Snowdon itself if that was what it took to elude the monster.

The beast took many long minutes to die, if dying it truly was. It never stopped lashing at Perceval, emitting grunting sounds that sometimes sounded human. Perceval wanted it to end quicker than that, in no small part because of the beating he took from the abomination's claws. It kept wanting to bite him, too, and even took his thigh in its jaws, but remained unable to pierce the chain link.

Llascoit, in some circles, would receive more of the credit for the unholy extermination, taking full advantage of the beast's distraction with Perceval. He never received more attention than the continually flailing legs, which did knock him down several times and bruise him about. But Perceval was the one who delivered the blow which sent shrieks into the wind and left both knight's ears ringing until well into the following day, as they made their way back to the camp where their companions waited. Yvaine and Galahad had taken a different path when the beast finally produced alternating sets of tracks, and Dindraine and Llio had watched the campsite.

There were no remains of it, other than those last terrible sounds, and the sticky evil blood of purplish hue on their

Dreamers of the Grail

swords and armor. It was as though the thing never lived. In a sense, it never had, at least not a life that the people who saw it, fled from it, or finally destroyed it could understand. Perceval and Llascoit's report was greeted with unspoken skepticism by some, intrigued concern and conjecture by others, and deadly seriousness followed with gladness by fellow knights, especially members of the Round Table. Most folk knew nothing at all of the horrors some of them had faced, the worst cases being the most recent. Gossip got out and spread anyway, to the point that tales grew of dragons imbued with fiery breath, trolls whose severed limbs regenerated with grotesque rapidity, and even otherwise plain humans possessing supernatural skill, weaponry, or strength. The knights neither confirmed nor denied such stories, knowing that their reputation was ironically enhanced through their telling, and they didn't wish to speak of such things themselves, genuine or imagined.

Camelot was astonished, whatever the truth behind the beast might have been. Arthur considered the prospect of advancing Perceval to the Table; only Gawaine, Lancelot, and Trystan made it there faster upon the heels of their new spurs. Yet the golden name plate on the table had been engraved, or engraved itself, if one believed issues of prophecy literally, with the appropriate name.

And it wasn't the only such gold plate to do so at that time.

Some years prior, a tradition had begun in the grand hall of the Round Table, which remained otherwise strictly forbidden for non-members, servants notwithstanding. Arthur saw it as a way in which the grandeur of both the place and the events and politics which were discussed therein could be spread by sources perhaps more accurate and less boastful than the knights themselves. The member knights enjoyed the expressions the fortunate recipients displayed in the presence of the Table and its brethren.

The tradition was that a new initiate could bring along one additional person who could stay for the opening minutes of the new member's first meeting. Lovers and betrothed were often chosen. In the absence of these, maybe because a knight's affairs of the heart and the bed were often of questionable length and devotion, sometimes family members or even close friends won the honor.

So when Perceval's name appeared, to the mixture of approval and chagrin of Llascoit, who swore to gain entry to the fraternal sanctuary someday himself, his choice was quite easy.

Galahad was the most elated Perceval had ever seen her, and the King felt most pleased for the choice as well. It was the only method he had to test that which he never doubted: the accuracy of whatever person or spirit or power which informed him of his next membership decision, sometimes before he felt completely confident of it himself.

The meeting itself was actually poorly attended. Knights across the land had reported the need to be at their homes, seeing to this or that concern. Arthur bemoaned the number of them who confided their fear that there was more trouble awaiting them than they looked forward to. Banditry, poverty, mysticism, pestilence, practices which would offend both Pagan and Christian, and strange sightings and happenings were all on the rise just about everywhere beyond Logres' secure borders.

Perceval knew better than to even suggest to Galahad that she leave her sword behind. She wore it proudly beneath the same robe she wore when she drew it in anger against her father. She barely noticed Lancelot's own absence that day.

Galahad would not later clearly recall details of the sizable hall itself, only its contents. The table might have looked ordinary without its meticulous restoration (old Leondegrance once thought of using it for emergency firewood during a particularly difficult winter when Guinevere was barely into her teens, but later was delighted to have saved it). Its legs were reinforced with silver brackets, to add strength and shine. Its circumference had been polished at the expense of much tired sweat, and coated with a varnish of fats and oils which protected it from knightly ale and wine spillage while still managing to reflect the bright flickerings from hundreds of candles and twin fireplaces spaced about the room. Each name plate was so perfectly fit into place that from the table's side it looked flat and smooth, and the plates seemed as so much golden paint from above. Each space had one; almost no place remained without a name engraved on it. Perceval, ever the agnostic, wondered who the fine engraver was, and what he did for the King when not embossing.

Galahad considered counting the seats, stopping after the first two dozen. There had to be over a hundred! And the chairs. The back of each stood quite high, of polished and carved hardwoods, some brought from oceans away. The seats and backs were velvet cushions with the suppleness of the finest fleece. She was surprised at how anything serious might be discussed in a place so cozy.

Galahad strode about the table, while some of the knights laughed with Perceval, who had begun to get used to his new duties. It was all he imagined and more still. Llio was intensely proud of him, so were his friends, and he felt more at home in this strange room on sight than he ever had in Cambria.

Kay made ready, at the room's sole entrance, to signal the meeting's official start. Since the King sat near the doorway, Kay and Galahad could hardly help but notice each other, instant recognition dawning in each other's eyes while both made quick efforts to look away.

Or, in Galahad's case, to move away also. In doing so she carelessly tripped in such a manner that made Arthur want to fall to his knees in humble prayer and thanks-offering.

She stumbled into the forbidden seat, known as the Siege Perilous. The seat the knights never touched, the one only used by commoners fortunate enough to have their pleas heard by royal ears.

And nothing happened, unless one counted Galahad's trepidation. She quickly decided that knighthood was just not in her destiny; she had defiled the ultimate physical manifestation of the order by seemingly to have the presumption, the very gall, to sit in one of their sacred seats! She wondered to whom it belonged, so she could prepare an elaborate apology and beg mercy. She could just imagine having to ask her father to champion her for such an offense!

In her moment of confusion, she didn't bother to read the golden name plate which lay just in front of her.

She misinterpreted the gasps and glares which followed her chaotic furniture usage, however. As if knowing their King's thoughts, some of them actually fell to their knees, bowing their heads penitently while Galahad fretted over the prospect of never leaving the room again.

"It has happened," said one knight, unknown to her. "So it is spoken," replied another. "And written," added a third, aware of the power of words in the land. Perhaps that was where the two chief religions of the Isles differed, in their assessments of the literal truth of sentences.

Perceval had not a clue what was happening. For a moment he thought that perhaps this was how they made a lady feel welcome, but when he saw the reverence for Galahad, which went beyond romantic adoration, he dismissed it.

Hearing even crusty Kay murmur, "The prophecy is true," and sounding as though he might gravely regret the statement's clarity, drew Perceval over. Since he had the vague impression that the others might be afraid to approach Galahad, he simply offered his hands to her where she sat, and helped her to her feet.

Again came the sounds of faith, awe, and incredulity. Arthur chose to speak. "Many marvels has your King seen in the course of just a single life, yet this latest surpasses them all. I have wondered about Lancelot's child for some years, but hardly expected she might come so far so quickly. Galienne," he gestured to her, as she stood nervously in front of Perceval, "come, sit again. Let the members of the Round Table serve witness to this."

Arthur remained the only one who Galahad never corrected regarding her name. Right then it didn't even cross her mind. She cautiously stepped over to the seat again, now realizing just what had transpired in the past moments.

The Perilous Seat, she thought. *So Lupinia's tale was true; it exists!* Lupinia was hardly the only one who ever mentioned the chair, and it was widely believed that no knight had attempted to master it for years, reserving it for the commons.

But her? Was she the chosen? Her visions never gave indication of this. And wasn't it really just a chair; how superstitious could Arthur's champions truly be?

Perhaps God withholds previews of the most glorious events of a seer's life. Or maybe He stopped sending the visions once she determined her own course.

Galahad let the King gently reseat her, at which point, instead of the faith-inspired drawing of breath, she was met with the sound of many knights clapping. Applauding for *her!* How well would men deal with someone who sat at their equal level, who was not even a knight, who even sat above them, in a sense, since she tamed something supposedly unattainable by any of them? Would it be said that a woman could do miraculous things of which no man was capable?

But she was getting ahead of herself. As Galahad watched, as awe-struck as any of the others in attendance, the others took their seats and awaited the King's or Seneschal's next command. Perceval remained duly fascinated. He could still hardly believe the honor of merely standing in this room, much less what happened since. He almost had to be led to his own seat. The meeting began, and Galahad was never asked to leave. The tales which would spring forth once the assembly adjourned would never lose their wonder to those who heard them. A woman at Arthur's Round Table. And Lancelot's daughter, no less.

Still busier times lay ahead of them, including widespread news that the Perilous Seat was tamed and its tamer made knight. Galahad knew many would protest a woman knight, and agreed with the King that the ceremony should be done in the Round Table chamber. Most of the members were present for that, although some felt a woman had no place in that room, alleged Perilous Seat prophecy or no. She didn't care, though. The highest honor she had dreamt of was hers! She was almost as pleased to be asked for a special favor by Perceval and Llio a short time later.

* * *

The wedding proved delightfully small and quiet. The King and Queen understood Perceval's and Llio's wishes for relative solitude, having felt overwhelmed with pomp and pageantry at their own nuptials years before.

It was after the revelations made at the first Round Table meeting attended by Perceval and Galahad that the former stole off to Jagent to officially ask Gornymant's "permission," even though he knew it was a moot point so far as his future wife was concerned. Indeed, Perceval had already asked her. He told them both he could not imagine spending his days with another woman, and that his love for her would never wane. He spent some of the money he still had at Gwern's Jewelry, the store he noticed on his first trip to Camelot, to acquire a simple ring of silver, and took it to Llio's bedroom in the apartment. On one knee, and beaming with pride and sheer joy, he asked for the privilege of marrying her.

She simply nodded, and jumped into his arms, biting his nose playfully and immediately making decisions about planning. They had already grown a bit wary of all the notice they got just by being seen about the city, and at once chose to keep the ceremony limited to royalty, family, and a few close friends.

It was all they dreamed of, surrounded by those who loved them. Guests had a hard time determining who wept more, Llio or her father. Baudwin himself officiated the ceremony, which was followed by a weekend of unadulterated carousing and merry-making.

The bishop had argued with Perceval about what would actually be said for the pair of them. Perceval never heard the traditional wedding vows of the Christians. He didn't like the sound of "until death shall you part," and made it known.

"With respect, Bishop, it will take something stronger than death to separate Llio and I."

Baudwin thought about it. "I see. What it really means is your physical life. Reunion in heaven is the goal."

"And I tell you that I'm convinced that this most noble and strong lady, who has given me the highest honor of sharing herself with the likes of me, shall never part from my side until she so desires it. Should one of us die first, then the earthly survivor will always feel the presence of the departed." Llio actually began to hurt Perceval with how tightly she gripped his hand.

That part of the matrimonial vow was thus altered. Llascoit and Galahad stood with them, as Dindraine brought in their hard-bought gold rings and helped Baudwin to bless them in the name of Creation.

They were all dressed quite simply. Perceval wore the white tunic which draped his body the day of his knighting, covered only by the surcoat Llio sewed him, with new hose. Llio was outfitted even more basically: a white gown showing no further finery or ornamentation. They wanted to keep it simple.

All in attendance listened solemnly to the prayers and recitations, proudly proclaiming their vows. The lovers swore to love each other forever, as each of them took a turn at describing what they felt for the other in the presence of their guests. Baudwin softly sang an old wedding verse to them, assisted by Dindraine, whose own strong voice helped carry that of the bishop.

Then Perceval leaned over and kissed his wife sweetly, Baudwin's ceremonial permission for him to do so falling upon deaf ears.

The celebration was joyous and loud; even Gornymant's sober students relished it, although Arthur kept a curious distance from the one named Mordred.

The couple moved into Gornymant's Camelot apartment, with the King granting the use of another for Dindraine, Galahad, and Llascoit. The five of them had grown all but inseparable.

There was another part of what so intrigued Perceval that last year, which was the way the stories took root and remained, no matter how the weeding practices of rational observers and experimenters, or faithful preachers and judges, tried to kill them off. At first this phenomenon merely amused him, as he heard reports of what the well-to-do, including him personally, had recently accomplished. He even took a liking to recognition, at least in Camelot. People knew his face and his doings and young boys and slightly older girls never tired of trying to talk with him, or the others, especially Galahad. He enjoyed this attention, always sharing it with Llio and the others, and he especially liked the time spent with the children.

But it was when he caught wind of the ugly rumor suggesting that Llio's sickness might have been caused by the Barking Beast, who wanted its own perverse revenge for what offense Perceval did not even begin to know, that he quickly grew to disdain gossip from those whose own lives didn't seem interesting enough to themselves. And he hated how he had begun that same way, always wondering what it would be like to be something else, somewhere different, never concentrating on the beauty and temporality of the fragile and dynamic present.

Llio began coughing again, and this time there was no obvious cause, and no apparent cure.

She fell into bed after the Eve of the Hallows, and at first all thought it just a cold. Llio kept reassuring them all that it was not the more dreaded lung-illness her mother had faced.

Dindraine immediately took over her care, ensuring that she received plenty of rest and privacy. She was tired herself from what had been a strangely-mixed evening of fervent prayer and welcoming of old spirits, depending upon one's faith. Samhain, too, was coming under the influence of the cross, though it didn't stop most folk from practicing old measures focusing on the new year and the mingling of the Two Sides, despite what the Christians had to say about the likes of faerie. She even retrieved a book from the King's library to help Llio pass the time, but as said time changed into the past, Llio lost interest and ability.

Perceval remained at her side daily, for as many hours as Dindraine would permit. Other friends visited regularly as well. Even Lupinia dropped by when she heard, full of support and her own amount of gossip, most of it about herself: Agrivaine had proposed to her and her father, and wedding plans were in the making. Lupy at least made sure to not recite such news in front of Llascoit.

Perceval sent word to Gornymant, who still kept busy in Jagent, and he quickly readied to head there at Perceval's request. The former pupil made no mention in the letter of how serious the condition seemed to be getting.

Dindraine was baffled, and sought the bishop's counsel. He, too, could think of no cure beyond what Kundry had imparted to her student. The symptoms were treated with a porridge consisting of an oatmeal base, to which was added dandelion, chickweed, hazel buds, and wood sorrel. When this failed, Dindraine opted for the heavier method, a potion made of ground ivy. While Llio chugged it down morning and evening, Dindraine offered prayers dating back centuries.

Dindraine turned to the bishop because his faith corresponded more directly with Llio's own. The healer's prayers were strongly Pagan, and her use of them was known only to her and Perceval, who would try anything which might work.

Gornymant made good time, arriving with his students, whom he dispatched to various parts of the city to run errands. Before he knew it, Gareth wandered into Pendragon Castle and somehow became the center of a request from a woman up north who had petitioned her cause: to have her few remaining lands rid of a villain knight. Arthur knew that region to be near or perhaps even overrun by the Wastes, and was hesitant to take her seriously, so he offered Gareth as questing errant. The King became fully aware of the lady's persistence at her hostile response to the "kitchen boy," who nonetheless displayed the same pride and purpose as Perceval did on his first visit to the grand hall of that castle. After Gornymant had seen his daughter, he was informed that his own new charge was already making ready to go on his first adventure.

It was then he learned that Llio's time was short, as were his own wife Arian's years before. He wondered what kind of evil affliction would target just one gender; his and his son's lungs were always strong.

Shortly after the Christmas-Yule, the defective lungs Llio inherited from her mother ceased working altogether, too filled with the poisons they themselves had produced. She died quietly in the night, with nary a sound. Perceval and Dindraine discovered her together the next morning, as they both entered.

Perceval tried to wake her, his custom in recent days. She slept more and more, until he had to remain at home with her most of the time just on the chance that he'd be able to spend some precious moments with her awake each day.

Dindraine and her brother felt the cool skin and pallid face and knew at once what happened. Perceval collapsed at the side of the bed and held Llio's hand, kissing her mouth one last time before he finally began to sob. He felt readied for this, but now that the finality had come, he found he could still shed tears. Dindraine kept her calm as much as possible; she had grown to quite adore Llio, her sister-in-law, during these months of their marriage, but right then Perceval needed a source of strength.

"We all did everything we could," she said to him simply, once the tears began to dry. He nodded, not wanting to speak.

When he calmed at last, never leaving Llio's side, he asked his sister, "Would Kundry herself have been able to help?"

Dindraine began to wrap the body in twin sheets, so Llio could be taken out of the apartment and prepared for burial. "I don't think so. I lived with her for many months. Do you think Gornymant taught to you all he truly knows, or might there be more to him than even you realized?"

He thought about it, watching the sheet cover the face, the face he would not have the joy of waking next to again. Not in this life. "I guess not. I think I see your point. I just can't help but wonder what could have prevented this. How little do we really know about ourselves," Perceval said, "if we can't offer anything for sickness other than potions and prayer?"

"It was a bad condition, Perceval. I've never seen any-one who so suffered from this illness than Llio did. Even if we'd noticed it earlier, I'm not sure we could have done anything with more results than we achieved." Dindraine was careful to stress Perceval's part in the treatment. His loyalty and attention to the deceased were unquestionable, and she remained com-pletely convinced that the mere presence of loved ones could help a person to overcome anything.

So the affliction had to have been inherited from Llio's mother. Llascoit told Dindraine the story of that shortly after they all first met.

Still, Dindraine had the itching doubt that perhaps something else was to blame. After all, Llio showed no sign symptoms for a long time, then suddenly developed a full condition.

Llascoit mentioned the incident regarding some odd smoke, too. She'd have to ask about that later. For now, someone had to find him and tell him his sister finally passed away.

Perceval was still lost in his thoughts. He stopped weeping as a single realization hit home.

He hadn't let Llio down. He gave her the best he had to offer. He would miss her terribly, for each of the rest of his days, but he had been true to her.

You'd be proud of me, Mother. I did well with this woman. Take care of her if the pair of you should find each other.

"What are you thinking? You're staring at the ceiling," Dindraine said.

He stood at last. "Dindraine, listen. I want you to know that if I ever get this distraught again, and say anything about you or your skills, I don't really mean it. What it will mean is just that I miss her."

"Thank you for your foresight. Come here," she said.

He collapsed about her. She had the vague notion that she had become something of a mother figure for the bunch of them during the previous seasons: Perceval, Llascoit, even proud Galahad.

She enjoyed that sensation, briefly considering if any of them would ever have their own children.

Perceval drew away. "She'd want a small funeral, wouldn't she?"

"I believe so. She never was much of a fan of the attention of strangers, even though we've all been settled here for some time."

The funeral did indeed prove small. Only close friends and family members attended. Gornymant saw that Llio's body was buried with the tablecloth that she once pulled out to welcome Perceval to Jagent. Baudwin gave an uplifting eulogy, praising Llio's devotion, warmth, and bright mind. The knights who attended other than Perceval all offered their finest knightly salutes: Galahad, Yvaine, Gareth (who came with his fiancée, the same woman who reprimanded him after she requested a knight to serve her). Perceval, Dindraine, Llascoit, and Gornymant lowered Llio's simple coffin into the ground.

When it was finished, Gornymant led the group in a timeless song originally conceived by the ancient bards. Dindraine learned it while with Kundry, and eagerly took up the tune. Even Baudwin sang along, for the music told of continual life without the classifications of redemption or renewal, of peace and joy and of the marvelous woman whose newly spiritual form awaited her lover and husband, to welcome him back to her side.

Only Perceval did not sing. He focused on the sky, thinking of birds, watching and listening for them.

A few more months passed, and for Perceval they were generally fraught with sadness and frustration. So often if felt like Llio was simply no more: gone, forever. Had he to rely on his eyes alone, he would have no choice but to conclude that she would remain unreachable by him forever since her body had been consigned to the earth. It was still a bound through faith for him to accept the prospect of continuous, or perhaps cyclical, life. He decided all he could truly do was keep Llio alive through the memories of her, and hope for the best as it came.

He got to thinking about it again when he recalled what Yvaine told him of his brother, Lamorak. Perceval had tried to avoid that subject since the night he learned of Lamorak's death, but he considered its implications.

If not for Yvaine and his constant travels, he might never have found out at all. The Knight of the Lion had headed home yet again, sometimes homesick himself. He was quite surprised to find the now almost legendary Taliesin performing in the court of Morgan and Uriens, the latter of whom was beginning to fail in health as well.

Yvaine happily sat through a night's feasting and entertainments for the privilege of being introduced to the bard who had made his name known in countless kingdoms. From him he acquired the knowledge of Perceval's background, including the direct blood tie to the late Sir Lamorak.

He wanted to ask how the bard found this out, then reconsidered. Taliesin would likely be the new arch-druid, at least in the minds of Pagans, and sacred knowledge was not discussed openly. But he never doubted for a moment the truth of what Taliesin imparted, and Yvaine vowed he would find Perceval immediately upon his return to Camelot.

Again, the question arose, though this time two knights asked it. What should be done about Gawaine? Neither of them wished a challenge, and besides, Gawaine had gone out of his way to help Perceval in the last stages of his errantry.

So at first Perceval let it lie. His mother had withheld something else from him all along! He spoke of it with Dindraine and Galahad, who likewise proffered no clear solution; they treated it mostly as a sad curiosity. And they reminded him of the past with the same logic invoked at Llio's deathbed: even if Perceval had known of his brother those years earlier, what might he have done? Family ties could not instantly overcome years of anonymity.

And there was more news from Yvaine, this part shared instead with Galahad, who then insisted they tell Dindraine and Llascoit.

An uncle fled the ill-omened Gwynedd, after Perceval's and Dindraine's mother abandoned one son to escape with an unborn one. A knight, Sir Pellam.

When Perceval broached the topic with Galahad, she was the most sober he'd ever seen her. "How can that be?" she demanded, almost angry. "I've been virtually convinced that old cripple has become the Grail's keeper, and now you mean to suggest that he's related to *you*?"

"Do you think it's really him?" Perceval said to her.

"How many Sir Pellams can exist? And what's more, if it's true, then the bloodline of the keepers has changed. All my life I'd known I was part of that line, and now it seems I am no longer."

His next remark left her stunned. "What if my ancestors were the keepers of the Grail, but yours were those capable of bringing the Grail out of hiding for the world to acknowledge, even to use and benefit from?" It was another of those half-formed thoughts of his, spoken before he understood its significance.

Galahad's gravity deepened. "What are you saying, that two clans have worked together all these centuries to keep knowledge of the Grail alive?"

"Perhaps not just the knowledge, but the potential to retrieve it. What do you suppose it might actually do for someone?"

Perceval had not seen Galahad cross herself for some time. "I've told you what I know of it already. It's not supposed to be intended for mortal eyes. It left us for the same reason we were banished from the Garden."

"But you're the one who thought we actually saw it that night, remember? The serving dish, the thing that looked so precious to you and like a soup bowl to me? And you already said you thought Pellam was keeping it."

She nodded. "I've thought of that night so many times, like when I was at Roche Sanguin. Do you know what Lady Ygerne said about Bridgnorth?"

He shrugged. "She thought we had a vision," Galahad said quietly.

Perceval unconsciously rolled his eyes, immediately setting Galahad on the defensive. "Look, I know how you feel about the mystical, but someday you've got to get this all figured out for yourself. I agree with Ygerne."

"What do I have to figure out?"

"What you believe. You need to know where your faith lies. I've never seen you place much of yourself in either magick or miracle."

Perceval didn't want to debate theology. He wanted to know more about the Grail. "Why is it so important to you what I believe?"

"Because, damn it, I love you and I'm worried about you! We all have to believe in something. It's what allows us to face whatever comes."

"Do you fret for me or my soul?"

"Both! But I don't even know if you believe in souls."

"I'll believe in whatever might allow me to be with Llio again."

"Is that why you ask me about the Grail?"

"That's part of it. Can it bring people back together?"

Galahad's mouth hung slack. "Surely you don't mean that..."

"I'm not sure what I mean! But this hurts too much! I've only ever wanted two things, and one is gone now. I think I understand why your father goes out of his way to so absent himself from Camelot."

She stiffened. Perceval tried to soothe her. "Oh, Gal, God, I'm sorry. I shouldn't have mentioned him."

"It's all right. But I'm still unsure what you mean."

"It heals, yes?"

"The Grail? Of course. How could it not? I mean, if it could be touched."

"Could it be drunk from? Like when Jesus made the wine?"

"Why not? But it feels like heresy to speak that way of it. And it's odd to hear such a holy sentiment from you."

"It's not faith, it's history. Or so you told me." Perceval felt his impressions and intuitions swirling about in his mind, each vying for the cherished status of belief. He knew he was close. And he wondered if religion could be based on something so simple as the Grail. He thought so. The heart of Christianity was salvation, the core of Paganism cyclical balance, so why not the cup or chalice?

"So you want to go looking for it?" Galahad meant it in jest.

"Gal, I want to ask you something, but I'm not sure how you'll take it."

"There's one way to find out." Despite her seriousness, she was in a good mood from their talk.

He looked around, almost guiltily. "Did you really have visions?"

She sighed, having not much cared who knew about that for some time. "I'm actually surprised you've never mentioned it until now. Yes. I believe I used to receive divine foreknowledge. I don't know how else to describe it."

"Were we looking for the Grail?"

That caught her off guard. "When?"

"In the dream we shared. Remember the hallway?"

She smiled. "I've never figured out who the other person was, or why we were naked." Just months ago, her last word would have made her blush.

"Maybe it will happen, though I don't know who the man was, either."

"It would be the greatest quest, if it actually could be found." Galahad allowed herself to dream.

"Think of what might be cured with it, if we sinful humans could touch it with our unworthy flesh."

"There you go again, with that Christian flair."

"I think I'm more Pagan, really. Probably just because my mother wouldn't approve."

She smiled at him. "I wonder what she'd think of us, or your uncle."

"Some day we'll have to try and find Pellam again. Do you want to go back into that forest?"

"I'm sure I can find Roche Sanguin, though you of course wouldn't be allowed there. I could leave you in the woods again, though."

"Brownie would love that." Perceval let Galahad keep the mare, who had always loved her. Besides, Styfnig was quite a load to care for.

Shortly thereafter, Arthur once again convened a Round Table meeting. The annual Pentecostal celebration was fast approaching, and the turnout for both meeting and festival were expected to be high indeed.

Presently, with Llio's burial behind them, Perceval and Galahad tried to brush aside how they would obviously be attending the meeting, but Llascoit would have none of it. He made them promise to share with him what details of the meeting they were allowed to; Arthur absolutely forbade, in the form of oaths from all member knights, the sharing of political and economic words from the meetings with anyone.

Llascoit could remain proud as he wished until he earned the same rank as his comrades. Perceval and Galahad felt their own pride as the meeting began, and it truly was well attended.

Galahad still received her share of looks whenever she entered the Round Table chamber. Most were curious, an occasional one seemed hostile or untrusting, and still others might have even suggested fondness for this woman who sat in what could be seen as the fourth highest place at the Table. The membership was not supposed to have any such hierarchy. Yet there was still no denying that despite equal say and equal heights and ornamentations of the furnishings, the King sat at the proverbial top, with both champions on his flank, and then the victor of the Perilous Seat, now usually called just "The Siege." Its magick seemed to have faded, replaced by the mix of feelings regarding the feminine interloper.

It seemed like every last one of the knights was here! Before the official commencement, Perceval and Galahad kept mostly to themselves, trying to pick out faces or heraldic emblems. They recognized Gawaine, Gaheris, Gareth, though the other Orkneys appeared absent. Lancelot arrived, receiving only a formal greeting from his daughter. Lucan, Kay, Bedivere, Dinadan, even Yvaine, and others met in recent months, mingled about. Some they didn't know had only heard about Galahad, and a few of these shifted glances between Lancelot and his proud offspring.

Kay had meanwhile actually gotten a bit used to being on guard against the latest of Dinadan's pranks. In truth, he was almost disappointed not to find another precarious water pail above the door or basket of stinky rotten eggs beneath his chair. The trickster opted to keep to himself this time, though most of the other knights laughed as Kay walked into the chamber and looked about anxiously.

"On my honor, I'm innocent, Kay," Dinadan shouted from across the room.

"Which is harder to believe," Kay answered in fun, "that you didn't trap the room this time or that you're a man of honor?" Many of the knights *ooh*ed, waiting a response. None came, other than Dinadan's smile, which usually meant he was plotting something.

Kay took over business. "Before the King arrives, I've announcements. Those of you who haven't need to get your lazy rears over to register for the tourney events. If it's not done by tomorrow noon then you're not competing."

"Oh, and no challenges within the ranks until the second round of the joust. The people wish to see the Round Table's finest defeat any potential decent fighters from abroad first, so keep your emotions in your drawers until you've had your first wins." Some laughter came at this.

Then Kay grew just a bit quieter. "Gentlemen, take your seats. His Majesty will be with us all shortly." He either forgot, or excluded, a reference to "Lady."

The assembly slowly sat in their respective places. Perceval, at the side of the table opposite Galahad, hugged her quickly then strode to his chair. It felt welcoming and yielding as he adjusted himself in its comfort.

Less than a minute later, Arthur appeared, with Kay just in front of him to make the announcement.

"Gentlemen, as your seneschal and the King's brother, it is my privilege and honor to proclaim this thirty-sixth annual Pentecostal commencement of the highest order of the Round Table, and the ninetieth meeting since our noble and true King assumed the throne of Logres. All shall rise and give hail to Arthur of the Britons!"

Applause rang through the room, echoing off the stone walls. They clapped till their ears rang, whistling and hollering for added effect. If nothing else, Arthur's men (and woman) were loyal and proud. The King tried to mask his own emotion, resting in the comfortable belief that his ideals might yet outlive him. He stood for several minutes before the fanfare died down. At least they all were in high spirits; with the news he and some of the others had to share, they'd need it.

Kay shut the massive doors behind his foster-brother, then waited at the King's side while he sat first. Then over nine dozen knights took their chairs at once as Kay gave the signal when he reached his own place.

"Thus convenes our latest assembling," said Kay.

Perceval and Galahad would never tire of this scene, even though it was routine to the older members: the glittering of polished armor, the thousand candles lighting the place well into the evening, complete with the wine and food that would be consumed while the affairs of Logres were discussed, debated, and decided.

The squires of some of the older knights had the privilege of serving the wine. Perceval requested a heady crimson vintage, the smell reminding him of a time he got drunk with Llio. They made love in the grass outside the city, down by the river Cam. Their sexual skill and comfort had grown leaps and bounds since a first nervous night in Worcester. They explored each other's glistening bodies while their mouths teased and tasted and savored faces, necks, fingers, the urges in their loins made them arch their backs and curl their toes in giddy ecstasy. All else was forgotten when Llio drew Perceval into her; they both could delay the inevitable frantic release for immeasurable lengths of time while they just enjoyed each other, talking softly and teasing each other. That last time they came together. Perceval would never forget it. They had listened to the frogs and crickets and turtles and fish, all jumping about and likely carrying on with one another with all the sweaty pulsing energy he and his late wife exhibited.

"– with new concerns," interrupted Kay. "The Orkney clan shall report first, representing the lands north of the Wall."

Gawaine took over the talk, his younger brothers eyeing him. "Pict attacks have increased again, extending into our own Lothian. Our mother the Queen has repelled them thus far, but our absences from court, and," he looked around, "those of our brothers will likely increase before it all ends." Actually, Gawaine knew his mother had some odd dealings with the Picts, but remained unsure as to their exact nature. Agrivaine and Mordred were home more often than not now, and Mordred had been so unapproachable since the Jagent tournament last year.

Gaheris took over where Gawaine's puzzled look left off. "In truth, my lord, there's little concern with them. Though the scouts have spotted Garmani ships that far north, there aren't enough convenient landing sites in Lothian to support a mass invasion, but their venturing so far beyond their normal reaches would seem to indicate a certain desperation." Gaheris knew mention of the Garmani would distract the listeners from the Picts, as his mother wished. He had Pictish friends as a boy, after Gawaine left to start his apprenticeship. Whatever his mother had planned, Gaheris wanted the King to look elsewhere for quelling disturbances.

"They've never been known to stray that far from Anglia and the east lands. They must be searching for new areas to settle." This concern came from Lucan, who could not even begin to count the number of Garmani he'd sent to Valhalla.

"Wouldn't it be simpler to just press inland again?" queried Kay.

"After Badon?" Arthur said. "They lost over half their numbers on the hill. They outnumbered us two to one, and we inflicted five casualties for each we took. Cerdic's dead, the other leaders the same or fled back to Germanic lands. What I want to know is whether they can support an invasion navy."

Every eye in the place looked to the King. "Navy, sire? One with enough men to overrun Logres?"

"Logres, or any other part of the Island from which they might gain the advantage they sought at Badon. Our own resources are stretched enough, and there's not land to go to all those who would have it." Arthur was proud of the diversity of his vassals and the remarkable tolerance they generally showed, but there inevitably came a time when there was too little to go around. Folk let their prejudices show at such occasions, and the memory of the Badon slaughter and of the "hairy barbarians of Kent and Sussex" was still fresh for many.

"Do you propose, your majesty, to construct our own fleet to meet them on the open sea?" The knights often made suggestions in the form of questions.

"No," Arthur said. "What I want is that to which you have all sworn yourselves: to be the fastest mobile force in history. I want you to continue being my eyes and ears all across the land. You all have done that for so many years I shudder to count for how many of them I've commanded you. You each need to be a symbol, now more than ever, of the Pax Brittanica. Our unrest continues to grow, and the people must see unity and strength here, of all places."

Nods and sounds of approval came from the knights. Then Arthur decided to speak of a topic which often had stuck in his throat, but he wanted it to be over with, especially since it had come to his attention that some people were talking about it, never mind it coming a years late.

He looked at Lancelot at his side, then addressed the group. "On the topic of unrest being met by strength, I have something to say, and know now that this shall be the only time I speak of it."

He cleared his throat, seeing Lancelot stiffen. So far as the King could guess, his friend was ignorant of what he would tell next. "I want it understood once and for all how I shall regard anyone I hear of who dares speak about my wife and her champion."

Lancelot looked up, concerned. Galahad felt the worst of emotions for him right then: pity. She had her visions of her father's "encounters" long before this day. "Simply put, there is nothing to tell. And erroneous slander about the King, the Queen, or a Round Table member, is regarded as treasonous. You all know this already. I reiterate because I'm damned tired of being the topic of conjectural conversation in my own kingdom. Is that clear, everyone?" Every head in the room nodded silently. "Good. Now, with that in mind, we can continue with our own news, and let us pray that there will be good encouraging reports to accompany this news from Gawaine. So, let us stay north for now, working our way down. What news of Gorre?"

"My mother sends her best wishes, my lord," said Yvaine, proud both to call the woman that and to be sitting in the room. "Uriens still holds his own."

"He may be old, nephew, but a good and strong man. How does your mother?" Arthur knew stressing the minimal relation between them helped keep the man bound to him.

"As fine as can be expected. She debates about setting up a regent, since I think she fancies governing herself. She makes few returns to home these days." Yvaine was careful not to mention Avalon. Those who would blame the Pagans for Britain's ills might well be in the majority.

"I hope she returns to Camelot soon," Arthur said, knowing the mood of his populace as astutely as Yvaine.

"She has no reports of Picts, Garmani, Irish, or anyone else who might pose a threat to Gorre. It would take more effort to capture the hills, granted, but things have remained quiet as of late."

"Speculation, gentlemen. Lady. Why would the Garmani and Picts only be interested in the eastern shores?" Arthur looked at Galahad as he said it.

Some murmurs followed, nothing concrete. Then Lancelot spoke. "Picture a northern invasion, Pict and Garmani fighting together, sweeping through one kingdom at a time until they stand poised to charge Logres."

The thought was sobering, but also comedic. "Why ever would the faeries band with Garmani? The Garmani use more iron than they can imagine. And Picts don't organize themselves cohesively enough on a battlefield." This came from one of the younger members.

"Neither do Garmani," countered Lancelot. "The reason they've proven such a nuisance in the past has been through sheer numbers and battle frenzy. Why don't you ask a Badon veteran how well he recalls the berserker cry, or the way they swing those double-hand, double-edged axes?"

"The question remains," Kay said. "Why the north, and the eastern coastlands?"

Arthur looked pensively at Gawaine, thinking about the real reason he had made Lancelot another champion and heir-apparent. The King did not trust his half-sister any further than he could spit, and the previous choice of Gawaine he could rack up to youthful immaturity and wishful thinking. He wondered how Gawaine and his brothers dealt with having that woman for a mother. And he wondered what Gawaine might have left out of his report on Lothian. He hated the art of politics, but had grown to live with its necessary counterpart of deception. Regardless of sentiment for his nephew, he was not about to give Margawse even the remotest claim to the throne.

"The Picts have never shown interest in conquering. What would they do with all the extra land?" asked Lucan. "They don't farm as it is. They wouldn't know how to work Logres if they had it."

"Maybe they only want the hills, down to the lake regions."

"I didn't pose the question to finalize a military solution," Arthur intoned. "I merely wanted you all to be thinking of its implications. Obviously the need to remain watchful is reinforced when we consider a joint threat, or multiple threats. But the Garmani has always come from the sea, before Vortigern gave Anglia and the other eastern provinces to him. It therefore seems worth considering that he shall come freshly from there yet again."

The meeting proceeded for hours in this manner, with the King hearing reports of goings-on throughout the land. The members learned of Gareth's upcoming marriage, and the hardships he endured during his first tumultuous quest. The enemy knight was beaten, but his kingdom was intimidatingly chaotic, poised to join an uprising should one begin.

They heard the story of Trystan's death at the hands of Marcus, for no other reason than jealousy out of control. Marcus was no longer considered an ally, and had fled to his and his wife's old holdings in Eire-land, leaving Dumnonia and Lyonesse largely to their own devices.

Also told was how a young minstrel named Taliesin had become arch-druid in reputation and knowledge, if not in name (though Merlin had no such title himself; it was a manner of speaking among those who placed faith in druidical tradition).

Arthur almost wept himself as he shared news of the (still) lack of an heir, and all present knew Guinevere was past bearing age. It was a grave confession to make. Already those who would oppose him cited the lack of central authority upon his demise, and the countless tribes and clans and churches and lesser kingdoms would not remain united without the Pendragon banner to either rally them all or keep them in check. The King offered some hope by emphasizing Lancelot as heir in the event no son could be produced, and Arthur would not even comment upon the supposed son who performed so brilliantly in Gornymant's Jagent tourney a short time ago, only to disappear afterwards. Mordred seemed to wear a mask to most, and had the passion and temper of one coddled by Margawse.

In truth, many present thought this part of the meeting a little dull, despite the colorful stories which gave a memorable feel, and those who finished reporting were free to start imbibing. The wine flowed freely in the chamber, as the news mostly exhausted itself.

"That brings us to announcements," Kay said. Those knights who had something to proffer the group made their intentions known by raising their goblets to gain attention. When they wanted more wine, they usually thumped said goblets against the table.

Yvaine spoke. "Congratulations to our lady member, Galahad, for taming the Siege Perilous." The applause which followed was mixed. Some were obviously eager to have a woman in their midst; others hesitated, offering their clapping hands because good taste demanded it. Galahad smiled, almost smirked. She sneaked a glance at Perceval, who whistled and cheered loudest of all.

Lucan shouted when it had died down, "Thanks to Bedivere for vanquishing the *afanc* in Norgales." More applause at this. Knights always cheered when others of their kind overcame obvious enemies. Bedivere would not comment on this; the Cambrian locals spoke of a menacing water spirit, roused to wreaking havoc when the foolish mortals had despoiled its home with wood burnings and waste. It looked like a giant animal, almost a monstrous beaver, though with a huge head and massive fangs. Bedivere was not that specific.

But on the topic of enemies, the fanfare roared out once again for young Gareth and his victory over a foe who had long been robbing caravans and capturing and humiliating knights. A few minutes were then spent listening to Gareth's description of the duel, after he journeyed through a portion of that rogue's lands which sounded as though the Wasteland had expanded even further. The trees were dead and barren, and used to hang the latter red knight's victims while still in their armor, creaking in the empty air for years on end. On his knees and waiting Gareth's executionary cut, this villain said he robbed and pillaged so many for so long because his crops had failed, his subjects had mostly died off, and so he turned to a life of criminality. Gareth finally killed him out of pity, not knowing what to do with the castle or the nearby lands, both of which were falling into ruin. The room fell silent during the telling, spoiling the mood. Everyone knew the wastes continued to grow, no one knew why exactly, and the idea that the whole island might one day succumb to the swelling pestilence was starting to make many edgy, to put it mildly. Part of Gawaine's vague report from his own home was that he felt afraid to confront the route to Lothian again. Too many stories like the mentally destroyed naked and bloody villagers and the torched church which spewed forth arrow-laden bodies had already come to light. What was still left wanting was an answer.

How do we heal the land? people wanted to know, not the least of them the great knights.

The announcements continued, helping a bit in restoring the mood. Congratulatory remarks went to those who fared well at the tournament Gornymant hosted. Entire circuits of tourneys had grown during the past decade or so, with the same places and persons hosting them year after year. It gave the knights regular venues to display themselves, show off their names and deeds, give less experienced knights chances for fame and fortune, and most importantly to Arthur, allowed venting of frustrations among them which otherwise had a tendency to erupt in bloodier violence. Yvaine never challenged his cousin, not even on the joust list. He just wanted to forget. And once again, he was already letting the wine at the table flow a bit too freely.

They heard other snippets as well. Dame Viviane had fallen ill, or so went the rumor. Nimue apparently became reigning priestess of Avalon, and was reputedly working side by side with the likes of Morgan and Taliesin, for what end remained uncertain. The Christian knights mostly scoffed at this.

Galahad and Perceval both refused to applaud, not caring if their insolence went noticed, at the mention of Agrivaine's impending marriage to Lupinia. The former two weren't sure whether to dislike Agrivaine for being such a bastard all the time or to fault Lupy for giving in to him. They felt quite convinced he was in it for dowry and sons, nothing more.

The man next to Perceval, Bors, a distant connection to the Continental Ganis clan, muttered softly in Perceval's ear how Agrivaine fortunately did not wreck the Jagent tourney like he had tried to do with others. Bors said the man was too full of himself to prove any worth to a wife, and his brother made a fine showing anyway. Agrivaine was probably jealous of his younger sibling; Mordred indeed fared well, defeating everyone he faced in the joust except Lancelot, who unhorsed him in the fifth of six rounds.

Perceval didn't really know Bors, other than just a face and name and the odd connection to Lancelot's blood. He had remained totally silent during the meeting up to that point, having looked quite morose when news of Trystan received voice. Perceval felt for him then; the pair of them must have been close.

Perceval snickered slightly at the description of Agrivaine, and could clearly see the older knight bragging about his latest conquest, be it by flesh or steel. He caught an incendiary look from Gaheris; Orkneymen were loyal to the last, no matter their indiscretions. He shifted his focus to Galahad.

She looked nervous up near Arthur, and alone. Maybe they could all take off for a while after the meeting, with Llascoit and Dindraine, perhaps Yvaine. It might prove rewarding to just disappear from city life for a time.

Except Perceval didn't know where he might want to travel this time. The urge was in his blood, surely, but where to start? Oerfa was already defunct, he heard, and it didn't surprise him. Dindraine had no greater desire than his to visit their old home, especially now that all which likely remained was a bunch of rotting wood. He knew little of the residents and their fates;

what tidbits he possessed heralded from the occasional wandering minstrel or touring merchant who in turn had heard something of someone.

Somewhere... Jagent, then, or Worcester? No, those would prove too agonizing for him. The loss of Llio still crashed over Perceval like one of the endless waves off Lyonesse, forever wearing it down.

That didn't seem to leave many places. The Continent, perhaps? Yvaine knew his way around the foreign lands, and Perceval had still never been on a ship. He saw himself and the others aboard a proud vessel like the formidable trader he and Galahad saw in Viroconium.

The time did indeed fly, like those geese on their way home from winter roost. He decided he'd better listen to the rest of the meeting, and not wallow in the melancholy of remembrance. He had the serving squires pour his goblet full, and sampled the cheese.

None of those present: king, seneschal, champions, lady, knights, servants, would ever reach consensus as to just what happened next. It caught them totally unaware, and that was part of its beauty.

At first Kay looked around angrily, ready to reprimand to whichever servant had been stupid enough to brighten the room so quickly. It wasn't until he noticed that such illumination was well beyond the capacity of the candles and fireplaces and sunlight permitted through the windows that he grew nervous instead, looking to his king for answers. When they were boys, Kay had always been full of answers; if he didn't know he'd make one up, until Arthur grew old enough to know better.

But now that those tables had turned, the King had no answers, either, only the look of awe on his face. No fear, only curiosity. No one in the chamber ever saw this man fear anything.

The others began to look about now, too. The light seemed to come from everywhere and nowhere; the room was already bright enough that they had to squint to keep seeing. They had grown used to the dusky setting of the chamber, and this new radiance was too much too fast for their eyes to grow accustomed. And it had no obvious source! Some of the knights joined the servants in panicking, though none would run for fear of being branded coward. Some of the others hoped they would see the light's source once their vision acclimated.

Who was it who spoke to them? They all wished to know. Some would later claim to have received a visit from one of the angels. Others would see a goddess image, strange and familiar at once. Whomever "she" was, "her" words came clearly to all in attendance. Like the light itself, the voice had no apparent source; it was in front of each person, around them, to the sides, now behind, but always warm and soothing, like the bedtime words of a loving mother as it spoke.

"Go you now to seek what is lost, find that which is absent from your physical lives and plant it in the Earth's breast. Each of you knows of what I speak, and you have never realized how close it truly is. Go then, those of you who will, and make peace with that which you fear. Follow your own passions, and reach for the divine."

That was how Perceval heard it. Alas, there would be no consensus regarding the phantom speech either, but everyone was clearly moved deeply by whatever they believed they actually heard.

More than one thought they recognized the speaker on a personal level. Some even could have sworn that Galahad herself recited the words. They stared at her, the only woman in the men's sanctuary. The chosen one?

It was over in seconds, of that Perceval was certain. He glanced toward Galahad. For the first time, he laughed as he watched her cross herself. He didn't even know why, it just felt good to laugh aloud.

Some of the others, including Galahad, glared back at him, a number of them wondering how he could possibly profane such a mystical experience. But, he told himself again, all he saw was a light, all he heard was a voice. It sounded familiar to him, too, but not like Galahad's. It was like the day after the Bridgnorth feast, when he thought he heard his sister.

And now the voices of the enraptured began, one after another. He couldn't tell who started it, as it grew into a chant. "The Grail," they said, first singly then as a group. "It is the Grail, and its guardian has spoken to us."

And they understood, even Perceval did; they had been shown the way. Galahad must have been right all along. From her very first story. And, Perceval almost shuddered, *she spoke of this day, just as it now happened!*

Tathan spoke to him now, in distant memory, from the time he and Dindraine used to roll down the hills near Oerfa, laughing and screaming in the sheer joy of being alive, the same joy which always seemed to die with age. *Why is that?* Perceval wondered.

And the slain warriors were placed into the Cauldron, from which they were made whole and breathing again. But this had a price, for none of those so revived could speak. Perceval could hear the bard as plainly now as he did then, relating another of the tales he had tried to ignore, but now it made sense. The Cauldron of his ancestors, the archaic vessel which took so many forms, from rebirth chamber to the source of druidical wisdom to the simple cooking pot which would only prepare dishes for those heroic enough to earn them. And the Grail, the chalice which inspired the Mass, which contained the remnants of Jesus' own blood, and which would grant knowledge or healing or perhaps other wishes to the chosen recipient. And Perceval heard Tathan's old words again. *All the gods and goddesses are one, lad. Anyone who claims otherwise is selling something, and who can possibly sell that which cannot be bought?*

Then does Pellam keep it, like Galahad suggested? Perceval wondered, knowing he would soon have to talk with her about it. *And if so, then under what circumstances? Everything I've heard suggests the Grail cannot be kept by mortals: it's too powerful, too large a responsibility.*

And besides, men like Bishop Baudwin and Abbot Uren had the task of reminding others that some things were just too tempting, too potentially corrupting, for mere humans to handle.

The mostly hushed discussion around the Table continued unabated. The King let them talk amongst themselves, having no conclusions to offer, and desperately wished Merlin was still around to help. He knew that sooner or later his knights would demand an answer to the obvious question. Quest. Question. Arthur had never before noticed how similar the words were.

Lancelot, perhaps the most passionate of them all, spoke first. "My lord," he said. "We have all served witness to the most marvelous of events! I beg your leave that I might pursue this quest, Sire." Many of the other knights grunted and cheered their assent. The voice reminded Lancelot of Nimue. Yvaine heard his mother Morgan speak the words. Arthur heard Guinevere, sounding as quietly knowing as the day they met, already carrying Excalibur and leading men like Leondegrance. Gawaine thought the voice like Ragnell's, and missed her once more. Gareth thought of his beloved, and imagined their first child grown to adult, having blessed the Table with her soothing words. And those knights who were not so overcome with the echoes of rapturous and glorious feminine intonations shouted and discussed what it all could mean.

The King raised a hand, signaling silence. When he had quiet, he spoke calmly. "My knights, far be it from me, a mere politician, to proclaim that which is deservedly marvelous or magickal. Yet I have been witness to so many truly remarkable happenings in the course of this life, and I tell you all that never have I seen or heard the likes of that." He took his time speaking, looking slowly around the table, making eye contact with as many as possible. Some looked thrilled, while others looked terrified. Bedivere, for some reason, appeared furious.

Arthur continued. "It is hardly news that the land is ill, and that my subjects, who have bent to my commands and policies these decades, have begun to live in the state of want and fear which preceded this reign. If riding forth on a quest, perhaps the grandest of all, promises hope of restoring the glory that was, then I would ride forth in its name myself were it not for my duties within Camelot."

Almost all cheered at that, reminded of what was great within their order.

Again he awaited their silence. Having their attention once more, Arthur said, "Then this is my proclamation. I want each of you, the symbols and instruments of this rule and its policies, to keep as visible as possible. I want you in the streets during the tourney, I want this celebration to be the greatest ever, I want you all on your most chivalrous behavior with everyone you encounter. And when the festivities come to a close, those who would do so shall ride forth in the name of the Quest for the Holy Grail. You will be my eyes and ears, and my noble seekers. Leave no forest, hill, cave, plain, or lake unsearched. Recover the glory we once had, for only then may your king pass in peace, knowing he gave all he could for the glory and fruition of Britain."

He knew how to motivate, no one would ever fault Arthur that. Many of them stood and applauded, whistling, clapping, so loudly it could be heard in the streets outside, and in the Queen's garden.

At this point only a few still looked apprehensive, among them Perceval, Galahad, and Gawaine. Bedivere wanted to storm out of the hall he was so angry, but the king, his personal friend, had spoken, come what would. This was not the time for bitterness.

But Bedivere could not help wondering: if so many of the knights were gone questing, who would remain behind to keep Logres' borders secure?

* * *

The snake scared Styfnig badly enough that he almost fell tail over goblet, and might have all but crushed Perceval, who at least finally learned what the hissing creature was.

Had Styfnig possessed the gift of speech, he would have complained how the long cold-blooded thing just slithered out from nowhere, and he promptly stomped it into scaly paste.

"What in the hells *is* that?" Perceval demanded of no one in particular.

"A snake, fool. Don't you have snakes back in Wales?" Llascoit said. "It was one, anyway." He dismounted, fascinated with the pulverized creature. Llascoit felt sorry for it, really; it did nothing wrong, and had probably been as terrified as the behemoth which jumped up and down on it with its hooves.

"Just a garden snake, harmless," he pronounced.

Llascoit's fascination with things dead brought bemused looks from Galahad and Dindraine, who made up the rest of the little band. No squires nor servants attended them, as they preferred to travel on their own.

"Llas, just leave it. Let's keep riding." Galahad quickly became the antsy, unofficial leader of the trek. More than any of the others, she knew Grail lore, plus a knowledge of things Biblical. She shared her curiosity with them after they left Camelot many days earlier, reporting that the Grail was mentioned nowhere at all in the Bible. Only the "cup," which Jesus used for so simple, yet so powerfully faithful an exercise. The vessel was merely the device of a doomed man.

And she didn't like snakes. No one intimate with the Good Book would likely be. Serpents had a negative connotation since the conclusion of Genesis and the beginning of human imperfection.

Llascoit climbed atop his charger. Only Perceval still watched the reptile. "A snake?" he said, finally answering Llascoit's question. He looked at his foster-brother. "And incidentally, it's Cambria to you. I'll not be called a foreigner in my own land, especially not by something so crude as that Garmani name."

"But it's not your home anymore. You told me that. And when was the last time you even saw a Garmani?" Llascoit never tired of baiting Perceval, the way Llio used to. The difference was, sometimes Llas didn't know when to stop.

"For that matter, what about you? Jagent is hardly infested with the bear-skinned followers of Wotan and Thor."

Llascoit sobered. "My father told me enough about them. They're treacherous beyond the worst robber knight, and they poison their axes. I've even heard of them using those, those, oh, what in blazes are those curved things with the ropes?"

"Bows?" asked Perceval. "We have those in Cambria. Who's the fool now?"

"Oh, give it a rest, why don't you both?" Dindraine was already tired of this. She wanted to be on the march again, along from curiosity and the desire to be on hand as a healer, if required.

Perceval recalled how the only bows he'd ever seen used had loosed their arrows at hunted animals, not humans. He watched the snake's carcass again. "Dindraine, what do you know of these snakes?" He had never seen one, except in places of which he was hesitant to speak, and he didn't want to hear Galahad's recitations of Bible stories again.

Dindraine offered the list based on her own experience. "They bleed like us, only it's cool to the touch, even when they first die. Their skin and eyes, even the poison of those which carry it, can be boiled or otherwise used in potions." She scanned the other faces quickly, hoping that Galahad was wise enough to know potions did not derive their power from demons and devils. Even Jesus turned water to wine; no alchemist could hope to duplicate that.

"Poison!" Perceval barked. "Some of these things can just kill you with one bite, then?"

"Not likely, though you'd still be very ill." She continued, "The snake is also a symbol, an omen sometimes. One alone can be bad luck, while two together, especially intertwined, are considered good." She almost laughed as Galahad and Llascoit looked about the area on the road for a possible second snake.

"An omen," Perceval said softly.

"What is it?" his sister asked, knowing her brother's moods and body language.

He smiled. "It think I'm starting to understand it now."

"What?" they all demanded.

"Gal, do you remember the weird dreams we had, when we first rode together?"

"Do I! Sleeping near you sent my mind to some fantastic places!" Llascoit laughed at that. He always laughed at whatever reminded him of the sex that, to the knowledge of the women with him, he still had not experienced. He knew otherwise, but chose to keep talk of his encounters with women of the sort pursued by the Orkneys (save young Gareth, of course) to himself and his male friends, including Perceval. He would have to hope that some treasure of a woman would still consider mating for life, since he had learned humans and geese were only alike during the art of sexual conquest, not afterwards. Besides, Llio's chastisement of him and his allegedly sexist views remained with Llascoit.

Perceval knew he had their undivided attention now. They all knew of the dream shared by Perceval and Galahad about the presentation of the Grail's likeness to the Round Table members, and the no less stunning story of the odd procession down some dank corridor in the nude, with an anonymous third party.

"Do you remember the one with the man and the boy?"

Galahad did indeed. The story had terrified her. She nodded.

"The man was Arthur! That's it. And there was one of these creatures," he said, pointing down at the length of flesh, now dead. "When I saw the snake, they went at each other!"

Perceval was elated. The others looked visibly disturbed. "Who's the serpent, then?" asked Dindraine.

"What?"

"I said the animal could be symbolic. Who's the figurative snake, the boy?"

"I suppose… He looked hateful, but also afraid, like he knew all along Arthur would kill him. I remember the sword the man had in my dream, and he wore a crown!" Perceval was delighted to now recall it so clearly again.

Galahad spoke. "If the boy is the serpent, we have to know who he is. He's the death of our King."

"Oh, Galahad, come on," Llascoit said, who always called the woman by her full chosen name. "You're saying that Perceval dreamt who would kill the King, and he did it before we even met him?"

"Let's just say I have some faith in a true vision," Galahad answered coolly. "And I think Perceval may have had one."

Llascoit didn't like this, but felt he was the only one. He opted to change the topic, just enough to put himself at ease.

He'd had enough strange dreams himself, and liked to hear how he wasn't alone. "Where was the tunnel?"

"The tunnel?"

"Or the hallway? Wherever you and Galahad were running around in your finest birthday garb." Galahad would have blushed once at such a comment. Now it amused her.

"I think we were on our search for the Grail," she said.

"Speaking of which, shouldn't we keep riding? It may take quite a while to find Bridgnorth again," said Dindraine, who enjoyed the traveling and talking for their own sakes. Like her brother, she never tired of seeing the world beyond the hills. And she was the only one who didn't see much urgency in their mission, other than to get away from the snake remains and keep enjoying the day.

They urged the four horses onward. Only Perceval turned to watch the snake as it became a sliver behind them, then faded into nothing.

* * *

"Sire?" came the plaintive but firm voice from beyond the bedroom chamber. Within, Arthur sat alone, staring beyond the city walls into Logres.

He of course knew Bedivere's tone at once. "Come," he commanded.

The door swung open cautiously. Bedivere knew the tale of how Agrivaine supposedly tried to find the Queen and Lancelot together in bed, and any time the former was in Pendragon Castle, he opened the more private doors slowly. He didn't want to know anything about the rumored affair, had always denied it stoically, but remained nervous about bursting in on an inappropriate scene.

"My lord," he said. "I request your ear concerning an issue I believe of prime importance."

"Cease the formalities. I would prefer to speak with my oldest friend casually." Arthur continued to look out his huge window. Unlike most keeps and castles, there was no shortage of outside light in the main chambers.

Bedivere closed the door. "Then why won't you look at me?"

The King turned, perhaps too quickly. "Because I know what you're here to say, and because I believe you're mistaken."

"We've let too many of them go, Artos." Bedivere was the only one who still called him by his adopted Latin name. "This place feels as empty as an Orkney bed the morning after one of their sex fests when everyone goes home, satisfied aside from the hangover. The city watch has even reported more incidents of crime. You'll have to hear those cases, people who stole or assaulted right under our noses."

"Because so many of the knights are gone. But Bedivere, they've always been free to go. Indeed they've had to; they are the ones who see to the divisions of government which I cannot. They're the hands and eyes and ears; this is the heart of Logres."

"The heart of Logres is you, not this place. That's what you've never understood." Only three individuals had ever spoken this directly to the King, the others being Guinevere and Merlin. "And in the past, there hasn't been this sweeping exodus as they left. We finished the annual or seasonal concerns, and they went home, slowly, one at a time. When they started this quest the whole world must have known. I've never seen so many colors flying at once!"

Arthur ignored the last, recalling the pride of witnessing his best announce to the world that there was nothing they couldn't accomplish, not even finding that which might not actually exist. "It's not focused on me alone. Merlin tried to tell me that, too, but I think it was really more about him."

"Why, because he saw the future? Because he ensured that you were begotten, and by particular parents?" A generation earlier, the then young King might have had someone's tongue for such crass boldness. Now he saw what the statements meant.

"Yes! Do you have any idea how many times I've felt like a pawn? The times I've truly felt free were when I was in the most peril. On the hunt, off to battle, wondering whether field and fate will send Garmani or disease to finally finish me off. Not even in my own wife's arms. That was arranged also!"

"So why is this new quest so important to you?"

"Because it's important to them," Arthur said, pointing out the window, perhaps to all civilization. "And because I ordered it. Merlin never mentioned the Grail. It was my own decision, and you heard how I said it. I just want something of what we've done here to last. All the fighting, the building, all the care and effort we've put into this way of life, and the peace and plenty which followed; I can't let that die. And the Grail is about things not dying but lasting."

Bedivere had listened to this man endless times, and knew how persuasive he could be, especially when he spoke passionately. Rarely did he speak otherwise. Showing emotion was a risky trait for a ruler, but Arthur pulled it off. His words, and those of his Queen, had soothed the thorns from all manner of issues and decisions, leaving the roses which flourished in their place.

But the man who grew up as friend to Arthur and Kay, trained and studied with them under the watchful eye of old Ector, Kay's blood father, still was horrified by the implications, no matter how noble the cause.

"Would you consider this, then? If there really is a sizable force out there waiting to engage us, it's hopefully too late to plan and mount an offensive this year. That gives us till next spring before we likely would have to be concerned. Do you think it can be found that quickly?"

"Ever since Gawaine brought back that green sash, we've always said 'a year and a day.' I don't know. How could we know?"

"Do Margawse and Mordred despise you enough to try attacking? We already know how groups of able men from every kingdom outside Logres, Garmani, Irish, Picts, whomever, have ventured off on unknown enterprises."

Arthur did not allow himself to wince at the mention of the two names which caused more trouble than anyone save the late Cerdic, leader of the impossibly large army crushed at Badon. "Yes. At least with Mordred I can understand it. He thinks he has a legitimate claim, but I'd sooner hand Logres to the Church. At least they'd keep some sense of order. Margawse is so spiteful and chaotic, she'd let it all just die, like that lump of coal she calls a heart. Do you know the worst part?"

Bedivere, the man known often as the Griffin for the way he hovered about cautiously before rendering swift judgment with his mind or his sword, simply shook his head.

"I honestly don't know why she hates me so much. And she did come to me that night, after the northern battles, but before Lot was killed. I thought she just wanted to teach him a lesson. It wasn't until later I learned that, that –"

Bedivere refused to shame the man by extending a helping hand or comforting word. He just waited for the iron will to regain control. That was what he did best.

"That she was my half-sister. Some wonder I got so drunk the next few nights. The other part that's so bad is that I've no way to know if Mordred's mine."

"Did you see him at Jagent?"

Arthur nodded. "He has my eyes. He even moves like I do when he fights. And he has that youthful frustration I did. He's not Lot's; Gawaine's brothers all look like Lot reincarnated just like the druids told. I don't know if I have a son, and what Camelot needs most is an heir. I certainly can't eliminate him now that he's become recognizable."

"We tried that once already, and things may have worsened for it." Bedivere clearly remembered the mission in Lothian, rounding up the recently born males and setting them adrift. Those who knew of it simply referred to the "May Babies," for the time of year. The great annual celebration in Camelot was partly an atonement for once again trying to live up to Merlin's expectations.

The old druid foresaw doom for the young king at the hands of a son in the north, and Arthur remained wary of so-called sooth-saying ever since. The King found dry amusement in the knowledge that the ploy didn't work; a particular male child had a name and a face. And an agenda, but that remained uncertain.

Bedivere felt guilty for pressing so, but knew Arthur expected and even demanded that from him. The former was the King's harshest judge, and always a realist. They didn't often disagree, but when they did, both did all they could to make sure the best decision was made.

The knight tried to soothe his king. "I would not worry about him. No one would accept a claim from Lot's land; he had too many enemies." Reminded of the past, he changed the topic, again trying to comfort. "It won't be like it was when we slaughtered them all."

"Why not? Wouldn't you crave vengeance if you were run off your land, had your farms and homes burned, your children killed?" Arthur learned at an early age that quelling a group meant forcibly ejecting them all from the land he needed safe for his own. There was far more to the King's rise to power than a sword, a wizard, and a battle for an otherwise drab and treeless hill just a few dozen miles west of the current Garmani borders. These three had grown out of proportion during this reign: the sword Excalibur, forged and used by the divinities, the wise old druid who had become seer, healer, and magician, and the battle "which felled tens of thousands of those looting Garmani dogs."

Power never came without price, that was Merlin's first lesson, taught to a boy who only saw how brightly the blade shone. And now the King felt his earlier decisions and policies might return to haunt him and his kingdom.

"Of course. And we were the ones seeking that retribution when we took back what was ours to begin with. Vortigern let them in, then couldn't control them. They would have swallowed us whole if not for Badon. Before that it was always turn them back here, reinforce a holding there, but there were always more. And to where would we have retreated? Eire? They still kill their kings by the time they reach your age there."

"Bedivere, I know all of this. I've learned never to forget my rationale for making decisions. But a whole generation has grown while we've sat in this keep and watched, and not just here, but everywhere. New Garmani. New Picts. How long can the central power maintain in the absence of a central force?"

"My point exactly," Bedivere countered, no longer trying to soften blows and remembering the reason for his visit. "Logres' central force is out now looking for something that's not supposed to be found."

"But dispatching them to all corners will remind the people! Logres would be nothing without the knights who charged with us, bled with us, overcame their own differences for us. They are the men who crushed the invaders, those who have no more legitimate claim to this soil than Margawse's child. Yes, Vortigern let them in, as mercenaries; they were not meant to stay, but they saw a rich land and sent envoys home to make more axes. But we've been here since the ice melted. And that's why this quest is so important. There's no villain out there that they seek this time, no evil to overcome, no legal judgment to make. I see the Grail as the representation of all we labored so hard to achieve here, and if I can't have an heir of my own, then damn it, let me find the Grail!"

Bedivere stood there silently a few moments, staring out the window and thinking of his own family: the wife who had graciously moved to Camelot, the children he had, their ages already numbering in the double digits. The idea of barbarians without honor edging closer to the ramparts of the gigantic hill-fort near the river Cam motivated him to speak. He knew all too well how the survivors of invasion were dealt with, and he could not sit with the idea of his family suffering in the absence of so much military strength.

No time to dwell on that, though. The knights have already left, on their greatest quest, or biggest folly. I wonder which. "What's this about the ice?" was all he could think to say then.

"Hmm?" grunted Arthur. "Oh. The Picts know that story, about how they've been here since a time when ice covered all the northern lands. The ice just makes me think of the inevitable."

"I have yet to see that which is inevitable, even in you. After all, what if you never pulled that sword? What if you never had the chance?"

"Do you think the sweeping of one people over another on this island is fated? It's happened so many times: Faerie flees from Pict flees from Cymru."

"Of course not. Did we leave when the Romans came? And you left out the Irish and Garmani, who don't go far to conquer and die before giving an inch. We're here to stay because we adapt and organize. What can you expect from the Picts, who spend their time hidden and only fight when they can ambush?"

"You sound like Gawaine."

"And the faeries? Please. They're a story. The Picts probably think they've descended from them, or some such nonsense. Some think they're even one and the same."

"Since you're so comfortable with fate, answer my original question."

Bedivere thought about it. "Which was?"

"Is what we did in the past about to catch up to us?"

"I suspect that depends mostly on the knights, now."

* * *

"Stop," commanded Llascoit coolly, trying to keep his voice soft. He wondered if they had really made such a wise decision after all. The forest hid them well, but could also hide others.

They had reached the depths of the Dean, now southeast of Viroconium. They elected to bypass the city entirely when they found an old trail to the east, where Perceval and Galahad had not ventured previously. All hoped it would prove a shortcut through much of the forest, getting them to Bridgnorth that much faster.

Perceval knew the tone, its hint of anxiety. "What?" he said as softly.

Llascoit gestured down the path with a slight nod of his head, not wanting to alert potential brigands by pointing. "We're not alone," he whispered, once Perceval arrived at his side.

"Are you sure?"

"It's just a feeling. And I trust my instincts. Something's in those trees." Again he gestured, and Perceval followed his glance.

Nothing. Just the dark labyrinth, the only sounds from birds and rustling ground animals.

Behind them, Galahad and Dindraine remained silent. Galahad had been anxious about this route also, recalling her lifelong trepidation for the forest.

But then Perceval signaled them to move forward. They thought it safe.

It was just before they reached the men that it happened. The blood-screams of battle erupted all around them, making every horse save Styfnig rear up in sudden terror. Then the unrecognized knights charged, four of them, each one formerly hidden behind one of the impossibly aged and thickened trees. They bore down on Perceval and Llascoit with open helms, their grins already visible.

Galahad and the men in front at once drew their blades, and she thought to return the charge in front of her, but then she heard Dindraine's own scream next to her. "Gal, they're behind us!"

Galahad wheeled Brownie with her knees, sword and shield in hand. Sure enough, a team of a half dozen footsoldiers came sprinting at them. She knew that to face them would likely doom her and leave Dindraine at their mercy. Victorious knights were bad enough; victorious bandits might let her bleed to death while raping her.

"Dindraine, come!" Galahad yelled, and to Dindraine's disbelief, they urged their horses to cover the fifty odd yards to Perceval and Llascoit.

Up ahead, the charge was almost met. "Who are these bastards?" Llascoit wondered aloud.

"When we have their heads on our lances, we'll try and find out. Llascoit, charge!" They both screamed, not seeing the women or bandits behind them, and lunged into their assailants.

Hooves pounding, horses' flanks lathering from exertion and the smell of fear, cold steel banging against more of its kind. The blur of a battle larger than an individual duel was something unknown to any of them. They imagined it would be just a group of smaller such duels, with themselves slashing and parrying their way from one to the next. Even in a small skirmish like this, the truth was uglier, the fear palpable.

Llascoit met the first and rode right into the second, barely meeting the man with his shield. He immediately lost sight of the first, but had no time to look around. He didn't notice his horse literally rub alongside his enemy's, could not afford to glance about for any identifying shield crest or other emblem. Recognition came blurry or not at all. And he remembered none of his training; there was no time for the formulation of exercises or combat theory, only conditioned muscles trying to survive while simultaneously allowing the sword to strike where it had to. Again, and again. Their opponents were determined.

Perceval fared little better, though he wounded his first with a gash to the arm, increasing the scream-noise by that much. He was just thankful they hadn't attacked in the open with lances; the forest precluded such large weapons. The second man got to his front and stayed there, trying at first to beat Perceval through his mount. The latter had to lean almost out of the saddle to ward off a blow aimed at Styfnig's head.

The death dance continued, persons yelling and oblivious to their hoarse lungs which would leave their throats sore later. Those who survived. There was only the blur, the only motion whatever chaotic swing or thrust or feint would get the job done. No tactics existed at this level; gone was the clarity which went into the planning of battles, even those the size of this small ambush.

The last place Dindraine wished to be was in the middle of the storm, and she was the only one clear-headed enough to hope the knights could be dispatched before the infantry closed the gap. She drew her own dagger while riding into the fray, mimicking Galahad's own furious and mad battle cry as she watched the younger woman raise sword above head, ready to spill the guts of whomever dared attack those she cared for.

Llascoit ignored his bleeding head, could not recall how it got that way. He kept maneuvering his own steed in between and around the attackers as best he could, never forgoing the few openings either of them left. His arm felt leaden and immobile, but he had to ignore it. He could not feel his left hand, so tightly was it gripped around the leather handle of his shield. And he hardly heard himself yell with delight as his blade found its marker at last, carving sickeningly through iron rings and the precious skin, meat, and ribs beneath them. The first knight slumped dumbly in his saddle, falling from it as his horse moved away.

Perceval had a fleeting image of a sword not his own caving in his shield, the blade rending the reinforced wood and leather and iron to find fleshy arm beneath. He was surprised a moment later to realize it had just been fantasy. The action had slowed down, he was certain; how else could he daydream so? It grew quieter as well, or was that the ringing in his ears? It made no difference. The only part he'd later recall was the comically stupid look on his enemy's face as frothy gray bits of brain oozed down its sides; Perceval thought he vaguely remembered landing his sword into the man's head, fearing his sturdy weapon might break rather than pass through helmet and skull.

Women screamed about him now. Where did they come from? They were beyond the range of whispers when this all began. Was that Galahad? She had buried her sword into the chest of a man whose name he did not know; Perceval almost felt pity for him.

Then he knew: there was a fourth. Quickly, what happened to the last one? The force of the impact and the view of the damp ground looming in front of him provided the initial part of an answer. When he landed, his only thought was, *there can't be this much blood in three men.*

"Perceval! He still has his dagger." Llascoit's voice went unheard, Galahad and Dindraine joining him in a drive to win through sheer numbers, though this meant that for the moment, the closing infantry went forgotten.

Llascoit freed the last knight's sword from him, and the knight responded by moving out of the way of the others and tackling Perceval from behind, to make an easy throat kill or perhaps even to hold the man hostage until his own reinforcements arrived.

Perceval's sword and shield fell from him as he landed, and his own drive told him he'd be dead before he found them. Only the other man mattered.

And he showed himself, diving atop Perceval and trying to force a dagger into his neck. *His* neck, his precious flesh! What manner of scum was he fighting anyway, that would ambush a smaller group? His own anger swelled, his companions still critical yards away.

Perceval always felt he was a better grappler than swordsman any day. Clenching his teeth, and growling at the other man, he brought his knee into the stranger's groin, then rolled over to be on top of him.

The two movements gave Perceval all the opening he needed. Before getting any other response, he took advantage of the knight's confused and pained state, and with both hands bent the man's arm so that his dagger forced its way into his heart with his own hand still gripping it. He stared at Perceval with the fading of his being, cursing him with silent mouth and hateful eyes.

Llascoit and Galahad were both relieved, but the sick tension returned when they heard Dindraine yell. "Six more of them!"

As always during such a lethal promenade, instinct gripped more tightly than fear, and Perceval was on his feet, scanning till he found his sword, ignoring his shield; there was no time.

Galahad and Llascoit were already there, perversely delighted that at least there were no bows or lengthy pole-arms, only a raggedy collection of maces and spears, the residual weapons of knights who preferred finer tools. Perceval, now the only one of his party on foot, ran at them, sword held in bloody hands.

Apart from the chaos for just a moment, he saw two of the infantry go down easily, their lack of training compensated by numbers. The survivors already looked terrified; one was even trying to flee whence he came, into the wooded sea.

Perceval decided to chase him down, while the others were surrounded and Llascoit and Galahad each ripped open another, leaving one in the circle of horses, on his knees and pleading for his life.

Perceval was amused by now, the adrenaline and strength from a childhood chasing creatures faster than himself giving him the extra speed needed to catch his quarry. He was a knight. For Arthur and Glory!

He dove and caught the man in the legs, hearing the wind leave the man as he met the unforgiving ground.

The footsoldier was too startled to try running again, and when he felt a blade nick him at the back of the neck just enough to bring a trace of blood, he slowly stood, trying not to wet himself. He was sure he was doomed, but he wished to die with some semblance of dignity intact.

"Come," commanded Perceval. The man obligingly walked with him back to the others.

Perceval took command of the situation as he led the man into the circle of Llascoit, Galahad, Dindraine, and their mounts. He figured since he was on foot, he'd try talking first. He didn't like how they would probably have to kill these sods: one less today meant one less to fight later. But who were they?

"Who sent you?" was Perceval's first question. "Tell me now, and I may just take your purses."

The survivor who had not been tackled by Perceval hissed at them all. "If our purses had anything in them, we wouldn't have had to attack you!"

"Those knights," Perceval continued, ignoring the comment. "Who were they? Don't lie to me or I'll make it quite unpleasant. I doubt my friends are any more in the mood for leniency than I."

The pair of them sat there, trying not to tremble. Their recruiter had promised them so much, and he left them there! Left them to die. These knights were a despicable bunch, no honor among them at all.

There was a quick *whooft* sound, ending when one of the men grabbed his leg and yowled in agony, not yet realizing a knife was sticking from his thigh.

All non-yowling heads turned to the sound's source, listening to the voice which followed. "Aye, that we are not," said Dindraine. "Now if I, the frail little woman of the bunch, will happily toss a knife into your more sensitive regions, just try and use your shallow imaginations to picture what these two men will do."

They looked at Perceval, then Llascoit, the wounded one gurgling with fear. The knights picked up Dindraine's lead, and grinned at the men maliciously.

"Twas Agrivaine, sirs! He commanded those you killed, and they commanded us. We were promised easy prey."

Dindraine jumped clean off her horse, and knelt beside the lame one, twisting the balanced dagger. "You mean we were easy! You thought your knights would kill our knights, leaving the six of you to fumble your way with us against our will, right? Answer me, or I'll cut off that which makes you want to rape and force you to watch until the ants have devoured it!"

"Yes!" he screamed. "That's what we were promised, so long as we saved some for the knights. Just let us live, sweet Jesus, I beg you!"

"Wrong deity to invoke in my presence," Dindraine said, pulling the weapon from him and using his own tortured cloak to wipe it clean.

Perceval felt ready to lose his last meal, small as it had been. Today's lessons would not be lost on him, and he realized that if he threw up now, the men would see his weakness and speak no more. "Where may we find Agrivaine?"

The answer came more easily than expected. "We don't know, sir. But there's a bunch of them somewhere."

"Where?" Llascoit demanded, seething just at the mere thought of the cold Orkneyman.

"They never stay two nights in the same place, always in the field. I don't know what they're up to, on my soul!"

A year ago, perhaps even yesterday, Perceval would have ordered them to Camelot for punishment as he had other men, but these weren't even knights. Yet he had seen enough bloodshed for one afternoon. "Go. Just leave. Don't ever let us see you again." The two men rose, and scampered as well as they could, one making good time down the trail, the other hobbling on his bad leg.

The four travelers were still breathing heavily, all disgusted by what they had done, finding little reassurance that they had no choice. "This is all I ever wanted," Perceval spat. "Are these a knight's duties, to kill or die? The King can solve his own damn problems, because the four of us are going to find the Grail!"

"Amen to that," added Galahad.

"Perceval," Llascoit said.

"I know, I'm just angered and shouldn't talk so of my lord, the source of my glory. But the source of my honor is here," he said, bringing his fist to his chest and leaving a blood stain, barely visible on his crimson surcoat, "and I feel I just drained it into the ground along with their blood."

Llascoit was in no mood for backtalk. "What you really just saw is what our good King has been up against his whole life. He's bled and been bled to carve out a country whose people will be at peace and safe, and can look forward to prosperity and living to see grandchildren. If this is the price for that, I'll gladly pay it. It's not all honorable, Perceval. To say so indicates immense ignorance, even for you."

Perceval was too drained to fight back. "I believe in the cause, what's good and right. The belief that we can still be of some use to the world no matter how much we destroy it along the way."

"That's all any of us believe in," Galahad said. "Else we wouldn't be with you now."

Perceval shrugged. "And where did you learn to handle a knife like that?" he asked his sister.

"If I'd thrown it before, I would have had to face at least another unarmed. And as for my teacher, I'll have to introduce you to her sometime."

The last time Perceval and Llascoit saw a forest fire, Llio was still alive, and Perceval charged through the smoke for help.

Except they could see the fire this time, and the thickened smoke was absent.

"What's the source?" Galahad wondered.

"It looks like just the one tree," Llascoit said.

"A forest full of combustible bark, and just one tree?" Perceval sounded dubious.

Dindraine offered her own suggestion, though she didn't think it would be taken seriously. "Maybe it's glamour, like the sword outside Camelot that day."

Galahad shot her a look just shy of hostile. "You don't believe that was prophetic, do you?"

"I didn't say that," said Dindraine defensively. "I just think that may be a glamorous fire."

"But who would leave something like that? I mean, it's right by this fork in the path, for all to see."

That was the part which disturbed them most: the tree stood at a junction in the path, and neither was anticipated by the group. How many people had to use such a remote trail for it to have branches?

"Well, I don't know what it means," grumbled Llascoit, still mad about the encounter with Agrivaine's hirelings, and that their boss was missing.

"What if Dindraine's right?" Galahad said. "Then the question becomes who did it, and why?"

"Magick like this is very taxing, and not performed lightly." Dindraine had no idea why it might have been left there. It had to be a message, but from whom?

"What if it's a guide?" she said. "Suppose it marks which path we're to take to reach Bridgnorth? We've already agreed finding Pellam's keep would be difficult at best."

They watched, barely listening to her, transfixed by how the tree kept burning slowly, without spreading. Llascoit rode closer to it, despite Dindraine's warnings, and they were all fairly convinced of glamour when he reported feeling no heat from it.

Llascoit wondered, Perceval frowned, Dindraine pondered, and Galahad crossed herself, still trying to resolve how what the Pagans called magick could exist within God's world. It seemed to violate His natural laws, and so had to be the work of the Devil, not some fanciful "other side" of existence.

The problem was that Galahad knew of magick which benefited others: Dindraine's potion-brewing, Merlin's work with Uther so that Arthur could be begotten. *Every act has good and evil within it,* she could hear the bishop say.

Perhaps it is God's way, a test. He makes all manner of wonder available to us, and we have to choose the path to reach it. She held her cross, the one Perceval got from his mother years before; her faith ruled her decisions.

"So someone went to a great deal of trouble to make sure we stayed on the right path. If that's the case, which way do we go?" Llascoit fidgeted. He wanted to be on his way. Finding the Grail would prove grand enough, but what he really hoped for was the chance to vanquish more of Arthur's enemies. That would likely give him a seat at the Table. Especially if he could help prove that Agrivaine was opposing him by hiring bandits to plague travelers!

Which path, then? Both led deeper into the forest, which was what they expected all along. The non-burning side of the tree indicated a side path, while the fiery one would keep them going straight, more or less.

Galahad was quick to answer. "We follow the clean path. The fire would indicate something evil awaiting us."

"Like more of those villains," Llascoit said.

"Or worse," Galahad added.

"What do you think, Dindraine?" Llascoit said, who would have loved to pursue whatever danger might lie down the one path.

"Um, I'm not sure. I know we're in a hurry, but I wish we could think this out some more."

"We should take the fire path," Perceval said, who spoke without the slightest hint of condescension. He was too forthright to seem patronizing.

"Why?" Galahad demanded, with whom he disagreed.

"Fire is cleansing, just like the Grail. I think that's the answer you would give if you thought about it."

She did, and found she couldn't argue with the logic. Fire was a universal symbol of rebirth through purification, destruction of the old.

"But that doesn't make sense," Dindraine said. "The Grail is supposed to be part of another sign."

The others looked at her, puzzled. "Remember the four basic elements?"

Llascoit answered, reciting the words his father had told him long ago. "Fire, earth, air, and water."

"Yes. Different things correspond to them, since they are, after all, the most basic forms of anything. You've read Plato; the men who taught him argued about which was the most important."

Galahad had no idea who Plato was, but made a mental note to study him sometime later. "Like what?" she said.

"They match the seasons, the four directions, even the Hallows."

"Tathan!" Perceval shouted. "What did he used to tell us about them?"

"There were four, and different from Britain's Treasures. There was a sword of prophecy."

"Excalibur!" Llascoit said. "Or Galahad's," he added.

"A spear –"

"That which gives unhealing wounds," Galahad answered.

"A platter, or stone. Even a table. This one's a bit vague."

"Could it be the Round Table?" Perceval hoped so; it would answer much.

"I suppose. The last is the cup or cauldron of plenty. The Grail, if you ask the Christians."

Galahad nodded silently. "The Grail."

"But that's what I don't understand," Dindraine said. "The Grail is part of the water sign, not fire."

"Fire is the opposite sign. So maybe the tree is to remind us to do the opposite of what seems the logical choice." Perceval considered it for a moment, then added, "I would think the non-burning path would lead us deeper into the forest, which might seem to bring us closer to Bridgnorth, but I really think my earlier answer is reinforced by this."

"Do the opposite of what Galahad suggests, in other words?" prompted a feisty Galahad.

Perceval laughed. "Yes! And I still say we take the fire path, if for no other reason than it's the more interesting. The mark seems obvious to me, and I vote we follow it."

They did, and reached the dark cabin by nightfall.

* * *

"Sons of Lothian. Report!"

The commands of Queen Margawse were not taken lightly, not even by her own blood. At her word, Agrivaine and a youthful Mordred relayed what they had received from their own subordinates.

"Pictish squadrons are formed and awaiting, Mother. Though we can only see some from here, so used to hiding are they." Mordred liked the Picts; they taught him a great deal about stealth, and better still, subterfuge.

Agrivaine reported proudly, "The combined force of Orkney, knights and tribal warriors ready to march and die at your word, are assembled, Lady. I shall lead them personally. King Marcus has only now just arrived, and brought two thousand of his own. To be led by Clamadeus are scores of others."

"Totals, lads?" coaxed the Queen.

"Just this side of nine thousand, Mother," Mordred said, computing.

"Excellent. Bring the field commanders to me. I should have a word with them now, before we ride south."

Margawse had watched her loved ones ride forth, gathering recruits taken from the disgruntled all over British soil. Mercenaries, errants, footsoldiers, peasants with halberds and knights with war-horses, bandits, cutpurses, those lured by gold and others by the promise of a new order, and of course those who, like herself, were in it for revenge. It took long years to get this far.

Anyone could loot and pillage. To acquire followers in doing so required statecraft, and a witchy, terrifying reputation didn't hurt. Uther's blood line would soon end, and Margawse would be vindicated. The north would remain free, and whomever held the lowlands, including Logres, Cambria, Dumnonia, and the Garmani lands, did not concern her in the least. She savored the irony of the Roman planners, who built their walls to keep folk from venturing south; now she would keep them reinforced and prevent anyone from heading too far north.

Let them tear each other to pieces in the south; the Old Ways would triumph in Lothian and all Pict-land!

She'd had her agents working for some time already. One killed many of Logres' knights, dangling them for the crows on trees whose spirits had fled the sight of mortals. She knew one of her youngest overcame him, but that did not matter now; the Red Lands were all but swallowed by the wastes, the great wasteland brought upon Britain by the likes of Arthur and his meddling druid.

At least Merlin was gone. Margawse never tired of hearing tales of how he departed, and remained satisfied that he was permanently out of the way.

She wondered which of her sons would still fight at Arthur's side, once they knew their own mother plotted his removal. She had found her allies in Marcus and Clamadeus, while Agrivaine and Mordred could hardly wait to claim what was theirs. She would let Mordred continue to rule Logres from Camelot until such time that it became imprudent to do so. There was an endless supply of foreigners who sought British soil.

Still, would Gawaine, Gaheris, and Gareth turn? Brother against brother? Margawse knew that passion could lead one to confront anyone. Only Mordred and Agrivaine saw her plans begin to come to fruition; the others she presumed were now too polluted with the pathetic "King's justice" and leftover scraps of Roman ideology and urban civilization to serve any use to her. If they came groveling later, she would welcome them home. But for the moment they had to be viewed as enemies. And Morgan, her dear sister: she was so concerned with little Avalon to even be consulted. Uriens would soon be dead, gone the way of the tiny foggy island, and Morgan could take care of herself.

Margawse thought she wouldn't care much for the fate of their brother.

Margawse's battlefield lieutenants had all assembled round her now, eager for the latest news or orders. She would speak and let her words spread like wildfire among all the hordes placed before her.

The saddle creaked slightly beneath her; Margawse listened to the light wind as it animated her lengthy shanks of hair. The mail rubbed her sorely but she wore it proudly, as would any knight. And she addressed them.

"Hear me, then, you brave men, who have entrusted your lives, your futures, your dreams, to me. You all know the nature of our divine cause. Arthur and his Roman brood have too long dwelt in warm halls, eating the sacred animals and farming the earth as though She were no more than a blushing maid."

The men were easily angered by that image; Paganism ran hot throughout Caledonia and Dumnonia. Neither had room for the cross.

"You, Sir Clamadeus, treacherously humiliated by one of Arthur's own. And that bastard not even a knight! What say you to this 'great peace,' when common thieves can freely impersonate knights and chivalry is made a mockery?"

Clamadeus, recalling how he should have razed the tiny fort in Worcester and been done with Perceval's woman, spat his answer into the wind. The disgust in the sound was palpable.

"Or you, Marcus, King of Dumnonia, now relegated to a mere puppet, and likewise humiliated by another false knight who thought nothing of the woman promised to you for having crushed your enemies. And where was Arthur during that? Ignoring your pleas for justice, while demanding you reinforce the Dumnonian coast against his own foes!"

Marcus sat impassive. Trystan had not been dead long. As for Isolde, he kept her at home where she belonged. Marcus was not used to being led by a woman, but he shared Margawse's vision.

"And who prompted the likes of Trystan?" Margawse raved. "Why, that bitch queen of Arthur's, of course! She and her court of love, trying to reconcile the natural desires that her religion damns with the guise of this society of brutes and beggars. Where are the men who remember the true nature of kings? Where may I find they who believe in the might of the sword, and the wealth of the herd, and the prophecy of magicks so vast as to make the Christian blush in impotency?"

"Here!" cried many of them. Southmen, northmen, freemen. Warriors who followed their passions and called upon the strength of their ancestors before heading screaming into battle, fearless in the shedding of blood because as the druids had taught forever, death was but a door to renewed life. Life was repeated endlessly, gloriously. The sham of Arthur's court was an obstacle to that freedom, and it would be smashed down.

"You can feed off your hate, my brothers! Look what is done to Mother Goddess by those who would rape the land to get rich, building castles and cities upon it and preventing its healing! Is it any wonder that all manner of evil plagues the lands to the south? What is the source of the great wastes?"

"Arthur!" shouted one. "The rape of the land!" harked another. "The false love of the Queen!" "The destruction of the wells and groves by the Romans and their descendants!" The commanders began banging their weapons together, and the scores of fighters behind them, who couldn't even hear Margawse, did likewise, working themselves into a frenzy.

"Then I call upon you all. Let nothing stand which tries to oppose us! Let us take back the home of our forebears, let the land be healed by the cleansing power of the righteous sword! Burn their churches and monasteries! Kill the younger Romans so that their terrible blood will be no more! Sack the cities so that the Mother's branches may reclaim what was lost!

And bring me the head of that man who likens himself king over us all."

The noise deafened. From so far they came, bent on a promise. Margawse had sent her instigators all over Britain. They marched from Cambria and Dumnonia, Eire-land and the Garmani settlements: those who never tasted the promises of Arthur, who wanted to ensure their way of life for their children's children, who wished to be free of the yoke of knightly tyranny and religious persecution, to measure their wealth in cattle and sheep instead of acres of exploited land. Each had their own reasons, yet one cause united them all:

They believed Logres had a stranglehold on its neighbors, militarily, economically, and most important, spiritually. The yoke had to be lifted.

* * *

"Who on earth would live way out here?" Llascoit asked of no one at all.

The others shrugged or murmured "I don't know" in a way which made it sound like a musical grunt. The hut was surely remote enough, so much so that even the likes of Agrivaine's mercenaries either ignored or couldn't find it at all.

"It must be abandoned," Galahad said. "Look how rotted this shack is." The archaic timber used to build the hut looked like the weight of mere rain might topple it.

"But I smell food," said Dindraine, curious as the rest. The place reminded her of Kundry's queerly-smelling but oddly safe-feeling home near Oerfa, with its endless assortment of philters and bizarre potion ingredients. She had not heard of her old mistress since she first arrived in Camelot.

"You're right," said Llascoit, leading his horse around back. They had to lead their mounts most of the time now that the woods grew so thick. "There's a big pot back here. It smells pretty good, like it had food in it recently."

They decided to wait for the owner to return, watering their mounts from a nearby stream and wondering if they would stay the night. It was almost dusk already, and they felt quite isolated in the forest. No other quest knights apparently came this way, and no one else seemed foolish enough to wander the vastness of the Dean. Or were they perhaps in the Arroy by now?

They also searched about the area, looking at as much as they could without feeling that the unwritten rules of hospitality were violated. There were some barrels inside the hut, and an assortment of various foods, mostly jarred to last until needed. There were a couple of cupboards, and some forlorn text in a tattered leather binding near them. A broom rested in one corner, looking little used. There was a small table and two chairs, one broken. It looked like a temporary home, at best, despite the preserved food.

On the table was a checkers board, like the kind Perceval and Gornymant's children used to play with in Jagent, with what little free time they had. Perceval smiled when he saw it, recalling how Llio usually bested him, and he usually bested her brother. He was pleased he could remember Llio now without automatically crying. It was more a feeling of peace, and it reminded him of how he felt when the leaves began to change before falling gently earthward. Thinking of her was like feeling that fall wind which blew the leaves about, painting the landscape; she was always there, just a thought and a feeling away.

"Llas! Look at this," he said. When Llascoit arrived, Perceval asked, "I haven't seen one since we left your father's."

Llascoit laughed, despite himself. "I hated that game! I never beat anyone at it. But what's with these different pieces?"

"I was wondering that as well."

"They're chessmen," Galahad said, who stepped inside the hut at the sound of the men giggling.

"What makes them different?" Perceval asked.

"It's a whole different game, though the object is still to capture each other's pieces. Why don't I teach you? We seem to have some time, if we're sleeping here tonight."

Llascoit and Dindraine finished seeing to their horses and exploring the place while Galahad instructed Perceval, who took an avid interest in the game at once, especially once he learned that knights and bishops and castles were all on the playing field.

"The first time I played this was with Lupinia," Galahad added to her list of explanations of how the pieces moved and attacked, "I thought about who some of these people might be. You look as though you're doing the same."

"Like how?"

"Like here's my king, and I'll pretend it's Arthur. And here's the Queen."

"Curious how the Queen can move much better than he can."

"Yes, but the game is really about him. You win by cornering that king."

Perceval nodded. "So would these be Lancelot and Gawaine?" he inquired, twirling the twin pieces carved to look like the heads of horses.

"Sure," she said, actually smiling at mention of her father. "Or Perceval and Galahad."

He smiled also, as Dindraine came over to watch. Llascoit rummaged about, looking for all the firewood he could carry. "Then these two must be Merlin and Baudwin."

That took her off guard, though Dindraine saw what he was getting to. "Why have them both as bishops?"

"Well, each one occupies and only seems to move on one set of squares, right? I mean, the checker board we used to play on was colored, alternating red and white like your shield. So couldn't each color be a different faith?"

Galahad never considered that before. Dindraine toyed with him. "You certainly got smarter once you left Oerfa. I'd hate to think I held you back."

He reached around and grabbed at her, trying to reach her ticklish spots. "You little hag! I was always smart, just, just —"

"Uninformed?" prompted Galahad.

"Yeah, Purse, or just plain dumb!" Dindraine screamed playfully as he stood and lunged his arms around her, prodding the parts of her stomach and arms which would make her giggle.

"Dumb, huh?" he grunted, as they tumbled about on the floor, rolling out of the tiny cabin and onto the earth.

"Children, children!" Galahad said, mimicking her late mother's best authoritative tone. "Please! Whatever will people say of you two?"

Then Perceval reached his one free arm out to her as well, pulling her into the fray. She yelped, then set about helping Dindraine to hold Perceval to the ground. It wasn't working; all the hours spent carrying weapons and wearing armor had strengthened him, and he was never a lightweight to start with.

"Is this a legal chess move?" Perceval giggled. "Taking on a knight and queen at the same time?"

"I'm no queen!" Dindraine squealed. "But we'll kick yours just the same, won't we, Gal?"

"Of course," she managed, still vying for control of Perceval's extremities. "The fool doesn't know when he's beaten."

Llascoit returned from his firewood expedition, and strolled over to the tumbling trio. He dropped the collection of branches and small logs near them. "Need some help there, old boy?"

"No, I can get them," Perceval said, himself trying to secure a wrist or arm or foot while limbs danced around him. "Trust me."

They continued grappling, laughing and exerting themselves enough to sweat. Finally a truce was recognized, if unspoken, while the three of them sat facing one another, panting.

"Is this the time to mention that one of you gets to build the fire, since I already did my job? By the way, the horses are tended for the night, and if they have any sense, will try and stay away from you weird souls." Llascoit was a bit jealous he'd been left out of the melee.

"You sound awfully serious," Perceval said. "Come sit by us."

"I don't know," he replied, "I'm not sure these two can be trusted."

"I'd trust a woman over a man any day," teased Galahad, reaching out with a flailing arm to try and catch Llascoit in the leg. He stepped out of the way.

"I think I probably would, too," answered Perceval, Llascoit's more somber mood catching up with him.

"Why is that?" Dindraine said. "Our mother, much as we loved her, was hardly trustworthy, and we learned from her first."

"Oh, because of Llio, and both of you. I thought I'd lost of you, and yet you both returned to my life." *If only I could say the same for Llio.* Perceval thought a silent prayer for her, wishing he could be with her again.

"I think trust must be earned," Llascoit said, finally sitting.

"Agreed," added Galahad, "but the catch is that in order to give someone a chance to prove their trustworthiness, you have to trust them. At least a little."

"Is that how it is with you?"

"Think about my father, Llascoit. There are details about me he'll never know. He followed me and Purse like some eager pup, and never came to our aid when we needed it. He barged right into Bridgnorth when we were there that time. So yes, it's difficult for me to trust the man. But we've come some way since. I once saw him weep over the loss of my mother, not so much for love, but because of the guilt, even though now I don't really hold him responsible."

"Lancelot weeping!" Llascoit couldn't picture it.

"Galahad, I wasn't going to ask this of you, but since we're talking of the mighty champion, is there some reason why we didn't think to ask him to come with us? He's such an excellent scout, and he probably could have helped us find Pellam's keep again." Perceval shared few words with the man, mostly from sheer awe.

"I did ask him."

Silence from the others. True, father and daughter made some progress in recent seasons, but this!

"And he wouldn't join us?" Dindraine said.

"He suggested to me that this quest wasn't so much an effort to find something as it was a test of worthiness. I truly believe that. And my father remains unconvinced of his own standing. I asked him once what made him such a magnificent fighter."

"What did he say?" Llascoit could hardly contain his curiosity.

"He said the only way to reach that level of skill is to absolutely not care whether or not you survive the fight."

Llascoit protested on behalf of the absent knight. "But he is the best, the bravest! How could he not live up to high standards, even God's own?"

"Far be it from me to sound the priestly judge," Galahad said, to responses of "Surely, you jest!" and "You? Never!"

She continued, "He feels he's committed too many sins to atone for with one last quest. He thinks he's betrayed everything he stands for."

"I'm not sure what you mean," Llascoit said.

"Llas, don't. This is hard enough for her as it is." Perceval still knew her better than anyone.

"But I'm just trying to understand."

"Llas," Galahad answered, "he turned his back on his faith. Do you know that he was studying druidry before becoming a knight?"

"I had no idea," Dindraine said. She ruminated on the possibilities of a warrior-druid, straight from the eldest Cymru legends.

"And," Galahad said, leaning into them and stealing a look around as though the residents of Camelot were just behind her eavesdropping, "you do know of not only my mother, but the Queen as well, don't you?"

"Gal, that's treasonous!" Perceval warned. But the reason he said so was his loathing of gossip.

"Is it treason to speak of one's own blood?"

"In that sense, no, but that whole business is better left alone."

"And all this time I thought it was just hearsay," Llascoit said.

"On the subject of blood," Dindraine began, not wanting to hear of the affair. "Wouldn't your father think he had a chance, since according to the story, you hail from Joseph of Arimathea's own line?"

"Sir Lancelot is indeed a descendant of Joseph, but even so, that doesn't pardon him from sin. Sin is what caused us to lose the Grail in the first place. And, as I told Perceval, I don't know whether that line accounts for Grail-keeping or Grail-seeking. Or both, or neither."

"Hey, it's all right," eased Perceval, seeing how worked up she was becoming. "It will be found."

The frustration came in a flood. "But doesn't it seem we're wasting our time? I know of no one with sufficient grace to find what was lost. It's like the banishing from Eden; we only get one chance to make that mistake."

"Wouldn't God, in His compassion, offer a chance to redeem ourselves?" Dindraine thought of her mother, then her teacher. *All the deities are one, child. The divine is simply that which cannot be understood, and must be taken on faith, the imposition of belief in the supernatural upon the natural. There is divinity in everything, you just have to open your senses to it and allow yourself to experience it. Only when you are compassionate, at peace, can this happen.*

"I hope so. If I didn't, I wouldn't be traveling with you now. And as for my father, he opted to stay behind. I saw him a few times with Bedivere before we left, and they both looked upset. But I trust they'll work out their own problems."

They sat for a few more moments, considering what they truly believed, who would hear their prayers in their most fearful moments when it really mattered. They didn't hear the barely perceptible sound from down the path.

"You found each other again, I see!" the scratchy voice said. "Dindraine, you look as vital as ever. May you never catch such illness as comes from a lifetime of doddering about in practices perhaps better forgotten!" She walked with a slight limp, holding her hands clenched at her sides.

Llascoit was irritated to be the only one who didn't recognize the haggard-looking crone. "Kundry!" Dindraine shouted. "Dame Kunneware!" Perceval and Galahad said simultaneously.

Dindraine stared disbelievingly at the others. They returned the gesture, ignoring the woman in their consternation.

"*The* Kundry?" Perceval said, more of his sister than the old woman. Both nodded. "So the woman who sat with us in Pellam's castle, and who accosted me on the road later, is the, the," His tongue began to numb. He couldn't quite utter the word *witch*.

Galahad distrusted her on sight. She'd been of no help during the feast and procession, and if she was Dindraine's tutor, then she deliberately deceived them all. Maybe. She wasn't quite sure. She just knew there was something unpleasant about the woman. *Of course, she is a witch!* Galahad fought the urge to cross herself.

"You're right, Perceval. It's 'Sir' now, yes? I do owe you all a bit of an explanation, starting with why I happen to be living in the middle of the woods."

"Is this where you came after you left Camelot?" Dindraine said, wondering where her teacher had gone for so long.

"Among other places," came the answer. "Actually, this has been deserted for decades, by the looks of it. I just took a liking to it for its isolation, like the old place near Oerfa." Perceval blushed a bit at that.

Llascoit decided to speak for the group. "Good lady, kindly accept our apologies for intruding upon your homestead. It was not our intent to disrupt either you or —"

"Oh, save your knightly verse for someone else, will you? An old woman hasn't the time." She made for one of the chairs, refusing Perceval's help in sitting. She was careful to hide her hands as much as she could.

But they didn't escape her student's attention.

"Kundry! Your hands. They've grown mottled."

Kundry rolled her eyes. "Now that you've noticed what I would have rather kept secret, what does your diagnosis tell you?"

Dindraine stepped forward, studying the wrinkled gray face. Then she took Kundry's hands, feeling no warmth in them. "The wasting sickness," she said.

"What?" asked Galahad.

"It's known more as leprosy now. Have you already tried the remedies?"

"Yes, but to what avail? A woman my age lacks the strength to concoct such an unguent, and the necessary parts are too rare anyway."

Dindraine looked at the ground. She knew what was in store for her teacher. "How much time?" she said feebly.

"Perhaps through the winter. Longer, if I could get some fresh blood."

Galahad tried to control her own gag reflex at mention of that. God! Witches drank blood, too?!

Dindraine saw her visibly disturbed. "Galahad, I'm sorry if this cure makes you uneasy, but I assure you, it is the only way to give my lady more time."

"I will not ask it of you, Dindraine. I can only accept if it is freely offered." Kundry was tired, the kind of exhaustion which precedes death for those to whom it comes gradually; knights did all they could to avoid such feeling. She felt ready to die and pass on to the next life, but she missed her pupil, and she had lacked the strength to reach Pellam again on her own. Two invalids, alone and unable to die, trying to find each other so maybe they could traverse the path of death together.

"But blood!" Galahad cried. "You can't possibly mean drink it!"

Dindraine turned on her. "That's precisely what I mean. I'd expect you to understand, really."

"What?! How can you even claim so?"

The young woman who had reset Llascoit's leg so it could heal properly, who had mended the strongest of men through terrible injuries, drove her point home. "This from one who drinks the blood of a god each Mass?"

Galahad sought a retort, but none came. She tried anyway. "It's Jesus' blood, the one true God."

"I thought he was the son of God."

"Ladies! We have a sick woman here. Now let's do what we can." Perceval wasn't in the mood for bickering. He had too many unanswered questions. He sat on the ground opposite Kundry.

"Sister, can this wait until tomorrow?" he said gently.

"Yes, but I'll have to stay with her. She'll be strong enough to travel again if I tend her." She looked at the old witch, who did not fit the preconceived image of one held by any of the group. "Is that what you want? My blood is yours for the taking, if you have the will to continue living just a little while longer. But you'll be stronger while you're still in this body."

Kundry simply nodded. "Stay, dear. Tomorrow I will accept your aid, and the others may continue."

"I'll stay, too," said Llascoit, worried he'd be as useful as a third wheel on a horse cart traveling with Perceval and Galahad. "With both of you in a weakened state, I'd be honored to have the duty of safeguarding you."

"Well now," Kundry brightened a bit, "maybe knights have their place yet."

The others tried not to laugh at that, but amused sounds escaped them all, even Galahad, despite herself.

"Now then," the elder woman continued. "I mentioned something of an explanation. You saw the white stag," she said, glaring at Perceval.

His face betrayed nothing. "And you put something in our water."

The others made a circle as Llascoit built a fire, and they listened.

"I apologize for that. There's much I'd like to make amends for, or atone, as you would have it, Lady Galahad. But we're running out of time."

"Why the urgency?" Llascoit said.

"The quest knights will miss the greatest threat the King has ever faced. Already is there a vast army poised to march straight for Camelot itself, burning anything in its path. I even saw some of the Orkneymen come through here. They paid no heed to an old crone once they saw I had nothing."

Llascoit growled. "Are they truly in position to threaten Camelot directly?"

A silent nod was all the answer he needed.

"We must warn the King! Arthur needs us."

"He needs the Grail more," protested Galahad.

"Grail, Grail! I'm sick of hearing of it! I only went on this quest to be with you. I'm not even sure it exists." Llascoit was scared; he found himself willing to believe a witch for the sake of his king, and he couldn't imagine the consequences of any ill befalling Camelot.

"My lady," he addressed Kundry. "With your permission, since I am now in your service, upon reaching your destination may I be given leave to ride back to Camelot and give suitable warning to the King's army?"

"What army, Llas?" Perceval said. "She just reminded us most of the army leaders are out looking for something you don't believe in."

"All the more reason for me to return, then, I say. One more good sword arm against the crown's enemies!"

"Go, then," Perceval prompted. "Return and warn them all. But the King himself would agree with us. Better to stay on this quest and see it through, come what will."

"How can you, of anyone, say that? This is all you've wanted, your whole life, to be a knight and serve the King."

"I do serve the King. And if there's any chance of finding his chalice, then I could offer him no greater service. He was the one who sent us forth."

"But that's stupid! Why send off all the knights like that if he knew there was an army coming?" Llascoit thought it over. "Did he even know?"

They all looked at Kundry. She shrugged helplessly.

"Llas, do you know what a wise man told me once?" Galahad's voice always sounded like calm reason to him, and she knew it.

Llascoit shook his head.

"He said that every action, and therefore every decision, has good and bad results. The King sends us on the greatest search in history, even though doing so leaves him vulnerable. He is our King, and we must respect his judgment." Galahad thought of both God and Arthur as she said it.

Llascoit turned back to Kundry. "Where do we travel?"

"To Bridgnorth. We simply arrive after the others."

"I shall be off once we reach the old man's castle, then," he vowed.

"Thank you for your assistance, Sir Llascoit."

With nothing left to stab at, Llascoit sat and watched the fire, listening.

"The water was necessary, or so I believed. I put my own concoction into your drinking and cleansing water to assist, that's all. Visions aren't unique to you, Lady Galahad, but they are still quite rare, and can be helped along."

"What's to keep from believing you worked some magick to rob me of my visions? And how did you know about me? Nimue did, too." Galahad still didn't trust the woman, even if she no longer missed her old "visitations."

"My intentions were good, and I never met the priestess before that night. As for knowing about you," Kundry paused. "Let's just say that I did all in my power to find out everything I could about the people Pellam believed might assist him."

"That's what I still don't understand," griped Perceval. "What happened to him? Why won't he talk of his infirmities, or the Grail?"

"Did you ask him?"

Perceval sighed. "No. I was too caught up in all that was happening. We ate extremely well, and the entertainment was amazing. But I have to ask Pellam about this, don't I?"

"Lad, I don't even know all of what has befallen Pellam."

Perceval decided to have it all out. It felt like the checkers move in which he hopped over several of his opponent's pieces and demanded to be "made king."

"Did you know he's my uncle? As far as I can tell."

"Wouldn't that make him our uncle?" asked Dindraine.

"Yes. Sorry. Well?"

There was so much to speak of, and then these two would have to be on their way. Kundry believed Pellam could still die, given his strange affliction, before revealing any more information. She had badgered him herself, but he always replied by saying he could only tell a certain type of person. That hurt the most, that she didn't meet some mysterious criteria.

"Yes," she said at last. "He fled Gwynedd when your mother made for the hills. With Pellinore gone, there was nothing to stop the tribes people from retaking what was theirs to begin with."

"Is that what will happen without an Arthur?" Llascoit said. "Will it all just fall to the next group to cross the sea?"

"It's not my place to answer that, even if I knew." Kundry tried to sound compassionate. She knew knights were emotional, and this one in front of her, with the wolf's and ram's heads on his shield, sounded so innocent in his pleas.

"May I ask, then, how all of this involves you?" This from Perceval.

"I suppose I should start by pointing out that magick shouldn't have this effect on anyone." Kundry indicated her slowly rotting skin. "It's been bad for more years than I can count, worse by far now than when your sister first came to me. Bless her for that." She took Dindraine's hand. It felt warm and strong. "She was the compassionate one for me whereas you must find it to be compassionate for Pellam."

Kundry brushed away a single tear. Perceval recognized the lone tear of a woman. "You were lovers?"

Kundry nodded. "Pellam didn't used to be so much of an outdoorsman, never mind his reputation. He was injured hunting and living alone when I found him. I was a refugee of sorts myself. Those were untrusting times, at least in the area we now call Logres. The new religion came to drive out the old, though I can't blame the Christians for the fate of my home."

"What happened?" asked Perceval, who thought of Oerfa, its palisade and buildings already crumpling the last time he saw it.

"The Garmani. I really admired Uther for warring against them, but they always kept on coming. They were convinced they had a right to the whole land, after only being recruited as hired fighters at first."

"So you nursed Pellam back to health. What of Oerfa?" Galahad never heard this story, though Dindraine had a number of times, and so she tended the fire and began preparing something resembling a dinner.

"Oh, that was years later. Pellam went on to his own fame. We were free spirits, not confined to anyone else's orders. He even wished for further glory under the Pendragon banner, but decided he was too old by then."

"So it runs in the blood," muttered Perceval. He felt pride in the dim recognition of his noble birth, even if it no longer mattered to anyone.

"Your family's full of knights, yes. Pellam and I went from one side of this island to the next, even to Eire and once to the Continent. The things we saw together! Though a white stag was never among them. Old places and new settlements. Pellam was so fascinated with anything which could elude him, and he worked until he became such an excellent huntsman. At his peak he could have tracked fish in a lake, for all I know. My own obsession lay in the old ways."

"Are you warm enough?" Dindraine said, listening to the eager crackling of wood and creation of embers. Kundry nodded.

It was dusk. The group knew they would spend the evening there, so they kept listening, vaguely aware of the oncoming night and the sounds of those who found darkness more livable than light.

"What of the white stag?" Perceval marveled at the creature. Galahad had never quite known what to think of it, and it bothered her.

"Just that one is rare in the extreme, and seeing one is a sign of good fortune, especially when seeking or hunting something. Like a goose. Very difficult to track, those geese. Pellam told me about chasing different creatures."

From the recesses of memory, the sound returned to Perceval. "You goose!" it had cried to him, as he left Bridgnorth.

"Finding strange animals is one matter; what about hearing things?" He never spoke of that voice, the one that sounded like all the women he cared for at once.

"Like voices?" Kundry said. Perceval looked at her, unsure of himself.

"I've never heard any before, that others couldn't as well, that is. Though perhaps they could be like Galahad's visions?"

Perceval didn't like that at all, since shortly after that he saw a goose slaughtered by a falcon, its blood dropping into the premature snow. If it was an omen, then who was the falcon come to do him harm?

Kundry felt the warmth of the fire, then opted to tell more. "I knew Merlin personally, even studied with him for a time. I could never get enough knowledge of such arcane matters, even when he warned me they came at a price. I always understood the cost to be measured in terms of labor and study and sacrifice, but there are other terms when dealing with the mystical. Pellam listened to all my ranting, for a time. But he was always more worldly than I. Or maybe my work scared him off. People drift sometimes. It's the way of things, like so much else.

"At first I blamed him for leaving, saying he was too caught up in his pursuit of fortune. I'd no idea how much the pelt of a lion or a weapon supposedly belonging to a faerie was worth, as I never looked at such in terms of money. He had already started refurbishing a great keep up north near the Wall. He wanted us to live there, but I wanted to keep exploring, to find every hollow hill and every stone circle and feel the Earth Mother's power come up through the ground and enter my being." She caught Galahad's unconscious eye-rolling.

"Good lady, whatever names we hang upon them, there are occurrences in this world that we can only begin to understand. Divine power is very real, as I know you believe. What matter whether we call it God's or by another name? The magick is the same either way, and faith is the key." Galahad never took her eyes off the strange old woman. She was a good storyteller, if a bit confused about the nature of true faith.

"I can tell what you're all waiting to hear. The essential part of it is that by the time I decided I had to settle somewhere and try to organize all I had learned, the only place that would let me near it was tiny Oerfa. My name was known by then, too. Sometimes I would still travel, though never for long, and my appearance had been ravaged by too much work and not enough rest for deeds some call evil. I sometimes helped the villagers, though. The bard brought me a sick child on more than one occasion for healing, when no other remedy worked. But there is a physical price to magick, Nimue and Queen Morgan could tell you that; they're the only ones who know enough to understand. Others are just charlatans, pranksters. Maybe a potion-brewer here and there, like Dindraine."

"So Oerfa came to reject you due to your appearance? They were afraid you were too powerful?" Perceval understood now; his mother would have had raving fits had she met the person in front of him now.

"That's right. When I traveled, I disguised myself. Always. And I would take another name, too. But I never forgot the man who once loved me. I tried to find him again, but his castle had grown more obscure. I simply had to wait for him to find me, which he finally did."

"Tell them how you tried to find him, Lady." Dindraine particularly enjoyed this part.

"I'm not sure they'd want to hear all that."

"Please," pleaded the others, Galahad included.

"Well, I journeyed on some occasions as a younger, healthier looking woman. Not the sort who'd attract the attention of anyone, especially the always lusty knights. I even found a young stallion of a knight and played something of a trick on him when he proved no help in locating Pellam."

"Who was this man? Surely not Lancelot!" Galahad said.

"Oh, no. The first time I saw the great Lancelot was in Bridgnorth, a much more modest holding for Pellam, when his servants fled the elder keep because they thought it bewitched. Some of them believed it to be the source or even the cause of the region being laid waste. But the knight was Gawaine."

"You knew Gawaine!" Llascoit said, who had forgotten his earlier frustration, enraptured with the tale.

"I did. And when he couldn't help locate Pellam I gave him a test. He was tested a great deal in those days. I heard of the other knight who fancied himself dressed in shades of green, much like the late Meliagrant favored red. Funny how colors speak volumes. I'm sure Galahad could tell you something of those colors."

"Some say they match to the deadly sins. Green of envy. Red for wrath. I grew up remembering because I saw them in the rainbows which came out at the end of angry storms. I thought God used the downpour to remind people of how He had been known to use rain to punish the worst sins we have to offer."

"Strange to say of something as lovely as a rainbow," Perceval said.

"Oh, they are beautiful. God's own light sent to remind us of our duties to each other."

"Well spoken," Kundry commented. "At any rate, I offered the Orkney heir a choice, giving him a sense of control over what was really my glamour. I called myself Ragnell at that time, and used the name for a while. It sounded dreary, and I wished to see what Arthur's knights were made of."

"Did Gawaine pass your little test?" Llascoit was intrigued by any knightly quest, no matter its nature.

"Oh, yes. He's very clever, that one. His problem is that he's always been trapped between devotion to his mother and loyalty to his king, knowing that the pair of them have been at odds since he was a boy and Lot still ruled Lothian."

Kundry paused again, rubbing her hands in front of the fire. She watched Dindraine preparing a meal, much in the manner that she'd taught her. She eyed the food: traveling rations of biscuits, sausages, apples. Simple food was best.

"The hills hid me, until Pellam was ready to find me once more. He bade me contact the pair of you," she said, looking toward Galahad and Perceval. "He wanted anyone he thought might be able to help him. Family counted in his eyes, as did anyone who exhibited their own unique traits. Galahad and your sword, Nimue and her enchantments, Taliesin with his poetry and music, and Lancelot."

Galahad could no longer stand the tension. "Lady, do you believe Pellam holds the Grail in his possession?"

"If he does, it would seem that he could use it to heal himself, if the tales of it are true. But I don't know. He told me he was unable to speak of it, that he could only tell someone who proved worthy enough to hear. That's all I know. I was angry at Perceval before, because he was the one Pellam wished to see the most, though he didn't even tell you the two of you were related, did he?"

Perceval just shook his head. "At least I know now why you berated me on the road. I knew less then. I apologize for not knowing how to act earlier."

"I accept, though there's no need for sorrow. I was more frustrated at Pellam's silence than anything else. He'd always change the subject, usually start talking about fishing. I hate fishing; slippery, cold things, fish are."

Galahad laughed. "Do you know the story of the bread and the fish?"

"I do. Jesus fed a multitude with very little of either, yes?"

"Yes. And when we ate in Bridgnorth, we all got whatever we liked best. I don't think he has the Grail, but he likes to play with people's beliefs for his own entertainment. He even got you to help, since he knew you had feelings for him still, after so many years."

Kundry looked concerned. "I don't know what he has holed up in that keep, only that I want to see him before I leave this life and demand from that tight-lipped bastard the answers to whatever questions he thought we should have asked him last time." She tried to laugh, but coughed violently instead.

Galahad wanted to laugh again, but held it in before the other woman's pain. "We'll find him. I have faith in that."

"Mistress, please eat," requested Dindraine. "Your healer thus commands."

Kundry smiled at her, and began eating, Llascoit and Dindraine joining her.

"Are you hungry yet?" Galahad said to Perceval. He shook his head.

"Then how about a game of chess, now that you know the rules?"

"I'd like that."

They kept playing as the pieces took on their own shadows in the firelight, the darkness surrounding them. Galahad checkmated him twice within the hour.

* * *

"Queen Morgan, I remain in your debt for this honor." Taliesin was pleased beyond words. For a second time, he would receive admission to the sacred island of Avalon. Morgan trusted him, even if he represented Mona and the male mysteries. She marveled at his breadth of knowledge, which went beyond poetic verse; he was a shrewd diplomat, a historian, fluent in every tongue spoken in the Isles, and the finest musician she ever heard. His name was respected or feared throughout the land.

"Don't thank me just yet," she said. "Nimue hasn't let you onto the island, nor has she given me authority to admit you."

"But I should at least be able to attain an audience with her, yes, even if we have to do it in Glastonbury?"

"I think so. Nimue has always had a soft spot in her heart for a bard, and there aren't many just roaming about anymore."

They had ridden from Gorre, complete with an armed escort of Uriens' knights and warriors. The old man was on his deathbed, Morgan knew, but there was no other way to get Taliesin this close to the Holy Isle. Besides, Uriens was too stubborn an old goat to die without having her hear his last words.

She would return forthwith; Taliesin could wander on his own once she got him to his destination.

"What did you and Nimue discuss when you were last on this road?" she asked him.

"That old Grail story, and the Cauldron."

"Ah, yes. My half-brother still thinks his men can bring it back, and restore the glory of Logres, something like that?"

"Surely you believe it exists, even if it's been perverted into something else by the Christians?"

Morgan winced. She didn't like talk of those Christians. In her mind, they were the outgrowth of the folk who brought the strange faith to the Isles in the first place. And she knew enough history to understand how petty and misogynistic those Romans were. "Yes, I believe in it. How could I not? I just don't think actually looking for it is very wise."

"I must agree with that. One should never deliberately search for a spiritual experience, much less try and locate something tangible as proof of the journey."

"My son went with them. That's the part which burns the most."

"But he is one of Arthur's own elite. He had orders to go. The other knights went also. The whole Table is probably empty right now."

"I want him back. He's needed at home. We've only lately been getting to know each other the way we should have done years ago, and now his father's close enough to Annwn to see its peaks and rivers."

Taliesin could picture the man riding about, asking questions. He wondered, as had Nimue about her magick, just what a person might ask another about this sacred relic. "Oh, just passing through, and by the way, you haven't seen a precious Grail lately, have you?"

"I heard he travels with Sir Bors. He's a kinsman of Lancelot's, though they're not close."

"I know," Morgan said. "Wasn't Bors the one who cared for Trystan so much? He must have hated Isolde, for her to always be on his mind. The way Trystan played those strings, you'd have thought he could fall in love with anyone."

"I didn't realize that about Bors. Perhaps that's why Lancelot feels no obligation to him. The remnants of their clan are Christian. Religion must truly be in the blood; I can think of no other reason for Lancelot to have left Mona."

Morgan felt the wind in her face, watched as it blew the hairs of her horses' mane, the green silk ribbons lovingly tied within fluttering without a sound. Change was in the air. The basic elements always indicated change; the trick was determining the shape of such. "If I get you into Avalon, do you think you can find my son and persuade him back to Gorre?"

"It's your candor one loves."

"I mean it, bard. You've heard what's said of me, and my sister, this far south. I hate that I have to ride with this many men. I think we both know that unless Arthur produces an heir, then all this will come to an end."

"But it won't. Do you understand that? It will not end, perhaps not ever."

"That's a defiant way to talk to your queen."

"My apologies, Lady. But I refuse to believe all the striving has been for naught. I think instead that all of us will live on in the memories of those who come after. What good is reincarnation if you have to forget everything? I think that if the darkness which has engulfed the Continent now that Rome has been sacked for likely the last time comes to these shores, we'll need to remember all of this to see us through to the other side."

"I'm trying to decide how Christian you sounded just then."

Taliesin laughed. "I'm willing to believe in my own ability to stick around forever. It's too much fun not to do so."

"I'm glad you're amused. What of my son?" Morgan thought the bard sounded like her offspring, before he saw too much. Yvaine was probably still drinking, now that he had

learned more truth than he wished to know. Truth was like the
Dragon of the Old Ones: it took many forms, did not like to be
discovered, and tended towards mercilessness when found.

"I'll find him and talk to him, but you know I cannot offer guarantees."

"That's all right. He likes you. And see if you can get
him to lighten up on those wine bottles. How can he watch a
lion if he's drunk?"

Taliesin considered carefully his next question. "So you
won't be returning to Avalon, then?"

Morgan sighed. "It was home for so many years. I miss
having Viviane run things, and I've never known Nimue as well
as I'd have liked. I feel like I've become a legend to them already,
like you suggested; I don't know any of the younger ones."

"They'll be safe there, that's for sure. There are some
places on this island which will always remain inviolate."

"Like Gorre. That's home now. Free spirits live there,
much like the folk in Eire. Though I have no wish to cross the
western sea." Morgan was content to remain up north, living
and teaching the Old Ways. Logres could come or go; the Old
Ways would linger.

"If your sister and the others win, you won't be able to
change your mind and head south. These roads will be infested
with the worst our kind has to offer." Taliesin rarely worried
about speaking candidly himself.

"A few years ago I might have taken offense to that. My
sister will do what she feels she must. I tried to stop all of this,
but she was adamant, and her underlings are hungry for blood
and what are likely pretended grievances. I stopped trying to
persuade when I reached two conclusions."

"What are those?" the bard said.

"First, I didn't want to so upset her that she'd turn on me
and march into Gorre."

"Surely she wouldn't!"

"I agree, but I had to consider it regardless."

"And the second one?"

"It is not my responsibility to either preserve or destroy Camelot. A place which has shunned me for years, simply because I'm a woman with power, deserves nothing from me but my inattention. I will not interfere with the natural course as Viviane might have, or Nimue probably has, or even you might, in your way. I've grown weary of the games of kings, and I know this will be my last journey south."

"Well spoken, Lady. May I have the wisdom to think as clearly as you."

Morgan stopped her mount, and pointed. "Do you see it?" she said.

Taliesin followed her gaze. A few miles further south, he could make out the silver crest where the divine haze forever hid a sacred place from prying eyes.

* * *

The thought bothered Galahad all day while they rode. "Do you think she's finished yet?"

"Who?" Perceval answered. The day remained quiet so far, and he was growing excited by how close they had to be to Bridgnorth. He could just tell somehow, he was sure of it.

"Your sister. Do you think she's finished with all that foul bloodletting?"

"Oh, Kundry. She's just trying to help. Can you offer a better cure?"

"Other than prayer, no. I'm just worried about it. Baudwin would say it's an evil practice."

"Healing hardly seems evil." Perceval scanned their surroundings. Still bleak and deep forest all around, few sounds other than their dialogue and the heavy breathing of Brownie and Styfnig.

"Don't patronize me! I'm worried. About Dindraine's soul, about Kundry being a witch, about what to do and say when we reach Bridgnorth."

"Dindraine and Kundry are responsible for their own souls. Do you know how close I think you really are to them?"

"How?"

"With matters of faith."

"But we're not," she protested. "They're Pagans. I love Dindraine like a sister, and perhaps Kundry is not so bad, but there are just some ways in which we can never reach one another."

Perceval stopped, listening to Styfnig snort and shake his head. "I want to show you something Dindraine showed me last year."

"Go ahead," Galahad said, trying to betray no anxiety.

"Give me your hand." She did.

"Now, I'm sure I don't need to show you the symbol Christians use to identify each other."

Galahad recoiled. "That's forbidden! It's a sacred sign!"

"If it was forbidden, then how could the survivors of the Coliseum have found each other?"

"Fine, point taken. But what's this about?"

He held out his own hand, waiting. As he took hers, he traced in her palm two arches connecting in the rough shape of a fish, symbol of Jesus' miraculous feeding of the masses. Galahad nodded.

Then Perceval sketched two additional arches, but these didn't overlap at one end as did the prior two. Galahad didn't jerk her hand back again, but she clenched it into a fist, nervously.

"What does that mean?" she asked.

"It's a Pagan sign. Dindraine taught me that, in trust. Either of those signs can only be given in trust, and those two adjacent arcs represent the Earth Mother. It's her birth-hole, the source of life, just like those of our own mothers."

"But I don't see how —"

"They're the same arcs, just positioned slightly differently. Do you understand?"

"I-I think so."

"Good. Then maybe you can explain it all to me."

She swatted him on the arm. "Dindraine calls you bonehead sometimes. I think I'll start, too."

"Then let's ride. Have you had any more thoughts about the last part of your worries today?"

"Oh, the keep. What do we say?"

"How about, 'Hey Pellam, where's that cup?'"

She leaned over to swat him again, the motion of the horses making it more difficult. "I'm serious."

"I don't know yet! We'll make it up when we get there, unless you have some great idea that just can't wait."

"I want to talk with Pellam, and ask him some questions."

"Then let's pretend. Let's say I'm him, and ask me something."

"Um, I don't know. That's why I'm worried about it. We can't get this wrong."

Perceval felt that same finality; they couldn't even be sure that Pellam was still alive, infirm as he was. And what if he had gone back to his older holding in the north, where they'd likely never find him? Gawaine and Gaheris were supposed to be up in that area again already anyway.

"Why do you think he won't even talk about it, then? I mean, I'm his blood, and I've no clue why we have to play hide-and-hunt with him."

"That's why we need to get this right the first time. Maybe I should talk with him first."

Perceval continued his original baiting. "Then tell me what you'll say."

"How about if I recount the Grail story, and ask him how he —"

"There it is! See?" She followed his excited point.

"Where? I don't see anything but trees."

"Through them, beyond the other side. We're almost out of this thick."

How did you see that? she wondered. But in a few seconds, she too could make out the faint outline of a small castle. The forest itself grew almost dark, thousands of trees lost in the shadows, but Perceval had seen the keep.

And now Galahad felt afraid for the first time on the quest, mentally assessing her own worthiness. Bridgnorth would be more comforting than another night in these woods, alone. The old fear of this area never fully left.

"Come on!" Perceval urged, squeezing Styfnig into a trot with his thighs.

Galahad urged Brownie accordingly, but still felt frantic, the fear rising in her throat like a lump of unswallowed food. *Something's wrong. There should be three of us, in a hallway. Naked.*

Her thoughts were forgotten as Bridgnorth came fully into view, the river cascading behind it. They could see Clellus awaiting their arrival at the gate.

All they could do was look at each other, knight to knight. Then back at Pellam's manservant, who patiently awaited the reins of their steeds.

"The Master has hoped for your return," Clellus said.

Feeling suddenly out of place and confused, Perceval asked feebly, "Has your master had much success fishing lately?" Galahad elbowed him in the ribs, giving him a glare clearly suggesting his idiocy.

"More than you might guess," the man said, showing a monumental lack of emotion. Clellus never sounded as though he felt anything.

They were inside the keep's walls once more, their armor feeling heavier than usual, like the responsibility they brought from Camelot. The place looked much the same: the relative absence of tracks near the gate, no surprise there, the stable, the tower with its thick doors.

And the mural on the tower, with more detail than it used to have.

Clellus tied up the horses. His guests noticed that water and hay were already set in the stables. They chose to look over the tower again.

The elaborate work neared its completion. The top portraits were already finished, and now Pellam had gone to work on the lower sections. The knights drank it all in, the glory of Camelot and its servants, the adventures undertaken. The green knight, the dragons that so frustrated Vortigern until Merlin proffered an answer to their riddle, fabulous opponents to test Camelot's mettle.

And there was a young man jousting a red knight to death. And a young woman with her angry hands on a sword resting snugly in the remains of a tree.

Had Kundry helped Pellam see all of this? Or had he gained his intelligence reports elsewhere?

No matter. The old witch could no longer help him, if help was what he even wanted. The King's knights sought answers.

"How soon may we see him?" Galahad said, speaking in the most femininely diplomatic voice her mother taught her, the voice which melted men.

But not Clellus. His armor was his formality. "We've prepared the same rooms, and you may both wash first. As you know, it takes my lord some time to prepare to meet guests."

The sweet voice disappeared in an instant. Galahad's fear and hostility came to the surface. "But you clearly knew we were coming, so why wouldn't he have had time already –"

Perceval did something he never tried before: he physically quieted a woman by covering her mouth with his gauntleted hand. Galahad bit him, getting nothing save a mouthful of chain link.

"Clellus, your master is fortunate to have a loyal right hand such as yourself. We would be honored if you would lead us to the rooms so we may make ready to meet him."

"Speaking of right hands," Galahad spat, tasting the metal in her mouth after getting the intruding extremity off her face. The taste reminded her of the rusty flavor of blood. Perceval didn't even look at her, which only infuriated her that much further.

"This way then, please," Clellus said, and led them into the keep.

The rooms were the same as they'd left them, and no sooner had the servant gone downstairs was Galahad in Perceval's room, and then in his face.

"What was *that* about? How dare you silence me like that!"

Perceval would have none of it. "Listen, how far do you think we're likely to get in here tonight with outbursts like that?"

"Outbursts? It was a legitimate question!"

"And a rude one! You know it's not proper to ask direct things of a host."

"Then what are we doing here, if we can't be direct?"

Perceval had an answer, but wanted to save it. "Do you trust me?"

That set her back a moment. "How could I not trust someone who showed me the vagina of the earth?" Her sarcasm was obvious.

"Then will you let me speak? I think you're too emotional about this. You've been telling the tale your whole life,
and your involvement in it. You're too attached to all this."

"What about you? Pellam's you're uncle, and you say I'm
too close!"

"Just trust me. That's all I ask. If I botch this, then you
can take over and say whatever pleases you. All right?"

"What are you hiding, Purse? You, Pellam? Why does
everyone in your family hide things?"

"Some things need to be kept until ready. Do you understand?"

She nodded, even though she didn't. She just wanted to
see and hear Pellam again.

Galahad went into her own room, washing herself with
the fresh basin of water. It had no scent whatsoever this time,
she was pleased to note. They both removed their armor in their
separate rooms, and primped as much as they could until they
would be received downstairs. Galahad admired anew Arthur's
gift: her own mail, covered by a white tunic featuring a prominent scarlet cross, Perceval's old cross still dangling on her chest.

When ready, they met in the hallway and shut their doors,
ignoring the intricate wood engravings laid in them. Clellus, as
always, was one step ahead of them, and extended Galahad a
hand to escort her into the main hall.

The place felt empty without its previous guests. Nimue,
Taliesin, Kundry, and Lancelot had their own schedules, and the
former pair had not been seen by Perceval and Galahad again.
Still, their absence seemed wrong. Taliesin's harp could coax any
feeling, and Galahad wanted to relax and not feel hostile.

Their old seats awaited them, just the two this time. The
table was set for a feast but the candles had not received flames
and the wine vessels stood full of nothing but air. Pellam was
nowhere in sight.

"Please be seated," Clellus invited. "He will see you at once."

The pair of knights watched as the man disappeared into the kitchen and store room, and remained standing.

"You don't want to sit at this table again either, do you?" Galahad said.

"I'm too nervous to sit. I haven't felt this scared of saying the wrong thing since I gave Llio her ring."

Galahad looked down at that. She missed Llio also, though she knew it could hardly compare to how Perceval felt about the loss.

Shortly, the lord of the keep emerged from the hidden rooms, carried by Clellus and one of the younger attendants.

He looked ancient! And so frail he might fall from his chair at any moment, a lifetime's strength finally expiring. Yet he still found his smile, offering it warmly to his guests.

"Not often we get repeat visitors to these parts," he said, coughing slightly.

"Uncle, may we speak freely?" Perceval said.

"I was hoping all along you would. There is much to learn, provided one asks the proper questions." His two guests bristled a bit at that. How many chances would they receive? They didn't dare ask; each word had to be measured.

"Let us help you," Perceval insisted, motioning to Galahad. Together, they approached the large chair, a virtual throne, at the sides of which Clellus and the younger man were clearly struggling.

They eased him down to the table's head. Pellam took a hand each from Perceval and Galahad, grasping them in his own. All blood-given heat had deserted them.

"Thank you, both. You're very patient, waiting on someone so damned infirm he can't even fish anymore. I have to watch Clellus do it from the tower. Now, will you sit, and speak whatever's troubling you?"

They retired to their assigned seats. "Actually, uncle, we came to inquire what might be troubling you."

"Just the dreariness of age setting in. Still, I can hardly complain. I've seen much in this long life."

Galahad looked toward her friend. Perceval seemed silenced by the answer he received. *It's not going to be so easy, is it, Purse?*

"My lord," she began, "could you tell us, please, about what we witnessed during our prior visit? The processional, the food and drink, the singing?"

Pellam stared at her with a largely blank expression. "I do hope the food and entertainment was to your liking. The salmon was quite tasty, if I recall."

But you didn't even eat any! Galahad thought angrily. *Old man, what are you hiding? Maybe I should ask you precisely that.* But she decided not to. She wanted to wait for Perceval.

What's he after? Perceval wondered. *There's more to this than what we saw that night.* He threw his head back, all but exasperated.

He glanced upward, seeing the mural of Camelot on the wall behind him. What would the King do were he here?

And in the painting, Perceval could just faintly make out the image of Arthur's crest above the gate leading into Pendragon Castle: the shield of blue with its three crowns.

Three! Gornymant, you old, wonderful, dear father-in-law! We've got three chances to ask the right thing, and Galahad's used one already.

He looked at her. She clearly wanted him to say something, but now with his sudden revelation he couldn't think of anything. Did he dare to share his insight with her, or would that ruin their chances?

Ruin the magick, more like. This whole place is magickal, it has to be. Some spell controls things here, not this man sitting as a false figurehead.

Perceval was instantly roused by Galahad speaking again. "I do recall that well, Sir," she said. "But if I may, what can you share with us about the serving dish, and that unusual spear?" *Perceval, I'm doing my best here. You said you'd thought this through already, and you're sitting there silent as a rock.*

Perceval stared at her, then broke a smile of his own. He admired Galahad's efforts, and her newly found self-control; she was playing the diplomat in a foreign kingdom quite well, actually. *But if you knew how foreign, you might never again take your hands from that cross I gave you. And that's two!*

He decided in an instant, choosing the direct approach. He was so spontaneous Pellam had only begun to answer. "As for the dish —" Pellam said.

Perceval stood, hospitality be damned. "Uncle, what ails you? Tell me. Tell us, and we will serve your needs."

The standing young knight mistook the source of Pellam's suddenly watering eyes, and for a slow moment thought he had wasted their last chance.

Yet as he watched, years seemed to melt off the sunken old face as though it emerged afresh from the womb. The eyes held their own life, glistening with the eagerness of a young boy exploring the secret confines of his lord's castle.

But not too much yet, and not too quickly. Was Perceval the one?

"It is an old wound, nephew. But the pain is already subsiding."

"How were you wounded?" Galahad asked.

"One could say in the same manner as was Kundry. You've met her." Perceval nodded. "Then please sit, Perceval. Let us talk frankly, the first time I've been truly able to since… Oh, I can't remember."

Perceval took his seat again. The mood in the room had changed. Even somber Clellus looked brighter, still standing at his lord's side awaiting the next command.

"To the Grail," Galahad offered, raising her goblet. Perceval heard a doubting tone in her voice.

"I'm afraid you won't find it in this place, Lady. I can offer you truth, but not prizes." Even Pellam's voice sounded surer, less gruff.

"But I thought —"

"That you did, and rightly so, at least at one point. It is long since departed from here, though. I lacked the worthiness to possess it."

"You?" That made no sense to Perceval. Who better to hold the Grail than Pellam?

If it *could* be kept...

"Of course. Galahad probably knows the story, if you don't. You're from a different bloodline than she." He gazed at her. "No one can actually keep it. I think the tale has been mistranslated over the years; the only way it can be 'kept' is from those who would abuse its power, or claim it theirs. It only appears to those who demonstrate the proper traits. I don't claim to know just what those are, nor does Kundry."

"But I thought if we asked the right questions," protested Perceval.

"That's a beginning. You have great compassion, Perceval. So much so, that you often forget your own needs. You haven't let anyone down, particularly the women you've known and loved."

The younger man's face smiled weakly. He saw enough in his time out of the isolation of home to no longer be easily surprised. "Did Kundry tell you that?"

"She said she encountered you on the road, and she knows enough to divine what men think from their words and actions. Some call that a type of magick."

"I've always been easy to read." Llio had told him that, and loved him all the more for it. "But this story of your being wounded. That sounds like one of the old Irish folk tales."

Thank the powers that be for Tathan. Perceval was surprised he suddenly recalled that detail.

"The old king who falls infirm and can no longer rule. Like our aging Arthur, I would think. And the important part is how the health of his kingdom is only as strong as his own. Why else would the heathens take such pleasure in slaughtering those who overstayed their welcome? No one rules forever."

"Who was it?" Galahad patiently awaited her first answer.

"Hmm? Ah, yes. The one I fought with, quite selfishly. He was another knight, like myself, who might have gone onto some measure of greatness had I not slain him."

"You speak quite candidly during this visit, Sir Pellam," Galahad commented. "The last time, we had little idea what to think of our host."

"I've been unable to have so glib a tongue for too long. I'd almost forgotten how it felt. But I'll get to that. First, the knight."

The audience knights listened, enraptured. They hadn't known what to expect, and what they heard went beyond their strangest imaginings.

"His name was Balin, though that hardly matters now. Not to me, surely. He even sat at the Round Table back when it was so wondrously new. I don't recall where he hailed from, though I heard he had a twin brother. Anyway, he was known for carrying out vendettas for any grievance, even ones he concocted from nothing. He went so far as to assault one of the Lake Ladies, right in front of Arthur's court! Said she was responsible for his own mother's death. Imagine! Raising arms in an infant Camelot while the young king was still fighting his own battles just to unify the land. Arthur banished him. He was too much a threat to what little stability existed at that time."

"How did you find him?" Perceval said. *I was right. It was three questions. Now I doubt we could silence this man if we tried.*

"My own hunts. I'd never met the boy king, and didn't really envision myself serving his banner. At that point he was just the next in line. For all I knew he might be slain and replaced, like so many before. But he had powerful friends. Merlin." At the name's mention, Pellam's face grew taut and he frowned into his wine goblet. He sipped some more, and continued.

"Anyway. News of not just the great druid but of how Arthur gained his kingship through the combined sword prophecy and the girding on behalf of the enchantresses swept through the land. Magick was alive, people said. Those of a more modern bent claimed God's hand was at work, showing approval of the new king and his ways. Whomever was right, the truth of the matter was that unusual and marvelous things *did* happen, all around. It was my own greed which led me to this keep."

"Why? Surely the Grail wasn't just sitting in here, waiting to be found by anyone who chanced by?" Galahad was still convinced the holy chalice had been here; she just felt it, but could not explain the sensation further. It held the same certainty for her that her visions once did.

"No, I don't think anyone was even seeking it then. Not in any literal sense. But there abounded all manner of stories about this or that fabled treasure. The Thirteen relics of the realm, the bony remains of saints, clippings of the tree Joseph of Arimathea planted near the church at Glastonbury; every faith held up its own artifacts, validations to the faithful, as existing somewhere beyond legend. I came here because this old place was rumored to hold one of the Thirteen Treasures."

Perceval immediately began to mentally inventory the items: supposedly, a ring which could grant invisibility, a cloak only wearable by certain properly-behaving women, a chariot able to whisk riders wherever they wished, and...

"Was it a spear? Or a cauldron?"

"I know of no spear among those Pagan items. And the cauldron was that which would cook only the food of heroes. I'm afraid I've long forgotten the names of the figures to whom they all corresponded."

So have I. "Then what?" *If it wasn't either of those items, then why did this place have its Grail associations?*

"A chessboard of gold, with silver pieces which would play by themselves. It sounded valuable enough, although I didn't believe in any such magick. And I can only imagine my humiliation were I to lose a game of chess to no visible opponent other than the men themselves."

Galahad looked over at Perceval, thinking of their games just the previous night. *One king was Arthur, you said. And you identified others, too, like you just knew them all. Who plays the opposing side, then?*

Pellam kept right on talking. "Balin must have heard the same. I can think of no other reason for him to have wandered into this part of the forest. And he wasn't about to give peace any chance when he saw me. He was here first, after all. And I thought he just wanted to keep the riches for himself. We fought throughout this place," he said, gesturing about at the tiny castle; its origins must have dated back longer than he cared to consider. "At one point I managed to disarm him. A good thing for me, too; I was already exhausted. But he found a spear, sure enough, Perceval." Pellam clenched noticeably at recollection of a pain which had kept him all but bedridden for many years. He spoke painfully. "And he managed to wound me in the thigh with it, and in another place I'll not mention in the presence of a lady. Suffice it to say I've not had certain manly urges for quite a while. At length I ran him through with my own sword. Clellus was my squire then; he dumped the body into the river."

"There's something I don't understand," interrupted Galahad. "How did you acquire your wealth?"

"I believe you know the answer already. Recall when Taliesin sat with you here. By that time I already possessed an impressive castle far north of here. That's mostly why I never had the interest in serving Arthur; he might have threatened my own humble kingdom, even if it lay far from his own home. I've not seen it since just after that last fight, and I tried to leave it guarded, in a way. The surrounding land was already dying, and I couldn't comprehend why."

The light which struck Perceval's mind could have blinded. "You! The wounded king and the wounded land, neither of which can be healed."

"I thought that was just another peasant story, until Merlin found me."

"Merlin?!" The younger knights were equally surprised as they exclaimed a name many had tried to forget, but never could.

"He knew all the legends. That old bastard came here trying to finish his collection. It maddened him that his searches for all those treasures I hinted at mostly bore no fruit. When he came here I was trying to make life bearable again. I painted some as a boy, though in Gwynedd where I hail from that was frowned upon. My father dictated that I would become a knight rather than an artist. Yet I rediscovered that here, as you can see on the tower. And I've come to love fishing, as you also know. A man who cannot die, even if he wants to, needs something to pass the time."

"Matters with Kundry had failed by then?" Perceval no longer worried about the boldness of his questions.

"Oh, before Balin even. She said I was too obsessive with my hunts, whether for relics or wildlife. And after my injuries I lacked the interest in women anyway. It was she who sought me out, when she learned that my old kingdom had grown not just dead but dangerous. And she managed to get

you all here. I asked her to help me find those who might be of
assistance in breaking the spell."

"What spell?" Galahad said, though she hardly needed
to.

The old man laughed, picturing the venerable druid forever imprisoned within a tree or beneath a rock, like local legend
suggested; the image brought no small joy. "The *geas* Merlin put
on me. He said some nonsense about my having violated the
sacred ways, including this keep, and that the only thing I consider sacred about this place is my brush work outside. He told
me that only a person who could prove instantly compassionate,
who truly wanted to heal the ills of whomever he could, would
manage to free me."

There were tears in his eyes when he turned to Perceval.
"Thank you. I can no longer offer much beyond my gratitude,
but in front of you sits an old man who owes you his life."

"Your life remains your own, Sir. Though like Galahad,
I still feel confused. Folk talk of the northern wasting regions as
though the land was the plague itself. How can just your injuries,
horrifying as they were, be responsible for that? How could all
of this have happened?"

"Since Lady Galahad is also a bit mystified, I'll put matters into her terms. Merlin laid his sins unto me. He fashioned
Logres, was instrumental in putting Arthur at its helm, but I
think he knew it was time for him to leave when he realized that
he was also the start of the discord in the land. Pagan against
Christian. Queen and Champion. The Round Table, symbol of
unity even though its members freely tore at each other's throats
when meetings adjourned. The seat no one could claim at that
same table, because the descendants of civilizing Rome forgot
the importance of the women they fought over. The lack of
a proper heir to inherit Excalibur. Merlin turned me into just
another symbol of instability, and with me as the focus of his
magick, the wastes took hold and grew."

"You mean to suggest that Merlin was trying to atone?"
That did not sound like the mighty wizard Galahad's mother
Elaine had bespoken.

"In essence, yes. I know little of Merlin really, but he
seemed to think he meddled in Britain's affairs for longer than
was prudent. I've not seen him again."

"Nor has anyone else, so far as we know," Perceval said.

"It's an almost funny thing about real power," Pellam
hinted, "it can stand invincible to so much, yet be undone so
simply."

"How do you mean?"

"You broke his *geas*. Someone of noble blood, Merlin
dictated, who could be spontaneously caring, without wondering what rewards it might bring. You're the one who met those
criteria, Perceval."

"That can't be all it took."

"But it was. When Kundry was studying each of you,
she knew you read the Greeks. Do you know the story of Achil-
les?"

Perceval shook his head. Galahad took up the slack.
"The hero who could only be wounded in the ankle, no matter
the quality of his armor."

"Yes. And think of our own Logres. Excalibur is the
mightiest of weapons, but even its glory seems surpassed at
times by that of a girl who received what is actually quite an
ordinary blade." *One probably recoverable by anyone with the bravery to
try.*

Galahad felt for the comforting hilt so often at her side.
The weapon remained in her guest room upstairs.

"Or a mighty king, to be undone by, what, then? Betrayal? Someone contending for the throne? What might topple
Arthur's rulership?"

"We'll have to find out for certain when we take our
leave of this place. But we still have questions." Perceval had

relaxed somewhat; the principal test seemed concluded, and he had passed! "If the Grail is not here, does it lie safely in a place you know?"

"Not that I know, my boy. Even my old finds are secluded in my keep up north. I should like to request you pay that dingy place a visit sometime, to ensure those things are never found." For the first time, the young knight did not mind the nickname "boy."

"Then it really is gone," mused Galahad wistfully. "Not even Arthur is a great enough sovereign to warrant its return."

Perceval, however, remained wholly unsatisfied. To have come so far for an answer like that! It galled him, and now the Round Table knights were spread so thinly. "What gives you this certitude?" he said.

"Because I've found or at least know of every genuine treasure on this whole island, and not one of them could heal me!" Pellam tried to contain his bitterness; thinking of Merlin angered him, but he felt better than he had in years.

"No, apparently only we could do that, by returning. Isn't that what you meant?"

Pellam looked at him coldly. "How so?"

"You indicated Merlin worked his own unholiness on you. Is it not then conceivable part of this 'geas' included the inability for you to heal on your own accord, given time? What other reason could there be? Either you could be cured by the knight who met Merlin's demands, or you could find the Grail, but you could hardly keep searching in this state. Merlin left you here to wither, but not die, like the dream of Arthur's kingdom. All you could do was wait for the impossible: for the Grail to just materialize for you, or for me to find you."

"Is it any wonder that I begged Kundry for aid when she was the one who actually found me?"

"Answer me this, then, uncle: could the Grail heal you completely?"

"I'm already as healed as I wish to be. I feel like I'll manage to walk on these feeble legs come morning. It's been a long life, and I've no urge to stick around past my time. Like Merlin. What he did must have cost him dearly."

"Then let us help our king. Tell us where it is. Please." Galahad added her voice to the plea. She hoped there was enough of the man left in the person before her to hear the requests of a woman.

"As I say, knight to knights, anything of value I might possess could be found far north of here, in a place I shall not see again. Despite the pain of these years, this remote structure has become home. But I warn you, and pray you heed me: gone Merlin may be, but there are powers in the world with which no faith is truly prepared to deal. Kundry could tell you that, lest you forget. It is best to confront the supernatural in the most non-threatening manner. Remember that, above all else; I would not have either of you live the way I have."

Perceval sighed deeply. Another lesson. "Thank you, Sir. Uncle. Now we are in your debt."

"Then consider us even. Balanced, if you will. It is good enough just to lay eyes on you. When Gwynedd was overthrown, I thought your mother perished. Just knowing she survived, bringing two more wonderful children into the world in her time, is more than I ever dared to dream."

"You should always dare to dream," Galahad said, though she was staring towards the keep's door as the words left her.

All of them spent the night further talking, political and mystical topics falling by the wayside as the wine soothed them. Even anxious Galahad knew she could hardly leave until morning for the darkness outside, and took delight in hearing the old man speak of his fabulous hunts. She had seen offspring of some of the creatures he described in the High Queen's menagerie.

The hours eventually caught up with them. Both guests felt excited and at ease all at once, and were eager to get on their way once the sun greeted them.

The only way to pick up a northerly road was to head back into the forest whence they came. Perceval and Galahad bid their farewell to Pellam at the river landing where their raft came to rest during their first intrepid visit. Nephew and uncle embraced while Pellam, indeed able to walk short distances now with the aid of a cane, eased himself into his fishing coracle. He insisted on venturing into the water alone for once, and didn't care if the fish would nip at his line or not; he felt released at long last! He suspected he would not see Perceval again, for his days felt numbered, but he welcomed that sensation, to know he might age and die like everyone else. And soon he might see his niece.

Perceval sensed the same, but held his head high, knowing he had to see the quest through, if for no other reason than to be able to look his king in the eye and say he had given his best effort. And Galahad was virtually champing at the bit to get going that morning, so they left as soon as they could make ready.

Dindraine, Llascoit, and Kundry found them just after the sun began its daily arc back down to meet the earth. Llascoit was the only one of them who looked to have any energy about him, but all three could have hardly missed the eager faces of their friends.

"You found it," Llascoit said. "Tell us you found it!"

Galahad shook her head. "No, but we know where it is." Perceval gawked at her. Up to that point, neither of them had dared to voice such a presumption, but they both prayed that whatever "grail" there was might be within Pellam's northern castle.

"Where?" Dindraine said. Her face was pale; after the previous day, the only mobility for her came from the back of a horse. Perceval answered her.

"But that's so far!" Llascoit complained. "How long till we can return to Camelot?"

Perceval had not yet shared his thoughts on this with any of them, but he had a plan. "Perhaps you should head back right away. Tell Arthur we know where the Grail is hiding, and that we've ridden to —" he almost said "claim."

"To?" Kundry said, who looked as frail as Pellam, though livelier than before.

"To see if what we believe is true. Lady Kundry, you and Dindraine could stay in Bridgnorth until we return. You'll be safe there, and Pellam would be thrilled with your company." Perceval turned to Llascoit. "You're the key. Keep up our king's hopes, and don't stop for anyone else on the road. Trust no one till you reach the city."

"Are you sure about this?" Llascoit said, trying not to let his eagerness betray him. The others all knew he itched to be at the King's side.

Galahad thought it over, and it made sense to her. She nodded with Perceval. "Just escort them for a few more hours to Bridgnorth, spend the night with my uncle's hospitality, and be off with the sunrise tomorrow. I'm sure you can navigate this forest again."

"Of course. I can't wait to see the look on Arthur's face. What do you suppose our king will do with his grail, live forever?"

Galahad cringed. "No. But perhaps it might afford us all a bit more time to solve Logres' problems." *It can heal, Mother said.*

"I mean it though, Llas," Perceval warned. "Don't travel with your guard down, not even on the royal roads. Trouble is coming to Camelot. Our king has enemies."

"You're not talking to some unseasoned peasant. Ladies, I would be proud to complete my escort while our friends turn north."

"Thank you," Dindraine chuckled. "But now that we know we're close and you won't leave until morning, can we ride a bit slower?"

Perceval and Galahad laughed, exchanging their embraces and promises for a speedy return with the others, then rode further east through the forest, until they reached the main road leading them toward the far reaches of Logres.

* * *

The two knights kept a good pace, noticing how sentiment through the land had grown tense. They passed no farm, manor, keep, town, or religious or secular settlement in which the prevailing mood felt comforting; Britain had ripened for civil war. Everywhere came talk of what would happen next, of who the key players were: the King and Queen, Margawse and Mordred, Morgan and Taliesin. No one spoke ill of Arthur's prognosis in front of Perceval and Galahad, but it was clear the people grew scared for the future. Most commoners cared little to nothing about who sat in which throne; what mattered to the majority was how the powerful affected their own humble lives. Arthur enabled prosperity and security for thousands of them; others held grievances, real or imagined, and awaited the next ruler as they might expect the next season.

And the knights had to tread lightly now, wherever they might go. Mention of the Round Table had lost some of its awe. The two travelers never heard a word from those who inexorably favored new blood in Pendragon Castle.

So they learned, and quickly. Galahad refused to believe her king capable of ordering the systematic drowning of mere babies, even when she acknowledged the strength of visions (it was the idea of such sendings interpreted through Merlin which

gave her cause to doubt; she distrusted magick more than ever).
Perceval had great trouble imagining Arthur rolling in bed with
his own sister. He'd have taken the head of someone accusing
him of the same with Dindraine!

What else didn't they know about yet? How much had
the High King atoned for, made reparations for? Galahad hated
to think in such terms, but she felt herself coming to imagine
whatever battles might lie ahead for Arthur as judgments. Like
Pellam indicated, rulers had to justify their right to power, and
remain fit. She guessed that fitness included not only the physical, for which Pellam paid too great a price, but the spiritual. She
crossed herself whenever she wondered about Arthur's worthiness.

Who judged the High King?

Galahad shared her trepidations with her companion.
Perceval could only offer an analogy to his mother, and the vows
he swore to her. Five of them, there were. They both wondered
what vows Arthur made, and to whom, and how well he had
lived up to the promise of each.

At one point fear got the better of Galahad. "Where
will we go, if we fail, if Arthur fails?"

"Some place will be safe. Always believe that. When
my mother's whole world crumbled at her feet, she found a new
home and a new life."

"But where?" she said again. The only homes she had
ever known were either Camelot or a town too close to the Garmani, who undoubtedly sat in the southeast grinning and grind-
ing new edges to their weapons.

"If we ever find Tathan again, perhaps we could go to
Eire-land." Perceval meant it as a jest.

"Eire-land?! Saint Patricus had barely begun to chase the
wickedness from that land, and he's gone. What chance would I
have?"

"Oh, come now. The cross has found a very solid foundation across the western sea. And you needn't convert anyone. Think of all the exploring we could do. I tell you, Gal, that land is the safest I know. Even the Romans couldn't reach it! And chivalry has made its way there, just not on the scale we know here. I think we'd fit fight in."

"Literate people, not just bards? And knights, not mere warriors?"

"Surely. I think the Irish know how to keep themselves safe, whatever dark times may lie ahead."

Galahad thought about it, too. If Arthur and the dream of Camelot were judged unfit to survive, the knights would probably return to their own lands, adopting the petty small-minded skirmishing and blade-rattling with which the late Uther had to contend. She and Perceval had no other lord to fall back upon; even Llascoit could conceivably return to his father. The barbarians would find easy pickings once again, remembering how their parents had suffered crushing defeats at the fury of Excalibur. No one could unite the masses like Arthur. That was what bothered her most. Someone had to keep the dream alive, if now wasn't the right time.

Days crept along, the frustration at the sheer distance between the knights and their goal mounting, but they knew when they reached far enough northward to have entered the wastes. Neither was sure what gave the region away: the odor of decay, or the terrain from which nothing grew.

Pellam warned them that navigating the dead lands would be challenging at best, but no words could have prepared them for the utter desolation they found.

Not a person in sight. No animals nor even trees, for that matter. "If we go in there, will we come out?" Perceval said.

"Do you think we have a choice any longer?" Galahad was concerned, too, but did not intend to turn back. She looked at the ground, listening to Brownie's snorting protest. Beneath rider and horse was still green grass, and the occasional flower and roving insects. Just in front of them, the grass was either dead or simply ceased to be, replaced by foul-looking gravelly dirt that smelled like carrion, though no crows dared to try landing on it.

So she didn't see what Perceval saw. "Riders!" he muttered. "Let's move."

"To where? There's no cover." Galahad's focus on their task included opposing those who might stand in their way. She followed his gaze, making out a faint dust cloud to the northeast.

"You're right. It looks like there's just a few: maybe four, no extra horses."

That meant they probably weren't knights. Not rich ones, at least. "Then we stand."

They didn't have long to wait. And their curiosity waned as just two riders could be seen. They easily recognized the arms of Yvaine and Bors.

Perceval hailed them, his voice sounding undeniably relieved. "Where do you ride from?"

Bors answered. "The east. We've been spying a bit on Lothian. The whole kingdom's all but deserted. We persuaded a Pict to loosen his tongue and he said a huge warband had marched south. Should be in the Midlands by now."

Yvaine looked white, his eyes noticing nothing, his hands barely grasping the reins. "What's happened?" Galahad said.

"We've had our own share of trouble. Margawse is gone from Lothian also. A good thing, too, since Yvaine here all but swore to kill her on sight."

"Why, Sir Yvaine?" Perceval said.

Nothing. The man stared vacantly.

Bors kept talking. "He's been like this, and getting worse, so I'm leading him back to Camelot."

"Camelot," babbled Yvaine, to no one.

"What news of the quest, then?" Galahad prayed the others had failed, if for no other reason that it would keep up her hopes.

"Lady, I've heard nothing of the object of our search. Anyone we've asked has proven indifferent or ignorant."

For a fleeting moment Galahad wondered at the relation she held with this man she barely knew. Was he close enough to be a cousin? Her father, even during their improving talks, never mentioned him. "The other knights, then?"

"None we've seen, not since Camelot. We need to reach the south soon, though; Yvaine has taken a nasty wound." Bors pointed at the other man's midsection. The knight of the lion, whose large cat was curiously absent, ignored the blood at his abdomen.

"From what?" asked Perceval.

"Bandits heading south to meet up with the army. At least that was what I learned from one survivor I questioned. Yvaine saved me, but he's getting worse."

Galahad surprised herself more than the others. "Bors, will you ride with us? We go into the wasteland, and I'm a great believer in the safety of numbers."

"Our brother knight won't last in there," he said grimly.

"Possibly. But if we don't try, he won't make it to Camelot either."

"Camelot," Yvaine again burbled.

"Try what?" Bors asked her.

"To complete the quest. We need you. We need our combined strength. What else is the Round Table about?"

It took but a moment's hesitation. "All right, then. We ride forth."

And they entered the wasteland. Only Yvaine looked calm about it.

The first night was the worst. They lost their way, argued back and forth about landmarks, only some of which could be found, and finally made camp, the three more coherent knights sharing shifts.

With the others dozing, Galahad nudged Bors.

"It's all right," he said, yawning. "I couldn't sleep."

"Who could, out here?"

"Why don't you try for some rest regardless. But tell me something: how are we to know this Pellam's castle?"

"In all this, I doubt we'll fail to identify it. It's just a matter of finding it."

"That's what your father said, the last time I saw him."

That roused her into heightened alertness. "When?"

"When we were all readying to leave the city. He knew where I was heading, and guessed you and Perceval might wind up in similar locales."

"I wonder how close he got," she wondered.

"A great knight like Lancelot? Probably pretty close."

"Why do you think someone like him might fail?"

"For the same reason I think I will myself. I, too, loved the wrong person."

Galahad hadn't been alert enough to sense that coming. "What does that have to do with the Grail?"

"Oh, Galahad, your father told me you knew something of Scripture. I've studied as well. Maybe I'll end up in a monastery after all of this. There's no way for someone like me to succeed here. The Grail needs a pure heart."

"You talk so freely, and you're the only other one I've met who sees this all as spiritual."

"How can God's own finery be found by us?"

She looked around them. "Pellam said worthiness, but couldn't explain it further."

"Maybe it's you. You have the purest heart I've seen."

"Me? But you barely know me."

Bors kept at it. "You sit in the Siege Perilous."

"But I don't know why. Because I'm a woman?"

"I don't claim to know. I only have my beliefs."

That piqued her curiosity. "I'd like to hear of them, if you don't mind sharing. Talking of such personal matters can be wanting with Perceval. He's a bit befuddled sometimes."

"Perhaps that's why you love him so much."

"I —" she started. "Yes, I do."

"But not in the usual way a woman loves a man?"

"Well, no. I guess not. Even if I did, he still misses his wife so much. Sometimes I hear him cry her name in his sleep."

"He's fortunate to have you. I don't have any friends like that."

That made her think on the matter. "Sir Bors, my father never has spoken of you. Not to me. Can you tell me why?"

He stared at the bleak landscape surrounding them. "As I stated, I loved the wrong person."

"Who? Was he jealous, in love with the same?"

Bors chuckled at that. "Oh, hardly. I don't think this person ever was willing to acknowledge my infatuation."

"Sounds like grand courtly love already," she said, mentally summarizing the stages of fine romance. It began with adoration from afar, virtuous rejection, wooing and deeds of honor and bravery as proof of love, acceptance, and then troubles, and ultimately, tragic ending. The woman was worshipped, the man brought to heroics in showing his devotion and desire. It irked Galahad to know that her father's love for Guinevere, no matter how painful and scandalous its results, had actually followed the so-called rules of love.

"It was never that, either, though it shared the trait of being forbidden."

"May I ask who?"

"It seems I'm not the only frank person at this camp."

Galahad shrugged. She rarely gossiped. Lupinia would have been proud.

He sighed. "I'll tell you, though I pray it won't drive a wedge between us."

"No wedges will do out here. We need each other to survive this place."

"Trystan," he said.

"You mean you loved Isolde from Eire-land? I can see how Trystan might have objected, but," she cut if off. *Another romantic affair gone afoul. Small wonder the Queen's love courts are likely surviving on borrowed time. Maybe she just wanted to justify my father.*

"Maybe there is somewhere my desires would be more acceptable. No, Lady Galahad, not Isolde." Bors cleared his throat. "I would not tell you this, but I think perhaps since you are a woman you may render less harsh judgment. Please don't tell the others, but my love was for Trystan himself."

Bors didn't like the silence. Nothing made a sound. There wasn't even the comforting crackle of a campfire, since it would give them away, and they never found suitable shelter from the elements.

"You mean my father shuns you because you're, you're —" she blushed at not even knowing the term for Bors.

"A man who loves men. There aren't many like me. Perhaps more would appear but for the fear."

"You're right about one thing. Scripture might damn you for this."

He drew away from her. "I thought you might respond this way."

But she took his hand. "It might also damn me for chasing a heretical, feminine object. We'll just have to take our chances with hell."

It was his turn to be shocked. After a moment, he said, "You see how I mean? The purest of hearts. Thank you, Galahad."

"You're welcome. I think you should follow your heart, no matter what my father says, or doesn't say."

"He said one other thing to me, that day in Camelot."

Galahad could barely see him in the darkness. Something about that made talking easier. "Yes?"

"You had already left with Perceval. So he said he wished you the wisdom to meet the quest. I think he's quite proud of you, more so than of me surely. But we knights aren't supposed to show feeling except for the lords who feed us and the ladies we try and win."

Galahad laughed. "Then someday may we rogues find appropriate men."

"Amen," he said, and bid Galahad goodnight, although neither could sleep.

* * *

She was right; Pellam's huge castle was easy to spot, even in the perpetual duskiness of the region.

It took almost all their efforts just to keep their horses from bolting, frantically seeking safer land or a place to graze. Food was almost gone.

Bors was all too aware of this. "We have to head back," he said. "We're too low on stores and water, and I don't know how much time Yvaine has." Yvaine had said no more than a smattering of words for the past two days.

Yet Galahad would not be budged. "We're low enough on food that if we turn back now, we're dead. We have to believe. Look! Pellam's castle is right in front of us." It lay just a few miles beyond now, at the reaches of their strained and hazy vision.

"How do we know it's Pellam's?" protested Bors. "This might be the place where Gareth almost died."

Perceval had his doubts, but knew they had to stay together. "Then if we see any trees dangling knights, we'll know otherwise. And Gareth fought alone, whereas we are four."

They urged their jittery horses forward, trying not to let their own fears show in any jerky motions; horses could be very sensitive.

The castle grew, becoming enormous as they rode within hailing distance. Bors led the cry to get someone's attention. Soon all but Yvaine shouted their own greetings, just wanting acknowledgment.

Silence was their only reply.

They kept trying. Uncaring minutes crawled by. They inched closer.

"The gate's locked," observed Bors.

They stared, then rode to it. Sure enough, the empty but sturdy gate tower stood uninvitingly shut. A badly rusted portcullis had been closed, though it still appeared strong. Behind this, massive wooden doors lay battered and broken.

"Is this the image you had when Gawaine and Gaheris talked of their adventurous castle?" Perceval asked them. They all nodded, having heard the story in the Round Table chamber.

"I forgot how they got out of here," he said.

"A tunnel," answered Galahad. "They found a long passageway leading beneath the whole courtyard."

"And it led outside," concluded Bors. "Let's find it."

They rode as a group, not caring that it would take longer. They felt blessed when they at last found an opening near one wall, heading into the side of the hill on which the castle stood, looking to lead from there past the walls.

"What did Pellam call this place?" Bors inquired.

"You know, that's strange," Perceval said. "We never asked him."

"So, who wants to go in first?" Galahad asked. The tunnel was black beyond comfort, and just high enough to get the horses through if they each dismounted, and then led their mounts in pairs.

"Yvaine," Perceval asked, feeling like he was talking to no one, "stay in back with Bors. We'll take the lead." He was already off Styfnig, while Yvaine remained oblivious, hunched atop his charger.

"Do we have the makings for a torch?" Galahad wanted to know, realizing they had no lantern among them.

"We do," Bors said, and he jumped down, rummaged through his gear until he produced a thick long stick, with old rags on one end, and some oil and his tinderbox for camp. He lit it quickly, even though no one else was in a hurry.

He handed it to Perceval, and they all walked into the tunnel.

They were all glad of two things: the tunnel was short, and light could be seen at its end. They took their time, though, calming their mounts as they walked. The walls were fairly smooth, but littered with cobwebs. It looked devoid of other life. Bors hoped there were no rats. He hated rats, bitten more than once as a child.

They all exhaled sighs of relief as they emerged from the darkness into the hazy light of the castle courtyard, but their brief sense of peace ended at once.

The place looked like it had remained unoccupied for generations. Slight gusts of wind filtered into the aging towers, howling. Dust and dirt were everywhere; already the bases of the walls showed signs of being buried forever as the wasted region swallowed it all.

"We should make camp in here, then," Galahad said, feeling giddy despite herself. This *had* to be the place! "If we don't find what we're after tonight, then we can leave tomorrow and search for more food." She didn't mention the Grail by name anymore. None of them did. It was as though they feared profaning it.

They eased Yvaine to the ground. His wounds had blessedly stayed closed for a day, but he could hardly move, and the others had to tend to him. *At least he's not awash in wine anymore*, thought Bors. *It must have been wine, to make him want Margawse's head so.* Bors could never comprehend so severe a hatred. Yvaine kept yelling how the Queen of Lothian would prove Arthur's undoing.

No more of that talk now, Bors thought, breaking out the requisite supplies to spend another night in oblivion. At least this time they would have the shelter of the walls, but none of them wanted to actually sleep indoors, especially after Perceval and Galahad returned from their scouting.

They went inside and roamed from room to room, finding the same places Gawaine found before, even the bed near which he was almost felled by crossbows. After his story back in Camelot, no one had ever wished to visit this place, much less spend time within it. The current visitors merely wanted the certainty of no one else's presence. They kept swords at the ready the whole time.

They found no one, and hardly felt surprised. When they found the kitchen, it reminded Perceval of Bridgnorth. He mentioned it to Galahad.

"Would this be where he kept it?" she asked him.

"I would think so. I wonder what it even looks like."

They searched cupboards and closets, pantries and furnishings, and found only dilapidated cookware and dishes. There were candlesticks, raggedy linens, and furniture which looked as though it would split apart from the pressure of anyone.

"It has to be here," Galahad insisted. "It must be." But there was no sign of anything which didn't look worn out, much less something holy. *What would it look like?* she wondered for the thousandth time, still caught up in the discrepancy between the precious ornamental piece she saw, and Perceval's carved dish.

It didn't matter. She believed they would know it if, *no, when,* they found it.

"Let's report back to the others," Perceval said. "There's just nothing around here."

As they left the kitchen, Perceval almost stepped on the small copper drinking goblet that Sir Gaheris wanted to keep before. It was so covered with dust and grime it had become as worthless as its surroundings.

At the campsite, Bors hovered over Yvaine, trying to keep him warm. The knight of the lion had begun to shiver.

"How bad is he?" Perceval asked, as he and Galahad noticed what was happening and came running.

"Hard to say," Bors confessed. "The wounds are open again, and I think he's losing consciousness."

The others gathered around him. Yvaine was trying to speak. "G-grail," he whispered feebly. "Camelot."

"Yes, we'll have you back home with the finest royal healers soon," Bors promised, hating himself for speaking emptily.

"H-heal," Yvaine said with a groan, and he his eyes closed.

"We're losing him," Perceval observed, wishing his sister was there.

"What can we do, though?" Bors said, questioning their efforts.

"We have to find it. Now. No more delays, no more philosophy or history or preaching." The others turned towards Galahad's commanding voice.

"It's not here!" Perceval yelled. "We've covered this god-forsaken place head to foot, and there's no grail here."

Galahad reached over Yvaine and slapped Perceval across the face, surprising more than hurting him.

"If God has forsaken this place, then it's our fault. All of us. It's here, it has to be. We've looked everywhere else."

"Why you, Gal?" Perceval said. "Everyone else has given up, declared either their own unworthiness or its nonexistence. All but you. Why?"

"Because it's in my blood! Yours, too. The seeker's blood is part of you."

"Then why can't I find it?"

"I don't know, but think! About all we've discussed, and guessed, and reasoned. Where could it be?"

"Didn't you once tell me of a dream you had of it?" Bors said, wanting to be part of the conversation again.

"Oh, that. It was so long ago. And it was so weird, because Galahad had the same one, or one like it. Do you remember?"

She sat as though he had struck her in return. "Why would you remember that now?" she mused, barely audible.

"What about it?" Perceval said, confused by her taking it so seriously.

"We had the same dream. We walked together, down a hallway, and there was some kind of light at the end." She turned back toward the tunnel they had recently traveled.

"Oh, come on," Perceval protested. "How can that be the same? And besides, we never knew if we dreamt of the Grail."

She almost crossed herself at the artifact's mention, but checked it. "But I had the dream after I first told you about Joseph of Arimathea."

Bors jumped in again. "Perceval, I thought you said you did know."

"But I don't recall it that way. Was I really talking about the Grail?"

"Yes. How could you not remember?"

He shrugged, feeling helpless. "What else do you remember?" He posed the question to Galahad.

"There were three of us, I think you were one, the other I've never identified, and I haven't had the dream since," she said. She felt no need to start missing her old visions.

"We were naked!" Perceval shouted triumphantly.

"What? At the Round Table?" Bors was clearly befuddled.

"No," Perceval said. "In the hallway. What dream are you talking about?"

"I thought the dream you both had was about the Grail when we saw it in the Round Table chamber."

"No," Galahad said. "This was a different one completely. No wonder Perceval couldn't remember it clearly."

"Then why were you all naked?"

They both looked around, feeling uncomfortable with the subject.

"Was I the third person?" Bors asked.

They stared at him, dumbfounded, then remembered the third person had a thick beard, like that of Bors.

"Look, both of you, there's a dying friend of ours right here, and we're running out of options. What does the nakedness mean?"

Galahad had an answer, amazed she had never thought of it before. "It's how we enter the world, totally vulnerable. No weapons, no armor, not even the ability to talk or reason."

"Is that the state you have to be in to find God's gift, then?"

Perceval was angry. The only person he felt comfortable running around with in a state of bodily freedom was dead, and this "grail," whatever it was, wouldn't be able to help Llio now. "What do you have in mind, Bors, to strip down bare and walk back through there, just because it reminded Galahad of the hall in our dream?"

"No. If we do that, I'm sure we'll be right back in the wastes, with nothing at all to help us. Maybe that region really is godforsaken. But in here, if the Grail ever was here, well, who knows?"

"All we can do is try," Galahad said, already steeling herself for roaming a strange castle in the raw with two men.

"But this is ridiculous," Perceval said. "Where do we look for it? I mean, surely you don't intend for us to search every room without so much as our drawers, do you?"

"No," Galahad protested, "not exactly. But what if the nudity we both dreamt of was symbolic, like it is for baptism, or for knighting? We lose armor and weapons first, then try," she swallowed, "completely naked, if that's what it takes." She hoped it would not.

Galahad rose, peeling off her surcoat and reaching for the buckles of her armor. "Let's try the feast hall. If there was ever a place for a lord to show off his prizes, it would be in there. Besides, it looks a bit like the room where we first saw it, back at Bridgnorth."

Perceval's mouth hadn't dropped so low since the day Llio first led him down to her father's pond for swimming instruction. He slept next to Galahad so many times, even saw her bathe, but never had she so unabashedly begun to remove clothing in front of him before. Bors was already joining her.

He willed himself to stand. He had to admit they had grown desperate, and the memory of the dream was potent enough he could still see the old, cold stone hallway. He took off his crimson surcoat first, lovingly folding it as always. It was one of the few treasures left from Llio.

He then placed the garment next to Yvaine, who groaned. His wound seemed to grow worse by the minute. Next came the armor and padding; all that was left were a linen shirt and leggings, worn next to the skin to prevent the mail from rubbing the skin raw. He took off the shirt to complete the ceremony.

Perceval now stood in little more than his underwear. Bors undressed quite quickly, standing before them. Galahad took one more look at them, then finished, revealing her own most basic clothes.

"You're sure?" he asked Bors one last time.

"Yes. Now hurry, if you please. It's getting cold!" Bors shivered slightly in the coming dusk, folding his arms and stamping his feet lightly on the ground. Perceval thought he looked quite foolish shifting his weight back and forth, extremities jiggling beneath the loose-fitting leggings. The man was in excellent health, however, and had more than his share of scars, visible through the light clothes.

Perceval had a fleeting glimpse of the young girl who had once been so shy she used to confess to bishop Baudwin, and could barely keep up with Lupinia's antics. Before him now, however, stood a radiant, unabashed, and proud woman, with a couple of scars of her own. He never took his glance from her face, even though he could see her entire body. He never noticed before how attractive she was, embarrassed and excited all at once to make out details of her under the light white garments she wore, like the men, beneath padding and mail. Her shaped hips and lean thighs looked anything but feminine when covered with mail, but her breasts had grown full and supple, and between her legs was a lovely shade darker than her own blonde hair. He couldn't help but notice, and swallowed hard to try and keep his own arousal in check. This was not the time! And besides, theirs was a different relationship. To the present Lancelot could hardly believe they had never made love together, especially after sharing so many beds.

"Stop staring and come on," Galahad demanded. She folded her arms like Bors. Her nipples were already hard from chilly breeze. Light clothing aside, it was damp from their sweat, and hardly insulating from the cold to begin with.

Perceval finished disrobing, his budding erection canceled by Galahad's words. He wondered if she spoke like that purposefully, as though she had sensed the mindless activity lurking beneath his breeches.

But no longer. Now they all stood almost naked, certainly feeling so without warmth of drier clothes and security of armaments, and silently made for the main hall, Bors carrying the torch. Yvaine moaned again as they left him with the securely tied horses.

Fortunately there was still a useful amount of light in the hall. Galahad went at once to the kitchens, partly from hope, partly from the cold.

Bors searched the table, looking for what he didn't really know. They all just sensed they would somehow know it when they saw it.

Perceval headed upstairs, no longer embarrassed. He found once regal quarters, fallen into dust and disuse with age. He looked in furniture, uplifted bedding and rugs, anything which might hide...

What, exactly? What did the Grail look like, really? Ornate silver cup? Large decorative serving bowl? Something else?

He was beginning to feel immensely ridiculous. He knew at least part of that feeling would diminish if he could wear more. How the hell was near nudity supposed to help him find anything other than illness?

"Purse!" came the female shout from downstairs. He was on his feet in no time and charged halfway down the steps until he could see them.

"What?" he cried, worried for their safety more than hopeful of finding anything.

"It's not here," Bors said gloomily. "Not in this building, it seems."

"I've all but ransacked the kitchen. Nothing."

"What's that you're holding?" Perceval asked of Bors.

"Oh, this. It was the only thing even vaguely interesting in the whole place. Just an old drinking goblet."

One fleeting glimmer of hope in Perceval's eyes: "Any jewels on it?"

"Hardly that. It's cheap, and filthy. Copper, I think. It's the only one like it here. The others must be lost."

"Maybe there were no oth-" Galahad began then stopped, frozen. She looked comical, standing there motionless and scantily clad. But her eyes widened in obvious fear.

The others followed her gaze. At the entrance to the keep stood a lion, licking its lips.

There was nowhere to run. They were exposed, trapped, and helpless.

"Oh, God, no. Yvaine," Bors whined, fearing the worst.

"No, look," Perceval said. "There's no blood on its mouth, though it looks like it just ate."

"H-how can you tell?" Galahad pleaded.

"Weren't you ever around cats? This is how they look afterwards. There were some in Oerfa."

"You mean this thing is just a big cat?" Galahad remained unconvinced.

"Sure. Yvaine could tell you that. This isn't his by chance, is it, Bors?"

"I don't see how it could be. We left Chat du Soleil in Guinevere's own little animal kingdom when we left the city."

"Then what kept it alive, if it's trapped up here? Nothing could get this far into the wastes without help."

Perceval didn't have a ready response to that. "It must have sneaked right by the horses."

"What do we do now?" Galahad wanted to know.

"We wait for that big golden boy to leave. And we follow him."

They didn't have long to wait, though it seemed a far more pronounced time to each of them. At least fear lessened the chill.

The lion then stood, and strolled casually for the stairs. Perceval was still on them, from when he answered to his name.

The others gasped. Perceval held his breath, wondering if he could just jump down to the room if attacked. He'd probably break a leg or two in the process, though it was better than getting mauled.

Or eaten. What did this creature eat? There existed no food for miles, other than what little the knights brought.

Galahad and Bors were almost as terrified as their friend, but they didn't dare say or do anything which might jeopardize his precarious position. They just watched, and waited.

And the lion casually sniffed Perceval, as though considering sampling a rare delicacy. Then it looked at his friends in the room below, and walked clear up the stairs, ignoring them all completely.

Perceval finally looked up after it, when he summoned the courage to do so. He felt a sudden urge to piss the stairs, despite the little water any of them had drunk for the past days.

"We have to follow it," he said.

The others were frozen in their positions. "You're mad," Bors concluded.

"We have to see where it goes, how it lives. How did it survive this long, and why didn't it kill me or Gawaine when it had the chance?"

No mere lion could crush the hope from Galahad. "When Joseph was imprisoned, the Grail nourished him. Do you think —" she started, then let the thought enter the minds of the men, asking them what she did not quite dare.

"Come on," Perceval said. He wanted to get upstairs.

The others made for the stone steps, still trying to ward off shivers. They joined him where he sat; he didn't want to go alone.

"How high?" Bors said.

"As high as it takes," Galahad answered. She gripped a hand of each man within hers, in the center of the trio.

They ascended the stairs, each wondering how closely the sight of them matched a pair of dreams almost forgotten. Again Galahad hoped the bare skin of their dreams would not have to translate literally, though she was past the point of truly caring; what was a little embarrassment in the presence of God?

They made slow time themselves. Each step felt cold and hard and unwanting as their feet touched them. Soon they would have no choice but to turn back, for they all felt the on-coming of shivers.

The prospect of starving kept them onward. Finally they reached the top landing. There was no sign of the lion, not even a trace it had ever been there.

Several doorways could be seen, though they had been checked already. At the end of the hall, they thought they could perceive another door.

Bors whispered. "Did you search all these?"

Perceval kept his voice out of his answer. "One's the master bedroom. There's a privy in another." He pointed. "That one is full of skins and furs, only some of which I knew, and that last is an armory, though the weapons and armor are worn and rusty." He paused. "But I don't remember that one at the end."

"Don't remember?!" Galahad exclaimed, her vocal chords squeaking in agitation.

"I thought we already had found all of these rooms, all right? Gawaine almost met his end in the bedroom alone! I might have noticed it if you hadn't yelled for me to come down."

Galahad looked toward the last door. She kept her ex-citement, though the source of it changed. "Look. Did you see that shadow?"

"What shadow?" the others said, their tongues finally finding their voices. What did it matter who heard them speak? The lion already knew they were here, and didn't care.

"Behind the door."

"How can you see behind the door, Gal?" Perceval wished to know.

"I mean, it crossed the light, coming from behind the door."

They peered down the hall. The outside dusk permitted little light inside, but then he saw the faint trace of it from behind the final door. Just beneath it. "There must be a window in that room," Bors offered.

"The others all have windows, too," Perceval said. "Pellam spent a king's ransom to build this place."

"Let's check the room on the end, then get out of here," Galahad voted. The men nodded, gripping her hands tightly.

They breathed in, summoning whatever composure remained. And they walked, ignoring the other rooms as they went. They had to stay focused now.

The air seemed to feel noticeably cooler as the door grew closer. Every other step, two of them could feel the hesitation of the third, as they each took turns fighting the urge to flee.

At last the door stood just before them. It was like the others, heavy, thick, with an iron handle and keyhole.

"I just hope it's not locked," Perceval said, as he reached for the handle.

It opened easily, given its mass, on silent hinges. The others, the knight recalled, all produced hinge squeaks from lack of maintenance.

Dusk had settled, going quickly into darkness. They had little time for a thorough search, and the torch Bors held wouldn't last much longer.

"What is this place?" Bors said, not expecting a useful answer.

"Some kind of reverence room," Galahad suggested. "Like a rectory. Maybe this was where Pellam came to pray."

"I wonder who heard his prayers," Perceval said, scanning the room. It contained a mix of symbols from around the world. A cross adorned one wall. A large cauldron sat in a corner, with the dusty remains of firewood beneath it. Dishes for incense or bloodletting, he did not know which, lined what looked like a small altar near the cross. There was an odd candlestick, with places for nine candles in a line, the middle one slightly larger, on a small table. None of them recognized this piece, nor what it might signify. Lovingly painted on the wall on either side of the door they entered were an assortment of sayings. Galahad easily noticed the Lord's Prayer as one of them. Others were more confusing, though Perceval's Latin background helped him read references to various Bible chapters, identified as such by Galahad as he read aloud. Other passages were in Greek, and even another language which none of them had any experience with, though some of the same characters appeared on the nine-tiered candelabra. After a full looking over, still another set of signs appeared, this last one using many curlicued symbols punctuated by dots. All told, it was an eclectic little room devoted not so much, it seemed, to fervent worship in any one faith, but rather to the study or perhaps comparison of many faiths. Every religion the interlopers knew of and more was represented here, and while each might scorn the symbols of the others, there they all were. More of Pellam's treasures he never took to Cambria.

While the men searched, Galahad took time to glance at a scroll rolled and tied on the altar. She read through it quickly, becoming disappointed with references she did not understand. Hebrew and Arabic details she found indecipherable, though each reference listed what appeared to be chapters, and she recognized still more biblical scriptures. The whole parchment was lavishly illustrated with images of strange creatures and important-looking persons.

And little pictures of a goblet, a simple drinking vessel, next to each listing of references.

They searched anew for one particular treasure, and within moments had found only two additional notable parts of the strange room.

A basin of clear water was in a corner by the window, next to where Galahad found the scroll. And the dirty skeleton of what could only be described as a large four-legged animal, in the opposite corner. The beast had obviously been dead for years.

"Where's the lion?" Bors said.

Perceval heard the question, but did not wish to offer an answer yet. He had never felt this way before. His body shuddered slightly, though he was no colder than previously. He even felt a bit warmer somehow, and he looked about helplessly, trying to etch every bit of the room into his memory.

Finally, he pointed at the bones. His brother knight did not agree with his consensus.

"Oh, come on, we just saw the lion. That's not it!"

"Then why don't you tell me where it went? How did it open up a door?"

"It must be in one of the other rooms."

"Then why don't you go check?"

"Gentlemen, please," Galahad insisted. "Instead of worrying about the lion, look at this water."

They both looked. Sure enough, it was a stone basin, waist-high, with water sitting in it. "So what?" Bors said.

"So why is it here, when everything else is dead or gone?" Perceval said, asking and explaining all at once. At least, that was how he felt. He kept looking around and taking his mental inventory. Somehow he knew he would never again see this place after the day was out.

"Stay here," he suddenly commanded, and dashed out.

"Where's he going?" Bors muttered, already tired of what felt more and more like a futile escapade.

"Who knows? He'll be back. But look at this again. Have you ever seen holy water?"

Bors looked at the basin incredulously. "What makes you so sure?" he said, his interest slowly returning.

"What else could it be, to have stayed here so long? *A fonte puro pura defluit aqua.* Joseph of Arimathea was kept alive by the Grail for a long time, so maybe this was what kept the lion alive, or –"

"Not that again. And what on earth did you just say?"

"Just that 'From a pure spring flows pure water.' Well, then what kept that beast around for so long, when we haven't seen any food for days, and it was nourished enough to ignore Perceval?"

They stared at the stone receptacle, letting their minds wander. A lion on its rear legs could easily reach the basin to take a drink, but that didn't explain the catly corpse behind them.

Perceval dashed downstairs, mumbling incoherently. He felt elated! He was in the middle of nowhere, shortly to die from either lack of food or too much exposure, and he couldn't have cared less. He all but flew down the steps; they no longer felt so cold, and he made straight for the kitchen again.

It had to be there. They were so close, it just *had* to be there.

He rummaged about the items they had looked through. Where had Bors left it?

There! On one of the chairs, the head chair. The little copper goblet found earlier. He took it and ran back to his companions, briskly searching each of the other rooms as he went.

"Where did you go?" Galahad demanded.

"I went to get something. Oh, and by the way, Bors, every room up here is empty, at least of lions."

"And?"

"I want to try something. I hope you'll both come with me."

"What's that?" Galahad said, warmer this time. Perceval showed her the cup. And he glanced out the window, out where Yvaine lay.

She understood at once, and gently took the cup from his hand. Bors looked befuddled, but she dipped the cup into the water with reverence normally reserved for the most devoted prayers, and filled it.

Then they walked out of the room, and back outside, keeping silent the whole way.

Yvaine still moaned occasionally, unaware of the approach of others. He was delirious, not even recognizing Galahad as she knelt at his side, gently lifting his head up to the cup she held.

Perceval stood back, wanting so much to believe...what? That a drink of water would save the man's life? Bors looked on but now understood. He knelt behind the others penitently, bowing his head and offering his own silent prayer.

Some of the precious drops ran down Yvaine's cheek and neck, but at last his lips parted sufficiently and he managed to swallow some. The others thought he might gulp it, but he took his time. They didn't like that; it was too suggestive of mortal frailty.

Only they were mistaken. Yvaine kept his eyes closed, barely listening to the now whispering prayers of his companions, and savored every drop as it passed lips and tongue and flowed delightfully down his dry throat, soothing and comforting the whole way.

He soon opened his eyes and looked at them. "Who stole your gear?" he said, sounding too strong for one so recently close to death.

They were too struck to speak, but Bors started laughing. "You hear that? He'll live! Good lord, the rotten knight of the lion is going to live!"

"Why would I do otherwise?" Yvaine said, looking a bit confused at his friend. "And don't you people know it's not only cold, but getting dark? Where's our camp?"

"How can you be asking questions so clearly like that?" Perceval demanded.

"How should I know? I remember now, when you and Galahad found us. I remember babbling and drooling like a baby."

"How can you sound so strong with that wound?" Galahad said.

"I don't know."

Bors probed gently at the man's abdomen, where his tunic and surcoat still bore the stained reminders of the horrible injuries he sustained. "That tickles," Yvaine told him.

"That's not all," Bors said, very seriously. "I can't find the wound."

The others all gawked at the knight's belly. The only sign of injury was the dried and drying blood; not so much as a scar told otherwise.

"Give me another sip," Yvaine insisted. Galahad obliged him, almost spilling the contents onto the ground. He had to steady her hand, and only the feeling of his new-found strength made her look away from his stomach.

Yvaine sat upright, looking as puzzled as the others. Before any of them drew conclusions, they all thought their silent prayers and related the events of the two previous days to their suddenly well comrade.

"I told you we should have brought Chat du Soleil," he laughed at them. "See how useful it is to have a lion with you?"

Bors, despite what he had evidenced, remained too much the skeptic to accept this blindly. "What makes you say so?"

"Lions are brave and kingly. Mine always made me think of the sun's brightness and fire."

Perceval gulped. "But the lion which helped us is long dead."

Galahad was the first to voice what the others felt, to varying degrees. "We have to ride. Daybreak."

"Why so soon? Are you so sure we've found it?" Bors said.

Galahad prodded about Yvaine's ruined clothing, noting again his newly perfect abdomen. "I need no more proof than this, and I say we ride."

"What's your hurry?" Perceval probed. "If we've found the Grail, shouldn't we take our time on the way home, perhaps heal those who need our help along the way? Isn't that what Jesus would have –"

"Jesus can't save us from those we might encounter. We ride, and we stop for no one till we reach Camelot."

Yvaine joined in the bewilderment his friends showed Galahad. "What makes you so afraid?"

"Who wouldn't kill to have the power we now possess? And our own lion awaits us in Camelot, with the poachers at his doorstep. Only the King can tell us what to do with this. Agreed?"

"Have we truly found it, then?" Perceval said, already believing.

"I think so. Now we have to protect it."

* * *

Dawn came as always, brighter and perhaps a touch warmer than previously in the dying land. The four knights broke camp, sharing the last remnants of their rations with each other and their mounts, who were just as eager to leave as their human riders. All four, along with the horses, drank several swallows from the cup, each feeling they could march tirelessly

for days. They wrapped the goblet, as they promised to call
it, not wanting to draw any careless attention to a "chalice" or
"grail," in Galahad's extra shift, and tied it as securely as they
knew how to Brownie's saddlebag. There it dangled, bouncing
slightly against the mare as they made off. Yvaine could hardly
keep his eyes from it; not only had it healed him, it reminded
him of the wine he oddly no longer craved.

When they reached the tunnel, Perceval stopped Styfnig, and took one last look about the castle. In another time,
the place must have been spectacular to behold, and inspiring
to call home. Now it was a dusty withering shell, a monument,
perhaps, to knights and their ways. The last of its riches had
been plundered. Perceval thought of Gareth and Gawaine and
Gaheris, the men who had been through these parts before, and
wondered if they knew how much each person who sat at Arthur's table had really contributed to the Great Search. He wondered where they were now.

The knights, and the other brethren of Orkney.

As they rode from the old castle, they could hardly help
but notice several patches of green beyond: grass. Just scattered little clumps at first, but as they made their way south, the
ground seemed to grow richer and livelier.

The land was healing.

* * *

When Perceval smelled the faint trace of such rank
smoke, he first thought of the utter foulness he rode through
after leaving Jagent. When Llio initially showed signs of illness.
He forced the image away. The others noticed it also, and urged
their mounts into a trot.

Soon it became a gallop. They had ridden for almost
a fortnight to get home, scavenging and lightly hunting, afraid
to abuse their newfound miraculous source of sustenance, and
were tough on their horses, still feeling rushed. The smell took

on elements of the strange sweetness of blood. They were nearing a battle scene. The burning might mean various things: pillaging of equipment not intended for enemy hands, razing of arable fields. Perhaps the timely disposal of too many bodies. Surely not that, they hoped.

But when they found the first corpses, recently cooled, they knew that whatever had transpired must have been enormous. Bits of hacked armor, shields, broken weapons, spent and unrecoverable arrows: all littered the hilly landscape. Almost subtly at first, then growing in number, along with the predominance of crow food. The black scavengers were already at their macabre feasting.

The travelers kept together, trying to maintain a vigil of their surroundings while passing mercifully brief inspections of bodies which would never again breathe, talk, walk, laugh, or love. Even the goblet was too late for them. Hatred never entered the minds of the four; all felt various degrees of shock, despair, and worst of all, helplessness.

Their alertness was wasted; nothing would move on this field till the scavengers finished their affairs. The knights wondered at the size a battle must have achieved to disallow any chance of burial or even pillage of the fallen. Possessions of the dead combatants remained in place; horses stood, here and there, licking their own wounds and still wearing their saddles and gear.

Barely aware they were following it, the knights kept to the trail of blood and bodies, trying to find its source. They noticed evidence of every conceivable method for weapons to kill; they could find examples of the destruction of every organ in the human body.

And for what? Almost blindly the four kept on, the miles passing, as the number of bodies grew from barely noticeable, to the point that they literally were piled on one another there. Even for veteran knights, it encouraged feelings of nausea.

"We have to find the King," Galahad said, knowing they were trying to.

Bors pointed to a young man who sported a spear from his stiff chest. "I knew him. Kid from Dumnonia." The others grunted; further dialogue seemed unnecessary and pointless.

At last Yvaine could stand it no longer. He wanted some answers. The group had just come to a trickling stream. Some of the blood had been washed away. "Where are we?" he asked them all at once.

"The Cotswold hills," Bors said. "See where the forest picks up south of here? Cirencester is to the east, and we could make Aquae Sulis within a day, Camelot within three."

"It looks like this fight continued south also," noted Perceval.

"I wonder if they went clear back to Camelot," Galahad added.

Yvaine felt just a morsel of relief. "At least the evidence goes in the direction we're traveling, so we can find out what in blazes happened. I can't say I relish the thought of riding past so many more bodies, though."

"Arthur awaits," Galahad said, urging them on once more. *I surely hope so*, she thought gloomily.

They camped that night two miles eastward. That was the necessary distance just to minimize the foul smells found that day. The next day they found Aquae Sulis deserted, and the largest grouping of corpses just south of the ancient city. Secure in the belief that the danger had passed, they took a chance on splitting into pairs and searching the area.

Bors and Galahad came back to report finding innumerable tracks in a pattern suggesting that the battle had gone well for those holding the southern part of the original field; from there they had pursued their enemies north, resulting in the devastation already encountered. But there must have been monstrous reinforcements for the invaders, driving southward those who previously enjoyed something of a rally.

Meanwhile, Perceval and Yvaine searched about Aquae Sulis, anxious but confident of Bors' estimate of their arrival time in Camelot, now that they, too, could identify more of the area. Arthur's city was assumed impregnable, and besides, they had not found the bodies of the more famous of their profession.

When the four of them met again and readied to ride south, Perceval led them on a brief detour, Yvaine amused with him.

"It may be funny, Yvaine," he said, "but it's on our way, and I just wanted to see if the others would think more of it than you."

"Listen," Yvaine replied, "I've learned enough just traveling this past time with you to realize your endless fascination with serpents. And why you want to slow us down to show off one you found is beyond me. I think it's amusing."

Galahad rolled her eyes. "Who cares about some dumb snake?" She had no wish to further explore their discussion of snakes, real or symbolized.

"It just seemed strange, is all. I noticed it was cut in half, right near the battlefield."

"So what?" Bors, too, had little patience with Perceval's intrigue.

"So why would a snake be hacked in half deliberately, in the midst of a battle so much larger than anything else we've ever seen?"

"Maybe it got in their way," Yvaine chuckled, picturing a mounted knight somehow afraid of a small inoffensive reptile.

"It seems like it was killed and then purposefully ignored," Bors noted, who began to notice the curious details. "Look at all the tracks. Everyone stayed away from it afterwards."

"Like it was bad somehow," Galahad said softly. The serpent made her think of a betrayer in Camelot, a Judas ready to open its doors to those who would ravish it.

Bodies still surrounded them, most no more than a couple of days gone. They watered the horses, covered their mouths with whatever spare cloth they each had, and forced themselves to continue.

Just a few more miles from their position was the worst of the fighting, and the most recent of it.

The scene would be a thieves' dream come true, if not for the presence of the newly-arrived knights. Everywhere were strewn pieces of equipment and personal valuables, no longer needed by their former owners. The crows had started even here, but remained hesitant about some of the dead and dying. Groans still emanated from a few of them.

"Maybe it's not too late," Galahad said, trying to sound hopeful.

"I agree," Yvaine answered. "Let's find survivors, anyone. We need to find out how it happened, and what transpired after this. There are so many tracks around here we'll never pin down where anyone healthy may have gone."

Galahad made sure she grabbed the goblet and her waterskin as she began searching. The others spread out, following the sounds of moaning.

Bors began something the others soon mimicked; as he recognized someone, he'd shout the name out for the benefit of the others, just so they began to get some idea of the magnitude of the conflict. Within a half hour they had identified Lucan, young Gareth, Kay, seven other members of the Round Table, and two others which made Perceval shudder to the core.

A malicious grin still on his face, the body of Clamadeus lay staring forever up at the heavens. One of his legs was missing, in its place a horrible mix of bloody mud.

"It should have been me," Perceval seethed. "I should have killed that bastard than let him live to plot another day."

"And then what?" Yvaine countered immediately. "You sound like your brother, Lamorak. I know firsthand that vendettas like that get you killed."

Perceval remained wholly unsatisfied, and the second bloodied and hacked man made him that much angrier.

Just enough reason remained to tell Perceval that at least Llascoit had succeeded in his last mission, and made it this far to give warning, probably giving the defenders the fighting chance they needed in the process. He wondered which of the nameless many, some literally faceless, killed him, as though it still mattered.

Perceval stared coldly at the shield, almost split in two from cuts, that his foster-brother painted that day. He felt his whole face constrict, and he had to look upward. The rage and the helplessness came out now, Perceval leading the way for them all.

All they could do, any of the four, was fall to the ground and sob. All but Yvaine retched, unable to control their bodies' reflexes. Time meant nothing now; they could hardly bring themselves to care about what became of their king. What was a king without subjects and an army which lay gutted and spread over many miles? Some of the living they found, only to watch them fade away.

But Galahad still plotted; she was the only one who thought there still might be time. And it was then she noticed another groan, from a body she almost tripped over.

"Father!" she said weakly, and crawled over to him. There lay Lancelot, the blood of scores of men mixed about his armor, clearly dying himself.

Perceval noticed her and ran over to them. Galahad was already unwrapping the goblet, making ready to pour into it some of the water they had taken in their skins from Pellam's rotting castle.

"Gal," Perceval said, his stomach still queasy, "Do we have the right?"

"Don't speak to me of right!" she spat at him. "This is my father! Wouldn't you save him if you could?" She knew his answer without him speaking it, felt it as he withdrew and watched her.

Bors and Yvaine began their search anew, walking about silently and dumbly, the spirit driven from them. They were disgusted at how the survivors would likely not make it, for the fighting had been so fierce that even this was not the last field of melee.

Galahad eased the cup to Lancelot's lips, and she had to force some of the cool water into his mouth. Like Yvaine, at first he couldn't even swallow, but then he began to gulp it, till none remained.

He opened his eyes, and saw the two oddest knights he'd ever met staring down at him.

"H-how long have I been out?" he said to them.

Perceval responded. "We don't know. We've only just gotten here ourselves."

Lancelot sat upright. "It's so quiet. Where are the rest?"

"Easy, Father. The others must have gone further south; up north are only decaying corpses."

"Then the King may yet live," he said, almost triumphantly. "He's not among these poor bastards here, is he?"

"Not so far as we can tell," said Perceval. "There's no sign of the Pendragon banner, nor of Bedivere."

"Then we head south, and finish this," Lancelot said, and started to stand, then changed his mind. "Hold. How is it I'm so free of pain, when I know how many wounds I took?"

Galahad showed him the goblet. It took Lancelot mere moments to understand what she meant.

"Is it true?" His disbelief was tempered by his loyalty to his king, which, even after all that had happened, still kept him going.

"If Arthur lives still, he may be likewise wounded," Perceval pleaded. "We have to get this to him!"

Lancelot began to nod, noting in utter shock how his wounds had simply disappeared, as though he dreamt the whole conflagration of war. Then he shook his head. "No."

"What?!" the others said together. "The King awaits! This is his prize, the promise of Camelot's endurance beyond all this treachery." It was Galahad's turn to try and convince him.

Yet he would not be stayed from what he had just decided. "I am Queen's Champion, and I order you both not to go anywhere near Camelot unless you first find out the King still lives and reigns."

"But why?"

"Because you've already seen the scope of this intrigue and treachery. We killed thousands in the last two days, and always more came. Margawse and Mordred hold immense sway with so many. Did you see either of them yet?"

They shook their heads.

"All the more reason to believe they live as well, which means Camelot remains threatened, which means the Grail cannot fall into the wrong hands."

"But we can help you, Father. Lead us into battle."

"No! I forbid you to take part in this. When Arthur's enemies are dead, I will send for you. Until then you find a safe place, where none of this despicable army can locate you."

"But," Galahad tried.

"Now," Lancelot ordered. He stood, readying his sword. From behind him he heard another voice. "Let me go with you," it said.

The Champion turned about to face Bors and Yvaine. The former had spoken. "Damn it, man, make your peace with me at last, and let us go and finish this. The others don't need me, and they'll be safe with the Grail." It was the first time Bors called it that.

Lancelot considered it, knowing he had to be quick. "Have you a healthy mount still?"

"Yes."

"Take mine as well," Yvaine added. "I'll escort the others." He was glad to not be riding forth, no longer feeling he had much to fight for.

Lancelot took the reins of Yvaine's charger, and offered his parting reassurance to the others. "I promise I'll take the heads of Mordred and Agrivaine myself, and split that bitch queen in two!"

"Long live the King, Lancelot," Perceval said.

"For Arthur and glory!" Bors shouted, and the pair of them rode south. Galahad watched them ride until they were completely out of sight.

* * *

Despite their orders to the contrary, the trio ventured south the next day. They had to know what else transpired. As it turned out, Lancelot's decision had good and bad results.

The positive news was that he slew Agrivaine personally, and his mere presence proved to be the final boost of morale needed to finish off the aggressors. But the defense had been so decimated that people were already fleeing, knowing Camelot could not be held against another invader, and rumors of Garmani swelling just miles to the east was enough to motivate most. They tried to find people they still knew. There was no sign of Lupinia, or Gawaine or the other Round Table members. Cabal had vanished, as had Yvaine's lion, along with most of the menagerie's other inhabitants. Perceval thanked God Himself that they had left Dindraine at Bridgnorth.

The three of them were hardly surprised to learn the more depressing news: Arthur found both his sister and his son, and finished them off, but not before Mordred delivered the King's death blow.

Or so it seemed. The folk they questioned outside the city said that several women had taken the King off to heal him. The three knights were nonplussed at that.

"To Avalon," the people said. "Morgan and the Lady of the Lake came for them." They could only assume Nimue was somehow responsible.

Perceval inquired about Arthur's mighty sword.

"Thrown into the water whence it came, by Bedivere" other folk told them. "It'll never be seen again, not till there's another worthy king," another added.

They thought of going into the city to learn more, but Galahad reminded them of her father's commands, so they left it behind. They had much to do and visit before embarking upon the course they had decided. Yvaine wished to speak with his mother, Dindraine had to be met, and some decision had to be made regarding the copper chalice that had become their life's work and ambition.

* * *

A fortnight passed, and Perceval presently sat alone; those who previously occupied the edifice to which he traveled had gone, and he had no idea how to find them. They would be safe in the hills, he imagined, like his family for so long.

So long, he thought. *Can it have been only these quick seasons since I met Yvaine and my unknown brother, running through the wilds with Dindraine?*

Yvaine and his sister would be waiting, as would Galahad. Bors had still not been seen, as he was off to defend the remnants of Logres against the hordes, or perhaps snugly shacked up, like the Queen supposedly was, within the confines of a monastic setting. Lancelot was rumored to be doing the same, which amused Galahad to no short end.

That was all right with Perceval either way, the knight and the queen. The chess match was resolved. The countryside was brimming with stories of how the Picts ventured south of the Wall, or how the Garmani had landed in Wictis, and other tales. He had seen enough evidence of that to last more than a single lifetime. *No more blood*, he vowed, wondering if such a promise could be kept.

He looked at the scroll case dangling unobtrusively from Styfnig's saddle. He was hesitant to read the letter again, though he supposed he must; the emotional drain was staggering, but he needed its reassuring tone to get him through the task he had chosen for himself. Galahad already said she didn't want to know where the final resting place was, especially since she didn't really feel it would be all that final. He reluctantly agreed with her; thus the hiding place. His original choice was Roche Sanguin, but Galahad protested, fearing the safety of the women's holding would be jeopardized. And besides, she would have had to lead him there. She tried to think positively about it; it would have been easy to just travel, using the wonderful healing the goblet offered.

But how long until such a gift corrupted them? Such was Galahad's sober conclusion. Could it offer life everlasting? Mend any hurt? Perhaps. But they all decided that such a gift could only be utilized by a person on one blessed occasion; any more seemed travesty, and Galahad had saved two human lives with it. So it would disappear, for now. If the powers in which they had come to believe were true, and they kept it with them and abused such an incredible potency, then Galahad would never reach heaven, Yvaine would never return as the lion he always fancied himself, Dindraine would not grow into the wise old crone that Kundry became, and Perceval... Well, Perceval's spirituality was still so privately muddled, but he still wondered about finding his beloved Llio again.

Padern gave him the letter in Worcester, about the only place Perceval ever felt really at home, beyond the hills he had so wished to leave. His love shared with Llio there was perfect, the people welcomed him as their champion, and treated him like a hero after he freed them from Clamadeus. He looked at his proud horse. And he had gotten Styfnig there! Worcester had to be seen again, and it was there he took his temporary parting from the others.

Gornymant was as vanished as so many of the others; that was the real reason it pained so much to read his letter again. Padern invited him to stay, all of them, but Worcester would have hurt too much also, and the others felt it was too close to Camelot anyway, and they had to live, to tell the tales. Perceval prayed that Taliesin's memory and music would preserve something of what they bled for, the great quests, the glory of Camelot.

So the traveler's destination would be as secure, with the additional attraction of being fresh and wholly new to them. Things had to be renewed periodically. Life grew stagnant otherwise. The other cargo Perceval had tied to his mount taught him that.

Best to get through it, then. A few moments reading, a few more digging and hiding, and he could leave Rhun behind forever.

He untied the scroll case, took out the letter, and read:

Perceval, my second son,
   My principle hope at this juncture in a life as old as mine is that you receive this notice, and are well. I am just glad I taught you to read, so you could once more partake of the musings of one tired of being alone.

You know how that feels yourself, do you not? You lost a lover, I a daughter, and another child who shed his fine blood defending Britain's most beloved and righteous King. So now, family gone, I find my only option is to once more serve our sovereign, and hold off the barbarians as we did before you were even born. I only hope Bedivere can find it in his heart to permit me the honor of carrying the dragon banner onto the field. Then shall we see who is the right: our noble Arthur, or his damned infernal sister and bastard. Thanks be to God for giving Margawse's other sons the wisdom to follow what is just and good.

Forgive me. My shaky pen flows with my rambling, an old man's privilege, I should hope. I've many things to tell, and already can I hear the trumpets rousing our best and bravest to the call of duty and honor.

It is most difficult, I think, to admit taking Mordred under my own wing. Believe me when I say, I hope so many can find it within them to forgive me that, especially you. Had I known… Dear Perceval, had I only known so much, but such is the course God plots for each of us. For a time, he was as bright and passionate as his brother Gareth, and I was proud of the progress I made with each of them. Perhaps it would be easier if I knew what went wrong, if his accursed mother poisoned him somehow, turned him against all of us. I once heard that at the tourney I hosted personally here in Jagent, someone with no noble intent on his mind informed the royal bastard of his true lineage. Had Mordred not known that previously, and I believe he was ignorant of such, I can only guess how it might have warped him. Not having a father is tragic enough; learning you are an unwanted prince besides must be devastating.

Perceval stopped and blinked back the first two tears, again considering the strange details his life and that of Sir Mordred shared. Then he kept reading.

Rebellion is everywhere now. I do not fault your absence in the least. You saw the greater glory of Logres, and not the butchery which preceded it and which, it now seems, may come in its wake. I wish and pray your safety, and of those for whom you still care. Do not waste tears on me. Find your happiness, wherever that quest may lead you.

Much talk of quests has filled the air around Camelot these past weeks. For your efforts you all will be remembered, and have earned the right to remain free of all the devastation the jealous and greedy invaders will bring. If the Grail can truly be found, remember it is not something to take lightly: the security of your soul depends on your treating it wisely. Above all, let it not fall into corrupted hands, and let it be said, still eons from now, that the reign of Arthur was that in which the greatest human endeavor and search took place!

I know well how Llio loved you. She used to go on about you while you and Llas were out pretending to run each other through. She adored you from the first day you arrived, fretful about your future and your recent deed. We all knew you to be noble from the start. She will always be in your heart and soul, and in mine as well. She was never the quiet sort, like her mother. Llio always had to be in the thick of it, never content to stay back or go unnoticed or unheard. Some say that is not appropriate in a woman, but I maintain it is a testament to her strength of character and her love of this precious life. She was the most giving, devoted soul I have ever known.

Incidentally, you silly goose, you never had to ask my permission! As we both know, Llio was one to make her own decisions. And she could not have found a more suitable mate.

As for Llascoit, you must not blame yourself. Yes, I know what happened. Mordred and his co-conspirators made it a point to boast of all the killing they had already done, especially if the name of a slain knight could be made public. Those bastards outnumbered him on an incredible scale, and still did he go down fighting, completing his mission of warning as well. Perhaps that, above all, was what drew me out of this retiring state; I have to know I helped thwart the plans of those who killed my son.

I do not know when you will have a chance to receive this, though I pray nightly you shall. Padern will keep it safe. I sent one of Arthur's own couriers since I was already in Camelot and learned of my son and of your quest. I have little fear you will have the insight to see Worcester once more before you leave, wherever you may go.

I have no doubt I'm leaving out some essential detail or bit of wisdom to offer in my passing. Never give up the quest, Perceval! Glory in pursuit and honor to yourself, above all! Never become so foolish you forget that.

I taught many what I taught you, and never did I have a pupil so quick and eager for more knowledge. May you find some place where the people have equal hunger, away from all this bloodshed. I will never falter in my love for you, just as my beloved Arian, Llio, and Llascoit remain alive within me. I heard you travel with that unusual girl of Lancelot's, and that you found your sister. This "Galienne" sounds a bit like Llio. I don't know your precise relation with her, though I know Llio would want your continued happiness, whether that includes loving another or no. May you remain safely together, wherever you call home.

Alas, the dream of the ancients must wait a little longer. Ever your proud teacher,

Sir Gornymant of Jagent, formerly of Worcester, in Deheubarth

Perceval wondered if Gornymant's body had lain with the others at that final, treacherous battlefield. There were so many that not all the bodies could receive proper identification. Still, he knew that his old master would have wanted it that way, to die at his king's side, sword still in his hand.

He sighed, readying to head to Gloucester, where he would board a tiny ship that the others would have hired by now. He could make the city by nightfall, and Yvaine, Dindraine, and Galahad would be waiting for him with open arms. The journey to Eire-land would be blessedly quick and hopefully enjoyable, on the chaotic Cymru Sea; the thought of the open water made Perceval edgy since he saw the white stag outside Bridgnorth.

Yvaine had already contacted his mother. Old Uriens finally died, though the kingdom remained safe and free, beyond the reaches of the invaders; he hoped no one else would have the staying power to venture so far inland. The wastes were gradually receding, and sites like Avalon and Mona would light the coming darkness, places where what happened would always be remembered. Yvaine's mother and her ways would remain safe, and Yvaine wished no part of that life of hiding; he wanted to be free, and only Eire-land sounded like it might meet that demand. The likes of Tathan and Taliesin would preserve the tales of Camelot, come what may.

Perceval put the letter away. He took a look around the place. Rhun had worn. He liked to think that Amlyn, Elffin, even Brugyn and Gwyn, found their own homes again in the wild lands he used to call home himself. Perceval smiled; he never did get the chance to best Gwyn in wrestling. The small castle was well on its way to becoming just an old landmark.

And a fairly well hidden one, at that. The chalice would be safe outside it: unnoticed, as Gornymant said, until someone needed it again. Perhaps a king? Who could tell? Arthur's dream would live, even if the Grail, if grail it truly was, could not help him directly.

Perceval admired the work he did. It looked almost like no earth had been moved at all to make room for such an inconspicuous little vessel. He buried it wrapped in soft silk, surrounded by a little wooden box purchased from the fine craftspeople in Worcester. The land itself was growing healthy again, Perceval wondering if this meager cup was the seed which needed to be planted within it. There it would stay until someone found it again.

He smiled. Had they found Christ's cup, or the more ancient Cauldron of wisdom and immortality? Something else? He knew now that it didn't matter, that the question was a pointless distraction. The Grail was what the seeker needed it to be, believed it to be, and that was enough. He loved the little chalice, swore he could feel some of its own spirit within him. Pellam said each seeker and keeper had to keep part of the wisdom of the mystery, and this bit was his.

Perceval rose and climbed onto Styfnig, taking his last glance at the tiny burial site. The Grail would be safe there, and it would return, like Excalibur or even the King himself, when the proper time came again.

Locales and Peoples within Dreamers of the Grail:

Cambria

This consists of all of modern Wales, plus portions of the adjacent English counties. For simplicity, it includes the sub-kingdoms of Powys in the midlands, Gwynedd in the north, and Deheubarth in the south. Several more small kingdoms came and went during this period, all the way up to the late Middle Ages, when Wales and England were more formally joined. The main Brythonic (Romano-British/Celtic) tribes in these regions included the Silures and Demetae in Deheubarth, the Ordovices in Powys, and the Decaengli in Gwynedd.

Logres

Arthur's kingdom, encompassing the rest of modern England which is not included elsewhere on this list. Here, the Celtic tribes include the Belgae, Dobunni, Coritani, and Catuvaellauni.

Dumnonia

The counties of Cornwall and Devon in southern England, inhabited by members of the Dumnonii and Cornovii tribes.

Anglia

A large portion consisting of the older Germanic settlements, including mainly Kent, Essex, and Sussex, and extending slightly further into modern England. The Germanic peoples emigrated here: Saxons, Jutes, Angles, Iclingas, Geats, Teutons, Varingas, and Trinovantes.

Caledonia

Roughly corresponding to southern Scotland. The northern portions were still inhabited by Pictish tribes, most notably the Votadini, Venicone, and Taixali, as well as Celtic peoples known as Orkney and Lindissi. Lothian and Gorre are the lands referred to most.

Cumbria

> Still the name of a northern English county, this is the general area of the Lake District. The small kingdoms affected most by the Wasteland are here (Rheged, Cambenet), as is the Wasteland itself, Listeneisse. The main peoples here were the Parisi and Brigantes.

Islands

> Pomitain is the old name for the Isle of Man, Wictis for the Isle of Wight, and Mona for the Isle of Anglesey.

Eire-land

> Ireland (the whole island).

Armorica

> Brittany, in France (sometimes called Less Britain in the old literature).

Gaul

> Roughly the additional area of modern France.

Forests, Hills, Mountains, Rivers

> Most old forests are long since clear-cut, but in the fourth and fifth centuries were huge and mysterious places. Cambria contained the Arroy and Dean. Logres had half of the Sauvage, most of the Campacorentin, Bedegraine, Roestoc, Deira, Landoine, and Arden. Anglia encapsulated the rest of the Sauvage, and Lincoln. The vast forest in Caledonia went by the same name. Hills referred to include the Brecon Beacons and Plimlimmons in Cambria, while Caledonia has the Highlands; the Cotswolds, Cumbrians, and Yorkshire are in Logres. And the main rivers include the Severn, the minor Cam which was placed here near Camelot, and of course the Thames.

Cameliard

> Fantastic; roughly at the border between Cheshire and Shropshire, with parts of each.

Lyonesse

> Fantastic; the now sunken legendary kingdom extending west off the tip of Cornwall.

Avalon

> Fantastic; the hills, formerly marshy islands, around Glastonbury, in Somerset.

Astolat

> Fantastic; in south-central England, west of London.

Camelot

> Fantastic; Caer Cadbury (Cadbury Hillfort), in Somerset.

Villages and Cities

> Camelot (*Logres*), Astolat (*Logres*), Aquae Sulis (modern Bath, *Logres*), Worcester (*Cambria*), Viroconium (modern Wroxeter, *Cambria*), Caernarfon (*Cambria*), Eburacum (modern York, *Logres*), Carmarthen (*Cambria*), Tintagel (*Dumnonia*), Quimper (*Armorica*), and Londinium (modern London, *Logres*).

This list uses a mix of old and legendary names, and most places on this list either did exist, or still do. The selection of names takes into account the influence of those who lived in or near these places during Arthur's time, the sixth century, at the onset of the period known as the Dark Ages.

Acknowledgements and Afterword

It seems more appropriate to me to give my thanks after the project, rather than at the start, when I think (and hope!) you're more inclined to dive right into the story, anyway. And besides, until you've finished, some of these comments are unlikely to make much sense. So what I have in mind here is a mix of traditional thanks, plus some insight about the sources for these ideas.

Clearly this is a work of fantasy first, and history a distant second. I love just about any and all renditions of the "Matter of Britain," though it feels that for the past several decades, the trend has been toward some sense of historical accuracy. As Parke Godwin points out at the onset of his novel Firelord, Arthur and some of the others are perfectly valid as historical subjects, just far less documented than many. Historical renditions make delightful reading, although this emphasis on "how it might have really been" seems to motivate the removing of magic and fantasy. A purely historical Camelot is something so far removed from us, both in terms of our common knowledge of the legends, and the lifestyle of fifth and sixth century Britain, that I sought to include more recognizable elements. This story is a mix of historical ingredients; what mattered to me was the tale itself. For background, however, the following unashamedly anachronistic details might assist.

Courtly love, stone castles, and knightly tournaments appeared during the 1100s. Stirrups were invented by the Chinese around 500, and two centuries passed before they reached Europe. Horseshoes to protect the mounts came about 900. The Normans introduced the method of couching a spear to use it as a lance, right at the end of the first millennium, and jousting began, curiously, at Winchester about 40 years later (just a quarter century before William and those Normans brought feudalism across the Channel). This novel also mentions potter's wheels,

Renaissance-style painting, weaver's looms, medieval heraldry, Christmas trees (a legacy of Martin Luther, from about 1500), and mechanical engineering and weapons (including the strange automatic crossbows which plague a certain knight). Plate armor came late, and was always ridiculously expensive and vulnerable to Welsh-inspired longbows and the later gunpowder weapons. Most folks in the "Dark" and Middle Ages stayed at or near home all their lives, and the movers and shakers were often those who left to seek glory elsewhere. Ireland was converted during the fifth century, and during the onset of the following two centuries, Christianity took root throughout Britain. These are all historical truths which nonetheless appear in my telling, because Arthur's realm is a society far ahead of its time. It was my intent, then, to bring out all the myth and legend I could, and give slightly less emphasis to what can be verified through the few historical pieces which survive from this period. What else could a story primarily about the Grail do?

What history remains is discussed in broad, sweeping terms, and most of it has to do with the lifestyle of the Celtic tribes, and the effects of Britain's various invaders, especially the Romans. When the Legions finally left in the early fifth century, the whole Island was too tempting to ignore. The Picts lay north of the Wall, the Irish raided the western coasts (specifically an Irish tribe known as Scotti, ancestors of modern Scots), and the Garmani, the German peoples, had already settled most of the eastern part of England and continued to threated the southeastern coasts. The Vikings did not appear until the 800s. Note the names here: Angle-land became known as England, and Wales was a Saxon term to refer to foreign land, so the Welsh were labeled foreigners in their own territory! The "Britons" were really the surviving remnants of the Celtic tribes known as Brythonic, mixed Romano-Welsh, and there was someone among them who held off the invaders for a few short decades, most likely operating out of southern Wales and western England.

Arthur and his colleagues probably hailed from either the Silures or Dobunni tribes, or some combination of the two. This raw core of loosely-documented history is likely where all this began. I chose to write about the ideal, of the legend which still offers such a pull: the mystical king, with his invincible troop of romantic warriors who bring peace to a scarred land and embark on the greatest of heroic adventures.

By the time the Roman Empire was finally crumbling and being assaulted by everyone from the Huns to the Vandals to the Visigoths, Britain, its northwestern-most province, had benefited from Roman civilization and security for four centuries. Caesar himself had launched a short-lived assault after taking Gaul, but the full invasion and pacification didn't really get going for another century. Like most imperial territories, there were those who welcomed the change (including Roman order, trade, affluence, and sheer military might), and those who would rebel, favoring their older society. Boudicca's revolt in Anglia in 60-61 revealed both the instability and occasional treachery of imperial life, and even one of the British Celts, Magnus Maximus (Macsen Wledig) was raised to the purple robes for a time.

So when it all came crashing down, and the Visigoths were running through Rome, and Hadrian's Wall in northern Britain was already in disrepair, and the emperor Honorius sent word to the British ordering them to take care of their own defensive needs (in the year 410), the Britons were at an utter loss. How could Roman civilization be maintained? More importantly, who would keep the heartlands secure, since central Britain was now looking at three simultaneous sources of trouble.

The precise identification of Arthur matters far less than what he represents: most take him as a fantasy hero, an historical oddity, perhaps merely a cuckolded husband, or even as a farcical character who never existed at all, but the important detail is that he is the historical link between Roman Britain and something called Great Britain. When he lived, there were no such entities as England, Wales, and Scotland; there was only Britain under continuous attack. Whoever Arthur was, he was most likely a Briton. It's important to understand this term in its proper historical context: the Britons as British Celts. Their modern descendants are the Welsh, not the English nor even the Scots, even though the term is still used colloquially to describe any contemporary British citizen. The main adversaries of these ancient Britons, referred to here collectively as Garmani, were actually a mix of Saxons, Angles, Jutes, as well as Danes and Frisians, coming from the lands now called Germany, Holland, and Denmark. Some members of these tribes had been chased from their homelands and were essentially wandering; by the time they'd made initial forays across the Channel, they realized Britain would prove an ideal homeland. The Britons were already there of course, so there were naturally conflicts. What exacerbated the situation was the actual invitation of numerous Garmani to come over and act as mercenaries against the more immediate threats of Irish and Picts.

The Irish hit western Britain repeatedly, and acquired a sufficient foothold that they eventually eliminated most of the Picts (who in turn became the even more ancient faerie people of legend). From what is now Scotland, forays could more easily be made, by a combination of landing in Wales and heading south, and overland past the decaying Wall. There originally were Legionary bases at York (Eburacum), Chester (Caer Legis), and Caerleon; these were the main outposts, aside from London (Londinium), in Roman Britain, and the Britons continued using them from which to launch counterattacks now that the Romans were gone.

After the Garmani rather treacherously murdered the Briton tribal leaders during what was promised to be a peace counsel (the "Night of the Long Knives," in 463), they proved themselves both more established and, to the Britons, untrustworthy, but by then the threats from north and west were largely in check. However, the entire eastern coast of the Isle was now Germanic; these were the ancestors of the English, and they were continuing to push westward. And the core of Celtic resistance likely came in the form of fast-moving cavalry units which could hurl themselves against the German infantry, and then disappear. Numbers were on the Germanic side, yet these Britons were the only people in western Europe who withstood the coming of the Germans. The Battle at Badon Hill (location unknown) probably took place approximately 515 or 518, with Arthur directing the defense; his success there enabled the British Celts to avoid extinction, and enforced a peace with the German tribes lasting some two decades.

        This is about all we know of the history. No descriptions are known to exist of Arthur or any of his entourage. The earliest Welsh tales describing him are violent and magical, and almost always contain reference to other major figures from the developing legends: Myrddin (Merlin), Gwynhwyfar (Guinevere), Bedwyr (Bedivere), Gwalchmai (Gawaine), Cei (Kay), Modron (Morgan), Owain (Yvaine). Geraint fought his famous battle at Llongborth slightly after the appropriate time period, but is remembered as a hero in his own right, eventually becoming Eric of the French story "Eric and Enide." Trystan and Essyllt (Tristram and Isolde) have their own legend, which really occurs during the latter 6th and possibly 7th centuries, so they likewise appear too late to truly be part of the history, and the same applies to Peredur (Perceval), who was a prince ruling at York, confirmed to have lived during the 7th century. Lancelot and Galahad, so vital to the later medieval romances, have no historical precedents; of all the key players on such a magnificent stage, they stand as pure literary creations. Camelot, Excalibur, the Grail, the Round Table, and all the decorations that have made the tales so gloriously detailed have little initial connection with this old Celtic warlord; Arthur wasn't even a king. He received the titles Duke of Battles and Count of Britain, but he was really a preview of the later medieval monarchs. A king never would have even worked: the Celtic peoples were always so hopelessly divided that other groups (especially the Romans) could overcome them simply by being better organized (witness the aforementioned hostility between the Irish, Celts themselves, attacking their cultural relatives in Wales in the Arthurian period). Someone needed to unite the Britons, and only an Arthur could meet the challenge.

What followed in the years beginning immediately after Badon was an explosion of literature, some historical, some fantastical, some conjectural, concerning what was growing into the "Matter of Britain." The literature might have remained more drab and purely of a semi-historical flavor if not for the tremendous input of mostly Continental rather than British writers, particularly the French troubadours and trobairitz, who came seven centuries later during the High Middle Ages. But why would they have cared? Indeed, there was already a "Matter of France:" Charlemagne and his paladins, who remain more historically grounded than Arthur and his knights. Some persons focus on the enmity between the English and French, but the Hundred Years War was still many decades away during the peak of the troubadour's influence (during the 12th and early 13th centuries). And many medieval British monarchs were actually Norman-French: the English court language was French, and English itself would remain an uncouth tongue until at least the 13th century. Even Richard I despised England, considering it a source of revenue for the Third Crusade, and might have sold London had he found a buyer. So the French influence was indubitable, with customs, foods, and manners having crossed the Channel with the invaders.

The "romances," then, were the poems and ballads composed in "romantic" (Latin-based) languages, including French, Spanish, and Italian, but also the non-Latin German languages. The troubadours and trobairitz were the popularizers and sometimes the authors of such dramas, the descendants of the wandering minstrels and court bards, recounting tales for sympathetic patrons. What made them different at this time was not just the inclusion of Arthur stories, but also a lessening of emphasis on the violence of the knights. Now there was love poetry, and praises sung and told in the name of chivalry. There were even alleged courts of love, including one supposedly set up by none other than Eleanor of Aquitaine, herself Queen of France before becoming Queen of England. Her daughter, Marie de Champagne, sponsored the works of Chrétien de Troyes, one of the three most important Arthurian writers. It was he who introduced Lancelot to the world, and elaborated on the details of courtly love and a Christian interpretation of the Grail quest. And Marie de France, a poetess in her own right, also composed Arthurian contributions. Love and magic were now celebrated alongside heroism and piety, while chivalry attempted to point the way to an ideal society.

Even the knights got into the written works near the end: Wolfram von Eschenbach and Thomas Malory finish the central trinity of romance writers, Wolfram in German (with his "Parzival"), Thomas in English (with "The Death of Arthur"), and both these men proved that warriors could also be writers. What had started out as drier, monastic histories including references to Arthur developed through the High Middle Ages into secular and adventurous stories known the world over.

Arthur is, again, a precursor to medieval kingship, inspiring politics as much as literature and history. Medieval rulers depended on him, not merely for ideals, but sometimes for their very positions. Henry II and the subsequent Plantagenets (the clan beginning with William I, the Conqueror, and lasting for four centuries) justified their rule in Arthurian terms, and it was during Henry's later reign that Arthur's and Guinevere's graves were allegedly found in Glastonbury. Richard I, the Lionheart, once offered as a gift an ornate sword he may have believed was

Excalibur, despite his aforementioned hostility toward England. His brother John helped ensure he would take the throne by ordering the death of his nephew, Prince Arthur (or perhaps getting his own hands dirty at the prince's expense; and curiously, there have existed several princes Arthur but none who ever would wear the crown as Arthur II). Edward I had the Glastonbury graves re-consecrated, so that the pesky Welsh he was trying to subdue (the true Celtic descendants of the historical Arthur) could go about forgetting the legend of him just hibernating in a cave somewhere so that he might come back and overthrow the English. And even at the end of this dynasty, when the future Henry VII landed in Britain to defeat the last Plantagenet Richard III, he, Henry, capitalized on his quarter-Welsh background and proclaimed himself another Arthur, in deed if not in name. Then as now, propaganda was a basic part of the political machine; it was easier to solidify and justify one's position if one could claim direct lineage to a loved and idealized forebear.

With the Tudors now established, Arthur remained influential as before: Henry's eldest son was another prince Arthur who died shortly after marrying his princess. She soon remarried another Henry, the forthcoming and far-better known Henry VIII. But after the Tudors, the Stuarts and Hanoverians largely ignored Arthur; how could he serve as a model for society in the face of the Renaissance, the Reformation, the English Civil Wars, the strengthening of Parliament at the monarchy's expense, the emergence of the Commonwealth, and the scientific and industrial revolutions, as well as the loss of those uppity New England colonies? So, just as in legend, Arthur lay somewhat dormant for a while; the Age of Reason was no time for superstitious old faery tales.

And then finally, in the 19th century, the Victorians rediscovered Arthur and glorified him into a virtual deity, capable of no wrong and offering the most perfect society imaginable. This was just in time to try and justify the objectives of the largest empire in history, when the sun literally never set on the Union Jack. By then, the old Celtic precedents were entirely glossed over; Arthur became the model Christian benevolent ruler, and in a textbook definition of irony, the King of the English (recall that the English were the historical Arthur's great enemies). He's sometimes criticized for being so malleable, but one can hardly blame someone who's been dead for fifteen centuries for the way his memory continually gets reinterpreted. Whatever the current time demands: monarchy, liberalism, social equality, economic reform, justified force, loving relationships, conquests, new moral codes… Arthur has been exploited and reshaped to answer all of these. He has remained omnipresent throughout British history, and as a result of Britain's influence, world history, for all these centuries. Make of him and his contemporaries what you will.

A similar line of thought involves what some will likely regard as a consistent misspelling of the word magic. The inclusion of the "k" on the end of that term was quite intentional. I wanted to make sure readers understood that when I refer to "magick," I am talking about something altogether different from magic as a post-modern stage profession. In fairness, there are genuine experts in this latter field, who thrill audiences with impressive feats of dexterity, illusion, escapism, and the otherwise unexplained. But this is not the traditional sense of the word. "Magick" is the "New Age" spelling, and refers to a much older practice.

Magick is, traditionally, a spiritual and religious activity. As Morgan points out, it is faith made real, whether one practices sacrifice or sacrament. Magick in this older sense has been with us from the very beginning, and takes varying forms: herbalism, shamanism, alchemy, glamour, divination, healing, praying for miraculous intervention, and others. One of the more unusual examples, the geas, comes from the old Irish Pagan tradition, and is a personalized taboo, the violation of which results in horrific death (or an unhealing torturous existence, in Pellam's case).

Magick began to get a bad name when theologians wanted to separate what they viewed as mere superstitious unorthodox practice from religious dogma and keep believers on the supposedly proper paths; "sorcery" and "witchcraft" thus became evil incarnate, rather than traditional activities. I describe many things in this novel as "magickal:" music, laughter, prayer, Nimue's glamour, Galienne's visions, ancient Christian and Celtic prophecies, Merlin's enchantments, the wasteland, Baudwin's blessings, and, of course, the Grail itself. Magick in this sense becomes a participation in the divine, in the unknowable, in whatever spiritual realm one believes to maintain its own unique reality and influence relative to the practitioner or casual believer. What one believes and thinks and feels is one's own concern, and faith is thus made the most magickal force of all.

With an educational background in philosophy, I could not resist the urge to put in a dose of the Classics. I loved the idea of Perceval studying the Greeks, and showing Pellam's guests debating the implications of the human will and the Pelagian Heresy, which was historically argued just over a century before the tale opens. The use of a free will is precisely what permits the heroes to succeed on the quest, so reference to it as its own subject seemed a prerequisite. As for the rest of it, well, I promise that's fiction, viewed through the eyes and experiences of your friendly neighborhood storyteller.

I think a storyteller is a social filter. It is impossible to retell a tale this old and influential without leaving my own stamp on it. With that in mind, I think it only fair that the Grail itself should have different "resolutions." Galahad and Perceval know it is the cup of Christ and the Cauldron of plenty. It has been a platter, a stone, a bowl, an emerald, a goblet, a woman, depending upon whose rendition of the tale one reads. It is a worldwide symbol of healing, vitality, freshness...the antithesis of the wastelands we create for ourselves.

I've hinted at a few other works which had their influence on me. Suffice it to say that this novel truly benefitted from the following sources:

Savage Mountains, by Greg Stafford and the folks at the Chaosium game company. This is a reference for Mr. Stafford's delightful and passionate role-playing game Pendragon, and details the marvelous land we now call Wales exhaustively. Many items in my own work referring to Cambria found their sources somewhere in this book.

Second is The Holy Grail, by Malcolm Godwin. This is the best introductory work I know of about this very involved artifact, and the legends, myths, and faith which let it grow into the ultimate symbol of Western spirituality.

Next comes Wolfram von Eschenbach's "Parzival," which offered inspiration for characters like Llio and Llascoit (even if I "Welsh-ified" their names), and taught me that the true strength of this story is that it transcends boundaries associated with gender, race, religion, and nationality. Chrétien de Troyes' "Perceval" and Thomas Malory's "Le Morte D'Arthur" were of course also invaluable.

Finally, there are of course those who deserve my gratitude, for their input, reading, encouragement, or faith (in some cases, all four!)

To my parents I owe my life and my love. Unlike Perceval's mother, they have always possessed the strength to see me off on my own quests.

To Sammy the Computer Geek, Jon the Sign Nerd, and Zollman, who have always listened to my stories, no matter how rational or ludicrous, your mootant loves you.

To John Beversluis, Paul Valliere, and Martin Schönfeld, you will always have my thanks for teaching me how to think.

To Uncle Dave, my savviest reader and one of my precious few relatives foolish enough to work in the entertainment industry and look good doing it, I give my gratitude for eager yet cautious optimism.

To Jon (again) and Caroline, for reading, editing, and critiquing several versions of the manuscript, I can only offer awe and wonder for having stuck it out this long.

And, thanks for believing: Kendra Wollert, Erin French, Wendy Giles, Tracey Scott, Sandra Van Bork, and Rhea Fleming.